Praise for *The Last Giant: Transgression, Part 1*

from Indie Book Reviewers

"...brilliantly imagined and fully developed...the writing was excellent...I'd love to read the next one!"

— Samantha Ryan

"...enough action and conflict and plot twists and descriptive fantasy world-building to keep you interested throughout...."

— J. T. Thomas

"...demonstrates a strong and almost addicting narrative style and great attention to detail...kept me eagerly turning the pages...late into the evening."

— Claire Middleton

"...one epic tale that I couldn't put down!"

— April Dawn

ABOUT THE AUTHORS

J. R. Hardesty is the husband-and-wife writing team of Johanna & Richard Hardesty. Johanna has several degrees including English, History, Archæology & Surveying. Richard has no degrees, but a lot of college credit hours. He spent some time with U. S. Air Force intelligence as a Russian linguist. After his USAF service, he spent several years as a computer programmer & systems operator and as a retail bookseller. He was also the proprietor of an antiquarian book business for several years. They currently live in NW Montana with their three cats and four dogs and get outdoors whenever possible.

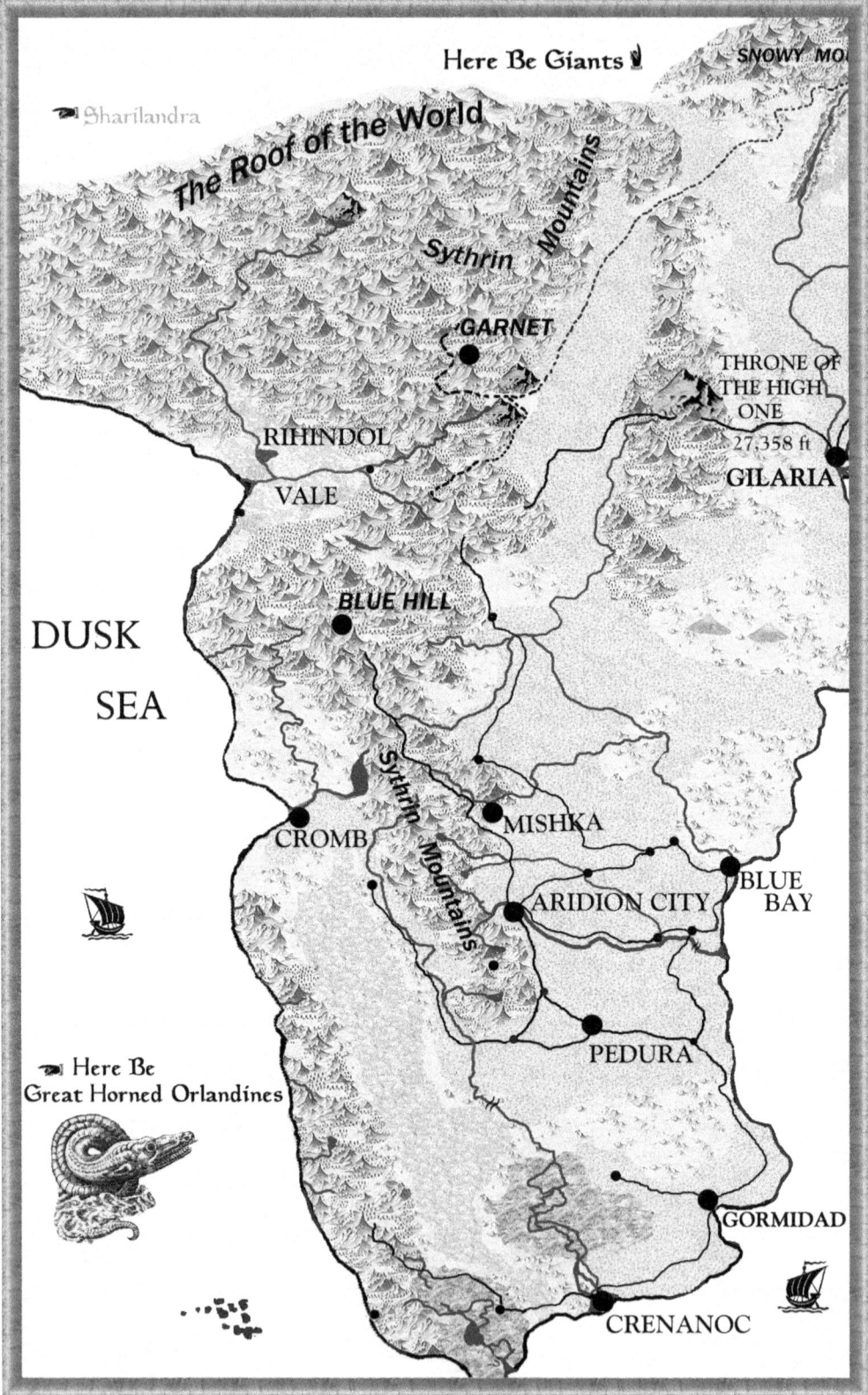

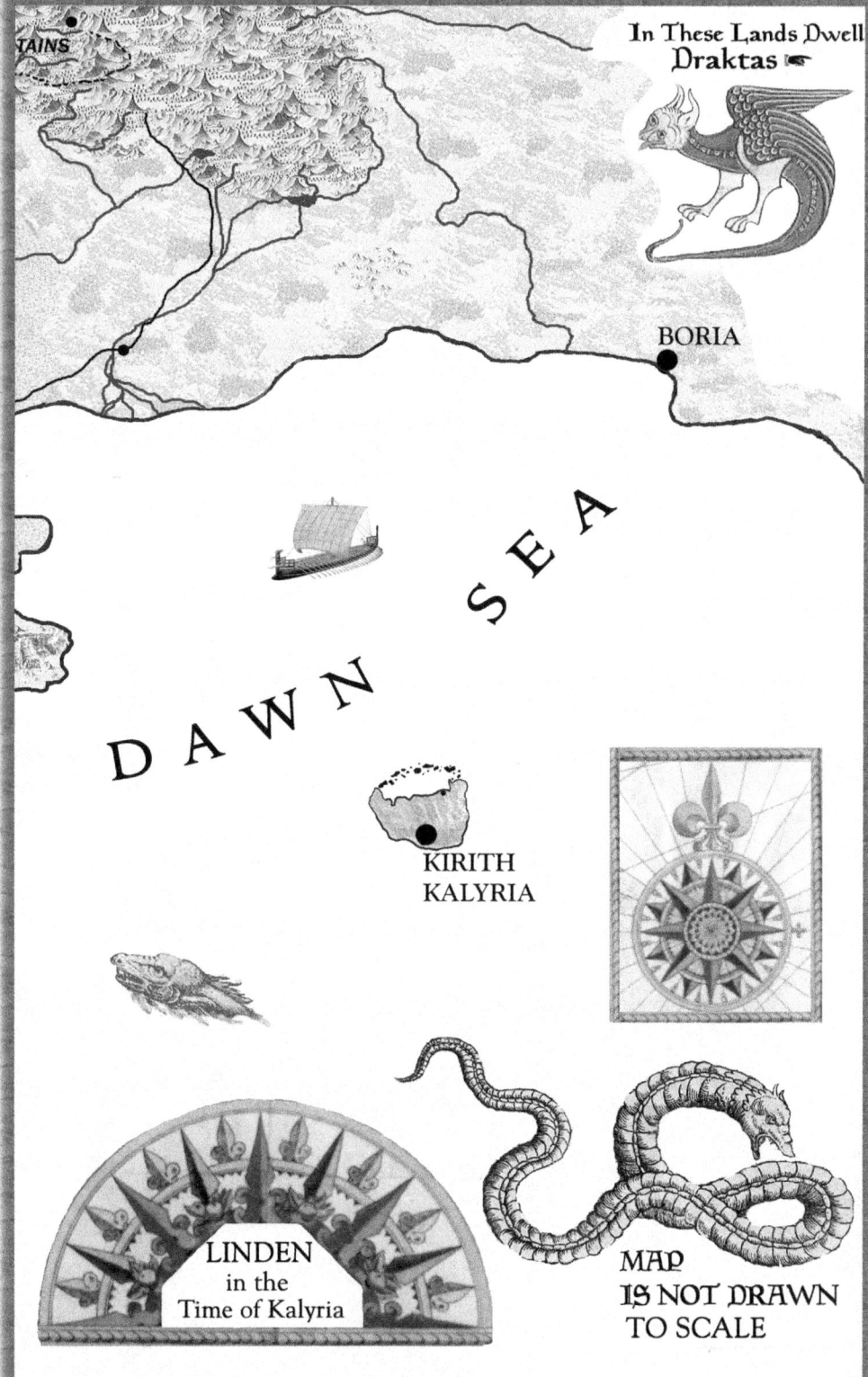

To Blackmore's Night whose music helped set the mood for writing and provided some inspiration. To all our beta readers. You told it like it was and we fixed it.

THE LINDENSAGA™

THE LAST GIANT
Book 1: Transgression

FORTHCOMING
THE LAST GIANT
Book 2: Retribution (Nov 2016)

THE GIFT OF THE HIGH ONE
Book 3: *Prince of the Teluri* (Mar 2017)
Book 4: *High King of the Teluri*

THE HARPER OF RHINDOL VALE
Book 5: *The Key of Tanguroth*
Book 6: *The Orb of Making*
Book 7: *The White Tower*
Book 8: *The Frostrill Stair*

Fifteen volumes in all are planned.

THE LAST GIANT
TRANSGRESSION

J. R. Hardesty

Book 1 of the Lindensaga

Hungry Horse
Golden Cocker Press
2016

Typography & design by Richard L. Hardesty at the Rising Wolf Press.

Lindensaga™ is a Trademark of Purple Mammoth Publishing LLC

Trade Paperback
ISBN-10 0-9907264-7-9
ISBN-13 978-0-9907264-7-0

Library of Congress Control Number: 2016911743

First One Volume Edition
Published October, 2016

First published in two volumes
Vol. 1 – December 2014
Vol. 2 – November 2015

THE LAST GIANT: TRANSGRESSION

IN THE BEGINNING, the High One created the World and all that is in it. He blessed it and called it good. One of the High One's previous Creations was a race of beings who lived with Him in the Heavens and served him willingly. But one there was among them who grew jealous of the High One and His power and thought to take for himself that which was not his and so rebelled against his Lord. For this, he was punished and exiled to the great Darkness and from there he plotted his revenge. The Fallen has been known by many names throughout the ages, but most often he is simply called the Evil One, and through him, evil crept into the newly made World of Linden. The history of Linden and its peoples' struggles to free themselves from the coils of the Evil One is recorded in the Lindensaga. There are many tales in that great book. This is one of them. It is the tale of the Last Giant.

CHAPTER I
(SUMMER OF THE WORLD 6996)

MENANNON STOOD ALONE IN THE HIGH HALL OF GATHERING, STARING THROUGH THE TALL MULLIONED WINDOWS AT THE CONSTELLATION TELURION WANDERER, THE SKY HUNTER, THE THREE BRIGHT STARS OF ITS BELT GLITTERING DOWN FROM THEIR FROSTY VAULT UNDISTURBED BY THE NEED TO CONTEND WITH THE LIGHT OF THE FULL MOON, HIS MIND FILLED WITH JOYFUL ANTICIPATION AND NOT THE LEAST TOUCHED BY THOUGHTS OF SORCERERS, MAD QUEENS, VIOLENT DEATHS AND WATERY GRAVES.

NOTHING TROUBLED HIS HEART, FOR THIS DAY WOULD SEE THE CULMINATION OF EIGHT LONG SUMMERS OF EFFORT. TODAY, HE WOULD ATTAIN THE RANK OF FULL JOURNEYMAN HARPER, THE FIRST GIANT EVER SO TO DO. THERE WAS BUT ONE STEP BEYOND THAT: PASSING THE MASTER'S TRIALS TO BECOME A MASTER HARPER OF THE HARPERS GUILD OF ARIDION, THEREBY HONORING HIS SIRE'S FAITH AND SACRIFICE, BUT THAT LAY IN THE FUTURE.

THIS DREAM HAD BEEN THE WHITE-HOT CENTER OF HIS LIFE EVER SINCE HE AND HIS SIRE HAD BEEN EXILED FROM THE GIANT LANDS OF LORNENNOG FOR THE CRIME OF LAUGHTER WHEN HE WAS BUT FIVE SUMMERS OLD. THEY HAD RETURNED TO THE MIGHTY ISLAND KINGDOM OF KALYRIA, LONG HIS SIRE'S DWELLING PLACE, AND THERE MENANNON HAD LEARNED OF HARPS AND HARPERS AND DISCOVERED IN HIMSELF AN EXTRAORDINARY TALENT FOR MUSIC.

WITH THE COMING OF THIS DAWN AND ITS RITUAL, THE YOUNG GIANT KNEW IN HIS HEART OF HEARTS THAT NOTHING NOW STOOD IN THE WAY OF ACHIEVING HIS DREAM, BUT HE HAD YET TO LEARN THAT SILENCE, LONELINESS AND FAILURE ARE THE BASTARD OFFSPRING OF HATE.

THE SUNLIGHT STREAMING IN through the hall's huge, mullioned windows gilded everything with intense light lending a dreamlike quality to the proceedings. The pews and benches were filled to capacity—even in the third choir loft high on the back wall. No surface of the great hall was left undecorated, from its intricately detailed marble floor to its fan vaulted ceiling held up by twin rows of hundred foot pillars. Despite the crowd, the acoustics of the hall were of such precision that not a soul present missed a single word of the ritual the Grandmaster was performing.

All the graduates had come forward to receive their honors in a jubilant blur of color as each discipline was called. By tradition, the new journeymen's robes were the color of their discipline: a drummer wore brown; a piper, blue; a harper, green; a singer, purple. Those who practiced the book arts wore crimson; lore masters, white; the smiths, rust and the healers, silver.

As the last new harp healer journeyman left the dais, amidst the applause and good wishes of the crowd, a hush began to creep through the pews. The moment all awaited had finally arrived. It was time for the harpers' first Giant to receive his honors. Anticipation ran through the crowd like the prickle before a lightning strike. The folk of Aridion City had taken Menannon to their hearts when he had first arrived, an all-elbows-and-knees eleven summers old child with naught to recommend him save a gift for harping and a determination to excel. They had watched him develop into a harper—whose skill some swore was fraught with the divine—and grow to a magnificent fellow who had to duck and go sideways through any door in the city save here at the harper hall alone. At nine feet, Menannon was the tallest living inhabitant of the city.

The young Giant strode proudly down the center aisle and climbed the stairs of the dais upon which stood the high altar and knelt respectfully in front of the Grandmaster's throne-like chair.

Rather than rising to continue the ritual as was usual, Grandmaster Blackmore eased around in his chair and leaned back comfortably to be better able to study his exceedingly tall apprentice. In so doing, he moved himself into a shaft of sunlight which gilded his white hair and showed his beardless face to be as wrinkled as a piece of vellum which has been cleaned far too many times. Despite his great age, being nearly six hundred five and thirty summers, his right eye held a youthful twinkle. His left was forever closed by the white scar of a long ago sword stroke, attesting to how the eye was lost, but not the circumstances. Blackmore was a short, sturdily built fellow of mixed Dwarf and Human ancestry whose parents had come from a small vale far to the northwest nestled along the Rhindolin River, sequestered between the Dwarf kingdoms of Garnet and Sythra on the east and the Dusk Sea on the west.

Not many of the Valinga, as this people were called, ever left the Vale, but the few who did had always proven of the highest worth to the lands of Aridion. Blackmore was no exception to this. He had been Grandmaster of the Harpers' Guild for over four hundred summers, his long age attributed to the Dwarven part of his ancestry, for the Humans of the Vale were as short-lived as were Humans of other lands, save for the People of the Long Ships. The Guild had prospered under his stewardship. How he came to the Guild was a story for the telling, if any knew it, but he kept it to himself to the chagrin of many a harper.

Blackmore continued his contemplation of the figure before him. The silence in the hall deepened as all wondered at this strange halt to the proceedings. He let them wonder, as he contented himself with looking long into the face of his Giant. It was a face well worth looking at: fine-boned and sensitive with high cheekbones rounding smoothly into the shadowed hollows beneath them, a strong nose and well formed, full-lipped mouth. Unruly collar-length blue-black hair curled about the high, broad forehead and a close-cropped beard softened the edges of a finely sculpted jaw line. Thick, slightly arching eyebrows and long lashes framed midnight-black eyes which, in the right light, glinted the same cobalt highlights as his hair and beard. Just now, those eyes were staring back at him with something of a wary expression.

Blackmore hid a grin at the self-conscious blush beginning to creep over Menannon's mobile countenance as the silence stretched on. The lad was too young to be totally in control of the incredible intellect with which the High One had blessed him and he still lacked the self-confidence it deserved. That would come with time, but for now, his emotions almost always overruled his judgement.

On the table near Blackmore's right hand still lay the sole remaining journeyman's cord on a velvet pillow. Unlike the rest of the cords which had borne the single color of the new journeyman's calling, this cord was entwined with all the colors of the Guild save healer's silver alone. Instead of rising, speaking the ritual words and threading the cord onto the shoulder of youngster's robe as he had with all the rest, Blackmore continued to silently sit there, looking from Menannon, to the cord and back.

At last, the ancient harper cleared his throat and stared hard at his very puzzled—and not a little embarrassed—apprentice.

"I'll give you this under one condition," Blackmore growled, totally ignoring the prescribed protocol. "I shall bestow this symbol of all your hard work—one you have justly earned— if and only if you give me your word you'll go home for six months and relax. Will you give me your word?"

Menannon, caught totally off-guard by this unexpected demand and break from tradition, nearly choked when he attempted to answer. The half-smothered snorts and chuckles he heard from the back of the hall where stood the other graduates did not help at all.

"I ... ah ... I so swear," Menannon stammered, his face now truly flaming.

"I didn't ask you to swear it, son. Your word would have been good enough." Blackmore grinned impishly as he finally stood up and signaled the youngster to lean down so he could thread the cord through the loops on Menannon right shoulder and buckle it into place. He then motioned him to rise and turn to face the hall. Blackmore hobbled to the front of the dais to address the gathering, his cane clicking loudly on the flagstones in the silence.

"Your Majesties, gentlewomen, worthies of the court, students, faculty, good folk of the city, all attend! For the first time in its history, the Harpers' Guild has been presented with an enigma: an apprentice who does not fit the normal frame-work of our guild. An apprentice whose talent, dedication and effort have so far exceeded all others who have passed through these doors that he has qualified to be made journeyman in all of the arts practiced by this Guild save one, and that through no fault of his own. To rightly honor this apprentice, the Masters of this Guild met in convocation to create a new rank among journeymen." Blackmore hobbled aside and pointed to Menannon with his cane.

"May I present to you for the first time, but surely not the last, Master Journeyman Menannon." Blackmore nearly crowed and the entire hall burst into spontaneous cheering, stomping and applause.

The young Giant stood still, not knowing quite what to do, the unusual cord glittering in the sun in stark contrast to the blackness of his robes, since his were still the color worn by the apprentices.

Dame Larisa, the Mistress of Seamstresses for the guild, had been hard-pressed to decide in what color to dress a fellow who was a journeyman in all of the disciplines of the guild, save only harp healing, as this question had never before arisen. She had wracked her brain for nearly the entire last summer of the Giant's training trying to come up with a suitable solution. She had finally thrown up her hands and decreed that such a fellow would wear black, stating as the reason that the creation of black dye required an infusion of all the other colors. The fact that it also emphasized the dark mystery of Menannon's eyes pleased her fancy as well, which of course, she was not about to admit.

As the crowd continued to cheer and Menannon still stood there in embarrassed silence, Blackmore could not help a twinge of fatherly pride, for he had personally refined and nurtured this extraordinary talent into being. It had taken a light hand at the reins. Only one thing remained now and that was for the lad to pass his master's trials, then the world would be his oyster and the Harper's Guild the more fortunate.

"Well, young man," the Grandmaster said with a grin, "don't stand there like a statue. Take a bow, if you will."

The young Giant and object of the crowd's pleasure took a bow as instructed, albeit a rather hasty one and made his escape, the sound of applause and cheering chasing after him like a determined bloodhound. At last, it was over.

OVERHEAD, gulls were wheeling and calling to each other, their very activity attesting to the nearness of dawn. Each bird seemed to have its own opinion of the deep-draft trading vessel below them, one adorned with a figurehead of a Great Stone Drakta. It was propelled by a square sail when the wind blew right, as it was now, and when it did not, by 50 oarsmen, 25 to a side in extended galleries built just below deck level, outside of the main hull to preserve the central space for passengers and cargo. Below-decks was partitioned into sleeping chambers and storerooms. The wealthiest passengers were given the cabin next the captain's own in the sterncastle in the shadow of the drakta's recurved tail.

Standing at the bow that he might catch sight of his beloved Kalyria that much the sooner, the salt smell of the sea air wafting over him was turning Menannon's head like fine wine. Until the ship had left port and gained the open sea six evenings ago, he had not realized just how homesick he had been or how much he missed the smell of the sea and the call of the gulls.

It had taken the best part of a fortnight to follow the road from Aridion City along the river Ari to Bridge Town and Koresh then north to Blue Bay, the port nearest the isle of Kalyria, his home and destination. He and several others of his fellow journeymen had set off the morning after graduation on a well-earned holiday before returning to the Master Hall in the fall. The majority of them would be posted to one of the far-flung harper halls that dotted greater Aridion, but some few, naught but a handful in fact, would be invited to stand the master's trials directly and of those, few would pass.

The harpers had joined a band of Dwarven traders to make the trip to Blue Bay. Upon reaching the port, all the rest save Menannon's best friend Leènoviilek, had taken ship for elsewhere. Menannon himself was heading east for the island of Kalyria and Lee, as his friends called the journeyman, had decided to accompany him, as that young gentleman had never seen the fabled island Menannon called home.

The great island lay in the midst of the Dawn Sea, a once mighty shield volcano that had long ago destroyed itself leaving behind a crescent-shaped island blessed by fertile soil and a mild climate beneficial for growing all crops, both good for food and pleasing to the eye. The white spires and golden roofs of its capital city, Kirith Kalyria, shone out from that island like a beacon, even in the darkest watches of the night.

Menannon stepped up onto the lower beam of the railing. He could not help himself in his eagerness to be home. From this slight increase in his vantage point, he strained his eyes to the northeast, but saw only azure blue sky with wisps of white cloud on the horizon.

One of the crewmen, possessed of iron-grey hair and a grizzled, weather-beaten face, paused momentarily in his task of mending a cargo net. His green over-tunic marked him as a senior seaman in the Guild of Mariners & Docksmen, one of the only craft guilds in all Linden not owing allegiance to the Harpers' Guild.

"Laddie, even if ya had the eyes of a drakta, ya wouldn't see it for at least a twoday more." the old fellow teasingly informed him. "If the wind holds, with this followin' sea, we'll have ya there by sunset on the third day hence."

Menannon stepped back onto the rolling deck, his high cheekbones coloring slightly.

At the sight of his blush, the old sailor laughed outright, his clear, blue eyes twinkling good-naturedly. "Do'na be ashamed lad. 'Tis normal to long for the sight of home. How long ya been gone?"

"Eight summers and a threeday," Menannon said without even having to think about it.

" 'Tis a long time, that. What ya been doin'? School, I'd warrant. From the look of ya, I'd say ya can't be more'n about twenty summers now."

"Nineteen, actually. I just finished my journeyman's training at the Master Harper Hall in Aridion City."

"So, 'tis a Harper ya are, then. A right honorable profession is that." The sailor nodded approvingly. "What ya specialize in? The drums?" he asked, tapping out a quick rhythm on one of the packing crates beside him.

"Nah," a new voice broke into the conversation.

Menannon and the sailor turned to see Lee coming towards them. Despite the heat, he still wore his brown Harper's robe over his clothes with his solid brown journeyman's cord prominent on his right shoulder marking him for a drummer in the guild. Menannon, however, had shed his harper's over-robe leaving himself dressed only in the loose-fitting white chemise, black hose and knee-high soft leather-laced boots which he normally wore underneath.

"He's a Jack," said Lee, grinning wickedly at Menannon, his white smile in stark contrast to his dark skin. His wine-dark eyes were alight with mischief. The light of the midday sun, highlighting his full-lipped mouth and hawk-like nose, showed that his dark brown hair cut warrior short was as curly as a new wool clip. All of these things marked him as being from the young city state of Crenanoc located far to the south beyond the

Watheran Wastes on the southernmost tip of greater Aridion, a city famous for its healers and horses.

"What's a 'Jack'?" The myriad lines around the sailor's eyes deepened in puzzlement.

"Why, a Jack-of-all-trades, of course." The drummer made himself comfortable on a crate near Menannon. "He couldn't make up his mind, so he specialized in all the arts of the hall and made journeyman in all of them."

"Some talent, is that." The old fellow whistled admiringly, slightly in awe of this young prodigy.

"Nah, in his case, it's just bull-headed determination." Lee grinned at Menannon who returned him a playfully disgusted look.

"I love you, too, Drum Journeyman Leènoviilek. Besides, I didn't specialize in everything. I'm not a harp healer."

The drummer turned back to the sailor. "Harp healing's not something you can learn," he said. "The High One either gifts you with the talent or He doesn't. The Harpers just help you perfect it. So he didn't have any choice in that one, but I still saw him going into the healer classes, so he at least knows the theory even if he can't practice the art. You mark my words, this boy is going to be Grandmaster Harper one of these bright days! Then the High One help us all, 'cause he'll expect all of us to be as overly conscientious as he is." Lee had himself barely scraped through the other required classes in history, lore, and the arts, due not to a lack of intelligence, but rather to a general lack of interest. His heart and love was for music and drumming alone and all else went in one ear and out the other and was not missed.

"I'm not overly conscientious. I just respect my guild."

"Oh, sure you do and didn't I see not only your harp in your kit, but your notes for studying for the Master's trials as well? And those aren't to be held until next June. And you're supposed to be on holiday and are under strict orders from Grandmaster Blackmore himself to relax and get drunk every night." Lee winked at the sailor.

Menannon snorted and shook his head at that suggestion. "He did not include 'get drunk every night' in that order!"

"Yes, he did," Lee assured the old sailor, who was very much enjoying the verbal sparring between the two. "And what, may I ask, is wrong with relaxing and getting drunk?" This last he addressed to the old salt.

"Nothin' I can think of." The old fellow grinned back.

"You see? He agrees with me." Lee turned back to Menannon. "So?"

Menannon leaned back against the railing and cast another quick glance to the northeast before answering. "Well, I can think of two very good reasons. The first is that I'm a Giant and Giants don't get drunk and secondly and far more importantly, my father would hurt me."

"And why should that make you cry off?" the drummer queried with great glee.

"You've not seen my father, my friend, or you'd not even think such a thing, much less voice it."

"So, yer a Giant, lad? I was wonderin'." The sailor finished his work and shoved a crate over and sat on it then pulled an old battered pipe from his belt pouch and began to fill and light it as he studied Menannon thoughtfully. "I was taken ya for a Teluri with as tall and fine built as ya are. Yer a sight handsomer than most Giants I've met and I've met my share." The old fellow pointed his pipe stem at Menannon and winked at him.

"I spent a winter in New Belitarra once. That there's a whole village of Giants inland from Gormidad. I'm not sayin' that Giants ain't a good lookin' folk, 'cause they're as good lookin' as any other folk and some of them New Belitarra lassies are downright breath terminatin', but you're better lookin' than any of the other fellows I've seen and you're a darn sight sh...." The old fellow gulped a bit and sort of mumbled to a halt, then took a long pull on his pipe. Menannon and Lee exchanged a grin.

"It's all right, you can say it ... I am a 'darn sight shorter' than any other full-grown Giant you've e'er seen." Menannon's smile lit his entire face, his black eyes twinkling.

"I was meanin' no offence, lad."

"And none was taken, sir, I assure you. Truth is truth and cannot give offence. I personally don't find my lack of height a problem, though what my father will think, I cannot say." Menannon glanced away a bit uncomfortably, then shrugged and looked back. "I can only hope he is not too disappointed at my size, as I am the same as when last he saw me, though I am three summers older."

"Disappointed!" the drummer burst out, incredulous. "The High One in glory, Menannon! You're as tall as a tree and as solid as a mountain. What more could he possibly desire?"

"Didn't you pay attention to the teaching scrolls? If you had, you would know that for my folk, I'm about the size of a half-grown lad of, say, thirteen summers. As our good sailor here will tell you, I'm a midget." He glanced at the sailor who nodded in agreement, a bit embarrassed at the admission.

"A midget? Surely you jest!" Lee's question came out a cross between a snort of disbelief and a chuckle.

"No," Menannon assured him with a serious shake of his head.

"Aye, he's tellin' ya the High One's own truth, lad."

"My father stands a full fifteen feet, three inches tall and he's just barely above average. I, on the other hand, stand exactly nine feet tall and that is two and a half feet shorter than the shortest Giant heretofore ever recorded. To give you a true idea of how tall my father is, consider this: you have about six feet in height, correct?"

"Six feet and two." Lee agreed, intrigued.

"All right, if you stood on top of my head and stretched up to your full height you would just about be able to look my father in the eye. Even on his knees, he's still over two feet taller than I." There was a long silence then as the three of them contemplated Menannon's words. Overhead, a gull flashed white in the sun as it wheeled and swung above the ship.

"A Giant from Kalyria." The old sailor mumbled to himself as he drew thoughtfully on his pipe. "A Giant from Kalyria ...." Suddenly, his eyes got big and he took the pipe stem from between his teeth and pointed it at Menannon.

"Yer Lord Gorlanndon's lad! By the Great Hornèd Orlandine, I've actually been talkin' to Lord Gorlanndon's heir an' I ne'er tumbled ...." His grin turned to a look of horror and he jumped to his feet as though he had been stung.

" 'Tis sorry I am to be sittin' without permission and bein' so informal. I'm beggin' yer pardon, me Lord."

The fellow's words nearly tumbled over each other in his haste to apologize for acting so in the presence of such an august personage as this young passenger. Beside him, Lee was staring at him in stunned surprise and Menannon could not decide whether to laugh or cringe.

"What are you talking about, man, not sitting in his presence? He's just a Journeyman Harper even if he is a rather tall one," Lee burst out.

"Nay, lad!" the old fellow interrupted him. "He's the heir of the First Councillor of Kalyria, the finest, most powerful trader in all the Dawn Sea. There ain't a sailor in these parts as what wouldn't give his left hind leg to be sailin' for Lord Gorlanndon. Why, lad, yer friend here is a prince, e'en if he don't have a crown. And ya'd best be treatin' him with the respect due his station on this ship!" the old sailor snapped.

"No, please...," Menannon began, but the sailor had puffed himself up with importance and was backing away with a salute.

"I'll just go an inform Cap'n and make sure Cook does us proud by ya." He nearly ran down the deck, calling for his mates, leaving Menannon and Lee to look after him in some consternation. Finally, Lee turned to his friend, one quizzical eyebrow raised.

"As I said, my father is very impressive." Menannon shrugged with a somewhat sheepish grin and led the way back towards the stern of the ship to prepare for what he knew was going to be a luncheon with the captain fit for royalty.

"A prince, the man said," observed Lee as they walked, "a prince! You? A prince?" Lee could not hide the laughter in his voice, nor did he try. Menannon's blush was all he needed to burst out in a full guffaw. "A prince! Now, that is rich. Wait 'til the gang back at the Hall hears this!"

Menannon just shot him a glare, which set Lee off even more, but he contained himself as they neared the stern and the captain's quarters. The meal went exactly as Menannon expected, and he could not free himself from the stiff formalities quickly enough.

THE MORNING OF THE THIRD DAY after his conversation with the old sailor found Menannon again standing on the bow rail, his eyes glued to the eastern horizon, squinting into the newly risen sun for a first glimpse of his home. In truth, though he was fond of his native island and preferred it to any other place he had lived or visited, it was his sire who was drawing on his heart so strongly. Since the hour they had come forth from Lornennog, they had been inseparable companions and friends. While it had been a great honor to be sent to the Master Hall for his training, the separation from his beloved sire had been the hardest trial yet in Menannon's young life and it had not improved over time.

Gorlanndon had made it a point to bring his flagship into port at Blue Bay and rendezvous there with his son during spring holiday each of the first five summers Menannon had spent in Aridion City. Then affairs at home had kept him close to Kalyria and he came no more to Blue Bay. This lack had begun to prey on Menannon's mind, filling him with a mounting anxiety he was not free to assuage in person. Menannon had received and sent many a letter, but naught else for the best part of three summers. The thing which loomed largest in his mind as a cause of his unease was the fact that his sire had not been able to attend his graduation, a failure that was wholly unlike him. The families of Lee and several others had even come all the way from far southern Crenanoc for the occasion, an arduous trip of many fortnights. Gorlanndon had explained his absence quite logically, if a bit too glibly. Now, however, Menannon was free to find out for himself whether or no all was well with his sire and his city.

As he reluctantly stepped back down onto the deck once more, a small voice within whispered to him, branding him a liar, telling him that it was not only his sire who concerned him. Nay, it told him, there was someone else ....

Without any willing on his part, deep purple eyes seemed to suddenly look back at him from the eastern horizon, eyes which had haunted his sleep and disturbed his waking hours all the long summers he had been gone, proving there was someone else on Kalyria who had a claim on his heart: Nirna. At the thought of her, his pulse quickened, leaving him in no doubt that his feelings for his former playmate were still there and, it seemed, stronger than he had realized. She was like a sister to him, and perhaps something more.... He halted his thoughts there, unwilling to take them further, firmly forcing himself to look across the waves again towards the horizon, towards home and his sire. Yet her face and her name intruded upon him, distracting him. Nirna...Nirna. Forever in his heart, yet never to be his.

Nirna was Human, and more, she was the Princess Royal of Kalyria and as such, far beyond his reach by both law and custom, though that had never stopped them being childhood friends and playmates. Now, however, both were adults and so this homecoming was going to be, well, a bit complicated. Despite that, Menannon was determined to see Nirna as soon as civilly possible. It would have to wait a few days, of course, until he could politely leave Lee to his own devices, as there was no possible way he was going to re-acquaint himself with his dearest childhood friend with another dear friend along. It would not be fair to either one of them.

It lacked but a little of mid-day when the sailor at the masthead finally called down, "Land! Land to the east, me lord." It had gotten around the ship like wildfire that Menannon was Gorlanndon of Kalyria's son and heir and he had been treated like royalty ever since, much to his embarrassment, but out of respect for his sire, he had born their attitude with good grace. The ship's master had accorded Menannon and Lee every courtesy, for he would not have it said that he failed in his duty to such a respected competitor as Gorlanndon. Besides, such failure might well have a very negative impact on the shipowner's business and thus on his own employ and he hadn't gotten where he was through lack of acumen.

"Where away?" Menannon called back. He stepped up onto the rail again and strained his eyes eastward.

"Ten degrees nor' east," came the answer and the Giant turned his gaze quickly in the direction given. Though his vision was sharper than a Human's, the curve of the world itself prevented him seeing what the sailor above could see. He waited impatiently, his gaze glued to the mark until at last he saw it: a dark smudge on the horizon like a low-lying cloud. He remained where he was for the greater part of the day watching as the island grew larger until it nearly filled the entire eastern horizon, floating like a great bird upon the waves.

"Well, I'd say we've almost reached our destination," Lee observed coming to the rail beside him. "What do you intend to do first when we reach port?"

"Report to my father, of course," Menannon said.

"Report to your sire? That's a rather odd way of putting it." Lee gave the Giant a quizzical look. Menannon grinned rather sheepishly.

"It's a holdover from the first time I sailed with him. I'd be skylarking in the rigging or something like when I was supposed to be studying or doing my chores. It never failed. I'd just get comfortably settled to watch for the albatross and I'd hear the first mate holler, 'Menannon! I see you! Report yourself to your sire, young man!' I've reported to him ever since then."

"So what would he do when you reported?" Lee could not help a grin at the thought of the responsible-to-a-fault Menannon ever being caught skylarking, even as a young boy.

The Giant could not help a slight rise in color at the memory of his child's self approaching his sire's cabin as though it were a drakta's lair. He cleared his throat and grinned.

"I'd go to his cabin with my knees knocking together. He'd be sitting at his desk writing in his ledgers. He'd stop and look at me. Never said a word—just looked at me—then he would motion me in and I'd sort of sidle up to his desk and he'd pick me up and stand me on an old parrot's perch he had in the corner so I could look him in the eye. He'd just sit there in his big chair and look at me, then he would get the most bitterly disappointed look on his face and my heart would drop into my boots and I'd start to cry and promise I'd try to be better. He'd nod as though we had just hand sealed a bargain, then start to turn away to go back to work, but he would always turn back. He'd grin and hold out his hands and I'd jump into his arms and he'd give me a great hug then stick me under his arm like a rolled up piece of vellum and stand up as straight as he could, given the low ceiling, and head for the door. Just as we were about to leave the cabin, he'd stop and look at me and say, "So, did you see the albatross?" and I'd have to tell him I hadn't, but then I'd assure him as how I would keep looking and he'd laugh his great laugh and we'd go out to the deck and he would get me settled to my work or studies."

There was a music in Menannon's voice Lee had never heard before as the Giant spoke of his sire. For just a moment, the drummer could not help a twinge of jealousy. He had a loving family complete with three mothers, five brothers and three sisters, but there was a closeness between Menannon and his sire Lee had never experienced and could only imagine what it must be like. He shook off his momentary lapse as being both unworthy and undeserved and grinned up at his friend.

"So, did you ever see the albatross?"

"No," Menannon chuckled, "but it wasn't for a lack of watching."

"Why were you looking for the blasted bird anyway?"

"Well, my father told me on our very first voyage together if I could spot the albatross over sea water, good luck would be ours for that voyage and always, because it would mean the High One was paying particular attention to us, but I think he just said it because I was a bit seasick and rather frightened of being surrounded by so much water, so he gave an imaginative five-summers old child something else to think about." Menannon could not help coloring slightly again at this memory.

Lee had to chuckle over that thought and went back to watching as details of the island begin to sort themselves from the general mass on the horizon.

The tip of Kalyria's Crown, the highest point of the island, was the first feature to stand out. It was the remnant of the last of the six original volcanic peaks that had formed the ancient island and it stood thirteen thousand four hundred fifty and eight feet above the surrounding sea. Next to appear was the great rampart of the Marble Cliffs that enclosed the Fields of Morr, the best ground for tillage on the entire island. The ship began its swing south and east to skirt the island and enter the mooring basin fronting Kirith Kalyria on the southern shore.

The captain kept his vessel well out from the land, as there were sunken ledges and pinnacles like teeth surrounding the entire visible landmass. The sun was casting long shadows beyond the bow of the ship by the time they cleared the western reaches of the Plain of Pelar and the City itself came into view.

Lee caught his breath in wonder. Two white towers flanked the mooring basin's mouth, set atop the Crescent which formed a natural breakwater for the city, their roofs, made of the finest gold, glittered blindingly in the setting sun. Beyond, the city seemed to well-nigh burn with white light as the sun's rays reflected from the gold and silver veined marble used in its construction where it lay like a richly woven carpet draped across the four hills upon which the city was built. There were so many ships within the mooring basin it looked as though an entire phalanx of clouds had settled down to the land. Even coming from a port city himself, Lee had never seen anything like this place. Beside him, Menannon was grinning slightly, enjoying his friend's reaction to his homeland.

"Beautiful, isn't it?" he murmured softly so as not to break the drummer's mood.

"Beautiful?" Lee turned shining eyes on the Giant. "To say Kirith Kalyria is beautiful is like saying the Throne of the High One is a middling tall hill rather than the highest mountain in Aridion! The tales do not do this place justice. The High One in glory! It's gorgeous!"

"Aye, that it is!"

They stood in silence for several moments, enjoying the sight of the city as it drew closer until they could just make out the green of trees and riotous patches of color marking the gardens and streets. Color and life were everywhere, all highlighted to perfection in the last golden rays of the setting sun.

The High One help me, it's good to be home. Menannon had to blink a mist from his eyes. He looked away quickly so Lee would not see the momentary lapse in his demeanor. He turned back again to the land and the city before them and looked hungrily up to the top of its westernmost hill, his eyes glued to the spot where he knew his sire's villa stood within its walled close and garden, though he could not yet distinguish it. There was a brief flash of light as though the sun had just glinted off from a newly cleaned window. Menannon stiffened and strained his eyes. Yes! There it was again! He lunged onto the rail and stretched up as high as he could and raised his hand in a salute.

"What's happening? Who are you waving to?" Lee looked hard to see what had caused his friend to suddenly wave at the city.

"My father!"

The joy on Menannon's face was breathtaking. Lee could not help an answering grin, but he was still puzzled.

"How can he possibly see you at this distance? We are just barely able to see the buildings of the city."

"Do you see that flashing?" Menannon pointed. Lee strained his eyes, but saw only the glitter of the city itself.

"Where?" he demanded.

"Up there to the left. Do you see it? There!" Menannon raised another salute, this time with both hands. "Do you see the flashing like the sun glinting from a window?" Lee followed along Menannon's pointing arm and finally caught the tiny flashes to which his friend was referring. They did indeed resemble sunlight glinting from newly cleaned glass.

"How could he possibly see you from there? It would be a wonder if he can even see this ship yet," Lee asked, incredulous.

"He is using his long-vision instrument" Menannon kept his gaze locked on the top of the hill from which the light still flashed intermittently.

"His what?" By now, Lee was beginning to believe his friend was having him on. Yet the look on Menannon's face was such a mixture of joy and relief he had to be serious.

Menannon looked down at his friend and grinned rather self-consciously and schooled his face back to the calm mien a gentleman was expected to display, but he just could not keep the sparkle out of his eyes.

"My father invented what he calls a Longseeker. It's like a series of spectacle lenses put together in a long metal tube which allows you to focus on distant objects and see them as though they were nearly within hand's reach. Each lens by itself can be used to make small things look large. As a child I was punished several times for taking the lenses in their metal circlets out of the tube and putting them over my eyes and holding them there with my cheek muscles to study tiny things like ants and beetles. In self defense and to prevent damage to an important tool, my father gave me some circles of glass and taught me how to grind lenses for myself. I used to be quite good at it."

Lee could not help a derisive snort at this. At the harper hall, it was positively axiomatic that there was nothing that Menannon was not 'quite good at.'

Beside him, Menannon grinned self-consciously at Lee's reaction and hurried on with his explanation. "When he's at home, my father keeps the Longseeker in the summerhouse behind his villa so he can watch his trading ships come and go from the mooring basin below the city. When he moves it just right, the sun flashes off from the last lens. See? Like that! He's still watching us." Menannon turned his attention back to the distant point of light.

"I'm coming, my father," he whispered. "I'm almost home."

Lee carefully hid his grin, not wanting Menannon to know he had overheard what was obviously a very private comment. Lee could not help turning his gaze from Menannon's intense face to the top of the far hill and back the entire time their ship was making its way beneath the mighty lighthouses and into the mooring basin alive with maritime traffic. The light continued to flash as they approached, proving beyond the shadow of a doubt someone up on that hill was as interested in their progress as they were interested in progressing.

It took a full turn of the hour more before their ship was able to tie up at a public wharf. Gorlanndon had his docks in another section of the mooring basin where others among the larger merchants had their private docks, wharves and warehouses. The deck came alive with activity as the crew saw to setting the ship to rights and the rest of the passengers gathered at the gangway to disembark. Lee gave Menannon a salute and went back to gather his belongings. The wharf whirled with activity and color as bearers came with sedan chairs and litters to escort returning masters and mistresses to their estates or sell their services to others and all other manner of sailors, hawkers, family, friends and total strangers came out to greet the ship and the rest of its passengers and crew.

Home at last!

CHAPTER 2
(SUMMER OF THE WORLD 6996)

MENANNON STOOD FOR A MOMENT undecided as to whether he should go back and get his belongings or disembark. A voice broke in on his thoughts and he turned to find the sailor of the cargo net grinning up at him.

"I told ya as we'd have ya here by sunset today, lad." The old sailor winked at him, then remembering himself, saluted. "Can we be of any further service to ya, me lord?"

"Well, actually, could you see my friend's kit and mine transferred to my sire's villa for me ...?" Menannon began, but the fellow cut him off with an even wider grin.

" 'Cause ya'll be makin' the trip up to the top circles that much the faster if yer not burdened with yer belongin's. Right ya are. I'll see to it personal and I'll make sure to hire a chair for yer friend as soon as he gets himself together, me lord."

The relieved smile on Menannon's face was all the thanks the old sailor needed. With a hasty 'thank you,' The youngster whirled and taking advantage of his great height, simply vaulted over the railing and landed with a thud on the wharf causing a small dark-haired girl selling flowers to shriek and nearly drop her basket.

Menannon dropped to one knee and steadied her with a quick hand. Her green eyes welled up with tears and her small chin began to quiver, but then something in the smile and slight wink Menannon gave her reassured the child and she smiled back at him. The little entrepreneur recovered quickly and held out a bouquet of freshly cut flowers. Menannon's smile widened and he reached a coin out of his belt pouch and deftly exchanged it for the flowers in her small hand. Her eyes got big with wonder as she looked at the coin and she immediately began to dig for change in the belt pouch of a rusty brown kirtle at least a size too big, but Menannon shook his head and gave her another wink, carefully tucked the flowers into his belt, stood and ran for the land, dodging the folk about the wharf. The entire transaction had been carried on in total silence.

Despite the growing darkness, the wide avenues leading up through the seven circles of the city were awash with shoppers and strollers, entertainers and those seeking entertainment. Members of the city guard were going about to ensure safety—more out of tradition than of necessity—and to open the Dwarf lanterns hanging from posts all along the avenues. Soon the main streets were as brightly lit as they were in daylight as the night life of the city got underway.

Even had there existed a conveyance capable of transporting even a small Giant such as he through the narrow, winding streets, Menannon was too impatient for such a slow mode of travel, so perforce he sallied forth on foot, dodging foot traffic, sedan chairs, porters and all manner of other folk on his way to the top of the Citadel, Kirith Kalyria's central hill where stood the government buildings and the Royal Palace, ancient home of the kings and queens of the Kalyrian Empire. From its lofty height, great bridges arched across to the other three hills: the Equian, whose heights and sides bore the great villas, orchards and vineyards of the city's wealthiest folk; the Idrian, where the main craft halls of the arts were found including the Harper hall—here also stood the great halls of the university founded by the Preceptors, a branch of the Harpers who specialized in the higher education of the sciences, engineering, husbandry and herb lore—and the Aureun, whose crown was graced by the great pleasure gardens of Kalyria, open to and adored by all the city's citizens..

Many was the hour Menannon had spent there as a beginning harper apprentice, using its exotic flora as subjects to practice the arts of illumination and painting. He also from time to time enjoyed the various entertainments to be found there, the outdoor concerts provided by the journeymen harpers from the local harper hall being his favorite, although, if pressed, he would admit to enjoying the jugglers and mummers almost as much. The Aureun was also the site of most of the larger trade halls of Kalyria's wealthiest businessmen including Menannon's sire.

The rest of the great city swirled about the lower reaches and the feet of her hills in walled concentric circles filling every available space with the houses, gardens, trade halls, shops, pubs and inns of its inhabitants. At least one road from each of the four hills had its terminus at the harbor, but the length of them varied with the shape and height of the hill. The main road up the Citadel was by far the shortest way to the top, as it switchbacked up the hill rather than spiraled around it as did the roads up the other three. From the top of the Citadel, it was an easy and quick route over the bridge to his sire's villa on the Equian.

He gained the top level of the Citadel in less time than it took to think about it, but it seemed to him an age and he nearly threw himself through the front gate of the wall surrounding the central plaza. He could not have made the trip at anything less than a flat out run if his very life had depended upon it.

"Here now! Slow down and show some respect." One of the doorwards, the light from the twin presence lamps in their accustomed glory on the pediment above the many pillared portico of the Council Hall glittering from his black and gold fish scale armour, stepped from his post at the lower steps of the Council hall and took him to task for his unseemly haste in such an august place. These lamps—the Eyes of the High One—had burned unceasingly since the city's foundations were laid, symbolizing the love of the High One for the people of Kalyria and they for Him. Their light was kindled by the High One Himself and no will save His alone could extinguish them.

Obediently, the Giant slowed almost to a walk and saluted the lamps as was proper, but he did not break stride as he went past the Council hall and the Queen's palace, where he could not help a quick glance at the lowest tower at the top of which where Nirna's chambers. The window at its top was alight. She was within. It was all he could do not to turn aside and go and throw pebbles at her window to get her attention as had been his wont as a boy, but the vigilance of the guards and the knowledge that his sire awaited him kept him to his course.

He passed the smaller government buildings and the monumental statuary reflecting the long history of Kalyria and was soon out the gate in the back wall of the plaza and off to the Mathematical Bridge at the western side of the hill at a dead run once more and hurled himself across the airy span to the crossroad where the Equian's three great avenues met. The central one went on up to the Equian's lofty height and the other twain went down, one to the left and the other to the right. Without a glance at the others, Menannon ran along the wide tree-lined central avenue winding between the high stone walls enclosing the gardens and buildings of the city's greatest villas.

He turned a last corner, breathing hard, and saw the high stone wall of his sire's close, but found to his surprise that the great wooden gate was closed and locked. This was very odd, for ever had it remained open to the street without fear of intrusion of any kind, for Kalyria was under the Peace of the High One, and crime was virtually non-existent. He slid to a halt in front of the gate and for the first time in his life, pulled the rope of the signal bell to be admitted to his own home. In his surprise and impatience, he pulled so hard he nearly pulled it down. The deep booming sound of the ancient bell echoed inside and in response, an embrasure opened in the center of the gate.

"Who goes?" a voice demanded as a gleaming Dwarf lantern was thrust through the opening to illuminate the visitor.

The porter looked out and then up and up again. There was a stunned silence for about half a heartbeat then the fellow's eyes rounded with surprise and delight.

"Master Menannon? The High One's holy tears, it's good to see you again!"

The fellow withdrew the lantern and slammed shut the

opening. Menannon could hear him yelling at the top of his lungs, "Master Menannon's at the gate!" even as the chains clanked and the main gate swung open.

"Come in, young Master!"

The porter proved to be none other than his sire's steward Skendrin, though why he should be acting as porter was a mystery which Menannon did not have the luxury of considering as the steward took hold of his arm and nearly yanked him through the gate in his pleasure.

"As The High One's my witness, you're a sight for sore eyes, lad!"

Menannon found himself confronted by the smiling face of one of his sire's longest serving employees. Skendrin's iron grey head came nearly to the center of the young Giant's chest as he was well over six feet in height. He was a lean-framed, long-limbed Human whose very leanness belied the sinewy muscles as strong as steel earned in a lifetime of serving aboard Gorlanndon's trading ships now hidden beneath his rather outlandishly decorated kirtle of orange and purple. Skendrin had reluctantly returned to dry land upon the death of his own sire who had served the Giant as his last steward.

"How do you know who I am?" Menannon could not help asking, as no one here at home had laid eyes on him since he had left for Aridion City eight summers since.

"Well, for one thing, we've been expecting you, ya young scamp! Your father sent word down to the house hours ago. And if that isn't enough, trust your own to always know ya. You don't have pointy ears, so you're not a Teluri and besides, you're too stocky for one of them anyways and you're too big to be anyone else. And you're the spitting image of your sire. Think, man! Your sire's been watching for you for the last twoday. He's in the summerhouse still. Been there for hours. 'Send him up when he arrives,' Himself said, and so I have. Now, go!"

Skendrin tugged him into the rapidly filling courtyard with cheering servants and liegemen all crowding in. Menannon found himself being greeted from all sides by folk he had known virtually all his life.

Gorlanndon's villa was actually fairly modest in size for the Giant, but for anyone else it would have been a major sprawling hall. Built of marble and roofed with slate, the central section's single story was thirty feet high held up by what appeared to be a forest of pillars, starting with those of the front portico. The left wing was far shorter, as it was built to accommodate guests of other races of whom there was never a lack in the Giant's home. His trading empire encompassed all the known world of Linden and trading partners from far lands were often guests in this house. In fact, a trader from the Heavenly Isles on the far side of Greater Aridion on the edge of the Dusk Sea was currently in residence, though he was departing in a twoday. The right wing housed the family chambers. Gorlanndon's therein at times doubled as an office. At the back, hard by the kale yard, were the kitchen, opulent servants quarters, the stillroom and all other chambers necessary to running a great house. On the near side of the courtyard, close to the gate, were the sheds, workshops and a large dwelling which was home to the Steward and his family. While Gorlanndon referred to the dwelling as a 'cottage,' it would have served as a villa to a wealthy landholder had it stood in its own courtyard. The close's ten acres were enclosed within a fine stone wall twenty feet high. Gorlanndon's home was the largest villa within the confines of Kirith Kalyria.

Menannon's gaze immediately jumped over the many pillared bulk of the villa, past the small orchard behind it to the top of the rocky knoll that had been included within Gorlanndon's close. There, glinting in the light of multiple Dwarf lanterns hanging from its eaves, was a structure that nearly resembled stone filigree, so delicately were its silver-veined marble walls carved. Its blinds and shutters were standing open to the sea breezes on all sides and it was roofed with sheet copper. To Human eyes, it would look a small tower, but for Gorlanndon, it was naught but a serviceable gazebo. The Giant had built it for his lady wife Julianna as her special retreat where she whiled away golden hours painting and writing poetry. When she had declined to return to Kalyria from Lornennog after Menannon's birth, Gorlanndon had claimed the summerhouse for his own special place and rare and privileged was the visitor who was allowed to wait upon him there.

It was just dark enough that Menannon could not see within, but his heart told him that his beloved sire was indeed still there and waiting for him. He started across the courtyard at a run, but brought himself up short and turned back, remembering to alert Skendrin to Lee's impending arrival accompanied by their equipage. He was surprised to see that the gate was flanked inside by gate wardens wearing tunics of his sire's colors of red and yellow over which they bore breastplates of beaten red kelandar, an incredibly hard and nearly priceless metal made by the Dwarves, with greaves and bracers of the same. At their belts they bore long, serviceable swords and each had a heavy ash-shafted spear leaning against the wall near at hand. The sight of such obvious protection caused Menannon to wonder anew just what exactly was happening on Kalyria, but he shook the thought aside and addressed Skendrin.

"A friend of mine with my kit is following me. Will you make sure to let him in and send him up to the summerhouse? Oh, and would you see that these are put in water and set in my sire's chamber?" Menannon took the flowers from his belt and handed them to Skendrin.

"Aye, young Master. All will be seen to. Now, get along. Your sire's waiting," Skendrin admonished him.

Menannon did not need to be told twice and he whirled away to throw himself around the villa and take the stairs up the hillside three at a time. At the top, he had crossed almost halfway across the level to the summerhouse when a huge figure burst soundlessly from it and traversed the space still separating them in two strides. Gorlanndon threw himself to his knees and took his son in his arms in a hard embrace that almost crushed the breath out of Menannon and well-nigh cracked his ribs. For just a moment, Gorlanndon held Menannon off at arms length to look him over with a quick glance, making sure there was nothing amiss with him, then he crushed him to his breast again and held him hard, whispering his name over and over. It was true dark before Gorlanndon could bring himself to loose his hold on his son and sit back on his heels to look him in the eyes.

"If I tried for a thousand summers, I could not begin to tell you how much I've missed you, boy!" The elder Giant had to clear his throat and blink several times against the mist clouding his vision.

"And I you, my Father!" Menannon nearly whispered, equally overcome with emotion at seeing his sire once again.

"Come! Come inside."

Gorlanndon stood and motioned his son to follow him. They reached the summerhouse and Gorlanndon went immediately to unshutter the Dwarf lantern hanging from the center of the ceiling. The light flashed from the polished tube of the Longseeker he had left on its stand at the window when he had emerged to greet his son.

The summerhouse had not changed in all the summers Menannon had been away. It still contained a large cupboard which held Gorlanndon's scrolls, codices and other oddments he used in his retreat and whose doors were painted with a delightful scene of children playing in a sunlit garden. The center of the room was dominated by a huge marble table set at the right height for the elder Giant to sit at comfortably. Thus it's top was nearly level with Menannon's chest. The whole was circled by a wooden bench made in movable sections all of which were far too high for any other than Gorlanndon to sit on comfortably. In the past, Menannon had spent many happy hours sitting on the table's top watching his sire work with his various inventions or listening to stories of the elder days of Linden read from the many volumes of lore housed in Gorlanndon's private library. Ever before, he had only been able to reach the top with his sire's help, but now he cast a quick glance and judged that with a running start he would be able to vault onto it unaided. His attention came back to the business at hand when his sire spoke.

"Pull the blinds, boy, and have a seat," Gorlanndon said over his shoulder.

"I would, if I could reach them."

Menannon spoke softly, his chest tightening with dread as the moment he had feared for the past three summers finally arrived. Ever since the hour he had realized that he was going to get no taller than nine feet, Menannon had feared his sire's disappointment.

Gorlanndon stopped and turned to look at him anew. Menannon indicated his own size with a self-deprecating shrug. For just a moment, Gorlanndon stood silently, truly considering him for the first time, having in the excitement of his son's arrival paid scant attention to aught but the boy's presence. Then he threw back his head and began to laugh.

At first, Menannon winced at the sound, but then he realized that what he had taken for mockery was but the sound of pure, unadulterated joy. His sire was actually laughing joyfully and so hard he had to sit down on one of the benches and wipe his eyes with a large handkerchief he pulled from his belt pouch. It took the elder Giant three tries before he could stop laughing enough to actually string two words together.

"Boy, you're perfect!" he finally managed to wheeze between guffaws.

He stood and lowered the blinds himself then sat back on the bench and waved Menannon over. The younger Giant came wordlessly and stood in front of his sire, well-nigh at attention. His mind reeled with confusion at his beloved parent's reaction to him for of all those he had envisioned, laughter had not been one of them. The look on his son's face sobered Gorlanndon instantly and he reached out and laid gentle hands upon his shoulders and looked deep into his eyes.

"I am so delighted to have you back, it never occurred to me that you should have attained your full height by now, boy," the elder Giant admitted with a slight heightening of his color. "I have that which I should have told you summers ago. Forgive me. I see by not telling you my secret, I have caused you needless anxiety. Just how tall are you?"

"Nine feet." The words came out in a cross between a gulp and a whisper.

"YES!! I thank Thee, High One, with all my heart!"

Gorlanndon could not help himself and he started to laugh again, hugging Menannon hard. When he finally gained some control over himself, he once again held his son off at arm's length.

"No, boy, I'm not crazed—even though from the look on your countenance, you're beginning to think so. Sit, sit. Here, on the table, so each may look upon the other so much the more comfortably."

Obediently, Menannon turned and took two running steps and was indeed able to vault onto the table. For several long moments, Gorlanndon sat with his eyes fixed on the closed blinds as though he could see in them a way to explain himself. While he thought, Menannon studied him.

The elder Giant was well fleshed, but not in anyway overly so, being a prime representative of his race. There was no trace of age about him beyond maturity despite his slightly more than two thousand summers of life. His hair was still the same blue-black as his son's, though he wore it considerably shorter than did Menannon so that it curled about his temples and over his forehead in lively abandon. He bore the same fine bone structure, broad forehead and high cheekbones with a slightly more beaked nose and a long, drooping mustache—adorned at each end with a single faceted bead of citrine—flowing about his full-lipped mouth. His midnight black eyes twinkled out from beneath thick, arching eyebrows nearly a match for Menannon's own, but there was a slight difference in that Gorlanndon's eyes were crinkled at the outer corners from staring out across a sun-sparkled sea for summers uncounted. His beard was worn close cropped, but less shaped than his son's, being allowed to grow farther up his cheeks and a bit more pointed at the chin. The Giant wore a sleeveless, thigh length kirtle of dark blue sorak, that costly cloth made from the cocoons of the fabled Blue Lantern beetle of Gormidad, much worked about its long neck closing and high collar with threads of gold and silver.

Beneath the kirtle, the long sleeves and the breast of Gorlanndon's white chemise showed in stark contrast. A wide, unadorned leather belt at his waist held a large belt pouch. Black hose and soft leather boots completed his attire. As Skendrin had observed, one look at Gorlanndon proved Menannon's paternity beyond all doubt. The two, save for Gorlanndon's size and Menannon's obvious youth, could almost have been twins.

Menannon found it interesting that his sire never wore the state robes of his office as First Councillor of Kalyria except when he was actually participating in a governmental function, being but newly come from the master harper hall in Aridion City where the robes of one's calling were worn at all times. His sire had always preferred, and obviously still did, to be taken for himself and not his office, a trait that Menannon heartily shared.

At last, Gorlanndon cleared his throat and looked up. "What I should have said is, you are the 'perfect' answer to my prayers."

"Why?" Menannon looked up into his sire's black eyes, seeking answers to his confusion. "Why would you pray that I would be a midget?"

"Not a midget. Never think of yourself as that. You're a blessing!" Gorlanndon shook his head, hastening to reassure his son that he in no way found him wanting in size. "Here is the way of it: when you and I came forth from Lornennog, I knew in my heart you would spend your entire life among the other races of Linden and not your own kind. You were small for a Giant child and I prayed then and every night since then, that you would stay small." Gorlanndon reached out and took

-47-

Menannon by the back of the neck and leaned down and kissed his brow.

"Menannon, I asked the High One to give you height sufficient that all would know you a true Giant, yet small as were the Giants of old to better fit into the world of greater Linden as the High One had intended. You see, Menannon, the High One created all folk to be comfortable in his world. We are the tallest of the races while the Dwarves are the shortest, yet of old both races were once sized to treat well with one another.

"You are a return to that. If you sit as you are now, you can treat with a standing Dwarf without either of you getting a crick in the neck, you from looking too far down or he from looking too far up. A Human could almost look you in the eye and you would actually have to look up slightly at an average Teluri. In other words, you personally fit comfortably into the High One's world with but a modicum of ducking and hunching. A Dwarf fits comfortably with only a bit of standing on step stools and climbing up ladders.

"Menannon, you are a true Giant who can walk through the door of a normal house and sit at a normal table to treat with any you choose in comfort and dignity. That is what I prayed for and the High One has answered me."

Gorlanndon's words were interrupted by Lee's voice coming up from the courtyard below.

"Menannon, are you up there?"

"Aye!" he called back, then turned to his sire, his mood lightening. "As I informed you in my letter, my dear friend and fellow journeyman, Lee, came home with me. May he come up and attend upon you?"

"By all means! Get him on up here." Gorlanndon's eyes twinkled with delight and not a little mischief, clearly anticipating the outsider's reaction to seeing a 'full sized' Giant for what was sure to be his first time.

"Come on up, Lee," Menannon called

The young Giant jumped down from his perch to open the

door and stood back, allowing Lee to enter. The drummer had made short work of attaining the summerhouse and already stood without.

"You folks live on the top of a mountain," he said to Menannon as he entered. He bore Menannon's pack, but his own and the greater part of their gear had been delivered to the courtyard below.

Menannon moved out of the way so he could make a proper introduction.

"Father, I present to you Leènoviilek of the House of Veriinal of Crenanoc, my best friend and fellow Harper."

"Welcome to my home, Leènoviilek of Crenanoc. You honor us with your presence," said Gorlanndon as he stood and gave a sweeping bow of welcome. "My home is yours and my staff yours to command."

Gorlanndon spoke softly, having long since mastered the art of modulating his voice for the comfort of his listener's ears. A full sized Giant's normal speaking voice would have been loud enough to leave any ears but those of another Giant ringing in distress.

Lee set down his burden and responded as required by protocol: "I am most honored, Sir. The High One bless this house and all that dwell within it." This benediction was followed by a graceful bow to his host.

It was to his undying credit that although his dark eyes did get a lot rounder than was their usual wont, he did not blanch at the sight of the awesome figure that was Gorlanndon. True, his voice did waver a bit, but he quickly recovered and continued normally, "I hope you don't mind my accompanying this scamp of yours."

"Not at all! Any friend of my son's is my friend as well. It is my honor to have the acquaintance of your sire, though I have not met him. I have corresponded with him both in my capacity as First Councillor of Kalyria and as a businessman. It is my pleasure to welcome his son into this place. Please, make yourself comfortable." Gorlanndon indicated the table. "It's easier for me to converse with you if you sit on the table."

"Oh, oh! Certainly." Lee immediately scrambled up onto one of the benches surrounding the table and from there to its top. He still felt incredibly small confronting the elder Giant. In fact, he had not felt this small since he had been able to ride about his family's pleasure garden astride his own sire's foot. He glanced out of the corner of his eye to where Menannon had moved to stand beside his pack and found himself heartily glad that his friend was a small Giant.

Menannon knelt and opened his pack and withdrew a large, heavily sealed scroll from its depths and handed it to his sire.

"Grandmaster Blackmore instructed me to give this to you the moment I arrived."

Gorlanndon opened the shutters on the Dwarf lantern farther and broke the seals on the scroll. The elder Giant had an amazingly delicate touch and, though the scroll was in fact too small for his comfortable use, he was able to unroll it with ease and turned its surface to the light. Blackmore had intentionally written his missive in a script several sizes larger than his normal hand so that Gorlanndon did not have to resort to his magnifying glass to read it.

While he read quietly for a few moments, Lee took the opportunity to glance up at the strange device providing light for the small chamber. He had never seen anything like it.

"It's a Dwarf lantern," Menannon's soft voice informed him. "They are lit by small crystals which glow of their own volition. The secret of their making is closely guarded by the Dwarves of Sythra and Garnet." The young Giant nodded to the lantern. "You'll notice that it gives no extra heat to the chamber as do candles and cressets."

Lee shook his head, knowing that this trip was going to be filled with wonders. He was suddenly doubly glad he had chosen to come along. He almost spoke again, but Gorlanndon's amused chuckle returned his attention to the elder Giant.

"He tells me, boy, to forbid you to study and do nothing but relax, since you possess the wit and skills to pass your master's trials with ease." Menannon's sire glanced up from the scroll with an appreciative grin for his talented son.

"He probably could, too," Lee nodded in agreement. Under their combined gaze, the object of these words turned beet red and glanced away uncomfortably.

"And if it is not against my will, he deems it to your benefit to get well and thoroughly drunk at least once while you're home ...."

"You see!" Lee crowed, interrupting Gorlanndon and pointing at Menannon, laughed gleefully. "I told you his orders were for you to get drunk!"

Gorlanndon shot the drummer an amused glance then continued, "He goes on to say you have been miserably homesick the entire time you've been in Aridion City and he fears you might not return thence to stand your master's trials and I'm to make certain that you do. For, he says, 'it would be a great tragedy if such a talent as his were wasted. Tell the lad if he wants to return to Kalyria after he has passed his trials, then I will post him to the harper hall there, but he has to return here this fall for at least eight months more'." Gorlanndon turned his gaze upon his son. "I'll send him a letter assuring him that you will be coming back in the fall, but for now, I think he has a very good idea. You do need to experience the 'Kiss of the Mistress,' as the Dwarves would say, so you'll know what it's like. Tomorrow evening, we'll sojourn to the Cokeyna and see if we can't get you well and thoroughly drunk." Gorlanndon smiled and laid his hand on his son's shoulder while he cast a wink at the drummer.

Later that night, after a goodly dinner and a semi-formal presentation to his sire's household, Menannon was left at the door of one of the larger sleeping chambers in the family wing of the villa. His sire had given him a silent kiss on the forehead and disappeared down the hall and around the corner to his own chamber. Menannon waited for the sound of his sire's door closing before he opened the chamber's door.

Within, much to his surprise, he found a chamber whose furnishings were exactly sized for him which answered the question as to why Skendrin had been late to dinner. Obviously the steward had been busy moving the best furniture from the chambers designed for the Teluri and setting up this chamber for his master's son.

Against the far wall was a long platform bed, made of rare blackwood from the jungles above Crenanoc, whose mattress was stuffed with down. The whole was heaped with feather pillows. On either side at the head were small blackwood tables adorned with graceful Dwarf lanterns whose shutters were open wide, bathing the chamber in clear, steady light. Just beyond the lefthand bedside table was a huge wardrobe of the same wood and at the bed's foot was an intricately carven clothes press. His few clothes and belongings had already been placed within the wardrobe and press save only his harp. This had been carefully left in its case and placed securely on his bed. A large fireplace occupied most of the near wall with a low marble topped hearth table topped and two comfortable chairs which completed the furnishings. The far wall was entirely made of sheet glass—a product unique to Kalyria—that had been formed into doors leading out into the family's pleasure garden. There were two small side doors made of solid oak, one leading to a private bathing chamber and the other to a small chamber lined with cases of scrolls and codices. Each sleeping chamber in the family wing and several of the guest chambers of Gorlanndon's villa were thus equipped with their own bathing chambers and libraries for the convenience of the occupants. These two doors and the rest of the walls and ceiling were covered in murals depicting ancient saga stories one of which included a flight of draktas circling overhead among painted clouds.

Menannon walked into the chamber and closed the door almost reverently. This had been his favorite place as a child and whenever he had been particularly good, his sire had let him play here amidst the almost breathing images of Linden's heroic past. The murals had, of course, been painted by his lady mother, which fact had only added to his childhood pleasure. He had expected to be housed in one of the Teluri guest chambers rather than being given such special attention. His heart warmed anew at his sire's love and thoughtfulness.

MENANNON SPENT THE NEXT DAY enjoying the pleasure of his sire's company and giving Lee the chance to accustom himself to the ways of Gorlanndon's household. The drummer had spent the greater part of the day in the chamber assigned him, claiming fatigue from the journey, but Menannon suspected that it was merely his friend's way of allowing him to spend this first day home alone with his sire, for which the young Giant was grateful.

The blue shadows of evening, however, found Lee totally recovered from his claimed fatigue and the three of them walking down the grand avenues to the harbor. At Gorlanndon's insistence, both young harpers wore their robes for the occasion.

Gorlanndon's small group this evening included four of his household guard in full armour who would await their master's pleasure outside the pub. It was the custom of Kalyria's wealthiest families to employ household guards from among the ranks of swords-for-hire, but Gorlanndon's guards and gate-wardens were not of that ilk. They were men who had long served him and had proven their loyalty to him many times over. This highly trained professional force was far more of a personal war band than mere guardsmen. Known as the Red Death from both the color of their armour and their skill at arms, they were known, respected—and greatly feared in some quarters—along all the coasts of the Dawn Sea.

The chosen destination for this evening's stroll was the Cokeyna, a small pub nestled between the city's wharfs and the tradesmen's warehouses. The Cokeyna had several claims to fame, one of which was that it had been built by the Dwarf, Kinrok of Garnet, a famous adventurer who had retired to Kalyria. He had built his pub to be "big enough to fit all me friends comfortable like" and so its single story consisted of a great hammer-beamed room that was open to the rafters a full thirty feet above the floor. Its door was twenty feet high and nearly that wide, but it opened with the slightest pressure due to the ingenious use of counter-weighted hinges. The entire wall on the seaward side was made of sheet glass yielding an uninterrupted view of the Crescent and its lighthouses. There were tables sized for all heights of customers and wares from all ports of call. The interior was almost garishly lit by a veritable galaxy of hanging Dwarf lanterns.

Despite these wonders, the Cokeyna's greatest claim to fame was volnaka, a distilled spirit made from potatoes and other, secret, ingredients which gave the drink its unique flavor. It was a specialty of the tiny village of Cromb on the far western side of Greater Aridion on the shore of the Dusk Sea. It was rarely exported, and, in fact, the Cokeyna was the only place outside of Cromb where it could be obtained on a regular basis thanks to a trade agreement that Gorlanndon had arranged on behalf of Kinrok. The spirit did a remarkable job of getting anyone drunk with alacrity. It also worked well as a combustible in lamps, as paint remover, was a marvelous antiseptic and was singularly effective at erasing any memory of ever having imbibed it.

When Gorlanndon and the two harpers arrived, this fine establishment was already riotous with laughter and noise and nearly filled to capacity. There were all manner of sailors, tradesmen and artisans from many of the city's guilds as well as members of most of the leading families. The Cokeyna was nothing, if not egalitarian in its clientele. At the back of the establishment, there was a small musicians' stand near the great bar, which at the moment was being used by several itinerant minstrels among whom was a Dwarf piper—an unusual sight, as Dwarves rarely performed outside their delvings. Even the Harpers' Guild had far more Dwarven craftsmen than musicians.

The fellow was a typical representative of his race, being just under five feet in height, broad shouldered and powerfully built. His long, ginger colored beard was intricately braided and tucked into a wide leather belt. The pipes he played looked rather more like fugitive plumbing than a musical instrument, but their sound was bewitching. Along with the musicians were three minstrel girls: two dark-skinned beauties from Crenanoc and a Borian girl with eyes the color of polar ice and hair as gold as ripe wheat. Her presence was surprising, for her homeland of Boria, located on the far eastern coast of the Dawn Sea, was one of the only areas where slave trading was a legal occupation and was therefore not the most popular place. Its inhabitants rarely came forth to peacefully treat with the rest of the world. All three girls were whirling with tambourines and flirting with the customers at nearby tables.

At the back near the windows, Kinrok had provided a table especially for Gorlanndon's use, one that the Giant himself had designed. The table was split down the middle with one side raised about two feet higher than the other. On this side a platform had been built several feet below floor level. Gorlanndon's massive chair was set in the middle of this platform and was reached by stepping down two large steps. This whole arrangement allowed Gorlanndon to converse comfortably with any who chose to join him at table. Gorlanndon made his way to his place, the youths following close behind. Three old friends of the Giant—two tall Humans and a Teluri—were awaiting them expectantly.

One of the Humans was a fellow of florid countenance of indeterminate age whose brown, pointed beard heavily mixed with white and long, drooping, bejeweled mustache did little to hide the fact that his once firm chin had gone rather soft and jowly from high living and comfort. The fellow's eyes retained a hawklike sharpness that hinted at a previous adventurous life.

He was dressed in a golden robe fringed in indigo, marking him as a member of Kalyria's royal council. Beside him, the other Human was a tall, lithe and sinewy, dark haired clean-shaven fellow in his prime, obviously a soldier, even though he was dressed in a simple brown broadcloth tunic, woolen hose and long boots.

The Teluri looked markedly like a Human at first glance. He was amazingly short for one of his race, being only just over six feet in height and much more squarely built and heavily muscled than the Teluri of Gilaria with whom Menannon was familiar from his sire's trading expeditions. In all other aspects, he was a normal Teluri as he bore the upswept brows and delicately pointed ears of his race and wore his ivory colored hair in waist length twin braids over his chest as was the custom of his people. He, too, was dressed simply: a thigh-length sleeveless kirtle of unadorned rust-brown sorak over a chemise of the same shade and material with a broad leather belt from which hung a sheathed malinir. His legs were bare and his feet encased in open leather sandals. The malinir drew Menannon's attention, for its quality belied the plainness of the rest of its owner's garb.

The malinir was the traditional personal weapon of Teluri of both sexes. Their blades were slightly curved and had no guard. They came in all sizes, from a small knife with a blade no more than four inches in length to be carried in a sheath on the belt of a child or in the bodice of a lady, up to a blade of two to three feet in length. These last were effectively short swords, and were often used by Teluri warriors in combination with the longer war sword in combat. No Teluri willingly went anywhere without a malinir. Even on the most formal of occasions, malinár were in evidence. Of course, the more important the owner, the more ornate the weapon and sheath. This particular malinir was one of the most ornate Menannon had ever seen, making him wonder exactly who this Teluri was to be carrying a weapon so obviously worth a king's ransom.

"Gorlanndon, old friend!" the sound of the councillor's

voice brought Menannon out of his musings with a start. "Your message cheered me immensely. It's been too long since we four gathered here. What brings us together this eve?" The fellow smiled up at the Giant.

"I'm celebrating a homecoming!" Gorlanndon laid his hand on Menannon's shoulder, drawing him towards the table. "You remember my son, Menannon, of course. He has just returned from Aridion City a fully trained journeyman harper and this is his good friend, Lee."

The Teluri stood and offered his hand to both young men. "I have the honor of being Irenos, son of Ilenar King, of Blue Hill, and this stalwart gentleman is Firod, captain of Kalyria's Guard," he said, indicating the soldier who stood and inclined his head, but did not speak. "And this," the Teluri indicated the robed lord, "is Lord Lonier of Kalyria." Turning to Lee, he addressed him politely, but with a warmth beyond mere courtesy for the Teluri above all others honored the Harpers, "Welcome harper. Is this thy first visit to this fair island?"

"Aye, sir. The glories of Kalyria have been ringing in my ears ever since I was a child and as Menannon was returning here for holiday, I thought to tag along to see whether this land and city was all that I have been told it was. It has, by the by, met and exceeded my expectations and I have but arrived! As Menannon's sire has been kind enough to not throw me out for my audacity, I look forward to seeing the rest." That statement brought a grin to all.

"I judge you to hail from Crenanoc or the western dales of Rhonndia, for you bear the height and look of those worthy folk," Lord Lonier said, speaking for the first time, and offered his hand to the drummer, though he did not rise.

"Aye, sir. Crenanoc, sir," Lee said as he took the councillor's hand. His smile was wide in return.

"So, you've finally decided to once more grace us with your presence," Lonier said, turning his attention to Menannon. "I must say, it's about time! We've not had the pleasure of seeing your sire's eyes glow this much since you left for the hinterlands."

"I hope he still finds my presence as satisfying after I've been here a few days!" Menannon grinned rather self-consciously and Lonier guffawed and slapped the arm of his chair.

"Glad to see you haven't lost your sense of humor over there on the mainland!"

At that comment, Menannon colored nicely, causing Lonier to laugh all the louder. He then rose to his full height, turning to address the gathering.

"Gentlemen and ladies: all attend! We are graced this evening with not one, but two corded harpers. Give them their due, one and all." With this, he turned back, placed his hand across his breast and gracefully inclined his head. Everyone else in the common room stood and followed suit.

Being new to their positions, neither Menannon nor Lee were used to this honorific formality as applied to themselves so that they both stood flame cheeked with embarrassed pleasure, not knowing quite how to respond.

Irenos rescued them from their predicament.

"Join us," he said, moving his chair aside and pulling another one up beside it. Menannon borrowed another from a nearby table and joined them at table between Lee and his sire. Everyone else returned to their interrupted conversations and occupations, allowing the harpers to return to the anonymity of the crowd.

Menannon was familiar with Lord Lonier, though he had always seen him ere this with the full jeweled collar of the Counsel General gracing the shoulders of his robes. He briefly wondered at the change, as the fellow was not old enough to have needed to step down from that august position. Captain Firod, he had also known as a child, but though Irenos was personally unknown to him, his name was not, as it was recorded in the King Lists kept in the Master Harper Hall in Aridion City.

The young Giant's musings were broken by the blonde minstrel girl suddenly appearing at his side and sitting upon the arm of his chair. She was playing a rebec and singing softly, as if to him alone. From the sweetness of the melodic line and her body language, Menannon knew the song was a love song, though he did not understand the words. It was not a new experience for the youngster to have a young lady or serving wench attempt to seduce him, yet it made him uncomfortable, particularly in front of his sire. Beside him, Lee was grinning broadly at his discomfiture, which did not help matters in the least.

Firod relieved him of the need to dislodge the girl. He gave her a stern look accompanied by a flipped coin as he jerked his chin, indicating she should be about her business. She glanced at Menannon and sighed wistfully, but obeyed and was soon sitting on the lap of a friendly sailor, although she still kept making eyes at Menannon from time to time.

"That's what you get for being so devastatingly handsome, my friend," Lee leaned over and whispered to him, still grinning. Menannon rolled his eyes in response. A guffaw of laughter accompanied by the smack of a dainty hand applied to rough skin came from the table where the minstrel girl had gone. Her new conquest, attempting to steal a kiss, had been severely chastised for his cheek. The girl flounced back to the musicians' stand where she resumed her place, disdain clearly written upon her countenance.

"So. Gentlemen, what is your desire?" Lonier asked as he started to raise his hand for service. Gorlanndon forestalled him with a smile and a wink. The Giant turned towards the bar and hailed one of the barkeeps.

"Davy, would you be having any volnaka on hand?" The barkeep was a tall, spare Human whose nose was far too large for his face and only managed to be balanced by an equally large adam's apple, both of which made him look like a turkey gobbler resting atop an animated scarecrow, all arms, legs and odd angles. When he came over to the table, Menannon was not sure whether he walked or flapped, as his legs seemed to arrive several seconds before the rest of him.

"Aye, me lord. Would ye be wantin' enough for the whole table or just enough fer yerself?" the fellow inquired politely.

"Just enough for one, but 'tis not for me. It's for this young fellow here," Gorlanndon said, slapping Menannon on the shoulder and winking at the barkeep, "and I shall have wine. These other gentlemen will have what they will have."

Davy nodded and grinned in understanding, took the orders of the others and departed, shortly returning with a large decanter of clear liquor and a small chalice about the size of a large mushroom cap and placed them in front of Menannon. He filled the chalice to the brim from the decanter and stepped back to be replaced by two of the potboys. One of them deftly placed a chalice of wine in front of Lee and refilled the chalices of the others while the other boy pushed a wheeled cart upon which sat a mug of wine so large it resembled a small rain barrel. It was, in fact, a smallish wine keg to which a handle had been attached. Filled, it was far too heavy for the boy to lift and so he left it on the cart and Gorlanndon served himself, though he flipped the youngster a coin and was rewarded with a gap-toothed grin ere the boy scampered back to the bar. The Giant turned back to the table, a rather impish grin lighting his face.

"There you go, boy, just as your master ordered!" the twinkle in his eye getting brighter as he grinned down at his son who was looking at the liquor with open curiosity.

"Volnaka ...," Lee began, scandalized.

"... is a most interesting drink," Gorlanndon cut him off with a smile. "Go on boy, try it."

Menannon picked up the chalice and eyed it doubtfully given the way Lee had said the word 'volnaka,' but his sire smiled at him encouragingly, so he shrugged his shoulders and downed the contents. It burned all the way down, hit his stomach and exploded. Menannon set his chalice down and started coughing, hardly able to breathe. Gorlanndon laughed good-naturedly and slapped him on the back.

"Unique, isn't it?"

The only answer Menannon could return his sire was a reproachful glare, his vocal cords being temporarily paralyzed. Many minutes later, when he regained the power of speech, he held up the decanter and eyed it dubiously.

"What is this stuff?" he managed in a strangled whisper. "It tastes precisely as paint stripper smells."

Irenos and Firod exchanged expressive glances with Gorlanndon.

"It's an acquired taste," Lonier informed him affably. "By the time you've downed a couple more of those, you'll see it differently." As though to encourage him, the councillor raised his chalice and saluted all around. "Your health and may your homecoming be a memorable one."

Everyone raised his chalice in response, including Menannon. The councillor was right. This time the liquor went down smoothly, hitting his stomach gently with a warm glow that slowly moved outwards into his limbs. *A delicious feeling, that. Perhaps it is not as bad as it first seemed.* He tried another sip. *All right, it's actually not bad at all. I could get to enjoy this stuff.* By now, his fingers and toes began to tingle, a pleasant feeling, to his mind. He was unaware of the grin now gracing his face.

That there was a new volnaka drinker among them this night spread quickly and all of the patrons of the pub took great pleasure in encouraging him in the task of finishing the entire decanter.

Lee alone was not among that number and a couple of times actually tried to keep Menannon from drinking any more of it, but he was booed down by everyone else. Gorlanndon kept giving the drummer reassuring glances which he read to mean the Giant would let no harm come to his son even if he was encouraging him to drink the most insidious liquor in the world. The drummer did not envy his friend the hangover he was going to have. Lee had himself once overindulged in volnaka at the occasion of his eldest brother's wedding feast and the result had been neither pretty nor pleasant.

By the time Menannon finished the entire decanter, he was

well and thoroughly drunk, so much so that he had taken off his harper's robe and climbed on one of the sturdy long tables with the girl who earlier had been sitting on the arm of his chair, intending to dance with her, but as she was no match for the height of the young Giant, he solved the problem by picking her up and placing her on his shoulder, the green of her tunica contrasting nicely with the white of his chemise. Together, they did a marvelous job of providing the entire pub with a night's entertainment that would not soon be forgotten.

"Well, Grandmaster Blackmore," Lee murmured to himself, "you wanted him drunk and there he is. I wish you could see it. If a person didn't know he doesn't usually dance on tabletops with a wench on his shoulder, they would not know he's drunk. He's the only fellow I've e'er seen who can even get drunk with dignity, excepting that silly smile." Lee shook his head with a grin and saluted Menannon with his chalice.

Another decanter later and Menannon was blissfully asleep on the flagstones of the floor, said "silly smile" frozen in place upon his now florid face.

Before they faded with the dawn, the last twinkle of the stars saw Gorlanndon and Lee wending their way a bit tipsily back up the broad avenues to the Giant's villa. Menannon made the trip home slung over his sire's broad shoulder humming softly to himself, much to the amusement of their personal guards.

VOLNAKA PRODUCES the worst hangover imaginable and for nearly a sevenday after his homecoming party, Menannon lay in his bed so sick just blinking his eyes made him retch, so he had to do it verrrry slowly. Several times he begged someone to kill him and get it over with. No one acceded to his pleading and he was left to wallow in his misery. It did not help that his sire, for some strange, twisted reason, found his condition amusing. He later confessed to his son he was remembering his own first overindulgence in the demonic drink known as volnaka.

On the first morning he was able to rise from his bed without having to immediately throw up in the ash bucket, Menannon put a vexing question to his sire: "To what purpose would Grandmaster Blackmore want me to go through acting the fool and then being so ill I wanted to die?"

Gorlanndon grinned at the question and motioned his son to join him at the summerhouse table where he was breaking his fast. During Menannon's indisposition, Gorlanndon had ordered several sections of the wooden bench surrounding the table to be raised so that they could sit at table together and converse comfortably. These new sections were also equipped with a short flight of stairs so that their occupants need not be gymnasts to sit on them.

Menannon gratefully settled in, though he still refused the breakfast his sire offered, being not quite sure of the temper of his stomach.

"I believe he meant for you to develop a bit more empathy for your fellows, boy," Gorlanndon mused after his son was seated. "We Giants can be rather too stuffy at times and I'm sure that you now understand a bit better how others feel when hung over. I'm sure that he also desired you to know the warning signs of nearing inebriation in yourself so that you can use drinking as a tool. The art of getting someone drunk without oneself succumbing is a very good skill to possess, for a person's true personality comes out when the restraints of sobriety have been lifted. A happy fellow gets happier, a talkative fellow gets more talkative and a fellow prone to being morose becomes either a bit suicidal or dangerous without restraint. Many has been the time that I have been glad of the insight into a business partner's heart that drink has afforded me." Gorlanndon's eyes twinkled. "You must forgive me for using volnaka on you, boy, for it does produce by far the worst hangover there is. Ale, mead and wine are much milder, but then, they also take a far greater amount to produce total drunkenness."

Menannon could not find it in his heart to be angry with his sire at this revelation, for he had been as good as his word and had stayed with his son through everything, even holding him gently while he was absolutely, utterly sick and begging to be put out of his misery.

"Have you e'er been drunk?"

"Aye, I've been drunk several times, but it is not wise, for when someone my size is drunk and stumbling, we can be very destructive. You, on the other hand, are only comical."

Menannon could not help coloring in embarrassment at the blurry memory he had of himself dancing with a minstrel girl. He vaguely remembered swinging her onto his shoulder and twirling about on a tabletop. More than that, he could not remember, which was a strange sensation, for Giants are blessed by the High One with perfect memories—anything seen, heard or experienced is forever etched upon their minds. To have blank spaces in his memory was a bit unnerving.

Gorlanndon saw the look in his son's eyes, recognized it for what it was and hastened to reassure him. "You did nothing to be ashamed of, boy," he grinned. "You were no trouble and you caused no trouble. I wished to be with you when you got drunk so there would be nothing to regret." He paused, his grin growing wider and chuckled, "You were, however, most amusing.

Menannon colored with heartfelt embarrassment, thinking it was probably a good thing he did not remember much of that evening. "If you don't mind, I deem I shall not repeat the experience. One such is quite enough, thank you very much." Menannon grinned rather sheepishly and his sire threw back his head and laughed while giving him a gentle tap on the shoulder which was still strong enough to rattle his bones and make his still recovering stomach a bit queasy. 🐛

CHAPTER 3
(SUMMER OF THE WORLD 6996)

MENANNON SPENT the next couple of days wandering about the city showing Lee its many marvels and rediscovering them himself. Not the least of the things most wonderful to the Crenanocian were buildings five and six stories high. On the mainland, the way had yet to be found to build structures with usable floors more than three stories, as anything of greater height fell down of its own weight. Here on Kalyria, there was actually one structure that stood seven stories and the view of the bay from the garden planted on its roof was breathtaking. The manner of accomplishing these amazing constructions was something that the Kalyrian builders were careful to keep to themselves for now, as it enhanced their position as the greatest city in this part of the world.

Of all the buildings they toured, the one that Lee would never forget as long as he lived was Gorlanndon's place of business. The second day of their sightseeing, Gorlanndon requested that they take a scroll to his warehouse manager Issilandur at the trade hall in the Serpentine Way. Menannon gladly acquiesced, for he had been looking forward to showing the building to Lee.

Lee was enchanted with the Serpentine Way halfway up the Aureun, with its long, sinuous curves lined by the trade halls of many of Kalyria's wealthier merchants including Gorlanndon's establishment and lined with flower filled boxes, large shade trees set amidst the paving stones of the street and the pedestrian walk fronting the buildings on each side. He found much of interest in the small shops that graced the lower floors of most of the halls. The entire street was awash in color and movement, a bedazzling display of life, prosperity and humanity. He could easily spend the whole day wandering here.

About halfway along its length, just short of their destination, they entered a small plaza often used for displaying wares that were a cut above the things available in the common markets of the waterfront yet not so fine as to warrant a place in the High Bazaar near the Royal Palace. This day, they found the plaza filled with the booths of artisans from all corners of the empire and overflowing with all manner of offerings. There were exquisite carvings, paintings, sculptures, jewelry, stained glass, all manner of finely embroidered clothing and accoutrements—almost anything the heart could desire if one had a deep enough belt pouch to afford the luxury.

In the midst of all, Lee noticed an ancient chapel whose white rotunda was dwarfed by the buildings around it. It rather appeared as a magnificent pearl within a shell of taller, yet somehow lesser, buildings.

"I don't know why, but this small chapel seems much larger than it is," Lee said in a hushed tone, not quite sure why he spoke so.

"It is because of the High One's presence within. There are many such chapels dotted about the city's landscape for the use of her citizenry, for here on Kalyria, the High One is never far from any who seek Him and His Presence has always been manifest within the walls."

Lee nodded in understanding. "We don't have anything like this back home, but we should. We have only the local harper hall." He felt drawn to the place and determined to return there when time allowed.

Menannon and Lee rounded the furthest curve of the Serpentine to see the trade hall they sought, the sight stopping Lee dead in his tracks, stunned by the splendor and sheer size of the place. It was the largest single building in all of Kalyria, a massive monument to free trade in a free market economy. Only the Royal Palace was larger, but it was an accretion of several buildings of varying age.

"It is rather impressive, isn't it?" Menannon paused to let Lee take it all in, seeing it anew himself through his friend's eyes.

"I had forgotten just how magnificent and overpowering it really is."

Lee had to agree to that last comment and realized the simplicity of the architecture, a simple rectangular design, was a perfect foil for the intricate stone façade constructed of a pink granitic rock with decorative trim and patterning of rare, icy silverstone from the Teluri quarry deep in the mountains of the Roof of the World.

Seeing it again after so long, Menannon could not help but find himself impressed anew by the place. "The silverstone used here is it's only application outside of the Teluri kingdom of Lilientharien, you know. It is positively stunning, is it not?"

The pink granite stones acted as a canvas for the silverstone which was placed to form stylized moonflowers at full bloom. The corners of the façade were also of silverstone, but of blocks smaller than the pattern blocks. The windows were also trimmed in small, alternating pink granite and silverstone squares. The silverstone flowers were carved in high relief and set out above the surface of the surrounding pink granite. The result was that they leapt from the surface as if they were gigantic and very real moonflowers. The result was beyond words, and Lee could but stare at the building, utterly enchanted.

After several minutes, Menannon nudged his friend and said with a grin, "Let's go on in and find Issilandur. You're gawking like a Sotaran farmer."

"I can't help it. I consider myself no rube, but every time I turn around here, I am reminded at just how provincial I really am. Everything here is grander, bigger, finer than anything I've e'er seen. Back home in Crenanoc, the Kafiq's palace is considered a marvel with its gilded domes and arches, but this … this merchant's entrepot makes it look like a squatter's hovel."

They crossed the street to the stairs which led down to the sunken plaza several feet below fronting Gorlanndon's establishment. It was paved with stones of many colors laid in a geometric pattern of great complexity incorporating portraits of birds, animals, fishes and flowers.

Lee almost hated to walk upon it, such was its beauty, but perforce had to, as Menannon led the way down the stair and across the plaza to the grand entrance flanked by polished black basalt columns twenty feet high, veined with a lighter mineral that on close inspection resembled gold, and which was in and of itself a work of art. The effect of these columns against the pink and white of the façade was startling.

Gazing upon the enormous double doors made of solid and intricately carven blackwood, Lee wondered aloud who could have made such things.

"Teluri craftsmen from Taaliron high up in the Sythrin Mountains near the southern end of that range. They are renowned for their woodcarving skills and Father has long been a friend to their king."

Lee noted the carvings were a series of scenes which related Gorlanndon's life, beginning with his childhood at the bottom of the left hand door then moving upwards to the top, across to the right hand door and ending at its bottom. The final scene showed Gorlanndon overseeing the building of this very structure. A biography in wood, it was, the scenes carven in extreme high relief of intricate and exquisite detail. He looked them over carefully and was soon lost in the detail of the carvings, his pleasure and enchantment punctuated with indrawn breaths followed by "Ohhhhh..." and other expressions of childlike delight. Menannon waited patiently, knowing full well Lee was experiencing what he had himself felt when he was a young boy and, he allowed, still did.

After a half turn of the hour, however, he got his friend's attention. "We need to be moving on."

"But...," began Lee.

"You'll have plenty of time later to come here and gaze to your heart's content. And, you'll keep finding things you missed as I still do." He chuckled softly. "When I was a boy, I suspected the Teluri of sneaking in at night and adding things to the doors because I would e'er be finding something new that I would swear had not been there before."

"I can well believe it," commented Lee in awe. "The workmanship of these carvings is beyond anything I've e'er seen, anywhere. Almost inhuman."

"Well, they were carved by Teluri...," said Menannon mischievously.

"That's not what I meant. I mean, well...it's just that...." His voice trailed off, at a loss for words to describe just what he did mean.

"I understand. I still feel that way. It's as if the Teluri craftsmen were directly inspired by the High One Himself, as if He was here, directing their work."

"Yes! That's it!" Lee was nodding excitedly as he spoke. "When you look at these doors, you feel as though the High One is looking over your shoulder."

Taking one last look at the magnificent doors, Menannon pushed them open and they entered into the atrium. Despite their massive size, the counterweighted doors opened easily. The building was literally of gigantic proportions, for the master of the establishment had access to all parts of it. Thus it was that all enclosed chambers had ceilings of thirty feet as Gorlanndon liked the airiness of such a ceiling although it made all but the tallest of the Teluri feel as though they were but children again playing hide-and-seek in their grandsire's villa.

The atrium was open all the way to its glass roof supported by delicate arches with balconies on the second and third floors. It was two hundred feet square and in the direct center was a magnificent multi-level fountain topped by a life sized statue of Kalyrinon, the founder and first king of Kalyria. The base of the fountain was formed into a circular bench whose seats were padded for the comfort of visitors. This was a popular gathering spot not only for merchants intending to do business with Gorlanndon, but also for the citizens of Kalyria for relaxation and conversation. It was open to all and sundry and it was thus not at all unusual to see a serving wench from the docks rubbing elbows with a high born dame from the palace. All were equal in Gorlanndon's eyes and all who entered these premises entered as guests and acceded to his rules.

The atrium's foundation was the bedrock of the island itself and was home to numerous flower beds wherein grew exotic plants from around the Empire, the light from the glass ceiling being sufficient to provide for their growth. These plants included flowers, bushes and even several large trees, the largest and in Menannon's mind, the most beautiful, was a large Blackwood tree, the only specimen outside of its natural home in the jungles of Crenanoc. Its broad, shiny, bright green lanceolate leaves contrasted with the rich black of its bark, the brilliant carmine flowers now in full bloom shining out from the rest of the tree as brilliant rubies in a green and black setting.

Around the edges of the atrium and the balconies on the upper floors were chambers varying in size wherein samples of the merchandise in which Gorlanndon dealt could be seen. The breadth and depth of the goods offered beggared the imagination. It was said that if Gorlanndon did not have an item or could not get it, it did not exist. Each room had a clerk eager to take orders to be fulfilled from either the warehouses on the lower levels of the trade hall or from his other warehouses scattered about the city.

Lee was visibly impressed by Gorlanndon's business workings and as he began to realize just how massive his business empire must be, a puzzling thought came to mind.

"Menannon, might I ask of you a question, which I deem may well be impertinent? 'Tis about your sire's business."

"I cannot see how such a question could be impertinent," said Menannon frankly, if a bit puzzled.

"Well...your sire has been in business a very long time and could easily have developed total control of all trade into and out of Kalyria, yet he has not. I know many traders in Crenanoc who have, over time, contrived to control trade in certain goods and even over several routes. Granted they are minor routes, but yet they have grown fat on the trade. Given the chance, they would cheerfully control all trade through Crenanoc. They are not in the same league as your sire, to be sure, yet traders tend to desire control. He, however, appears not to."

"Ah. Many do not understand my father's business methods. He has been in business for a thousand and a half summers and he is very good at it. That he does not have a monopoly on trade to and from Kalyria—or throughout Aridion for that matter—is entirely due to the fact that he is a complete stranger to greed. He feels competition is healthy for all concerned, so he has always encouraged others to go into business for themselves and has often aided them in that endeavor. In fact, most of the merchants doing business from Kalyria owe their start to my father or to someone whom he aided. I have heard him say more than once that there is enough trade for all and to spare."

"That is very unusual, but it fits, for I have seen for myself that he is in so many ways an unusual man," Lee said, truly impressed.

"Joram & Sons, one of my father's major competitors and now under the direction of Sadram Joram—often a guest at my father's table—and is in its sixth generation. They got their start with my father's assistance. Sadram continues to apply my father's business philosophies, for he himself has helped several young men build successful businesses, some of whom have become serious competition to both Sadram and my father in certain areas or goods, to the satisfaction of all. Such is the way of the merchants of Kalyria, with only a few exceptions, for as my father has often stated, greed is ever the bane of lesser men. But come, let's be moving. I still have to deliver this message to Issilandur. There is, however, just one thing more I'd like to show you before we do."

Lee followed Menannon as they made their way to Gorlanndon's surprisingly unostentatious office along the back wall of the first floor. His door was usually open to any who wished to speak with him and many was the time when he got little work done for the steady stream in and out of his office. When he did not wish to be disturbed, his door was closed to all save his senior clerks and the warehouse manager. In the middle of the back wall sat his vast desk and chair, placed to face the door. There was more to the building behind his office, so there were no windows. Situated about the office were comfortable chairs of various sizes to accommodate whomever had business with him, be they Dwarf, Human or Teluri. There was also a table of a size to accommodate his visitors, one half of which was lower than the other so that the Dwarves were not asked to sit on outsized chairs.

The walls of Gorlanndon's office were strikingly bare of all decoration, save for a large portrait which hung directly behind the desk and above the pigeonholes holding the scrolls of his business affairs. It was of a Giantess, of slim and delicate build, dressed in a robe of light peach sorak with roses entwined in the long curls of her black hair. It had been commissioned of an itinerant portrait artist who had been in vogue with the Kalyrian court many summers past, but whose name had been forgotten by all save Gorlanndon. So struck with her beauty had the artist been that he had poured into her portrait all the skill and artistry he possessed as well as his very soul, "for," he had said, "such beauty deserves no less than all that I have, and even then, I fear, I have fallen short and have not done her justice. I fear no man could." With that, he had packed up his brushes and paints and betook himself off, never to be seen or heard from again.

Lee was enchanted. "Who is she?" Although he suspected the identify of the subject, he wanted to be sure. His voice quavered, overcome with unexpected emotion, as were all who saw the portrait. Who could remain unmoved in the face of such beauty?

"My mother, Julianna. I have not seen her since I was five."

The tone in Menannon's voice was such that Lee held his tongue, leaving his friend his privacy.

They stood there for several minutes, gazing upon the portrait, each lost in his own thoughts, then without a word, Menannon abruptly turned and left the office. He was almost out the door before Lee was aware of his departure and he had to scramble to catch up.

Lee quietly followed Menannon, waiting for his friend to break the silence as they headed for a large and very odd opening to the left of his sire's office and further along the back wall. It was ten feet wide and extended up the wall to just short of the balcony overhead. It was about ten feet deep and had an open gate across it that extended only four feet above the floor. Another, similar gate was just beyond it on the other side of a gap in the floor. Here, Menannon halted.

"This is what my father calls a lift. He developed it from the simple hoist common around Linden and it is used to bring goods up from the floors below. It works by ropes and counterweights in the walls, although it is more complicated than that. There are two floors above us and the twelve floors below have been carved from the island itself, the bottom one opening upon the wharf. Goods are offloaded on the wharf and then brought into the warehouse and from there are brought up to the appropriate floor using one of these lifts. This is the only one that comes up here, though, and we'll take it down two floors where Issilandur has his office. He is the warehouse manager and has been with my father for a good many summers. He is a Teluri from Lilientharien. My father says that having an immortal Teluri for his warehouseman is a stroke of good fortune because he doesn't have to train in a new one every fifty summers or so."

"A good point. It would simplify things, wouldn't it?" Lee had to admit that immortality had its strong points, and that would be one of them. It allowed Gorlanndon to maintain continuity in his business affairs.

"My father has said on more than one occasion that Issilandur knows more about his business than he does," Menannon commented with a chuckle. "Well, let us discharge our mission. The sooner done, the quicker gone." With that, Menannon pulled a lever set into the wall next the door, and the gates sank noiselessly until the tops were even with the floor of the lift. They stepped in and Menannon pulled a lever inside and the gates returned to their normal places, thereby securing them within the lift. He then pulled a third lever and the lift began to slowly descend. At its first movement, Lee grabbed instinctively for the wall.

"Don't worry. Its descent is well controlled," Menannon assured him. After a few moments, Lee found he could relax and enjoy the experience. He noted that Menannon kept his hand on the third lever at all times. Outside the gate, the floor they had just been on passed them by and then another opening began to appear. It grew to full size and then began to shrink again as the Giant continued to hold the lever. The floor of this next level passed and a third opening began to appear. Just before they came even with the floor of this level, Menannon let go of the lever and the lift slowed to a stop, perfectly aligned with the floor. He opened the gates and they stepped off. He then pulled the lever set into the wall outside, closing the gates, leaving the lift ready for the next user.

Lee had all sorts of question as to the operation of this most interesting device, but Menannon was already in motion and he had to forego his questions until some other time, as the Giant was moving quite purposefully down the hall. He stopped in front of the third door on the left and knocked. There was no answer, so he turned the handle and stepped inside. The office was much like Gorlanndon's, but rather than a portrait its back wall was covered by a large map showing all of the Giant's vast holdings and trade centers throughout the known world.

Menannon stepped up to an immaculate desk and laid his sire's scroll in its exact center, then turned to leave with Lee close on his heels. At the office door Lee halted and drew Menannon's attention to a small wooden box hanging just to one side. It had a lever on the side which could be pulled down and tubes running from its top and disappeared into the ceiling.

"What is that?" he asked, wondering if it could be another lift or some such.

"It is a communication device. By pulling down on this lever," Menannon said pointing to the metal handle attached to the side, "a signal is sent to a twin device in the office of my sire's master of the flagship launching crew in the village of Waterdeep on the far side of the island."

"Surely you jest!" Lee glanced up at his friend sure that he was having him on.

"No. It is another of my father's inventions. Ask me not how it works, for that knowledge it is not within my scope." Menannon held up his hand, leaving Lee's rain of questions unspoken. "But come, there is much more to see here on the Aureun."

Yet of all the wonders Lee experienced on Kalyria, the greatest was a simple thing, but positively incredible to the drummer. On Lee's first night, Menannon had insisted on accompanying him to the bathing chamber in his assigned quarters. Why, Lee could not imagine until the Giant opened the door on a room of wonders. It was a medium-sized chamber, roofed, walled and floored in marble. Four marble pillars held up its ceiling and supported Dwarf lanterns. All this he was coming to realize was not that unusual, but what he saw in the center of the chamber was.

Lee's attention was drawn to a huge sunken area in the marble floor which had a seating bench all around inside, although there were no cushions. It seemed an odd place for a conversation, but all right. He walked over and inspected it. Strangely, the area was marred by a large hole directly in the center. It was a shame, for it disrupted what would otherwise have been a marvelous mosaic depicting a garden under the sea. He was about to ask what it was going to take to repair the damage when Menannon walked over and tapped a small metal statue of a dolphin with his foot and it began to spew forth water from its open mouth. If that was not enough, the young Giant tapped a second such statue and hot water began to spew from its mouth, steam rising instantly from it! Then Menannon turned a handle set between the two statues. The hole in the center closed and the water began to pool in the sunken space.

Lee nearly jumped out of his skin in surprise. He looked down into the water and shook his head. A self-filling bathing pool? He looked up to see that Menannon was grinning at him, for the Giant well remembered his own reaction as a child when Clarinda, his sire's Housemarm and Menannon's erstwhile nursemaid, had first introduced him to the joys of automatic plumbing, something not present in his native village. He stopped the water and turned the handle so the tub would drain and silently motioned Lee to follow him into a small side chamber where there was what seemed to be an ordinary garderobe for relieving one's self. Again, Menannon motioned him over and pointed into the marble basin. To his surprise, there was clear water standing in it, filling it about halfway.

"Watch," Menannon said softly and pulled a handle situated within easy reach of someone using the garderobe. The water swirled away and was replaced by new which, as soon as Menannon let go of the handle, settled into stillness waiting for the next use. Lee was stunned. Beside the garderobe was a small basin with two more dolphin statues that Lee assumed had to be for washing your hands and face though he had only ever used a basin and pitcher to perform such ablutions.

The final wonder was a small freestanding room in its own side chamber. One could walk all the way around it. It bore three walls made of marble and the fourth was a sheet of glass made into a door, itself a wonder to his eyes. This small room was equipped with a single dolphin statue set high on the back wall with two handles directly below it, though there was no handle to close the center hole in the floor. He glanced questioningly at Menannon.

"You step inside and close the door then turn the handles and it sprays you like a waterfall. You use it to get clean ere you take a soak," the Giant informed him as they returned to the outer chamber. "Well, how do you like it?"

Lee just shook his head, absolutely speechless, causing Menannon to laugh outright and slap him on the shoulder.

"There are towels in that wardrobe and a sleeping tunic." He pointed to a large ornate rosewood wardrobe standing on the far side of the chamber near windows that were made of glass which appeared to be permanently covered with winter's frost. "Oh, and by the by, a full turn of the hour of running the hot water will deplete the reservoir and it takes another half turn of the hour for it to reheat. Enjoy!" Menannon closed the door softly behind him leaving Lee to one of the most wonderful evenings of his life.

THE MORNING AFTER THEIR VISIT to Gorlanndon's trade hall found the journeymen enjoying a sunrise stroll through the gardens atop the Aureun. It was a particularly popular time of day to be in the gardens for there were not a few exotic flowers which bloomed only at sunrise or sunset and then for mere minutes only. A small planting of one such flower was clustered in the center of the Speakers Grove, a place designated for public speaking. Any who chose to speak, unhindered by law or custom, could freely air his opinion there and none could gainsay him. There were curved marble benches and a low wall set to demarcate the edge of the grove and a magnificent fountain made to look like a forest grotto at the back, the sound of its water tending to soften the edge of the many opinions voiced here.

Menannon and Lee rounded the small clump of night blooming Peridüs trees which formed the outer edge of the Grove only to be brought up short by the magnificent display of hornflowers gathered gracefully about the plinth of the statue of Kalyrinon King. The flowers were fully budded, but their long trumpet shaped blossoms were still hidden by their sepals. They awaited but the slightest touch of the rising sun to unfurl and show their faces to the world. Each blossom bloomed for no more than a half turn of the hour ere they would furl, never to open again. The plant itself, however, continued to produce new buds throughout the summer into the fall.

All about the Grove, small groups of people sat or stood waiting for that rare moment. Menannon touched Lee's arm and silently pointed him to a spot no more than three paces from the largest of the plants, then stood back so that the drummer could view the coming marvel unhindered. Menannon himself had seen the flowers several times in his childhood in the company of his dear friend Nirna, but he never tired of the sight.

Across the island to the north, the tip of Kalyria's Crown began to glow soft rose, then slowly it lightened until it seemed about to burst into flame once more. As the sun rose above the summit, it flashed like a beacon and sunlight flooded across the city as it cleared the eastern peaks to illuminate the Aureun gardens. The sunlight broke through the surrounding Peridüs trees and touched the first bud of the waiting hornflowers. At its coming, the buds on three of the plants unfurled, opening their delicate faces to the sky. The blossoms shaded from deepest scarlet at the base of the throat to a bright golden yellow at the very edge of the trumpet. As the sunlight washed down across the small garden, more and more of the rare flowers unfurled. The air was instantly filled with an indescribably heady fragrance.

A cloud of tiny lace-winged insects appeared as though out of the very air itself, hovered about the blossoms but briefly, then dropped down upon them, crawling deep within the trumpets. The deliriously feeding insects flew from blossom to blossom, extracting the nutritious nectar while pollinating the flowers they visited. The insects had little time to accomplish their endeavors and each insect attempted to reach as many blossoms as possible in that time. Pollinated by their winged visitors, new seed would soon develop and thus perpetuate these wondrous plants. As for the two-legged onlookers, everyone stood silently, enchanted by the sight and the wonderful fragrance of this rare flower. No one moved, nor even seemed to breathe, lest a single sensation of this moment be lost. The light grew in intensity as the minutes passed, then it was over as almost as one, the delicate blossoms curled back within their sepals, never to open again. The insects disappeared as quickly as they had come.

About them, the people murmured and sighed and began to talk as though they had just awakened from an enchantment.

"I thought you had taken leave of your senses to rouse me from my bed before first light and insist that we take a stroll, but your timing was perfect! I've ne'er seen them open before." Lee was on his knees where he had been studying one of the hornflowers, a look of pure delight on his face. "There is no fragrance like theirs in all the world." The drummer sat back on his heels and looked up at Menannon. "My sire was gifted two of these beauties by our late king in thanks for a lifetime of service to the royal house."

"A truly princely gift," Menannon nearly whispered, finding it hard to speak normally in the aftermath of such an incredible event. He swallowed hard and cleared his throat. "Your family's specimens are two of only a handful of such plants yet in the world, for the small island these beauties called home was volcanic in origin and it blew itself to the High One nearly a hundred summers ago, leaving only its memory in the few hornflowers then in captivity. The folk who care for these gardens have set upon a mission of breeding as many of the flowers as they can, but it has proven no easy task, for they must breed and propagate the insect as well, for without it, there is no seed. The insect itself, it was found, is entirely dependent upon the flower, and spends most of its life in immature form within the plants they pollinate. They have managed to produce a few dozen—those you see here, the few that were sent as gifts to vassal kings, such as the ones your sire was gifted and their breeding stock in the arboretum—and all have come from the few specimens they possessed at the time of the island's annihilation. But come, there is much more to see." Lee obligingly stood and followed Menannon farther into the depths of the Aureun gardens intent upon discovering more of their wonders.

It had been the decree of the third queen of Kalyria, Tyra, that the gardens be created for two purposes: the enjoyment of the citizenry and the preservation and propagation of rare plants and trees. To that end, the folk of Kalyria had set out to gather specimens from all parts of the known world. It had become rather fashionable to spend one's holidays on such expeditions, a pastime which Gorlanndon had indulged to the fullest and many was the collecting expedition on which Menannon had accompanied him before he had left for Aridion City. Rightly, the Aureun Gardens were considered one of the wonders of the world. Lee was sure he could spend a lifetime here and not see all of their secrets. By the end of the day, he was more than willing to put the experiment to the test. He had never in his life been in a place so beautiful as this.

FIRST LIGHT TWO MORNINGS LATER again found Lee up and dressed, only this time he had arisen of his own volition and was seated on a deep window seat in his chamber, his arms resting on the sill, watching the sunrise and enjoying a magnificent view of the city and the harbor below. The chamber was on the end of the south wing of the villa and was specially furnished to be of a comfortable size for Gorlanndon's Human guests. As in Menannon's chamber, a large platform bed, this one made of a medium grained rosewood with a feather mattress so soft it was like sleeping on a cloud, was complimented by a tall wardrobe of the same wood and a large clothes press. A large, nearly walk-in fireplace dominated the wall which included the door, with two low comfortable hearth chairs flanking a round table topped with green-veined white marble set in front of it. The opposite wall was almost solid windows impossibly made from continuous sheets of glass. Most were solid framed, but two could be opened by means of releasing a latch and pushing a notched lever outward until the desired notch caught a pin protruding from the frame. This allowed fresh air into the room, and Lee greatly appreciated that feature. He was puzzled, however, as to how these sheets could possibly be made, as heretofore he had never seen glass windows made from anything other than small, mouth-blown panes of glass set within muntins and separated into windows by mullions. On the mainland, if one wanted larger, unbroken windows, one had to make them of highly greased vellum or sheets of thinly sliced marble, both of which were incredibly fragile and therefore only used sparingly and neither substance gave a clear view as did these Kalyrian windows. Despite several attempts to export this Kalyrian sheet glass, no one yet had succeeded, as it did not survive the effects of rough seas and rugged roads without extensive packing which rendered it too costly to export.

Every other available wall space had been decorated with exquisitely lifelike murals depicting life on Kalyria. Even the ceiling bore a mural of the sky at first light which made the chamber seem roofless. Though the drummer came from a highborn, wealthy family in Crenanoc, he had never experienced the luxury and taste shown in every facet of Gorlanndon's home. No wonder Menannon had such refined tastes in music, art and culture.

As though the thought of the young giant had conjured him, there was a soft knock on the door and Menannon's deep voice sounded through the heavy wood.

"Lee, have you arisen yet?"

"Enter," the drummer replied over his shoulder, but he did not change his position, so caught up was he in the wonder of the vista before him. Menannon opened the door and ducked through, for even the doors in this wing had been made Human sized. Gorlanndon could not have entered any of them save on his knees.

"You live in the most beautiful place in the High One's entire world," Lee said, not taking his eyes from the sight of the growing sunlight glittering in stages, unveiling the city as though Kirith Kalyria were a beautiful woman disrobing for her husband's pleasure.

"The city is magnificent, but I think you will value the countryside just as much." Menannon glanced out of the windows appreciatively. "And to aid you in gaining that appreciation, I have come this morning to invite you to accompany me on an errand inland for my sire. Do you feel like going riding for a few days?"

"Riding? Do Giants actually have horses?!" Lee burst out, glancing up at his friend and taking in his attire. Menannon was indeed dressed for riding having a short woolen cloak over his usual day clothes, a small pack slung over his shoulder. "I mean," he continued, "how could you ride ... I mean, without ..." Lee's voice trailed into silence, his consternation having been the source of great amusement to his friend.

"Of course we have horses." Menannon's grin at the look on the drummer's face grew even wider. "My sire has a small holding just without the city walls where he keeps a few head of saddle stock for the convenience of Skendrin and others who perform tasks for him at various points on Kalyria. He, of course, has not been able to ride a horse since he was a small boy, but I still can." He crossed to the wardrobe and reached inside to secure a small pack that hung on a hook at the back. This he tossed to Lee. "Select enough clothing for a sevenday."

"But ...," Lee began, thoroughly bemused by the thought of Giants on horseback.

"Don't talk. Pack," Menannon grinned.

Lee did as he was bid and, with Menannon's help, soon had the pack filled and closed. As he took off his harper's robe and replaced it with a light cloak and pulled on calf-length soft boots, the drummer returned to his subject.

"There are horses big enough to bear you!? Oh, now this

wonder I must see with my own eyes! Why, my eldest brother stands nearly seven feet and he can't ride a horse, and he's not nearly so, well, 'stout' as you are."

"You're thinking of horses the size of your small desert stock. Swift and sure they may be, but they would be hard pressed to bear even you for a great distance." Menannon motioned Lee to follow him and led the way out of the chamber. He continued to explain as they went. "The Giants were at one time great horse breeders and our clan in particular developed a breed out of the Calish Barb, the wild horses of the High Plains of Cala. Though the breed never got large enough to bear a normal Giant, breeding them was a passion at one time, as they made good beasts of burden. In these later summers, they have become playthings and pets for children. Rather like the ponies your folk breed."

"A horse big enough for you? This I really must see!" Lee grinned and shook his head again, following Menannon into the kitchen.

The villa's light and airy kitchen lay at the back of the building hard by the kale yard and orchard. It was one long chamber with many windows that let in plenty of light to aid in the preparation of everything from meats, breads, soups, vegetables and sweets to wines and simples. Lee was astonished at the size and complexity of the place, beginning with a long marble-topped table running down the middle of most of the length of the chamber. There were three hearths: one for baking, one for roasting and one for simple cooking.

The third was called a kettledor, which was something Lee had never seen before. It was a tall, narrow hearth set into the wall which boasted its own chimney. It was set with a deep fire pot at the base and a tall, hooked wooden crane attached to one side, like a large sign post, where cauldrons of all sizes could be hung and swung into the kettledor. The crane was fitted with a heavy chain attached to a crank so that the cauldron could be raised and lowered to adjust the amount of heat.

Along the same wall was the main meat oven with its

rotating spit. Nearby, was a fellow sitting on a stool peeling potatoes into a large tub and turning the spit with a pedal that moved up and down to the pressure of his sandaled foot. All along the sides of the chamber were marble-topped shelves and counters overflowing with foodstuffs and utensils. There were two side chambers: one a wet sink where produce could be washed and readied and the other a cold room with a constant flow of water through stone-lined troughs in which sat wine jars and milk jugs and all manner of other things that needed to be kept cold. The source of the near freezing water was a deep well just outside of the back door whose pumping system was run by a wind sail, so there was never a shortage of water.

The kitchen was a whirl of activity as a small army of serving folk prepared to feed the household, its myriad of guests and dozens of liegemen. Despite all, the truly marvelous thing to the drummer was the huge sink for washing up with its hot and cold running water. Here again, dolphin statues stood ready to be turned and produce the desired temperature.

Amidst all of this stood Clarinda, her iron grey hair tied up neatly in a bandeau of bright red sorak and a long length of white linen tied about her stout waist to protect her dark brown kirtle from the ravages of pot and pan. She was a sweet-faced lady whose every wrinkle was a laugh line, but the snap in her hazel eyes warned one and all that she was not to be trifled with. To assure that she was not, she flourished a large wooden spoon like a rod of office in one chubby hand. It's bowl was used to stir what needed to be stirred and its stout handle was used liberally to smack the bottom of any luckless helper who did not move smartly enough for the old Dwarf's liking.

Clarinda had been born in this place and overseen the kitchen and the stillroom since the hour she turned sixteen and had begun to aid her own sire in the same position. From position of kitchen helper, she had risen to the rank of Housemarm and now had charge over the food, cleanliness, health and upkeep of the entire villa, a position she was more than capable of fulfilling. In many ways, this was more

Clarinda's house than it was Gorlanndon's and she was fiercely protective of all that was hers, most particularly her beloved master and his son.

When Menannon and Lee entered, she immediately faced them with kind authority and a smile. At the sight of their riding attire and packs, she turned to a helper chopping leeks and garlic near the wet sink doorway and beckoned her.

"Two sacks filled with touring victuals, if you please," she ordered and smartly smacked the girl's ample bottom with her spoon when she showed more interest in staring at her master's son than doing as bidden. The girl squeaked and scurried away, red-cheeked, to fulfill her mistress's desires. Before Lee could ask Menannon what 'touring victuals' were, Clarinda returned her attention to them.

"Now, lads, you'll be wantin' to break yer fast, so move along to the table." She waved her spoon towards a small table set comfortably near the back of the chamber within a section of wall that bowed out from the rest.

There the wall was again made from ceiling-to-floor glass panels through which the morning's first glow was just peeping. Only afternoon's strong sun would come through them directly. Obediently, the two young harpers did as they were bid, Lee half suspecting if they had not moved smartly, they twain would also have been assisted along by the application of the good lady's spoon. As they settled into chairs at the table and set their packs on the floor under it, Clarinda went to the cooking hearth herself and in a twinkling had produced two mighty omelettes, cooked in olive oil and smothered in peppered honey sauce. These she set in front of them with a flourish along with large glasses of cold milk.

"Eat, eat! You'll be needin' yer strength to handle those great beasties in the wilds." Clarinda stood with her hands firmly planted on her hips waiting for them to take the first bite.

All around them, the kitchen went strangely quiet as everyone seemed to wait in breathless anticipation of their reaction to the food. Both Lee and Menannon forked up large portions of the fare with alacrity. The omelettes were marvelous and Lee's eyes lit with greedy delight as he dug in for another mouthful.

That was enough for Clarinda and she patted his shoulder approvingly before turning back to her duties, bidding her helpers to "Stir, don't stare!" Instantly, the kitchen came alive with noise and activity again.

"Is she always like this?" Lee questioned softly, glancing over his shoulder to make sure he would not be overheard.

Menannon nodded and swallowed a bite before he answered. "Always! You should see the way she bullies my father," he grinned, then dug back into the omelette with an almost guilty start.

Lee glanced out of the corner of his eye to see that the good lady was watching them from across the central table even as she supervised her helper who was busily filling two huge sacks with food the sight of which reminded him of his question.

"What does she mean by 'touring victuals'?"

"She has menus worked out for every contingency," the young Giant explained softly. "Touring victuals are the food-stuffs she always prepares for camping trips outside the city. When I was a child, she used to prepare me 'touring victuals' on the nights, my father allowed me to pitch a tent out in the orchard and pretend I was on an adventure with Rhindolier, the famous Teluri explorer." Menannon quickly glanced to see that Clarinda was busy, talking to the fellow turning the spit where a great shoulder of beef was cooking for tonight's dinner, and lowered his voice even more before he continued. "She always sets out enough touring victuals to feed an army. If I hadn't been growing so fast, I'm sure I would have wound up twice as wide as I was tall, even though I did camp out only infrequently."

With a grin and a shake of his head at the memory, Menannon returned to his food and both of them finished up. When Lee finally pushed his plate away and downed the last of the milk, he felt as though he would need to spend the rest of the day chopping wood or something like to work off the amount he had eaten. "By the by, how do you get the milk so cold? It's like drinking snow."

"It's sent up new each evening and stands in clay jugs overnight in the water flowing directly from the well through the keeping troughs. There is no water colder than that which is drawn from the deep wells of the Equian," Menannon informed him with no small amount of pride.

They retrieved their packs, arose and crossed to where Clarinda was busily stuffing into the sacks the food her helper was still fetching for her.

"And don't be forgettin' those meat pies. They just have to have some of those. They're in the green crock!" Clarinda called after the girl as she disappeared into the cold room again. The Dwarf turned to look them up and down. "Did you get enough to eat?"

"More than enough. We thank you!" Menannon said, a bit too hurriedly for politeness, almost interrupting her, but he was nearly terrified that the good lady would find something else he needed to eat before he left. Beside him, Lee nodded on vigorous agreement and patted his stomach.

"I don't think I've been this full in summers uncounted!" he grimaced, wishing the waistband of his hose was a little bigger. "The omelette was incredible!" he added hastily so as not to accidentally offend its creator.

She smiled at the complement, a small dimple appearing in her cheek, then turned serious again as her helper came back with two sacks of meat pies and two sealed jars of wine. These Clarinda added to the already bulging bags, causing Menannon to hold up a hand in protest.

"Clarinda, we're only going to be gone for a sevenday or a bit less...," Menannon began, but the Dwarf cut him off decisively.

"And a sevenday is a good long time and I'll not have you starvin' on me and have to be answerin' to yer Da for yer deaths!" It took two helpers to hold the sacks closed while

Clarinda laced thongs through their rings and tied them off. "Now take yer vittles and be off with you!"

Menannon just shook his head, with a what do you do? look for Lee and gave her a kiss on the cheek, swung his pack onto his shoulders and took up the two sacks which even he found a bit awkward to carry.

They hurried out of the back door of the kitchen before the good lady could think of any other victuals they 'just had to have.' They emerged into the kale yard and quickly made their way along the path between well-ordered rows of vegetables and herbs and around the end of the villa intent upon attaining the courtyard in front. Just before they reached the end of the north wing of the villa, Lee heard the sound of Gorlanndon's voice, though not the words.

Contrary to the drummers previous expectations, the elder Giant's speaking voice was surprisingly of a higher pitch than his son's. Whereas Menannon had a well-modulated bass speaking voice, Gorlanndon's was far closer to the tenor range. It was neither thin nor squeaky, but of a much higher pitch than one would expect from someone his size. This went far towards showing that the Giants were specifically designed by the High One to be the size they were and were not just over-stretched anomalies as were any Humans who had the misfortune of displaying gigantism with all the ills and strained parameters that attended upon such a thing. Though he had never thought about it before, Lee was beginning to realize the reason Menannon had always seemed so normal to him—if a bit tall—was because he was normal.

The young Giant was as light of foot, graceful and as well-coordinated as any other created being. He was not hampered by the ills besetting anomalous Humans. Menannon's spine had regular bone structure and was not burdened with too much space between bones not meant to be so located. He did not lurch and lumber, because his muscles were not strained beyond capacity in attempting to move a frame they were not designed to move. Menannon's organs, muscles and bone structure were all perfectly suited to his physical size and he was thus able to walk, run, ride and dance as easily and gracefully as any other person in Linden. His vocal cords were not stretched beyond their capacity and so he did not growl and grate when he spoke. While his speaking voice was indeed bass, his singing voice was a magnificent baritone. Were it not for his height and good looks, one would not notice him in a crowd.

They rounded the corner of the villa and emerged from beneath a trellis of climbing roses already in full bloom to find Gorlanndon seated on a long bench set between the gate and one of the outbuildings, talking to Skendrin. At their appearance, the Giant instantly ceased his speech with a soft "we shall continue this later," and turned to Menannon.

"What's that you carry?" he asked, indicating the sacks Menannon bore on his shoulders.

"Clarinda is convinced we'll starve ere we return from the 'wilderness' of rural Kalyria," Menannon grinned, his eyes twinkling despite his curiosity and not a little concern over his sire's continual halting of obviously important conversations whenever he made his appearance.

"She has ne'er been without the city walls in all her long life and I suspect she is convinced that no good can come of going anywhere beyond the market place and of course her answer to all is food … in great quantities." Gorlanndon chuckled, then sobered, a slight frown furrowing his brow as he picked up a large heavy scroll from the bench beside him. "Give this to Georgi, my Master of the Horse, will you? And tell him that he needs to prepare me a complete list of all breeding stock." He handed the scroll to Menannon then turned his attention to Lee, his face clearing again.

"So go with the High One and enjoy yourselves!" he said.

"Have a good sevenday," Menannon nodded to his sire with a smile and was rewarded with a wink. "Shall we depart for the terrifying wilderness?" He turned to Lee who immediately headed for the gate. Menannon grinned at his friend's enthusiasm and followed him.

At the gate, the porter and one of the wardens were speaking in low, almost angry voices, but instantly ceased, just as Gorlanndon had, as soon as Menannon and Lee came up. They bowed to their young master and his friend and the porter let them out the gate and closed it after them.

Menannon heard the sound of the bolts being closed and was puzzled. Why are so many conversations suddenly cut short when I come within hearing? It's as though Father and his folk are all determined to not speak of some things in my presence. And why do they lock the gate? What is going on here? Maybe I'm just being suspicious, but I get the distinct feeling that they're keeping something from me. I don't like it, not at all. Beneath the spellbinding beauty of this rose and gold morning however, his concerns receded into the background and he shrugged away his unease. It was too beautiful a day and too wonderful a place to harbor dark thoughts and it might well be coincidence anyway.

The two friends set off down the Equian and turned left at the crossroads to descend its western branch wending down the slopes of the hill opposite the harbor and through orchards just coming into full bloom. All about them, the soft pink of the apple buds vied for notice with the white of their more open fellows, the rose blush of the cherry and the vibrant carmine of the robust peach. The scent of this profusion of blossoms wafting about them as they walked was quite intoxicating. Amidst the orchards, the grape vines were blooming as well, but their small blossoms were hardly noticeable amidst the opening leaves. The vines would get their due in the fall when their great clusters of purple fruit commanded the attention of one and all—including the sea gulls that were always about. Scaring the gulls out of the vineyards was a veritable cottage industry among the less well-to-do children on the island.

The way led them past the walls and impressive gates of the large villas of Kalyria's wealthy. Everywhere, they were hailed and greeted by all manner of folk, both common and high born. Some, like themselves, were rising early while others were wending their way homewards after a night of frivolity or employment. One such fellow was intent upon having a conversation with everything he passed, including the lantern-posts and flowerpots. His several friends, nearly as inebriated as he, were having a merry time attempting to get him along home. It was taking an incredible amount of time to disengage him from his pastime as he kept turning back to the last object that had taken time to listen to his opinions and continuing his diatribe unabated. At the rate they were moving, Lee figured that they just might have sobered up by the time they reached their domicile. Lee was amazed that the life of Kirith Kalyria seemed to be equally lively no matter what the hour as both work and play seemed ubiquitous here. On the mainland, sundown was the limit of activity in most places save the inns and pubs of the harbor districts, but even there, dawn was rarely seen save right side up.

At the foot of the hill they found themselves once again amongst the shops, stalls and humbler homes of Kirith Kalyria's smaller merchants and craftsmen. Even at this early hour, the owners were opening their awnings and setting out their wares, for there were many early customers intent upon obtaining the best. It was a case of first come, best served, although the less discriminating were content to sort through the less expensive dregs later in the day.

As Lee followed Menannon around a last corner towards the gates, he heard a familiar rumbling: farm carts. They emerged from the foot of the Equian way to find themselves amidst the morning traffic from the surrounding countryside, huge farm carts and a veritable army of basket carriers bringing in the morning's produce and wares. Even here, Lee was surprised, for all of the drivers and bearers seemed more courteous than he was used to in either Aridion City or Crenanoc, where it seemed the common belief that the louder one yelled and the harder one pushed, the faster one got to one's destination.

Menannon dodged around a particularly large farm cart driven by a young woman whose dark complexion and waist-length brown curling hair proclaimed her a descendant of Crenanoc and made his way to where the city gates stood wide. Behind him, Lee could not help being transfixed by the cart's comely driver and stood watching her as the cart rolled by him. The Giant came back to collect him and could not help casting his own appreciative look at the lady, who apparently was enjoying the regard of two such handsome youths, for she turned around on her high seat and gave them a wink and a saucy toss of her chin before returning to directing her horses to the fast filling market.

The usual dusk of Lee's face turned to full midnight as the drummer blushed hotly at being caught staring. Menannon grinned broadly and tugged the drummer towards the gates. With a rather dramatic sigh and an expressive roll of eyes, Lee followed, but with one more quick glance at the retreating wagon. For just a moment, he had a flash of homesickness, for the lass brought to mind the twin sisters whose sire's lands ran next to his family's properties. He was suddenly glad he was not required to report back to Aridion City with Menannon in the fall. The indecision he had been suffering as to whether to go back to the hall early or to go on to Crenanoc for a month or so was instantly banished as he decided that a further and more thorough acquaintance with the twins might just be in order. He turned and caught up with Menannon as the latter reached the gate again.

The gates of Kirith Kalyria were more a formality than a requirement for even closed, anyone smaller than a full-sized Giant could easily pass through their delicately filigreed panels. Stationed at their small gatehouse, the wardens, members of Captain Firod's city guards, seemed to be acting more as tour guides than as guards, for they simply waved the harpers through with a slight nod and turned back to giving directions and settling minor disputes. This startled Lee, as on the mainland, city gates were just that: gates. Their intended function was to limit access to the city at need, but apparently here on Kalyria, there was no need for such precautions. He chuckled to himself at his own gawpishness. A regular country bumpkin, I am. Who would there be to keep out? Who, indeed? The Kalyrians had long since subdued any seafaring threat to their empire. The island was not even the home of any predatory beasts that might be feared by its two-legged inhabitants.

It was a walk of a matter of minutes to Gorlanndon's stable hold down a road lined with low stone walls and tall, conical evergreen trees. The holding consisted of a long, low, single story stone house with a slate roof and stable yard surrounded by a fine, dry stone wall. Beyond was a magnificent two-story barn and rolling green meadows with a pond at the far end near which Lee could just make out a small herd of horses grazing peacefully. As they let themselves through the yard's gate, a signal bell attached to it sounded. In response, there emerged from the house a tall Human whose iron-grey hair and squint-lined face bespoke his age and experience. The material of his brown sleeveless tunic strained across the breadth of his chest, hardly needing the broad leather belt and pouch to hold it at the waist. He stood nearly a head taller than the drummer and his massive legs encased in brown cross-tied woollen hose and soft ankle-high boots rather resembled tree trunks. He moved with the smooth grace of one who is comfortable in his body. This was not a fellow to be tampered with lightly.

"Master Menannon! We heard you were comin' home. Welcome, lad! You're a sight for sore eyes and no mistake!" he boomed affably, offering his hand to Menannon who lowered the sacks to the ground and shook the hand thus proffered.

"Lee, this is Paulus Muellen." Menannon turned to the drummer and made the introductions quickly. "He and his wife have served my father for longer than I have been alive. Paulus, this is my good friend, Leènoviilek. We call him Lee."

"You're most welcome here as well, lad. You'll be from Crenanoc, then. Lovely place. Spent some time there in my youth. There was this lovely lass ... ah, but that was many summers ago, and I was young and carefree," Paulus informed him as he and the drummer shook hands. "I suppose you young gentlemen are here to find horses?"

"Aye, my father sends us to Georgi Grimmaxe with instructions," Menannon informed him.

"Ah! So the time has finally come, has it? Himself has been none too quick in makin' up his mind," Paulus nodded and turned to lead the way into the barn.

"The time has come for what?" Menannon inquired, puzzled by the comment, his unease of the morning re-awakening.

"Och, your sire has had in his mind a new breeding scheme for some summers now and 'twould seem he's finally goin' to set it into motion, that's all, lad." Paulus answered promptly enough, but there was that in his manner which made Menannon suspect he was not quite telling the truth, yet without openly accusing the man of lying, there was no way to find out more. He let it go for the moment and followed Paulus into the hay-scented barn.

The interior of the barn was open all the way up to a hammer-beamed ceiling nearly forty feet above their heads. There was a large hayloft at the back below the window opening in the peak and two rows of huge box stalls down either side of a central isle. At their entrance, several curious heads came up over the sides of the stalls and Lee found himself looking up into the faces of horses so huge they actually looked down on Menannon!

"The High One Almighty! Those aren't horses! They're draktas with hair!" he blurted out, incredulous at the sight and stopped dead in his tracks. Menannon could not help laughing outright as his friend reacted more strenuously over the size of the horses than he had at the size of Gorlanndon. But then, he thought, one expects Giants to be tall.

"These are just the small ones," Paulus assured him with a grin and a quick hand to pat any soft nose reaching his way, "but we've a couple at the back more to your size, lad."

He lead the way to the farthest reaches of the barn where a comfortable box stall of normal proportions awaited their inspection. Within it were two large, but not huge, dapple grey horses. They looked up curiously as Paulus opened the gate and entered the stall, signaling Lee to follow him.

"Here, me beauties," Paulus reached out a couple of carrots from his belt pouch and gave them to the drummer. "I'll leave you to make friends while we see to callin' in Kane."

He nodded to the drummer and let himself back out of the stall, leaving Lee to the gentle machinations of two beauties with limpid brown eyes and the softest noses he had ever felt on a horse. Being a member of a horse-loving culture, Lee was ecstatic and set about making friends with a will.

"Come on, then. Let's go call in your special friend," Paulus said to Menannon.

They headed out the back door of the barn which opened upon the rear of the stable yard with its smaller tack shed. Directly facing them, another gate interrupted the back fence of the yard and opened onto a meadow. Paulus strode to the back fence, opened the meadow gate and stepped through, followed closely by Menannon. He halted, indicating that Menannon should whistle in his mount. Obligingly, the Giant pursed his lips and whistled a loud series of notes which ended on a high clear pitch. He was immediately answered by a shrill whinny and the thunder of hoofs. Paulus closed the gate.

"He's been pinin' for you, lad. So you'd best be prepared to get royally greeted," the old horse handler grinned and stepped out of the way.

Menannon stood his ground and watched as a large piece of one of the meadow's hills seemed to detach itself and thunder towards him. The very ground shook to the thunder of hooves the size of battle hammers smashing down like catapult loads. This behemoth soon resolved itself into a huge black stallion with flowing white mane and tail and equally long, draped fetlocks. The fellow stood seven and twenty hands high at the withers and positively towered over his young master as he slid to a halt in a cloud of dust, stopping just barely in time to avoid completely flattening Menannon. As it was, he still managed to knock the young Giant back a few feet with his shoulder. The stallion stood stomping and blowing, nodding and shaking his great head in the excess of his excitement. Menannon stepped towards him.

"The High One's holy blood! Don't get near that thing! He'll squash you flat without even knowing he's stepped on you!" Lee's was nearly terror-stricken at the size of the horse and the power that size represented. The drummer had come out to see what had made the rolling thunder that seemed to come in answer to Menannon's call. "The High One in paradise!"

"Not to worry. This is Kane. I've ridden him since I was five summers old. Though I must admit, 'ride' is not exactly an accurate word. 'Hung on' would be more appropriate. I'd scramble up onto his neck, grab his mane and hope for the best while he went where he would. Did I not, old friend?" Menannon reached up and scratched the stallion's forehead and was rewarded by a playful butt in the chest that knocked him flat. Kane then came over to where Menannon lay and proceeded to nuzzle his face.

"All right, you big lummox, enough." Menannon wiped his face with his sleeve as he scrambled back to his feet. Kane whistled and stomped and made as though to butt him again, but Menannon jumped back and the horse settled for rubbing his face against the Giant's chest.

"He has still ne'er let any ride him save you or your little lady friend, lad. So he's bound to be a bit frisky at first," Paulus warned as they returned to the stable yard, closing the meadow gate behind them, while Paulus headed for the tack shed.

"Nirna has ridden him, then, as she promised?"

"Aye, lad. She's come every sevenday, as faithful as an albatross, all the summers you've been gone," Paulus assured him as he came back out of the tack shed with a saddle and bridle proportioned for this colossus and handed the tack to Menannon.

So Faeori kept her promise, Menannon mused to himself as he proceeded to saddle the stallion with no trouble at all as the horse took the bit of his own volition. Once he had the gear in place, Menannon led Kane through the side gate and out into the main stable yard where he had put the food sacks and held one out to Paulus.

"Clarinda was overzealous of our food needs, as usual. So, if you wouldn't mind, we would appreciate your relieving us of half the burden," he said.

"Surely, lad. The wife will appreciate not havin' to argue her way through the markets for a while," Paulus nodded, accepting the heavy sack with an appreciative grin. "You'd best be settin' a goodly pace, as it's near seventy miles to the Holt. That's a good three days ride even for Kane's long legs."

Lee went back into the barn and made short work of saddling one of the greys and led him out the front door to join Menannon. Both young men swung up onto their mounts with ease and took up the reins. These saddles bore no provisions for feet, so they simply hung on with their knees. Having been ridden often and regularly, Lee's mount was as biddable as the drummer could desire and he was thoroughly enjoying being back in the saddle again though the horse was bigger than any he had ever ridden. He kept his horse well out of the way, as he was not sure what Menannon's Kane would do and he had been involved in a goodly share of wrecks caused by another's horse as his brothers all seemed to have a penchant for riding half–broken desert wildlings.

Despite having ridden rarely over the last ten summers—in fact, not at all since he had attained his full adult height—the young Giant was equal to the antics of his mount, who spent the next few moments playing and doing exactly the opposite of whatever Menannon wished him to do. After something of a wrestling match, Kane settled down with a final shake of his mane, and moved off just as pretty as you please. Paulus let them out of the hold, back onto the road with a wave and went back into the house to finish his interrupted meal. 🐛

CHAPTER 4
(SUMMER OF THE WORLD 6996)

THE FIELDS AND FARMS of Kalyria's people rolled away from the city wall across the Plains of Pelar in a well-ordered landscape of fine stone walls, wood lots, ploughed fields ready for planting and orchards in the full bloom of spring surrounding well kept farmsteads, crofts and numerous villages. It was a good land and treated her people well. Even the poorest folk on Kalyria were housed and fed better than many a yeoman farmer on the mainland.

Beyond the settled sections, the land gave way to rolling hills heavily dotted with sheep and cattle and wooded slopes that climbed up to the lower reaches of Kalyria's Crown and her seven sisters, ancient volcanoes all. From where he rode, Lee was fascinated that he could see both the sparkling blue of the sea and the pristine white of Kalyria's only glacier which was draped between two of the smaller peaks near the Crown. The lower slopes of the mountains were dotted with small villages and not a few mines which he could discern from the tailings stacked in regular mounds at their mouths. Nearer at hand, perhaps three miles distant, was a range of low hills completely clad in dark evergreens though the smoke rising here and there through the trees showed where a few villages or holdings lay sequestered within the forest.

Noontide found them eating fine meat pies at a small inn in a village totally surrounded by fields of sunflowers, whose green shoots would by autumn spring eight feet in the air and turn their multi-rayed blossom to the sun they resembled. This time, it was Lee rather than Menannon who was being made to feel uncomfortable under the attentions of the innkeeper's daughter, a circumstance which the Giant found exceedingly funny as it put the shoe on the other foot for once. They ate a leisurely meal, but then Lee fairly sprinted back to the horses at its end while Menannon settled the account. The girl in question followed him out and stood watching in the courtyard until they turned the corner and disappeared from her sight. When they were safely around the corner, Lee glanced back and heaved a sigh of relief at which Menannon just barely managed to stifle a grin

"You shut up!" Lee growled

"I said not a word," Menannon held up a hand as though warding off a blow and Lee turned back to riding with a nod and they rode in silence for a few moments. "But I was thinking it!" Menannon informed him wickedly and kicked Kane up with a whoop and galloped off, leaving the drummer far behind.

"Some friend you are!" Lee called after him disgustedly and kicked up his grey in turn.

There was a network of roads, all shining white in the rays of the afternoon sun, crossing the lowlands in a regular grid pattern. They, like the one the harpers followed, were made of large blocks of low-grade marble fitted so tightly together it would be difficult to slip a piece of vellum between them. These roads ran as straight as their builders could contrive and were wide enough for two wagons to pass with ease. Any obstructions had been mastered. Hills had been cut down to fill dales and bridges thrown across small streams and marshes. Nothing to aid the ease of travelers had been left undone even to the building of small pavilions every two miles so any who wished could rest. Lee was fascinated to see such engineering in pristine condition. There were in his land naught but the remains of such roads, ruins of the ancient Teluri kingdom of Haal scattered about the landscape above Crenanoc.

The landscape of Kalyria was fascinating to the drummer as he was used to the wild, nearly impenetrable overgrowth of the jungles of southern Wathera or the sand and sun of the Watheran Desert and the steppes and jagged peaks of Rhonndia—lands with a bite to them whose colors ranged from drab to shocking with no transitions and where death awaited the unwary at every turn. Kalyria was a tame, well-watered land, a place where towering beech groves guarded natural forest glades, the colors jewellike and delicate, flowing gracefully one into another. Here the only danger was thoughtlessness and stupidity. In order to die on Kalyria from the land itself, one would truly have to strive for such an outcome.

As the sun set the first evening, they made camp on a small hill crowned with a tall beech with her attendant hornbeams arranged along the far edge of the hill's top like a queen with her ladies-in-waiting. The queen made a lovely roof above them while the ladies formed a perfect wind screen against the breeze that would come in from the sea at sunset. A large, old log formed a good backrest near to a fire pit that had obviously served wayfarers for many summers to judge by the blackening of the rocks around it. The harpers flipped a silver penny to see who would cook and who would clean. Cooking fell to Lee and cleaning to Menannon who immediately dug out a large jug and headed down to the crystalline, spring-fed stream gurgling along at the foot of the hill.

True night found them leaning back against the log, warmed by a cheerful fire and contemplating the stars winking overhead, goodly cups of golden tea in hand. Lee had managed to cobble together an excellent repast from just a few of the ingredients in Clarinda's bag and the washing up had been a matter of moments. Behind them, at the far end of the hornbeam grove, Kane and the grey were ground hobbled and grazing contentedly on sweet grass and yellow clover.

"Have you ever noticed how bright the stars are without a cities walls?" Lee murmured. "Look! There's a shooting star!" He pointed to a streak of light flashing across the southern horizon. They followed the flash until it disappeared into the darkness. "You know, I've not seen one of those since midwinter festival three summers ago. Remember?"

"The shooting star or the festival?" Menannon queried with a grin.

"Either one." Lee shrugged and took a long sip of his tea.

"I remember the star and how could I possibly forget the festival?" Menannon reached over to the tea pot where they had left it on a flat rock near the fire to stay warm. He refilled his mug and settled back. "That was the one where I started playing the wrong music and could not help wondering why no one joined me, as I was not supposed to be playing a solo."

"Oh, yes! I remember. And Grandmaster Blackmore waited until you had done and then said, 'Thank you for that marvelous introduction, Apprentice Menannon, but now could we kindly get back to the planned program?' " Lee chuckled at the look of chagrin on his friend's face, as even three summers later, the young Giant was still embarrassed by his mistake. "Come now, you played so well that no one would have known it was a mistake if he had said naught about it."

"Well, it was a mistake and he was right to take me to task." Menannon quickly rose to Blackmore's defense which caused Lee's grin to widen and Menannon to color nicely when he realized that the drummer was just ribbing him. "It would have been better if he had rebuked me in private, but he didn't," he commented.

"You have grown so serious this past summer, my friend." Lee refilled his mug and considered the Giant over its rim. "Whence has gone that fellow that used to sneak out of the dormitory window with me and raid old man Tolindor's apple trees?"

"Well, I...," Menannon began, but Lee cut him off.

"Do you remember the time I fell off from that old vine we used to climb down from our window and nearly landed on top of Drum Master Nikodemus and you hollered down, 'I told you not to try getting that harpstring back for me, Lee! You could have gotten yourself killed?' " Lee nearly crowed. "Talk about a fast thinker!"

"Aye, and I remember the look on his face, too. Of course he didn't believe either of us, but he was willing to go along so long as you came right back into the hall as though you actually had just fallen out of the window," Menannon reminded him with a shake of his head.

"Now that was truly an embarrassing moment. My pride was definitely deflated."

"That wasn't all that was deflated. If I remember rightly, you had a hard time sitting down for the better part of a sevenday, as you had landed on your 'pride' rather forcefully." They both chuckled over the memory.

"Oh! Oh!" Lee gestured quickly halting Menannon's half-formed thought. "How about when you were so intent on studying that painting you were working on, you stepped back to get a better look at it and fell over backwards right off the dais landing square at the feet of old Sigismund King when he was walking through the hall with Blackmore?"

"Aye, and I remember how hard Grandmaster Blackmore was trying not to laugh when the king patted me on the shoulder as I was sitting there in front of him wondering how I had gotten there. He almost couldn't hold his composure when the King peered at me in his nearsighted way and said 'I appreciate your enthusiasm young fellow, but really, you should have used the stairs to come down here to make your obeisance.' That was one of the more embarrassing moments of my life."

"If you want to talk about embarrassing moments, I've got one for you." Lee shifted around and rested his arm on the log so that he could study Menannon more easily. "Do you remember the midwinter festival I had to miss in our third summer because I had to go home to take part in the ceremony honoring my sire when he retired from active court life?"

"I remember. It was just after your thirteenth name day when you left," Menannon nodded.

"Well, part of the ceremony was to bring a large ewer of blood-red wine down to the Kafiq so that he could bless it and then my sire would serve it. It is traditional to have the youngest son of a councilor carry the ewer and I carried it with all proper dignity right up to the point where I tripped over the first step of the dais and fairly flung the ewer at the Kafiq, who was, of course, wearing his white prayer robes. He caught the thing, but most of the contents wound up on the front of his robes."

"You never told me that."

Lee looked consideringly into his tea before raising his eyes to Menannon's. "Well, at first," he said, "I was too embarrassed and then I didn't have the courage to admit even to you that I had ruined my sire's ceremony."

"Why? I would never have chided you for having an accident."

"I know that," Lee hastened to assure him, "but you see, I knew how much store you set by your sire's good opinion of you that I didn't want you to think I had done something to forfeit my own sire's good opinion."

"That would never have crossed my mind."

Lee drained his mug and they sat for nearly a half turn of the hour each remembering other such moments from their childhood separately and together. At last, Lee screwed his courage to the sticking place and turned to his friend in all seriousness.

"You know, Menannon there is something that I have wondered about ever since we first were assigned beds next to each other in the dormitory. It's rather personal. Do you mind if I ask now?" The drummer raised an inquisitive eyebrow.

"No, of course not. You can ask anything you like. You have earned the right many times over," Menannon assured him with a smile and refilled his mug. "Would you like a refill?" Lee shook his head and Menannon set the pot back down and settled more comfortably against the log and awaited his friend's good pleasure.

"Don't take offence...," he began, which elicited a look of impatience from the Giant. "Ok, ok. You have always been the most talented of us and the hardest working and there was once that I overheard Grandmaster Blackmore telling Dame Larisa that you did not want to disappoint your sire. Would you please tell me why your sire's good opinion means so much to you that you have driven yourself mercilessly for the past eight summers to not just learn and pass every class and skill, but to excel to the point of mastery as just an apprentice? I realize, after having met him, that your sire is an incredible fellow, but he doesn't strike me as someone who would demand the impossible of anyone, not even his own son." There was a long silence after Lee ceased speaking. He wondered if Menannon would answer him or whether his friend had in fact taken offence at the question. Overhead, a nightjar called and was answered by another somewhere down by the creek.

"I'm not really sure that I can explain," Menannon said at last, clearing his throat. "I've never really considered my motives in learning the skills and offerings of our guild. It just seemed the thing to do, but I suppose you're right that the root of it does lie with my father. You see, Lee, I owe him everything because he gave up the truly most important thing in his life for me: my mother."

Lee gave him a long, startled glance, but said nothing, not wanting to interrupt the flow of his thoughts. After a few moments, Menannon continued.

"I caused my father to be cast out of his home village and be branded a dangerous deviant."

"What...how??," Lee nearly whispered, puzzled as to how that could be. He was also horrified at the idea of being an outcast from one's own people. For the Crenanocian, the concept of such a separation was unthinkable, as the core of his personal identity came in large part from his people and his land.

"It started out as one of those embarrassing moments we've been discussing," Menannon continued, his black eyes gazing deeply into the fire as though it were his past. "Father had always warned me not to do a certain thing in public and one fine fall day, I not only did it in public, but in the very council hall itself."

"What on earth did you do!?"Lee sat up, startled, expecting some horrible crime, the exact nature of which eluded him, for what could a mere child do?

"I laughed," Menannon said softly.

"Laughed!?! All you did was laugh? The High One's holy

tears! You were making me think you had murdered someone or something." The drummer sat back with a sigh and a shake of his head.

"To Giants, I believe that would have been preferable." Menannon glanced at him, then turned his gaze back to the fire. "You see, to them, laughter is—literally—a capital offence."

"Surely you jest! Laughter's no crime!" the drummer was sure his friend was having him on. "No one ...."

"Among the Giants, it is." The directness of Menannon's gaze brought Lee up short and he snapped his mouth shut, his mind reeling.

Menannon settled more comfortably back against the log and sought to explain what seemed even to him totally inexplicable.

"The Giants of old were fiery and emotional to a fault, easily brought to laughter, tears, love, hate ... they were so emotionally unrestrained they fell into total anarchy and over time, nearly wiped themselves out in clan wars and blood feuds, and so the clans scattered to the four winds, hoping that isolation from one another would save the race.

"After the clans had separated sometime during the Dim Times, a sage arose in Clan Sommilthraka by the name of Zilronen. This sage preached that isolationism was not enough, that it did not preclude the possibility of clan warfare, that the Giants needed to do something more. Something that would take away all possibility of bloodshed among them. For the sake of their very survival as a race, he taught, they must learn to purge all strong emotion from themselves and live by the tenets of law and order alone for 'emotion kills as surely as a sword,' or so he said. And above all, they must foreswear the Way of Rock and Blood, the traditional practices of weapons mastery and war. To this end, he devised a new philosophy, the Way of Stolidus, a philosophy which embraces total pacifism and in which the rule of law is paramount. Zilronen traveled far and wide among the clans proselytizing his new philosophy. This went well with their innate legalism, for wherever he went, the Giants laid down their weapons and embraced his new world view. They set about purging and criminalizing all strong emotions, teaching themselves and their children the Way of Stolidus. By the tenets of this new philosophy, Giants are not allowed to show more than a slight smile if they deem something uproariously funny and a slight frown if something is worthy of a murderous fury. Any more than that is considered dangerous and deviant."

"Did all the Giants choose this way?" Lee wondered almost more to himself than to Menannon.

"Yea...and nay," Menannon said, shaking his head. "There were those who said it was against the will of the High One to forsake the Way of Rock and Blood. They held that the Giants were taught these arts by Lornennir himself, the sire of their race, at the beginning of the world and his teaching should be honored. Yet, even these bowed to the wisdom of emotionless living, though they were forced to leave the clan lands. The village of New Belitarra above Gormidad was started by such a group from Clan Belitarr. There may be others, but I know naught of them."

"But, Menannon, both you and your sire laugh...." Lee's voice trailed off into the stillness, transforming his statement into a question. The delicate way the drummer was probing for further information without truly asking made the Giant recall that his sire always said the Crenanocian diplomats were the most skilled in the world. He could not help grinning at the thought and quickly cleared his throat and began to answer his friend's non-question.

"It has to do with Father's basic nature," he said, turning thoughtfully serious again. "He has always been of a curious bent, never taking anything at face value. He began asking 'Why?' as soon as he could talk and has never ceased. His curiosity led him to defy the laws of the Giants and look beyond the confines of his clan village and travel the world to find the headwaters of rivers and the source of anything and everything. I swear he has searched in the darkness under stones to see if the darkness is an effect of the stone or of itself alone. He has become an inventor, a scientist, an artist, a merchant, a horse breeder—the list is endless and all due to an unquenchable curiosity. It has led him to put together the largest and most comprehensive library in all of Linden, a collection which includes some of the oldest, most ancient scrolls still extant as well as newly completed manuscripts. He even invented the bound book—the codex —that we so take for granted today. You know, he says he could loose his business and everything else without regret, but losing his library would kill him, for it contains the history and culture of this world. His inventions, he said, he could reconstruct as long as he had the library, for within it are the plans of all the things he has created." He paused, then continued, "I'm sorry, I digress."

Lee gave Menannon a slight grin and motioned to him to continue.

"Among all the things my father has done or become, the most important to his life and mine is that he has become a heretic, for in his travels, he observed how Humans, Dwarves and Teluri all are able to live full and successful lives while experiencing and showing emotions. He also noticed that the warriors among them were not murdering monsters ravening the battlefields like wild beasts.

"Most importantly, he found a complete copy of the Word Hoard of the High One, not one that had been edited by Zilronen. In that unexpurgated copy he found such verses as *Thou shalt love and serve thy fellows with all thy heart and all thy mind all of the days of thy life* and *The valor of thy hand shall protect the weak and helpless*. He could not help but wonder, if the High One Himself did not consider love a crime, how could the other emotions be crimes?

"Leaving Issilandur in charge of his business, he and my mother left here and went back to Lornennog so that he could observe the Giants and the first thing he noticed was that all Giantish children are born with emotions and use them and that they have to be taught that emotions are wrong. So, he wondered, as the High One had so obviously created the Giants complete with emotions, why was it a crime to display and feel them? He came to the conclusion that Zilronen had chosen poorly when he sought to purge emotions from the race of Giants rather than teach the children to control them.

"While they were sojourning there in Lornennog, the unbelievable happened. After centuries of happy, but childless marriage, the High One saw fit to bless my parents with a child. This could not have been better timed as far as he was concerned. Now he would have a child with whom to experiment. So when I was born, he refused to let my lady mother train me to not have or display emotions. He desired to move back here to Kalyria where it would have been easier, but my lady mother refused, wanting me raised among their own kind. Father reluctantly agreed, but continued his experiment despite all. She pleaded with him, but to no avail. When Gorlanndon of Lornennog decides on a course of action he believes in, nothing can dissuade him from it. Though we continued to live among the Giants, he deliberately did not allow even his own parents and siblings around me so that no one would teach me that laughter, crying, love and even anger were wrong.

"My poor mother suffered my childish kisses and hugs with good grace. She even suffered through my laughter so long as Father made it clear to me that such behavior was only acceptable at home and then only when we were alone. Not even the servants were to know about it. To better keep the secret, all but the oldest, most loyal retainers were let go and my lady mother became my nurse. So my deviant behavior was hidden as if I were a madman chained to the attic wall. The plan was successful until I was allowed, in the fall of my fifth summer, to attend the Harvest feast held in the Hall of Councils. Father warned her against it, but my lady mother insisted that I had to be allowed to mingle with other Giants and a large gathering would be the very place for me to mingle, yet still be lost in a crowd. And so we went.

"All was well until one of the servants tripped over a dog near our table and wound up on the floor with the soup pot he had been carrying on his head like a helmet with soup dripping down his face. He pretended that he had fallen as part of the entertainment. Naturally I laughed at the sight." Menannon glanced over his shoulder from where he had been poking the fire with a long stick.

"I have never in my life heard such silence. I doubt anyone even breathed. Then another little boy, a toddler, laughed as well and was cuffed and silenced for it. Everyone turned to my father to see how he would react to my behavior. He just looked down at me and winked and kept eating. I swear he was the only person in the hall daring to move, much less eat. For a moment, nothing else happened, then my mother scooped me up—I was very small for my age—and ran out of the hall with me. I remember that she was in tears and I did not understand why.

"The next day the council held a meeting and my parents were called to stand before it. They walked there together, holding hands, and Father carried me in the crook of his arm. I'll never forget that meeting. All twelve Elders were there in their finest robes. All were seated in their great chairs on the raised dais at the upper end of the hall. All those of the village who could had squeezed into the chamber. So many came the crowd overflowed into the square outside. As my parents walked through them and into the building there was that same thundering silence that I had heard the night before. We halted in the only clear space, directly beside the great fire pit in front of the Elders. That scene is burned into my brain.

"The High Elder broke the silence: 'Gorlanndon, it has forcibly come to our attention'—by the by, the High Elder is my father's father—'that you have not obeyed our laws. Your son has been allowed to regularly commit … a foul crime.' He could not even say the word laughter, it was so abhorrent to him. 'Due to your high standing in this community, you have been allowed freedoms that none other has been allowed and I see now that this was wrong. You have flouted our traditions and laws for your own gain, though until now this has endangered no one but yourself and your lady wife. But with this last, you have endangered us all. To raise a Giant who knows no emotional restraint is a crime against us all and none will sleep safe in their beds until that creature you are raising has been sent to the council school for proper training and this madness stamped out! What defense do you offer?' Everyone turned to my father. There were tears in my lady mother's eyes when she looked down at me and then back up to my father's face.

"He looked at everyone in the hall and thence to my lady mother and barely shook his head. He then looked down at me and with a grin and a wink, tickled me. Of course, I began to giggle despite the palpable strain in the air. From everyone's horrified reaction, you would have thought they were hearing the shrieking of the fiends damned to Outer Darkness. I saw that reaction and didn't feel like laughing any more. My father knew what I was in my heart. 'It's all right boy,' he whispered to me. He swept his arm to indicate everyone in the hall and said in a voice meant to carry to the far corners of the square outside: 'Look at them, boy! See how silly they are? You laugh, my son. You laugh and ne'er let anyone say you nay!' Pandemonium broke out and the High Elder had to slam his staff of office into the flagstones repeatedly to restore order.

"The High Elder fairly shouted, 'Gorlanndon, as you do not seem to comprehend the gravity of this situation, I give you a choice: Train your son properly or be cast out from among us forever!' That form of capital punishment is second only to beheading, so grave an offense is laughter considered among them. Anyone so cast out is forever shunned by all Giants everywhere and any who acknowledge or succor them in anyway will suffer the same punishment. Father stood there for several long moments, looking nowhere but into my lady mother's eyes. She looked up at him, then down at me and burst into a flood of tears and fled the hall. The gathered folk opened their ranks for her to pass then closed back together again as much as to say, she is ours but you are not! My father watched her go until she had disappeared into the throng, then turned back to face the council.

"He said in a strong voice, staring straight into his sire's eyes, 'A choice which allows no choice, is no choice. I follow the teachings of the High One and not of Zilronen, as does my son.' He turned me around to face the High Elder and pointed at him and the entire Council. 'Remember these faces, boy, and know that they will one day regret with all their hearts that they have denied the will of the High One Himself and followed a false prophet. It will be their undoing.' With that admonition, he tickled me again and threw back his own head and began to laugh himself. It was such an incredibly loud, glorious sound. It shook the walls of the council hall, causing everyone in it to cover their ears, cringing. To me, he sounded so happy I took heart and began to laugh again and laughing together, we left the council hall, the village and the Giants and came back here to live." Menannon tossed the stick into the fire and sat back.

"That is, I suppose, why I have worked so hard to make him proud of me. He walked away from his village, his family, his very people so that I could live a true follower of the High One. How, then, could I do any less than I have done?"

Lee swallowed hard and after a while, asked softly, "What happened to your mother?"

"She stayed with her folk," Menannon replied matter-of-factly, almost as though her actions had nothing to do with him. The look on Lee's face caused him to try to explain further. "She came with us to the edge of the Dawn Sea and then departed. She had not the courage to go against the laws of the Giants, so she chose to leave us and return to Lornennog and as far as I know, lives there still. Perhaps she has chosen another consort and has had other children, as her marriage to my father was dissolved by the Elders upon our departure. I truly hope so, for to live totally alone is a cruel fate I would not wish on anyone, least of all my own blood."

Lee sat quietly, considering Menannon's words. He had never known a Giant other than Menannon, and now his sire, so he had not realized that as a race, they were supposed to be emotionless, though there was a saying in his city, as grim as a Giant. The drummer had always thought that sometime in the distant past, some Giant had simply had a good grouch on, rather than it being the description of the race itself. And how anyone could abandon their own husband and child out of fear of ridicule or censure was totally beyond him.

"Come, it's time we got some sleep. We need to make an early start in the morning." Menannon threw the last of his tea away and emptied the pot, took his bedding from behind the log and laid it out on the soft grass. After a few minutes, Lee thoughtfully followed him. Silence fell gently, returning the night to the sounds of the crackling fire and the whispering of the night wind through the leaves of the beech far above them.

BY DAWN, they were already riding through the last of the settled country and beginning to ride through lush forests riotous with creepers, bushes, ferns and all manner of flowering plants. The woods were alive with multicolored birds and replete with squirrels and other small animals. There was also plenty of evidence that there were hoofed creatures here as well. Lee drew Menannon's attention to the marshy edge of a small lily mead beside the crystalline creek along which they were riding, the brilliant scarlet of the lilies a startling contrast to the surrounding green of the meadow. There in the mud, very clearly and so new they were just filling with water, were the tracks of cloven hooves.

"Spiralhorns," Menannon replied to Lee's unasked question.

"Spiralhorns! Surely you jest!" The drummer halted his horse, incredulous. Spiralhorns were things of legend and saga, not real creatures to walk under the rays of the sun and leave hoof prints in the lily meads.

"Truth!" Menannon grinned at him, halting Kane at the same

time. "There is quite a healthy herd on the higher slopes here and on Kidron and they often stray down here in the spring. They are particularly fond of plum blossoms. As I have it, the progenitors of the herd were brought here by Rhindolier the Wanderer as a gift for Kalyrinon King just after the settlement era. Where he obtained them, I know not."

"But ...," Lee began to protest.

Menannon halted him with a swift hand and a gesture of silence. He spoke softly. "Make no sudden movements. Look over your right shoulder and you will see the very creatures near the skirts of the forest. They but wait for us to depart to return to their interrupted drink."

As slowly as he could, his heart pounding, Lee turned his head and beheld a wonder. There, in the dappled shadows of the forest's edge, stood three delicate creatures who bore some resemblance to deer, though they were slightly larger and their glossy hides shaded a dark tan on their backs with soft white underbellies. Their foreheads were crowned with two horns, pale golden and spiraling upward. He was entranced. Never had he seen such delicate beauty.

The spiralhorns stood still, their long ears swiveling as they tested the morning for sounds, their eyes fixed on the youths. Just as it seemed they might return to the more open creek bank, the unmistakable creaking of a farm wagon came from the road hidden in the forest ahead. As the noses of the great work horses pulling it broke from the shadows, the spiralhorns faded silently into the deeper forest as though they had never been. Lee shook himself and blinked. So awed was he, it never occurred to him to be disappointed that the wagon had interrupted his vision. The eyes he turned on Menannon positively glowed.

Menannon just gave him a smile and a shrug as he directed Kane out of the wagon's way.

"Good day t'ye!" the driver bellowed from atop his high seat and saluted them with his whip. He seemed to take the sight of the mountain of a horse Menannon was riding as nothing unusual, but as the fellow was a burly black-bearded Dwarf, it would have been beneath his dignity to show surprise. Lee did, however, see him cast a quick glance over his shoulder as soon as he was past them and he could do so without losing face. Lee grinned and kicked up his grey to catch up with Menannon, already disappearing into the shadows of the forest.

As the day wore on, the road began to wend through a forest so dense it seemed to be encased in a green tunnel though broken here and there by a meadow carved out of it for a farmstead and grazing ground and the remains of last fall's charcoal clamps. For the first time, Lee found himself getting a bit nervous, for on the mainland such a forest would have been the perfect place to encounter outlaws and brigands.

He glanced out of the corner of his eye at the Giant, truly taking in his gear for the first time and realized he bore no weapons, lacking even a belt knife. On the mainland, no one, not even Menannon for all his great strength and height, traveled anywhere unarmed. As a matter of fact, Lee suddenly realized that he had this morning seen another wonder: a Dwarf without an axe! Perchance the fellow had placed his axe on the seat, but no. Lee pictured the wagon to himself and realized he had been able to see the entire seat area and there had been no visible weapon of any kind, unless one considered the whip a weapon, but to a Dwarf such a thing would have been a toy of little use.

Menannon saw the puzzlement on the drummer's face and easily divined its cause. "There are no brigands on Kalyria," he hastened to assure him. "Nearly a thousand summers ago, the captain of the king's guard set out to rid the land of a growing band that was headquartered at Waterdeep, a village above Watermouth bay. They were captured and executed to the last man and a law was enacted that any other such brigands would suffer the same fate with no hope of reprieve. There were a few bold fellows after that who sought to test the law and were dispatched with alacrity. There have been none since, though I will allow that the unwary fellow and his goods can be parted fast enough on the waterfront, but the methods used there are gambling and wenching and the quick change of prices...."

"...which methods, while not exactly illegal, are certainly questionable and found in every port along the sea shore," Lee finished for him, feeling much better about their surroundings, but he just could not help glancing about surreptitiously until they had cleared the forest and were riding up the rolling rocky hills leading to the Marble Cliffs.

These ramparts were made of almost pure marble which had formed alongside the magma flows of the volcanoes, the remnants of the limestone from which they were formed still visible in places as small outcrops surrounded by the expected calcareous soil which supported a plant community unique to it.

They now came upon the large tunnel through the very fabric of the cliffs themselves that made communication and travel between the Fields of Morr and the city much easier. While it was high enough to accommodate large farm wagons and their drivers, it was not made for Giants on horseback, so Menannon was forced to dismount and lead Kane through. In sympathy with this, Lee dismounted and led his mount as well. He could not resist taking advantage of the situation to learn more about these wondrous strange horses.

"You said your clan first bred these beauties?" he asked, indicating Kane.

"Aye." Menannon nodded. "During the first summers after the High One created the world, Kyr Beastmaster, another of the twelve kings of the Teluri, bred the i-Kyriani from Kyrian Firehoof, sometime messenger of the High One and a most unusual beast as you well know from our studies. The result was a line of horses far taller and faster than normal horses, being on average six and twenty hands at the withers. They are also possessed of long life, usually living to three hundred summers. Well, the sires of my clan thought to mix the blood of the i-Kyriani with that of the wild horses running the High Plains of Cala. These wild ones were a particularly large breed that has long been used for battle chargers and plow horses. The fellows pulling the wagon that just passed us and your grey are of that breed. They set about breeding for size, speed and heart. Thus was born the Calish Barb. My father is the only breeder left, as even Kane here could not bear an ordinary adult Giant. According to his calculations, Kane is about as large as it is possible to breed them and still retain their speed and strength. Any larger and they would begin to suffer from the same ills as Humans who grow beyond their body's inherent capacities."

"Who could possibly want a horse taller than this fellow?" Lee said, indicating Kane. They walked for several long moments in silence, Menannon lost in thought.

Thinking of the long-departed and unlamented brigands of Waterdeep had turned Menannon's thoughts again to the strange undercurrents he had been noticing at his father's villa: the suddenly halted conversations; the gates that had never been closed which were now not only closed, but locked and guarded; late night visitations by folk who came with the darkness and left before dawn. His father had never been one to socialize overmuch as he was so busy tending to business, although the day-to-day tasks were left to Issilandur, and in studying and inventing that he tended to forget there were other folk in the world, but he had always attended a few entertainments and banquets at the palace or other villas in addition to his official duties as a Royal Councillor. Strangely, he had apparently not attended any such social functions in more than two full summers according to Clarinda who had been complaining to her young master that his "sire did nay get out enough any more." As the dear lady was an inveterate gossip, Menannon had made it a point to renew his acquaintance with her baking and thus was able to listen to her complaints as well, though he was sure the practice was going to mean Lee would have to roll him onto the ship when they went back to Aridion City in the late fall. His hose were already getting a bit tight about the waist.

One of her favorite laments was his father's new practice of sequestering himself in his office for several turns of the hour almost every day with Captain Firod. When the good captain was present, the office door was always locked and thus she was unable to insist that her master eat his luncheon at a proper turn of the hour. There were times, as Menannon had observed himself in the past few days, that a goodly number of the other members of Kalyria's council came to call, not as councillors, but as private citizens, almost as though they held clandestine meetings at the villa. All of these things were making Menannon's hackles rise with the fear that all was not well with Kalyria and from that thought, he immediately made the leap to Norilendra Queen and Nirna, the Princess Royal. If there was unrest, what was happening with the royal family? Gorlanndon had served four kings of Kalyria and was now serving her Regent, the Queen, but even so, he would not hesitate to go against Norilendra's wishes if he deemed she was wrong and the good of the people hung in the balance.

Lee's low whistle of admiration brought Menannon out of his dark thoughts with a start to find that they had reached the end of the tunnel. They had come out of its darkness into the full light of a glorious evening on the plateau above the Fields of Morr to be rewarded with a magnificent view of a long sweep of emerald green fields flowing down to a sea so clear a blue one could actually see into the depths a hundred feet or more.

"The High One's holy tears," the drummer whispered in awe. He turned to the Giant and shook his head. "If you ever try to say that your homeland is not the most beautiful place in the High One's world, I shall call you a liar to your face and ne'er speak to you again!"

"Far be it from me to disagree with words spoken from the heart," Menannon smiled and joined his friend in silent reverie as they looked at the beauty spread before them.

The road entered the Fields in a long smooth sweep then turned at the base of the cliff and cut straight as an arrow's flight across to the small village which nestled in the very center of this agricultural wonderland. To the farther side of the Fields, Menannon could just make out their destination: a hanging valley perched precariously on the side of the enclosing cliffs.

Menannon was reminded of the last time he had gone riding, just before leaving for Aridion City. He had ridden double on Kane with Nirna mounted in front of him. He could not quite suppress the wish that it was Nirna who rode with him now rather than the drummer. That thought settled it. He had put it off long enough and as quickly as possible upon their return, he would have to find time to call upon her even though it would mean abandoning Lee for a day and facing the Queen's disapproval. That resolution firmly made, Menannon remounted and they headed down into the valley to make camp.

WHILE MENANNON AND LEE were abroad on their camping trip Gorlanndon spent the time catching up on work demanding his attention at his trade hall, often staying late. On one such eve as he sat at his desk near the mid-of-night, the clear light of a Dwarf lantern shining upon several large scrolls in a neat stack upon his desk and one rolled out flat held so by the weight of its spindles and the silence of the place was itself a sound, he heard the front doors whisper open and feet come across the atrium. Moments later, a small, freckled face peered around the side of his office doorway.

"Come in, child," Gorlanndon smiled, laying his brush into its holder and motioning for the youngster to enter, "and be welcome. What brings you here long after you should be tucked in bed?"

"Grandmaster Blackmore did b...b...bid me come," the boy stammered, sidling into the chamber, his apprentice robes catching around his bare feet. The red mop of hair sweeping into his eyes could not disguise the look of awe at the sight of the Giant. The lad was from an outlying village on the farther side of the Plain of Pelar and though he well knew of Gorlanndon, as did all upon the island, he had not before set eyes upon him.

"What does your master require of me?" Gorlanndon asked, keeping his voice light so as not to discomfit the child any more than he already was.

"He...he wishes you to attend upon him up at the hall, master." Though a bit shy in the Giant's presence, the little messenger was nearly popping with importance at having not only seen, but spoken to two of the most august people in his world in one night! The other lads were going to be pea-green with envy that he and not they were Master Penor's runner. Until now, the rest of the apprentices had rubbed it in that he was at Penor's beck and call, as no one at the hall liked the Master Harper, but now they would have to admit the position did have its advantages. "N...now, if it please ya, Master."

"Hold then a moment. I come." Gorlanndon grinned at the lad and quickly rolled up his scroll, placing it and its fellows into their pigeon holes in the wall behind him. He set his desk to rights and closed the lantern, plunging the chamber into semi-darkness now lit only by the moonlight coming through the atrium roof. He strode out to the front door and halted, as the child had to run to keep pace with him. From the dirt clinging to his feet and the hem of his robes, running was just what he had been doing in his whole search, as he would have gone first to the villa and then to the trade hall.

"By your leave young sir, may I give you a ride on my shoulder as we'll reach your master that much the faster without your having to run all the way?" Gorlanndon looked down, one inquiring eyebrow raised, deepening his resemblance to his son.

The apprentice nodded vigorously, blue eyes round and tongue tied with delight. With a soft chuckle at the reaction to his offer, the mighty Giant picked the lad up and perched him on his shoulder and left the hall.

At first, the lad clung to the collar of the Giant's kirtle as he had never been this high in his life, not even in the trees he had climbed in the forest near his parent's cottage. Soon, however, the smoothness of the Giant's stride and the thrill of the ride claimed him and he relaxed, giving himself over to an adventure he would remember and tell his children, grandchildren and great-grandchildren until death claimed him.

All too soon for the apprentice's liking, they arrived at the harper hall and Gorlanndon set him down at the bottom of the portico steps, for even here at the harper hall, he was forced to bend nearly double to negotiate the door.

The lad obligingly ran up the steps and opened the doors for him and he managed to duck through for it was only ten feet high and just wide enough for two Humans to fit through together. Even inside, he could not stand upright as the ceiling was only twelve feet high.

"Come this way, master." the lad scampered off to neither the hall's office nor even the High Hall of Gathering, but to the enclave's walled garden. Gorlanndon followed as silently as only a Giant can, for he had been summoned thus many times before and the Valinga had always come in secret, even from the Master Harper here in Kalyria. In summers past, the Valinga had come down to the trade hall to meet, but in the last fifty or so Blackmore had begun to summon the Giant as he could no longer walk so far. Exactly how he arrived on the island Gorlanndon had never known, but that it was by Mythrian magic was obvious as the harper had refused the offer of the use of the Giant's flagship, the Julianna, saying that it was too slow to serve his needs.

They twain came to the garden door and the lad reached for the lowest of its three handles.

"Grandmaster?" The lad pushed open the door and called softly.

"Here, lad." Blackmore's voice wafted quietly across the garden from near an ancient wisteria trained into a tree where stood the "Seat of the High One's Men." There was such a seat in the garden of every harper hall reserved for the explicit use of the Grandmaster should he deign to visit. There in the moon's shadows, Gorlanndon found Blackmore awaiting him.

"My thanks lad" the old fellow nodded to his apprentice. "Now go and tell no one of this night's work. If asked, say only that you were sent with a message to himself," he indicated the Giant. "Tell no one by whom." The old Valinga smiled benignly at the child who obediently scampered off, satisfied with a job well done and appreciated. When the door had closed behind him, Blackmore addressed Gorlanndon.

"Now if you please, set me up there on the wall and we shall converse." Blackmore pointed to a spot on the surrounding stones that was clear of ivy and close to ten feet high. Gorlanndon obligingly picked him up and settled him comfortably on the desired spot. He then leaned next to him so that their heads were now close enough together for easy conversation. Not one to waste time, Blackmore got right to the point of this visit.

"Old friend, I have had reports that not all is well here on Kalyria," he said softly. "Can you enlighten me?" In the moonlight, the ancient harper looked all of his great age and more, his good eye clouded with concern not only for his guild, but for all of the High One's children, for he was the spiritual father to all of Linden, the Harpers Guild counting among their number the priests of the High One as well. Thus, the Grandmaster Harper also bore the weight of the office of High Priest.

"Great evil has come among us," Gorlanndon said answering directness with directness.

"I see," Blackmore's voice held knowledge far greater than his mere words would imply. "How came this?"

"Norilendra Queen made a good will voyage east three summers ago to Hardura, Boria and Silimon. Upon her return, she brought with her a new councilor and confidante whom she had already named Counsel General in place of Lonier. She announced him at the first full meeting of the General Council. I well remember her exact words: 'You will come to value him as I have. We are blessed with the knowledge and services of Counsel General Azuron!'

"I will not tell you that we all took this announcement in

good faith and good will for that is not so. Especially not with the sight of him standing there at her side as though he owned the spot. While none of the rest, save perhaps Ambassador Solumin of Hardura, had e'er seen him before, all felt the strangeness of him. I, on the other hand, have seen him before and not as a bringer of good counsel and benign service." Gorlanndon turned his gaze directly to meet Blackmore's good eye.

"Blackmore, he is that Azuron known as the Black Sorcerer of Boria!" There was a deep resounding silence in the garden as both of them thought back to the wars in Boria fought nearly five hundred summers ago when the ancient line of kings was overthrown by a prince of their house with the aid and counsel of a Teluri sorcerer whose bald head and smoky eyes were forever burned into their memories. When the fighting was over, a new order had been established in Boria whose economic basis was slave trading and piracy and whose spiritual awareness had turned form the High One to Khalandria, the Black god of Death.

"I will not insult you by asking if you are sure that this is he,"Blackmore said, breaking the silence. Unconsciously, he rubbed the scar closing his left eye as he spoke. "What think you he intends here?"

"The same as has been intended everywhere else." Gorlanndon turned and looked out across the wall and down at the twinkling lights of the lower city. He began picking small pieces of stone from the wall and flicking them into the night.

"I have watched a path of desecration and destruction move across the lands of the East for the last thousand summers and always it leads back to a mysterious source. A mystic or sorcerer who suddenly appears at the left hand of the king promising peace and prosperity, but bringing death and desecration." He turned back to the Valinga and lowered his voice still more. "And now it is our turn."

"I fear I believe in my heart of hearts you are right," Blackmore nodded. "I'm sure its roots lie as far back as the Dim

Times when the forces of Khalandria were defeated by the followers of the High One or earlier .... I suspect even the rise of Zilronen among your people was from the same source, for he was able to turn your folk away from being the High One's intended Guardians practicing the Way of Rock and Blood to pacifists, thus robbing our world of its appointed defenders"

"Aye!" Gorlanndon agreed. "As the leader of our clan, my own father is Zilronen's staunchest adherent. On Zilronen's counsel, he ordered our clan to follow the new philosophy, the so-called 'Way of Stolidus.' The greater fools, they." There was an edge of disgust in Gorlanndon's voice as he spoke of these things. Another long silence was followed broken only by the cry of a nightjar and the barking of a far off dog.

"What do you intend to do?" the Grandmaster queried at last.

"I fear I know naught what course to take," Gorlanndon sighed, turning to look back down at the city. "I have already attempted to persuade Norilendra of her folly, but to no avail. She is totally in his power. Short of overthrowing the government myself ...," the Giant let his words trail off with a shrug of his shoulders.

"No, indeed. That would break the covenant between the High One and Kalyria with disastrous moment." Blackmore agreed with Gorlanndon's unspoken assessment. "Have you informed Menannon of all this?"

"Nay! Though he has nearly caught me talking to others on several occasions. I know he suspects something is afoot. I do not want him involved in any of this. The High One has greater plans for him than to loose him to the machinations of evil. Azuron knows full well I am the only real impediment to his plans and Menannon to be my one weakness. No, my son must be kept clear."

"He will worry and perchance act rashly if he learns only pieces of the truth," Blackmore warned, knowing his volatile journeyman all too well.

"I know, but be that as it may, if he learns the truth, no power in the High One's world would keep him from my side and then Azuron would have the weapon he needs to defeat me." Gorlanndon turned back to look at Blackmore once more. "Old friend, you know I have given up everything truly dear to me—my homeland, my people, even my beloved wife—so that Menannon could grow up a true follower of the High One, free of the taint of Zilronen's evil. Azuron knows this for Norilendra has always known it and all that she knows, he comprehends most thoroughly. Threaten Menannon and he threatens me. Control Menannon and he controls me. The more ignorant of the truth my son is and the farther away I can keep him, the safer we all are. So long as I am free of impediment, Azuron will have to be cautious of his actions. The more time he has to take, the greater the possibility of his making a mistake that will allow me to take him down without breaking faith with the High One."

Blackmore nodded his head in understanding, though not without reservations. "Well, my friend, it is late. I leave you to do what you may. I will do what I can. Call upon me at need."

"I shall. Safe journey, though I know not how you come and go," Gorlanndon said as he set the Valinga upon the ground.

Blackmore grinned at him and winked. "There are few who do. Not even Pennor."

With that, the Grandmaster of the Harpers of Aridion departed for his quarters many leagues away in the West. He arrived just in time for the prior evening's meal.

IT TOOK LEE AND MENANNON most of the next morning to ride across the Fields, as they stopped so often to admire some view or speak with a stout crofter. The villages dotting the Fields of Morr were nearly deserted save for a few of the oldest and youngest inhabitants, as all the rest were out in the fields and orchards taking advantage of this beautiful day to both work and bask in the sun. They rode through the quiet high streets of each village with their tidy homes and shops, clean cobblestone streets and on out the other side with only a nod or two from a grandsire or grandam seated on the front porch of a well-kept, slate-roofed, stone cottage keeping a weather eye on grandchildren playing in the garden. By mid-afternoon they found themselves riding up the long switchbacks to Gorlanndon's holding in the hanging valley where the bulk of his stud was kept.

The road crested a final rise only to be halted by a strong gate made of solid pine fourteen feet high, three feet thick and closed—no decorative filigree here! From Kane's broad back, Menannon sat high enough to see over the wall. Here again, the holding sported a solid, single story stone house with a slate roof and a large pillared portico fronting on a slate-paved stable yard. Along the south side was a garden already brave with vegetable starts and roses. A pond with a fine gaggle of geese completed the home area. To the rear and dominating the courtyard was a large barn, basically the twin of the one at Paulus' holding, the main difference being that the rear fence did not open onto a meadow, but into a cleft in the mountainside which led in turn to a fine box canyon that was home to Gorlanndon's main stud. Menannon looked about carefully and noted little activity in the main yard, only two small children playing with a basket of puppies and several hens intent upon finding any seeds which might have been dropped by the gardener. Of any adults, there was no sign, yet Menannon knew they were being watched and very carefully so.

Casually, so as not to arouse any suspicions, he threw his leg over Kane's ears and slid to the ground. When Lee made as though to dismount as well, Menannon shook his head and stepped up to the arched gateway where he pulled the bell pull and heard the deep thrum of the signal bell echo within the barn and the lighter tinkle of the house bell. There was no answering sound for several minutes then, just when Menannon had decided to pull the rope a second time, he heard footsteps on the other side of the gate and the thunk of a bolt being withdrawn. A small embrasure opened in the face of the gate.

"Stand ye back so's I can be seein' ye," a gruff voice ordered, much less than politely.

Obligingly, Menannon retreated until he was standing far enough back he could be seen clearly through the embrasure which was less than halfway up the gate.

"Humph...as yer ridin' Kane an' bearin' the looks o' himself, ye must be his lad an' as such I'll be lettin' ye in. But one false step and ye'll wish ye hadna made it. Right smart, now, and don't tarry!"

With that admonition, the embrasure slammed shut and the sound of chains rattling announced the opening of the main gate. Lee and Menannon exchanged a puzzled glance, but did not hesitate in entering the holding. Gorlanndon's son or not, Menannon was sure if they tarried, the gate would be slammed in their faces.

The gate arch was high enough that Menannon could have ridden through, it having been made to allow Gorlanndon easy access, but he did not remount and instead, quickly led Kane into the main yard. Lee followed close behind. When they halted just within the grounds, the drummer carefully dismounted and stood beside Menannon, not quite sure what to do next. Behind them, the gate suddenly slammed shut with a great bang and a burly, ill-tempered Dwarf marched around in front of them and halted, his thumbs thrust into a broad belt which sported a large war axe and a good sized short sword. He wore a full boiled leather breastplate and greaves over his dark grey tunic and woolen hose. His intricately braided, grey streaked, black beard thrust into his belt was nearly bristling with distrust as he planted himself belligerently in front of his visitors.

The children and puppies had disappeared as if by magic, and a tall willowy Human woman just past her prime to judge by the wings of grey beginning to form in the dark hair above her temples, now stood quietly on the portico watching them. In her, Menannon recognized Sandrina Grimmaxe, Georgi's lady wife. While it was not uncommon in greater Aridion to find Humans married to Dwarves, it was something rarely seen on Kalyria and in fact, this was the only such match of which Menannon was aware on this whole island though he was sure there were more. Menannon inclined his head to her. Lee followed suit. The Dwarf followed their glances and waved his wife back into the cottage, she disappeared instantly and he turned back to them with a glower.

"Well, state yer business an' be quick about it," Georgi growled without preamble and with no deference paid to his master's son and heir. Lee started to bristle at this insult, but Menannon gave him the slightest of warning frowns and bowed gracefully to their reluctant host.

"Is it my pleasure to be addressing Georgi Grimmaxe?" he inquired formally just as though he had not known the Dwarf as a child and the welcome had been mannerly rather than churlish.

"Aye," came the flat answer.

"Then my sire did bid me give you this scroll and tell you to begin making him a list of all breeding stock." Menannon withdrew the scroll Gorlanndon had given him from the breast of his kirtle and held it out to the Dwarf.

The fellow fairly snatched it from his hand and broke the seals. He read quietly for a few minutes then looked up at Menannon consideringly. "Have ye read any o' this?" he asked, his manner fairly dripping with suspicion.

"Nay," Menannon shook his head. "It was sealed ere my sire gave it me. Of its contents, I know naught." He maintained his formal manner which puzzled Lee further. While Menannon was known for the evenness of his temper, he was not one to suffer insult mildly, yet here he was being insulted right and left by an ill-humored hireling and not reacting at all. Even having to cool their heels in the courtyard while the fellow read his mail had no effect on him. The Dwarf read for a few more minutes, then re-rolled the scroll and thrust it under his arm and looked up riveting him with a glare.

"Air ye sure yer Da said exactly them words: 'a complete list o' all breedin' stock'?" The Dwarf slapped the scroll for emphasis.

"Aye," Menannon assured him, rather puzzled.

"All right, be off wi' ye. We've got work to be doin' an' there ain't no time fer entertainin'.'" Grimmaxe stomped back to his cottage and slammed the door, leaving the two harpers to exchange puzzled shrugs and let themselves back out the gate.

When they were remounted and riding back down the switchbacks, Lee finally questioned Menannon about the Dwarf's attitude and conduct.

"I know not why he's being so very rude this day," Menannon shrugged. "Georgi Grimmaxe has always been less than polite and somewhat taciturn, but I've never known him to act like this. Something certainly has his saddle on sideways and no mistake. Another thing I find odd...and unsettling: he's armed and armoured." Menannon turned his attention back to the road, struggling to set aside the worry that was beginning to crowd in upon his mind again. He had no intention of darkening Lee's visit, but his sire was going to be answering some questions, and soon.

They reached the lowest switchback above the valley and halted, coming to a parting of the road. The way they had come turned and went on down into the valley, but a small, little used trail branched off and began wending its way steeply up the mountain to a saddle high above. Menannon could not resist a spur-of-the-moment change in plans. He glanced up at the sun. They still had plenty of time before evening darkness closed in. Without a word, he turned Kane's head into the new trail and headed up the mountain. Lee followed behind, a bit puzzled. The trail was indeed steep, so much so that Lee was not sure he would have been able to get up it on foot without a stout walking stick and a rope. The horses, however, were used to such things and made their way easily. In a much shorter time than the drummer would have credited, they reached the saddle. The trail widened out in the flat area between the two mountains which sported not only a small traveler's hut, but a large stone platform obviously meant to be an overlook to the north.

Menannon dismounted, ground hitched Kane, and walked out onto the platform to look down the other side. Lee followed him, though he took the precaution of flopping the reins of his mount over a limb of a convenient tree whose wind-warped presence attested to the determination of plants. It was obviously a full-grown fir tree, but its topmost branches came just to the drummer's shoulder, most of its branches laying low along the rocky ground.

The wind must get to hurricane force up here, Lee thought and could not help whistling at the thought of wind strong and steady enough to shape a tree's growth pattern. All about were other such trees and low-lying plants which all formed cushions and rugs of green rather than attempt to raise flowering stalks into the air as did their lower elevation cousins. Luckily, this day the wind was contenting itself with being just a stout breeze.

Lee took hold of his flapping cape and stepped onto the platform beside Menannon and looked north to be rewarded with a breathtaking view. The side of the mountain fell away in a straight cliff down to the great Watermouth Bay lapping the rocks a full thousand feet below them, its water a deep aquamarine and again so clear one could see the great fish swimming within it. Beyond the bay, the Dragon's Teeth thrust up, the white wave heads frothing about them as the tide was coming in. They were the remains of the north edge of the caldera of the ancient volcanic island that was Kalyria. Closer along the feet of the mountains to the east, four small villages lay between the water and the rock. Lee could see their fishing boats and nets hauled up after the night's work. Farther along, about half way around the edge of the bay, was Waterdeep Town, the fifth and largest village clinging in several levels up the side of Kalyria's Crown. Above this village and further to the east, a great dark maw showed in the mountain's side out of which sprang an incredible waterfall, its water gushing in torrents and sparkling mist into the bay far below. Beyond the waterfall, a long artificial construction caught Lee's eye. It dropped down the rocky face from the waterfall to the very shore of the bay and even into the water there.

"What is that?" Lee questioned pointing to it. Menannon followed the drummer's gesture and saw the source of his perplexity.

"That's the Waterdeep inclined plane." The Giant informed him.

"The what?" Lee turned a puzzled frown on his friend. Menannon grinned and pointed back to the strange construction.

"It is called an inclined plane and is used to raise and lower ships. My father invented it. Many summers ago, he discovered that a series of water-filled lava tubes runs across the island from a central basin, or lynne, beneath Kirith Kalyria to the side of Kalyria's Crown above Waterdeep. Several underground streams feed into this system. The water pools in a deep lynne on this end as well before it flows over the side into yonder waterfall. The tubes are large enough to accommodate great ships, so he decided to put them to use and created a mooring basin within the Citadel beneath the palace and this mechanical device to then lower the ships into the sea. He uses it to harbor his flagship."

"How does it work?" Lee was intrigued.

"If you look closely at the mouth of the tube, you can just see a huge, long, half-cylindrical water-filled container." Lee followed Menannon's pointing finger and could barely see a large vat of some kind within the mouth of the cavern. "My father sculls his ship along the lava tube from the city and enters that container through a series of gates, and then the whole thing, container, ship, water and all are winched down the long rails you see and into the edge of the bay. The water is deep enough there that the rails can reach down far enough into it so the ship can sail out of the container when its gates are opened at the bottom. He has been using it for many summers, as his personal ship is so huge it causes major traffic jams in the city's own harbor."

"Your sire is an amazing person," Lee shook his head in wonder.

"He is, isn't he?" Menannon agreed with a smile. "If you are lucky, perchance he will have need of launching his ship while we are here and you will be able to witness it in use. But come, we must head down or we'll not reach the valley floor ere dark and I, for one, don't like pitching camp in darkness. I've managed to set my bedding down on too many thistle patches and cactuses in my time."

Lee glanced questioningly at the stone hut.

Menannon replied with a grin, "The roof leaks and I do not like the wind up here. It is loud and fierce."

Lee said nothing, but his dark eyes shown with wonder as he glanced one more time over the cliff edge. As the sun really was beginning to wester far towards evening, he did not linger, but followed Menannon to the horses.

CHAPTER 5

(SUMMER OF THE WORLD 6996)

THEY ARRIVED BACK AT THE VILLA at the end of the sevenday, to find Gorlanndon hosting an intimate banquet attended only by Captain Firod with his children and the members of his own household. Menannon could not hope to get the chance to speak privately with his sire under these circumstances, so resigned himself to enjoying the evening and worrying about the odd actions of Georgi and others later. As he washed and dressed for dinner, he promised himself he would corner his sire at the first opportunity and not take "No!" for an answer.

When Menannon entered the dining hall, Firod's children were already seated at a small child-sized table to one side of the banqueting chamber near the hearth for their comfort. They were being shepherded by their eldest sister, as Firod's wife was still in confinement after the birth of their eighth child, a boy. Both mother and son were doing fine. Firod himself was seated near the head of the table to the left of his host where he was keeping a weather eye on his children as well. To his left sat Skendrin and his lady Mariett, the latter deep in conversation with Clarinda who always ate with the rest of the family when she had finished superintending the meal's preparations.

The hall was small enough to be intimate, but large enough to accommodate quite a gathering should its master wish. Here as well, the walls and the ceiling were alive with exquisite murals. Sitting at the table, one felt as if they were seated in the center of a high mountain meadow surrounded by white-tipped peaks and thousands of wildflowers. A ceiling painting of a clear blue sky overhead completed the illusion. All along the sides were sideboards for serving and innumerable cases holding all manner of oddments of stone, statuary and specimens both botanical and zoölogical collected over hundreds of summers by Gorlanndon in his travels. It was essentially a utilitarian cabinet of curiosities.

Menannon circled around the table and took a seat next to Lee at its foot. The chairs about the table were of varying heights set to accommodate all races. Lee was beginning to come to expect this of his host. Gorlanndon nodded to him from his seat at its head where things had been arranged neatly so that his guests could converse with him comfortably. As at the Cokeyna, his great chair stood within a sunken area of the floor and the end of the table was raised a bit so that he was more of a height with his guests, but also did not have to lean to get to the table himself. There was space beside Gorlanndon at the head of the table for another chair and place setting, though none was set. Menannon knew that this had been his mother's place during the nearly seven centuries she had lived here. Her influence was still felt throughout the villa and grounds.

At Gorlanndon's signal, the kitchen staff began to serve the courses. The meal was enjoyed amidst much merriment and laughter. There were sufficient courses and sweets afterward that even Firod's middle son, in the midst of constant growth-induced hunger, was satisfied. As the staff cleared away the remains of the feast, Gorlanndon glanced thoughtfully to where Menannon sat in soft conversation with Lee.

"Boy!" he hailed him. "Could we persuade you to play for us this evening?"

"Most assuredly, sir." Menannon's face lit up at the request and he quickly excused himself to go and fetch a lute from his chamber, as that instrument better fit the informality of the family dining hall than did his harp.

"Does anyone perchance have a drum or even a stout leather bucket?" Lee enquired as they awaited Menannon's return. "I fear I did not bring my drum on this holiday and I would accompany Menannon if there is something I can play." As there was no drum in Gorlanndon's home, a good stout leather bucket and two heavy wooden spoons were produced with alacrity. Thus he was ready when the young Giant re-entered the banqueting hall. Menannon stopped short at the sight of the odd instrument.

"How do you think I practiced after lights-out when we had examinations coming up?" Lee grinned at him and tapped out a rhythm on the bottom of the bucket held upturned on his knee. It gave out a satisfying, if a bit flat, hollow thunk. Menannon grinned and shook his head. He quickly regained his place at the table and set about tuning his lute.

"What shall we play?" He gave a questioning look around the eager group which was, he noted, larger than when he had left to get his instrument. It seemed the entire household had gathered into the spacious dining hall to hear them play.

"Something about draktas!" one of Firod's smaller sons called out while his littlest sister bounced in her seat and clapped her hands in eagerness.

"Draktas, eh? Hmmm...Ah, I know!" Menannon turned to Lee. "Do you remember *Finicky's Fussiness* from our first apprentice class?"

"Of, course! That will do nicely," the drummer agreed and started off with an impressive drum roll despite the primitive nature of his instrument and odd drumsticks. Menannon quickly joined in and soon the chamber was filled with the music and story of a particularly inept Fæorlinga, Finicky by name, one of the nature guardians of ancient Kaalamar whose efforts to control the weather in his small patch of forest proved so annoying to a greater stone drakta that the beast agreed to serve him for one full turn of a summer if he would only stop making it rain. Finicky had actually been trying to make the sun shine on a particular patch of forget-me-nots and had succeeded instead in calling up a rain cloud which did nothing but spin about the drakta's head and drench him continually no matter where he went, even in his cave.

The children were delighted with the song and when it was done began shouting all sorts of other suggestions. The rest of the evening was spent in the enjoyment of music and laughter as Menannon and Lee played everything from sea chanties to love ballads. Menannon noted that the audience was constantly changing as staff came and went quietly to partake of the entertainment for as long as they could before their duties required them to leave. For the better part of three turns of the hour, the two Harpers entertained the appreciative assembly until the drummer finally hit his bucket with a bit more enthusiasm than he should have and a spoon snapped in half, bringing the evening's entertainment to an abrupt close. Although another spoon was proffered, it was agreed that it was late and time to bring a halt to the evening's entertainments. There was an enthusiastic round of applause and some sounds of disappointment, the loudest from the children, when the harpers retired their instruments, Menannon's to the side board and Lee's to the mop closet.

As soon as everyone had returned to their drinks and conversations once more, Firod's eldest daughter stood from her seat at the small table, crossed to her sire's side and spoke softly, her bright gold hair glinting in the gleam of the Dwarf lanterns. Darya was tall for fourteen summers, already showing the beauty of her mother in the fineness of her bone structure and the figure that was beginning to show beneath the folds of her robe. A few more summers and Firod would have to guard his gates well, Menannon thought with an inward smile as he watched the two converse. He noticed that the other children were watching their sire with great intensity and he wondered about the subject of the conversation. Her voice was pitched so that none but those directly at the head of the table could hear her. The twain carried on a soft conversation for several moments during which she indicated herself and her brothers and sisters. Firod glanced over his shoulder at his children, then turned back to Darya.

"Azuron has called a special session of the Privy council for tomorrow. We'll be in council the entire day if things go as usual," Gorlanndon interrupted the conversation, his voice carrying clearly to the rest of those at the table. Firod nodded and turned back to his daughter and spoke to her.

Darya looked very disappointed at his words and she quickly replied. From her body language alone, Menannon could tell as plainly as though he could hear her words that she was saying, "… but Papa, you promised." Firod shook his head and she sighed and began to turn away when Gorlanndon raised his hand, halting her. She looked up at the elder Giant questioningly.

He spoke for a moment to Firod who nodded and then turned his attention to Menannon. "Are you free for the morrow, boy?" he questioned, frowning in thought.

"Yes, sir," Menannon answered, wondering if his sire intended to ask him to attend tomorrow's council as had been his wont when he was a child. Instead, Gorlanndon's face cleared and he exchanged a quick glance with Firod.

"I have a favor to ask of you. Could you perchance be persuaded to take these imps of the good captain's for an outing to Clear Lake above Black Falls? Their sire will be otherwise occupied and must therefore be foresworn on a promise, but you can keep it for him, if you will."

"Right willingly, sir!" Menannon replied, his enthusiasm for the idea plainly showing in his voice and the way he sat up a bit straighter. "It would be my pleasure."

Darya looked greatly relieved at his reply, then blushed prettily and lowered her eyes. Several of the other children exchanged excited murmurs. In the short time he had been home, the young Giant had already managed to become a great favorite with everyone who frequented Gorlanndon's holding. Lee was reminded again that Menannon was one of the only apprentices or journeymen who never objected to being assigned to care for the child oblates at the harper hall or the orphans at the alms house. The drummer's thoughts were interrupted as Firod continued.

"You need not take them all. The youngest, Shira, should remain home with their nurse, for she is too small for such a long outing," the captain hurriedly assured his surrogate escort.

At the table by the hearth, the object of Firod's words gave her sire a very resentful look.

"At your word, sir, but she would be no trouble," Menannon assured him with an eye to the look on Shira's little face.

"Nay, she will stay." Firod shook his head.

"Good! 'Tis settled then," Gorlanndon turned back to Darya. "Take your siblings to the guest wing and settle them to bed as you might as well stay the night. Then have yourself and your siblings gathered in the courtyard in the morning and my son shall meet you and serve as escort for your outing. Does that suit?"

"Most agreeably," Darya smiled at Menannon and dropped Gorlanndon a pretty courtesy then nearly ran back to the children's table and began to shepherd them from the chamber and off to bed, as they would need a good night's sleep.

Gorlanndon spoke softly to one of the servers standing near the door, "Go find the bearers and dismiss them as the children will not need the sedan chairs tonight. Menannon will see them to their home after the outing." The man nodded and left followed closely by all of the children, save for Shira who lagged behind, her stuffed toy dog, Pin, clutched in her hand. As the other children disappeared, she halted and turned back and walked determinedly to Menannon's end of the table. Carefully circling around Lee, she came and stood beside the young Giant's chair. She was so small none but Lee and Menannon could see her. Pretending to be deep in conversation with the drummer, Menannon watched the child out of the corner of his eye, wondering just what she was about. Shira stood on tiptoe to reach up as far as she could towards Menannon's knee and tugged on the leg of his hose.

"Hello…hello…hello…."

Menannon glanced down and raised an expressive eyebrow. "Hello." Beside him, Lee hid a smile and moved his chair back, giving her better access to her quarry. At the other end of the table, Firod started to speak, but Menannon forestalled him with a quick grin and a slight shake of his head. He turned his attention back to his imperious visitor.

"I come too...yes!" Shira's dark brown eyes snapped with determination and her little voice carried clearly to everyone at the table as she pointedly informed Menannon of her intentions. The curly-haired moppet was having to lean so far back to speak to the Giant she nearly fell over backwards. He reached down, took her up and stood her on his knee to ease the task.

"Hmmmmm," Menannon frowned at her consideringly. "You're awfully heavy and perchance I shall get tired carrying you all the way to the lake ...."

"I not!" came the indignant answer. "Papa says I a feather!"

"A feather?! A feather from a roc, mayhap, and those are very, very heavy," Menannon assured her, his look quite serious.

"Nu-uh!" Shira was equally serious and shook her head solemnly for good measure. Around the table everyone was having an incredibly difficult time not to laugh as this tiny mite gave as good as she got. Even Firod's usually stern mein was twitching with suppressed laughter as his small daughter treated with the young Giant.

"I deem you are a roc," Menannon nodded. "So, you're definitely too heavy to carry all the way to the lake. I'd better leave you home...."

"Nu-uh! I a girl."

"How do you know?

"Papa told me," she said with all the assurance of childhood when a sire's every word has the veracity of gospel.

"Well, I still deem you're a roc. Do you know how to tell a roc when you find one?" Menannon asked totally straight faced.

She shook her head, her brown curls bouncing.

"Well, you sneak up on them and then ...," Menannon moved his left hand to steady the child on his knee then took his right forefinger and tickled her tummy. Shira immediately shrieked and giggled with laughter and tried to push his hand away. "... you tickle them and if they giggle, you know they're a roc." He tickled her again and she giggled even louder. "You see! You're a roc. Nay, you're too heavy to carry all that way."

At that Shira looked around at Lee as though she would find the answer to her dilemma somewhere in his face. Her small brow was furrowed in thought for several long moments, then her face cleared and she turned back.

"You not carry me. I walk!" she said happily at finding a solution to his objection.

Menannon gave her a skeptical look, "How far have you e'er walked?"

"I walk to the palace. That two whole miles!"she assured him, stretching up on her tiptoes as though the added height would add weight to her words. Menannon managed to swallow a grin so as not to discomfit the child who was being very serious.

"That's a long way. Two whole miles, you say?" he asked.

"Uh-huh!" was her stout reply.

"In that case...hmm...." Menannon glanced down the table one eyebrow raised, silently seeking Firod's permission to add his youngest daughter to the outing. The captain just shrugged and nodded with a grin. Menannon turned back to Shira. "All right, you can come along. Under one condition: if I get tired, you have to carry me. Is it a bargain?"

Shira looked Menannon up and down her small mouth screwed up in thought. "Uh-huh, I carry Pin, I carry you," she assured him solemnly.

"Shake!" Menannon held out his hand and she was just able to get her small fingers around his thumb and they hand-fasted the bargain, after which he set her back on the floor. She skipped from the room to rejoin her brothers and sisters, Pin the stuffed toy puppy, bumping along behind, firmly grasped by one foot. As the door closed, the entire chamber dissolved in laughter.

"So would you like to accompany me on an outing under the imperious leadership of one mite?" Menannon questioned, turning to Lee.

"I wouldn't miss it for the world," the drummer grinned in enthusiastic response. "It should prove very entertaining."

AS THE SUN SLIPPED ABOVE THE HORIZON the next morning, all seven of Firod's older youngsters stood in the courtyard awaiting Menannon. Lee glanced out of his window as he was dressing to see them giggling and nudging each other as they waited under the watchful eyes of the two gate wardens. It had been arranged the two harpers would take the children to an eating house for breakfast. Lunch was to be carried along as a picnic. Of course, Lee had not realized the children would be ready quite this early and he could not begin to imagine what eating house would be open at this hour. He could not help grinning at their enthusiasm and hoped Menannon did not keep them waiting overlong. He started to turn back to his dressing when he spied movement out of the corner of his eye and turned his gaze to see the young Giant already emerging around the corner of the villa, a large pack on his back and an equally large picnic basket in his hand. Clarinda had obviously provided one of her 'touring victuals' to prevent the children from starving on such a 'strenuous' outing. At the sight of him, little Shira began to jump up and down and clap her small hands. Menannon reached the group and scooped her up. The long fingers of his hand nearly reached all the way around the waist of the four-summers old child and she shrieked and giggled in glee as he tossed her up onto his shoulder from which dizzy height she looked down at her brothers and sisters, positively grinning from ear to ear. The other children crowded around him, all talking at once.

"Lee! Come on, slug-a-bed," Menannon called as he caught sight of the drummer looking out at them. Lee raised a hand and turned away to hurriedly finish dressing. He emerged in the courtyard a few moments later, still tying the breast of his tunic.

"Where are we going to find a place to feed these hungry urchins?" he asked as soon as he joined the group.

"The Cokeyna starts serving breakfast long ere the sun is up, as there are always hungry sailors about. We'll stop there," Menannon assured him with a smile and a wink for his young charges. It took but a few more minutes to organize the small troop and a very happy crew were let out of the close and seen on their way, fishing poles in hand.

LATE AFTERNOON FOUND THEM RELAXING on the shore of the small lake nestled above the village of Black Falls. They had found a fine stretch of beach with a firm sandy bottom in a small bay, perfect for swimming. A bit farther around, the shore turned marshy, a haven for water birds and fish, though a great deal of laughter and mud had resulted from trying to catch either creature. All were happily worn out from fishing and swimming. Even little Shira had been able to go swimming perched high upon Menannon's shoulders as he cut cleanly through the water. She had been the proud winner of the first race of the day in just such a manner. The other children had cheered her roundly. As the day wore on, all of the children had found that a floating Giant makes a marvelous diving platform, rather like a floating island, yet it could be unpredictable, for no one knew when that same Giant might just suddenly roll over and dump everyone into the water. Lee, being from a largely desert homeland and therefore no swimmer, had stayed on the shore and laughed until his sides ached watching the antics of these Kalyrian lunatics playing together.

When everyone had their fill of swimming and mucking about in the water, as much of their clothing as modesty allowed were laid out to dry on the bushes and rocks. They built a fire and had their picnic lunch augmented by the few fresh fish they had been able to catch. Now, the children were resting in the shade of an ancient willow whose long branches trailed into the water causing small ripples to glitter across the surface of the lake with every passing breeze, all but Shira, who was instead sleeping comfortably ensconced on Menannon's lap where he sat relaxing against a rock. The child had her small thumb firmly in her mouth. They made a picture of pure contentment.

Lee could not help grinning at the sight. He, too, lounged against a comfortable rock. The young Giant appeared to be half asleep, but from long experience, the drummer knew—as many an apprentice had learned to their chagrin—let there be the slightest hint of trouble and Menannon would be fully awake and dealing with it before the culprit knew what was happening.

"You know, you're going to make some lucky children a great sire someday," Lee observed with a grin as he watched Menannon ease Shira's thumb out of her mouth. The child sighed and snuggled more comfortably into his lap.

"My future is in the hands of the High One and as He wills, so shall it be with me." Menannon smiled. Though he did not say it to Lee, there was one particular Human he would trade all the world and everything in it to be able to marry and raise a family with. Alas, that was not to be, as it was his understanding that the High One forbade marriage between Giants and Humans, yet he could not help wishing that He did not. To distract himself from that line of thought, he glanced over the lake to see that the sun had westered far while they had been resting.

"I deem it's time to get these children home," Menannon said, feeling the need to change the subject. He gently laid the sleeping Shira onto the ground, then stretched muscles stiffened by long sitting, donned his chemise and tunic and, picking up the sleeping girl, began the task of shepherding the other tired children home. They left the lake amidst evening's blue-fingered shadows, with both Lee and Menannon burdened by small sleepy bodies and a line of happily bedraggled youngsters trailing behind. Darya brought up the rear.

CHAPTER 6
(SUMMER OF THE WORLD 6996)

MENANNON'S DILEMMA as to how to arrange to meet with Nirna in private was resolved very nicely when an invitation to a Royal banquet arrived at Gorlanndon's villa within the sevenday and was accepted. Menannon bided his time impatiently.

The evening of the banquet, cool and fine after the day's heat, found Gorlanndon dressed for once in his councillor's robes of golden sorak fringed in indigo. He and his small party walked along the central avenue between the garden walls of the great houses amidst the sweet smell of flowers and the exotic odors of spices wafting through the air attesting to the dinner hour. Lee walked beside the Giant, his brown harper's robe serving as a warm contrast to Gorlanndon's bright attire. The drummer was lost in the enjoyment of his surroundings. As usual, they were accompanied by four of Gorlanndon's household guard in full armour, but this time, Menannon was not with them.

When the drummer had inquired after his friend, Gorlanndon had assured him that his son would be along anon when he had completed the task set him. They made a long leisurely stroll of their walk to the Citadel and its crown of government buildings, even stopping to admire the view of the city offered by the span of the Mathematical bridge. Kirith Kalyria lay peacefully bathed in the last rays of the setting sun. A single, early star spangled the sky, hanging just above the point of the roof of the westernmost lighthouse. Lee was firmly convinced he had never seen anything as peaceful or as beautiful as the city of Kirith Kalyria and the golden crescent of its harbor. Almost reluctantly, he moved on across the bridge and into the vast plaza surrounding the council hall, palace and the buildings which housed the various government offices.

The home of Kalyria's rulers stood on the highest point of the Citadel—well above even the great council hall—its ornate towers seeming to nearly touch the sky. It was constructed of huge blocks of blackest granite interspaced with nodules of volcanic glass that glittered in the evening light causing the entire structure to glow and was not only a testament to the stonemason's art, but one of the most magnificent buildings the drummer had ever seen. There were four levels to the building, the bottom most having a tower at its each of its four corners. The upper levels, each one smaller than the one below it, also possessed a tower at all four corners, the walls between the towers being arched and crenelated interlinking them like gems on a necklace. Each level was filled with rooms and chambers of unimaginable size and intricacy. Surrounding this layered structure was a pillared portico whose forest of columns bore a groin vaulted roof of symmetrical perfection.

Doorwards stood on the steps leading to the great portico: at the foot, the middle landing, the top step and finally, a pair flanked the palace doors themselves. Each wore a breast-plate, greaves and bracers of black fish scale plates constructed from the metal Kelandar and were armed with a silver-chased ash spear and a very un-ceremonial sword. The helms they wore covered both head and face with protective metal. The face plates were fine latticework which rendered the wearer anonymous and therefore more greatly to be feared, for no foe could gauge thought or action by movement of eyes. The arms and armour of the guardians of Kalyria's kings and queens were gifts of the Dwarves of Starkhad and of Garnet.

As Gorlanndon and his small entourage mounted the steps, from beyond the closed doors of the palace, the sound of merriment and revelry spilled out around them, tumbled down the stairs and flew away on the evening breeze down to the harbor and on out to sea to be faintly heard by a few late-returning fishing boats.

The great doors of the palace were opened with alacrity for

Kalyria's ancient councillor and Gorlanndon was announced and bowed through into the high-ceilinged reception hall with all the respect due him and his station. A short walk along a many-doored hallway and up a grand staircase brought them to the palace's great banqueting hall where he and his party were announced to the assembly. The doors were narrow, but tall, and Gorlanndon easily entered though he had to turn sideways a bit. He could stand to his full height within the chamber whose groin vaulted ceiling soared three full stories above his head. He did, however, have to mind the chandeliers with their glittering Dwarf lights appended.

The farther doors of the hall had been folded back to create a huge chamber over a hundred feet in length, the near end of which had been laid with tables for the banquet and the farther end cleared for dancing. The high, arched windows along the south wall bore long glass panels allowing an unprecedented view of the city and the harbor below. The interior walls were gay with multicolored murals depicting the long history of the island nation. The whole was awhirl with dancing, music and conversation. At the far end, hard by the doors leading to the inner wards of the palace, a harper's gallery was filled to capacity with harpers playing myriad instruments: drums, bells, cymbals, rebecs, all manner and sizes of pipes and lutes and, of course, many-stringed harps. Near it, the Master of Kalyria's Harper hall, Penor, fluttered back and forth between the edge of the dance floor and his harpers, constantly mopping his forehead with his scented kerchief, his golden robe billowing about his corpulent figure and his beringed hands flourishing as though upon his efforts alone rested the success or failure of the banquet. Despite his supercilious arrogance, his kohl rimmed blue eyes missed nothing that might prove of use to him in assuring position or ascendance for himself.

The dance floor was a crush of whirling couples performing a lively country dance. All were brave in their finest robes and tunics, kirtles and hose, gold and jewels encrusting every possible surface of their attire and persons, particularly the braids and curling locks of the ladies' hair: a dazzling display of dandies and demoiselles. Even the men—particularly the younger ones—had affixed jewels to the edges of their stiffly pointed beards and the drooping ends of their mustaches. The few Teluri, with their jewel-free hair and smooth faces and the foreigners attending, stood out in stark contrast to the garish crowd. Lee, with his close-cropped hair and beardless chin, was unusual for his age group, even among the harpers present.

Gorlanndon made his way past the banquet tables to the sideboard where a large contingent of Dwarves was acting as barkeeps and potboys for the evening, their great beards intricately braided and tucked into conspicuously axe-free golden belts. Lee followed the Giant closely, as the crowd parted in front of him to make way for their very impressive councillor. By following the Giant so closely, Lee was safe in the backwater and at no risk of getting lost in the crowd. At the farther end of the refreshment table, Lord Lonier stood in conversation with several Teluri, including Irenos. Standing, the old fellow was still a formidable figure despite his ample girth and tendency to overindulge in the fruits of the vine.

With this group also stood a magnificent woman who, though she was slightly past the prime of her life, was still tall and slender and moved with an easy grace. Her long, intricately braided and bejewelled hair was a deep chestnut brown only slightly streaked with silver. Her face was still full and had not yet developed the thinness so often associated with ageing. The gown she wore was actually a simple floor length shift made from a single piece of deep blue brocade woven in a circle and clasped at the points of her shoulders with shield brooches of ancient, intricately worked gold. The seeming simplicity of the garment was belied each time she moved, for it flickered and burned with its own inner light, its entire surface being encrusted with tiny rubies, sapphires and diamonds. The creamy length of her arms, the long, slender column of her throat and the turn of her cheek glowed in lovely contrast to the darkness of her hair and raiment.

Gorlanndon joined the group, knelt, and bowed to this lady, before gently pushing Lee to stand in front of him. "My Lady, allow me to present Leènoviilek of Crenanoc, youngest son of First Minister Viilekoniirac and also a newly-corded Journeyman Harper. Lee, you have the privilege and honor of greeting her Royal Majesty, Norilendra, Queen Regent of Kalyria."

Lee bent into his best sweeping courtly bow, long practiced and perfected in the royal court of Crenanoc, but there his composure ended as the Queen offered him her hand for the kiss of a favorite, a nearly unheard of concession.

"Of old, I knew your sire and have always thought well of him," she said with a voice possessed of a deep, smoky timbre which added a quality of intimacy to her words that left Lee unmanned as he retained only enough mind at the moment to take the proffered hand and kiss its soft back. He looked up for a instant into a fine aquiline face just beginning to recede into the angularity of age, finding himself arrested by the most startling feature of all: a wide, clear gaze of lapis lazuli which seemed perfectly capable of reading mens' very souls. He found himself so dazed and dazzled that Gorlanndon had to nudge his arm to recall him to the fact he was still holding the queen's hand. He let go and straightened, blushing clear to the tips of his ears. Norilendra inclined her head to him with a soft smile and a gleam of understanding lighting those glorious eyes as she turned back to the Giant.

"Where is your son? Came he not with you this night? Nirna will be sorely vexed should he not attend," she said by way of greeting.

"Rest assured, my Lady, he will come anon upon completion of a task I set him," Gorlanndon assured her affably. "He has been greatly anticipating reacquainting himself with both you and your daughter."

"And well he should be. Nirna has talked of nothing else since mid-winter." The tone of the queen's voice hinted at her irritation at this preoccupation of her only child. While his education had withdrawn the young Giant from the princess's circle, it had not, it seemed, taken him from her heart.

"The young always remember their early acquaintances with too kind a regard," Gorlanndon agreed with alacrity, fully recognizing an impending fit of pique on the part of his monarch and maneuvering to prevent it.

Behind her shoulder, Lonier gave him a warning glance. Their queen was in a chancy mood this night and they had all better be on their guard. Gorlanndon nodded to her, obtained a huge chalice of wine and stood to make his way to the farther end of the tables near the dance floor, where an immense chair was set for him at the foot of the queen's table. It was, as usual, set several feet below the rest of the floor on a sunken platform. Lee sat at a table directly to the Giant's right from which he had a clear view of the dance floor and its occupants. He was soon joined by Irenos.

"Good even' to thee." The Teluri inclined his head to the drummer. "Wouldst thou mind company?"

"Join me! I was starting to feel a bit lonely as Menannon is not yet come. His sire set him a task that, it seems, has taken the better part of the day."

"Sons needs must get used to their sires' whims." Irenos nodded and grinned at his companion. "Not an easy task, I assure thee." The Teluri was dressed—a bit somberly for a gathering such as this—in a dark blue sleeveless kirtle over a sky-blue linen chemise, adorned about the neck opening and side slits with double rows of faceted gems set amidst knotwork of silver and gold threads. He was barelegged with naught but the slimmest of sandals on his feet. He, of course, bore his malinir at his belt even here in the presence of Kalyria's royalty and none would have had the temerity to say him nay.

It was perhaps a full turn of the hour more when Lee stood and crossed to the refreshment table to refill his chalice of peach-laced honey mead and a hush began to fall across the assembly. He glanced about to see the cause and discovered that Menannon had entered the chamber and was standing quietly just inside the doors. Person after person caught sight of him and stopped in awe and fell into silence at the sight. Menannon was incredible. He was dressed in a long-sleeved thigh-length tunic of crimson sorak over which he wore a black velvet kirtle of the same length, much worked with gold thread and fine gems, mostly blood-red rubies about the high collar and long throat opening, as well as the hem and elaborate side slits. Down the sides of its narrow, bell-shaped elbow length sleeves and around their cuffs, more rubies glittered from their framing of golden thread work. About his waist, a long sash belt was intricately tied. Its gem-encrusted surface, twinkling in the strong light, fell well past the hem of the kirtle almost to his knees. Nearly skin-tight black hose flowed without a wrinkle into knee-high black boots made of the softest of leather and laced up the fronts with lacings of black leather thickly intertwined with pure gold wire. The clothing, combined with Menannon's dark good looks and his nine feet of stature, rendered the young Giant breathtaking—and not only for the ladies present.

Lee stopped with his newly filled chalice half-way to his lips and stared at his friend, then gave a soft whistle of appreciation. A prince the old sailor from the ship had called him and a prince he looked and no mistake. Menannon continued to hesitate in the doorway, waiting to be announced, his black gaze surveying the gathering. Though indiscernible to any who knew him less well than the drummer, it was plain to Lee that the young Giant was suffering from what his friend always referred to as an attack of the shys. Lee could not help but grin. Menannon was unused to attending entertainments as a guest instead of working them and was therefore not a little uncomfortable at gatherings such as this which always caused him to retreat behind the mask of his face.

This very remoteness inevitably defeated its own purpose, as rather than allowing the Giant to comfortably disappear into the wall covering, his aloof manner caused him to be all the more mysterious and therefore attractive, resulting in his becoming—

and remaining—a center of attention. Somewhat surprisingly, the gentry of Kalyria did not seem to know their own as well as did the tradesmen and shopkeepers of the city. Here for the first time, Lee found people who did not recognize the young Giant for whom and what he was. How odd! Speculations ran races around the chamber as to who this paragon could possibly be. A Teluri prince? But no that could not be, as his hair and close-cropped beard shone blue-black in the light of the Dwarf lanterns. But his height ... he could not be Human, could he? A Human prince from some unknown land?

Lee managed to keep a straight face as Menannon continued to stand just within the doorway and the speculations became all the more exotic. The drummer looked across to where Gorlanndon was conversing with Lord Lonier, who had joined the elder Giant at table, and found, as he suspected he would, that Menannon's sire was finding the speculations about his son vastly amusing. He seemed to even be encouraging them as he only shrugged when someone wondered aloud near him as to the identity of this paragon. Lee doubted that Gorlanndon had had this much fun at a royal banquet in many a summer.

All speculation came to an end when the late-arriving guest was announced to the assembly. The functionary, a bit put off by so late an arrival, was embarrassed at his failure to promptly announce the guest, who by his appearance, had to be someone of importance. He was, therefore, also somewhat disappointed when the majestically turned-out guest was revealed as not a visiting dignitary from some exotic foreign land after all.

After a quick consultation with the new arrival, he turned to the assembled guests and announced in full voice which, although not loud, carried surprisingly well throughout the hall, "Presenting Master Journeyman Harper Menannon, son and Heir of the Governor-General of Rhonndia, Lord of the Port and Chief Councillor, Gorlanndon of Kalyria."

Ignoring the buzz of surprise and discussion which exploded after that announcement, Menannon caught sight of his sire halfway down the chamber and moved to greet him. He reached the table and gave a nod of recognition and deference to Lord Lonier and his sire a respectful inclination of his head.

"Your son and servant, sir." His voice was low. Menannon could not help but hear some of the chatter from the crowd as everyone began to speculate as to how old he could possibly be, for he was only the height of a half grown boy! Gorlanndon's son? It couldn't be! How long did it take for a Giant to reach full height anyway? The more knowledgeable among the speculators instructed that Giants achieved their full height in their late teens as did all the races save the Teluri alone and as Menannon must be at least twenty summers, he had to be full grown. Wonder-of-wonders, he was a midget!

It only added to this impression when Gorlanndon stood to greet his son and everyone could see that Menannon's head came barely above his sire's elbow. Lee could not help wondering why Gorlanndon seemed to be going out of his way to make Menannon conspicuous, first by seeing to it he came late and dressed royally, then by seeming to go out of his way to make sure his lack of height and thereby his implied lack of worth was plainly seen by all assembled. To any who did not know him, Menannon would easily be mistaken for a gussied up brainless popinjay who sought to cover his lack of stature, and perhaps even intelligence, with velvet and gold and grand entrances. It was almost as though the elder Giant sought to have his son seen as of non-account amidst this world of position-conscious courtiers. Piqued, Lee hurried to join his friend and show the gathering that at least the Harpers valued their own. He greeted Menannon a little more warmly than was necessary, a gesture which the young Giant instantly recognized and obviously appreciated. As Gorlanndon's heir and one of Aridion's harpers, he was unused to being belittled and felt the sting of the assembly's growing disdain more acutely than otherwise as it was coming from folk he had always deemed his own people. As his sire had required him to not wear his harper's robes this night, he was being judged on his own merit and was obviously being found lacking. It made him wonder if something had changed in his sire's status among the council to thus lower the level of respect due his heir.

"Well, boy, you might as well go treat with the queen and have done."

Gorlanndon's voice broke in on his thoughts and he looked up to see his sire grinning down at him with a knowing look. Menannon glanced over to where the queen was standing amidst a crowd of smitten courtiers, her inner circle, and gave a slight sigh.

"Those who treat with Norilendra Queen must be accomplished serpent handlers." He raised an eyebrow at his sire and shook his head.

"I take it you would lief as not do it?" Lee questioned surprised, as he was still under the spell of Kalyria's queen and could not imagine that anyone would rather not treat with her.

"Needs must when evil drives, as the saying goes." Menannon shrugged, acknowledging his reluctance, but also the inevitability of the situation. "I was never one of her favorites."

"No, boy, but Nirna favored you and still does, it seems, so go give your greeting to the mother so you may treat with the daughter at leisure this evening." There was a slight emphasis on the words this evening that caught Menannon's ear, but he had not the time to speculate as Gorlanndon gave him a slight push to start him on his way, causing a ripple of laughter at the table nearest them.

Menannon crossed to stand near the queen's party and awaited his turn to greet her. It came rather sooner than he would have liked, but she had been watching for his move and turned to gaze up at him in cold hauteur. The others between them cleared out of Menannon's way and he gave her a courtly bow fully as elegant and polished as Lee's had been, though he in no way came under her spell as he had long since recognized the steel behind her eyes. As her daughter's favored playmate, though unworthy of such a place in her mother's opinion, he had garnered more than his share of her ill will and once felt, the lash of her scorn was never forgotten. There was that even now in the depths of the drowning blue of her eyes which was subtly reminding him of his place. Though most of the gathering appeared to have fallen for Gorlanndon's ploy, Norilendra was under no illusion as to the mettle and mind of this young harper. Small he might be for a Giant, but a force to be reckoned with he surely was.

"It must be of great moment to your sire that you have finally come home to him." She addressed him as protocol dictated, though her tone clearly indicated that Gorlanndon alone should be pleased with his son's advent. "How long will we be graced with your presence?"

"I must return to the mainland in the fall, your highness." Menannon spoke politely, but there was a certain coldness in his voice as well that was not missed by the courtiers surrounding Norilendra. They shuffled a bit and inadvertently opened a place at the queen's back which was instantly filled by a strange Teluri, the likes of whom the young Giant had never seen. Where exactly the man had come from was unclear as at his height, Menannon was able to plainly see all those surrounding the queen and the Teluri had definitely not been among them only an instant before.

The fellow was tall, a good seven feet in height, and spare to the point of emaciation, his long face rendered even longer by his total lack of hair, for he was strangely and completely bald, though whether by nature or design, there was no way of knowing. He was dressed in a long sorak robe woven of all the colors of the rainbow save red alone and had golden rings set with large stones on every finger of both hands and an ancient, intricate torque lay about his neck, to which was appended a medallion portraying a black sun rising from a blood red sea. About his shoulders lay the jeweled collar of the Counsel General. The strangest thing about him was that this Teluri, unlike the rest of his race present, did not bear a malinir, a fact Menannon took note of in surprise, but almost instantly forgot as he caught sight of the look in the fellow's smoldering black eyes which shifted restlessly, never truly resting upon anything. The look clearly said, She likes thee not, nor do I, so be warned. Seeing the look and recognizing its truth, Menannon instantly stepped back, retreating to the physical edge of the queen's presence, removing himself from the area only to be occupied by her inner circle. Though his movement was in acquiescence of her wishes, it did not compromise his own dignity or rightful self-value, which nuance was not lost upon her. Norilendra gave him a slight smile that was both acknowledgment and dismissal and turned back to speaking with her circle. Menannon instantly left her proximity with an inward sigh of relief. At the sight of his retreat, many titters of slightly malicious laughter came from the queen's inner circle which he pointedly ignored and took his place beside Lee at the small table. He was used to being given the cold shoulder by the queen's favorites, there was nothing new in that, but open hostility had never been shown him before. He could not help but wonder as to who this strange Teluri was that he wore the collar of the Counsel General, whence and when he came and how he, Menannon, had come to engender the man's enmity.

"Highness, who ...," he began addressing Irenos, but that worthy gave him a quick burning look which instantly silenced him, leaving him even more perplexed. Before anything more could be said, the gong sounded and the banquet began, giving everyone a chance to change their attention from the subject of Giants to that of food. The chamber was flooded with laughter and speech again and Menannon was forgotten for the moment.

As the courses were served by the kitchen staff, Menannon, having performed his obligatory duty of contacting the mother, took the opportunity to look about the chamber for the daughter. Though he had not seen her for eight summers, and she would have changed a great deal just as he had, he was sure that he could recognize the Princess Nirna, but there seemed to be no young woman of eighteen summers or so who fit his mental image of his former playmate and boon companion. There were myriad young women at table who were approximately the right age range, but none chimed the chord of his memory.

He finally espied Gooddame Matilda, Nirna's nurse and chaperone, among the diners not far from the Queen's left hand sitting between an empty chair and a tallish Dwarf who, from the costly furs adorning his black velvet kirtle, must be the ambassador from Starkhad resident here on Kalyria. The gooddame was talking animatedly with him, her plump face wreathed in smiles beneath the white sorak veil covering her iron grey hair. She was wearing a round gown of autumn brown sorak whose sleeves, attached with gold medallions at the shoulders and at intervals along her arms, ended in a point over the back of her gesticulating hands. Thus arrayed and animated, Matilda looked like someone's favorite grandam, but as Menannon well knew, let anything in any way threaten her nurseling and she could turn into a full-rigged war galley in a moment with her brown doe-like eyes flashing fire and brimstone. One did not cross Matilda where Nirna was concerned.

The empty place beside the gooddame proved that Nirna was not present. So where was she?

Beside him, Lee was in great form entertaining their table mate with hysterical stories of the trials and tribulations of life in Aridion's Master Harper Hall. One particular story dealt with the nervous jitters that accompany the thought of standing the journeyman's trials which must be passed in order to graduate. The story reminded Menannon that Nirna had suffered from the same jitters at official dinners, so he carefully chose a small meat pie from his plate and put it quietly into his table napkin. Under cover of the appreciative laughter following Lee's story, he excused himself and strolled nonchalantly over to the windows. He chose a window close to the rear of the chamber whose heavy ceiling-to-floor damask curtain was only partially drawn aside and stood looking out across the bay to where the towers stood upon the ends of the crescent. The sounds of the banquet washed over him slightly muffled by the heavy cloth beside him.

"It is said the more things change, the more they remain the same," Menannon spoke softly and held the wrapped pie into the space between the curtain and the glass. Almost instantly, a very shapely feminine hand reached out from the depths of the cloth and took it from him. Before he could speak further, the curtain beside him suddenly flung out to engulf him in its folds and he found himself facing a piquant face, crowned by masses of blond curls so pale they were nearly white falling to just below her waist. Dark purple eyes regarded him with unfeigned delight.

"Playfellow, you've finally come home!" the Princess Nirna whispered and tugged him still farther along the window into the depths of the curtain. She laid his gift upon the broad windowsill and turned to throw her arms around him in a heartfelt embrace. Due to his lack of height for a Giant, the top of her head reached comfortably to slightly above the center of his chest. Nirna had fulfilled the promise of childhood and was tall, even by the standards of Kalyria's royal bloodline, being nearly eight feet in height, though still so slender as to be almost ethereal. Menannon easily could, and did, kiss the top of her head. They stayed thus entwined for several long minutes, silently filling the emptiness left by summers of separation. At last, Menannon gently unclasped her hold about his waist and stepped back to arm's length.

There was nothing of her mother in her face and bearing. Nirna was sealed with her sire's seal from the top of her head to the tips of her toes. She was the very image of Ronirinen King, Norilendra Queen's late husband and the third of that name to rule Kalyria, and she looked every inch the Princess Royal in her elaborately fringed gown. It was made from a single rectangular piece of pale coral brocade, edged with tassels spun from gold and silver wire. The nether end was secured to a beaten gold ring brooch on her left shoulder with the last of its length hanging down behind her nearly to the floor. The rest of the cloth then wrapped around her lithe young body in complete circles allowing the fringe to spiral upwards around her. The whole was secured by a golden girdle about her slender waist. Her right shoulder was left bare, as were her delicate arms, thus acknowledging her unmarried status, as only married women or widows wore double brooches.

Despite the summers that had elapsed since their last meeting, there was no need to ask if her feelings towards her 'playfellow' had altered. The look on her face was eloquent answer. He was reminded of their first meeting. It had been but a little since he had first come to Kirith Kalyria and he had been wandering on a voyage of discovery which had inadvertently taken him through an open wicket in a stone wall and into a magnificent garden. Within it, he had discovered not only wondrous beauty in the form of rare plants and trees, but under one ancient tree, he had discovered a being so slender and sprightly he was instantly sure he was seeing a Fæorlinga. He had approached her cautiously, fearing she would flee from him into the tree, but instead the being had raised her head and regarded him the same way she was now. A single glance from those lavender eyes had taken his measure and his heart. Without a word, she had reached out a hand and pointed to a watering can near where she was planting hibiscus blossoms in her own small garden. Right willingly he had joined her gardening efforts and from that instant they were fast friends and boon companions. A half turn of an hour later, Gooddame Matilda, her nurse, had returned and found the stranger contentedly following the commands of his heart's general and had set to send him away only to be brought up short by her princess's first Imperial edict.

"He is allowed to attend upon me any time he desires. He is my playfellow!" The edict and the name had stuck. For his part, he fixed upon her the name Fæori. As a very young, sensitive boy, he was never quite convinced she was a real person and not a Fæorlinga. This night, she resembled far more the Princess Royal than she did his well-remembered playmate. However, the regal illusion was instantly broken as she turned and clambered up onto the broad windowsill and, taking up the pie, began to eat with delicate relish.

"I'm nearly starving! Nothing has changed. My stomach still gets upset to the point I can't eat at table at my mother's state functions. I was afraid I would starve to death. You came so late and took so much time to bring me something." The confidence in her voice showed that she had never thought to doubt that her playfellow would remember his normal service. Menannon grinned and leaned against the windowsill. She still was, and always would be, his Fæori.

"I see your sire's prayers have been answered," she smiled and tilted her fine head as she always had. She studied him candidly for several long moments then nodded to herself and went back to eating and quickly finished her pie. "I am so glad you're not a great, hulking brute like your sire." She gave him a mischievous smile knowing full well he would bridle at her so calling his sire.

Menannon just shook his head, too nonplused by her revelation to take exception to her words. "How did you know of my father's prayer when I did not?" he could not resist asking, although it revealed a small lack of communication between himself and his beloved parent.

"I went out of my way to find out everything I could about Giants while you were away. I will confess that I shamelessly pestered your sire until he told me many things. Some, like his prayer, I've no doubt even you don't know." The lavender of her eyes darkened mysteriously at this statement and her smile was rather private, a thing which puzzled him greatly. She considered him thus for a moment then threw back her head and laughed softly at the look on his face. She laid a shapely hand on his arm.

"Seriously, Playfellow, I'm surprised you did not hear my sigh of relief when you came through yonder door this evening without turning sideways, striding in tall and magnificent and in no way hampered by excess size. You, sir, are perfection itself and won't all of the rest of these supercilious puffballs be jealous!" She jerked her shapely chin in a disdainful thrust at the bejewelled courtiers reveling just beyond her curtain. "There isn't one of them who can fill out a tunic and kirtle the way you do much less do anything else, though they are all very well practiced at groveling." There was a distinct sneer in her voice at this, for even at her slender size, she was a deadly archer and accomplished rider, though she could not embroider to save her life.

"There is little I do well, either, save play a harp," Menannon reminded her with a grin, as his sire had refused to let his son join the princess and the rest of the children of Kalyria's nobles in martial training.

"Well, then, when we are old and grey together, I shall hunt and prepare our dinner and you shall serenade me with harp song the like of which has not been heard since Kaalamar was withdrawn from the realms of this world. Does that suit?"

"Most admirably," Menannon agreed, easily falling back into their play that they would always be together. They had once promised each to the other to grow up and grow old together and always stand shoulder to shoulder against the world. It had been a beautiful dream. Their peace was interrupted by a high titter of laughter and the noise of diners rising to their feet. The banquet was ending. Nirna subsided into stillness and turned to look out of the windows with a blank stare.

"What is it, Fæori?" Menannon asked softly, leaning closer to better look into her face. She had gone pale and was biting her lip, but did not answer him. Very gently, he took her chin and turned her face up to his. "I cannot serve my liege lady if she confides not in me," he said using a turn of phrase which had always made her smile. This time, there was only the most fleeting of smiles before she turned back to the window and began twisting the table napkin between her shapely fingers. When at last she spoke, her voice was very soft and he had to lean close to hear.

"I'm afraid, Playfellow. Mother's new councillor is evil. I can feel it when e'er he comes near me."

"Which one is he?" Menannon's stomach tightened at her words.

"Azuron, the bald Teluri. He came back here from Boria with my mother three summers ago and has wormed his way into her confidence, pushing aside all other councillors, even your sire and Lord Lonier. She dotes on him and will listen to none other. She has even demoted Lord Lonier from the office of Counsel General and appointed Azuron to it instead. I have tried to tell her there is something wrong about him, but she only laughs and pats me on the head and tells me to run along like a good child. Playfellow, she could call me a mewling babe if she wished if only she would listen to me or to someone. Listen to them. Do you hear the fear?" She fell silent, her head cocked, listening to the sounds of laughter and revelry. She was right. There was something wrong here. It was not overt, but it was there in the voices of the councillors and their consorts and their laughter, all a bit too loud and a bit too high. There was a current running just below the surface that he could have sworn was indeed fear, but fear of what?

Nirna turned and opened a crack between two curtains and pointed across the chamber to where her mother was standing once more in conversation with the bald Teluri.

"Keep your distance from him, Playfellow. I would that you were never even introduced to him, for I trust him not."

Menannon looked where she pointed and beheld again the bald Teluri. Azuron stood a little way behind the queen, but there was that in his demeanor as he treated with her or watched her talk to others that reminded Menannon of the master of the mummers puppets at a village fair. He could almost swear that if he looked hard enough he would see strings leading from the queen's limbs back to the Teluri's hands. He blinked and shook his head at such a fancy.

"But enough," Nirna said, straightening her shoulders with determination and gracefully slipped down from the window-sill. "I am letting them taint our first evening together in over eight summers. It is in fair to the both of us." She turned to look up at him. "Come, it's time we danced together as we did of old, only this time we shall do it for all the world to see." Resolutely, she set down the cloth and took his hand to lead him out from behind the curtain to the dance floor where a new set of dancers was just forming up. Many had been the childhood evening when they had opened the window of her chamber, after all the children had been sent to bed during a banquet, but before the dancing had begun. The music and laughter had floated in upon the breeze and they had danced together with none save her nurse, Gooddame Matilda, to see. This night would see that changed.

Lee glanced up from his honey mead, startled as Menannon walked past his table hand in hand with one of the most beautiful women he had ever seen. The drummer glanced quickly at Irenos, his eyebrow raised in question.

"Nirna, the Princess Royal," the Teluri informed him softly, a disapproving tone in his voice.

Lee looked back, wondering what could be wrong in Menannon dancing with the princess. He cast a glance at Gorlanndon to see a disapproving look in the Giant's eyes. Neither man, it seemed, desired that Menannon be seen associating so intimately with Kalyria's Princess Royal. He wondered why, as Menannon had himself informed his friend that he and the princess had been playmates before he had left for the mainland. Why should it be so strange that he would renew the acquaintance? He watched as they took their places with the rest of the dancers. As the music started, Lee mentally shrugged and settled back to watch his friend dance. Menannon and the princess danced gracefully, moving as one as though they had often practiced this art. Despite Menannon's great height, Nirna was tall enough to comfortably dance with him with only the minimum of stooping on his part. As the dance progressed, Nirna's mood lightened and her clear bubbling laughter could be heard throughout the chamber as Menannon picked her up in the lifts required by the movements of the dance.

"Why, it's just like flying," she informed him breathlessly when he returned her to the floor from the latest such lift. "I love you, Playfellow. I'm so glad you're home!"

At her words, Menannon glanced towards Norilendra and found that both the queen and her shadow, Azuron, had heard the princess' words and neither approved. While the queen's look bespoke volumes of her displeasure, Azuron was staring at him with open hatred as he continued to twirl Nirna lightly through the intricate steps of the dance. Why? Did the Teluri have designs upon the princess? Menannon caught again the look and knew instantly Azuron had plans for her in which he, Menannon, had no place.

The dance ended and Menannon bowed gracefully to his fair partner and led her to her mother's table.

"I'd best take my leave, Fæori," he whispered. "Your lady mother is going to suffer a fit of apoplexy if we spend any more time together this evening."

She nodded in understanding as he pulled out a chair for her at the table.

"Ride with me on the morrow," she whispered as he made to step back.

He gave her the slightest ghost of a wink then stood to his full height, his mind a whirl with the prospect of spending a day alone with her as had been their wont of old when they could slip away from her nurse. A thing which, when you came to think on it, had been suspiciously easy to do. He mentally shook himself back to the here and now and bowed to her.

"Thank you for the dance, Princess," he said loudly enough for everyone to hear, then turned and bowed to the queen and withdrew to his table, where Lee waited, all questions and good humor. Irenos had moved along to join Gorlanndon and Lonier, leaving the drummer on his own.

The evening was nearly spent when Menannon took the opportunity to move along to the harper's gallery and listen intently to the music and watch the techniques being employed by the various harpers. Lee had long since found his way to the same place and had actually played several sets with them.

Irenos' attention was drawn to the Queen Regent who was in close consultation with Azuron, not unusual in itself, but what concerned him was that they kept looking at Menannon and that boded ill. He voiced his concern to Gorlanndon, who gave the dark pair a hard look and realized that events were about to move in a direction he wished to avoid.

Gorlanndon saw that his son was looking in his direction and summoned him with a gesture, intent on sending him home on some excuse or another to remove him from the spotlight. He knew that Norilendra was suggesting something to Azuron and he feared how the dark one might bend it to Menannon's—and therefore his—detriment, but if Menannon was gone, those plans would come to naught.

Menannon had just reached his side when Azuron's voice spoke up, conjointly silky and sinister. Irenos straightened with a jerk. Blue Hill's prince glanced at Gorlanndon and shook his head in warning. The councillor stepped away from the queen and faced the Giant, his manner punctilious to the point of near insult. It was clear there was no love lost between these two Royal Councillors.

"Sayest thou not that this son of thine is forwarded for his master's trials next spring?" Azuron's voice was poisonously polite.

"Aye. So his master writes." Gorlanndon nodded affably.

With growing alarm, Irenos whispered to Gorlanndon, fearing a challenge, and knowing the new Counsel General, expected that it would be one that Menannon could not meet.

"Nay, have no fear. This boy's skills are up to any challenge," the elder Giant assured his friend with a grin. Too late now to send his son away from the danger, he could do naught but ride the currents where they led.

Azuron continued, "Then I deem I have the perfect musical request. With your permission?" Receiving an indulgent nod from Gorlanndon, the Teluri turned to Menannon with a challenging look in his dark eyes. "Wouldst thou be so kind as to play the *Lay of the World's Beginning*? I've not heard it played in more summers than I can count."

"The High One above, sir!" Lee exclaimed, stunned into speech by the pure absurdity of the request. "There has not been a harper who could play that lay solo save its own composer, Taalinōth, and he a Teluri king with thousands of summers to perfect his art ere he wrote the piece! At the Master Hall we have all learned it, though what we play is an orchestrated version which takes six good harpers to accomplish."

At Lee's objection, the harper's gallery erupted in a sympathetic protest at the request and the ballroom burst into a cacophony of murmurs, exclamations of surprise and speculation.

Many protests were heard, including from Elder Journeyman Davin who engaged Menannon in a quiet but intense discussion quite obviously attempting to talk Menannon out of accepting the challenge. With a final shake of his head, the young Giant halted Davin in his speech and the Elder Journeyman slumped his shoulders in defeat.

Lee continued, straining to be heard over the crowd. "If it is truly your wish to hear it, allow us to fetch ...."

"Enough!" Menannon halted Lee's protest with a smile and then turned to Azuron with a courtly bow. "I would be honored, sir, to play it for you, but I will require one grace."

At this, the Teluri's countenance began to take on a knowing leer, but Menannon did not allow him to complete his triumph and embarrass Gorlanndon by embarrassing his son.

"Nay, sir, do not mistake me. I would but ask a moment's indulgence to send to my father's villa for my own harp, for I know it better and can trust its voice to sing me true. And," he added, "it is better suited to the task."

"A right reasonable request," Lonier boomed out heartily before Azuron could say him nay. "I deem the slight wait will but enhance the enjoyment to come. Send, boy, send!" Lonier waved him away and turned back to his interrupted conversation with a stalwart Dwarf from Gormidad who sat at his end of Gorlanndon's table.

This brought new life to the chamber as speculations began to fly as to whether this particular journeyman harper could actually do what no other harper in over a thousand summers, not even the Grandmasters of the guild, had ever been able to accomplish. Most thought he would fail for they had taken his measure and found him a dilettante rather than a serious harper and thus easily dismissed, causing a flurry of wagering to begin immediately even as Menannon turned to one of the apprentices and spoke softly, sending him to fetch the harp. Some few, however, had the perspicacity to see in Menannon one who might just meet the challenge, but they kept their counsel and quietly wagered in favor of the young Giant and ignored the taunts from the less observant who gleefully accepted their wagers.

Even Norilendra Queen, it seemed, could not resist a wager on her daughter's favorite playfellow. Whether it was for or against him, only Penor knew for sure as she whispered in his ear and handed him a small, though heavy, purse. The master harper had seen a golden opportunity and was taking all bets. He cast a pitying glance at Menannon where he stood near the door waiting for the boy to return with his harp, his usual equanimity firmly in place to all appearances. Beside him, his friend, Lee, was not so calm and many were taking their cue from the drummer, as though his manner proved Menannon's lack of skill. Automatically assuming the worst, they were betting accordingly.

The wait was not long and soon the sound of feet could be heard on the stairs. The boy returned, accompanied by one of Gorlanndon's strongest gate wardens, as the harp was far too heavy for a young boy to carry. Even Gorlanndon's man was a bit winded. Menannon grinned his thanks and gave the youngster a coin for his troubles. He did not even hint at paying his sire's man, as that worthy would have been mortally insulted by the gesture.

"Would you set me a stool?" he whispered to Lee as he took the instrument from its bearer and began to untie its wrappings.

Half the folk in the chamber began to jockey for position to be the first to see the harp as it had been long whispered that Gorlanndon had paid the equivalent of a small country's mercantile trade for an entire summer for it. There was an expressive sigh all around when Menannon revealed it.

The instrument was magnificent. It was constructed entirely of blackwood, even the sounding box, hand-rubbed to reveal the stunning grain of this rare wood, cross-strung with strings of gold alloyed with kelandar. It's twin necks attached to a narrow X-shaped double pillar and its only decoration was a single blood-red ruby the size of a man's fist set in gold where the pillars crossed. It had forty three strings on the neck on the player's left and thirty one on the right hand neck. Anyone other than its owner would have to set it on the floor to play it, but for the young Giant, it was a lap harp. It was unique. Menannon valued it beyond all other possessions not for its cost, but for the love it represented.

Lee quickly set a tall stool directly in front of the harpers' gallery for Menannon's use and then retired to stand near Gorlanndon, mentally crossing his fingers and silently uttering several heartfelt prayers. He knew in his heart of hearts that Menannon, the most accomplished harper the Guild had turned out in centuries, would be unable to play the Lay of the World's Beginning unaided.

Menannon took the stool and began to tune the harp. Beside Lee, the elder Giant seemed equally as calm as his son save for the very odd shape his chalice had taken on in the last few minutes. In the Giant's hand, the vessel was no longer round, but rather oddly elliptical. Gorlanndon caught the direction of Lee's gaze and shrugged, yet still managed a confident enough wink. To reinforce everyone's knowledge of his confidence in his son, Gorlanndon waved one of the other journeymen harpers over and handed him a heavy purse.

"I wager all of this on my son to succeed," he said making sure to speak loudly enough so that all heard him over the hubbub in the chamber. "Oh, and what odds does Penor offer?"

"Ten to one in favor, two to one against, Lord Gorlanndon," the harper replied with some trepidation.

"Excellent!" Gorlanndon's shout of satisfaction was heard all over the hall.

The harper delivered the wager to Penor who took it and wrote it down with a sneer. It was the last wager offered or accepted.

Silence fell, everyone turning to watch Menannon as his love for and skill with his instrument made even the mundane process of tuning into artistry. When he was satisfied that the harp was as close to perfectly tuned as it is possible to get a harp—there is no such thing as a perfectly tuned harp, as every apprentice quickly learns—he raised his head and locked eyes with Azuron.

"It is customary, when a harper is set a challenge, that his instrument be examined so that there is assurance that no extra advantage has been taken and that the instrument is regulation with no more than a double set of strings and no hidden accoutrements. Master Penor, would you examine this harp and see that there has been no tampering?"

Even while making this request, his eyes never left Azuron's emaciated face, his black gaze unreadable.

Penor immediately looked to Azuron for guidance and the Counselor nodded. With little grace, the harper laid aside the scroll and pen he had been using to record wagers and flounced over to the Giant where the harp sat upon the floor awaiting him and took up the harp, the look on his florid face bespeaking volumes of his distaste for the job. Yet the harp had its due, for even Penor found himself affected by its magnificence and his whole demeanor changed. Suddenly, the ghost of the true harper he had once been seemed to inhabit him and he handled the instrument with reverence, examined it closely and, in a voice which quavered slightly, pronounced it a clean, cross-stringed harp, quite within regulation, if unusual. He gently and carefully handed it back to Menannon and scurried back to his table, now not quite so confident in the wisdom of his wagering.

"Lee, would you be so kind as to narrate?" Menannon turned to the drummer who nodded and came to stand beside and slightly behind him.

To add to the coming drama, Norilendra Queen softly ordered all the dwarf lanterns in the hall shuttered save one, plunging the chamber into gloom save for a single pool of brilliant light surrounding the young Giant.

Menannon bowed his head and prayed silently. High One, if it be not against Thy will, aid me in this so that my sire be not shamed in front of his people. In this as in all things, Thy will be done. He raised his head, took a deep breath and laid hands to strings in a soft chiming note.

"Let the outcome of this challenge be according to the will of the High One, as in all things," Menannon said, speaking the ritual words spoken before all such challenges.

He did not notice the dark look that crossed Azuron's face upon hearing them.

Beside him, Lee cleared his throat nervously and began the narration: "In the time of Creation, the High One walked the lands, speaking all things into being."

With a single melody, the harp began to sing the words of the High One and its listeners heard the softness of that first morning. The great instrument walked them in the very footsteps of creation over hills but newly green, along crystal stream and sunlit sea. It whispered the love of the High One for all his creation.

"Upon the land did He bring forth the sires of the Four Races: first, the Teluri!" a second melodic line began to sing along with the first.

"The Dwarves!" and a third melody joined.

"Men!" A fourth melody sang higher now, above the others.

"The Giants!" Now the fifth and final melody joined, its deep resonance creating a vibration that was almost more felt than heard.

Beside Lee, Menannon played, eyes closed to better concentrate, his hands fairly flying upon the strings, incredibly keeping all five melodies sounding separately and together, their lines perfectly harmonizing with each other as once did the races themselves and with the High One in the time before darkness had descended upon the world.

As he continued to play, Menannon's concentration became so intense, so deep, he lost all sense of himself as though his whole spirit was becoming one with his harp, his fingers moving of their own volition. He no longer heard Lee telling the story or was aware of his audience. He was aware of nothing but the music. Even the physical connection of his fingers with the strings was lost within the song of the harp. Minutes became turns of the hour, time flying by as together the harper and the drummer told the story of the building of the first city and the life of the High One's creation under a new made sun. The harp's voice sang the joys and sorrows, the laughter and tears of all the races as they lived their lives following the ways of the High One. It sang of the Dwarves in their halls of stone and the Teluri building their cities of marble gleaming in the sun. About these twined the lives of the Giants and Humans all in perfect harmony. Then the voice of the harp changed. A sinister sixth musical line joined the others: the Evil One was come to challenge the High One for His new-made world.

Now the melodies were torn apart, separated into their own distinct lines, jarring against each other even as the races had been torn apart in the battles of the Dim Times when the very existence of the world had hung in the balance. Impossibly, Menannon continued to play the *Lay* note perfect as it had originally been written, a single harp and harper playing all six melodic lines as they fought and challenged each other for control of the High One's world. The voice of the harp was leading its listeners through the epic of the Dim Times. Sweeping them towards the climax, a battle that had left the world forever changed.

His entire audience was on its feet now entranced, held within the music, as their very vision changed and before them they saw not the dimly lit chamber, but the battlefield soaked in blood. They saw the armies marshaled for the last great thrust: nefrangs, Teluri, Giants, Dwarves, Humans, draktas and Fæorlinga. They saw the charge and felt the earth shake. They smelled the dust and blood and heard the screaming. They saw the sun darken and felt the fear stalking the land as the Evil One and his lieutenants marshaled their forces to sweep the field and claim their victory. Then everything stopped as though the earth itself stood still and the dust settled. A small force was revealed to be standing against the horde: Beldronnen, tallest of Giants with his sons and clansmen; Gandomar Earthshaker, greatest of draktas; Telurion Firstborn, sire of the Teluri; Kyr Beastmaster, eldest of his sons beside him with the other eleven ranged behind; Kyrian Firehoof, the High One's own messenger; Kalyrinon King, master of the Men of the Long Ships and his house guard; and the Dawn Greybeards, the sires of the Dwarves. By the power of the harp's voice, they saw them all standing to the last, in defense of all they held dear, refusing to yield, preferring death to slavery. A single high clear note sounded like a clarion call and it began.

Menannon threw his head back, his lips parted slightly as he gasped for breath. He was nearing utter exhaustion, yet his fingers flew without a single mistake, not a note was missed nor a single tone garbled despite the fact his face ran with sweat and his fingers bled. Beneath his hands, the harp roared the battle rage of the great drakta and shrieked the death cries of the nefrangs—the evil one's unnatural grotesques—and cried the pain and loss in Gandomar's soul as Kyr fell from his shoulders, the final arrow of the Evil One through his noble heart. The harp thundered the drakta's fury and trumpeted the battle horns of the Dawn Grey Beards. All came together in one final clashing crescendo, then all the rest was silence, broken at last by a single clear note as the High One's golden sun rose above a field of victory, the Evil One and his minions fled back to Hella and Outer Darkness.

For just a moment, there was total stillness in the chamber as the last note faded and was gone. Menannon opened his eyes to see that Azuron alone was unaffected by the power of the harp. The councillor stood frozen, his strange, smoldering gaze riveted on the harper, his displeasure evident in every line of his body. Then he seemed to master himself and shook off his mood like an incubus and began the applause. At the sound of the applause, the gathered councillors and all the rest blinked and started as though waking from a dream and all began to applaud and cheer the indescribable display of harping they had just experienced. Azuron gave Menannon a mocking little bow as though acknowledging first blood to an enemy and eased back into the crowd and disappeared.

As Irenos had feared during this impromptu concert, the Queen's favorite councillor had taken the true measure of Gorlanndon's son and knew his worth. He had also seen for himself exactly what store the elder Giant set by his son and divined in truth what a weapon he could make of him. At Azuron's departure, Menannon blinked and nearly fell from the stool as his exhaustion washed over him. He was being deafened by the noise and pummeled by Lee who, in the excess of his relief and joy, was literally pounding on him.

"You did it! By the High One's holy tears, you did it!" the drummer was crowing. "I deem you just passed your Master's trials!" Lee was laughing so hard, he was nearly crying. "If only Grandmaster Blackmore could have heard it!"

Menannon managed a slight grin in response.

"If you will excuse me," he whispered and stood, setting his harp on the stool, deliberately placing the drummer's hands on it as there was no possible way he could have found enough voice to ask him to hold it for a few minutes.

Menannon smiled at his well-wishers and began pushing his way towards the door, knowing full well he had to get out and somewhere private before he snatched defeat from the jaws of victory by passing out cold in the middle of the floor. Just as he managed to reach the door, there was a heart-rending shriek behind him which drew everyone's attention and allowed him to make good his escape.

Even as the door closed, he heard further wailing followed by loud guffaws and the sound of his sire's hearty laughter, but he was too exhausted to even wonder at the sounds. He was barely able to make his way down the hall and let himself into a small antechamber and lock the door before his body finally betrayed him and he measured his full length on the floor, gasping for breath, his senses reeling, blood still oozing from his lacerated fingers. Three and a half turns of the hour of the most intense playing had exacted a heavy toll.

He lay still, fading in and out of his senses, for several minutes when he heard a key turn in the lock, the door open and two people come into the little chamber. One was light and fleet of step while the other was slower, steadier.

"Playfellow!" Nirna's voice seemed to come to him from the other end of a field as she knelt beside him and wiped the sweat from his face with a lavender scented handkerchief.

Menannon kept his eyes closed for the simple reason that when he opened them the chamber began to reel about him, nearly making him heave.

"Leave him be, lass," a strong, motherly voice commanded her. "Don't be makin' him talk just now. Help me with this wine."

He recognized the voice of Gooddame Matilda, Nirna's nurse.

"The High One's tears, Mati, his fingers are bleeding," Nirna's voice sounded stricken and Menannon wanted to reassure her, but he was too tired. The gooddame did it for him.

"They're all right. Just a little scraped they are. We'll tend them in a nonce."

Menannon vaguely heard a cork being pulled from a wine bottle and the sound of liquid being poured. Then he felt an arm begin to slide under his shoulders and the cold edge of a metal goblet against his lips.

"Hold his head, lass. Here now, laddie, drink this, it'll make ya feel better."

By instinct rather than desire, Menannon swallowed the herb-laced wine and nearly retched at the horrible taste, but he managed to keep the liquid down.

"Good on ya, lad. Now, just rest." Matilda eased him back to the thick rug and set the goblet aside. "Now let's be seeing to his fingers."

Again, Menannon felt the nurse's firm, but gentle hands. This time, they were raising each of his hands, presumably so that she could inspect their lacerations. In a twinkling, she had dressed each of his fingertips with a soothing ointment and wrapped them with soft linen strips.

"There, lass. He's as good as can be done, so just let him sleep. Watch with him a bit while I go and tell his da he's all right."

Menannon heard Gooddame Matilda heave herself to her feet and briskly leave the chamber. Nirna knelt once more at his side and took hold of his hand, being careful not to disturb the neat bandages. Whether she knew he was awake or not, she spoke softly to him.

"I love you, Playfellow. I'm glad you're home. Do you remember the shaman woman from the market when we were children? She was from the horse clans of Cala, remember? And I got her to read our futures. She told me that I would know both great sorrow and great love and you, she said, were touched by the High One for his own use. Do you remember? She said that in your hands rested destiny."

Destiny. Menannon could hear unshakable faith in him in her voice and words. Destiny? But to what end? It was obvious that his Fæori was sure he could stand between her and that which she feared. Even as the nurse's medicinal took effect and he was falling into a deep sleep, he could not help but wonder about the blindness of love.

CHAPTER 7
(SUMMER OF THE WORLD 6996)

B REAKFAST AT THE VILLA the next morning was a lively affair as Gorlanndon recounted the happenings at the banquet after Menannon left. In the excess of his pride in his son's accomplishments, Gorlanndon had opened his retreat to one and all and had breakfast served in the summerhouse. Firod was present as was his wont and of course, Lord Lonier had come up for his daily discussions with his fellow councillor. Unlike everyone else, Firod had not been present to witness Menannon's harping having been on duty the night before, so the rest were taking great delight in informing him of the event, much to the young Giant's embarrassment.

"You should have heard Penor wailing. It would have done your heart good," Gorlanndon chuckled. "He had taken all wagers, expecting everyone to wager that the boy here would fail save for a few so he gave short odds on that and long odds on his succeeding. Well, there were several wagers in favor of him. Three that I think are of interest and mine of course."

Turning to Menannon, he added, "I put a substantial sum on you to succeed, my boy, a princely sum, I should say."

Turning again to Firod, he continued his tale with some glee.

"Penor's Elder Journeyman Davin wagered in favor of him more to spite his master than thinking he would succeed. Princess Nirna wagered for sheer friendship's sake and Norilendra Queen wagered a handsome sum on him to succeed ...."

"The Queen!?" Menannon was stunned at this revelation. "Why would she wager in my favor?"

"Well, she may not approve of your friendship with her daughter, but she obviously recognizes your mettle, boy, because her wager alone nearly paupered poor Penor. Had not so many others wagered against you, Penor would have been de-feathered completely. As it was, he had to go crawling to

Azuron, who had agreed with Penor to guarantee all bets. The bald one was, ah, most discomfited." Gorlanndon's great laugh filled the summerhouse and he slapped Menannon gently on the shoulder. "You are a true treasure boy, a true treasure."

Menannon swallowed all this praise a bit uneasily, much to Lee's inner amusement. Most harpers would have been basking in the praise, taking it as their due, but the young Giant was embarrassed. To his mind, he had simply done his best, as was expected of all harpers. That his best was far beyond any other living harper had not occurred to him. He was, in fact, modest to a major fault.

Lee could not help adding fuel to the fire and turned to Firod, grinning from ear to ear.

"Captain, the audience was so impressed with this lout's performance they are demanding that the harper hall here learn the piece."

Lee grinned at his friend and shook his head. He was still mystified as to how the young Giant had been able to actually play the piece alone.

Menannon saw the question in his eyes and shrugged.

"I was terrified that I would indeed fail, so of course, there was but one thing for me to do: pray. I prayed hard and asked the High One that if it be His will, to give me the strength and skill to succeed and then I relaxed and left it in His hands. Had I done otherwise, I would have failed miserably."

"Skill had nothing to do with it, I suppose?"

Lee gave him a playfully exasperated look under which Menannon colored intensely and hurried into further explanation to cover his discomfiture.

"Of course it does, but that skill was given me by the High One, so praise Him and not me."

"Be that as it may, last night was a great coup. Davin has asked me to attend upon him this morning to discuss matters. I think he's a bit afraid of you as he was hesitant to request your presence, though as he outranks us, he could have simply ordered it," the drummer's grin was one of pure bliss. "Would you like to accompany me and scare him silly?"

"Nay! I thank you!" Menannon's replied instantly, as the mere thought of a whole hall full of harpers eager to praise his playing positively petrified him. Even this familial praise was making him highly uncomfortable and leaving him wishing there was something else to be talked about.

Gorlanndon understood his son as no other and gave him a sympathetic grin and changed the subject for him. The elder Giant turned to Lonier and cleared his throat and broached a subject he knew would change the discussion.

"I understand the arena is coming along nicely," he said with an innocent twinkle in his eye for Firod who just shook his head as Lord Lonier immediately rose to the bait.

"Damned waste of the treasury, if you ask me!" the old lord snarled. "There are far better things to spend the kingdom's money on than arenas and circuses! Were I still Counsel General, this would not have happened!"

"Arenas and circuses?" Menannon questioned and the old lord turned blazing eyes on him, his jowls fairly quivering with outrage.

"Aye! The kingdom has just finished building an arena down near the docks hard by the foot of the Idrian for the express purpose of holding circuses, wrestling matches, foot races and all other games of strength and endurance so that our people can waste their hard earned money in betting."

"So our puzzlement is answered," Menannon whispered to Lee, as the two of them had been wondering what was the huge edifice being built not far from the Cokeyna. He turned back to Lonier and addressed his next words to the old lord.

"Games of chance have always been held in the establishments along the waterfront, sir." he said. "So why ...?"

"Because the royal house has never organized them ere this! Since the Queen is the one who built the arena, it will seem the bond and duty of every citizen no matter how penurious he may be to go to that arena and bet on the games! There will be games or circuses there all hours of the day and night until everyone is either broke, engorged or too stupefied to care about whatever else is happening in the kingdom!"

"I, for one, have more faith in our people than that," Gorlanndon broke into the conversation overriding Menannon's half-formed protest. Menannon nodded at his sire's words.

"Besides it is being organized and run by the Orlando family whose circus has been performing throughout the empire since time out of mind. Taratillo is a decent, honorable man who has always run his establishments fairly."

"Aye, but that was as a legitimate businessman, not as a government factotum whose take will be vast and the temptation of easy wealth even vaster."

Lonier lapsed into a sullen silence which quickly spread to the rest of the gathering. Before it could become too stifling, Menannon stood and stretched.

"I believe I shall go riding, as I've been shamelessly neglecting Kane."

Besides, Nirna might just manage to keep her appointment to ride—a small hope he kept scrupulously to himself, though a rather odd glance from Firod suggested the captain was suspicious of something. Briefly, Menannon wondered what might have occurred at the palace after he had awakened and been aided home.

"Well, I'll go bask in your glory for you then," Lee winked at him and rose.

Both young men nodded to their elders and headed for the door, Menannon intent on achieving the stable holding as rapidly as possible. Out of the corner of his eye, he saw Firod lean across to speak to his sire.

"You must speak to him ere this goes any farther," he heard Firod whisper. The only answer he heard from his sire was a gusty sigh. Even as Lee went out and Menannon was in the process of closing the door, Gorlanndon called him back.

"A word, boy, if you please."

There was that in his sire's tone that did not bode well. Menannon nodded to Lee and returned to the table, careful to close the door behind him. He stood before his sire, his stomach tightening with a dread he could not name. Gorlanndon studied his son thoughtfully for several long heartbeats, then cleared his throat. Beside him, Lonier had mastered his mood and he was sipping tea nonchalantly, but his hawklike gaze was riveted to the younger Giant, totally belying his assumed ease.

"After we departed last night, there appears to have been a discussion concerning the princess Nirna and yourself," Gorlanndon glanced at Firod and the captain nodded confirmation. "It would seem that our queen has made an edict this morning that her daughter shall not keep fellowship with you at any time, either alone or in company, even with her nurse as chaperone."

"Why?" Menannon demanded a bit more hotly than he intended and he immediately glanced away and took a deep settling breath, not wanting to let the others see the true depth of his feelings for Nirna.

"Our queen's motivations are none of your affair, my boy," Gorlanndon informed him a bit curtly. "Suffice it to say, you will abide by her edict and mine, for I, too, forbid you to attend upon Nirna. That is final. You may go."

Despite this dismissal, Menannon held his ground and looked his sire straight in the eyes.

"I understand this not, sir. The princess and I have been friends life long and while this was not necessarily to her lady mother's liking, it was ne'er forbidden. Why now? There is nothing improper in our friendship."

"What is allowable in childhood is not necessarily a good thing as adults."

Lonier spoke softly, setting down his tea cup. "Nirna is the Princess Royal and she has reached marriageable age ...."

"But, I am in no way a suitor so why ...?" Menannon interrupted, nonplused

"In your mind perhaps, but you are her dearest friend and as such, are at least an impediment to actual suitors. Perhaps her mother does not want you seen as competition."

"But … how …?" Menannon almost stuttered to a halt, truly puzzled now.

There was a brief silence during which all three older men glanced at each other. Finally Firod cleared his throat and spoke.

"It is your size, Menannon." His words were soft but the tone was steely.

"My size? But what has that to do with anything?!"

"Nirna is of the blood royal and is therefore taller than normal Human women," Firod continued as though Menannon had not spoken, "and in fact she is taller than all other women of her house save her grandam. When you were dancing together last night it became very obvious that she is tall enough to make you a wife. Speculations began to foment out of all proportion that you are already her chosen and approved Prince Consort as she has always favored you to the point of having no other friends—not even women friends—in all the summers you've been gone."

"But … but … she's Human! I'm Giant." Menannon spluttered suddenly wondering if he had gone mad or if everyone else had. "The High One forbids …." he struggled to a halt and looked to his sire for understanding. Gorlanndon was sitting quietly, his face closed.

"The High One does not forbid it, lad," Lonier informed him gently. "It is just that such a relationship would be impossible between a Human and a normally sized Giant such as your sire. Had you returned home a fifteen foot monolith as is your sire, this would ne'er have come up. But you did not. You returned here a magnificent nine-foot fellow whose height makes it entirely possible for you to be the consort of an eight-foot princess and therein lies the whole of the issue."

"But…." Menannon began again, beginning to feel like his sire's ancient parrot constantly repeating the few words he knew. "I…."

Lonier held up his hand halting him.

"Let me explain a bit further. As the sire of five daughters, I can tell you that you're turning many a feminine head here on Kalyria. Though you may not think of yourself in this way, you are something of a paragon. You have height, build, looks, talent and you're the son and heir of Kalyria's richest, most ancient, most trusted councillor. There is not a single living soul on this island—save the few resident Teluri—who was alive ere Gorlanndon of Lornennog came here. Your sire has been the prop and stay of this kingdom for so long most folk here feel as though he is a member of the royal household. Though neither he nor you are of the Blood Royal, in the minds of the populace—and some of the nobility—that is insignificant, so it is to be expected that you would be considered as a suitor of the princess. To most minds, that fact almost goes without saying. In fact, young man, though you don't seem to see it, you are Kalyria's most eligible bachelor."

"But the Queen thinks not so," Menannon muttered despite himself.

"Nay, lad, she does not. For whate'er reason, she has always disapproved of you and that disapproval is fast turning into hatred. So for all our sakes, stay away from Nirna. Your friendship with her is part of your past. Keep it that way."

There was kindness in the look the old lord was bending on him and some understanding of what he was asking Menannon to sacrifice.

Gorlanndon spoke up, "It should not be too difficult to stand by my rules and the Queen's wishes, boy, as you will be returning to your life on the mainland soon enough."

His tone almost made it sound as though he expected Menannon to go back to Aridion City and stay there, never to return to Kalyria. The elder Giant nodded to his son and waved him on his way, deliberately turning to converse with Firod.

Menannon inclined his head and left the summerhouse, his mind reeling in confusion. As he was closing the door behind him, he heard his father speak.

"Gentlemen, I fear Azuron now knows ...."

The rest of his words were cut off by the closing of the door and the lowering of Gorlanndon's voice. It was apparent he did not wish his son to hear his words, leaving Menannon to wonder. Whatever it was that Azuron now knew, Menannon was certain it did not bode well for someone and he felt sorry for whomever it might be.

Silently, he sought his chamber and donned a rough service-able tunic and good woolen hose with knee-high leather boots as his riding kit. He threw a cloak over his shoulder as a precaution, not knowing how late he might return. Several of the household staff bade him good morn, but for once, he did not hear them, being too fraught with his own inner turmoil to attend to what was happening around him. He went to the kitchen where he found Clarinda had set out travel victuals for him and a bottle of good peach wine on the back table. How she had known he would be in need of such he neither knew nor cared at the moment, but took it up gratefully and one of the under cooks let him out the back door. He circled the villa to the front gate where the gate wardens unlocked the portal and waved him through, locking it again behind him.

It was still early and the soft rose light of morning glittered across the city and the sea beyond promising a beautiful day, but this time he did not stand to admire the view, being intent upon attaining his sire's stable holding as quickly as possible. He arrived without any delays or distractions, withdrew a small key from his belt pouch and let himself in the side gate as there was no need to disturb Paulus. He whistled in Kane and waited for the horse, attempting to keep his mind blank as he desired to not consider the implications of his sire's ban, or more importantly, Lonier's words, but they echoed in his mind: *You returned here a magnificent nine-foot fellow whose height makes it entirely possible for you to be consort to the princess…consort to the princess…consort.* He clamped firmly down on his spinning thoughts. Heretofore, he had never allowed himself to consider marrying Nirna. She was his beloved Fæori, but she was Human and he, Giant. The High One forbade such a relationship, didn't He? Well, apparently not, if Lonier was right. That was a heart-stopping thought and one that would have to be researched as soon as he returned to Aridion City's harper hall and its great library.

Kane thundered across the pasture and came to a clattering halt in the courtyard where he stood snorting and blowing playfully at Menannon's hair, full of his usual hijinks, putting an end to his young master's speculations for the nonce. He followed curiously as Menannon went into the saddle shed and searched out the stallion's tack. Back out in the courtyard, Kane allowed himself to be saddled and bridled with his usual ease, though he could not resist butting his master in the shoulder every now and then just to keep him on his toes.

Menannon had almost finished his task when there was a thumping on the top rail of the fence. He looked up from his work and beheld a tall fair lad looking over the fence. He was dressed in the drab cote and hose of a dock worker with the wide-brimmed hat of his occupation.

"If we were vera good, would tha be willin' 'ta take we fer a ride?" the fellow enquired in a rather high voice for a lad.

"Fæori, you'll have to practice lowering your voice should you truly desire to be taken for a youth."

Menannon ducked his head to give himself time to breathe a sigh of relief that she had come and to rearrange his face into some semblance of normalcy. There was no reason to disturb her thoughts with his speculations. When he could trust himself, he looked back up with a grin.

"I must say you have old Corin's dialect down perfectly."

Corin had been a gardener at the palace when they were children and both of them had been fascinated with his mode of speech. He was a Dwarf from Starkhad in the far north of Aridion and though he had spent many summers in service to Kalyria's king, he had never lost his home speech pattern.

"Well, can we have a ride?" she asked, again attempting to lower her voice, as she climbed over the fence.

"Most assuredly, my boy."

Menannon grinned and raised an expressive eyebrow to her as he stood to help her into the saddle. With only slight aid from him, Nirna clambered up onto Kane's back. The horse did not mind her presence, a testament to how faithfully she had kept her word to exercise him while his young master was away.

"Oh, my! I'm always amazed how tall he is!"

Nirna giggled a bit breathlessly as Menannon mounted behind her, being amazed anew in his turn at how tall she was and how well they fit together. Perhaps the High One had made him only nine feet tall for this very purpose.... Menannon again forced his mind away from such speculations.

"You know, of course, we are forbidden to meet, Fæori. My sire and Lord Lonier gave me your mother's edict this morning," Menannon said to give her the chance to not go against her mother's wishes should she so choose, speaking softly so as not to be overheard by Paulus' lad who had just come out into the courtyard.

His stomach tightened whist he awaited her response. He need not have worried, for the words had barely left his lips when she raised her head in imperious denial.

"You mean Azuron's edict!" She looked up at him, fairly hissing the Teluri councillors name. "He is controlling my mother's thoughts and actions more and more and he is determined to control me as well, but he will not! I am the Princess Royal and my sire's daughter. I'll not be bidden by a mere upstart councillor, even if he does have the queen's ear. You are my dearest friend and I'll not give you up and that is final."

She tossed her head, her hat nearly unseating at the movement.

"I would not give you up even were this edict actually from my mother. Now, I have no further desire to talk about my mother's pet. So don't you dare even mention his name again this entire day!"

This last she said with sweet venom and turning back, settled her hat more firmly in place.

Menannon refrained from saying the obvious that it had not

been he who had been speaking of the councillor. Wisely, he just clicked to the stallion and Kane started just as prettily as you please with no hint of his usual hijinks. As Kane moved, Menannon resisted the temptation to take Nirna about the waist to steady her as this would not be something he would do with a youth of her seeming age. Such a stripling would be expected to fend for himself even if he did ride in front rather than behind. Paulus' lad let them out the gate and secured it behind them.

They quickly left the hold behind, turning southeast at a ground covering lope. All about them, the colors of high summer strode the land and the fields were already velvety green with their life-giving treasure soon to turn golden under the High One's sun. Despite the early hour, they were hailed and greeted on all sides as they crossed the settled lands and even when they entered the forests beyond, for the charcoalers were out gathering sticks and fallen limbs for their charcoal clamps. They circled the skirts of the old forest and headed southeast on a less-used road which took them to a favorite haunt of old—a hidden cove nestled securely in a curve in the southern shore. Many had been the expedition they had made here together especially the last summer before he left for the mainland.

It was a small cove with a sweet spring bubbling above it and falling in a delicate waterfall down the cliff face straight into the sea. A fine trail led down the cliff giving access to the cove. In the center of the cove itself a small island lay. It was a drowned tongue of stone thrusting away from the cliff with a delightful stretch of black sand forming a small beach on its seaward side. For two adventurous children, this had served as pirate galley, mysterious uncharted lands, homestead and even the mystical land of beginnings, Kaalamar itself. It had been almost as far as two healthy children could swim to reach it then, now it was still a goodly swim to achieve, a great enough distance from shore one could lie on its beach unseen by any who happened by above. Though this part of Kalyria was unfrequented by any save fishermen, it had still added an element of adventure to their play to be able to be thus unseen.

They arrived at the head of the cliff trail and Menannon drew Kane to a halt and they sat looking down, each recalling the last time they had been here. Nirna gave a great sigh of contentment. She had long since abandoned her boyish disguise and removed her hat, allowing her riotous curls to cascade over her shoulders. The gentle breeze wafting up from the water below played with her loosed hair, causing it to glint in the sun.

"Long have I dreamed of this day, Playfellow, the day you would return and bring me here, to our private place."

There was a distracted quality to her voice as she spoke, almost as though her thoughts were lost in a private dream.

"Came you not here whilst I was gone?" Menannon asked.

"Nay, it would have been so lifeless without you, it would have saddened me greatly."

Her words chimed a like chord within his own heart. He would have shunned it as well for much the same reason.

"Well, Fæori, as we are both here, shall we return to Kaalamar?"

"Aye, with all my heart!" she turned and smiled up at him, her eyes glinting purple mystery in which he could have lost himself.

In that moment, it struck him with all the force of revelation, that if the High One did not forbid the union of Giant and Human, Nirna was truly far more to him than boon companion. What had once been in his mind was now also in his heart of hearts and it shook him to the core of his being. In the depths of her eyes he saw the truth: She was his and only his as he was hers and only hers! In near panic, he forced himself away from that truth and quickly headed Kane down the trail and onto the beach below, returning to a place beloved to them both in childhood. Once there, he did not stop, but rode Kane directly into the sea until the water was lapping at the horse's belly.

Then as unceremoniously as though they really were

children still, he took hold of Nirna's boot and neatly flipped her into the sparkling water. Her indignant protest was cut off by a mouthful of seawater. Menannon's laughter at Nirna's expense was short lived as, thus relieved of his feminine burden, Kane reverted to his usual self and casually dumped Menannon into the sea as well. The young Giant landed with a great splash and the stallion whinnied at him and shook his mane, turned smartly about and took himself back out of the water and up the cliff trail to the top where he began contentedly cropping grass.

"You great booby!" Nirna fumed and began splashing Menannon with great handsful of water as fast as her arms could move.

"All right! All right! I surrender and as penance, I'll go retrieve our repast."

Menannon chuckled and held up a dripping arm. He scrambled out of the water before she could drown him and ran back up the trail. By the time he had succeeded in securing the large basket from behind Kane's saddle and returned to the beach, Nirna had come out of the water and doffed most of her clothing and hung it on the bushes to dry, leaving herself dressed in naught but her white chemise.

While this garment was great for swimming, as it reached only to her thighs, wet, it did nothing at all in providing for modesty though it was a marvel at highlighting her very feminine charms. She moved along the small beach as freely and innocently as a sea nymph. Perhaps she really is a Fæorlinga, Menannon found himself musing and shook his head and firmly set himself to making a hollow in the sand and kindling a fire from the driftwood studding the beach.

Had he desired to kindle an emotional fire, he need only have glanced down the beach to where Nirna was looking for shells. Dressed as she was not, she was doing a marvelous job of kindling his fire without any help from him. In that moment, his world went slightly out of focus as he imagined himself, married to Nirna and the two of them raising a family together. In his mind's eye, he suddenly had a vision of a beautiful girl slightly taller than Nirna herself with the black hair of her Giant sire cascading in waves to nearly her knees and the violet eyes of her Human mother considering him across her shoulder as she walked away through a field of wild flowers. Resolutely, Menannon shook his head, clamped down on his emotions again and tried to concentrate on his work. Even so, the world did not quite return to focus, yet seemed to retain a soft, rosy glow.

When he had the fire burning, so that it would make a good bed of coals for cooking, he took off his wet boots and tunic and tossed them on a nearby bush, leaving himself dressed in naught but his hose, the better to swim. He glanced down the beach to see that Nirna had her hands full of shells and was busily reaching for a conch shell caught in a small pool formed atop a rock during the last storm.

"Last one out to the island has to cook," he called, grinning at her mischievously. He dove into the water and struck out for the small island.

"Trickster!" she shrieked indignantly and dropped her shells, diving in after him and nearly beat him to the island. Both of them climbed up onto the rock, breathing hard. Menannon barely caught his wind before Nirna was off again into the water daring him to catch her. For the next almost full turn of the hour, the clock turned back and they played as though they were indeed children until they were both happily exhausted and they crawled out onto the little island's beach to rest.

The sun-warmed sand felt marvelous after the cool of the sea and both of them stretched out comfortably in companionable silence. Overhead, the clouds floated white against an azure sky. High above, a white bird attracted Menannon's attention. He sat up and studied it as it wheeled and soared above them. Menannon caught his breath. It was an albatross! At long last, he was actually seeing the fabled albatross over sea water!

"Look, Fæori, the albatross! See how her feathers flutter with the speed of her flight?"

Nirna followed his pointing finger and could just distinguish a beautiful white bird riding upon the wind. How much better a Giant's eyesight was than a mere Human's! Nirna could see farther than most of her race, but more than the bird, she could not see. That he could see her individual feathers at this great distance was a miracle of the High One.

"You know, Fæori, according to the lore of the Giants of Lornennog, as we have now seen the High One's albatross over sea water, we shall be specially blessed all the days of our lives."

"I believe that," she whispered in reply, but she was not looking at the albatross as she spoke.

They lay back down and watched the bird until it flew beyond even Menannon's sight. Peaceful silence settled over the little beach.

At last, Nirna propped herself up on one elbow and studied Menannon as he lay on his back, his hands behind his head, eyes closed, nearly asleep. Nothing and no one had ever seemed more beautiful to her. She studied him almost hungrily as she searched her heart for truth. Her mother's edict and the thought of losing him made her consider things far more closely than she ever had ere this. What did she really feel for this playfellow of hers? She well knew already that he was more than a friend as she would rather do nothing with him than do anything in all the world with anyone else. Had she not proven that to herself over all the summers he had been away, as no one else had taken his place nor even interested her in spending time with them. He alone could make her laugh or cry. He alone stirred her passions. In short, she found that her childhood liking for Menannon had grown and matured onto a very adult feeling indeed. She loved him with all her heart with a passion as fixed as a star in the firmament.

She could not help herself. She had to express that love. Very shyly, she leaned over him and kissed his lips, tasting the salt of the sea and more. Menannon came fully awake with a start to find Nirna looking down at him, her whole heart in her eyes. His heart matched hers and would not be gainsaid. Her shy kiss set fire to his already smoldering senses and he rolled over and took her in his arms, returning her kiss for kiss, her skin feeling warm and smooth under his hands and lips, his body following where his soul led as his love burned suddenly white hot, nearly consuming them both.

In the one small corner of his mind still capable of rational thought, alarm bells began to ring imperious warning. This was wrong! With an effort that nearly shattered his soul, Menannon forced himself to stop mid-kiss. He rolled as far away as the little stretch of sand would allow and sat up.

"What is it?" she whispered, reaching for him.

He leaned back onto his elbow and took her searching hands and held them in both of his own.

"We must not do this thing, Fæori," his voice was rough with a combination of passion and fear. "We would be stealing from the High One Himself by taking a blessing granted only to the marriage bed. It is wrong to so besmirch ourselves."

"But, I love you, Menannon, and only you and I realize now I always have. I want to be yours. How can this be wrong?" she slipped one delicate hand from his clasp and ran her fingers through his hair, smoothing the stray wisps away from his brow. "I want you to claim me for your own. I have never belonged to another and I never will. The High One does not forbid two people in love from cleaving unto each other."

He could have drowned in the depths of her eyes at that moment. Almost, he gave in, but for both their sakes, he fought for control and won a precarious victory.

"The High One does not forbid this blessing within the vows of marriage, Fæori," he nearly whispered.

"But if we truly love each other, it should not matter...."

"Yet it *does* matter, for the very act of cleaving each to the other is a giving of all that we are and this must never be done lightly. Once two souls are joined in this way, they can never be whole again unto themselves, for each now possesses a part of the other's very spirit. This blessing must be warded and hedged about as much as possible, for to so join before time or with the wrong person for mere cravings of the body leaves one's soul forever marred."

She lay still thinking upon his words for several long moments before turning to him to touch the side of his face.

"All right. If our loving is forbidden outside of marriage ... we will soon be of age ... then we can marry and none can ever say us nay again."

Her voice held the lilt of one who has finally achieved the answer to a long-sought question.

Menannon's pulses quickened anew at her words, but he forced himself to think. He was not absolutely positive that the High One did not forbid a Giant to marry a Human and until he could research the matter, he chose silence as his answer. Only yesterday, he had been dreading the return to Aridion City, but now he welcomed it.

He spoke no word, but gave her a loving smile. Her answering smile was as bright as the sun breaking through rain. She bounced to her feet and held out her hand to him.

"Come my beloved, the coals should be ready to cook upon and your future wife longs to serve you."

Nirna raised her head high, her eyes sparkling.

Menannon let himself be swept into her enthusiasm and rose and bowed to her.

"I sincerely hope you cook better than you embroider."

"Just you wait!" She sprang away and dove into the water heading for the beach, her clear laugh challenging him to follow.

Menannon dove in after and caught her just as she rose from the water. He halted her with a swift hand, leaving her standing in place and went down the beach to where she had been collecting shells. He found the conch shell where it still lay in its cradle of water atop the rock. It was beautiful, its coral pink throat glowing nearly the color of Nirna's cheeks where the afternoon's sun had kissed them. He picked it up and returned to her.

Despite his resolve to make sure their union was legal in the eyes of the High One, he could not resist securing it a little and cleared his throat a bit self-consciously.

"It is customary to bind a pledge by exchanging hand-fasting gifts. So to honor that tradition, I give you this conch shell as a pledge of my love."

He bowed to her and handed her the shell. She took it with shining eyes.

"Wait, I have that which I would give you as well."

Nirna ran swiftly to where her clothes lay draped over the bushes and separated out a long sash of pale peach sorak she had used to tie her hair under her hat. She returned to him and held it out.

"I give you this sash as a pledge of my love."

Menannon lowered his head, enabling her to wrap the soft cloth around his neck. For just a moment, they stood quietly, their eyes speaking everything their hearts were longing to say. Then together they walked hand-in-hand to the fire pit where its still-glowing coals aided them in their dream. They spent the rest of the afternoon and well into the night until the stars were long glinting overhead, talking and dreaming of the future. For this day, love alone ruled their lives.

IT WAS WELL PAST THE MID OF NIGHT when Menannon finally entered his chambers and crossed to the table near the windows where he opened the small Dwarf lamp just a crack, the low light suiting his mood the better. He took off his cloak and draped it over the back of one of the hearth chairs, then stood still for a few moments before slowly untying Nirna's sash from about his throat. He drew it off almost reverently, then impulsively held it to his lips before he laid it carefully on the table. Menannon turned to enter the bathing chamber, took one step, then froze.

His sire was sitting in the darkness near his bed, silently staring at him, his eyes glowing slightly red. The two Giants faced each other wordlessly for a single heartbeat then Gorlanndon's voice broke the stillness in a low grating whisper.

"I ordered you to stay away from the Princess, boy! Why did you disobey my direct command?"

Menannon straightened, standing nearly at attention. He had seen his sire's eyes burning red with anger just once before. Though it had not been at him, his heart had turned to water then, as it was threatening to do now. He took a deep breath, then forced himself to answer as calmly as he could though his hands were shaking.

"She is my dearest friend and I refuse to give her up just to please some pointed-eared son of a thrice-damned sea slug! You know as well as I that the Queen's new councillor is behind this edict of hers. Nirna deserves better than that, as do I!"

There was that in Menannon's heart that bordered on total rebellion. His own anger began to rise and he looked his sire straight in the eyes.

"I will meet with Nirna whene'er it pleases us and no one will say me nay, not even you!"

Gorlanndon rose from his chair and crossed the chamber so fast Menannon hardly saw him start to move before he felt the back of his sire's hand connecting with the side of his face with a sickening crack. The blow sent him crashing into the table behind him, shattering it and depositing him on the floor among its splintered remains. He lay stunned, the taste of his own blood in his mouth. His mind barely had time to register the pain of Gorlanndon's blow when the elder Giant was on him, jerking him up by the front of his tunic until they were nearly nose to nose.

"You are my son and you will do as I bid in all things. Nothing has changed my rights over you!" Gorlanndon's eyes were glowing fiercely now, even as he spoke, his Giantish temper coming rapidly to the boiling point.

"I respect your will in all things but this," Menannon managed to force past the constricting collar of his tunic where his sire was holding it so tightly it was nearly strangling him. "I will not betray Fæori's trust in me...."

Gorlanndon gave a growl deep in his throat and raised his free hand to strike again.

"You may beat me to death, Father, but you will alter not my feelings, nor my mind."

"Why is her friendship so dear to you that you are willing to risk all our futures for it? Answer me, boy!"

Gorlanndon shook him hard.

"I love her." Menannon spoke softly and from his heart.

Gorlanndon froze, the red going instantly out of his eyes as his son's words sank into his mind.

"You're meddling with forces you don't begin to understand, boy! Nirna is not an ordinary woman," he nearly snarled, setting Menannon back down on the floor.

Menannon tore himself out of his sire's grip and lurched over to the window.

"I am not a fool, though some might beg to differ with me. I am aware that Fæori is the Princess Royal and that there will be complications, but I love her and there is naught I can do about it. Eight summers and all the pains, heartaches and triumphs of growing up have not changed my feelings for her, nor hers for me. My heart is in her keeping."

He turned back to face his sire, locking eyes with him, willing him to understand.

Gorlanndon spoke no word, just stood there looking at his son, watching the blood drip down his face from a gash over his eye, where a splinter of the table had torn his flesh. *How has it come to this,* the elder Giant wondered silently, *that I have allowed myself to succumb so far to fear of this sorcerer and his possibilities that I can strike my own child with pure savagery when he has done no more than fall in love?* The elder Giant had no words to breach the impasse.

Menannon waited a few moments more then inclined his head to his sire.

"Should you seek me, sir, I shall be in the soaking chamber."

He managed to keep his voice steady when he really wanted to scream at him, demanding to know what he had done to deserve losing the regard of his beloved sire just because he had acknowledged his love for Nirna. When Gorlanndon said nothing in return, Menannon inclined his head again and turned to the door.

"I foreswore the woman I love for the greater good," Gorlanndon said to Menannon's retreating back, his voice soft in the air.

Menannon stopped at the door, his hand on the knob and turned back at his sire's words, but the elder Giant was looking out the window. Did he see the night without or perchance did the beautiful face of a Giantess linger in the darkness just beyond the glass? Menannon left the room silently, closing the door behind him.

A full turn of the hour later, Menannon returned to his chamber dressed in a sleeping robe, to find his sire gone and the remains of the table cleared away. Nirna's scarf was hung carefully over the back of a chair. He stood looking at it for a long moment, then threw himself onto his bed and fell into a haunted slumber.

The last stars were going out for the night when Menannon was awakened suddenly by the feel of something warm upon his swollen face. He jerked into a sitting position to find himself looking at his sire's chest where Gorlanndon sat at his bedside, a basin of warm sage tea in one hand and a soft cloth in the other.

"Hush, boy. All is well. Go back to sleep,"

Gorlanndon soothed him and pushed him gently back down and smoothed the blankets back around his shoulders. The elder Giant set the basin down on the bedside table and re-soaked the cloth in the soothing mixture and laid it back on the side of Menannon's face. Menannon lay stiffly, keeping his gaze turned from his sire. The silence had strained between the two of them almost to the breaking point when Gorlanndon heaved a gusty sigh.

"All right, boy, that's enough of this," he said removing the cloth from Menannon's face and, taking a hold of his chin, forced him to turn his head and look at him with his right eye, as his left was swollen shut. "Now say it and have done!" Gorlanndon's voice was a low growl.

"Say what, sir?" Menannon kept his voice inflectionless.

Gorlanndon sighed again and shook his head.

"Giants! I swear to the High One we'd rather die than admit to a hurting heart."

He leaned down and looked Menannon straight in the eye, his face stone serious.

"All right, if you won't speak your mind, I will speak it for you. What you say is this: My father, after tonight's doings, I desperately need to know if I have forfeited your love."

The darkness almost hid Menannon's blush, but not quite, as his sire literally took the words straight out of his heart. Gorlanndon nodded and raised a knowing eyebrow which deepened his son's blush even farther. He cleared his throat and continued.

"What I say in return to your question is this: Nothing in all the High One's world could e'er make me turn my love from you. Nothing! Menannon, you are flesh of my flesh and bone of my bone. I love you more than life itself. I always have and I always will. You must trust me as you have e'er trusted me. I may not always approve of what you do, but that will ne'er change the way I feel about you. Don't ever doubt me, boy."

There was silence in the chamber then as Gorlanndon waited, giving his son the time to think about his words.

Menannon lay still, looking into the darkness, his emotions swinging wildly between childhood and manhood. Part of him wanted desperately to throw himself into his sire's embrace and the rest wanted to find some way of expressing verbally the relief and love he felt. At the last, he could think of no words or actions that could truly express what was in his heart so he gave up and settled for saying something totally irrelevant.

"I finally saw the albatross over water today, sir," he almost mumbled.

Gorlanndon sat looking at him for just a moment, then

threw back his fine head and laughed his great booming laugh, awakening the entire household with the sound of his mirth. When he could get himself back under control, Gorlanndon, being long mature and knowing full well what expressions his manhood could withstand, reached down and took his son up in his strong arms as easily as though he were still a child and held him in a nearly bone cracking embrace.

"You and that benighted albatross," he chortled against Menannon's hair. "So, you finally saw her after fourteen summers of looking and now the High One's blessings will be upon you all the days of your life according to the legends of Lornennog. The High One alone knows how much I love you, boy!"

MENANNON EMERGED from his chambers later that morning, his face still swollen greatly and his left eye showing most of the colors of the rainbow. He was not a pretty sight.

"What in the High One's holy world happened to you?" Lee whistled and winced at the sight of his friend's battered face. The drummer was enjoying a late breakfast with his host while he waited for Menannon to emerge. "Did Kane kick you in the head?"

"Ah ... no."

Menannon held his hand against his lip to keep it from splitting again as he could not help grinning at his sire. He sat in the chair next to the drummer at the dining room table and began to serve himself from the covered breakfast dishes.

"No, it wasn't Kane," Gorlanndon informed his guest with a wink at his son. "It was something rather larger."

"Larger than that horse? That would take some doing!"

"Take that as a warning, youngster. You never want to be in the wrong place at the right time when a Giant is expressing his opinion," Gorlanndon informed him with a wide grin.

Menannon just shook his head, coloring nicely as he saw understanding widen Lee's eyes. Needless to say, the drummer changed the subject rather hurriedly and spent the rest of breakfast regaling them with tales of how his time had been spent the day before at the harper hall.

CHAPTER 8
(SUMMER OF THE WORLD 6996)

MENANNON AND LEE SPENT the next few sevendays of their holiday either camping and fishing or wandering the city and enjoying its distractions. It was a bit disconcerting for Menannon that the fame of his harping had spread through the city and he could not go about without having someone congratulate him or at least mention his great ability. Lee of course found the whole situation exceedingly funny. He was sure that it was good for his friend to receive the accolades as he would need to be able to accept such things gracefully should he indeed become the Grandmaster Harper.

Despite the prohibition against it, there were many times Nirna was able, with her nurse's aid, to meet Menannon, perforce always in the company of the drummer and ever were they careful to not mention their day at the cove in anyone's company, nor to give voice to their hopes and dreams. Yet they could not quite prevent their eyes from betraying them, particularly Menannon, for he was not as skilled at dissembling as was Nirna whose life within the palace had schooled her in the ways of intrigue and politics. As Lee could read his friend like an open codex despite Menannon's best efforts to remain closed, he always felt that he was intruding upon them and usually found some plausible excuse to give them their privacy.

One bright day, however, intrusion was not an issue, as they were exploring the rough and tumble world of the open markets near the docks. The blended market was alive with buyers and sellers. The many booths, brightly colored awnings and flags nearly shining in the sun, displayed wares from all parts of the empire and even beyond. There was one Borian trader, a most unusual sight, whose wares included carven ivory from the tribal lands of far southern Goth where the folk wore sealskin clothing and hunted walruses upon the ice floes.

Amidst these settled booths were hawkers who carried their wares upon trays suspended from leather ties about their necks and flower sellers with baskets of beauty clutched in their hands. The place was alive with performers and acrobats, mummers and artists and even stilt-walkers advertising the nightly circus. Everywhere one looked, there was movement and color and noise. The whole was crowded with folk strolling, buying, arguing, debating, and generally enjoying all the delights the market had to offer. The dock markets were also the place of choice for rendezvous when one would prefer not to be noticed, whether it was seedy looking fellows talking in the shadows or a wealthy lass taking advantage of the crush to meet her beau and steal a kiss or two behind the booths out of sight of her nurse's watchful eyes. The markets were the perfect place for secrets.

It was said that all the world and his wife met at least once in the market places of Kirith Kalyria and Lee found himself believing it. He wandered along behind Menannon as he strolled from booth to booth taking an inordinate amount of time looking at wares in which Lee knew full well he had absolutely no interest. The drummer was only briefly left to wonder at his friend's unusual activity as they had no sooner reached the far end of the booths and begun to turn for another round when Lee spotted Gooddame Matilda coming down the main avenue, a large basket on her arm, her white sorak head covering floating out with the light breeze blowing in from the sea. Lee stopped and watched the lady and when the breeze let the head covering fall for a moment, he saw what he expected see: the Princess Nirna followed her nurse closely, her fair ringlets shining unmistakably against the claret sorak robe she wore.

Beside him, he felt Menannon stiffen and he glanced up to see the Giant was looking hard towards a group of palace guards lounging in front of one of the myriad pubs fronting the market. They were obviously having a small nuncheon washed down with an ample amount of wine and enjoying a game of dice. It was well known throughout the city that Nirna and the Giant's son were forbidden to keep company, a ban the palace guards had been ordered to enforce. However, Lee did not think the guards would interfere with this chance meeting in an open market. Needless to say, Menannon slowed his pace so that they twain by all appearance were innocently perusing the goods at a booth selling basketry hard by the closest entrance to the market when the ladies arrived at the same booth.

The Giant picked up a highly decorated basket and was examining it carefully, his attention seemingly fully engaged so that when the princess walked past and bumped into him, his reaction of surprised delight seemed totally natural. Lee could not help a grin at how well they had maneuvered this meeting, though when they had planned it was beyond his ken. He suspected that Clarinda might well have had a part to play as that good lady was as loyal to her Menannon as Matilda was to Nirna. It was well known that the two ladies were as thick as thieves, having been long thrown into each others company by the childhood friendship of their charges.

"Princess. My lady."

Menannon stepped back and inclined his head to both ladies acting purely as one should in such a course: respectfully polite and no more. Lee himself could not resist giving them a full court bow, which act caused Nirna to giggle behind her peacock feather fan.

"Well met," Matilda called out her greeting rather more loudly than necessary, "for I have need of a long arm and a strong back this day and yours will do better than another's."

She unceremoniously thrust her basket into the young Giant's hands and began to circle the market.

The three youngsters looked at each other and shrugged. They fell in with the gooddame, Menannon being careful to walk with her so perforce Lee became escort to Nirna. This arrangement lasted for most of a half turn of an hour with Menannon obediently reaching out for her inspection the fruits, vegetables and herbs Matilda pointed out and carefully placing them in the basket should they pass muster.

Nirna engaged Lee in an animated discussion of his plans for when he returned to Crenanoc, a city with which she was very conversant, though she had never visited it. Although he took great pleasure in talking with the princess, for she was a fair and comely companion of surprising knowledge, the drummer was curious to see how she would arrange to switch partners in so public a place. She did not seem to be in any great haste, which the Crenanocian took as a complement—that and the fact she did not do him the discourtesy of asking only after her erstwhile playmate, though the drummer was the perfect person to be so questioned. A quarter turn of the hour more and they were at a confectioner's booth hard by the pub where the guardsmen were still enjoying their nuncheon. Here Nirna chose to make her move. As a slightly stronger breeze blew through the market she gave a slight gasp and jerked her head away from her fan as though its feathers had struck her face.

"I've something in my eye!" she exclaimed, taking hold of the nearest arm: Menannon's. "Please, get it out. It hurts."

Obediently, Menannon set down the basket and turned to look at Nirna's upturned face.

"I can see nothing, my Princess," he said, shaking his head.

"But there must be something there. It still hurts!" she exclaimed, waving her hand as though she were resisting rubbing her eye.

They were standing in the shadow of the awning which gave Menannon the perfect excuse to take Nirna's fan from her and drop it in the basket, then take her arm and tug her into the sunshine.

"Here, my Lady, turn your head," Menannon gently took her chin and turned her to face him so that the sun fell fully on her eye.

He looked closely for a moment then held her eye open and blew gently.

"It was a bit of your feather fan," he said offering her a clean handkerchief from his belt pouch as her eye was watering for real now having been exposed to direct sunlight for a moment.

"Thank you," she sighed, wiping her eye. "That is much better."

Nirna took his arm and smiled up at him and he inclined his head with the slightest ghost of a wink. They turned back to join the others and Lee hastily retrieved Matilda's basket. When they returned to the ladies' shopping, they had neatly changed partners.

Lee glanced out of the corner of his eye to see how the guards would react. They had watched the little drama as had most of the shoppers in the market. One of the younger men apparently had asked what they should do thereby prompting the eldest among them, a grizzled veteran of indeterminate age, to glance disinterestedly over his shoulder in appraisal. He waved a dismissive hand. Obviously, what his princess chose to do was her business and not his. All of them went back to eating their nuncheon and playing their rather boisterous dice game.

As they continued to circle the market, Matilda tugged surreptitiously on Lee's arm until they were walking just far enough behind Menannon and Nirna to allow them a bit of privacy without sacrificing decorum. Matilda also began talking to Lee about Crenanoc, a city with which she was well acquainted having served there many summers as the nurse to Nirna's sire when his own sire was yet the Prince Royal and serving as Kalyria's Governor-General to that section of Aridion. Matilda was replete with stories of her life and adventures there which she began to recount to him with exceeding relish, causing the drummer to immediately divine that here was the source of Nirna's great knowledge of his city. The gooddame even told him how she had once been courted by a member of the Crenanocian royal family, but it had come to naught and she had returned to Kirith Kalyria with a sadder but wiser heart. Despite that unfortunate event, she was still an incurable romantic and thus a willing accomplice to Nirna's activities.

They had nearly finished the ladies' shopping when

Menannon's attention was caught by a high nasal voice raised petulantly.

"No! I like these tomatoes not at all. They are obviously inferior and terribly overpriced."

Menannon turned to see that the speaker was none other than Master Harper Penor who was standing in all his be-ringed and pomaded glory beneath the shade of an umbrella held by a young harper apprentice barely big enough to hold it. He was arguing with the proprietor of a vegetable booth.

"And I'm sure they are at least a sevenday old."

"I assure ya sir, t'ey were just brought in from t'village only t'is mornin'," the proprietor, an elderly farmer, assured him, his rheumy old eyes darting around nervously to see if Penor's outburst had been overheard.

The ill will of such an august personage as the Master Harper could ruin his business.

"No, no! Look at this one. It's moldy I say!" Penor obviously grabbed a tomato at random and shook it under the man's nose.

"T'at's only a slight bit of dust easily cleaned."

The man took the tomato from him and wiped it carefully with a small towel.

"Here, t'en, d'ya see? A fine specimen of a tomato."

They were beginning to draw a crowd. Penor looked askance at the newly cleaned tomato, set it down and reached for another one. Before he could disparage this new one, the proprietor grabbed several and thrust them into a draw-stringed sack and handed it to the harper.

"Here, sir! Take t'ese with me complements. T'ey're the finest tomatoes, I assure ya."

Penor took them with a sneer and rolled his eyes, but he placed the sack in his basket with alacrity and moved away, obviously having achieved his goal.

Menannon and Lee exchanged a disgusted glance and shook their heads. Not only had the master harper cheated the goodman out of his due, he had caused him to loose face for, despite the harper's departure, other shoppers were noticeably avoiding the vegetable booth. If something was not done to change their focus, the fellow's business would be ruined for at least the day. Menannon glanced, around wondering what might give the crowd a new sensation to latch onto. There did not seem to be anything unusual in the offing. He glanced back to where Nirna was looking out for a sweet to serve after dinner in her own chambers, as she avoided eating at her mother's table whenever possible. Lee was standing in the shade of the booth's awning casually swatting at the few flies buzzing about while Gooddame Matilda had moved several booths away and was looking at a beautiful shawl made of the finest wool, spun gossamer fine. It was unusual to find such an item here at the docks. Things of such craftsmanship were usually reserved for the booths in the Serpentine where the money pouches were better filled. She had her basket near her feet where the drummer had set it for her convenience.

Seeing that the gooddame was well occupied, Menannon turned his attention back to Nirna who for some reason had become almost as finicky as Penor had been, but without the spite. It gave him an idea. He glanced at the seller to see he was a jovial looking middle-aged farmer with twinkling blue eyes and a ready smile. It was likely he would not interfere with Menannon's plan. In fact he was obviously beginning to feel a bit ill-used as the Princess fussed. Though of course he would never say anything to Kalyria's royalty, as it was an honor to have their patronage, but she was preventing other shoppers from purchasing his wares and there were after all, other fruit booths in the market and he was already losing trade to some of them. At this rate, he stood to loose half his day's earnings. Nirna was being so fussy about the quality of the plums she was choosing, she had already picked up at least half of them and set each one down with a distinct shake of her head and an upturning of her nose. At last, she found one with which she was satisfied and set it down on the tray the proprietor had handed her for the purpose.

Now was Menannon's chance to draw attention away from

the vegetable seller and have a bit of fun at the same time. The Giant looked over Nirna's head and gave the seller a wink and motioned for his silence then moved to stand at the Princess' side where he picked up the plum and examined it and shook his head pursing his lips and looked over at Lee.

"No, no this is definitely not a prize plum. You'd best find another," he said, pitching his voice high and through his nose in a marvelous imitation of Master Harper Penor, a counterfeit not missed by the shoppers nearby as there were several muffled giggles to be heard.

Not quite sure what was happening, but more than willing to play along, Lee nodded vigorously in agreement. Menannon set the fruit back on the pile of its fellows as though it were wormy and fastidiously wiped his hand on the towel hanging in the booth for the purpose.

"What are you talking about it? It is a marvelous plum."

Nirna looked up at him, puzzled, and put the fruit back on her tray.

"Oh, no, no, no, your highness ...."

Menannon shook his head and removed it again. Nirna started and grabbed it back, which of course resulted in Menannon removing it again. At about the fifth time of this Nirna, grabbed the plum again and almost smashed it down onto her tray.

"I will have this one and none other!" her violet eyes were beginning to flash dangerously.

Menannon pursed his lips and gave her a long-suffering look.

"I simply cannot allow you to soil your tray and thus your tummy with such a poor quality specimen."

He removed it once more waving his fingers in another perfect parody of Penor. A louder laugh rippled across the growing audience about the fruit seller's booth.

"Why, you supercilious jackanapes!" Nirna shrieked, took up the plum—which by this time was looking rather the worse for wear—and threw it at him, bouncing it juicily off from his cheek.

"Oh, its to be war then, is it? Well then ...."

Menannon instantly grabbed up another plum and threw it at Nirna, bouncing it off her nose from whence it fell onto her sorak robe, the color of its juice nearly matching the cloth.

"OH!"

Nirna raised the ante by grabbing up a ripe peach and bouncing it off the Giant's chin. The fruit stayed there for just a moment, the juice running down Menannon's beard in a positive cascade before it flopped off and landed in the dust at his feet.

Nirna's anger melted into laughter. That was all it took and instantly the air was filled with flying fruit, most of which was dodged and thus wound up pelting other shoppers and a great deal of the market. The seller stepped back out of firing range and joined in the general laughter as the gathered crowd watched their princess and cheered her on. It was all right with them if her ladyship would rather wear her fruit than eat it. Nirna landed another ripe melon on the side of Menannon's head with a soft explosion and a great cheer went up.

Lee stood back, laughing his head off at the antics of the two. Nirna looked over, her face running with the juice from Menannon's latest shot, and took in the drummer's clean face and tunic and immediately threw a ripe melon at him which burst in all its seedy glory in the middle of his chest, his brown harper's robe making a beautiful contrast to the yellow of the seeds. Lee joined the battle with a will.

During all of this, Matilda had been so concentrating on a conversation she was having with a chance met friend that she was totally oblivious to the unseemly behavior of her royal charge and her companions until the sound of Nirna's high, fluting laughter caught her attention and she looked up to be horrified by what she saw. She rose with a full wind in her sails and moved into the fray like a war ship, her shoulder lowered to butt aside any onlooker in her path. She reached the center of the ring surrounding the laughing fruit throwers only to be narrowly missed by a good-sized melon which landed at the feet of a small flower seller who stood on tiptoe to watch the fun.

"Princess!" Matilda called aghast. "Stop that this instant!"

"Aw, don't be scoldin' 'em Mistress," a small voice halted her as she took lung to shout again. Matilda looked down to see the flower girl grinning up at her.

"But this is unseemly! She is the Princess Royal and he a fully corded harper, for the High One's holy sake! They're acting like foolish children," Matilda spluttered, her eyes snapping angrily as she tried to see past a stout fisherman intent upon the fray.

"But they air children, ain't they?" the little business girl observed. "Our Princess ain't but eighteen summers an' he cain't be much more."

She cast a quick look at Menannon with something close to hero worship in her green eyes as she spoke of him. She was the self-same flower seller he had bought the bouquet from when he had landed in the spring.

"Aye, but ...." The nurse began, but was interrupted as another melon sailed past them to the sound of another cheer.

"My ma always says as a child should act like a child oncet in a while, as there'll be plenty o' time fer actin' proper when yer old," the small philosopher informed her stoutly.

That halted Matilda mid-move as she had been about to dodge around the fisherman.

"Ye must have swallowed wisdom with tha's porridge this mornin'," she smiled, falling back into her childhood brogue, having to agree despite herself. "But still, such behavior in the market is a bit past it, don't ye think?" Before the child could answer, the nurse pushed past the fisherman with an "Out of my way, young man!" and moved onto the battlefield where she stopped, her hands on her formidable hips.

"Princess! Gentlemen! Will you three act your age and not your sandal size! Ye're making a scene and ruinin' this goodman's wares!" Gooddame Matilda scolded tartly.

The youngsters halted their activity mid-throw and stood looking about at the havoc they had wrought. The entire booth was empty of its wares save for a few ripe pears which had so far been missed by the expedience of being in a small basket at the side. All three combatants were liberally covered with seeds, pulp and juice and the entire area was awash in the casualties of the battle. There were crushed and splattered fruit carcases everywhere. Lee and Nirna looked at each other and Matilda a bit shamefacedly and set down their ammunition in contrite haste.

Menannon, instead of setting down the melon he had been about to lob at Lee, stood tossing it on his palm and looking at his sandaled feet. At last he looked up at Matilda, his black eyes as guileless as a spring sky.

"In my case, dear Mati, I would think you'd prefer me to act my sandal size rather than my age, for then I would be acting four and thirty and be too old and responsible to throw melons in the market."

Matilda looked up at him her mouth open to reply when he gave her a grin and a wink. Her mouth snapped shut, her eyes sparked and she grabbed a handful of the ripe pears which she began to throw at him with telling accuracy. Menannon dropped his melon and fled the scene, tossing a well-filled coin pouch to the fruit seller as he left. The man caught it with a great smile and a bow. Menannon's laughter echoed through the market place.

Behind him, his ploy having had, its desired affect everyone returned to their several occupations, shoppers to shopping and sellers to selling, including the old vegetable seller whose booth was soon crowded with buyers and those who wanted a recitation of the fruit war, as he was the closest remaining witness, the fruit seller having happily hung up his closed sign and taken himself off to the Cokeyna with a pouch full of gold coins worth the price of his entire establishment, not just his day's wares.

The incident provided many a story and a hearty laugh in the time to follow, even eventually reaching the ears of Grandmaster Blackmore in Aridion City as traders spread it along their routes.

Gorlanndon had a visitor later that evening when the fruit seller stopped by the Giant's office in the Serpentine and returned the extra coins.

"I'll be keepin' payment for me wares," he said "But I'll nay make the lad pay more, as he gave me one o' the best laughs I've had in me life. That be worth more than gold."

Gorlanndon accepted the coins, thanked the man graciously, but made no further comment.

At the end of his day, the closed his office and he and his escort headed home along strangely quiet streets. He reached the villa, bid his men "Good evening," and went in search of his son and found him settled in the atrium playing Fox and Hounds with the drummer. Gorlanndon watched the two for a few minutes as they challenged and counter challenged each other, rolling the long sticks in their hands and in Lee's case moving his game pieces with a whoop each time he bested the young Giant in a toss. The game they were playing had been ancient when Gorlanndon himself was a child and while it seemed simple, it was deceptively so, for a good hounder had to learn to throw the sticks so that they fell to his advantage. The Crenanocian was obviously a very good hounder as the tally board showed he had beaten Menannon seven games to one.

After another successful throw on Lee's part, Gorlanndon cleared his throat, interrupting the play. Both young men immediately rose and stood politely beside their chairs waiting for him to speak, Lee with obvious pleasure, but Menannon with a slight hint of trepidation. The younger Giant was plainly expecting to receive a rebuke from his sire as he had caught sight of the coin pouch Gorlanndon had made no attempt to hide.

Gorlanndon waved them to their chairs and set another for himself. He settled into it with a sigh and set the pouch on the table in front of him. It settled with a well filled thunk. He relaxed back into his chair and he turned his gaze upon his son.

"I understand there was quite a disturbance at the dock markets this afternoon," he said, one quizzical eyebrow raised. "The details, however, have not come to my ears. Would you care to enlighten me?" There was neither rebuke nor approval in Gorlanndon's tone. Not yet anyway.

Menannon glanced from the pouch to his sire's face and back then made as though to rise.

"No, boy, this is not an inquisition, just a question." Gorlanndon said, but Menannon rose anyway finding it easier to face his sire standing.

"As you obviously already know, sir," he began, glancing once more at the coin pouch, "I caused a fruit fight in the market."

He straightened his shoulders and looked up into his sire's eyes.

"It wasn't just Menannon, sir." Lee sat up straighter and confessed, "I'm just as guilty."

"I assumed as much, as it does take at least two to accomplish such a 'fight,' " Gorlanndon said with a slight grin in his voice, though his face remained totally neutral.

At the tone, Lee's dark complexion turned several shades darker with embarrassment.

"Now that we have established the culprits, shall we establish the reason for this display?" Gorlanndon's voice remained even, but still conversational.

"It was Master Penor, sir," Menannon almost snarled, his anger and indignation still hot. "He falsely accused an old vegetable seller of trying to palm off half-rotten tomatoes upon him, forcing the fellow to gift him with a sack of them. He left then, but the damage was done. All within hearing were persuaded that the seller was indeed dishonest. It would have ruined his business. I simply sought to distract the shoppers ere the situation got any worse. You know how skittish folk can be. If the Master Harper," Menannon's voice took on Penor's simper once more, "disdains something, then all and sundry will follow his lead."

The young Giant finished his explanation with something of a disgusted snort.

"Is that why you started picking on the Princess? I wondered." Lee burst out enlightened. "Penor certainly is a ..."

"... supercilious jackass!" Menannon finished for him.

Silence fell then as Gorlanndon considered what his son had said. Both young men stirred uneasily in the silence. Gorlanndon let them. The Giant had to agree with his son: Master Harper Penor really was a supercilious jackass and had been a very poor choice as the replacement for Master Kor when that good old man had passed away four summers ago. He still wondered what had been Grandmaster Blackmore's purpose in making such an assignment, as the Valinga never did anything without reason. He found himself heartily wishing that Penor had still been in the market when the fight broke out and had thus been the target for some well-aimed and well deserved fruit. The vision of Penor dripping fruit juice down his kohl decorated face caused Gorlanndon to laugh inwardly though he made sure that none of his mirth showed upon his countenance, as it really had been unseemly for the three culprits to disrupt the market, even for so good a cause. He waited for a few moments longer until the timing was just right. When his offspring was beginning look slightly contrite, he rose to his full height and stood looking down at them then gave his decision. It was not what Menannon was expecting.

"It would seem you had just cause for your little display," his sire spoke solemnly. Gorlanndon smiled at last, his eyes twinkling and tossed Menannon the coin pouch. "Here's your change."

His son caught it with less than his usual dexterity, causing the elder Giant to chuckle aloud. He started to leave the table, but turned back and laid his hand on his son's shoulder.

"I might suggest, however, that it would have been a bit less messy to simply have had Nirna move on to the fellow's booth and buy something with slightly louder and heartier than normal approval. If the Princess Royal approves, who is the

Master Harper to disapprove?"

Gorlanndon raised an expressive eyebrow, causing his son to color nicely despite the approval in his sire's tone. Menannon remained politely standing and Lee rose beside him until the elder Giant reached the door where he halted and turned back.

"Well done, gentlemen. I'm not going to enquire as to how the Princess got involved." Gorlanndon left the chamber, closing the door with a soft click. With its shutting, he obviously could not hold his mirth any longer and they heard him walk away laughing outright.

Menannon let out a deep breath he had not realized he was holding and both young men returned to their seats and interrupted game. They played quietly for a few rounds then Lee looked up and glanced at the door to make sure it was still closed.

"It might have been less messy, but it wouldn't have been nearly as much fun," he whispered with a grin.

Menannon grinned back, the twinkle returning to his eyes. The game regained its former gusto.

As the days passed and autumn began to settle upon the land, the strange, almost furtive behavior Menannon had previously noticed in his sire's villa seemed to manifest itself in the population at large as he began to notice a growing unrest among the people. Where before the folk of Kirith Kalyria had been open and friendly to one and all, they began noticeably to shun each other, never quite meeting eyes as they spoke or passed one another in the street. Even in the market places and pubs, people seemed preoccupied and, yes, even nervous, conversing in low voices with many a leery glance about to see who might be listening. Almost, Menannon would have chalked this perception up to his own inner turmoil over Nirna had he and Lee not had a very strange experience in the Aureun gardens a fortnight ere they were to depart for the mainland.

They had left Gorlanndon's villa in the pre-dawn twilight intent upon witnessing the opening of the last few hornflowers of this season. Gentle silence reigned over the city broken only by the happy twittering of the birds and the far off creak of wagon wheels as the morning's farm carts with the day's wares began coming in from the countryside through the outer gates. There were a few early folk about, some heading down towards the markets and others coming back from a night's employment or revelry. As they passed each group, the harpers received a slight nod or a soft greeting, but here as well, no one looked them in the eyes. Strangely, as they actually approached the entrance to the gardens, few strollers out became none, which was odd, for never before had the blooming of the hornflowers failed to command a considerable crowd. Menannon found this lack very unsettling, but he kept his concerns to himself not wishing to darken Lee's memories of Kalyria with what might well be naught but his imagination. As they walked, the drummer chatted away about things that had happened during their holiday and the things he was planning to do once they had returned to the mainland. Menannon walked silently, letting Lee's voice wash over him almost, but not quite, unheeded.

They entered the gardens just as first light was beginning to glow above Kalyria's crown. As they approached the Grove, they began to hear sound coming from it. Menannon and Lee rounded the clump of peridüs trees at the edge of the Grove only to be brought up short by a considerable gathering. Most oddly, no one was paying any attention whatsoever to the hornflowers which were about to bloom. Rather, all of those gathered stood listening intently to a tall fellow, cloaked and cowled, standing on the plinth of the statue of Kalyrinon.

The fellow's cloak was black with a deep shadowing cowl hiding all of his face save his mouth and beardless chin. The cloak was marked with a crest on the left shoulder bearing the image of a black sun rising from a blood red sea. Menannon had only seen one such crest before and that was on a medallion worn by Azuron at the banquet. To what race the speaker belonged was impossible to tell from his swathed form and shadowed eyes.

Instinctively, Menannon stepped back, drawing Lee with him, and gesturing for silence. From behind the screening branches of the peridüs, they observed the gathering and the object of its interest. There was a strange sort of buzzing hush on the crowd that felt rather like the stillness before a storm. The cowled figure was speaking loudly and with great vehemence, but his voice was strangely silky, almost soothing, flowing with an hypnotic undercurrent. It was rather hard to concentrate on his words from where they stood, but even at that distance they were affected by his speech.

A feeling of near bliss crept over Menannon and from the look in Lee's eyes, over the drummer as well. The Giant shook his head and blinked. His mind cleared instantly and much to his surprise and chagrin, he found that the two of them had not only joined the crowd, but were near the front, almost directly below the speaker. Menannon's heart skipped a beat. What was the power of this fellow that he could so mesmerize with his mere voice—or was it something else, some strange sorcery or incantation just below the threshold of hearing? What ever it was, the entire crowd was under its spell.

Menannon glanced back to find the cowl turned directly towards him as though its wearer knew he alone, of all those assembled, was no longer under his control. Menannon could barely discern the glint of eyes within the shadows. The mouth took on a grim tightness as the sinister figure studied the Giant. A slight, foreboding shiver went up Menannon's spine, but he forced himself to smile and bow slightly which act seemed to mollify the cowled one a bit and he returned his attention to the crowd. Menannon tried to listen to the words being spoken, but again the feeling of bliss began to fog his mind. He balled his fist behind his back so hard the fingernails began to pierce into the flesh of his palm. By this pain alone could he keep his mind clear and the words finally made sense.

"... Divinity is within us! Look within thine own spirit and see that Divinity! We are one with the Divine! Therefore, we are the Divine! By the power of our own Divinity shall we throw down the old and reshape this land in our image and bring forth upon it the most powerful, the most wonderful, the most magnificent kingdom of all time! Together we shall remake our very world!"

The cowled one's voice now took on the timbre of a true zealot.

"Our world will not be bound by laws and rules as dead and lifeless as the scrolls upon which they are inscribed. It will not be ruled by visionless fools. It will shine beyond the confines of the old. In our world, there will be only one law, The One True Law... DO AS THINE OWN HEART WILLS!"

The cowled one was shrieking now, his arms raised to the skies as though he would bring about this glorious revolution by himself alone.

Menannon shook his head trying to clear the muzziness from his mind. Surely he must be mishearing what this person was saying. Surely he could not be saying that the minds of mere created beings were more powerful, more enlightened than their Creator?! To look to ones imperfect self as the font of all wisdom was as foolish as launching a ship without sail or steering oar into a hurricane! An imperfect being can create naught but imperfection. This fool was not just preaching folly, he was preaching insanity and calling it sane! All about Menannon the crowd shrieked and screamed in agreement and ecstasy, including, to his dismay, even Lee.

How long had this fool been spreading this stupidity among the people of Kalyria? Was this the cause of the unrest he had been feeling? Menannon knew that many of the ruling class of the island, particularly its sons and daughters, were feeling jaded and dissatisfied with things as they were in their land. They had reached the pinnacle of wealth and power and their kingdom was now resting on its well deserved laurels and serving as the guide and arbiter for the rest of the kingdoms of greater Linden. Yet for many, this was not exciting enough, they needed more. They needed change, excitement, anything so long as it was different even if it was folly, but this new doctrine was not just folly, it was insanity and disaster!

All about Menannon, the noise had risen to a near deafening level. The cowled one allowed this tumult to reign for a few minutes more then he held up his hands for silence and the noise subsided as instantly as a well trained choir will follow its director. He began to speak again.

"There are those among us who would stop us from bringing this Divine excellence into being. Those who would cling to the superstitions of the unenlightened past. There are those who are too dull witted, too indoctrinated to see the plain truth right in front of them. These must be taught to have better minds so they may be welcomed among us and become worthy of living in our new and enlightened world."

Totally bewildered, Menannon turned from looking at the crowd to find the cowled one once again staring at him. There was a brief moment of silence during which the gloved hand of the speaker rose slowly and with studied deliberation, pointed straight at Menannon!

"Thou, son of Gorlanndon, are one such. Thou must learn!" The hooded one's voice fairly shrieked, "Teach him!".

As one, the crowd turned on the Giant. Beside him Lee, turned with the rest, his eyes showing the same glazed look as the others. Menannon fled. Only his great height and inhuman strength allowed him to escape the unarmed crowd, but even so, he reached the entrance of the Aureun gardens with his kirtle torn and his face bleeding and bruised, his cheek having been broken open by a precisely aimed rock. He held his hand against his left side as his ribs were aching where he had been slammed into the edge of a solid stone wall by a well-placed foot. The ribs were bruised, but not broken. He thanked the High One that there was no greater damage done. Strangely, the crowd stopped at the entrance of the garden and turned back, leaving their erstwhile victim to puzzle even more over what was happening in the city.

Too stunned to be more than confused at the moment, Menannon moved along the street circling the west side of the gardens until he reached a small pub, whose doors were open despite the early hour, and ducked inside. The proprietor was a tall ginger-bearded Dwarf who took one look at his torn clothing and battered face and pointed him to the bathing chamber. There were no other patrons this early. Menannon took his time washing the blood from his face then toweled off and removed his kirtle, which he folded carefully so that the rips did not show, and came back into the common room.

Wordlessly, the Dwarf motioned him to come behind the bar and through a heavy curtain. Menannon followed and was led into what was obviously the family's living quarters. There he was motioned to a stool at the table. He sat and watched the Dwarf search through the cupboards and take out a large goblet which he filled with a goodly measure of wine and a great pinch of herbs from a small jar on the counter. Menannon recognized the label of the herbalist whose shop stood near his father's trade hall. The Dwarf handed him the wine, then reached down a small jar that proved to contain an herbal paste used to heal minor cuts and abrasions. The fellow sat down across the table from him. So far, everything had been done in silence. Something in the fellow's deep-set brown eyes reassured Menannon and he drank, draining the goblet in three large swallows, the wretched taste of the drink confirming that it was a pain medicinal. The Dwarf took the goblet from him and set it on the counter then smoothed some of the paste onto Menannon's various hurts. That done, he closed his jar and setting it aside, settled back and studied the Giant as though he were trying to decide something. At last he nodded, cleared his throat and spoke softly as if the very walls had ears.

"Ye'll have been noticin' 'tis nay longer safe t' enter the gardens at dawn. No," the Dwarf help up his hand forestalling any comment from Menannon, "I'm knowin' that's where ye came from as yer nay the first t' be comin' in here bloodied. Those who're after needin' shelter be welcome here."

"What's going on?" Menannon kept his voice equally low.

"I'll nay be sayin' as those who say too much are experiencin' an ill wind in Kalyria these days. Take me advice an' be goin' back to the mainland as soon as may be as this land o' ours is in for heavy seas. I'll no be sayin' more to ye, only advisin' ye to follow me example an' leave this place, especially as yer Lord Gorlanndon's lad."

"Why?!" Menannon demanded, all his suspicions coming instantly to the fore. "Why me in particular?"

"I'll just be sayin' ye'd best be leavin', an' the sooner the better." The Dwarf cast him a level look into which almost anything could be read.

Menannon's stomach tightened painfully. "Are you going then?"

"Aye. Me, the wife an' the youngins are set wi' passage on the *Sparrow* three days hence. An' I'll no be breathin' easy until we're on board an' under sail."

With that admonition, the Dwarf stood and waved him back into the common room where he motioned Menannon to halt by the bar while he walked back to the door and looked out. He stepped outside as though to adjust the awning over the window all the while looking both ways. In a few minutes, he came back in.

"Ye can be goin' now, as the hornflowers will have closed fer the day an' the Doomcriers gone on about their business like good an' peaceable citizens."

The Dwarf's voice fairly dripped with his contempt for those he was naming Doomcriers.

"Doomcriers?" Menannon made a question of the name, as he had never heard it before.

"They're a risin' faction whose only words air doom an' gloom an' whose only actions air mindin' other folks business under the guise o' helpin' 'em. They number considerable among those as serve the new Counsel General Azuron, which

I'm thinkin' ye'll not be findin' surprisin'.''

The Dwarf glanced outside again.

"There's another laddie standin' down near the gate lookin' a wee bit confused. I'm supposin' he's lookin' fer ye."

"Aye," Menannon nodded. "He and I went into the gardens together, but he was caught up in the speech and was not required to make a hasty exit."

The Dwarf caught his meaning and shook his head. "Ye've a strong will laddie, seein' ye was able to resist the Honeybreath o' the Black Teluri."

"Black Teluri?" Menannon questioned startled. "What mean you by Black Teluri?"

"Why, did ye not notice as how the fellow talkin' was black-haired an' black-eyed?"

"Black-haired? There's no such thing as a black-haired Teluri …," Menannon began to protest, but the Dwarf cut him off.

"There are here."

The Dwarf looked him square in the eyes, unblinking. There was no doubting the sincerity of his words.

"There's Teluri here whose hair is as black as midnight under an old log an' ye'd best be avoidin' 'em as clear as possible as they've got the queerest ideas ye've e'er heard an I'd no be trustin' any o' 'em. Now get ye gone an' be heedin' me words."

"My thanks for your aid and I'll remember."

Menannon reached into his belt pouch to retrieve some coins, but the Dwarf held up his hand, halting the movement.

"Nay, laddie. Harpers are honored in me own place. Anyone o' yer callin' will ne'er pay a farthin' t' me."

With that statement, the Dwarf gave him a quick salute.

Menannon inclined his head in thanks and ducked back out into the street and the door was shut firmly behind him. He stood there, his mind reeling with confusion. Doomcriers? Black-haired Teluri? Never in all the sagas he had studied had there ever been mention of a Teluri possessing black hair. The speaker in the gardens had been close-cowled, so there was no telling what color his hair had been or even if he had been a Teluri. On the other hand, was it possible that Azuron possessed black hair and was shaving his head and eyebrows to disguise that fact? But why? Why should black hair on a Teluri head be cause for secrecy and disguise? It was unusual, certainly, but why hide it? And why would a Teluri with black hair be any less trustworthy than a Teluri with any other color hair?

Menannon shook his head. The only thing he knew for sure was the speaker in the grove had been a follower of Azuron. The evidence was clear: there was the crest on his cloak and the fact that the fellow had instructed the crowd to attack him was a thing well within the scope of the situation. Azuron could easily have given his followers the order to discomfit the Giant at any opportunity. There was no need to search further for any other more arcane reason behind this morning's attack upon himself, yet, according to the Dwarf, others had been attacked in the same way. Again, why? Had they, too, fallen afoul of Azuron in some way?

Menannon sighed gustily. There were too many questions and not enough answers. He shook his head again and headed back to the gardens.

"Where did you go?" Lee called when he caught sight of his friend coming down the street.

Menannon said not a word, only walked past him and re-entered the gardens. Lee, puzzled, turned and followed him. He strode quickly to where the cowled speaker had been and found no trace of the crowd or its insidious master save only one thing: all but one of the rare hornflowers had been trampled to death beneath myriad feet and left to lie shattered in their beds. Menannon's already dark mood darkened even further.

Lee stood stunned at the destruction as Menannon took a quick glance around the rest of the grove for what, he knew not.

"What happened? What's going on?" the drummer inquired, confounded and disturbed.

"Not here," Menannon almost growled and again moved

past him to lead the way back out of the gardens and down the Aureun, back to its bridge.

Lee nearly had to run to keep up with his long strides. Neither spoke a word until they reached the villa and Menannon was pulling the bell rope for admittance.

Lee grabbed his friend by the arm to get his attention. "Menannon, what happened back there?"

"Not now!"Menannon spoke over his shoulder his gaze remaining fixed upon the still closed embrasure.

"Why not?"

"Lee, what do you remember?"

Menannon turned and looked his friend square in the eye.

"Well, we were listening to this cowled fellow, then I found myself outside the garden with neither you nor anyone else in sight. Rather bizarre, that."

Lee's face showed all his puzzlement and not a little worry.

"That's all?" Menannon nearly snarled his question.

"Yes, that's all I remember. Now, tell me—what happened?" Lee demanded, his own anger beginning to rise.

"Later, when we're alone."

"But...," Lee's protest at Menannon's unexpected response was cut short by the arrival of the porter.

"My father is going to answer some questions and he is going to answer them now!" the young Giant growled to Lee and stormed through the gate as soon as the porter began to open it.

The fellow had to scramble out of the way or be knocked flat. He cast a quick look at the drummer for explanation, but Lee could only shake his head and shrug and quickly follow after the Giant.

Menannon marched into the villa determined to discover what was going on, neither breaking stride nor acknowledging greetings, until he had attained the family wing and stood without his sire's chamber, its door slightly ajar. He slapped it open with the flat of his hand and strode in crossing to the windows where he dashed aside the curtains letting the morning sunlight stream in and threw his kirtle on the back of one of the chairs. Only then did he turn and acknowledge his sire's presence where the elder Giant still lay upon his bed, dressed in a lounging robe and propped up with pillows, reading his early dispatches, his morning goblet of sparkling water on the bedside table.

"You owe me an explanation! What in all Hella is going on in this city?! I demand to know and I demand to know now!"

Menannon snarled without preamble, his voice low and biting. He was so angry he was nearly hissing through his teeth.

Lee hovered near the door knowing he should retreat for politeness sake, but unwilling to, as he was determined to know anything that meant good or ill for his dearest friend.

Gorlanndon lowered his scroll, raised his head and locked eyes with his angry offspring. Several silent moments passed during which it became apparent that Menannon was in no mood to back down. Gorlanndon glanced at Lee a questioning eyebrow raised, but all the drummer could do was shrug and shake his head again as he knew no more about the cause of his friend's ire than did his sire.

"It would seem that you have forgotten your manners this morning, boy," Gorlanndon murmured as he turned his attention back to Menannon who still stood glaring at him.

This comment brought no change in his son's demeanor causing Gorlanndon to take note that he was talking with his son, the adult this morning, and not the youth. He mentally nodded to himself and treated with him on that basis.

"There is an element among our people who have chosen to follow a new…philosophy…and are intent upon indoctrinating the rest of us. A mere difference of opinion…."

"I would hardly call this a mere difference of opinion!" Menannon snarled, interrupting him. He jerked his belt loose and tore off his chemise, which he threw on the floor, thus revealing the massive bruising beginning to darken along the left side of his ribs.

Lee's low whistle and Gorlanndon's "Humph" sounded

together.

"Where did you come by that little decoration?" Gorlanndon asked in an offhanded manner which surprised the drummer, as Lee had become accustomed to Menannon's sire being rather solicitous of his son's welfare.

"In the Aureun gardens this morning, where one of those little 'indoctrinations' was apparently going on!" Menannon snarled, determined to give no ground this time. "Not only did I gain this little decoration, but the hornflowers have been murdered, trampled to death by a witless crowd!"he finished.

This last statement brought a look of surprise and consternation to the elder Giant's countenance, quickly masked.

"It would seem that you ran afoul of a group which was a bit more active than usual," Gorlanndon observed drily and he settled back more comfortably on his pillows. "It is normally their wont to aid elderly folk with their shopping and clean the streets, all the while regaling everyone within sound of their voices with words extolling the new ... divinity ... and decrying the backsliding of the kingdom. Gloom and Doom! Ay me," he shook his head and sighed. "Rest in peace; the status quo ennui rises apace.

"Now...," Gorlanndon held up his hand forestalling an angry retort from his son, "enough discussion of the stupidity of a dissatisfied minority. Shall we adjourn to the summerhouse to break our fast and plan your farewell party, which I am afraid will have to be brought forward a full sevenday as Firod's lady wife has taken it into her head to take her entire brood on holiday to her parents' home in Pedura. She is intent upon letting her parents see their new grandson and celebrating Shira's nameday at one go. So all of you will have to leave two days hence in order to achieve this intent, as there are too many of the youngsters to make a sea voyage in safety under only the watchful eyes of their mother and nurse. I fear you twain have been drafted into service once more."

"But...," Menannon began, immediately suspicious of this oh-so-conveniently scheduled trip.

"We must please the ladies to keep peace in the household."

Gorlanndon winked at Lee as he rose and put on his sandals.

"She has already prevailed upon me to launch my flagship rather than wait a third day for the sailing of the *Sparrow*."

Before Menannon could say any more, his sire opened the bedroom door and waved Lee through, following the drummer with suspicious alacrity. The elder Giant stopped with his hand on the door and turned back.

"Clarinda said she was going to work in the stillroom this morning, boy. Get her to attend your hurt ere you come to table at the summerhouse. We'll make sure to save you something."

He turned and left, closing the door with a soft thud.

Menannon was left to again don his chemise, pick up his kirtle and follow, totally unsatisfied with the outcome of this dis-cussion. As he passed the bedside table, he paused to see that his sire had also been perusing the morning broadsides and one of the announcements was the sailing schedule of a number of ships bound for the all ports of call on the mainland. Among them was the sailing date of the *Sparrow* bound for Blue Bay. Was this a convenient coincidence or had he actually been looking for that information before Menannon had so unceremoniously entered his bedchamber? There was only one way to tell and that was to head Firod off when he arrived for the usual morning meeting ere his sire could talk to him and ask the truth of the planned trip.

He ran lightly down the hall and out through the kitchen door, dodging kitchen help as he went, hoping to reach the steps to the summerhouse before the captain, but in this, he was to be thwarted as Firod was already standing at the door of the summerhouse in conversation with not only Gorlanndon, but Lonier as well. Lee was standing a respectful distance behind them so if they were speaking softly, the drummer would not be able to tell him if the subject of the proposed departure had been newly broached. Reluctantly, he turned and re-entered the villa in search of Clarinda.

IT WAS NOT UNTIL LATER THAT EVENING, just prior to retiring for the night, that Menannon felt comfortable in discussing with Lee the morning's events.

As they were preparing to retire, Menannon signaled Lee to follow him and they retreated into the Giant's chamber and sat by the unlit hearth.

With the very solid door closed tight and thus secure in their privacy, Menannon again inquired of Lee what he remembered of the morning's events, and Lee repeated what he had said earlier outside the front gate.

"Lee, that speaker, whoever he was, had you and the crowd under some sort of spell or compulsion. It was only with great effort that I threw it off, and because I was able to, he ordered the crowd to attack me, and they did. And Lee, you were right in there with them, wholly under his direction and oblivious of what you were doing."

"Impossible! You're my best friend. I would not attack you."

Lee was incensed at the thought that he could have been compelled by anyone to commit such a treacherous act.

"Yet you did...and you have no memory of it. Lee, you weren't yourself, nor were any of the others. They were all under the spell of that speaker." Menannon stood and began to pace restlessly about the chamber.

Lee was silent for a while, thinking over what his friend had said.

"Well, I can't dispute what you say, because I truly have no memory of it. But if I did attack you ...."

He stopped, and he shuddered at the thought that someone could so manipulate him.

"It makes my skin crawl, to think that someone can control me—or anyone—like that. Something is very amiss here."

"Yes, something is amiss, and my father refuses to tell me precisely what it is, and I resent that with all my heart. Does he not trust me?"

Menannon halted at the window twitching aside the curtains and glanced out into the darkness.

"Perhaps, my friend, he is trying to protect you," the drummer suggested mildly.

"So he sends me away, leaving himself unprotected." Menannon jerked the curtain back into place and resumed pacing.

"Uhhhh, he does have a very impressive company of guards, you know. I wouldn't say he's unprotected." Lee reminded him.

"Even so, I wish he thought enough of me to tell me the truth and not hide it from me. I am not a little child, you know. He says he loves me, and I know he does, but yet he hides things from me. I would lay down my life for him."

Menannon came back to the hearth and threw himself in his vacated chair.

"I know." Lee kept his voice low and earnest. "And maybe, just maybe, that is precisely why he won't tell you anything and is sending you away."

Menannon had no answer to that and retreated deep into his own thoughts. Lee quietly got up, departing for his own chamber.

CHAPTER 9
(SUMMER OF THE WORLD 6996)

THE FAREWELL PARTY WAS HELD at the new arena as Firod's children had been given the choice of venues and they had chosen the circus, so the night before their departure found Menannon and Lee seated high up on the western side of the great marble amphitheater surrounded by Firod's children. Firod himself and his wife had also accompanied their offspring, as had Gorlanndon.

Charina sat between her husband and the elder Giant, totally dwarfed by both as she was of diminutive stature though half her folk were originally from Crenanoc. She had the dark skin of her sire and the smoky grey eyes of her Gormidadish mother. Theirs had been a marriage of peoples which had, as usual, produced offspring of greater beauty than either.

The children sat near their parents with Lee and Menannon sitting at the end of the row. Shira was, of course, perched upon the young Giant's shoulder the better to see the spectacle spread out before them.

As Gorlanndon had predicted, the Orlando family was running the circus well. While there were indeed betting and games of chance aplenty carried on at booths in the many-arched palisade enclosing the arena, none were allowed inside. Taratillo was making sure that the main attraction was real circus.

On the floor of the arena, four rings were laid out, each filled with its own activity much to the delight of all assembled. They whirled and sparkled with trained animals, gymnasts, contests of strength, flame dancers and sword wielders and those who nearly walked on air as they negotiated a single rope strung across the very top of the arena.

Enclosing the rings in a great circle was a racetrack, used for foot races, horse races, wagon races, dog races, ostrich races and even chicken races; though the latter were more for fun than excitement. The building was open to the sky save when inclement weather forced it to be roofed with a huge expanse of oiled sail cloth. Over all this Taratillo presided, striding grandly upon his eight-foot stilts. Menannon found this feat the most spectacular of all.

The Orlando family was famous for its stilt walkers. Yet even among them, only a few children could master the art, as the stilts they used were strapped to the feet as a full extension to their legs rather than the more familiar style used by shepherds in marshy country that were platforms about halfway up a large wooden pole upon which one placed a foot—one stilt for each foot—and manipulated with the hands on the pole.

For the Orlandos, balance alone was the key and upon these stilts they walked, ran, tumbled, jumped and danced. To achieve this, stilts were strapped to the babes feet even before they could walk and those who proved able were gradually raised to longer and longer stilts until they reached their maximum capability, usually somewhere near the eight foot height. Though Turanio, the eldest son of Taratillo's third wife, had achieved the nearly unheard of height of eleven foot stilts, making his highest walking stature almost a full foot taller than Gorlanndon. These high stilts were used only during performances and the rest of the time, he used more manageable ones of four feet in length.

Tulio, Turanio's younger brother by Taratillo's second wife was even now, at a mere fourteen summers old, using a form of stilt that few had been able to master even in the Orlando family: stilts which were hinged to form a knee. The boy had already mastered the four foot version of these and how much higher he would be able to go was in the hands of the High One.

Despite his misgivings about conditions in his homeland, Menannon could not help being affected by the children's enthusiasm and found himself enjoying this particular outing marvelous much. Beside him, Lee was entranced by a particularly beautiful rider whose dancing stallion seemed to almost fly rather than trot or gallop. While her mount performed, the girl danced upon his back and together they nearly brought the house down.

For Shira, the highlight of the evening was when one of the rope dancers performing overhead called down and motioned Menannon to stand and hold the child up. The young Giant was just tall enough that the dancer could reach down and present her with a rose he seemed to have pulled out of thin air. Her new cavalier saluted her and danced on, leaving behind him an awestruck child who from that moment on was a lifelong lover of circus.

There was but one interruption to the evening and that was when Azuron entered and made his way to the special box set halfway up the opposite side of the arena for the use of the Queen and her chosen companions. Though he was alone save for Penor who minced a respectful step behind him, almost half the audience rose to its feet and began calling his name and stamping. The Teluri inclined his head and raised his hand rather nonchalantly in acceptance of this accolade. On the floor of the arena many of the performers joined in this salute.

"I suppose they all feel beholden to him, as I understand it was this Azuron of yours who insisted the queen build this arena," Lee whispered to Menannon, who looked around sharply to see if anyone close to them was paying them any heed, feeling slightly uneasy for no reason he could fathom.

It was just a prickle quickly passing. No one seemed to be paying the least bit of attention as all eyes were fixed on Azuron as he made his way to the box and took his seat, seeming to fill it as though he were the king of Kalyria and not just its Counsel General.

Beside the Teluri, Penor could be seen to be basking in the reflected light, for after all, was he not the one sitting beside the great man and no other? Firod made a disparaging sound in his throat at the sight. Charina quickly shushed him, glancing around with what Menannon could have sworn was fear in her eyes. Menannon found his gaze drawn back to the rings below where, oddly, the members of the Orlando family and their own circus folk were not joining in the accolades for Azuron.

Briefly he wondered why, as surely they had benefitted the most of anyone in the building of this magnificent arena. The answer came to him as he noticed something strange about the people saluting Azuron, almost in mass they were wearing red; red robes, red kirtles, red tunics or if nothing else at least a red sash about their waists! Was this a mark of this new sect, the Doomcriers, as the Dwarf of the pub near the Aureun gardens had called them? The sheer numbers of folk thus dressed was amazing. This new philosophy must be spreading rapidly, despite his sire's seeming dismissal of it.

Obviously, the Orlando family was not a convert to it as their silence confirmed. Menannon glanced down to the other end of their small group where Gorlanndon had conveniently placed himself so that his son could not assay to continue the conversation he had been attempting to have for the last two days. Gorlanndon was gazing around at the crowd, probably noting the numbers of red-wearing attendees. As Menannon watched him, his sire looked across the arena and nodded to Azuron who almost preened at the look. Menannon was not quite sure what to make of the exchange.

When the stamping and shouting began to cause an uncomfortable lull in the circus, Azuron raised his hand, expressively signaling the performance to go on and settled back with obvious pleasure at the warmth of his reception. The noise ceased instantly and the choir that belonged to the circus itself could be heard once more as the performers resumed their interrupted occupations.

When all of the children had fallen asleep save Darya, an end was called to the party and Gorlanndon's small group left for the night though behind them, the entertainments were really just getting started. None seemed to notice their departure, save Azuron alone who watched them until the last of the children disappeared through an archway.

Outside, games of chance, wrestling matches and all other such entertainments were in full swing along with all manner of merchants hawking their wares and food booths abounded. It was a market place gone mad where one had to nearly step on revelers and hawkers alike to make any progress. This was what Lonier had been expecting of all the activities at the arena, but happily only here, without, were his dire predictions coming true.

Menannon raised the sleeping Shira to his shoulder again and employed his great height to open a pathway for the rest. When it seemed that many of the red-garbed Doomcriers were determined not to give way, the Giant simply plowed them aside like a mighty ship cutting through waves. The method was effective and his party soon found themselves on the edge of the grounds where things were calmer and Gorlanndon's guardsmen awaited them as they were not allowed on the grounds while on duty.

Menannon halted and turned to count heads. All were present save for Gorlanndon himself. Menannon instantly raised his eyes to see where his sire had gone and was surprised to see the elder Giant standing near some of the most disreputable of the gaming tents visiting with several of their seedy proprietors. His great laugh could be heard over the other noise. His son turned to Firod, who had been walking beside the elder Giant, a questioning eyebrow raised.

"He told me he held an interest in seeing if any of them were bringing in Borian spices and that he would be along anon."

The captain shrugged at his friend's known taste for these very rare and expensive spices which were seldom legally available on Kalyria, as they were grown and processed by slaves in Boria.

Since slavery was banned in Aridion and Kalyria, it was illegal to purchase spices from any but the few authorized dealers who obtained them from small family farms. To purchase the spices from these legal sources was so expensive that it took the value of the entire annual mercantile production of a fairly large country to buy a few ounces. Even Gorlanndon rarely indulged. Menannon reluctantly accepted this excuse and turned to lead their small group home leaving all four of his sire's guards with the command to await their master and see that he got home safely.

⁂

LATE THAT NIGHT, the tables were turned and Gorlanndon entered his chamber to find Menannon seated in the darkness awaiting him. Though his eyes were not tinged with red, the younger Giant was clearly agitated. Gorlanndon sighed, bowing to the inevitable and crossed the chamber to open the shutters on the bedside Dwarf lamp. He removed his cloak and placed it within the wardrobe, taking a moment to gaze upon the small portrait which hung on the inside. He nodded slightly to the delicate features of his wife depicted there, closed the door softly, then went to the shelves occupying almost half the wall opposite the chamber's door and removed a small box. He stood there for a long moment, studying Menannon where he sat staring fixedly at him, his hands resting on the table top, fingers laced together obviously attempting to contain his impatience.

Gorlanndon's gaze took in the strong cut of his son's features, the way he held his head and the shape and size of his hands. In them alone did he find any trace of the lady who had birthed him, for Menannon bore his sire's stamp so strongly none would even suspect that Julianna of Lornennog had carried him beneath her heart. Yet while his sire had bequeathed him his look and depth of mind, his lady mother had bequeathed him his creative spirit. It was visible there in his hands, in their long tapering fingers, graceful motion and delicate touch. The hands of an artist.

Gorlanndon glanced down at his own hands, taking in their broad palms, blunt fingers and large knuckles. The hands of a warrior. To take the hands of the one and turn them into the hands of the other would be a perversion of the High One's work. No! Menannon was going back to the mainland, returning to the world to which he belonged, the world for which the High One had suited him. The battle for Kalyria was not to be his.

Gorlanndon came over to the table, settled into the chair

-236-

opposite Menannon and laid the box between them. Menannon still said nothing, only looked at him, his look alone demanding answers and explanations. Gorlanndon cleared his throat, but said nothing, and simply continued to sit sort of hunched over the table, staring at the box. A strained silence lay between them broken only by the sounds of the watch changing without and a subdued argument coming from the kitchen where Clarinda was supervising the packing of the victuals she deemed necessary to allow her lord's son and his companions to survive the crossing back to the mainland, as none had ever been able to convince her that a ship had victuals and a galley of its own.

Menannon waited impatiently for his sire to come to the sticking place. Gorlanndon, for his part, took a great deal of time to open the box and finally withdraw an object from its depths. It was the small case that Blackmore had sent him. The laid it on the table top, being careful to align it just perfectly at right angles with the box from which it had come. He kept fiddling with it until Menannon was about to explode with impatience. At last, Gorlanndon began to speak, his voice low, almost a whisper, the small case still between his fingers, unopened.

"My son, I have no intention of discussing with you the situation politic here on Kalyria. We have more important matters with which to deal."

Gorlanndon held up his hand halting the words struggling upon his son's lips.

"Nay, I'll not be gainsaid in this! Boy," he continued softly, "I have not been entirely truthful with you. While I did indeed pray that you would remain small to ease your life, there was more to my desire than that."

He took a deep breath, glanced up, then returned his gaze to the case and began to fiddle with it once more as though he were giving himself time to think. At last he nodded to himself, sat up straight and squared his shoulders, then decisively opened the small case and withdrew from within a twin of Menannon's own harper's cord. This he laid upon the table between them where its many colors gleamed in the light of the Dwarf lantern.

When he continued speaking, his voice had changed and now, rather than being contemplative and uncertain, it was strong and sure. Menannon was suddenly positive that his sire had changed what he had been going to say and wondered why.

"Boy," Gorlanndon said, "the High One has gifted you beyond all others of our race. You are a true Giant. You have and use emotions, you are the right size for this world, you are a gifted illuminator, scholar and harper. This cord bears witness to all that you are. It is a symbol of the High One's gifts. You will return to Aridion City on the morrow and stand your masters trials and you will become what the High One intends you to be. Though I know you have a heart to stay here on Kalyria with me, I will not allow it. You will not waste the talents the High One has given you. And perhaps, one day you will even be the Grandmaster of your guild. Now go to bed and possess yourself in the knowledge that, unlike the rest of your race, you are perfected in the will of the High One."

With that, Gorlanndon rose and left the chamber. The harper's cord lay where he had placed it, silent witness to the truth of his words. His footsteps faded into silence.

Finally, Menannon rose and took up the cord and putting it into the breast of his kirtle, left his sire's chamber. He wandered through the villa and out into the yard via the kale yard, his thoughts too chaotic to even consider sleeping. At last, his steps led him to the top of the hill behind the summerhouse and the lowest point in the wall of the villa's close, which he climbed easily enough and sat down on the top, his long legs dangling down its face. From this vantage point he could see all the way to the mooring basin and across the bay to the crescent where the lighthouses shone forth their warning and welcome. He took out his harper's cord and held it loosely in his hand, considering all that it represented.

So, his father thought it possible that he could become the Grandmaster Harper. That probably was a possibility, but in reality it was likely to be mere wishful thinking on his beloved parent's part. Even if it was certain that he would attain such an august position in the guild, it was not as important to him as was his sire's safety and well-being. There was some evil brewing here on Kalyria, he would stake his sacred honor on it. What if that evil broke loose into violence while he was gone on the mainland and his sire was here alone? Menannon stirred uncomfortably at the thought. His sire was an inventor and merchant, not a warrior. Though he knew Gorlanndon had been born before the teachings of Zilronen had taken full hold in Lornennog, Menannon had never seen any evidence nor heard any spoken word to make him think his sire had ever had any martial training and Gorlanndon had been adamant that Menannon himself have none.

What if his sire's villa was attacked? They did have their personal guard and the place was defensible. Most importantly, it had its own well rather than relying on the city water pipes. They could defend it nearly indefinitely, especially if there were two Giants here rather than just one. Even if neither of them could wield a sword properly, their size alone should count for something.

There was also another being who needed protection here on Kalyria, someone dearer to his heart even than his sire: Nirna. What would happen to her if violence broke out on the island? Yes, there was Firod and his men, but Nirna was counting on him, as she always had, to do her whatever service was necessary, whether it was planting childish hibiscus blossoms in a pretend garden or standing shoulder to shoulder with her against all comers. Had she not reminded him not very long ago that the shaman woman of the Horse Clans had said that in his hands lay Destiny. If the destiny of his sire and Nirna lay in his hands, he had better not be in Aridion City when he was needed. His reach was not that long.

Menannon sat silently for many long turns of the hour weighing the possibilities in his mind and finally came to the conclusion that his presence here was more important than fulfilling his sire's dreams for him, a conclusion which was utterly at odds with everything he had believed in and done before, for his sires wishes had been his commands. He would send a letter to Grandmaster Blackmore informing him that he was resigning from the guild and staying here. Lee would deliver it, much though the drummer would hate the task.

As the decision crystalized in his mind, Menannon realized that it had already been made the day he left Aridion City to come home. In his heart, he knew he had never really intended to go back. Much though he loved his guild and all it stood for, he loved his sire more and he had instinctively known there was something amiss here even before he had arrived. What he had seen, heard and experienced since he got back had only served to confirm his suspicions. He sat looking down at the lights of the city long after his decision was made, his stomach tied in knots wondering if his love was clouding his thinking. He was young enough to still be vulnerable to uncertainty: that terrible 'what if?'

Lee found him sitting there even as the first birds began to sing their good morning song, though darkness was still complete.

"What are you doing?" the drummer came to the base of the wall to stand looking up at his friend. "You should have been in bed hours ago. I came looking for you when I heard your sire make his way past my chamber, but you were not in yours."

"I've been contemplating." Menannon replied, his voice quiet, almost gentle, its very tone telling his long friend that he was troubled.

"Contemplating what?"

Lee reached up and laid his hand on Menannon's foot. Menannon looked away towards the open sea again and wondered how to explain to his dearest friend the turmoil in his soul. How could he make it clear to someone who valued the harpers' guild more than anything else in the world that to him, there were far more important things and he had decided to leave it. At last he took a deep breath and let it out slowly. He owed Lee nothing but the truth at all times, so he cleared his throat and spoke.

"I have decided not to return with you. I'm going to resign from the Guild."

Menannon looked down to find that the drummer was not the

least bit surprised by this announcement. In point of fact, he was nodding.

"I knew you would so decide, though I did not expect you to take so long to come to the sticking place," Lee replied, his own voice softly serious.

"But ...," Menannon began, his surprise at the drummers reaction or, rather, his lack thereof, lighting his mobile face, causing his friend to chuckle.

"You are as a brother and I know you as I know myself."

Lee climbed up on the wall and sat, crossing his legs comfortably. From here he could better study his friend's face.

"Upon the instant it became obvious there was something amiss here, I knew you would choose to stay, for e'er are you ready to rush in and set things aright or die in the attempt, and I know it would ne'er occur to you to seek aid nor to expect any to be offered."

Lee frowned and shook his head, forestalling the comment obviously struggling on the young Giant's lips. He looked away at the city below for a moment, trying to find a way to explain what he was feeling. He knew full well that this was probably one of the most critical turning points in his friend's life and he needed to make sure he spoke true. At last he looked back at the Giant and studied him with a penetrating gaze. When he spoke again, his voice was as thoughtful as Menannon had ever heard it.

"My grandsire always said that there are certain souls made of the stuff of kings who have the ill fortune to be born to lesser folk. Such a one either stays a misfit who withers under the lash of futility or carves his own place in the world, a hermitage which allows him the freedom to not be ruled by men a thousand times less his own worth. Menannon, this is something you must comprehend for all our sakes. Yours is such a soul. Being so born is no easy burden to bear and I can tell you standing friend to such a one is no easy task, either."

This last statement caused Menannon to color nicely.

Lee grinned at this, but continued.

"I've always known it. Hella, we've all known it. You are a

prodigy in all you touch, from the harp to the illumination brush. You're brighter and more gifted in all ways than any of us, and it's born in you to lead and protect. You have the worst case of Noblesse Oblige I have e'er seen! That old sailor on the ship last spring had the right of it. You are a prince. Though it's not because your sire is rich, it's because the High One made you that way, a prince without a kingdom, but He has not left you a misfit. He has provided you with a ready made hermitage ... the Harpers' Guild!"

Lee's voice became more ardent and his dark eyes began to glow with inspiration.

"Menannon, our guild is the oldest and most powerful in all Linden. The Grandmaster of the Harpers' Guild is answerable to none save the High One alone! Even the masters of the other guilds are answerable to him. Do you not comprehend that Grandmaster Blackmore wields more power with his merest word than do the Kings and Queens of Kalyria with all their wealth and armies. He rules kings! He makes empires tremble, for he speaks with the authority of the High One himself. He is above mere kings and emperors because he is the High One's own man."

Lee stopped speaking for a moment and looked long into Menannon's troubled eyes. When he continued, his voice was low and earnest.

"You can be that man as well! Blackmore won't live forever and he will be replaced by someone of the High One's choosing. And my dearest friend, all jesting aside, I deem the High One intends you to fill that vacancy when it comes."

"I deem not the High One is planning to set a nineteen summers old outcast Giant at the head of His most powerful guild." Menannon's words came out in a self-derisive snort.

"You cannot know that," Lee returned levelly, locking eyes with him.

Menannon was the first to look away.

"And if you turn away now, you will ne'er know."

A brooding silence fell between them as each thought about the implications of the drummer's words.

"If you truly wish to be of use to your sire, then come back to

Aridion City now and stand your master's trials and at least be ready to answer if the High One calls."

Lee spoke softly, cutting to the heart of the matter even as the first pink glow of dawn began to gild the eastern horizon.

"You remember what Grandmaster Blackmore told your sire in his letter? He said he would be willing to post you back here as soon as the trials are over. Then you may return here with all the power of our guild at your back and defend your sire with some real might, not just love and dreams."

"Prophets come in all shapes and sizes," Menannon murmured at last, a slight smile easing the worry from his countenance as he put the cord back into the breast of his kirtle.

"And ages." Lee raised an expressive eyebrow with a grin.

Menannon just shook his head. He then let out a sigh, took a deep breath and released it, then nodded.

"Well, I guess we had best go prepare for this voyage."

By the look in his eyes, the drummer could tell by that statement, the Giant meant more than just the crossing of sea water. Whether he had said the right things to change his friend's mind completely or just caused Menannon to decide to give himself a bit more time did not matter. At least he was going to return to Aridion City for the moment. Lee carefully kept his grin of relief to himself.

The two young men climbed down together and made their way back to the villa to gather their belongings and prepare for the coming voyage. They passed the silent summerhouse unaware that Gorlanndon had been sitting there, a quiet witness to their conversation. As the sound of their footsteps dwindled away towards the villa, he rose and opened the blinds to the dawn's first light.

"No truer words have e'er been spoken by friend or foe, young fellow," he murmured saluting the drummer with the last of the wine in his chalice.

THE FULL LIGHT OF DAY found a small army leaving Gorlann-don's villa to make its way down the road, across the Mathematical bridge and around the far side of the central plaza behind the Council hall. Firod's company had spent the night in Gorlanndon's villa as it was much closer to the lynne and his flagship than was Firod's own quarters and it was simply more convenient to leave from the villa. The group consisted of Firod and Charina, all eight of their children—the youngest carried in his nurse's capable arms—Menannon burdened with his smallest admirer, Shira, who slept comfortably in the crook of the young Giant's left arm, a warm blanket tucked securely around her to ward off the morning chill. Skendrin and his wife, Mariett, who had decided to accompany Charina, followed close behind them. Completing the group were Lee, Gorlanndon and a veritable cohort of the household staff burdened with boxes, bags and small crates containing the foodstuffs Clarinda had ordered. The cook herself brought up the rear to keep a watchful eye on two of the younger kitchen helpers who carried between them a very special farewell confection, covered with a white cloth bearing Gorlanndon's crest. From the size and the trouble the boys were having in carrying it, the confection must have weighed at least twenty pounds. Following the caravan were four of his sire's household guard in full armour.

The group moved quietly, the children being too sleepy to do aught else and the adults seemingly burdened by a sense of disquiet, though Menannon could not tell whether this was his own interpretation of the mood or whether the others felt the same.

Lee alone seemed light-hearted this morning, understandably, as he was going home for a short visit to his family in Crenanoc ere he returned to Aridion City. Unknown to Menannon, Lee's cheer was almost totally caused by his friend's decision to return to stand the trials.

They crossed the Mathematical bridge where Menannon could not resist stopping for a moment to look down across the awakening city. His gaze followed the descending streets and out across the harbor to where the light towers atop the Crescent were sparkling in the light of the morning sun.

"I still say yours is the most beautiful city in the world," Lee murmured at his shoulder, taking a deep, satisfied breath and letting it out slowly. "I may just have to request Grandmaster Blackmore post me here for a few summers. With you as the Master here and me as the Elder Journeyman, Kirith Kalyria's harper hall will be the crowning glory of our guild."

With a wide grin and a wink, the drummer turned and moved to catch up with the rest of the party. Menannon shook his head with a slight smile and followed him, his determination to return as soon as this round of master's trials were completed firmly settled in his mind.

They entered the Citadel's close and walked past the steps to the council hall where the Eyes of the High One glowed brightly. The doorwards saluted Councillor Gorlanndon and his party as they circled around the side of the building moving to where an open stone palisade stood guard over a break in the fabric of the plaza.

There the shadows still clung so that Menannon could see the glow from within the opening which highlighted a single stair. Should one not know of the lynne beneath the Citadel, the use of the stair would be a total mystery. The initiated knew it was the head of a stair descending deep into the bowls of the Citadel which alone of Kirith Kalyria's four hills was not completely freestanding. Nearly halfway up its northern side, the hill was hooked to the cliff face circling behind the city like a wall by a natural dyke cutting across the Kidron gorge forming a saddle within which the great lava tubes ran connecting the lynne beneath the Citadel with the spectacular waterfall above Watermouth bay. The stair provided access to the anchorage and launching path for Gorlanndon's magnificent flagship.

Skendrin began the descent into the mooring basin, all the rest lining up to follow him. Gorlanndon himself joined his guardsmen and brought up the rear. Just before he began the descent, Menannon glanced up at the back of the palace rising high above the plaza and wondered if Nirna was awake and watching for them. He had only been able to send her a note rather than meeting with her one last time, so no such arrangement had been made.

There was a small loft over the brattice circling the topmost level of the walls in which they had played as children when they wished to be free from Gooddame Matilda's watchful eye. It overlooked the rear of the palace and therefore the head of the lynne stair. For just a moment, he thought he saw movement there, but he was not sure. It could have just been a trick of the light. Behind him, his sire cleared his throat and, reluctantly, he turned away and began to descend the stair.

The stair clung to the wall of a cylindrical chamber whose domed ceiling was a full hundred feet above its base. An iron grating covered a large air hole in the apex of the dome allowing air and some light to reach the depths of the chamber. At the bottom, a wide platform and a circling walkway covered about a third of the space. The rest was water. Thanks to the open Dwarf lanterns hanging all along the stair and at strategic points of the roof, the place was nearly as light as full daylight without. Nearly all the available area for mooring was taken up with a marvelous great ship whose drakta-headed prow almost touched the roof of the lava tube opening behind it.

Lee set down his kit and stood to examine the ship. He let out a low whistle of appreciation and turned shining eyes to her master.

"She's a beauty sir. I've ne'er see anything like her. How big is she?"

"She'll carry four hundred crew and passengers plus cargo and a hundred head of livestock with room to spare," Gorlanndon informed him proudly. "She'll withstand the worst storm and keep sailing as her hull is Snow Cedar from Lornennog, full plank thick. I'll defy even a Great Hornèd Orlandine to sink her. I named her the *Julianna*."

The Giant's eyes glowed with justifiable pride as he studied the star of his merchant fleet. At a time when most water craft were shallow draft galleys bearing a single square sail, two and thirty rowing oars affording space for seventy men or less, all told, plus trade goods, Gorlanndon's ship was a colossus. It bore two masts, each sporting a triangular sail, allowing it to beat against the wind without the necessity of rowing oars. Rather than using oars, the ship was instead sculled with its mighty steering oar when there was insufficient wind to fill its sails.

There were three cabins for passengers in the forecastle and two more larger cabins in the sterncastle. These last two were for Gorlanndon and the captain. The bow and stern decks were reached by stairs set to either side of the cabins. The stairs themselves were of a unique design as they had landings every fourth step. Thus both Humans and Gorlanndon could use them comfortably; Humans stepping on the full stairs and the Giant on the landings.

The deck between the fore and stern castles was pierced in three places with hatches leading to the lower decks. Down the center of the main deck was the rack which held the masts along with their ingenious lifting system. To raise the masts and sails all one needed to do was untie the rope holding them down and they would swing up and latch into place of their own volition. The steering oar lay along one side of the sterncastle and its extension on the other. When the ship was in the lynne both masts were stowed in their racks as the roof of the lava tube was too low to accommodate them upright. Thus the ship had to be launched by sculling it with its oar. The entire ship shone like a mirror in the glitter of the Dwarf lanterns

"Very, very impressive!" Lee grinned and took up his kit again, following Skendrin on board to take a quick look around ere they departed.

Menannon found himself avoiding his sire's eyes as there were many things his heart was clamoring to say, but in public was not the place nor this departure the time. Suffice it that when he returned after the June master's trials, he'd give full rein to his feelings and opinions whether Gorlanndon wished it or not.

Menannon ran lightly up the gangplank to find nearly the entire after deck space covered with boxes, crates and piles of the necessary items Firod's lady deemed requisite to her family traveling in safety. Issilandur and a select group of his warehouse staff had spent the previous two days crating and hauling Lady Firod's chosen belongings to the ship and were now finishing their tasks under the watchful eye of Charina's lady, Piia. She was a tall formidable Crenanocian who was very solicitous of her lady as she had been with her all of her life, first as her nurse, then as her governess and now as her companion. Piia was busily ordering the Teluri and his staff in the task of moving the family's goods and gear into the large aft cabin which Gorlanndon had turned over to their use, while the children would be sleeping in the second aft cabin. The ship's captain would be bunking in with his second this voyage. Menannon and Lee would occupy one of the forward guest cabins. Menannon glanced at the piles of necessaries and gave a low whistle. To his eye, these belongings looked suspiciously like the entire contents of Firod's residence save for the largest pieces of furniture. No wonder the captain's family had stayed the night at the villa. Their own home must be nearly empty of comforts and thus virtually unlivable.

He laid Shira on an enormous pile of pillows and blankets, near Piia and retreated out of the well-ordered chaos to the ship's side and stood looking down to where Firod and Charina were shepherding the rest of their children on board. All of the children were in awe of the great ship and hurried up the gangplank and along to the afterdeck where they moved to stand quietly near their sleeping sister, their eyes round and curious as the crew moved to and fro readying her to sail.

Firod and Charina stayed at the head of the gangplank waiting to speak to Gorlanndon who was last up. They walked with him to the afterdeck, their conversation unheard save by the three of them. With a final word Firod nodded to the then turned and took Charina aside and spoke softly to her alone. Gorlanndon moved away, coming to a halt but a few steps from Menannon so that the couple could speak unheard.

Though he would not have overheard the parting words between a husband and wife for any provocation, Menannon could not help watching them as there was that in their manner which bespoke a parting that would be life-long rather than one of just a matter of a few months. Charina wept softly and clung to Firod, seeming as though she begged something of him that he was either unwilling or unable to agree to as he kept shaking his head, though he spoke no further words. At last, he took her in a fierce embrace and kissed her long, then unclasped her arms from about his neck. He signaled to her waiting woman and slowly, tenderly, forced her into Piia's hold. Piia briefly nodded to him and took the weeping woman into the aft cabin. The door closed with a deadening thunk.

Firod then turned to where his children still clustered about the blanket pile. He visibly squared his shoulders and arranged his face into as gentle a mien as his fierce features allowed and motioned them to come to him one at a time. Darya woke Shira so the youngest sister would not miss speaking with their sire. Firod knelt on one knee and spoke long and earnestly to each, then gave the child a strong embrace and sent them after their mother, Darya going last and the most reluctantly. When she departed, Firod stood and watched the closed door for a long heartbeat then turned and wordlessly left the ship and the mooring basin. Strangely, he did not wait for the sailing ritual that always began any voyage.

"Why ...?" Menannon began, his suspicions flaring anew, and turned to where Gorlanndon still stood not a yard behind him as he spoke.

Gorlanndon smiled and shrugged, cutting him off.

"He is a fond sire who has ne'er been separated from his family before," he said, then turned and began instructing his crew in getting the rest of the gear stowed away, forestalling anything else Menannon had to say, all the while looking about as if in search of someone. Spotting the object of his search, he took his son by the arm and headed in that person's direction.

"Come, my son. It is time for you to meet the ship's new captain and he, you. He's been with me many summers and served me well on many a ship, so I put him charge of this one not quite three summers ago."

Menannon saw they were approaching a tall, dark-skinned man of obvious authority, bearded and garbed all in brown.

"Captain Spero," Gorlanndon called out.

The man Menannon had spied turned to them, and with a deep bow, replied, "At your service, my Lord."

"Captain, I have the honor of presenting to you my son, Menannon."

Spero bowed to Menannon as well, although not as deeply as he had to Gorlanndon, which was to be expected.

"Welcome aboard, young lord. We are honored by your presence and we shall be certain to extend to your all the courtesies we would extend to your sire, whose ship I have the honor of commanding."

"All right, you old pirate. Don't overdo the proprieties! We've spent too many days at sea together for all that nonsense," Gorlanndon said with a chuckle.

Turning to his son, he said, "Captain Spero is the only man I would trust with this ship. He knows every plank, rope, peg, nail and corner of it. You'll be in good hands, son. None better."

"Save your own, that is," the Captain said with a large grin which was matched by Gorlanndon's answering one.

When all cargo was stowed, possessions stored and the decks cleared, the first mate set a small table in the center of the main deck and everyone gathered around it forming a ring which included Firod's children with Piia and their nurse, though Charina did not emerge from the cabin. Even the warehouse-men and villa staff who would not be sailing joined the ring. Lee took his place next to Menannon. On this table Clarinda had the boys set the farewell confection which she left covered and then nodded to Gorlanndon and stood back, a very pleased look lighting her plump features.

Gorlanndon stepped into the ring and knelt on one knee at the table where he bowed his head. All the rest bowed their heads as he spoke:

"O High One eternal, hear our prayer. Thy will alone rules the world and all within it. Thou who didst hang the stars and bind the seas, be it pleasing unto Thee to take this ship and all who sail within her under Thy fatherly care and protect her whereso'er she goes until safe haven receives her at the voyage's end."

The Amen was heartfelt all around. As soon as its last echoes had faded, Gorlanndon withdrew the covering from Clarinda's masterpiece. Everyone exclaimed in awe and delight as the large farewell confection was revealed. Unlike the normal such confection which was simply made of a single level of braided savory bread and shaped in a large oval, this one consisted of several levels of braided bread mounded into the likeness of the ship.

As was traditional, Gorlanndon now relinquished his place to Spero who took the large knife offered him by Clarinda herself and cut the masterpiece. Each person sailing and all her present well-wishers were given a piece to eat for luck. Those who were to go were given another, wrapped in fine vellum to place in their belt pouches, to carry with them for the length of the voyage as a talisman of the High One's love and protection. Beside Menannon, little Shira carefully tore her vellum wrapped piece in half and tucked one half in the pocket of her tunica and the other under the collar of Pin the stuffed puppy. The remaining undivided portion of the confection would be set afloat when they reached Watermouth bay and set their sails west.

The ritual now ended, Gorlanndon signaled to all who would not be going on this voyage to disembark. Issilandur, the warehouse manager, came to stand beside Gorlanndon. He proved to be a tall red-haired Teluri whose height made his head reach nearly to the elder Giant's elbow. He was dressed in a simple tunic of beige sorak with a broad leather belt about his waist from which appended a huge bunch of keys, a small belt pouch and, of course, a malinir. His legs were bare and his feet were encased in plain leather sandals. Despite the simplicity of his raiment, this Teluri was, by his very bearing, almost regal. His hawklike face wore a dour expression and there was something of a watchful stillness in the grey eyes that turned to survey the ship. Clearly nothing escaped the fellow for long, if at all.

Skendrin said his goodbyes to his lady wife, then left the deck and returned to the platform below. After a brief conversation with his master, Issilandur motioned to his crew and they headed back down the gangplank followed by Clarinda and the rest of the staff from the villa. She went in high good humor knowing that all would now be well with her beloved young master and his companions as she had said special prayers with every turn of the braid as she worked most of the night on the confection. Issilandur himself circled the lynne and, withdrawing a large key from his belt pouch, unlocked the sea gates opening the way into the lava tube.

The huge metal gates swung easily into the channel and thence against the sides of the lava tube. There were ropes and pulleys appended to them which enabled them to be closed with little effort even in the spring when the current was stronger. This time of the summer there was very little current in the water, so Gorlanndon ordered the gangplank hauled aboard then went to the roof of the sterncastle and unlimbered the mighty steering oar and locked it into place. With a final salute to his warehouseman, he began to easily scull his huge craft into the tube and along its launch path.

Two of the crewmen ran forward and opened the drakta's eyes and the light of two large Dwarf lanterns shone forth from either side of the figurehead to light their way as the illumination from the mooring basin lanterns was soon left far behind. Just before the ship entered the tube, Menannon's eye caught a shadow overhead and he glanced up to see that Firod stood above looking through the grating as the ship slipped by. Menannon shook his head and turned his attention to the tube they were entering, pushing his questions to the back of his mind. There would be time enough once they were truly underway to seek information from Firod's lady wife as to the real reason for this voyage. With that determined, he made his way forward to where Lee stood just below the figurehead, all attention and excitement.

The great ship slipped into the darkness of the lava tube where

Gorlanndon was able to hold it easily in the middle of the languidly flowing water. Between the current in the water and the Giant's sculling, they set a goodly pace. Overhead, the arching tube was streaked with glittering pockets of obsidian and many colored crystals, its surface uneven almost as though it was made from a huge pile of ropes that had been tunneled out. In fact, part of the tube had been altered in the making of the water course to launch the ship, for there was a pathway running all along the west side of it, where even a horse the size of Kane could walk comfortably. The light from the Dwarf lanterns in the draktas' eyes glittering back from the water and the tube walls caused a soft glow all about them.

Menannon felt a tugging on his boot top. He looked down to see Shira staring up at him, obviously wanting a better vantage point from which to see what was happening. He reached down with a grin and scooped her up and perched her on his shoulder. The rest of the children had come back out of the cabin and crowded around the young harpers and their cries of delight at each new clump of crystals echoed back from the walls and water.

After several hours, even the children began to tire of the wonders of the tube and they settled down as the excitement wore off. Shira was the first to tire and was soon fast asleep in Menannon's arms. The noon meal was served to the passengers to the delight of all and the children—all but the oldest—were soon enjoying a post-prandial nap. The evening meal was followed by an announcement from the Captain that they would be arriving at the end of the tube shortly before dusk.

Somewhat sooner than expected, the way ahead began to glow with outdoor light as they reached their first destination: the inclined plane. As they neared the end of the lava tube, four of the sailors made ready at the bow where four heavy drag stones tied about with coils of rope swung pendulously from their capstans. At Spero's call of "let all go!" they heaved on the latching mechanisms and let the stones loose to fall alongside the ship, slowing her forward progress. At the same time, Gorlanndon swung the ship to starboard with the sculling oar acting as a rudder. She headed into a side channel and came to a halt at a massive gate while the waterway they had just left continued on until it went over the cliff as the impressive cascade known as Highfall.

There in the side channel, she floated for a few moments while the drags were retrieved and a loud blast on a ram's horn was sounded. At the call, a fellow stepped out onto a ledge above them and signaled to someone beyond the gate from whence immediately came the sound of rushing water. Lee and the children crowded around Menannon at the bow, eager to see this odd system that would launch the ship into the ocean lapping at the base of the cliff.

There was a wait of nearly a half turn of an hour then another blast on the horn was heard and the gate swung open revealing a gigantic sluice leading to a trough filled with water to the same level as that in the lava tube. There were huge ropes attached to the sides of the trough connecting it to an intricate pulley system. Another call from the ram's horn and Gorlanndon sculled his ship easily forward through the sluice and into the trough. The gates closed behind it with a sodden thud and click as the locking mechanism engaged.

For a moment nothing happened, then the horn sounded for a final time, ropes tightened and groaned under the weight and the trough, ship and all, began to move towards the cliff edge. It reached the edge and seemed to hang there for a moment, then it slipped over and began to move down the long slope towards the sea, its speed controlled by the pulley system whose winches were turned by mighty horses all nearly the size of Menannon's Kane, plodding in their precisely measured circles on the sand far below. The trough was built upon a huge gimbal which turned as they descended keeping all level. Firod's children all shrieked and laughed, clapping their hands each time the ship lurched and turned on its journey. Their excitement was contagious and everyone found themselves awed by this wondrous strange method of launching a ship.

With a last thud and a splash, the trough sank into the clear water of the bay. The four sailors of the drag stones leapt from the bow to the top of the trough's wall and ran lightly along it to where the gate on the far side awaited. This they opened with alacrity and Gorlanndon sculled his ship out and into the water of the bay where it rocked gently as they waited for the trough to be withdrawn back up onto the beach where it would await the ship's return. With its launch cradle out of the way, Gorlanndon quickly turned the ship's head and sculled her across the bay and laid her alongside the wharf below the village of Waterdeep. His crew secured it and hastily lowered the gangplank. The first part of their journey was complete.

Lee looked up at Menannon, a great smile lighting his face.

"No one at home is e'er going to believe me when I tell them about this. Incredible!"

"I knew that you would find it interesting," Menannon grinned. He started to say more, but his sire's voice broke into their conversation.

"Come one and all and we shall have one more night ashore ere you depart. The Cormorant is a fine establishment with a few sleeping chambers and serves an excellent repast as well."

Gorlanndon led the way down the gangplank and across the small waterfront to the pub where they were met with delight by the landlord and his family. Captain Spero and part of the crew had elected to stay aboard as did Captain Firod's family, Piia thinking it would be easier to keep the children in their new cabin rather than moving them to an inn for naught but a single night.

The elder Giant entertained the rest of the crew and the two harpers this night with stories and tales from far and near gleaned from his many centuries of questing about the High One's world. As Menannon sat near his sire and listened, summers seemed to fall away and it was as though he had never left Kalyria for the mainland. In his mind's eye, he was once again a boy at his parent's knee whose whole heart and soul belonged to the sire he loved. Beside him Lee was entranced with tales of places about which he had only dreamed. It was a merry crew who sought their beds in the old inn's upstairs.

They were all once more aboard ship at dawn's first light. Despite the early hour, Firod's children were up and happily clamoring for the harpers' attention. Menannon scooped up Shira and perched her upon his shoulder as was fast becoming a tradition between the two. Lee leaned upon the railing pointing out several kinds of fish that could be seen swimming about the ship's hull. There were giggles of delight at each new kind thus seen.

"Menannon, attend."

The young Giant heard his sire's voice over the noise and handed Shira to her eldest sister then excused himself and quickly dodged across the deck to the head of the gangplank where his sire waited. All about him the hurried yet orderly business of getting the ship ready for the open sea was going on.

"Your son and servant, sir."

Menannon spoke softly as he reached Gorlanndon's side and stood respectfully, awaiting his pleasure.

The mighty Giant turned to him and drew him aside out of the way and knelt upon one knee the better to treat with him. He laid a gentle hand on his shoulder.

"I have enjoyed your company, boy, more than you know."

He spoke softly, his words coming from the heart.

"I want you to understand that I am more proud of you than I can say and I would that I could come the rest of the way with you and witness your master's trials, but there is much work to be done here that cannot spare me at this time. However, either I shall come to you in the summer or I'll send for you, as I know your master will spare you to me again if I ask it of him. Will that suffice?"

Menannon took a deep breath and licked lips gone suddenly dry before he could answer.

"If you give me your word that all will be well with you until then and you make our meeting not later than Mid-Summer's Day, I shall abide by your will."

"Done!"

Gorlanndon laughed and slapped Menannon gently on the

shoulder then took him in a near bone-cracking embrace.

"I love you, boy!" he finished in a whisper then stood before Menannon could speak further and left the ship.

"Captain Spero, the ship is yours. Take her out!" Gorlanndon stood on the wharf and saluted the Captain.

The crew pulled in the gangplank and loosed the ropes. At her stern, four stout sailors unlimbered a long extension to the steering oar which when locked into place would allow them enough leverage to take Gorlanndon's place and steer the ship. Menannon moved out of their way and stepped to the aft rail.

"The High One be with you always and bless you with a strong wind and a following sea," Gorlanndon called across the widening space of water as the great ship answered her steering oar and began her long journey.

"May He keep you in the hollow of His hand, my father!" Menannon called back then stood at the aft rail until the shoulder of Kalyria's Crown cut off his view of the bay called Watermouth and the wharf upon which his sire still stood, unmoving.

A good crossing took this ship four days to accomplish and this proved a particularly good crossing as the weather remained mild and the sea calm with only a brief flurry of excitement when Firod's eldest son swore he sighted a Great Hornèd Orlandine shadowing the ship. The lad was spending a great deal of very pleasurable time with the lookout in the crow's nest atop the central mast. That fellow swore he saw no such thing as he had been looking forward instead of aft at the instant the creature surfaced. Thus was the lad able to keep the illusion of having seen a sea monster in the flesh. The question of whether or not such a creature actually existed and whether the lad had, indeed seen one, was left unattended. The sailor, who may or may not have seen what the lad saw or did not see, was thereby able to keep face with his fellows below decks, for all knew that Orlandines are myths, tall tales told over mugs of ale. Yet, some few there were who claimed to have seen the beasts following a ship in its wake.

The other children had soon settled into the routine of the ship, their eagerness for the trip and its prospect of attending upon their grandparents quickly pushing aside their sadness at being separated from their sire. Shira did not think twice about the sire she was leaving behind as she immediately attached herself to Menannon who was not averse to watching out for the small family as that occupation allowed him to stop pondering the situation on Kalyria and thereby worrying about his sire's future.

Of Firod's lady wife, Menannon saw nothing for the first two full days of the voyage. It was not until the evening of the third day that she emerged from her cabin in the company of her lady, Piia. In the clear light of the setting sun, Charina looked very small and vulnerable, almost as childlike as one of her offspring despite the twin shield brooches fastening the shoulders of her robe of yellow sorak denoting her status as a wife and mother. There was a wistful sadness about her that puzzled him. She stood at the rail looking to the northeast back the way they had come and her lady leaned over her, talking earnestly in soft whispers the sound of which carried to where Menannon and Lee were teaching the children to play Fox and Hounds amidst the ropes coiled on the roof of the stern castle. The whispers carried, but not the words they contained.

At the sight of Charina, Menannon excused himself, leaving Lee to teach Darya the finer points of throwing the hounding sticks and descended the stairs to the lower deck and approached her to stand respectfully a few paces from her, awaiting her pleasure. At his appearance, the conversation between the two women ceased and Charina turned to him. Menannon inclined his head politely.

"My Lady, I have a question I would ask of you," he began, but Piia gave him a warning frown over her head, obviously having read in his look his intention to ask about Firod. Menannon took the warning and changed his subject.

"I was wondering if you would be met at Blue Bay by a representative of your family?" he asked, blurting out the first thing that came to mind.

"No, it has not been so arranged, as I fear this trip is something of a whim," Charina glanced at Piia and took a deep breath then forced a smile which did not reach her wine-dark eyes. "I'm certain we shall be all right."

Menannon immediately sought about in his mind for a solution to this new problem as he could not in all good conscience let this small family go overland to Pedura unescorted.

"Would you object, then, if I claim the honor of escorting you to your family's holding?" he offered with a solemn inclination of his head.

Charina's eyes lit and her face eased, only to cloud again as a new thought occurred to her.

"Would this not make you behindhand in your return to Aridion City? Surely your leave does not extend so long."

"Grandmaster Blackmore would have my hide should he learn that I returned to my duties leaving you and yours to the mercies of the road simply to save myself a reprimand," Menannon smiled, attempting to cheer her. "Besides, I understand that your family is one of the prime horse breeders in all Pedura, a not inconsiderable accomplishment. I would love to see their stock."

"You would love them," Charina's eyes sparkled slightly for the first time since they had left the circus on Kalyria. "Though my sire's stock is not nearly large enough for you to ride," she hastened to warn him.

That statement brought a wide grin to his face.

"Few horses are, my lady, but that matters not, as I still appreciate fine horses even when they are to me but ponies."

The vision he conjured with that statement did bring a true smile to her lips.

"Ah! Then I right willingly accept your gallant offer and will assay to have my sire send your master a missive explaining your continued absence. Perchance with will ease his ill will?"

She looked up at him hopefully.

"Dearest lady, Grandmaster Blackmore is a reasonable man and that will more than appease any ill will he might possibly harbor towards me. With that, I will bid you good night and return to my game, though I fear your children are already far more adept at Fox and Hounds than I and are beating me soundly."

Menannon inclined his head once more and departed to inform

Lee of the change in his plans, still wondering why a trip that began as a whim should so sadden the lady.

Late evening of the next day saw them tacking into the small harbor at Blue Bay, an anchorage almost too small to accommodate Gorlanndon's flagship. Even at that, the harbor master had to require two smaller ships be pulled away from the dock in order to let the Julianna get close enough to disembark her passengers and cargo. Captain Spero immediately sent his first mate ashore to secure accommodations for his passengers at the small inn near the docks. The fellow was tasked as well with obtaining wains enough to carry all Charina's belongings. Everything was done with efficiency and speed so that none, most especially the master's son and heir, would be in any way inconvenienced.

Menannon stood on deck watching his sire's crewmen move about the business of landing like a well crafted machine. They were quick, efficient and effective as was everyone who served the elder Giant. For a moment, Menannon's stomach tightened as he thought once more of his sire and Nirna and what was really happening on Kalyria. There was no profit in such thoughts at this pass so he resolutely pushed them aside and concentrated on the task at hand: getting Firod's family safely to Pedura. Lee came up to stand beside him and looked to the west where the setting sun was obscured by tall thunder heads.

"I certainly hope that holds off a few more days, else you'll have a wet trip," he observed, nodding to the clouds on the horizon.

Menannon looked at the smaller vessels lining the port and saw none that would not be tossed about like cork in a good storm before he replied.

"Yours could get a bit rough as well."

"Well, think dry thoughts then, and we'll both fare well," Lee grinned. He was eager to get off the ship and find another to take him south to Gormidad and Crenanoc, yet reluctant to leave Menannon's company. Almost he asked the Giant to come with him and thought briefly of proposing that he come along to

Pedura and then the two of them return to Blue Bay and go south together. It was a nice thought, but impractical as he knew there was not enough time since Menannon was required back at the hall within the fortnight to begin the process of final training for his master's trials while Lee himself still had two months of holiday, as he was not to be forwarded to the trials for another full summer. He stood quietly, wondering what his friend was thinking as they watched Charina and her family disembark and follow their guide to the inn. As soon as the last child disappeared through the old inn's door, Captain Spero came to report to Menannon.

"Your transportation has been arranged, lad," he said coming to stand beside the young Giant with a jaunty salute. "Four large freight wagons and two covered wains will be loaded and at yer disposal on the morrow. The lady and her youngest children and nurses will share one wain and you and the older ones can share the other."

"My thanks for your care," Menannon nodded, rather puzzled as to the number of wagons. Surely Charina had not that much in goods and gear.

"Why so many wagons?"

"Your sire has that which he is sending to your master at Aridion City." Spero nodded towards several large crates Menannon had not seen before just being swayed out of the aft cargo hold.

"Your sire instructed me to give ye this for your master and asks ye to tell him that he is sorry it has taken so long to accomplish things."

The captain took a large scroll out of the front of his kirtle and handed it to Menannon. It was indeed sealed with Gorlanndon's personal seal showing his crest, the likeness of two mythical Great Hornèd Orlandines, their long necks entwined over a long ship, with a crown G above all. He placed it into the breast of his own kirtle and nodded his thanks.

"I have taken the liberty of stowing all of your personal gear in those wagons as well, lad. All, that is, save what ye still have in your cabin. Oh, and by-the-bye," the captain continued, now addressing Lee, "we'll be sailing with the morning tide for Gormidad and parts south, as I have an errand to Rhonndia to accomplish, so if you're of a mind to stay aboard, I'd be pleased to take you on to Crenanoc."

He nodded to both young men and left to continue overseeing the unloading.

"That suits me just fine," Lee grinned, much relieved at not having to find another, lesser ship to take him south. "Now I see where you get your gift for attending to everything at once. Your sire is quite a fellow."

"That he is," Menannon nodded a bit absently, as he was still wondering what his sire could be sending to Grandmaster Blackmore and more importantly to his mind, why was he sending whatever it was now? They stood watching a few moments longer then both turned to gather Menannon's few personal belongings. It took them nearly no time to perform the task and they were back at the railing ready for Menannon to disembark before a quarter turn of the hour had elapsed.

"My time with you has been most pleasant and I have learned much," Lee grinned. "I have many wondrous tales to tell my folk when I arrive and I've no doubt they won't believe the half of them."

"Well, try to keep them somewhere near the truth," Menannon grinned and held out his hand to his friend. "I'm glad you came along and I'll see you the beginning of winter classes. Try not to be late as I'd lief as not be saddled with all the new apprentices by myself."

"Count on it. Now you'd better be on your way as Shira won't go to sleep without the rest of that bedtime story you started last night." Lee took Menannon's hand in a strong grip. "Take care of yourself."

"And you!" Menannon nodded and then shouldered his harp in its protective case and took up his personal bag, then strode down the gangplank to the dock where he turned and raised a hand to see Lee standing at the top of the gangplank with a rather odd look on his face.

"Ummm, are we not getting ahead of our horses, my friend? This ship leaves in the morning, does it not?" Lee enquired of Menannon.

"Of course." Menannon paused, then scratched his head in chagrin as he realized the implication of Lee's query. "Ah, yes, we are indeed being a bit hasty. Let us repair to the inn together and take our leave in the morn."

The friends laughed together at their gaffe, and repaired to the inn with haste, eager to catch up to Menannon's charges and most content to spend one last night together before going their separate ways.

CHAPTER 10
(SUMMER OF THE WORLD 6996)

THE SMALL CARAVAN LEFT BLUE BAY with the dawn after seeing the rest of Menannon's belongings—save his harp and a few changes of clothes—loaded on the wagons bearing the large crates destined for Grandmaster Blackmore. Mariett, Skendrin's wife, also went with the baggage wains to Aridion City to join her family whom she had not seen in many a summer and who would be grandly surprised by her unexpected arrival. These would take the shorter route to Aridion City through Koresh and Bridge Town and be at the harper hall many days before Menannon arrived.

That same dawn had also seen Gorlanndon's great ship head back out to sea to complete her voyage to Gormidad and Crenanoc, bearing Lee homeward. That had been a sad parting for the children as they had all grown fond of the drummer and were loath to be separated from him. Only Menannon's reassurance that he would not leave them as well, and would in fact accompany them all the way to Pedura had eased their morose condition.

The remaining wains bearing Menannon and Firod's family set out on their overland travel with mild weather providing them dry roads and a pleasant journey and they reached Pedura without incident. While the plan had been that only the older children would ride with Menannon in the second wain, Shira had put paid to that idea with alacrity. She had firmly declared her intention to ride with her friend and that was that. And so she had, keeping him so busy answering questions, singing and playing games that they had been within sight of Pedura for nearly the full turn of an hour before he even realized they had arrived.

Pedura was a small city located at the far southern end of the Plains of Aridion. Charina's parents possessed a large villa and holdings just without the town where they raised both riding and draft horses famed throughout the region, no small thing in a province dedicated to the breeding of fine horses. The small caravan circled the town proper and made its way to a long hill overlooking it from the northwest atop which stood their destination. The road to the villa was long and lined on both sides with tall, conical evergreens and myriad rhododendron and azalea bushes whose leaves had not yet fallen for the coming winter. In the spring and summer, this place would be a fountain of flowers.

They drew up at the entrance to the villa, a large pillared portico raised six steps above the beaten earth of the courtyard. Beyond the central building were several large outbuildings, obviously horse barns, storage barns and dormitories for the estate's workers. Menannon was surprised that here there were no walls nor gates to be shut in case of attack. This fact pointed to the peace that Pedura had obviously known for so long that such things had been dispensed with. He wondered at this, for even Aridion City itself lay within a huge wall pierced by five gates and two water gates which could be closed at the ringing of an alarm bell.

As soon as the wagons' wheels stopped turning, all the children made short work of disembarking and scrambling inside in search of Ninna and Pedda as they called their grandparents. All save Shira, that is, as she remained in the wain reluctant to go inside knowing that the parting with Menannon was near at hand.

"But you must go, Sunshine," Menannon urged, "for they set great store by you and would be greatly disappointed should you not go to see them."

Shira had looked at him as though he had lost his mind, but she had obediently climbed down. It was not until she was halfway up the steps to the portico that he had realized how strange he must have sounded to her as she had never seen her grandparents before, being far too young to have even been a twinkle in her sire's eye the last time those worthies had made the voyage to Kalyria.

More to give Shira the time to settle in than from any actual fatigue, Menannon claimed the need to take a couple of days to rest before he departed for Aridion City. Everyone was delighted and made him more than welcome. His stay with Charina's family was most pleasant, but all too short.

When the day of his departure finally arrived, there were many tears, most especially from little Shira who insisted upon giving him her stuffed puppy, Pin.

"I give you Pin. He a good friend an' will keep you from being sad," she told him with a smile, but then burst into tears and ran back into the villa.

It was almost more than he could do to pick up his harp in its case and walk down the road to the main track, there to join the small caravan of Dwarven wool merchants he would be traveling with. The sound of Shira's crying echoed across the still morning, making him feel like a traitor.

Charina, sensitive to Menannon's mood, sought to ease his discomfort.

"She will be fine. She will never forget you, and the sadness will pass in time and she will return to the merry urchin we all love."

He reached the main track in a very lugubrious mood and found the merchants already waiting for him. They were somewhat disgruntled by his tardiness, but not so much as to forego a little humor at his expense, they being less taciturn that many of their race.

The caravan's leader, one Orin Goldfoot of Mishka, greeted him with crossed arms and a glare.

"Took ye long enough, lad. We've been waitin' for ye for two days. Another few turns of the hour an' we'd be long gone." He followed his pronouncement with a gruff "Harrumph."

Menannon blushed to the roots of his hair, and began to stumble through an apology when the Dwarf burst out into a great guffaw.

Nonplused, Menannon stared at the Dwarf in confusion.

"Ah, lad, we'd to wait anyway, for me cousin Norin here was slow in joinin' us wi' his load and wi'out him we couldna start."

The rest of the dwarven band broke out in great snorts of laughter at Menannon's discomfiture and Orin slapped him on the back good-naturedly as he commented, "Besides, 'tisn't often we ha' the pleasure o' the company of a harper such as yerself. Welcome, lad, welcome!"

With that, he bowed to Menannon, giving him the proper and respectful greeting due a harper.

As he climbed aboard the lead wagon, Menannon remem-bered that he had never had the chance to speak to Charina about her future plans and he had no better idea now as to what was happening on Kalyria than he had when they sailed. This irked him and he was rather disgusted at himself for his failure.

The caravan he was joining was returning to the Dwarves' home and point of departure, the village of Mishka, by the shortest route which would take them through Aridion City and then north along the foothills of the Sythrin mountains. Mishka was a Dwarf realm famous for its garment trade, most especially walking jackets made from boiled wool. The making of the cloth for these jackets was a well-kept secret handed down with the kingship, and the current king, Kricklan the Eighth, was carrying on the tradition.

The caravan's leader, Orin Goldfoot, a well set up fellow with a magnificent red beard tucked into a belt resplendent with gold findings all along its length bespeaking his success at his chosen profession, was indeed more than delighted to take on a journeyman harper for the remainder of their trip. For him, that was the crowning achievement of a more than usually successful trip. The Dwarves had been accompanied on the former part of their trading venture to Gormidad and Crenanoc by an itinerant minstrel who had immediately found a reason to stay in Pedura when it became known that a journeyman of the Harper's Guild would be joining the company.

Though the minstrels could and at times did claim membership in the harpers' guild, they were considered at best second-rate musicians who were either lacking in sufficient talent or too restless to have begun or stuck to the summers of training and discipline required to become a full-fledged member of the guild. From their ranks came the street musicians and pub players who enlivened the entertainments of the everyday folk. Usually, they avoided all contact with corded harpers by whom they were almost universally looked down upon, though Menannon cared neither way. The Giant considered there was a place for all musicians and let the argument be carried on by those who loved to argue. However, with the minstrel's departure, he would now be called upon to perform each evening of the journey by himself rather than having someone with whom to share the load.

The fall rains set in with a vengeance the second night on the road out of Pedura transforming what normally was a hard wagon journey into an extended and excruciating one. The hard, driving rain soaked nearly everything, making a fire impossible and rendering the roads nearly impassible morasses into which the wagons kept sinking nearly to their axles. While Orin had been thinking it was going to be a pleasure to hear the journeyman play, it turned out that Menannon was far more useful in extracting the wagons from mud hole after mud hole. It was the first time in his life he found his brawn more useful than his brains. He hoped it would be the last. That the rain precluded his performing served only to worsen his mood. By the time they reached the environs of Aridion City they were all thoroughly filthy, tired and heartily sick of rain and mud.

The incessant rain had lightened to a slight drizzle as they reached the crest of the ridge overlooking the valley in which lay Aridion City, so the caravan halted for a brief rest. Here, within five miles of the city wall, the road changed from dirt to stone as it was in the process of being paved. It was the plan of Gilderon IV, the current king of Aridion City, to pave all the roads within his writ to aid both his people and his army. Menannon was definitely a supporter of the plan after having experienced the roads of greater Aridion in all their muddy glory for the full sevenday past and more. Below them, the road moved through well-tended fields and orchards, each delineated by low stone walls that crisscrossed the valley, marking the boundaries of the small holdings and great villas that swore fealty to the city.

Just beyond these estates rose a huge wall whose veneer was

made of individual megaliths raised side by side so tightly that not even the thinnest sheet of vellum could be slipped between them. This wall strode the land sixty feet high and forty feet across, encircling the city. It had been built by Beldronnen, mightiest of Giants, at the end of the Dim Times to protect a single building: the so called Harpers' Haven. This small holding was started by one Gimdaruk and his few students, wandering minstrels all. To this one man, the High One had given the task of bringing together and codifying all the arts and crafts, history and lore of the war-scattered peoples of Linden. From this first small group, Gimdaruk organized the Harpers' Guild and created the far flung network of its halls with Harpers' Haven growing into the mother house of the guild. Around the hall within the protection of Beldronnen's wall grew a mighty city, Aridion.

Below where Menannon sat upon the seat of the lead wagon, the city spread out in a vast complex of streets and courtyards, all laid out like a starfish. There were five main tree-lined thoroughfares that moved away from a huge central plaza to end at the first set of five gates. These gates were flanked by huge draktas made of stone, one on each side. Each gate opened onto another section of city, offset a small amount from the previous section so that the thoroughfares all angled left a hundred yards ere they straightened again to move in another straight line to the next set of drakta gates from which they angled back right forming a multi-angled snake that wove back and forth across the arm. Any attacking army that might breach Beldronnen's wall, considered by most an impossibility, would find conquering the city a hard slog.

Each arm of the great starfish that was Aridion City had its own smaller wall enclosing the dwellings and shops of its inhabitants with numerous courtyards and great halls aplenty. Some of these halls were splendid dwellings while others were obviously the mother houses of the various guilds of greater Aridion. The buildings of the city were almost universally built of light blond Aridion stone, one of the most sought-after building stones in greater Aridion as it was immensely strong, yet still carvable. The space between these arms provided shared ground for tillage, thus enabling Aridion City to feed its inhabitants in good times and bad.

The huge water meadow which had once occupied both banks of the river Ari had been successfully drained on the south bank several centuries earlier to provide additional building space. The north bank meadow lay yet undisturbed. The river had been shaped and molded for many centuries along its length, and now was considerably wider and deeper than nature had made it, although only the sharpest bends had been straightened out to help keep the current from becoming too strong. At the shore of the Dawn sea, the Ari terminated in a spectacular waterfall rather than the gentler deltas the other rivers along that side of the continent sported allowing for port cities and maritime trade.

Unlike Crenanoc, Gormidad and Blue Bay, Aridion City was therefore effectively landlocked, the solution to which situation had eluded Gilderon and his ancestors until now. That solution had come, it was hoped, in the form of a wide tow path presently being constructed along the north bank of the Ari from Aridion City to Koresh. This was to accommodate horse drawn barges which would haul wares to and from the city to Koresh and thence overland to Blue Bay thereby allowing her to have a certain level of maritime trade of her own, for the port at Blue Bay gave access to all the ports along both the Dawn and the Dusk Seas. To facilitate this plan, long wharves, warehouses and shops were being constructed in Aridion City and Koresh as well as along the bank of the river to receive the goods, both coming and going.

These facilities would stand between the long garden lands running from huge villas down to the water. Some of the wealthiest families of the city yet lived hard by the water gates despite the danger of seasonal flooding. The barges would begin to ply their routes in the spring after the dangers of high water were done and one and all would learn if the king's grand plan was going to work. Against all of this, the building work was going on at a prodigious rate in an attempt to have all done in time for the first shipping season the following Spring.

The heavier than usual fall rains in the lower Sythrins were causing the Ari to rise and it was threatening to jump its banks thereby putting a temporary halt to the building efforts. From where Menannon sat, he could see that the river was showing dark and fast. He was heartily glad that he was coming in from Pedura rather than Bridge Town as that road crossed the river just above the city via a rope winched ferry, not a crossing to be trusted with the river rising the way it was. Overhead, the lowering skies once more decided to open with a heavy downpour, putting paid to further sightseeing. Orin clicked up his huge greys and they plodded on down the road.

The cobblestone pavement snaked its way down the ridge switchbacking across its face to aid wagons in the descent. Despite that, both horses and wagons had a tendency to slide on the wet stones and the teams had to be held back by main force to keep them from spooking as the wagons veered and swung. One particularly steep spot had formed a small river of its own as mud and water gushed across the road from above down a rapidly eroding swale. The lead wagon nearly slid into the inside drainage ditch as Orin attempted to negotiate the curve.

"Hold there."

Menannon took Orin's arm as he was about to urge his frightened horses forward for a second try.

"Let me see what I can accomplish."

"Right ye are, me lord," Orin agreed right readily.

The Dwarf's reply was nearly drowned out by a crash of thunder almost on top of them. The right leader rose in the traces pawing and shrieking with only the rock-steady wheeler behind him managing to hold the team in place long enough for Menannon to throw aside his sodden cloak and leap down. He waded through water already running well above his ankles to take the leader by the bit and pull him down. Even his great height and strength were almost overcome by the terror of the horse. With dint of massive effort he was finally able to wrestle the horse down onto all four hoofs again and tear off his own tunic with which he blindfolded the beast. The horse stood still then, trembling and breathing hard.

"Orin! Come lead them down while I hold the wagon back!" he yelled to make himself heard over the storm.

The Dwarf leapt down from the high seat and bulled his way through water almost to his knees to take hold of the bridles of his horses with arms of iron. Menannon nodded to him and moved back to the front of the wagon just behind the wheeler. He put his back against the box and shoved. When he was set, he reached up and loosed the brake. The wagon jerked forward, nearly knocking him down. Instinctively, the young Giant let himself go heavy and the wagon instantly halted.

He mentally thanked the High One and his sire for the ability and training that allowed Giants to manipulate their body mass at will. A Giant trained in the art could so manipulate the life force within him that he could make himself lighter or heavier at need. To ease his life in the outside world where things were not made for the use of Giants, Gorlanndon had long since trained his son in this practice. To make himself the same mass as a Human or even a Teluri of his size had become so second nature to Menannon that it was now his body's normal state and he could hold it even when he was asleep and thus was able to sit on chairs and sleep in beds without splintering them instantly. The only time he reverted to his actual mass and weight was when he was unconscious or intentionally willed it. Only once had the Giant ever willingly used the ability to go heavy and that was on the playground as a child when he had been involved in a tug-of-war game. He had quickly discovered that using this ability was tantamount to cheating and had eschewed it ever since. There in the mud and downpour, he could not help grinning as he found a legitimate use for his natural ability and happily applied it.

Foot by foot, Menannon let the wagon roll forward to the apex of the curve where he halted with both feet braced against the retaining wall and shoved the wagon on around the curve and down onto the gentler stretch of road below. From there, the road ahead was relatively easily negotiated even in the rain. With one wagon safely down, Menannon resolutely trudged back up the road to start the next of the remaining five down the road. He instructed the drivers to each take their turn leading their teams while he handled the wagons.

By the time all six wagons were safely on the last switchback, Menannon's chemise was in tatters and his left shoulder and back well filleted and bleeding sluggishly from the scraping of the rough wood of the wagon boxes. At least the heavy rain had washed most of the mud from his clothing and hair, but battered, bedraggled and soaking wet was not the way he would have chosen to appear at his homecoming. Menannon trudged forward to the lead wagon, swung up onto his place on the seat next to Orin and gratefully accepted the soggy blanket the Dwarf held out to him. Even with its load of water, the wool was still far warmer than the rain. When he had it well wrapped around himself, Orin nodded to him and clicked to his team. As a precaution, they had left the right leader blindfolded so, despite the continued thunder, there were no further mishaps.

Due to the lowering clouds and storm, night came earlier than usual this day and the city gate was closed and its lanterns lit by the time the caravan reached it. They pulled to a halt on the large cobblestone apron without the guard hut with its bell pole. Menannon swung down to ring the admittance bell. Everything, including the bell and its rope, was running with water. Within the small hut the flickering of firelight shone through the window curtains attesting to the guard's presence. Menannon pulled the rope and the bell rang nobly enough, though he had half expected it to gurgle rather than ring. It took a few moments, but then there was the sound of a chair being pushed across the floor within and he heard the watchman grumbling to himself as he came to answer the summons.

"I'll be blinked if'n a fellow can't even eat his dinner in peace."

The grumbled words of the disturbed guard came clearly to Menannon despite the noise of the rain and the stamping of the horses behind him. There was a crash and further mumbling as the guard must have knocked over a piece of furniture. The door jerked open, startling the Giant, and an arm and hand holding a shuttered storm lantern emerged.

"Ye'd better have a good reason to be disturbin' a fellow out o' his vittles …."

The lantern flipped open and the light shone directly into Menannon's eyes, temporarily blinding him. He instinctively threw up his right hand to ward it off. Menannon lowered his hand and tried to look beyond the light, but could see only the guard's silhouette against the firelight spilling from the hut. When his eyes adjusted to the light, the guard was revealed to be a grizzled one-armed veteran of middle height wearing the black and gold armour of Aridion City's army.

"What d'ya …" the fellow began, looking out at his visitor. Out, then up, then up some more.

For a moment, he stared at the person before him, his face tightened into a frown. Then his brow cleared and his face broke into a smile as, despite the rain plastering his hair and beard and soaking all his clothing into a nondescript mud color, Menannon was recognized for who and what he was.

"Master Journeyman Menannon! 'Tis about time ya was gettin' back. Himself has been in a fine takin' that yer gear arrived without ya, an the carter could nay tell him as to where ya were other than that ya'd gone a different way. He's had his runner down here lookin' fer ya every couple o' hours day and night fer the last threeday. The lad's plum wore out with the task!"

The fellow set down his lantern and, taking an oil cloth from a peg behind the door, threw it over his head and shoulders and stepped out into the rain to open the postern and let the harper enter the city. Only when he got outside did he notice the horses and wagons arranged across the cobbles behind the Giant. He stared at them for a moment then recognized Orin.

"Goldfoot! Yer runnin' a bit behind! Ye must've had a successful trip!" he called over his shoulder as he took the gate keys from his belt pouch and flipped through them to find the right one.

"So 'twas! Well worth the trouble, even with this infernal rain," the Dwarf's voice rumbled through the murk. "Though I'm not knowin' how we'd've made it through wi'out the help o' this young fellow. He's a mud grubber o' the first water!"

"Hey, watch who yer callin' a mud grubber," the guard snapped indignantly, rising to Menannon's defense. "This here's Menannon, the finest journeyman in the whole harper craft, so don't ya be insultin' him!"

"I was meanin' no insult ...," Orin began, but Menannon cut him off with a chuckle.

"And none was taken!"

He glanced down at the guard and winked his thanks for the man's care for his rank and reputation.

"I'm always up for learning a new skill, though 'mud grubbing' as you call it, will ne'er be a favorite, I assure you," which statement brought a hearty guffaw from the great Dwarf.

"Yer as game, lad, as ye are tall," he said reaching down to pick up Menannon's discarded cloak. "Here ye be, lad and don't be forgettin' yer harp an' pack! They're under yer seat safe and sound. Oh, an' yer tunic too. It's still on the horse."

Menannon took the cloak and doffed the blanket, ready to hand it back to its owner.

"Nay, lad. Ye be after keepin' it. Ye've got a goodly walk yet over t'the hall an' tis as fine pneumonia weather as I've e'er seen. So be keepin' the blanket an' be warm."

"My thanks."

Menannon gratefully wrapped the heavy wool blanket back around his shoulders then reached up and retrieved his harp, safe in its carrying bag. He slung it and his pack and cloak across his shoulder, then pulled his sodden tunic from the horse and saluted the Dwarves.

"What do I owe you for the trip?" he asked starting to reach for his belt pouch.

"Nary a coin," Orin held up his hand forestalling him. "Ne'er let it be said that Orin Goldfoot took a farthin' in payment from a corded harper, much less one who's had to be doin' more than his fair share o' work along the way."

There were answering calls of agreement from the rest of

Dwarves overriding the protest the young Giant tried to make.

"Well, I guess ye've been told good and proper," the watchman said with a grin.

"Again, my thanks!" Menannon inclined his head with a smile. "What are your plans from here?"

"We'll be after headin' to tie up at the horse fair across the river an' be headin' out at first light."

"Yer nay goin' to be able to do that," the guard came back to stand looking up at the Dwarf. "The Ari's floodin' over yonder an' the ferry's been hauled out for the nonce. So ye better be circlin' yer wagons in yonder copse an' hobblin yer horses then come on back an' spend the night in my place. There's plenty o' floor space to throw yer blankets an' I've a bucket o' good stew on the hob."

Orin looked down the line of his wagons to see that all the drivers were nodding their agreement with this proposal. He turned back and nodded.

"We'll be doin' just that then an' see what the dawn brings. Round 'em up!" he called and raising a hand to Menannon in a final salute, turned his team and rumbled away headed for the indicated copse.

The others followed, each with a salute for the harper. When the last wagon had left for the copse, Menannon blinked the rainwater out of his eyes and followed the guard to the gate where the fellow opened the entire left panel rather than just the postern so that the Giant could walk through without ducking.

"Good night to ya now and the High One's blessing be on ya," he heard as the gate swung shut behind him.

"And upon you!" he called just before the outer gate clanged shut, closing him back into the place where he had grown to manhood.

He turned away and began to walk through the long gate tunnel. It was barrel-vaulted and the stones of its ceiling had been laid dry with small spaces left between many of them. These spaces acted as murder holes and in time of war they would allow defenders to pour boiling oil and send arrows down upon the heads of any attackers foolish enough to try and force the gate. To facilitate this defense, at ten foot intervals along the way there were portcullises that could be dropped, trapping between them any within the tunnel. On this peaceful night, it was well lit with torches at either end. Menannon made short work of the tunnel and soon faced the inner gate.

Here again there was a traveler's bell which, when he pulled the rope, echoed in the tunnel with authority. It was answered quickly by the opening of an embrasure through which an inquisitive eye peered. The consideration lasted only a moment then the embrasure snapped closed and again the whole side of the gate opened. The gates were designed to oblige mounted men and great wagons so they accommodated a normal sized Giant with ease. Menannon stepped through and was saluted silently by the duty guard who simply closed the gate and returned to his warming hut. Menannon grinned at the difference in greeting and turned towards the center of the city and walked on into its western arm wherein the harper hall stood within its close. Despite the rain, the city was alive with light and noise, dogs barking, people laughing, the sound of music and merriment pouring from its pubs and inns and many of its houses as well.

By the time Menannon reached the last turning of the street leading to the close surrounding the harper hall, the rain had lightened to a cold drizzle which would last the night. He turned the corner and the great bulk of the hall loomed out of the murk, standing tall above its surrounding wall, its windows alight as the dinner hour was just coming to a close. The student body would still be in the refectory for the full turn of the hour of free time before they returned to their chambers for the evening study period before lights out. The noise could be heard even out here in the street. The gate stood open and a light shone in the porters small office which occupied the gatehouse arch that joined the fore and nether ends of the close's enclosing wall, though the fellow himself would be in the hall at table. Menannon walked under the gate arch and halted looking with pleasure on the place he had called home for the last eight summers.

The Master Harper Hall of Aridion was an impressive sight with its central hall rising more than a hundred feet in the air with flying buttresses all along to bear the massive weight, allowing its walls to be pierced with huge traceried windows made with multicolored glass set within mullions of stone. This was the High Hall of Gathering where all ceremonies, concerts and celebrations were held and was the first building built by Gimdaruk. Over the centuries, other sections had been added. Jutting out from the east end of the southern wall of the hall and at right angles to it was another building equally as tall which provided the hall with space for the grandmaster's audience chamber and a cloistered walk to the entrance of the High Hall.

At the front of this building was the entrance hall which provided access both to it and to the two-story refectory and the classroom building which stood across a nearly enclosed courtyard from the audience hall. Half of this courtyard was filled with the hall'
capacious kitchen. The walls of both were solid buff stone, but while the classroom building had mullioned windows full length on both floors, the audience hall had only its clerestory pierced all along with smaller versions of the windows in the High Hall, though these were of clear glass rather than colored, the better to provide working light. The entrance hall fronted upon the courtyard of the close and the main gate leading out to the rest of the city. Joined to the left side of this entrance hall was the three story dormitory wing which provided living space for all the apprentices, journeymen and masters living and working at the hall. Along the west wall of the classroom wing was a flower and vegetable garden, small orchard, an exercise yard and the outbuildings which included stables, sheds and the smithy devoted to the teaching of the blacksmith's craft.

In the forecourt beside a small garden was a long, low classroom building which housed the day school for the children of Aridion City. General classes were conducted here, but the specialty classes such as music, smithing and painting were taught in the harper hall itself. Nestled to the right of the audience hall was a cloistered pleasure garden. This garden extended to the side wall of the close and was overlooked by the three stories and squat tower of the king's palace. At a time when buildings on the mainland tended to be low and blocky even here in Aridion City, the harper hall stood out like an airy bird among turtles.

The hall had been designed by Gimdaruk, but the Teluri had actually found the ways to put wings to the grandmaster's dream and the Giants had done the work, molding stone to fit the plan. Though why the grandmaster had seen fit to have his hall built in the wilderness above a huge water meadow along a wild river backed by the foothills of the Sythrin mountains had been fodder for the wildest speculations for centuries in the more civilized places such as Kalyria and Gilaria. When questioned, Gimdaruk had only smiled and said that it was the will of the High One.

Menannon broke into a light run as he crossed the forecourt, his joy at returning overcoming his weariness. His quick steps took him past the small garden still brave with late-blooming asters and the fountain which had yet to be turned off for the season. He trotted up the seven steps to the hall's portico and halted in the shadow of the great pillars. The doors were closed, but their doorwards would be within ready to answer the ring of the silver bell hanging on the first great pillar to the right of the door. Menannon quickly reached over and pulled the bell's rope. Its clear ring sounded through the night, announcing to all the city that someone was asking entrance into the harper hall. The doorward responded to the ring instantly and the ornate doors swung open silently on their massive counterweighted hinges. Warm light and noise washed over him as the doorward stepped out to inquire of his business.

The fellow on duty this evening was Conar, one of the older journeymen of the smithing arts. He was a tall Human in his mid forties whose many hours at the forges had given him the build of an ox, his chest muscles straining the material of his rust colored harper robes. Conar looked at the newcomer for just a moment then his face lit with a great smile.

"Go tell the Grandmaster his truant has arrived," he called over his shoulder to the other doorward before he stepped back motioning Menannon to enter. "Come in lad before you catch your death. You've been missed."

Gratefully, Menannon stepped inside the hall and the doors were closed behind him, shutting out the cold and rainy darkness and allowing the delicious warmth of the hall to swarm around him, encasing him in its softness.

"Here let me take those," Conar indicated Menannon's harp and gear. Right willingly Menannon handed him the requested items. "I'll see this to your chamber," Conar said, slinging the strap of the harp case over his shoulder, "and this to the laundry," he grinned, holding the muddy cloak and tunic nearly at arms length. "Now get along with you. The Grandmaster will not be best pleased if you keep him waiting any longer."

"Where is he?" Menannon asked, glancing towards the hall leading to the audience chamber.

"He's still at table," Conar nodded his head towards where the noise was still booming from inside the refectory. Menannon nodded his thanks and headed across the entry hall towards the heavy refectory doors and the source of the noise echoing about.

The entrance hall was a veritable forest of pillars, traceried windows and fan vaulting soaring one hundred feet above his head. There was not a single square inch of wall, ceiling or floor which was not somehow decorated with frescoes, carvings and inlaid stone mosaics. The Master Harper Hall of Aridion City not only housed the leading artists and craftsmen of all Aridion, it was a functional work of art in itself.

The young Giant made sure to keep the blanket well wrapped around his shoulders to hide the condition of his chemise and the skin beneath and took hold of the upper of the refectory door's three knobs. He turned the knob and pushed it open. The noise within hit him like a wall.

The refectory was a long, low chamber set with all manner of tables and their benches from those small enough to be used by only one person all the way up to long ones running the entire length of the refectory along its eastern and western walls. The western table stood beneath the windows overlooking the vegetable garden and the eastern was closest to the kitchen. A side table held a huge barrel of fresh water with several stacks of mugs, tankards and even blown glass goblets beside it. At the far northern end on a dais raised two steps above the main floor was the long table set for the head masters of the various disciplines and at its direct center was the great throne-like chair of the Grandmaster, a chair that would have more than amply accommodated Menannon himself.

All of the tables were still crowded with apprentices, journeymen and masters, their various colored robes flowing together in a near rainbow. At the tables filled with the younger apprentices, game boards abounded and the noise level was nearly deafening. The game of Fox and Hounds was as popular here as it was on Kalyria and was being played with great and loud enthusiasm. Others tables were crowded with dice throwers and other games of chance, though no money was allowed to change hands. They played for colored stones which were returned to their boxes at the end of the evening and sometimes, though frowned upon, for special favors from one another.

At the tables where the older apprentices and journeymen sat together, the relaxation took the form of a glass of wine and good conversation or even debate of the finer points of their craft. A few of the masters sat with their students though most sat at tables of their own. One tall master with iron grey hair brushing the shoulders of a scarlet robe denoting his status as an illuminator was wandering about the chamber ever watchful that enthusiasm did not get carried away and turn into something more. He carried with him a long willow stick that could both tickle and smart at need. He was the Master appointed to the office of Disciplinarian, which responsibility rotated regularly amongst all the Masters at the hall, some of whom discharged their duties with great relish.

As Menannon entered, many a conversation was halted as he was greeted by all and sundry. When it was recognized that he was soaking wet and not a little covered with mud, many ribbing comments were forthcoming concerning his inability to come in out of the rain. The young Giant just grinned and rolled his eyes and kept moving, weaving his way between tables and well-wishers until he arrived at the head table where he halted and inclined his head to the masters there. They returned his greeting, but none tried to talk over the noise as there would be time enough on the morrow to talk to him about his holiday and Kalyria.

Menannon turned his full attention to where Blackmore sat surrounded by cushions so that he was more comfortable at table and could see and be seen by all in the hall. At the moment, he was leaning back in his huge chair surveying his returned journeyman with not a little pleasure sparkling in his blue eye.

"Grandmaster," Menannon inclined his head again then stood waiting his pleasure.

"Well, it took you long enough, young sir." The Valinga had to shout to be heard over the cacophony in the chamber. "You were to report back here a sevenday since."

"I beg your indulgence, sir. Did you not receive a letter from my host explaining I was tapped to escort a mother and her children from Kirith Kalyria to her family in Pedura? And upon my return, the weather became less than coöperative, slowing us down considerably," Menannon hastened to explain his absence.

"I can see the results of the bad weather," Blackmore grinned at him glancing down to see where the rain water dripping from his clothing and blanket was forming quite a puddle about Menannon's feet, "but, no, I received no letter."

Before Menannon could do more than color under the look Blackmore was bending upon him, the Valinga reached across the table to ring a small gong signaling the end of the relaxation hour. The chamber went instantly quiet as everyone hurried to return their games and glasses to the side boards and to leave in as orderly a fashion as they could manage.

The double doors were flung open to accommodate the flood of bodies as the students departed and pounded up the stairs of the dormitory, the journeymen and senior apprentices to the second floor and the apprentices to the third. The first floor was reserved for the masters and visitors. There were no stragglers. While

Blackmore was sirely to one and all, he was a sire who brooked no disobedience and was more than adequate to the task of dealing smartly with any recalcitrant members of his guild, be they apprentice, journeyman or even master.

By the most ancient laws of Aridion, he commanded absolute obedience from his guild and had the right of life and death over all within his writ. He was both judge and executioner up to and including the dealing out of capital punishment. Rarely did he have to use more than his voice—or at most the willow wand—on a miscreant, but he was fully capable of ordering and carrying out floggings, imprisonment and even executions if necessary, although the last such execution had taken place over five hundred summers ago, well before his time.

The cessation of noise was almost unsettling as the chamber now became utterly quiet and any word spoken seemed to reverberate from the ceiling. At a glance from Blackmore, all of the masters also stood and bid him goodnight and nodding to the journeyman, left the chamber. Blackmore's runner, Jondlin, a tall, freckle-faced apprentice from Delridion, a small hamlet northwest of Mishka, was the last person to leave. He gave Menannon a heartfelt look of relief and a grin as he left, closing the doors softly behind him. Menannon turned his attention back to the grandmaster.

Blackmore relaxed back in his seat once more and waved Menannon to join him. He waited until the Giant had pulled up a wooden chair that would not be damaged by his wet clothing and sat down.

"Have you eaten yet, son?" Not waiting for Menannon's reply, Blackmore eschewed the nicety of a soup bowl and simply pushed a large tureen of savory soup towards him and offered him a serving spoon. "Dig in."

As with all the food at the hall, the soup was delectable and Menannon ate with relish. The quality of the food served at his table was of the utmost importance to the Valinga. Many hardships and austerities could be endured for the sake of perfecting one's art, but unpalatable food was not one of them. As an army was known to march on its stomach, so did the harpers' guild perform and perfect on its own. Blackmore had come late to his calling as a harper, having spent his youth as a wandering minstrel and even a sword for hire, traveling to various places across the length and breadth of Aridion and many ports of call along the Dawn sea, so he had a great appreciation for varied cuisine ... well cooked. The hall's apprentices took their turns as potboys and dishwashers, but never as cooks. For that lofty calling, he had of late turned to the chefs of Breikka's Inn, a small hamlet situated on the north road to Blue Bay.

Five and fifty summers past, a stout Dwarf by the name of Breikka had left far northern Starkhad and built himself an inn which soon became famous for its fine cuisine, so famous in fact, that folk from far and wide began coming there to learn Breikka's ways. Thus a cooking school had grown up which never had any lack of students eager to learn and willing to pay for the privilege. The inn had turned from a hostel along the road to a destination in itself and one now had to make reservations over a summer in advance in order to stay there one night.

The whole was running smoothly save for one irritating issue: a feud with the bakers guild, more formally known as the Ancient and Honorable Company of Bakers and Confectioners, a feud which had begun when Breikka started teaching his students the fine art of making sweets, an area of endeavor the masters of the BC's, as they were known, deemed exclusively theirs. Breikka, being a Dwarf, was not inclined to pay them any heed and thus the BC's found it hard to take such insult. The feud threatened to involve the King, but so far, that had not been necessary.

Blackmore sat quietly watching Menannon eat, a relieved smile playing about the corners of his mouth. Until the doorward had run in and announced that the young Giant had returned, Blackmore had not truly realized how much he had missed him nor the depth of his worry at Menannon's uncharacteristic truancy. For Menannon to just disappear without a word was unprecedented and the fact that he had done so was ample evidence that the youngster was troubled, for prior to this he had adhered to guild laws with an exactitude only a Giant could manage. The grandmaster waited until his journeyman had finished eating his soup and washed it down with a large chalice of wine before he spoke again.

"Now then," he began.

Menannon set his chalice down and turned, one quizzical eyebrow raised as Blackmore's voice had taken on the tone of master addressing journeyman, Menannon straightened in his chair and waited his pleasure in respectful silence.

Blackmore cleared his throat and continued, "Ere I send you off to get cleaned up and rest, we must settle things between us. Since the entire hall is aware that you were absent without leave for slightly more than a sevenday and did not send word of the necessity of it when you had ample opportunity so to do, you must be punished, even though you made reference to a missive informing me of your circumstances which has not, unfortunately, been received here."

Menannon nodded, but did not speak, being fully aware that his truancy would have been sanctioned had he simply remembered the little detail of reminding Charina's sire to send that letter. Or better yet, he could have simply sent word with the carters who had brought his sire's crates. He would have been greatly surprised and almost disappointed had Blackmore not felt the need to punish him for his truancy, for he should have sent his own message just to be sure, and he had not. The responsibility was entirely his.

"What shall I do with you?" Blackmore settled more comfortably into his chair again and steepled his fingers against his lower lip, a slightly impish twinkle lighting his eye.

"It is not easy to punish you, you know, as there are very few of the activities in this hall which you disfavor. About the only thing I can think of that would actually ruffle your equanimity would be a few strokes at the whipping post, but I hardly think your small misstep warrants that."

The old man grinned at the brief frown that crossed the Giant's brow.

"Of course, were this a fortnight from now, I would simply assign you to teach the beginning harp classes to the new group of day school students. I know how much you dread that!"

He laughed outright at the shudder that passed through Menannon's lithe frame.

With his perfect pitch and limited patience when it came to music, the cacophony created by the beginning harp students from the local day school made Menannon's teeth ache and gave him a skull splitting headache not five minutes into any such class. He far preferred to teach the beginning apprentices who at least had some skill with their instruments before they were allowed to come to the master hall to train. That the local day school students had both the right and the need to have music as part of the curriculum taught them by the harpers, Menannon did not argue, but he fervently prayed to the High One to let him not be the one to teach it to them! Menannon brought his wandering thoughts back to Blackmore who was still speaking.

"But no. No, that won't do. Ah! I have it! I'll send you down to the alms house for the fortnight."

"But ...," Menannon began, but the grandmaster held up a hand halting further protest.

"I realize that you don't find the duty there irksome, but nearly everyone else seems to and the fact that you don't is not well known, as you have been assigned there so little of late. So by sending you there, everyone will be satisfied that you are being punished and so long as you manage to look put upon when anyone asks you how things are going, none will e'er be the wiser. Does that suit?"

"Aye, sir," Menannon grinned and shook his head at his grandmaster's ability to both mete out punishment and not to at the same time. Blackmore chuckled at his reaction.

"Now get you gone and attend to yourself," he ordered amiably. "I expect you to report to my audience hall at the hour of noon on the morrow and not a moment sooner." The Giant obediently pushed back his chair and walked around the end of the table, then came to stand on the floor below the dais, facing his Grandmaster. He inclined his head.

"Go, go! You're dismissed!" Blackmore waved him away when Menannon hesitated. The journeyman turned then and made his way to the door. Just as he reached it, Blackmore spoke softly. "I'm glad you're safely home, son."

"As am I, sir." Menannon inclined his head once more and left the refectory, closing the door behind him with a soft click.

"Sleep well, son," Blackmore spoke to the closed door and reached for the wine decanter and refilled his chalice. He settled back with a sigh and took a long sip. If it was the High One's will mayhap Gorlanndon would now be able to solve the riddle of Azuron unhindered by worry about his son ere the lad could pass his master's trials and return to Kalyria.

Menannon moved across the now empty entrance hall and turned to the stairs leading to the dormitories. He quickly went to his room and obtained a change of clothes, then returned to the entrance hall and took the smaller stair that headed down into the undercroft. Here as well, the way was well lit with brightly burning cressets. His soft boots were nearly soundless on the flags of the floor as he walked the long, barrel-vaulted hall of the undercroft past storerooms containing everything from foodstuffs and instruments, to all the raw materials needed for illuminating and any other craft practiced at the hall.

Here in the undercroft was the well-ordered work room of Dame Larisa, and her assistants, who undertook to keep the hall's inhabitants clothed and clean. The sight of her work room reminded him that he would have to bring his torn shirt down to be mended. Creating clothes large enough for even a small Giant was something of a daunting task and the good dame would not be best pleased that he had not taken better care of his attire. He made a mental note to add as a peace offering one of the small, unassigned gifts he had brought home to the one he had specifically chosen for her.

Menannon reached the end of the hall and entered the communal bathing chamber. There was no one else about at the moment, so he crossed the dressing room and went directly to the tub room. Here, large copper bathing tubs of all shapes and sizes were leaned up against the walls awaiting their next use. At the near end of the room was a huge water barrel from which one obtained the necessary amount of water to fill whatever bath tub was being used. At the far end was a huge pot hanging over a goodly bed of glowing coals which held the hot water ready to be mixed with the cold.

Menannon selected the largest of the tubs, one that Blackmore had ordered particularly for his use as a present on his seventeenth nameday, and set it on its eagle-claw feet in the center of the room hard by the floor drain down which the water would go when he was done. He tossed his blanket and clean clothing onto one of the wooden benches circling the room, got down one of the large ewers hanging above the water barrel and began to fill the tub with cool water. When that was done, he stripped off his filthy garments and tossed them in a heap on the floor beside the tub, before drawing an ewer of boiling water and pouring it into the tub as well. He stirred the water with a wooden paddle and added another ewer of hot, until it was just the right temperature for him.

He set aside the paddle and took a large towel from a neatly folded stack on a shelf near the hot water hearth. He settled into the tub and closed its lid to keep the heat in as long as possible. Only his head was still exposed to the air of the chamber which, despite the coal bed, was none too warm. This issue he resolved by wrapping the towel around his head. It was a usable method for achieving a hot bath, but it took a great deal of effort. Bathing was so much simpler on Kalyria where even the humblest of homes had running water and automatic plumbing. Though he longed for a good long soak, he had that which prodded at him and did not allow him to relax. After several minutes of trying to ignore the pricking of his conscience he emerged from the tub, warmer and cleaner than before. Throwing on the clean clothes he'd brought along, he left in a hurry, for the prodding had become a demand: he had to know whether or not Giants and Humans were, by the High One's will, allowed to marry.

He made his way quietly to the library and using skills acquired during his apprentice days, quickly gained entry into the now locked gallery. He thought the answer to his question would be easily found, but in this, he was mistaken. A full turn of the hour passed and he had made no progress whatsoever. He was hampered by his weariness, and finally gave up. He would have to return later when he had more time and wasn't so tired. Disappointed, he departed for his chamber.

Menannon slept long and deeply, under the watchful eye of Pin, the stuffed toy puppy who now occupied a place of honor upon the shelf above his bed having been rescued from the depths of his harp case. The sheer familiarity of the sounds and surroundings added to his relaxed state and he was asleep almost as soon as his head hit the pillow.

CHAPTER 11
(SUMMER OF THE WORLD 6996-6997)

THE NEXT MORNING, Menannon was awake early and lay in bed listening to the sounds of the hall as it came to life: the running feet of the apprentices in their great cavernous dormitory on the floor above him, the low-voiced, considerate conversations of the journeymen walking past his door, doors banging and laughter ringing out all quickly drowned in the general noise coming up from the refectory as the student body prepared for the day's classes and work. Rather than coming down to break his fast with all the rest, he gave himself the time to perform his morning exercises then read for a half turn of the hour from the Word Hoard of the High One, both activities he had been neglecting of late. Both things always helped to settle his mind and improve his attitude.

When he finally did go in search of food, the normalcy of life here in the hall had begun to make his fears for his sire and his worries about what might be happening on Kalyria seem much ado about little or nothing. Surely, if things really were as troubled on the island as he had been imagining, Grandmaster Blackmore would have been informed, not by Penor of course, but by Elder Journeyman Davin who was an intelligent, reliable fellow. Menannon was in a much better frame of mind than he had been in many sevendays as he finished breaking his fast and headed out of the refectory intent upon reporting to Blackmore.

He noted that Jondlin was not at the table just outside the Grandmaster's quarters which served him as a desk, apparently out on some errand for the Grandmaster. Behind it was an alcove bed built into the wall. At the moment, its doors were closed, but when he was at his station, they stood wide to allow easy access to the many scrolls stacked on the shelf above the bed.

The twelfth ring of the time bell in the entrance hall was just fading into silence when he knocked on the door of the grandmaster's audience chamber, his sire's scroll, retrieved from the side pouch of his harp case, clutched in his right hand.

"Come!"

Blackmore's voice carried softly through the muffling wood. Menannon opened the door and advanced to stand respectfully in front of the desk and await his grandmaster's pleasure. Blackmore was busily engaged in the massive correspondence required to run his far flung guild and did not look up for several minutes. Menannon filled the time by looking about the chamber.

The first thing he noticed was that the chair he had set in front of Blackmore's desk the last evening before he left for Kalyria was still there. Although it had been cleaned and polished with everything else in the chamber, it had only been moved to the end of the Grandmaster's desk rather than being restored to its original place along the wall. Menannon's attention wandered to take in the rest of the chamber.

Unlike the last sevenday, today the full sun of a fine fall day was streaming in the clerestory and side windows overlooking the garden. Due to its brightness, the curtains had been pulled over most of the glittering glass mosaics which hung on every square inch of available wall space of the lower floor, else the light within would have been blinding. These art works were all uniformly ten feet tall and six feet wide and hung so that their bases were barely an inch above the flagstones of the floor and thereby almost the entire chamber was lined with glass. Exactly what subjects they depicted had not been a study of Menannon's as he had never had the leisure to peruse them having always been engaged in other things when he was attending upon the Grandmaster. He had a general impression that they were landscapes of some sort, but knew no more than that.

Scattered here and there were low tables with large chairs drawn up and high stools set beside music stands. In one corner, the tables had been moved aside and their places taken up with four huge wooden crates. Menannon recognized them instantly as the ones he had seen being offloaded from his sire's ship. Among all of this were two harpers of indeterminate age dressed in beige robes with no shoulder cords busily applying mops and dusters, members of the service branch of the guild.

Finished with the scroll he had been writing on, Blackmore laid aside the spoon-shaped spectacles he had been holding by their crossed handles over the bridge of his nose. Having vision only in one eye, he could have used a single side from the spectacles, but he had never gotten around to having a pair thus altered. Both hands now free, Blackmore rolled up the scroll and sealed it with the ornate be-ribboned seal of his official correspondence and tossed it into a basket with several other such scrolls. That done, he looked up at his patiently waiting journeyman.

"So, are you ready to perform your penance at the alms house?"

His grin was wicked as he glanced to where the busily working cleaning staff was obviously listening to every word said. There were very, very few secrets in a harper hall.

"Aye, sir, but ere I leave, I was instructed by my father through his ship's captain to give you this."

Menannon laid the scroll on the desk in front of his grandmaster and stepped back. Blackmore slit the seal with alacrity and raised his spectacles again to peruse its contents with great curiosity and not a little pleasure.

"Ah! At last, at last!" He sighed immensely and closed the scroll, his old face wreathed in a very satisfied smile. "Your sire is a man of his word in all things, son."

He pointed with the scroll towards the stacked crates, though he did not offer any further explanation of its contents or theirs.

"Now then, down to business. I want you to take these missives to Lucca at the alms house and stop by the infirmary on your way out to take the re-supply of herbs and simples down to him as well. Report to me after dinner this evening and we'll talk."

Blackmore handed him several small scrolls then returned to his writing, dismissing Menannon with a wave of his hand. The Giant inclined his head and turned to depart. At the door he glanced back to see that Blackmore was once more reading his sire's scroll and had he not had to hold his spectacles on, the old fellow would have been positively rubbing his hands together in the excess of his glee. Menannon shook his head with a slight grin and departed the audience hall. He made short work of gathering the necessary items from the infirmary and crossed the entry hall.

Conar was once again on doorward duty and opened the great door for him.

"Don't be falling in with any of the shady ladies down by the docks now, youngster." he said as he saluted the Giant, his face totally serious, but his eyes twinkled with mischief.

"Only the most beautiful!" Menannon grinned and shook his head at the admonition he had been receiving from the blacksmith ever since he had first been sent to the alms house when he was but twelve summers old. It and his response had become a ritual between them.

He shouldered the sack of provisions, crossed the courtyard, passed under the gatehouse and walked out into the street. The gate itself stood open as always, for Grandmaster Blackmore was determined that nothing should stand in the way of anyone who sought council or sanctuary with the harpers. He turned south and made his way through the crowded central plaza of the city headed for the southeastern arm of the starfish and the docks.

THE SOUTHEASTERN GATE was flanked by two life-sized bas-reliefs of sand draktas, their scaly hides represented by the Aridion stone itself as they were sandy colored both on back and belly. Unlike their larger relatives of the northern climes, the sand draktas were approximately fifteen feet in length from the ends of their toothy snouts to the tips of their stubby tails with small, almost flipper-like wings and huge claws. Their heads bore large bony protrusions and eyes that were protected by transparent horny plates which the sculptor had represented with clear glass.

Not one of Menannon's favorite creatures, these statues were, as he remembered from his browsing in the library, based upon the description written down long summers ago by Liiall of Crenanoc who had apparently described them from life, he being one of the few people to have actually seen one and lived to tell the tale, for these draktas were rare, secretive and lived under the desert sands of the Watheran Wastes far to the south where they apparently swam through the sand itself as through water, only rising when hunting. According to Liiall's report, when an unsuspecting prey was heard walking overhead the sand drakta would leap out of the sand, ensnare its victim and drag it back down into the darkness where the drakta then dined at leisure. Menannon shuddered at the thought and said a brief prayer thanking the High One that Lee was not drawn to explore the desert lands north of his homeland.

The Giant moved slowly along, enjoying the sunshine and the fine weather which would soon enough turn snowy and bleak. The thoroughfare, wending its way back and forth across the southern arm of the city, was lined with buildings that contained shops, offices and pubs on their lower floors and the homes of their owners above and behind them. Down the alleys between these, he caught glimpses of gardens and heard the sound of children playing. Here and there, the sound of chickens and goats mixed with the other noises of the city as many of the garden lands also contained small crofts allowing the householders to be self-sufficient in most foodstuffs. All along, Menannon was greeted and politely saluted for the harper he was as well as for himself.

Despite his leisurely pace, he soon reached the end of the buildings and entered the open land which still lay between the city and the river. Here the street changed from cobblestone to beaten earth, delineated by small white stones and medium-sized apple trees that in the spring were a riot of blossoms, but were now bare having just been relieved of their crop. Beyond them, the grasses and wildflowers had taken on the brown stubbly look of late fall with only an occasional late blooming aster to add a spot of color.

Just at the river's edge, another set of buildings arose. These were the warehouses and stockades of Aridion's merchants and the inns and pubs dedicated to the river trade. Here as well were the craft houses of the less savory trades whose smell caused them to be segregated from the rest of the city, the tanners and vellum makers, among others. While their wares were highly sought after, the smell of their manufacture was not. Amidst these were also the dwellings of the poor. Hard by the tanners yardland also stood the solid two story alms house of the Harpers' guild in its own small close and garden.

The gate in the stone wall here stood open as well, its summoning bell brave on the post to the right of it. Just within was a small gatehouse in which someone was always on duty to let in those in need and to keep out those who sought to do them harm, either for sport or spite.

As was the rule here even when the gate was open, Menannon stepped up and pulled the bell rope. The silvery clang reverberated through the air. This afternoon Lucca himself sat within the shade of the house writing in his large ledger. He came out blinking into the sun and stood to his full height of seven feet and slightly more. He was a great tree of a Human, massive and burly, dressed in the beige robes of the serving arm of the harpers though his shoulder sported the gold cord of a Master of the Guild. His sleeves were rolled back from hands that were no stranger to either the sword or the pen. Lucca had been Infirmarer here at the alms house for longer than anyone knew save Blackmore himself and under his stewardship, its folk were well attended.

"There you are now, lad! How was yer holiday?" Lucca greeted Menannon, offering his hand to the Giant.

Menannon found his hand enveloped in a grip nearly as strong as his sire's as the fellow drew him inside.

"It was good to see my father again," Menannon informed him with a smile handing him Blackmore's scrolls. He had liked and respected Lucca from the first and was more than a little impressed with his capability and patience.

Lucca sat back down at the small table in the gatehouse and

quickly opened the first scroll, the one bearing Blackmore's personal seal and read it thoughtfully. Menannon stood quietly awaiting his pleasure. The small gatehouse was basically a windowless warming hut of unadorned stone having but a single room and an enclosed garderobe for the convenience of the porter on duty, though there was a tiny stove in one back corner and a bunk which folded against the wall for the night duty. Despite its size and serviceability, the gatehouse was still tall enough that the Giant could stand straight without having to mind the rafters.

Lucca's low chuckle brought Menannon's attention back to the infirmarer.

"So I see that yer here on punishment duty," he said glancing up at the journeyman with a grin, "though why Himself would consider this a punishment for ya, I don't begin to know. However, as I am cursed with yer services for a fortnight, I shall try to make the best of it."

Lucca grinned widely and stood. Chuckling to himself, he gathered the rest of the scrolls into the breast of his robe, settled his ledger under his arm and led Menannon out of the gatehouse towards the alms house itself, calling for one of his assistants to take over the duties as porter. There were a goodly number of the house's inhabitants out in the yard enjoying the sunshine after the sevenday of rain. There was just enough breeze blowing this day that the stench from the tanning yard was barely discernable.

Menannon glanced quickly at the folk moving about or lounging upon the building's wide portico not wanting them to see him staring. Here were the flotsam and jetsam common to most cities and civilizations, the lame, the sick, the blind, the simple and the homeless. All were greeted by Lucca by name as he moved through his small domain. Menannon recognized a few of the folk and nodded and smiled as they greeted him, but for the most part, the faces were new as the inhabitants of the alms house were ever changing, some leaving as they regained their health, others to move on to what they hoped might be greener pastures and no few into the arms of the High One.

There was a large and well-kept cemetery just beyond the walls of the close, its stone markers scrupulously maintained so that at least in death, these folk were the equals of anyone.

Menannon followed Lucca through the heavy doors of the alms house to find himself once more within a long chamber with a high, barrel-vaulted ceiling where he could stand comfortably. The first portion of the chamber was segregated into an antechamber of the infirmary where each person requesting a bed here was given a thorough examination for pestilence and allowed to bathe and dress in fresh, though simple, robes or tunica before they were allowed into the rest of the building. There had been no outbreaks of plague in Aridion City in over seventy summers, but Lucca was not remiss in any of his duty to these people or his guild. Beyond this antechamber the lower floor of the building was sectioned into three parts: the hospital, the adult dormitory and the dining chamber which also functioned as a workroom. Everyone living here, who was capable, did small jobs either indoors sewing or carving or the like or outdoor work on the home farm. No one in need was ever turned from the doors here, but sloth was neither justified nor brooked.

"Give the supplies to Nunc," Lucca ordered him, pushing open a door on the left side of the infirmary which led to a well- lit storeroom whose shelves overflowed with bags, pots, baskets, bottles and bunches of dried herbs.

The large desk, nearly dwarfing the fellow who sat behind it, was half hidden under such stacks as well.

Nunc, the herbalist here, was the physical opposite of his superior: a short, skinny almost spindly Human with nondescript grey-blue eyes blinking behind large spectacles he held over his high bridged nose and lank blond hair, but the mind under that hair was as sharp as a razor and no herb, simple or remedy—no matter how obscure—escaped his notice. Not a few of the remedies used here were of Nunc's own blending. Menannon deposited his burden into Nunc's capable hands and hurried back out to rejoin Lucca who was waiting to re-acquaint him with his duties here.

The infirmarer led him into the hospital proper where all

manner of folk lay upon clean mattresses made of linen filled with sweet-smelling hay. The long chamber running the full length of the left side of the first floor was separated down the middle with brightly woven hangings so that men and women could have their privacy. Menannon was amazed by the number of folk here at this time and the wide range of their maladies. There were already seven healer journeymen moving about among the beds seeing to the needs of the patients, their silver robes glinting in the sunlight streaming in the windows added a touch of cheer to the room. Each of the young men bore a shoulder cord made of silver twined with aqua marking them as herbalists rather than harp healers whose skills were more for the healing of the wounded and broken rather than the diseased.

"It's the rain has driven them in, lad," Lucca whispered in answer to the look on the young Giant's face.

As they moved along the rows of beds, Lucca again spoke to each person by name and took a hand no matter how hideous the condition of the patient and introduced Menannon to those who did not already know him. Many were blind or missing limbs or parts of fingers or disfigured with running sores but newly dressed. This was the place of last resort for most of these, for they had come here from begging in the streets and sleeping in the hedge rows and hay ricks. As he moved among them, Menannon's heart went out to these misfortunes and in his youth and strength, he could not help but whisper a silent prayer thanking the High One that he himself would never be one of them. It was the same on the women's side of the chamber as disease and poverty is no respecter of sex or race for there were several Dwarves among the Humans, but no Teluri, for diseases such as these did not touch the immortals.

Near the farther end of the women's side, an old lady, who had long ago lost the use of her legs and had thus been here for many summers, was sitting in a wagon chair beside an open window. She was reading to someone he could not see due to the pile of pillows surrounding her. At the sound of Lucca's great growl the woman looked up and caught sight of Menannon walking behind him. She immediately dropped her scroll and let out a noise that sounded like a cross between the caw of a crow and the shriek of a cat whose tail had just been stepped on.

"Beautiful! Ye've come back to see old Meg!" She held up her arms, delightedly waving her hands in the air and laughing.

At a nod from Lucca, Menannon stepped around him and went to Meg's side where he dropped to one knee and leaned down to her. She threw her arms around his neck.

"Ye haven't forgotten yer best girl?!" she crowed in her high, cackly voice.

"Nay, sweet lady! How could I forget you?"

Menannon smiled at her despite the fact she was half strangling him. He glanced over her shoulder and froze as his eyes fell upon the woman to whom Meg had been reading. She was young to judge by the color of her hair and what little was left of her face. Disease had left her with naught but a single eye and a few shreds of flesh. The usual wrappings had been removed for a turn of the hour to allow air to reach the sores. Menannon kept his face straight by dint of sheer gut willpower, but he had to look away and convulsively swallow the bile that rose up at the sight. Luckily, old Meg gave him the excuse to look away by pulling his cheek around so she could plant a great kiss upon it.

"Are ye goin' to play for us, Beautiful? Are ye?" she asked, sounding like a child begging a sweet.

"If Master Lucca gives me leave," he said forcing himself to smile down at her.

Meg clapped her hands.

"Kinra, this here's Beautiful an' he plays the string box so shockin' sweet it makes ye think ye'd died and gone to Kaalamar," Meg said, looking around at the other woman.

This time Menannon was better prepared for the sight and he was able to smile and incline his head to her at the introduction. The name chimed a chord in his mind and he suddenly remembered one of the 'shady ladies,' as Conar called the women for hire down here at the docks. She had been about three and twenty and had a hard though beautiful face and an air of superiority. Some said she was a rich man's daughter who had run away from home and others said she was a rich man's by-blow, but whatever she was, she had considered herself a cut above the others of her profession and had charged accordingly. From the remains of her face, he could not tell if this dying husk was she and he suddenly did not want to know.

"I've got to go back to work, Meg, but I'll ask if I may bring my harp on the morrow. Does that suit?" he ask turning back to the old lady.

"Oh, aye, an' it does!" she crowed and clapped her hands again as he stood to return to Lucca who was waiting to take him upstairs.

Menannon managed to walk back to the infirmarer when he would rather have run. Lucca gave him an understanding and approving smile then turned and led him into the dining chamber and up the stairs at its near end to where the sound of childish laughter was ringing out loudly: the orphans' dormitory and schoolroom.

The orphans here at the alms house ranged in age from babes being cared for by wet nurses from the city to one lovely lass of thirteen who was soon to be apprenticed to Dame Larisa at the hall. There were five and twenty children in all. Here, life and happiness reigned though there were reminders of the disease and poverty from which most of these had come, for even the orphans had their share of maimed, but there was no hint of sadness here as there was below, for none of these children would leave this haven save to be well apprenticed, adopted or released when of age and for these, the future was as sure as it could be for anyone in the High One's world. Those who were released were not just sent out into the world to fare as best they might, but were released to a waiting position, either in the community or within the Guild itself, and their place in the world was thus assured, at least for a while.

While yet they lived within the orphanage, they were learning the one great lesson of life: for those who truly believed in and followed the will of the High One, all things turn together for good. Lucca left Menannon with the children and returned below to his other duties. Later in the day, the young Giant would serve at table for those able to come to it and help the rest who could not, but for the remainder of the afternoon, he was the contented prisoner of the orphans of Aridion City.

As night was closing in, Lucca walked Menannon out to the front gate. Across the river to the west, the last light of evening was turning the mountaintops to fire and the western sky to cloth of purple, edged in gold. They stopped in the shadows of the gatehouse and Lucca turned to look up at the Giant consideringly.

"I know yer willing to treat with the children and serve the sick here, lad, as though you're just an ordinary journeyman, but yer not and they all know it. Though they are perfectly happy to have you spread the salve and spoon their frumenty, these folk would far rather hear you play and sing. That would mean more than any other service you could render them. Bring yer harp on the morrow and let a bit of the High One's light into their lives," he finished with a grin.

"It would be my pleasure, Master Lucca." Menannon inclined his head to Lucca and the infirmarer clapped him on the shoulder.

Unfortunately, it was his left shoulder whose abrasions had been cleaned, but not treated in any other way and still pained him a bit. Menannon's face stiffened for a half turn of a second then he relaxed as quickly as possible, but it was not soon enough, for Lucca was looking up at him with a slightly irritated look on his face.

"So you've ailments of yer own you didn't see fit to tell me about." He shook his head and pulled Menannon into the gatehouse by the arm. "Off with yer robes and chemise lad! Lets see what's the matter," Lucca ordered and lit a lamp with a brand from the hearth.

Obediently, though with slight embarrassment, Menannon unfastened his robe and tossed it onto the back of a nearby chair. He drew off his chemise and turned so the abraded shoulder was exposed to the lamp light. Lucca gave a low whistle.

"What were you doin' to achieve that? Wrestling too long and well with the children?" Lucca quipped as he reached up to examine the wounds.

"Nay, but I would rather that was the cause. Instead, I was arguing wagons down the southern road in the rain yestereve and they nearly got the better of me on that last switchback."

"Aye, that piece of road can be treacherous, especially now its been paved," Lucca nodded as he pulled a small jar from his belt pouch. "Sit down so I can reach you the better," he ordered, pulling out one of the stools from the table with the toe of his boot.

Menannon sat. The infirmarer opened his jar which proved to contain a greenish ointment. He began to spread its soothing contents across Menannon's abrasion. The salve started out a bit cold, but soon warmed and began to ease out both the stiffness from the muscles and the sting of the hurts themselves. Lucca felt Menannon relax under his ministrations and grinned.

"Aye, it feels good," he said, but did not cease smoothing and kneading the knotted muscles in the Giant's shoulder. He spoke as he worked. "It's a concoction of my own making. It helps the healing of the body and soothes the muscles as a side advantage. I put in comfrey to help the body's strings to knit back together, arnica to relieve pain, horsetail to build the muscles back and witch hazel, calendula, marigold and plantain to take down the swelling and stop the bruising and a few other things for good measure." After a few more minutes of expert massage, he spoke again, "Well, I'm done with you."

Lucca stepped back and wiped his hands on a clean piece of cloth he had in his belt pouch for the purpose. Menannon rose and flexed his shoulder experimentally. It already hurt far less than it had.

"I thank you. It does feel much better."

Menannon accepted the chemise Lucca held out to him. The infirmarer waited until the journeyman had donned his clothing then handed him the now closed jar of salve.

"Take this along, lad, and keep it with you as you never know when it might come in handy. I'll write down the ingredients and amounts for you and have it on the morrow, but for now off with you, else the grandmaster will have Jondlin down here after you."

"I thank you again."

Menannon accepted the jar and placed it into his belt pouch then stepped back out of the gatehouse. True dark had fallen while they had been within and the porter was busy lighting the lanterns flanking the gate. Lucca waved him on his way and turned back to the alms house. Menannon saluted the porter, who was now lighting the archway lamps, and took the road back to the city in long swinging strides that carried him back to the harper hall almost as quickly as a normal Human would have made the journey astride a trotting horse.

THE REFECTORY WAS JUST QUIETING DOWN when he entered and took a seat near the water barrel. One of the kitchen staff served him a goodly portion of roast beef, steamed vegetables and hot rolls with new butter. This was followed with a mint pudding so light it nearly floated from the plate. Menannon wondered if Breikka had ever written down any of his recipes, as he was sure that Clarinda would adore such a collection since she was ever trying to find new things to tempt his sire's palate. He finished his dinner with a contented sigh then deposited his dishes and cutlery on the sideboard and went in search of Grandmaster Blackmore.

Jondlin was seated at the low desk table, the doors to the alcove bed now open. He looked up as Menannon approached and smiled in recognition.

"He left orders that you are to come right in as soon as may be, master journeyman," he said, nodding towards the chamber's door. "He's been busy since early this morning, so try not to stay over long, though I doubt not that he'll try to keep you most of the night."

Menannon and the boy shared a grin as both recalled many

a sleepless night of speech with Blackmore.

Menannon knocked once and pushed the door open. Blackmore was seated at his desk reading from the large scroll Gorlanndon had sent him and making copious notes, to judge by the pile of vellum sheets stacked at his elbow. His spectacles glinted in the light of the single cresset on the wall behind him. All the rest of the chamber was dark save for the moonlight coming in through the clerestory. By the soft light, he looked old and tired, but exceedingly happy. Menannon came to stand respectfully in front of the desk.

"Have a seat, son," Blackmore glanced up with a welcoming smile, indicating the large chair.

Menannon took the proffered seat feeling a bit awkward at thus being seated at the end of Blackmore's desk as though he were sharing it on an equal footing rather than sitting across from him as was customary.

The Valinga eased around in his chair and leaned back comfortably. Blackmore cleared his throat then addressed Menannon.

"You left your sire in good health, I trust?" he said as a way to ease into the subject of Kalyria.

"Aye, sir. His health is excellent, but I deem his state of mind is somewhat disturbed. Though perchance I do but read into things my own apprehensions," Menannon replied with a shrug.

"Why so?"

Blackmore studied Menannon, his eyes narrowing, wondering how much of what was happening on Kalyria the lad had been able to divine. The journeyman sat silent for a few heartbeats, his eyes fixed upon his interlaced fingers where he rested his hands on the desktop. At last he looked up, his gaze troubled.

"There is a group of malcontents on Kalyria whom the folk there are calling Doomcriers, the subject of their diatribes being naught but doom and gloom and the rejection of the High One. My father does not seem to regard them as overly important," Menannon informed him with a sigh, "nor does he seem overly concerned with the Queen's new councillor, a Teluri by the name of Azuron."

"Ah, yes, the bald one!" Blackmore nodded. Making no mention of his visit with Gorlanndon, he continued, "Davin informed me of his coming and the fact that Norilendra seems a bit besotted with him. That is to be expected, as she has been a widow for nearly two decades and a lonely heart is easily influenced. Is there aught else you noticed while at home?"

"Only that Master Penor is somewhat less than adequate as the Master Harper on Kalyria." Menannon spoke softly, attempting to not allow his dislike of the man to show through.

"You might as well speak your mind, son." Blackmore's eye twinkled at this delicacy on the part of his journeyman.

"I am perhaps not the best person to evaluate Master Penor," Menannon hedged.

"Why say you that?" Blackmore demanded, not unkindly, but not allowing him to get away so easily.

"It is because I cannot abide the fellow, and should therefore not be a judge of his capability," Menannon informed him, sitting up a bit straighter.

"Now we're getting somewhere," Blackmore nodded, "and why can you not abide him?"

Menannon glanced away and sighed, but the grandmaster was looking at him pointedly and he found he could not answer with anything less than the truth.

"By your leave, Grandmaster, he is a supercilious dissolute and it is beyond my comprehension why you assigned him to the Head Master's position there—or anywhere for that matter," he finally blurted out, coloring nicely at his own bluntness. "I'm sorry, sir, but you asked me to speak my mind," he finished a bit lamely.

"You have the right to your opinions, son," Blackmore grinned at him, which only served to deepen Menannon's blush causing the Valinga to chuckle outright. "You also have a right to know my reasoning."

"You need not justify yourself to me, Grandmaster!" Menannon interrupted him aghast at the mere thought.

"I have no intention of justifying my actions to anyone," Blackmore informed him quietly. "But my reasons are another matter. I assigned Penor there in the hopes that he would regain some of the quality of his calling. He is a fine musician and was once an Elder Journeyman of some note. He is from Sotara and served there well, but as sometimes happens, when he passed his master's trials, he changed and his underlying tendency to dissipation and arrogance surfaced. I sought to send him to a post whose orthodoxy was assured and one which had fewer resident apprentices so that he could have as little impact as possible while he settled down again. I will not set up any man to fail and to send Penor to a busy or difficult hall would only have fed his ego. If a man fails in this guild, it is by his own hand. It saddens me that he has not settled down, which Davin believes—and I agree—is due to the coming of this Azuron three summers ago. An ill-timed arrival, for Penor himself had but newly arrived there taking up his duties only a few sevendays since.

"Take this as a lesson son. Despite all your best intentions, there are times that it is impossible to save someone from themselves. As for these Doomcriers, at the moment I think we need not worry overmuch about them. They seem to be a small cult that is being encouraged by this Azuron and he is not in a position at the moment to do much more than charm Norilendra. I think the political situation on Kalyria can well be left in the capable hands of your sire and the Kalyrian council."

He finished with an inward sigh of relief that Gorlanndon had been able to keep his son ignorant of the worst of the happenings in his homeland.

"Now, however, we have more pressing matters to concern us: preparing you to be a master of the Harpers' Guild."

This the Valinga said with a distinct twinkle of pleasure in his eye. He sat forward and began to rummage in the drawers of his desk. Menannon sat back and awaited his pleasure.

After a good deal of searching, Blackmore withdrew a huge folder filled with various sizes of vellum sheets and set it on the desktop. He stared at it for a few moments as though deciding how best to begin his instruction. At last he looked up and rested his gaze upon Menannon consideringly.

"Now, son, you and I, and everyone else in this guild, know that you could pass your Master's Trials with your eyes closed and both hands tied behind your back even if they were held on the morrow. As a matter of fact, according to Davin, you already passed the harp trials by playing the *Lay of the World's Beginning* alone and flawlessly at that. That accomplishment by its own merit is enough to earn you your first cord. I wish I could have witnessed that."

Blackmore grinned at the embarrassment that crept into Menannon's demeanor at this mention of his recent recital, but the old Valinga continued speaking without commenting on it.

"I know that you are equally skilled at all the other disciplines of our guild, therefore, I shall dispense with the totally unnecessary assignment of further practice and study on your part and begin instead to train you in the ways and means of ordering harper halls."

The young Giant looked a bit startled at this announcement, but kept his council, as he should have plenty of time during his leisure hours to practice and study as much as he deemed necessary, which was obviously more than Blackmore deemed, as he lacked the Grandmaster's opinion of himself.

"First," Blackmore continued, opening his folder and holding his spectacles over his nose, "you will report to me each evening after the dinner hour when your other duties are finished and I shall see to your instruction. Shall we begin?" the Valinga glanced up at his journeyman. When he did not respond, he raised a quizzical eyebrow.

"Surely, Grandmaster, you've more important things to do than instruct me ...," Menannon began to protest, but the curt shake of Blackmore's head brought his words to a halt.

"If your instruction e'er becomes a burden, I shall so inform you." Blackmore briskly dismissed his protest and turned back to the folder.

"The first thing you need to study is the mathematics of a

harper hall, so attend."

With that statement, he began Menannon's course of instruction which continued each evening for the next several months and covered all aspects of managing a harper hall from the logistics of feeding and clothing its members to the art of evaluating the potential of a possible apprentice. The oddest thing Blackmore required of him, to Menannon's mind, was that he memorize the names, background, strengths and weaknesses of each and every journeyman and master currently belonging to the guild. This entailed the study of endless sheets of vellum and a quiz each night in which he was asked to recite the list verbatim. More than once in the months to come, Menannon would find himself thanking the High One that He had blessed Giants with perfect memories.

As PROMISED, the next morning Menannon brought his harp to the alms house where he set it in Lucca's office until he was given permission to play, which was not long in coming, as old Meg had seen him come in with the harp case over his shoulder.

"Beautiful! Did ye bring yer string box? Did ye?" she cackled excitedly, her eyes as shiny as any child's at the thought of his playing.

She rolled her chair down the isle between the beds and would have knocked right into his shins in her excitement had he not caught the chair's arms and held it off.

"Aye, good lady. I brought it," he grinned and glanced over to where Lucca was standing by the door, but before he could say anything to that worthy, Meg pulled him down on his knees and was kissing his cheek, happy tears streaming down her face. As soon as he could gently disengage from her, he stood and nodded to the infirmarer, one expressive eyebrow raised.

"When our breakfast is completed and all is cleared away, you may begin," Lucca informed him with an approving smile.

The news that Menannon would be playing was spread throughout the alms house and yard seemingly without a word being spoken. Never had breakfast been prepared, eaten and cleared away so quickly in the history of the alms house and in a twinkling, all who could had walked and hobbled into the common area. Those who could not come on their own were wheeled in and one—the lady Meg had been reading to yesterday—was brought in, bed and all. Lucca and two of the journeymen moved one of the tables around for the Giant to sit on as none of the chairs or benches were high enough for his comfort.

As soon as all were settled, he fetched the harp from Lucca's office and uncovered it. A soft sigh of wonder passed through the gathering at the sight of it. He sat down and began to tune it.

"Now ye'll hear the High One's own music! Beautiful plays like the High One's own messenger. Just see if he don't."

Old Meg cackled and rocked back and forth in her chair in anticipation.

Menannon struck the first cord and a hush fell upon his listeners. Even the youngest child held in the arms of her nurse, turned to look at him, her big brown eyes wide with wonder. The young Giant always played as well as he could no matter who he played for, but for this small group of the world's forgotten, the harp sang doubly sweet, for true beauty was so rare in their lives that it was almost pain. No musician had ever had more attentive nor more appreciative listeners. He played folk tunes and love ballads, concert pieces and sea chanties. Some he sang to and some they all sang to and some they just listened to as though they truly listened to the music of the spheres. After a full two hours of playing, Lucca laid a hand upon his shoulder, calling a halt much to the regret of all present, including Menannon himself. To be able to bring such joy to another heart was a gift that was given back to him tenfold.

"You can play again after supper," the infirmarer promised him and there was a hearty round of cheering and clapping accompanying Meg's shrieks of joy.

"I told ye he play's like the High One's messenger, I told ye, I told ye."

She rolled her chair through the thinning crowd and laid her head on Menannon's knee and burst into tears. He quickly set down his harp and slid off from the table to take her into his arms and pat her gently on the back until she recovered herself. Then he rolled her back to her small bed at the end of the women's section and helped her into it to take a much needed rest. When he had her settled and was smoothing her blanket about her shoulders, she took his hand between both of hers and held it against her withered cheek.

"I love ye, Beautiful." she whispered so no one else could hear.

"And I you, Sunshine," he whispered back and gave her a quick kiss on the cheek.

Her eyes closed in sleep even as he gently disengaged his hand and closed the curtain around her bed. As he turned to walk away, Kinra blinked her one remaining eye at him over the bandages once again swathing her face. Music and beauty need no words. Menannon smiled and nodded to her then moved back into the common room to join Lucca and see what else he was assigned. As he walked down the row of beds, he was heartily thanked from all sides which caused him to make up his mind then and there to request Grandmaster Blackmore make arrangements that someone would come here at least once a sevenday to play for these people. In the common area Lucca was setting his people to their tasks. He gave Menannon a wide "I told you so" grin and motioned him on upstairs to work with the children where he stayed the rest of the day until evening's dark shades fell without and he played again. Thus was set the pattern of the rest of his punishment time at the alms house.

The promised letter from Charina's sire explaining his truancy finally arrived three sevendays after Menannon's punishment was completed and he had returned to his normal duties at the hall, which timing caused Grandmaster Blackmore a great deal of mirth at his journeyman's expense.

ONE OTHER EXERCISE was added to Menannon's training and that was to teach himself to play a soundless instrument resembling a wooden box with a single row of levers along its face which could be depressed and held down. All Blackmore told him was that the scale of the levers was the same as on his harp though it represented but two octaves whereas Menannon's marvelous instrument bore six. This whole assignment was rather puzzling to the young Giant, but as Blackmore never did anything without reason, he did as he was bid by humming the missing music as he played.

The mystery was at last resolved one fine autumn day when Blackmore called a holiday and bade all members of the hall—even the serving staff—to attend upon him in the front courtyard at noontide. Each master was to order his journeymen and apprentices by ranks on the pavements and remain with them. The sun shone brilliantly over the city, illuminating the proceedings with that kind of thin, golden sunlight which gives great beauty to anything it touches, but provides little warmth. The gathered harpers had all taken the precaution to add an extra cape to their robes this day. Everyone shuffled in expectation as they waited for the grandmaster who did not keep them waiting over long. Blackmore soon emerged from the hall's great doors dressed in his fur-lined cape, his cane clicking firmly on the pavements of the portico. He stopped on the top step to address the assembly.

"Thank you one and all for joining me this day. As many of you know, the journeymen instrument makers and the silversmiths under Master Bellin have been working long and secretly on a special project of mine."

A murmur of assent passed through the assembly, as many an inquisitive apprentice had been foiled in his efforts to discover just what the best wood and silver smiths had been doing for the last couple of months. Blackmore waved them to silence and continued.

"I have a great treasure which has been given to this guild by Councillor Gorlanndon of Kalyria, sire of our own Master Journeyman, Menannon."

Many inquisitive glances were cast at the Giant and not just by the apprentices present, but he could do nothing save shrug, as he was as ignorant of what his sire and Blackmore had been up to as were the rest of them. The old Valinga's voice overrode the murmurs again.

"This treasure was long in the creation and almost as long I fear in the assembling, but at last it is finished! Come with me one and all to the Grotto of the Winds to see it!"

With an enigmatic smile for all and an impish grin for Menannon, the old fellow came down the steps and entered his sedan chair borne by four of the blacksmith journeymen, an honor everyone in that branch of the guild coveted highly and vied for with good natured gusto among their fellows.

Menannon walked directly behind the sedan chair, since as Master Journeyman of everything, he was not really a part of any particular branch of the guild and was therefore under no master save Blackmore himself. The rest of the hall followed along by ranks. They were watched and needless to say, followed by, many residents of the city as well. Whatever the harpers were up to in such numbers was bound to be of interest and few who had the time to spare were going to miss whatever it was and most particularly, the boys from the day school who had been given the day off due to the festive assembly. Thus the size of the army which bore down on the gatewardens was nothing less than eye-popping to those worthies and all four of them took refuge on the top of the great arch to watch in wonder as it flowed through the gateways and out onto the apron without the walls. Blackmore and his throng reached the city gates in a very short time as no one wanted to lag behind on this expedition. With Blackmore leading the way, once through the gates, they turned sharply left onto the side road and moved smartly along towards the grotto.

The Grotto of the Winds lay some two miles up river from the city reached by a well maintained side road which luckily did not require crossing the Ari, as that would have taken several hours to accomplish given the size of the rope pulled ferry and the number of people needing it.

The grotto was a small pleasure garden which had been built by the Teluri for the pleasure of the first queen of Aridion City. It consisted of a natural shallow grotto with a small, but vigorous, waterfall flowing over it into a deep pool which emptied into the Ari flowing nearby and a beautiful grove of cherry trees whose blossoms heralded spring in a profusion of sweet-smelling pink fountains. Beneath these, flowerbeds had been arranged so that, once started, blooming color was never lacking beginning with the first anemones in Spring and finishing with the last asters of Autumn.

The garden had been augmented with but one artificial addition: four life-sized statues of wild cranes atop tall marble pillars, their wings outspread as though about to take flight. The cranes were so constructed as to start singing when the gentle breeze of either sunrise or sunset flowed down the Sythrin mountains to the west and passed over the grotto. They whistled and sang their airy songs as long as the breeze lasted. Thus the name Grotto of the Winds had been given the spot by the delighted queen and thus it had been called for all the centuries since.

Today, however, something else had been added. Between the pillars bearing the westernmost cranes and within the grotto itself, was a strange construct of wood, silver and stone. It consisted of what appeared to be a wide, wooden box resting upon four great marble legs with a row of four and twenty silver pipes along its farther edge ranging in descending size from several feet in length to one small pipe just a few inches tall. The nether side of the box bore a long, horizontal line of levers just like the silent 'instrument' Menannon had been practicing upon. The waterfall, at a much reduced rate of flow, was now diverted into two channels each of which flowed down the grotto's face, one to each side of the strange construction. Facing this side of the box was a tall wooden bench and all about the garden was a hastily built grandstand for the audience just come from the city.

Blackmore softly instructed his bearers to set his sedan chair down as near to the strange construction as the garden and pool allowed. This they did and he stepped down to hobble to the bench and then turn to face his following. The bearers quickly moved the chair out of the way as more and more harpers and townsfolk came into the garden. Blackmore signaled Menannon to his side.

"Stand here, son, while I get them settled," Blackmore instructed then raised his hands for attention. "Take seats one and all," he called out, the grotto itself aiding in his task of speaking as it magnified his voice beautifully. "Have a care for the garden, if you please."

It took nearly a half turn of an hour for all to find a place to sit on the grandstand, the garden's benches and all of the nearby boulders that afforded.

When all were seated, Blackmore turned to Menannon and spoke softly.

"It was invented by your sire and he calls it a hydropipe. I heard him play it once many summers ago in Lornennog and fell in love with it. Now it is for you to play, so sit you down and play. You know how."

"But...!" Menannon started to protest in horror, glancing at the huge audience surrounding him in hushed expectation of something wondrous. "I...."

"Trust yourself, son," Blackmore interrupted him, grinning, his blue eye twinkling with delight.

He turned and settled himself in the chair his bearers had set for him, leaving the young Giant standing in front of a crowd of hundreds and feeling as naked as a babe. He had not the slightest idea how to play this instrument and was in near mortal dread of making a fool of himself in front of the whole guild and half the city.

Menannon ran a distracted hand through his hair and briefly wondered if this would be a good time to resign from the Harpers, but the lure of his sire's creation was too strong. Quite undone by this sudden turn of events, he made his way to the bench where he stood looking at the lever board while taking off his cloak to give himself time to calm down. He laid his cloak on a rock beside the bench, totally unaware that it was now lying half in the stream of the left hand waterfall. Resolutely, he squared his shoulders and sat on the bench facing the instrument. It was perfectly sized for him, but in his distracted state, he did not notice that fact. Behind him, the crowd was nearly as stunned as he and all waited silently save for one member of it. A small thrush flitted into the grotto, perched upon the tallest pipe and began to sing. Menannon could not help shaking his head and grinning at the High One's songster. At least there was some music in the grotto, even if he were not making it. Menannon sat for a moment longer, his hands clasped in his lap to still their shaking, then he screwed his courage to the sticking place and pressed down on the far left hand lever, the one below the tallest pipe.

Three things happened at once: the grotto was suddenly filled with a low clear thundering note, the thrush flew up into the air an indignant ball of feathers—protesting the stream of air that had just blown him from his perch—and Menannon was so startled he jumped away from the instrument, turning over the bench with a crash in the process. The instant his hand left the lever the sound stopped. Menannon stood, his heart pounding and exchanged a glance with the thrush. Well, that was one horrendous way to start a concert. The bird flew off with an indignant squeak and Menannon became aware of Blackmore's soft chuckle behind him. All about them, the gathered harpers suddenly relaxed from their astonishment and began to laugh and then applaud. Menannon glanced at them, then turned a disgusted look at his master before righting the bench and sitting down once more. He stretched a crick out of his back and took a deep breath then started again.

He set his hands to the levers and experimentally pressed each in turn finding them incredibly light to the touch. As he moved down the row the pipes got smaller and the notes went higher. He suddenly realized that what his father had created was a lever operated panpipe, though how the air was being driven through it, he could not begin to comprehend. Upon this realization, his nervousness fell away and the purpose behind his playing that soundless lever box for Grandmaster Blackmore was suddenly clear to him. He was quite put out at himself for not having realized it sooner, but he excused his lapse by the fact that he had been taken unawares.

Now that he understood that he did indeed, as the grandmaster had told him, know how to play this thing, he began to pick out the notes to a simple tune, much to the delight of all assembled. Soon, he was playing it as though he had been all his life and the afternoon was filled with the music of a huge set of pipes, the likes of which had never been heard before in this part of the High One's world. At last, his hands began to tire with the unaccustomed motion and he brought his impromptu concert to a close. When the last note faded into the distance, the gathering sighed and then Blackmore started the applause. Menannon jumped at the sound, for he had long since forgotten he had an audience, so lost had he been in the wonder and delight of the new instrument and its music.

"Bravo, my boy! I believe you just passed your master's trial for the pipes," Blackmore said, grinning.

Everyone else was shouting congratulations at their finest fellow harper. After several minutes, Blackmore held up his hand for silence and ordered all harpers to return to the hall and get ready for dinner, save only Menannon, Master Bellin and five of his journeymen. When all save a few curious townsfolk and Blackmore's sedan bearers had departed, the grandmaster stood and came to Menannon's side.

"All right son, ask away," he grinned up at the Giant.

"How does it work, sir?" Menannon asked even as he knelt on one knee to better converse with the Valinga.

"It plays by aspiration," Blackmore informed him. "If you look closely up there," he indicated the back top of the grotto. "You'll see a pipe coming down from the waterfall above. There is a smaller pipe connected to it, that has one end open to the air and the other firmly in the water. The force of the falling water draws the air into the lever chamber and is released through the pipes when you play. This spot is perfect for the process as the long drop of the water supplies a very forceful suction and thus the vast amount of air available to you. It is both deceptively simple and incredibly complex at the same time," Blackmore concluded with satisfaction.

"As are all my father's inventions," Menannon nodded.

He understood the theory now, but until he had the chance to actually study his sires design drawings, he would not truly understand the workings. He could not resist running his hand lightly over the levers. There was an answering whisper of sound as though the instrument was sighing in contentment as well.

"Come then, shall we return to the Hall? I, for one, have conceived a huge appetite," Blackmore grinned and slapped the young Giant on the arm.

He turned and entered his waiting sedan chair and was borne back to his hall in a high good humor. Menannon could not resist staying and watching while the artisans closed up the hydropipe. One climbed up the escarpment to the top of the falls where he shut off the water supply while another opened a large valve and drained the water from the body of the thing and covered it with a large oil cloth cover sewn to its exact shape and size. The others, under the direction of Master Bellin worked quickly to set into place a strong gate and decorative grating which would protect the whole from the curious and avaricious. When they were done, they picked up their tools and also departed for the hall.

Menannon shook himself as though waking from a dream and looked around for his cloak. He spotted it and started to reach for it only to realize that it was lying in a large pool of water that it's very presence had diverted from the waterfall. The young Giant stood for a moment, then shook his head and, grinning at himself, picked up the dripping mass of wool. He squeezed as much water out as he could and threw it over one shoulder, knowing full well there was no way he could carry it without getting the rest of his clothing wet. He turned and headed for the city just as the sun was about to set behind the Sythrins. The evening breeze arose and the cranes began their nightly song as Menannon felt the first of the water begin to run down his chest from his cloak. With a snort of muffled laughter he broke into a light run to catch up with the retreating harpers. Behind him, the cranes' song rose in triumph. The High One always had the last laugh.

CHAPTER 12
(SUMMER OF THE WORLD 6997)

WITH THE FIRST FLAKES OF WINTER SNOW came also the returning journeymen who were to continue their training at the Master Hall, all the rest having been posted to the various harper halls around the length and breadth of the land. Lee returned with the rest full of good cheer and not a little news of his own. The evening of his first night home found him firmly ensconced with Menannon in their chairs by the hearth in their own chamber, each regaling the other with their adventures since they parted at Blue Bay.

"And how did you find the twins?" Menannon finally asked with a wide grin.

"As beautiful as ever," Lee informed him with a sigh. "Both have grown out of mind since last I saw them. I asked my mother to have the women of the House of Rasid come to the villa for a sevenday so that we could get better acquainted. She was a darling and brought it off beautifully, including an evening of Fox and Hounds at which I was able to partner with the girls against two of my sisters and their husband. It was a wonderful evening." Lee grinned, his eyes glowing a bit brighter with the memory.

"They actually managed to put up with you for an entire evening?"

"Put up with me!" Lee bridled instantly. "Both are devoted to me! They are my jewels!"

"In your dreams!" Menannon's quick reply caused Lee to blush nicely, having been caught easily in his friend's trap.

The Crenanocian really was smitten with the twins, though he was not ready to admit it, even to his best friend. Lee settled back in his chair and turned his gaze to the fire.

Safira and Emerelda were the eldest daughters of the House of Rasid, there being seven and twenty children in all. They were five summers younger than the drummer and had watched him from their sire's pleasure garden each time he came home from Aridion City, especially when he was training and riding his beloved horses. From the first, it had been a mutual observation, for Lee had noticed them dancing in their garden in their tenth summer, just as they were beginning to blossom with the first blush of the grace and shape of womanhood. Lee had been exercising his sire's favorite stallion along the fence line of the farthest pasture and had heard trilling laughter coming from beyond a tall rhododendron hedge. Curiosity had overwhelmed him and he had dismounted, climbed the dry stone fence and made his way through the hedge and found himself facing the pleasure garden of the House of Rasid.

Within, two delicate creatures had halted mid-twirl at the sound of his approach and stood frozen in place for a mere second, ere they ran giggling into the protection of the shuttered gazebo. It had been a brief encounter, yet it was enough to start a slight smolder in the hearts of all three young people. That he had forgotten to tie his horse allowing it thus to return home without him did not dampen the young harper's new-found ardor at all. In fact, the long walk home had allowed him to contem-plate in glorious detail the visions he had beheld, even embroi-dering the interlude with all the eloquent things he would have said had he been given the chance.

The smoldering had been fanned a bit three summers later when, by either luck or familial design, Lee had been home when the twins had turned thirteen. Thus he had been available and had been applied for and allowed to escort both girls at their formal presentation to the Kafiq. Having one escort for two young ladies was unusual but not unheard of when one household had two daughters ready for their coming out summer. This presentation marked the beginning of a summer's-long line of parties, outings, balls and entertainments designed to show the girls off to their best advantage and garner them worthy husbands who would deal with them gently and support them in the manner to which their birth had accustomed them. Having applied to the House of Veriinal, the household of First Minister Viilekoniirac, for a suitable escort and having been approved and provided with one showed Crenanocian society two things: one, the House of Rasid was willing and able to aim for the highest ranks among them for husbands for its daughters and two, that Quiintanin Rasid was cognizant of the swaying of his daughters' hearts and was of a mind to indulge their wishes. This demonstration, that so powerful a personage as the Patriarch of the House of Rasid held his women in such high favor, gave warning to all prospective suitors that they needs must do the same or face a wrath better left unkindled.

Menannon sat quietly watching the firelight play across his friend's face. Lee was obviously equally smitten with both Safira and Emerelda and in his culture that was permissible. It puzzled the Giant that anyone could actually be in love with more than one woman at a time. Attracted to, yes, but to be actually in love with them? He just could not make sense of that. He knew that plural marriage, rare in greater Aridion, was peculiar to Crenanoc and some of the northern tribes, such as the Horse Clans of Cala. While not illegal elsewhere, the practice of having multiple wives was frowned upon among the followers of the High One in greater Aridion as it tended to reduce women to the status of mere property, a thing forbidden in the pages of the Word Hoard of the High One.

In the early summers following the Dim Times when the southern clans had banded together and formed the kingdom of Crenanoc, Grandmaster Gimdaruk had pled the case to Crenoviilek, the first Kafiq and vassal to the fledgling empire of Kalyria, saying that it was unfair to women to force them to share their husbands with others. Crenoviilek had agreed in theory that this indeed might be so, but that the practice had grown out of necessity as so many of their men had been slain in the wars of the Dim Times that there was an excess of women to be provided for and the simplest way to do this had been to allow plural marriages. Now, of course, the clans were stronger and had their own city and the population was more balanced and so the practice could be abandoned.

"Howe'er," Crenoviilek had continued, "though I am perfectly willing to give up my other six wives and keep only she who is my head wife, I am not willing to tell them. You inform them and I shall acquiesce."

Thus had ended the one and only true attempt to change the laws of Crenanoc and ban the practice of multiple wives. Of course, the practice was only found among the very wealthy, as those of lesser means could not afford the luxury of many women running their households and the numbers of children that inevitably needed to be provided for. Lee's own sire had but three wives, of whom his head wife had borne his eldest and his youngest sons, and he was one of the wealthiest citizens of the country.

"So it seems that Grandmaster Blackmore will have to provide you with a villa at whatever harper hall you are sent to, as you will be supporting two wives," Menannon finally broke into Lee's thoughts teasingly.

"I assume I will have to resign from the guild if I marry more than one wife," Lee replied seriously, straightening in his chair.

At this comment, Menannon frowned, startled.

"Why should that be? There are several married masters from Crenanoc among the harp healers as well as elder journeymen within the guild and most of them have more than one wife."

"How came you by that knowledge?" Lee demanded, his hopes growing anew. "There are no married Crenanocian masters here save only Master Beelin and he has only one wife."

"The nightly study sessions with Grandmaster Blackmore I told you about are proving very enlightening. There are all manner of things about this guild of which you and I ne'er had an inkling as we have been concentrating on growing up and learning our craft. In this case, our guild is sworn to provide not only for the harper himself, but for any near kin including parents if needs be. Also, I have found out something about Grandmaster Blackmore: he is widowed from a wife by the name of Kandis, who dwelt here for nearly three hundred summers and was in charge of the seamstresses. In fact, as I understand it, Gooddame Blackmore trained Dame Larisa in the craft and some of her designs are still used in our robes and other furnishings. She was also a fine singer and composer who wrote several songs which have become stock in trade for us, such as *The King to the Castle Came*."

"That's one of my favorites," Lee responded, "but I did not know the composer was the Grandmaster's wife 'til now."

A sharp knock on the door interrupted their conversation. Menannon rose to answer it, to find Jondlin standing there, a very cross look on his face. At the sight of the runner, Menannon colored nicely and hastily turned to Lee.

"Speaking of the Grandmaster, I've totally lost track of time and am indeed late for that self-same instructional session. If you'll excuse me," he turned back to apologize to Jondlin, but the boy had disappeared as if by sorcery, leaving the hall empty save for a passing journeyman who gave the Giant a jaunty salute.

"That's all right, as I intend to seek my bed and dream of a plethora of feminine pulchritude." Lee grinned at Menannon's retreating back as the Giant closed their door behind him.

So, multiple marriage was not forbidden to master harpers, Lee thought with satisfaction. That was good to know, because his love for music and his guild was just as strong as his love for his sire's Crenanocian style home and family and it would have been a wrenching decision to have had to choose between the two. He fell asleep quickly and dreamed of feminine laughter, beautiful eyes, ruby red lips, long hair and soft, compliant curves. He was sound asleep with a silly grin on his face when Menannon returned from his evening's study.

WINTER'S FREEZING BREATH blowing down out of the Sythrins quickly brought a halt to Menannon's playing of the hydropipe, as the gathering ice in the waterfall necessitated the draining of the instrument and its wrapping for the season. The cessation of the hydropipe concerts did little to ease the burdens of the Giant as he had been set to teach not only beginning harp to the incoming apprentices, but also advanced illumination and metal casting to the upper level journeymen as part of their continuing studies. These activities along with his nightly sessions with Blackmore were enough to keep him busy.

Lee had, of course, gone back to teaching music at the day school which he enjoyed immensely much to Menannon's relief, as that meant he did not have to be one of the journeymen who rotated duties at the school. Lee had also been assigned a chamber of his own as was befitting a journeyman and had thus moved from the chamber he and Menannon had shared for over four summers. Time flew as the routine of the hall moved flawlessly along. Midwinter's Eve and it's snow festival came and went, highlighted this time by something totally unrelated to it.

On mid-winter's eve, the mail delivery at the evening meal included Lee's usual missive from his family along with many presents and treats to share with his friends. This time it also contained a separate letter from his sire. Lee stepped out into the entrance hall with the scroll and broke the seal a bit nervously. Menannon watched him carefully for any sign of distress since, like all high level government factotums, Lee's sire never wrote anything unless it was of great importance. Chatty conversational missives were not for First Minister Viilekoniirac.

As his friend watched, Lee read the scroll quickly, then looked startled and read it again then immediately read it a third time. This last time was apparently the deciding one, for the young harper's face suddenly wreathed with a sunlight smile and he threw the scroll into the air, caught it and again waved it around as he did a little dance. At last, he thrust it into his belt pouch and returned to the refectory to rejoin Menannon.

"What is it?" Menannon whispered lowering his head and glancing around to make sure they would not be overheard.

"I'll tell you later," Lee said, then changed his mind. "No! Better yet, read it for yourself!"

He snatched the scroll out of his belt pouch and thrust it into Menannon's hand then returned to his interrupted supper with great gusto.

Carefully so that no other could see its contents, Menannon unrolled the scroll and read the following words: *Greetings to you my son. I have the privilege of informing you that the House of Rasid has asked for you as the desired husband for its twin daughters, Safira and Emerelda. I am even now negotiating the marriage settlements on your behalf. I assure you that the girls are well dowered and Quiintanin Rasid will not stint in his provision for them ....*

"Congratulations, my friend." Menannon slapped Lee on the shoulder and re-rolled the scroll.

"You see! I told you they adore me!" Lee was nearly bouncing on the bench and, with just the slightest encouragement, would have indulged in a little dancing on the table tops without the aid of volnaka.

"But remember, you have to pass your master's trials or be posted to a hall as an elder journeyman ere you can officially wed," Menannon reminded him as he handed him back the precious scroll.

"Once the settlements are agreed to and the contract signed, all is done and then it's just a matter of time and I'll be wed. You have to stand up with me of course," Lee turned serious for an instant and looked up at his friend hopefully.

"If you desire it...," Menannon began, but Lee cut him off, nearly shouting.

"Desire it? I won't do it without you there!"

"All right! Be assured that I will be at your side when you wed your jewels," Menannon assured him and Lee settled the scroll back into his belt pouch just as Blackmore rang the bell announcing the end of the meal.

They all rose and went out to gather their instruments and cloaks ere they proceeded to the city's central square where they would perform for the annual Snow Festival. As they went out, Menannon was not sure whether Lee walked or floated. He shook his head and grinned as he followed his friend. The only thing that would have made the Giant happier than this news for Lee would have been to have received such a missive from his own sire informing him that he was to be wed to Nirna, a thought which reminded him that he had been unable to do his research on the marriage laws between Giants and Humans and which he must do at the first opportunity.

THAT OPPORTUNITY ARRIVED sooner than expected, as Grandmaster Blackmore relieved Menannon of some of his teaching duties, declaring that he should have some time to call his own and that rest and relaxation were as important to one's well-being as were hard work and study.

Menannon wasted no time in repairing to the guildhall library. While Blackmore had intended the Giant spend his newly acquired spare time in relaxation, Menannon spent it in research, which to him was relaxing. Though familiar with the Word Hoard of the High One and able to quote from it extensively, he knew it would be easier to pursue such a study by consulting the various glosses, concordances and extensive commentaries on the library's shelves.

The high, fan-vaulted ceilings of the library boasted square columns forty feet high and the shelves between them were thirty feet in height with three levels. Each level was attained by a spiral staircase at the end of each bank of shelves and had a catwalk along it with a rolling ladder to allow access to the higher shelves.

The thousands of codices and scrolls contained within this massive library represented many centuries of acquisition and included both originals and copies of many ancient Teluri treatises and works of literature, ancient writings of the Dwarves and Humans and even of the Giants, gathered by dedicated scholars from all races and times. The history and literature of a world rested within these walls. The only place to rival it was the Royal Library in Kirith Kalyria and Menannon suspected that even that great house of lore fell short.

The library was a place which encouraged one to linger and absorb the atmosphere of centuries and millennia. Menannon was quite at home here. It was a perfect place to study, meditate and reflect.

He determined it was best to begin with Glamm's concordance, which was by far the most thorough and comprehensive subject guide to the Hoard and the starting point for any serious study of that sacred text. The library had in its collections Glinford Glamm's original manuscript whose unique hand was not always easy to follow, but as Menannon had referred to this volume many times in the past, he was familiar with its peculiarities of letter forms and abbreviations and had no trouble reading it. There were available other copies made by several scribes in more modern scripts, but Menannon preferred the original with all its oddities as it better suited his antiquarian bent. It was not, however, in its customary place on the shelves. He checked the catalogue to be sure it had not been moved to another part of the library, but it had not. It appeared to have been misplaced. He would have to hunt for it.

After several days search, he serendipitously and to his relief found Glamm's original manuscript on one of the highest shelves near the rear of the library. How it came to be there, he neither knew nor cared. He quickly returned with it to a large table beneath a window and began his quest.

He could have removed the massive volume—which at some time in its past had been re-bound in codex form making it much easier to use—to his room, but preferred the ambiance of the library with its massive columns and book-filled shelves. The aroma wafting through the library was itself an attraction to him and he reveled in the wondrous odor which spoke of ancient things. There is nothing quite like smell of old codices and scrolls. Those who love books understand and those who do not, cannot.

Some sevendays passed before he was satisfied that he had, indeed, found the answer he sought and it was very encouraging: the High One had not forbade interracial marriages to Giants! It did not often occur simply as a matter of practicality, but it was not forbidden. There had been, in fact, several marriages between individuals of his own clan and Humans that he had found in some ancient genealogies from the very early days when, as Blackmore asserted, Giants were Menannon's size. It was true that few of these inter-marriages yielded offspring, but that was not important. No, what mattered was that he could marry Nirna! Yet there was that which still nagged at him. Marriage between them was possible, but what might happen if she became with child? He was nearly her size it was true, but his parents and their ancestors back many generations were not. What did that portend? This was a road down which he did not wish to travel. What would he tell Nirna? What, indeed?

WITH THE COMING OF SPRING came also a heightened tension to the hall, most especially among the few senior journeymen who were to stand their master's trials in June. There were also a few journeymen who had come in from outlying halls. Most of these had stood the trials once or even twice before and having failed them, had been assigned to an outlying hall for more experience. Those who had stood them twice before were particularly on edge since this, their third time, was their last chance. Should they fail, they would forever remain Elder Journeymen, which though honorable, was not as prestigious as Master. Elder Journeymen could and did act as master to many an outlying harper hall, but to be only an Elder Journeyman was thought by some to be a failure. Of course, there were those who chose to not take their master's trials, being content to serve in the ranks, as it were. The rank of Elder Journeyman did not preclude a harper from being ordained a priest of the High One or most other posts in the guild, but it did bar him from serving as the head of his discipline in the guild and also from being a candidate for the Choosing when a new Grandmaster was needed. Only Masters of the Guild were eligible and only they had voting rights in the Choosing.

Grandmaster Blackmore now kept Menannon so busy he did

not have time to be overly concerned as to whether he would pass his trials. What worried him more was that he had not heard from his sire since the winter winds had subsided and the seaways between the mainland and Kalyria were clearing for the season. There were strange rumors among the traders about odd ships and black clouds sighted near Kalyria but they were just rumors and could not be tracked down to actual sightings. They were the stuff of My brother's sister-in-law's best friend's brother saw such and such, so I'm sure it is true. No one with even a modicum of intelligence believed such evidence, but still he could not help wondering, for where there is smoke, there is fire, even if the hard facts are elusive.

A mere fortnight before the masters trials were to begin, Menannon finally received a communication from his sire, but not in the manner expected. It came not as a scroll at the dinner hour, but as a summons in the wee hours of the morning from Conar—again doing his turn as gatewarden—to attend upon him at the front gate. It was not yet light as Menannon made his way down the dormitory stair and out the main doors. He arrived at the gate to be confronted by a caravan of six large wains draped in oil cloth each pulled by a team of ten sturdy oxen and under the command of none other than Issilandur himself.

The Teluri stood talking softly with Conar while they waited for Menannon. He was wrapped in a long, hooded cloak and booted for riding the restive horse from which he had just dismounted. The young Giant halted mid-step at the sight of his sire's warehouse manager here in Aridion City, then forced himself to finish crossing the courtyard and bow to the Teluri.

"Your servant, sir." He inclined his head to his sire's man.

"How goes, it with thee, young master?" Issilandur smiled his greeting in return.

"I am well," Menannon replied, if a bit stiffly. "What are you doing here? You never leave the trade hall," he could not help blurting out rather rudely.

The Teluri did not blink an eye at the words or manner, but answered in the same calm tone he had used before.

"I have brought a large donation from thy sire to this guild and by his instruction am giving it over into thine hands to see it properly inventoried and placed."

"What?" Menannon was instantly suspicious. "What ails my father that he sends you for this mission rather than coming himself?" he demanded.

"Nothing lad. Thy sire was in fine fettle when last I saw him. I asked to accompany his gift myself as I desired to take a long overdue holiday and visit my kindred in Lilientharien upon completing this task. He granted my boon. Spring is a busy time of the summer for his business ventures and either he or I must be at the trade hall at all times, so doth he remain behind whilst I sojourn. Is there somewhere we can write in comfort?" Issilandur asked, turning to Conar. "I have a receipt which needs to be signed ere I relinquish these wains"

"Aye, the gatehouse has a fine table," the blacksmith nodded and indicated that the Teluri and Menannon should follow him.

He escorted them into the small gatehouse and lit the cressets for their convenience. Menannon moved with alacrity hoping that he could question the Teluri further as to the happenings on Kalyria after the formalities had been concluded. Once inside, Issilandur took a seat and withdrew a large scroll, sealed with Gorlanndon's seal, and a much smaller, thinner one from the breast of his tunic, then indicated that Menannon should be seated as well. Conar returned to his duties at the gate to allow them privacy.

"This is a list of the contents of all six wains," the Teluri said, tapping the large scroll. "Thou needs must sign for them."

He broke the seal and began to unroll it, but Menannon stayed his hand.

"You don't need to show it to me now. If I cannot trust you to have delivered all that my father intended, then no one in this world is trustworthy."

Menannon reached to the sideboard and withdrew a brush and ink from one of the shelves. Issilandur grinned at his impetuousness and the complement paid him, then quickly reversed the scroll's roll so that the end was free with its lines for signatures. Menannon quickly dipped the brush and signed his name and Issilandur followed suit. The young Giant blew gently on the ink and when it was dry, re-rolled the scroll.

"Keep that, young master, as thou wilt need it to take inventory of the wains when thou dost unload them." Issilandur then unrolled the small scroll and spoke again. "Place thy signature upon this receipt which shall be returned to thy sire anon and we are concluded."

Menannon did as he was bid and Issilandur placed the scroll back into the breast of his tunic and started to rise.

"Now, tell me of my sire," Menannon halted the Teluri with a quick hand upon his arm. "What is happening at home?"

"Thy sire is well, lad, and nothing unusual is happening on Kalyria." Issilandur shrugged. "The politicians debate, the queen grows more fond of her Counselor General, the traders trade and the people go to the circus. And the Princess Nirna grows prettier and more petulant everyday. Some say that is thy fault and others that she is bored and needs a husband."

The Teluri removed Menannon's hand gently from his arm and stood to his full height.

"Kalyria is as she has always been, lad. Now stop worrying and pass thy master's trials."

Issilandur grinned and raised a hand when Menannon would have questioned more.

"Nay, lad, I must away, as the traders with whom I shall be traveling are to leave at break of day, which, to judge by the bird song in thy garden, is not far off."

The Teluri turned and left the gatehouse giving the young Giant no choice but to follow.

Back at the gate, Conar untied Issilandur's horse from the first wain and held the reins until the Teluri was comfortably settled back into the saddle. There was nothing more this ancient servitor was going to tell his master's son. Menannon bowed to the inevitable, closed his mouth on his questions and raised his hand in farewell.

"The High One be with you on your journey," he said, "and thank you for a service well rendered, as always."

"My pleasure, lad." Issilandur inclined his head then clicked up his horse and road back towards the city gates leaving Menannon with six wains of whose disposition he was uncertain.

"You lot pull around behind to the stable yard and see to your cattle there," Conar ordered the drivers coming to Menannon's rescue with a wink. "I'll be around to help you in a moment as I see my relief coming even as we speak."

Menannon glanced towards the hall's main door to see that there was indeed another doorward coming down the steps chewing the last of a breakfast roll as he came.

"Go on in and seek out the Grandmaster and let him know what's afoot," the blacksmith advised and crossed the courtyard to meet his relief and have a word before he followed the wains which were even now creaking their way into the close and heading around the hall towards the smithy and stable yard.

Menannon stood undecided for a moment longer then turned and headed for the hall at a run, intent upon finding out what Blackmore knew about this gift of his sire's. He made his way quickly up the steps and into the hall. Rather than going to the refectory which even now was beginning to fill with the hall's early risers, he turned and headed down the hall to the Grandmaster's audience chambers to inquire of Jondlin as to where Blackmore might be found. The grandmaster's runner was still sitting on the edge of his unmade bed trying to wake up when the Giant arrived.

"Of what are you in need this morning?" he asked Menannon rather pointedly, as he was very protective of his master and did not like having Blackmore disturbed ere the old Valinga had shown himself for the day.

"I have need of speech with the Grandmaster. My father has sent another gift to the guild." Menannon replied almost as curtly as Jondlin had spoken. The runner raised his head and stared up at the Giant, his determination to protect his master warring with his curiosity as to what new wonder the elder Giant had sent.

"He will see you at the normal audience hour, Master Journeyman," he finally growled, his curiosity losing the battle. "As it is not a dire emergency, there is no reason to deviate from the rules."

Menannon took breath to say more, but then his own predisposition for law came to the fore and he turned on his heel and strode back down the hall to join the carters in the stable yard. He found them settling their cattle into the hall's large stable after having parked the wains side by each along the north wall of the barn.

Conar glanced up at Menannon's approach and signaled him over.

"I told them to stable their beasts to rest 'em while they make use of the guest hall themselves. They'll be having to find a return load going back to Blue Bay, else loose money on this deal, so they may be here a few days. Also it looks as though it'll take us a bit to unload and store this lot." The blacksmith nodded towards the wains.

So the carters are just hirelings, Menannon thought in disappointment. There would be no information to be gleaned from them. He took a deep breath, shrugged and moved to the tail of the first wain and began to untie the oil cloth. He climbed up onto the wain and threw back the loosened cloth to reveal stacks of wooden crates, bales of cloth and assorted oddly shaped bundles, all packed with precision and all marked with his sire's seal. Beside him, Conar gave a low whistle.

"He must've sent half the trade goods on the whole island!" he observed dryly as Menannon climbed down to fetch a prybar from the nearby smithy.

Having found one, he climbed back onto the wain and chose a large crate near the tail and set to. He soon had the lid off exposing a great stack of linen-wrapped objects nestled in insulating hay. Menannon set down the crate's lid and reached out the first package. It proved to be an ancient scroll of herb lore penned hundreds of summers ago by Rhindolier himself. Menannon's hands began to shake and his heart race as he looked again at the many crates in this wain alone.

"High One Almighty! He's sent his whole library," he whispered, stunned.

Menannon swallowed convulsively against the fear rising within him and carefully placed the scroll back in its covering, returning it to the crate before jumping down. He grabbed the prybar and wheeled for the second wain.

"What's wrong, lad?" Conar grabbed his arm, halting him, his dark eyes alive with concern as the young Giant had blanched nearly white to the lips.

"He's sent his library and who knows what else!" Menannon replied shaking loose from the blacksmith's hold.

The young Giant made short work of loosening the coverings on all of the wains and opening sample crates from each one. When he had done, the newly risen sun sparkled from an assortment of scrolls, codices, metal wheels and gears, sheets of glass and the taxidermy of a full sized spiralhorn. Menannon set down the prybar and stepped slowly down from the last wain almost too stunned to speak.

"The High One's holy blood," he muttered, looking from one wain to another.

Quite a crowd was gathering in the stable yard, as news of this new sending from Menannon's sire had gotten around the hall like wildfire. There was a festive air among them all, save Lee who had come out to see what was happening and had made his way to the back of the first wain, his cup of breakfast tea in his hand. The drummer alone was in a position to realize that this was not an auspicious moment—he and those few who could see the look on Menannon's face.

"Again, lad, I ask you what is wrong with this gift that you face it as though you were facing your own execution," Conar inquired, greatly puzzled by Menannon's behavior. He kept his voice low so as to no draw attention.

"You don't understand, Conar. My father would not be parted from his inventions and collections save on his death bed."

Menannon turned pleading eyes on the blacksmith then

reached up into the wain and withdrew the gleaming tube of the Long Seeker from its wrappings.

"And from his library, not even then!"

"But that Teluri who brought all this assured you that all was well with your sire!"

"He lied!" Menannon snarled, thrusting the instrument into the blacksmith's hands. "Set a guard. Don't let anyone touch anything. I've got to talk to Blackmore."

Menannon whirled and thrust his way through the bewildered crowd and ran for the hall. Lee thrust his cup into the hands of the startled journeyman next to him and pounded after the Giant. Behind them, Conar climbed up on the tail of the wain the better to be heard and addressed the crowd.

"All right one and all. You've all got chores and lessons to be getting on with. You'll get the chance to see these things in due time. Now on your way."

Conar was one of the Elder Journeymen who had decided not to take the masters trials and was thus of respected enough position that even the masters present took his word and began to send their apprentices on their way. Soon the stable yard was empty of gawkers and everyone else had gone back their own business, leaving the blacksmith to stand vigil alone.

Menannon and Lee arrived at the grandmaster's audience hall almost at the same time. This time, the Giant did not follow protocol in the slightest and simply turned the handle of the door and thrust it open despite Jondlin's protests. Lee stayed a moment to explain things to the runner while Menannon stormed on into the chamber. The desk was empty as the Valinga, who normally broke his fast alone in his chambers, had not yet come forth. Menannon halted in the center of the large chamber and simply called out Blackmore's name at the top of his lungs, causing the glass in the mosaics to sing in protest. When the Valinga did not appear he tried again.

"Grandmaster, I need to speak to you. NOW!"

There could not have been a single person in the entire hall from the deepest undercroft to the highest reaches of the dormitory who did not hear Menannon's words. Lee, who had finished speaking with Jondlin and come into the chamber, was momentarily deafened despite having his fingers and part of his sleeves stuffed into his ears. Menannon waited a moment and was taking lung to try again when the section of the wall to the left of the grandmaster's desk sunk in and slid aside. Blackmore stood in the opening highlighted by the sun streaming in the clerestory. His robes were immaculate and he was totally unruffled by the unusual behavior of his journeyman.

"What is it, son?" he calmly inquired and stepped out into the chamber, allowing the door to close behind him.

Menannon crossed the chamber in three strides and threw himself to his knees in front of his master the better to speak to him.

"My father has sent his library, collections and inventions to the guild as a donation ...!"

"Lower your voice, son." Blackmore admonished him. "You're speaking so loudly I can't hear you. Now, what did you say?"

Menannon forced himself to take a deep breath and moderate his volume as best he could under the circumstances and tried again.

"Grandmaster, my father has sent a new donation to our guild. It arrived this morning under the care of Issilandur, his warehouse manager. It consists of ...."

Blackmore held up a hand, halting him, and turned to his desk where he limped up the steps and settled himself into his chair.

"All right, son, come over here and sit down. And you as well," he said, motioning to Lee. "You won't get any taller standing there hovering at the door."

The drummer made haste to obey him and was seated across the desk from him before Menannon had gotten up from his knees and taken his usual chair.

"Now continue." Blackmore instructed and sat back, steepling his fingers against his lips.

"Grandmaster, my father has sent his entire library, his specimen collection gathered on a lifetime of travels and his inventions. He has even sent his Long Seeker, an instrument he has heretofore employed every day in his business affairs."

A pleading note crept into Menannon 's voice as he continued.

"Issilandur swears there is nothing amiss with him, but that cannot be true ...."

"Why not?" Blackmore interrupted again.

"My father's entire life is wrapped up in those things. He would not part with them for any cause short of his death bed. And from his library he would not be parted at all."

Blackmore glanced at Lee who nodded his head in vehement agreement. There was silence in the chamber for a few moments as Blackmore considered the import of Menannon's words. At last, he sat forward and placed his hands on his desk, his fingers interlocking, and looked from one youngster to the other.

"So, what is it you desire of me, son?" he turned back to Menannon alone.

"I need to be given leave to attend upon my father and see for myself what is amiss with him."

Menannon spoke as levelly as he could manage.

"No," was Blackmore's quiet reply.

"Why not?!" Menannon demanded, rearing back like a hawk about to take flight, his voice rising to near thunder.

"You have too many things to do here right now ...."

"But ...!"

"I will send to Journeyman Davin and have him enquire as to your sire's situation and will so inform you of his answer."

Blackmore held up his hand, halting Menannon's angry protest.

"I have given you my word. Now go about your affairs and take this ragamuffin with you. You twain are to see to settling your sire's belongings into the grain barn. And have the smiths change the locks on the door. I trust my people, but I do not want to tempt any of the boys or even their elders to get themselves into trouble. Once we have the goods and gear properly cared for, such extra precautions will not be needed. Now off with you."

He waved them away and selected a set of vellum sheets from one of the pigeon holes in the wall behind him and began his day's labors, thereby putting an end to the interview. Both journeymen went, though Lee had to pull on Menannon's sleeve when the Giant would have turned back for one more word.

The drummer forced his friend to go to the refectory and break his fast before the two of them organized a work crew from among the serving men and apprentices and set to unloading the wains and settling Gorlanndon's collections in the grain barn. The barn was actually a huge empty hall which was used for gatherings and dances and was called the grain barn simply due to its size and lack of windows.

It took all of two days to unload and make a cursory check of the contents of the crates, matching them to Issilandur's list. As was to be expected, everything was accounted for and in good order. No sooner were the wains empty than the carters took their leave. They had been able to find a large load of wool and a lot of general merchandise in need of moving to Mishka and Deep Delving to the north. From there they would have no trouble finding a load to take back to Blue Bay, since the Mishka wool merchants shipped their goods all over the known world.

Among the rest of his sire's crates, Menannon found one thing totally unexpected: a portrait of his mother. It was the one that had always hung over the fireplace in Gorlanndon's bed chamber. Painted by Julianna herself, it was his sire's favorite. She had laughingly given it to him with the admonition that "Now I can be in two places at once and you need never be without me either at home or in your trade hall." The painting was probably the most treasured of all Gorlanndon's possessions. The sight of the portrait confirmed Menannon's worst fears and nearly made him storm back to Blackmore's audience chamber for another go at trying to get leave to go home.

"Let him fulfill his promise," Lee admonished him. "If there is aught amiss that you can do anything about, he'll let you go. You know that. Now come on. Lets take this painting up to your chamber and hang it there. I don't think the guild will miss this item from the collections."

Menannon hesitated for a few more minutes then shook his

head with a resigned sigh and took up his mother's portrait, hidden once more in its wrappings, and followed Lee out the door. The drummer carefully locked it behind them. It was late evening and the bell for studies was just sounding when they entered the hall. Wisely, they waited just inside the great doors until the flood of students and masters had made their way out of the refectory and into the dormitory before they ventured up the stairs to Menannon's chamber with the precious portrait. Lee opened the door for him and Menannon set it on his bed until they could obtain the wire and nails to hang it.

"Come! I crave sustenance!" Lee slapped Menannon on the arm and headed back out the door.

Menannon followed, more to appease the drummer than from real hunger. They entered the refectory and sat down near the kitchen doorway where they were soon served a goodly dinner of beef stew and new vegetables fresh from the hall's own conservatory. There were a few other late diners as well, so they ate in silence, not wanting to share their misgivings with the rest of the guild. They had just finished eating—second helpings in Lee's case—when Jondlin came into the refectory and stood just inside the door looking around. The runner quickly caught sight of Menannon and motioned him to come. The Giant nearly turned over his chair in his haste to obey the summons. The boy said nothing, only turned and led him back to the audience hall where he opened the door and announced him.

"Master Journeyman Menannon, as you ordered, sir," he called across the chamber then stepped out of the Giant's way and closed the door behind him. Menannon walked across the chamber and stood across the desk from Blackmore who was perusing a scroll, his good eye half closed in thought.

"Grandmaster, you wished to see me?" Menannon spoke softly to get the Valinga's attention.

Blackmore ignored him, still deep in his scroll. Menannon could not help fidgeting. At last, Blackmore looked up and frowned.

"Sit down. You're making me nervous and you're late for your lessons. Where have you been 'til this hour?"

"I was finishing seeing to my sire's belongings."

Menannon sat down, trying hard not to show his disappointment at this summons having nothing to do with his sire, but instead being only a reminder of his studies. Almost reluctantly, he reached over to the pigeonhole assigned to him and got out his work folders. He had just opened the first one when Blackmore set down his spectacles and rolled up the scroll which uncharacteristically, he almost threw back into his correspondence basket.

"Is there aught amiss?" Menannon inquired softly.

"No, no everything's fine," Blackmore replied rather distractedly then sat for several minutes looking into space.

Menannon set quietly to work. Eventually, Blackmore shook himself from his thoughts and began his nightly instruction. Soon they were deep in the workings of harper halls. It was near the mid-of-night when the Valinga at last called a halt to their work and stood up. Menannon closed his work and returned it to its pigeonhole and rose to incline his head to the grandmaster and take his leave. He had gotten halfway across the chamber when Blackmore's voice halted him.

"By the by, son, I received Davin's report on your sire this evening."

Menannon whirled and returned to the desk alert with anticipation, but greatly puzzled as well that Blackmore had already gotten word from Davin. It had been only two days! How was this possible? It was well known that Blackmore had his secrets and this was clear proof of that. He forced himself to stand silently and await the Valinga's pleasure. Blackmore did not keep him waiting long.

"Davin went down to your sire's trade hall this afternoon and spoke with Gorlanndon himself as I knew you would not countenance second hand information. He said that your sire appears to be well and in good spirits and up to his ears in work. He thanked him for the donation of such an incredible collection and as politely as he could, asked his reasons for making it. The reply was so like your sire," Blackmore grinned, as he greatly appreciated Gorlanndon's sense humor.

"What did he say?" Menannon blurted out.

"He said that having all of those things taking up the space in his home precluded him from having the excuse to obtain any more which was taking much of the fun out of his hobbies. So he desired to find a good home for what he had so he could begin anew. He also said that he has included one of your mother's portraits in the collection as a special gift for you as he was beginning to feel guilty and selfish at his having two and you having none. There you have it. Now go to bed and stop worrying."

Blackmore waved him away and sat back down to re-open the scroll which he had been reading when the Giant had first entered the chamber. Menannon glanced at it and saw that it had been sealed with the seal of Gilaria's king, Lindren. He briefly wondered what ill news it bore to so disturb the Valinga's usual calm, but he refrained from asking and left the chamber. Going silently past Jondlin's alcove where the runner was sleeping soundly, he arrived at his chamber to find Lee sitting by the hearth waiting for him.

"Well?" the drummer asked the instant the Giant entered the room and before he even had the chance to close the door.

"Davin has spoken to my sire who says that he simply was doing a major housecleaning so that he can have the fun of creating the collection all over again."

Menannon shrugged and sat down on the edge of his bed to take off his boots, not sure whether to believe his sire's excuse or not. It did sound exactly like him, though.

"He also said that he had sent this portrait to me personally as a gift." Menannon indicated the painting still lying on his bed.

"Parents!" Lee snorted, stood with a shake of his head and left the chamber, stopping at the door. He faced Menannon with a puzzled look. "Davin, you say? How ...?"

Menannon shrugged and said, "I have no idea."

Lee stared at him a moment, shook his head and muttered,

"Grandmasters!" He left then, closing the door with a soft click.

Menannon grinned at their shared befuddlement and decided to let go of his anxiety. He carefully took up the painting, unwrapped it and placed it upon the mantlepiece for safekeeping until he could actually hang it. He quickly readied himself for bed, crawled gratefully under the covers and fell asleep under the watchful eye of his lady mother.

THE REST OF THE SEVENDAY passed quickly and saw the end of lessons for the day students and the newly-corded journeymen readying to depart for their homes on their post-graduation holiday. For those about to take their masters trials, it had passed far too quickly. The trials would start the first day of June, which momentous occasion was far too close for comfort.

The night after graduation found Menannon, Lee and a number of their closest friends celebrating their release from teaching for a while at the Drakta & Stone. The pub was on the lower floor of a two-story stone building just within the first large plaza of the eastern arm of the city, the one guarded by the bas-reliefs of Greater Stone Draktas. The pub consisted of one long, low windowless room where Menannon was forced to mind his head to keep from hitting the rafters until he was safely seated at one of the back tables not too far from the high bar. Strangely, the establishment belonged to one of Aridion City's resident Teluri, one Dorinen by name.

Everyone wondered why he had not built his establishment with a higher ceiling, for even he had to be careful to avoid the central chandelier with its burning candles. The answer was, of course, that Dorinen and his family lived above and given the somewhat primitive construction capabilities used in greater Aridion, he had been forced to choose where added height would be best used and had chosen to put it in his home rather than his business. Then, too, Dorinen was a member of the House of Lyria and thus stood only six feet and three inches in height. In truth, he was but an inch shorter than his prince, Irenos, a fact Menannon had only noticed this summer on his return from Kalyria. Had Dorinen not had pointed ears, upswept eyebrows and worn his hair in the normal twin braids down his chest, everyone who met him would have assumed from his build and demeanor he was Human and not Teluri. There were a few who wondered if he were actually wearing a disguise, but there were enough patrons who had been thrown out of the pub for fisticuffs who were in a position to assure all the rest that there was nothing unreal about this particular Teluri, most especially the strength of his arm and the accuracy of his fist.

There were as many tables crowded onto the pub's flagstone floor as could be managed and still let the serving wenches make their rounds. The place was filled to overflowing nearly every night not only because of the quality of its mead and ale—of which its proprietor was justly proud, as he was his own brew-master—but because it was a great place to hear all the latest news and rumors circulating the city. It was frequented by harpers of every level who were old enough to drink, the tradesmen and shop keepers of the city, the servitors and guards from the palace and even some members of the royal family. Prince Delanorian was a regular customer here.

This night, the pub was filled to bursting with celebrating harpers and a large group of equally giddy traders just up from Blue Bay. This sevenday had also marked the arrival of the inaugural teams of horse-drawn sail barges from Koresh. They were the first to use the newly built tow path and horse barge their goods from Koresh to Aridion City. The whole system had worked wonderfully and they were celebrating.

There was a small contingent of carters at one of the larger tables, who were not so happy about this success since it meant the loss of a great deal of cartage for them. So far, there had been no bad blood between the two groups, but it was yet early. While some of the carters had seen the way the wind blew and had invested a goodly sum of their earnings from the last few summers in sail barges rather than wains, there were those who either from stubbornness or lack of funds had stayed strictly with wains and they were not happy.

Menannon, Lee and the rest had been toasting each other several rounds in Dorinen's good apricot mead when the Giant caught a comment from one of the trader's tables that gave him pause. Lee started to say something to him but he waved him to silence and turned an ear to listen over the other noise in the pub.

"Why'd ya be thinkin' that? Kalyria's always one o' the best runs," a burly local Dwarf was questioning a chance-met friend from among the newly arrived bargemen.

"Well, I was after waitin' at Blue Bay fer a ship to get in from Gilaria wi' a load o' furs I'd contracted to barge up here an' I got to talkin' to Dorlock. Yer knowin' him?"

"Aye, he an' me brother air good mates," the local nodded.

"Well, then, ye'll be knowin' he ne'er takes his ship out o' harbor wi' out a goodly load. Well, he had such a load o' sorak out o' Gormidad to take out to Kalyria. Only he did na do it."

"What! Yer jokin', right?" the fellow from Aridion City started to guffaw, but halted when his friend shook his head.

"Nay, 'tis truth, I tell ye. Dorlock took the Dingle out, but he nay got her to Kalyria to unload. He ran afoul o' the strangest weather an' could nay get near the island!"

"I've been after hearin' others ...." The two Dwarves lowered their voices then and Menannon could hear no more.

The Giant turned a puzzled glance on Lee, but the drummer just shrugged his shoulders.

"Sailors are a superstitious lot and perchance this Dorlock took fright at something," Lee suggested and turned back to their unfinished toast drawing Menannon with him.

A few minutes later, the Dwarves were joined by more traders and the conversation changed to the trials and tribulations of using the king's new tow path.

The rest of the evening passed uneventfully and the newly risen moon saw Menannon and Lee helping several of their inebriated fellows back to the hall intent upon getting them into their beds.

Tomorrow would start the countdown to the masters trials and everyone needed their wits about them, even those who were not standing the trials, as they would be called upon to help their fellows do their last minute cramming.

CHAPTER 13
(SUMMER OF THE WORLD 6997)

THE NEXT MORNING'S BREAKFAST was a much quieter affair than usual as the graduated journeymen had all left the hall yesterday and the younger apprentices were very cognizant of the looks on the faces of the three and twenty journeymen who were to stand their trials, so they all ate as quietly as possible and then departed the refectory as soon as they were allowed. Of the journeymen, only Menannon was his usual relaxed self, as he was convinced that if he did not know his craft by now, a sevenday of frantic studying would not help.

When all had finished eating, Blackmore himself came in and took his seat at the high table. He surveyed his masters and journeymen then nodded to the heads of each discipline starting with the healers, followed by the harpers, the pipers and so forth, ending with the blacksmiths. Each master in turn called off the names of the journeymen in his discipline who would be taking their trials. Along with each name, another was called who would be helping him study. When all had been called save for Menannon, Blackmore dismissed them to study where and how best they saw fit. They all departed along with their assigned tutors.

Lee went with a tall drummer who had been the Elder Journeyman and acting master at Ft. Santir for nearly ten summers and was to stand his trials for the first time. Ft. Santir was an outpost of civilization more than halfway to the northern Dwarf kingdom of Sythra and had thus only rated an Elder Journeyman to lead it. Lee found himself fervently hoping that the experience would aid the fellow to overcome the case of nerves that even now had his hands shaking so badly he had dropped his eating utensils at least a dozen times during breakfast.

At the departure of the rest of the journeymen, Menannon rose to go about his business but Blackmore halted him with a raised hand. The Valinga finished speaking to his masters and dismissed them as well before turning back to the waiting Giant.

"You had a visitor last evening while you were out and he left something for you in the stable yard."

Blackmore's good eye studied his journeyman intently.

"He also left you this."

He reached down beside his chair and took up a large pack and set it on the table, indicating Menannon should come and claim it which he did with some reluctance. The Giant was becoming leery of unexpected visitations.

"Open it here or elsewhere, at your pleasure."

Menannon glanced from the pack to Blackmore and back, then gave a sigh and opened it. It proved to be filled with scrolls and a large codex, none of which he had seen before. He took up the codex and swiftly opened it. It was the breeding register for his sire's horses, something that was irreplaceable should one wish to continue the stud. Menannon looked back at Blackmore and wordlessly showed it to him.

"Who brought this?" Menannon asked at last when he had finished a quick examination of the scrolls. Each one he opened bore the individual bloodline of one of the top breeding stallions or mares. Even Kane was included.

"An impressive gentleman by the name of Paulus Muellen. He said that he and Georgi Grimmaxe and both their families have moved the stud to an estate in Rhonndia on your sire's orders and that you are to keep the master copy of the breeding register and they will send you updates as needed."

"Did he say why my father had made this decision?" Menannon kept his rising worry in check by main force of will.

"He said that the stud had outgrown their valley and needed more space and as your sire has that magnificent estate just above the Great Falls of the Rhonn going completely to waste, the horses were a perfect fit. This Paulus also said that since you are the only member of the family who can ride them, the horses are really of more use to you than to your sire, other than as a hobby, so the closer they are to you, the better."

Blackmore ceased speaking and leaned back in his chair to better study the young Giant's face. Menannon was obviously trying to decide whether this move of his sire's boded ill or not. At last he settled on neutrality ... for the moment.

"You'd best be on your way to the stable, son and see what else is going on."

Blackmore waved him away and rose from the table and hobbled from the refectory, his cane clicking loudly in the silent chamber. Menannon stood looking at the scrolls for a few moments more, then resignedly placed them back in the pack along with the breeding register and settled it on his shoulder and left the refectory himself to seek the stable.

Before he even reached its huge doors, he heard a loud thumping and neighing going on. The young Giant entered the stable and saw exactly what he was expecting to see: Kane. The stallion was standing in a box stall barely big enough to accommodate him and voicing his displeasure to the stablemen at the top of his lungs. One large hind hoof was beating a tattoo on the wooden wall behind him. All of the stablemen had gathered outside the stall to see this monstrous horse who had come unannounced among them. Menannon shook his head and walked up to his stallion.

"Hello, old fellow. This isn't exactly what you're used to, is it?"

Menannon kept his voice low and soothing. At the sight of his young master, Kane immediately settled down and began to whicker soft complaints deep in his throat. Menannon reached up and scratched Kane's forelock, before turning to Deelen, the chief stableman. The fellow was a short, squarely built Borian with ice-blue eyes and hair the color of ripe wheat. He was something of an anomaly here and how this one had gotten to Aridion City and become a member of the Harpers Guild, no one knew save Blackmore alone and all were content to leave it at that, since the man himself was not inclined to talk.

"He is as docile as one could wish unless a stranger tries to ride him," he informed Deelen, "but he will need a larger stall if Grandmaster Blackmore gives me leave to keep him here."

"Find out then, Master Journeyman, and I'll start building."

He looked around at his assistants and the apprentices assigned to him and scowled.

"Show's over! Back to your duties."

Turning again to Menannon, he added, "The tall drink of water who brought him said he was excessively fond of carrots and oats, so I assume you'll be wantin' him fed such things on a regular basis along with his normal provender."

"He'll be your friend forever should you see to that," Menannon grinned despite his misgivings over the horses in general.

He patted Kane once more then headed back for the hall to obtain Blackmore's permission to house the horse permanently in Aridion City.

Later that evening after dinner and a short meeting with the Grandmaster, Menannon found himself free to return to his chamber where he discovered Lee sitting in one of the hearth chairs reading another letter from his sire.

"Well, he has signed the nuptial agreement," Lee crowed before Menannon had even had the chance to close the door. "Safira and Emerelda are mine as soon as Blackmore settles me where he wants me."

"It would seem that you're up for the master's trials next summer for sure, then," the Giant grinned and tossed the pack he had brought in from the stables onto the hearth table.

"Yes, and I hope I face them with better heart than Elder Journeyman Ginks is," Lee said.

"He is your charge?"

"Aye and a more nervous rabbit you'll not find if your life depended on it." Lee almost growled and shook his head. "I don't understand it, Menannon. The fellow has been running his own hall for the last ten summers, yet here he is acting like a new apprentice at his first solo!" The drummer set his letter on the table. "I worked with him all day and all he managed to do was drop his beater every time he attempted anything beyond the simplest roll or flair. The High One above! My first term day-schoolers can do better than that!"

"He is apparently discomposing himself at the mere thought of the trials." Menannon shrugged and sat down in the other hearth chair with a sigh. "Some fellows simply cannot handle examinations, and the more important the exam, the worse their panic is. It would appear he is one such."

"So it does. Now, what have you there?" Lee asked indicating the pack.

"Paulus Muellen brought it to the hall last night when he delivered Kane to me."

"What! Your sire sent Kane here?" Lee sat up straight and stared at Menannon, his dark eyes wide with astonishment. "Why in the world would he do that?"

"That's not all he did. He has sent the entire stud to Rhonndia and both the Muellen and Grimmaxe families with it."

Menannon opened the pack and shoved it towards Lee.

"And he sent me his breeding register and all of the horses' pedigrees to boot. I don't begin to understand his motives in any of this."

Menannon rose and began to pace the chamber while Lee started looking through the scrolls.

"Everyone assures me that all is well with my sire and gives good plausible reasons for the things he has done. Yet it doesn't ring true. Why now? Why does he send Kane here when he knows I'll be coming back there as soon as I pass my trials and Grandmaster Blackmore posts me?"

Menannon kept pacing and wondering aloud while Lee looked through the pack. He was amazed at the how thorough the elder Giant had been in his breeding project. Each line was distinct and well managed. No wonder Kane and the rest were such marvelous creatures. The drummer dumped the scrolls from the pack onto the table and began to look through them. They all seemed to be the pedigrees of the individual horses, but there was one thicker and heavier than the rest. It bore a simple wax seal with no device on it. Lee's curiosity got the better of him and he broke the seal and began to unroll it. It proved to be a very long, very badly written poem.

"Menannon, look at this. Who wrote it?"

He turned the surface of the scroll towards the Giant who came back to the chair and took it from him to hold it closer to the fire the better to see it.

"This is odd," he muttered. "Someone is less than a stellar poet. I wonder ...."

He quickly unrolled the cumbersome object and looked at the end to find the signature. There was simply a stick figure N and nothing more.

"Wait a moment." Menannon looked over at Lee with a frown. "Faeori and I used to write poetry to each other that had a very simple code within it. We used it so that Gooddame Matilda would not know what we were saying to each other. Of course, I'm sure she could read it as easily as we, but it added an element of adventure to our play. This appears to be from Faeori!"

He turned to the large double desk he now used alone, lit the lamp, spread out the scroll and weighted the corners down. He sat down quickly and taking out a sheet of vellum and brush, began to write out what the code would say if this was indeed a coded poem as of old. There was silence for a few minutes broken only by the crackle of the hearth fire and the swishing of his brush. At last he set down his brush and took up the missive he had created. It was indeed a coded poem and Faeori's disguised letter read thus:

Dearest Playfellow,

I hope this finds you well and know that I am also. However, all is not well here. Azuron and his Doomcriers are taking more and more control. He has charged his Doomcriers with the enforcement of his laws and measures. He has not disbanded Captain Firod's guardsmen yet, but it can only be a matter of time as the General Council is split almost directly down the middle with half following your sire and the other half following Azuron. That is not all. Anyone who speaks out against him in the Council is being done away with! Not two days since, Lord Normanus called for a vote of no confidence and demanded Azuron's resignation. A fight broke out and Lord Normanus was assassinated right there in the chamber. One of the other councillors drew a knife and stabbed the good old man. Azuron of course swears he did not see which councillor did it, but he has been hinting that it was either Lord Lonier or your sire and threatening them both with arrest. Mother agrees with him in all things! Even this horrible senseless distrust of your sire. Playfellow, I don't know which way to turn. I'm so frightened. Please come home. We need you here. I need you here. Your sire needs you here even if he does not say so. Please come home!

All my love, Nirna.

There was a profound silence in the chamber when Menannon ceased reading, the kind that rings in the ears as well as in the spirit. The Giant found himself holding his breath and let it out in a convulsive gasp that was almost a sob.

"High One Almighty," Menannon whispered.

"Are you sure you've transcribed it right?" Lee questioned, stalling for time while he struggled with how to respond properly.

"Of course I'm sure!" Menannon growled. "We always used the simple code of using every third letter for the true message. It makes for easily readable code but lousy poetry. The High One help me! I knew he was in mortal danger. There could be no other reason for him to send everything dear to him off the island. He is trying to make sure that if he is assassinated, nothing of his falls into Azuron's clutches. Don't you see? I should never have let you persuade me to come back,"

Menannon snarled in frustration and threw down Nirna's letter and began frantically pacing back and forth across the chamber, his robes billowing about him. Lee sat still, watching him pace, not quite sure what to say or do at the moment.

"Menannon, your sire is over fifteen feet tall. Don't you think he can take care of himself?" Lee finally said, trying to keep his voice low and composed.

Menannon wheeled on him, his words hissing between clenched teeth.

"Of course he can, but the question is, will he?"

"What do you mean?"

"You heard me. Will my sire take care of himself or will he

choose to let them kill him?! My sire is a philosopher and inventor, not a warrior. I fear he will allow those monstrosities to murder him without even attempting to defend himself. High One damn me to Hella! I should be there!"

"You're no warrior either, you know. What exactly do you think you could do if you did get there?" Lee pleaded reasonably, his stomach tied in knots.

Menannon stopped dead in the center of the chamber and leveled a such an intense look at Lee that it nearly knocked the Crenanocian drummer from his chair. When Menannon spoke again, his voice was low and dangerous.

"Were I there, I could at least force my sire to defend me, if he will not defend himself, and in said manner, he would be saved from this mess as well."

"Or he could simply die attemptin' to save his son."

The quiet voice of Grandmaster Blackmore broke into their conversation.

Both youngsters whirled to find him standing in the doorway, his one eye staring at them fixedly. How long he had been there, neither of them knew. They had been so intent on their conversation they had not heard him arrive. He hobbled into the chamber, his cane clicking on the flagstones. Lee jumped up and offered him his chair which the old man accepted with quiet dignity. When he had settled himself comfortably, he looked up at the young Giant towering over him. Menannon was so agitated that, even though he was standing stone still, one had the impression he was prowling the chamber like a wild cat in a cage. There was something about him that had suddenly gone feral and dangerous. Despite himself, Lee edged away from the Giant, retreating until the back of his legs hit the bed behind him, so strong was his reaction to the pent-up anger of the Giant. For the first time, Lee realized just how dangerous a Giant might be, even a small one.

"Come here, Menannon and sit. I would have some speech with you." Blackmore spoke softly, but quite firmly.

Menannon visibly forced himself to come and sit in the other hearth chair facing his master, though, to Lee's mind, his position in the chair seemed rather more like some great bird of prey perching on a rock.

Lee shuddered, then caught himself and shook his head angrily. This is Menannon, he mentally snarled at himself, not some fire-breathing drakta. He took a deep breath and forced himself to come back and pull up the wooden desk chair, though it took all of his courage and his great love for his friend to do it. Blackmore glanced at him and gave him an approving wink which did much to settle his nerves.

Again Blackmore spoke to Menannon, his voice soft, but firm, his very calm settling like a benediction upon the chamber.

"Compose yourself, son. We are not your enemies. Take your time and settle ere we speak."

Almost, Menannon seemed about to rear back and take flight, but then he dropped his face into his hands, his elbows braced on his knees, his breathing shallow and rasping as he tried to regain control. Finally, the rigidity left his shoulders and he took several deep breaths then raised his face to his grandmaster. His eyes were haunted by a terrible fear. His whole body was trembling. Blackmore sat quietly staring at him, watching as he wrestled with himself. It was taking all of Menannon's considerable will power to keep the seat of his hose to the seat of the chair. Finally the silence drove him to lurch to his feet and begin pacing again. Blackmore immediately called him back.

"Sit down, Menannon. I cannot speak to you if you're circling around me like a vulture."

Menannon took a deep breath and returned to the chair and again, the Grandmaster simply sat looking at him. Again, the Giant could not stay still and was on his feet even faster this time than last. Lee started to say something to him but Blackmore shook his head stilling him.

"Menannon! Sit down!"

The Giant let out an explosive breath and rolled his eyes, but came back to the hearth for a third time.

"No, not in the chair, right here at my feet," Blackmore

pointed to the wide hearthstone. "I want you where I can smack you up the side of the head with my cane if you do not pay attention to me. Now, **SIT DOWN!**"

The last two words were said with all the trained lung power of a concert singer and thus had the desired effect. Menannon sat down on the hearthstone and forced himself to clasp his hands about his upraised knees and await his master's pleasure.

"That's better. Now, I came up here tonight to appraise you of a few facts, some of which you have already been informed."

Blackmore pointed his cane to where Nirna's scroll still lay on the desk. He turned back and took a hold of Menannon's chin, forcing him to turn his face to him.

"I have had a conversation with Davin this evening about the current state of affairs on Kalyria. The rest of what you need to know is this: first, all trade between greater Aridion and Kalyria has been suspended, so there are no merchant ships to take you there at the moment. Your sire is rich enough that I'm sure you could find some fishing craft willing to take you east this time of the summer for the seas are usually temperate in the good weather months and spring is well along. You should be able to get there in safety even in such a small craft as a fishing boat.

"But that brings up the second point. My Master Harper in Gilaria has informed me not a full day since that a strange wall of mist has formed about Kalyria and none can approach her from the water. There is some power in the mist that prevents any access. Every ship Lindren King has tried to send there has entered the mist only to find itself exiting at exactly the same place it entered and the captains swear by their life's blood that they did not change their course.

"Third, Lindren's captains have seen several ships attempting to leave the mist and before their fantails clear the stuff, they are drawn back as though by an invisible hand."

Blackmore let go of Menannon's chin and sat looking at him silently, his single eye boring into the youth's eyes as though he sought to read his very soul.

"So. You want to go to an island that no one can get to and no one can leave. Is that correct?"

Menannon nodded.

"I said, is that correct?" Blackmore's single good eye bored into Menannon's twain.

Menannon had to clear his throat before he could answer and when he did his voice was a half-strangled croak.

"Aye."

"WHY?" The word cracked through the chamber like lightning.

Menannon flinched at the sound, but he did not turn his eyes from the old man's face.

"Because my father and F...others...I love are there."

The way in which he spoke those words made them argument, justification and conclusion all in themselves.

Blackmore said nothing further, yet he did not dismiss Menannon. Lee continued to sit where he was, essentially an invisible and silent witness. The silence in the room continued without break. All that could be heard was breathing. Grandmaster Blackmore's breath was slow and very deep, Menannon's was fast and shallow. As for Lee, his was slow and shallow, for he was concentrating on being the little man who wasn't there.

The silence within contrasted with the sounds without, where the bells rang the end of the post-supper relaxation hour followed immediately by the sound of pounding feet as the student body hurried about returning to their chambers for the night, the very normalcy of which seemed to accentuate the stifled anxiety in the chamber. Silence reined in the chamber for a full quarter turn of the hour, while Blackmore wrestled with his heart trying see which was the lesser of two evils: to send Menannon back to Kalyria where he would again become a pawn in the chess game of the island's fate or keep him here and watch him drive himself to madness with worry as the news coming from Kalyria became ever darker. Either way, the risks were beyond imagining. Finally, Grandmaster Blackmore broke the silence his voice low and steady.

"What you are tryin' to tell me is that you'd rather die there with your sire than live anywhere else in the High One's world without him," he said, carefully ignoring his journeyman's stumbling inclusion of others. "Is that correct?"

His look brooked no lies from his youthful journeyman.

"Aye. He and I once swore an oath to ne'er be parted from one another," Menannon whispered.

He set his jaw and had to blink a mist from his vision to keep himself under control.

"You do understand what you are throwing away if you don't stay here and stand your master's trials? If you wilfully choose not to stand them now, you will not be given a second chance. You can fail them twice, but you cannot turn them down when called. That is guild law. You do understand this, do you not?"

"Aye," Menannon whispered again and looked down at his clasped hands.

"I wonder if you really do."

Blackmore tapped Menannon on the shoulder with his cane to get his attention back.

"Do you stand your trials, you have a bright future in this guild. You are the most gifted journeyman it has been my privilege to train. You have excelled in all the arts of the guild and understand down to the finest detail the discipline of healing. You are without doubt the finest illuminator that the Harpers have ever produced and when you are granted your master's cord in all of these arts you will be the only journeyman to have ever achieved this. With a few more summers under your belt, you will be ready to stand the Choosing and perhaps become the Grandmaster of this Guild when the High One calls me home. Unders-tanding all of this, do you still desire to return to Kalyria now? Will you not even consider waiting the sevenday until the trials?"

"What if I wait that sevenday and the fortnight of the trials themselves adding all three to the other sevendays it will take to reach Kalyria and my sire is dead when I get there?"

The young Giant's eyes were haunted.

"How would I live with myself then? How could I justify such treachery?"

"Not many youngsters would say that and truly mean it,"

Blackmore murmured with a heartfelt sigh. "It's tearing your guts out, isn't it?"

"I can vouch for that," Lee spoke softly from where he sat, startling them all with the sudden unexpectedness of his comment, so well had he succeeded in becoming invisible,

Recovering from his startle, Blackmore added, "And if he did stand his trials in this mental state, he would fail half of them anyway. Can you conceive of his attempting to illuminate a carpet page or facet a gemstone for a scroll spindle with hands shaking that badly."

The old Valinga nodded to where Menannon's hands were clasped about his knees. They were trembling violently, hard though he was trying to keep them steady. Menannon colored nicely under the look his master bent upon him. Blackmore sighed.

"Come, gather your belongings and report to my audience chamber in a half turn of the hour."

The Grandmaster stood and began making his way to the door. To Lee's eyes he looked uncounted summers older than he had when he entered the chamber. Blackmore left without another word.

Menannon sat staring after him, his face a study in confusion. At last he looked up at the drummer.

"Gather my belongings? What did he mean by that?"

"I suspect he meant you to get your things together, you big lout. I cannot fathom what is going through his grandmasterly mind, but apparently he thinks he has some way to get you to Kalyria, so you'd best make tracks."

Lee reached out a hand and helped Menannon to his feet.

For just a moment, the Giant stood looking about the chamber as though he wished to burn it into his memory, then he and the drummer collected the few belongings he chose to take with him and put them in his old traveling pack. Menannon carefully took off his journeyman's robe, folded it and laid it into the press from which he had just pulled a few of his clothes, then almost as an afterthought, he placed his journeyman's cord there as well. He closed the lid of the clothes press very slowly as though he were closing the door on this part of his life.

One last thing needed to be attended to. Menannon crossed to where his black harp stood upon its stand. Almost reverently, he reached out and ran his long fingers across its strings, drawing forth a soft chord. He let his hand drop and the vibrations faded into silence. Menannon cleared his throat.

"Will you keep this for me and exercise Kane whene'er you have the time," he questioned Lee softly.

His voice sounded normal, but he kept his gaze averted as he spoke.

"Most assuredly, though I'll have to take him on a lead as I couldn't ride that monster if I tried."

Lee gave him a slightly lopsided grin.

"He'll bide well enough with that and this should be played once in a while,"

Menannon turned to look at his friend a slight smile upon his lips.

"Perchance it might even be able to improve your harping."

"I doubt even your magnificent harp can manage to perform that feat! But I'll take it to my chamber as soon as you've departed and put it to the test."

It was only then he realized Menannon fully expected to die in his city at his sire's side. The drummer swallowed against the lump suddenly forming in his throat. He turned quickly so Menannon would not see his face until he was able to get himself in hand once more. It took more effort than he expected to compose himself. Having accomplished his composure, he walked calmly to the chamber door, opened it with more force than was really needed and led the way out.

They made their way quickly down the long hall past the myriad doors of the other journeymen's chambers. The cressets were still burning, having yet to be damped for the night, their light glowing back from the highly polished wood paneling and pooling on the flagstones of the floor. Their footsteps echoed as they went down the stairs, the echo adding a ghostly third to their company. To Lee's ear, it was as though the footfalls of disaster were following them. He glanced up into Menannon's tight face to see that his friend was paying no heed to their spectral follower. He shuddered and hurried on.

They reached the lower level and made their way across the immense entrance hall, past the closed doors to the refectory, now dark and peaceful after the dinner hour and turned down the hall leading to the Grandmaster's audience chamber. Jondlin's alcove was open, but of the runner, there was no sign, likely gone on some employment or another. The audience chamber's door was closed, though there was a dim light stealing from beneath it attesting to its use. Menannon took a deep breath, squared his shoulders and knocked.

"Enter," Blackmore's voice came softly through the door.

Menannon pushed the door open and entered the great chamber. Moonlight streamed through the small panes of the mullioned windows of the clerestory, lighting the interior and falling upon the glass mosaics whose curtains had all been drawn back. The chamber fairly glowed. The single cresset burning behind the grandmaster's great desk added its yellowish light to the room. Grandmaster Blackmore was nearly obscured by the stacked slates, scrolls and music scores littering its surface all awaiting their use in the coming trials. He sat writing on a great scroll, its large wooden spindles holding it flat open upon his desk.

The two journeymen closed the door quietly and crossed to stand at the desk and await his pleasure. Menannon lowered his pack to the floor with a slight thud, startling an echo in a chamber whose only other sound was that of Blackmore's brush softly swishing across the vellum. This gentle stillness returned to the chamber for many long moments. Blackmore looked up at last and grinned at both of them then turned his attention to Lee alone.

"Not you, ya scamp. You'll ne'er be more than the best drum instructor this old hall has seen in many a generation, but the High One has other plans for this long fellow here. So, say your goodbyes and depart."

Blackmore waved a dismissing hand with a wink which took the sting from his words and returned to his writing to give the two youngsters a bit of space. They stood for a few tongue-tied heartbeats then both began to speak at once, only to falter to an embarrassed halt.

"You first," Menannon grinned, though for once his smile did not reach his eyes.

"You watch yourself, hear?"

Lee looked down at the toes of his soft boots to give himself time to form the words his heart was clamoring to say. He desperately wanted to find a way to tell this remarkable friend just how much his friendship had meant during the trials and tribulations of their apprentice summers together. To make him understand that no true blood kindred could have stood for him any stronger or be bound any tighter to his heart. At last he gave up and looked up with a lopsided grin.

"Stay out of the Cokeyna. That minstrel girl sure has her eye out for you," he finished lamely.

The comment brought a true twinkle to Menannon's eyes. Lee colored hotly under Menannon's look.

Menannon himself hesitated finding it no easier to conjure up the words he needed, so he simply solved the whole awkward situation by reaching out and taking the drummer in his arms in a hard swift embrace that said all that needed to be said between two who were brothers under the skin. Menannon let him go with a nod and a gentle shove to start him on his way. No further words were spoken in the chamber until the door closed behind Lee and Menannon turned back to face the grandmaster.

Blackmore sighed and put his brush carefully in its holder before looking up.

"Ere you make yer final decision to go or stay, I've something to show you and to say to you. Leave yer things, son and come with me."

He stood and hobbled to one of the only portions of the chamber's wall not decorated by a mosaic. Menannon followed a respectful pace behind. Blackmore reached out and touched something that was obviously the latch for this strange door, for at his touch, part of the wall detached, sank into the surrounding wall and slid aside. He motioned Menannon to follow him into his private quarters which consisted of three rooms, one of which was a small ante-chamber which had been made into a library reading room complete with a large fireplace and a low table set beneath a high mullioned window flanked by two comfortable chairs. Upon the table rested an open scroll next to a tall lantern whose wick had been newly trimmed, awaiting it's next use.

The second, larger chamber, in which they now stood, was a sleeping chamber, again with a large fireplace set about with two hearth chairs and a low table between them. Against the far wall stood a tall bed platform of turned blackwood. Beside it a wardrobe and a sturdy clothespress dominated a large section of wall. All of the furnishings were sized for a normal Human, though there was a small set of movable steps beside the bed to better allow the Valinga access to it. The third room was a bathing chamber.

Menannon looked down at Blackmore a bit puzzled. At the look, the old Valinga's face lit with an impish grin.

"Come this way, if you please."

He motioned Menannon to the end of the bed and pointed to the wardrobe.

"Pull that out," he said and stood back out of the way.

Menannon did as he was bid, only to discover an ornate door hidden behind it. It reminded him of the door to his sire's trade hall, only the bas-reliefs depicted not the life of one man, but the life of the world itself. Its surface was covered with scenes of mountains, deserts, forests and all manner of transitions in between. It even had one scene which reminded him of a painting he had once seen of the great ice sheets of Goth. Strangely, the door had but a single handle at the exact height for Menannon's comfortable use.

Blackmore let him study the door for a few moments then cleared his throat.

"If you'll be so kind as to open it ...," the Valinga said as he turned and hobbled over to the bedside table and took a small lamp from it which he lit with a brand from the fire.

Menannon opened the door and Blackmore again led the way, the light from his lamp revealing another, much larger, sleeping chamber. Menannon followed him into it and halted, looking about in wonder. It was as though he had walked into his own chamber at home on Kalyria. Everything in this chamber—the bedframe, the wardrobe, the clothes press, even the hearth chairs and table—were sized exactly for him, though the design of the furniture was strange to him, especially the bed which possessed tall posts at each corner holding the sleeping frame well above the floor and a wooden canopy at their tops which covered the whole. If one were to add curtains on all four sides the bed would become a small chamber all of its own. It would certainly be warm in winter.

"I understand nothing of this," Menannon whispered, looking down at Blackmore, nearly bursting with confusion. "Why is this concealed here? And why is everything sized so oddly?"

Blackmore just grinned at him and returned to the reading room. Menannon followed wordlessly, shutting the door and returning the wardrobe to its place as he did so. When he entered the reading room, Blackmore waved him to a chair and waited for him to sit as well as his agitation allowed before he spoke.

"Son, you have now seen one of the two great secrets of this hall—the Grandmaster's chambers—and you have seen that they were not meant for a Human, a Dwarf or even a Teluri, though one of that race would be more comfortable than the rest. That chamber was built at the same time this hall was built and furnished over two thousand summers ago and it has not been changed since. The part that I and every other Grandmaster use as a sleeping chamber was really meant to be a sitting room where the Grandmaster could enjoy his visitors in private. It has never been used thus, for no one has ever been tall enough to use the furnishings in the inner bed chamber.

"Why do you think the High One inspired the first Grandmaster harper to build his halls as he did? The Giants of his day were already monolithic, yet Gimdaruk had this hall built with all ceilings only twelve feet high and all doors only ten feet high and just wide enough for two Humans to enter them abreast and have three handles when only two would suffice, as the Teluri are only slightly taller than normal Humans. All the harper halls of Aridion are built to those specifications, and yet that one door, of all doors belonging to the Harpers of Aridion, has but one doorhandle. That bedframe in there is exactly eleven feet long. Why? While those sizes would not accommodate one of the inbred, monolithic Giants such as your sire, they do perfectly accommodate you, a normally sized Giant. Yet, how could anyone ever suspect that there would ever again be a Giant born in all of Linden who was of normal size? It has always been a moot point anyway, since there was never a Giant apprenticed to this guild in all the summers of its existence ... until now."

Blackmore ceased speaking and looked out the mullioned window for many long, moments. Menannon waited in restless silence, his mind awash with a confusion of thoughts.

At last, the Valinga turned back and looked up consideringly.

"When my master harper on Kalyria sent me word of his very unusual apprentice, I knew that something momentous was happening. So I watched your progress at home and then I had you brought here. When you arrived and took to all the disciplines of our craft like a seal enjoying a spring ice slide, I suspected that indeed the High One had plans for you. Then, in your seventeenth summer, the impossible happened. You reached nine feet and stopped growing. Beyond all hope, our world was once again home to a normal Giant! Why do you think you were allowed to take any classes you chose, even the healing classes though the High One did not gift you with the art of healing? Why do you think the masters here volunteered to tutor you when you ran out of class hours in the day?"

Blackmore halted staring at him.

"I know not," Menannon whispered at last when the silence was becoming oppressive.

He was not sure he really wanted to know the answers to those questions. Something inside him told him he was on the brink of a mystery, one that concerned him, and he was afraid of what it might portend.

Blackmore continued almost as though he spoke to himself.

"There is something for which this hall has been waiting for over two thousand summers. The coming of its Giant! A Giant who can stride these halls with dignity, who neither has to stoop nor kneel to be comfortable here. A Giant fit for our world and all that is in it.

"I'm old Menannon, far older than normal for my folk and I've seen enough of this world to fear for our Guild and all of our folk. Times are changing. When Kalyria falls—and she will—the old order will be swept away and a new world will grow upon the ruins. The Teluri are retreating into their own realms and the Giants have long since turned their backs upon the rest of us. The Dwarves are active enough, but their interest is in trading and smithing, not the arts, history and teaching. That leaves only the Humans to shape this new age of ours. I'm a Valinga and have both Human and Dwarf blood in my veins and I know both my folk. Our memories are short and our past easily forgotten. Our great men have their hour upon the scene, then they fade and within a generation or less, they're forgotten and their grand plans and brilliant ideas disappear beneath the weight of the next grand plan and brilliant idea. And so it ever goes with the works of Humans and Dwarves." He turned his single eye back to look squarely at Menannon.

"The youth of our world is over. I want to die with the comfort of knowing that someone is at the helm of our guild who will be able to guide it and give it stability for many long summers to come."

"Should not that honor fall to the finest master of his generation as it always has? Such men have always done well guiding our guild, through the desire to do what is right in the eyes of the High One."

Menannon's voice was very soft, but in the stillness it almost echoed.

"Meaning Master Oliinier?

"Yes."

"I agree Master Oliinier would be an exemplary Grandmaster in ordinary times, for he is intelligent, highly skilled and canny, but these are not ordinary times. These are times of change and sudden upheaval. These times need clear thinking and careful planning so that what is good from the old order will not be lost. We do not need just an intelligent, highly skilled, canny person to follow me as Grandmaster of this guild. We need someone who is far more than that: a person who can build bridges and adapt to change not be swept along by it. The Harpers' Guild is the repository for the arts, the lore, the laws—all of the accumulated knowledge of this world and it needs to be helmed by someone to whom those things are living, breathing disciplines, not just dusty relics of a by-gone age. And that someone, my dearest Master Journeyman-Jack, is you."

"Me?!" Menannon was truly and utterly stunned, as his fears were being proven well-founded.

The old man chuckled softly at the total confusion writ large on his journeyman's face.

"I ask again. Why do you think all of this was built the way it was? It was built for you, my magnificent nine-foot tall Giant. The High One has prepared this guild for you and sent you to it at this hour because you are exactly the person who can guard and guide His harpers into this new age. You have the talents, the knowledge, the depth of mind, the fortitude and most importantly, the life-span that our guild so desperately needs. The hour of the Giants has come, the call gone forth. Will you answer it?"

The silence in the small chamber was smothering as Menannon wrestled with his conscience. What he had feared was not just a Mystery, but Fate, and his conscience rebelled at the implications. His sire needed him. Faeori needed him. His guild needed him. Whose need was greater? Events and hopes seemed to be gathering about him like gulls about a fishing fleet. He was beginning to feel like a lone rock in the midst of a troubled sea, but what could a rock do against the sea, save endure for a time?

Blackmore sat quietly watching him, seeing the indecision and pain wash over his mobile face. As he watched, the old Valinga nodded to himself and took a folded piece of vellum out of his belt pouch and held it in his lap.

At last, Menannon stood and walked over to the window. As did the window in the audience chamber, it opened onto a view of the inner garden with its great bench under the cherry tree. The bench was nearly beneath the window, so close he could almost touch it. The moon shone full upon it causing shadows to dance across it as the soft breath of the night wind blew through the branches of the tree making them sway gently back and forth, casting the bench into darkness, then revealing it in flashes of silver light. It seemed to mock him, thus offering itself and then withdrawing as though daring him to take it. *I am The Seat of the High One's Men* it seemed to be saying to him. *Are you one of them? Are you fit to be Grandmaster of this guild?* Lee had hinted at such a thing the night before they had left Kalyria and now Grandmaster Blackmore had said it straight out. He tried with all his heart to envision himself seated on that moonlit bench wearing the robes of the Grandmaster Harper, but all he could see was a vision of his father looking back at him with accusing eyes. He knew as well as he had ever known anything in his life that should he stay here, and should his father and Faeori be lost to the darkness that was devouring Kalyria, he would never be able to live with himself. On the instant that thought entered his mind, a cloud scudded across the moon, plunging the bench and its garden into shadow. Cold fingers seemed to creep up his spine and a shudder passed through his lithe frame. He turned hurriedly back to face Blackmore.

"I'm sorry Grandmaster. I cannot stay. I owe my Guild my allegiance, but I owe my father my life," Menannon nearly whispered.

Not to mention Faeori, my heart. The thought remained unspoken, but from the look in the Valinga's eye, his master knew it.

Blackmore cocked his head to one side and considered his very conflicted journeyman.

"I knew even as you walked into my audience hall this night what your answer would be, but the question had to be asked and the choice made. Come. Time is short and we must get you to Kalyria while the way is still open. Gather your things."

Blackmore stood and led the way back into the audience hall. He hobbled to the far wall and up to a magnificent mosaic depicting a golden city rising from the sea. It seemed to glow with its own inner light.

Menannon retrieved his pack and came to join him, not quite sure what was going on. He instantly recognized the city in the mosaic. It was Kirith Kalyria, but why were they now standing in front of a piece of artwork, glorious though it was?

Blackmore thrust the folded vellum he had been holding into the Giant's hand and spoke without looking up.

"That contains the word of command which will open the gate in the harper hall on Kalyria and the step pattern you must walk to return here. Now listen carefully, for your very life depends upon your following my directions to the letter. You are going to tread the Straight Paths to Kalyria."

Blackmore held up his hand, halting Menannon's half-formed question and continued as though there had been no interruption.

"The Straight Paths are a series of mystical trails which tie together every harper hall in Aridion and all of the Teluri realms as well. They are reached through a series of gates such as this one."

He indicated the mosaic before them.

"The whole network was created by the Teluri at the request of Gimdaruk. Three of the kings of the ancient Teluri houses—Liliénthar, Tanguroth and Gilarian—designed the gates and the Straight Paths between them. Tanguroth could not resist turning the gates into beautiful works of art, as it was not in his nature to create anything purely functional, hence each gate here is a magnificent mosaic depicting the destination to which it leads."

Blackmore waved his hand to include all of the walls of the

audience hall, indicating the exquisite mosaics.

"While the Teluri kings and their High King can travel between their realms and this place, only the Grandmaster Harper and those whom he himself teaches know all the secrets of the Straight Paths and the words of command used to open their gates and can travel wheresoever they desire through these gates. This is the second great secret of the Harpers and a sacred responsibility with which I am burdening you, son. I've instructed none of my masters as to their use, nor even of their existence, so you are the only person alive other than the Teluri kings and myself who know of the Paths and will be able to use them."

Blackmore raised his hand and spoke a word of command and the mosaic before them split down the middle and ground open allowing fierce cobalt light to flood the audience chamber. Instinctively, Menannon threw up his arm, shielding his eyes from the light.

"You'll get used to it," Blackmore informed him. "Now, you must enter the gate and walk four paces forward and don't worry that your strides are longer than mine. The Paths seem able to take size into account, for no matter what the stride length, the patterns are always the same. Turn left and go four more paces then walk widdershins. Turn dul deiseil and go four more paces then turn tuathal and go six paces then you will find yourself in front of the gate to Kalyria's harper hall. Take one pace straight towards it and it will open for you. Remember, you must keep the pattern clear in your mind, else you could end up anywhere in all Aridion or nowhere, unable to go forwards or back, lost for all eternity unless you are found by accident. Should you desire to bring anyone with you, they must hold tightly to you and then they will be able to move along the Paths as well. Now go and the High One go with you."

Blackmore stepped back so that Menannon had clear access to the gateway. He hesitated a moment.

"Grandmaster … I …" he began, but Blackmore cut him off with a shake of his head and a slight smile.

"Someday, the High One willing, we will face each other

again, but for now, go and give my regards to your sire … and the others."

Menannon entered the light and the gate closed behind him leaving the room far emptier than it looked.

"Ay, me! How long will be the hours until your return?" Blackmore whispered to the closed gate.

Menannon held in his mind the pattern given him with a fierce concentration. He could see nothing as he walked along, surrounded as he was in a fiercely radiant nimbus of cobalt light characteristic of the Mythrian magic which made the Paths work. His eyes ached and teared with the radiance. He had the impression of other paths intersecting with the one he trod, but he paid them no heed and soon found himself facing a large metal gate whose surface was incised with ancient runes of power. In its exact middle was carven the word Kalyria. He halted uncertainly, facing the gate. As he stood there, he could almost hear Blackmore speaking softly, *There is a choice. You can still turn back, the way is on the vellum I gave you.*

"No, Master, there is no choice. I must go to them and do what I can, though it cost me my life," he whispered aloud and took the fateful last step.

CHAPTER 14
(SUMMER OF THE WORLD 6097)

MENANNON STEPPED FORWARD into the unknown. The gate cracked down the middle and ground open. He stepped through and it closed behind him, shutting out the cobalt light, leaving him almost blinded in a chamber dark and silent.

A quick glance around revealed he had emerged in the sanctuary deep within the solid stone walls of Kalyria's harper hall. There were no openings to the world outside, and it was lit only by the vigil lamp hanging above the high altar, its light almost lost within the groin of the great vault above it. For all the warning of his heart, the presence of the High One's consecration created a peaceful hush in the great chamber and calmed his fears for the nonce. As long as the vigil lamp burned, nothing truly evil could enter this place.

He looked about and found nothing amiss. The sanctuary was just as he remembered it from his apprentice days here. There was a small side door almost hidden in back of the titular throne set behind the high altar for the use of the priest officiating at the services. This door led to, among other places, a tunnel built into the very wall of the sanctuary and thence to the rear of the building hard by the east side of the Kidron Gorge. Were he ever in need of total secrecy in entering or exiting the harper hall, that is the way he would use, but for now, he did not wish to call any attention to it and so chose to leave the hall in the normal manner.

He bowed to the lamp acknowledging the High One, silently asking for His protection and guidance and thanking Him for bringing him back to Kalyria. Now he must seek out his sire and satisfy himself that all was well with him. If all was not well …nothing would be able to protect Azuron. With that resolve burning in his heart, Menannon turned and hurried to the chamber doors. There he halted and listened intently. There was no sound from without.

Kalyria's harper hall was a day school which housed very few members of the guild itself. Only the Master, his few journeymen and serving men actually dwelt in the hall, as most of the students and apprentices returned to their parents' homes at the end of the day. The few exceptions to this were the small group of students from the outlying villages of the island. These boys alone slept in the dormitory wing.

The young Giant eased open the door to find the outer hall deserted, though there was the sound of a low-voiced conversation coming from around a sharp curve in the corridor which led to the classroom wing. He quickly darted across the hall and out the front doors into the shadows of the tall pillars supporting the portico. He was just in time, for the door had barely closed when the sound of feet could be heard just beyond it and the panel nearest him began to swing open.

Two figures emerged—one a harper in full robes, Elder Journeyman Davin, and the other a workman in the cotte and leather apron of a tanner. Menannon willed himself to be unseen in his shadow and watched as the twain passed down the wide front steps, made their way across the close and disappeared out of the gate into the surrounding night. He breathed a small prayer of thanks and set himself to follow in their footsteps as silently as only a Giant can.

His stomach tightening into knots again, Menannon hurried silently up the Idrian way and across the connecting bridge to the Citadel. The thought that he would soon be in his sire's presence after all these months of uncertainty lent wings to his feet. He halted in the shadows of the bridge's guy rope pylons, wondering which was the safer course...to follow the King's road on up to the top of the Citadel or stay on the thoroughfare and cross the hill's face past the humbler shops and homes gracing its sides? He needed to reach his sire's villa unseen. Despite the lateness of the hour there were lights aplenty at scattered points along the thoroughfare. Though there would be actual guards on duty at the Citadel's crown there would be fewer eyes to stray in his direction as the wealthy watched not the darkness without for their store of gossip and information. They were their own source of such entertainment and thus sought no farther than their own villas. Of what interest to them was a lone figure striding along in the night. Menannon turned right and set his course upward.

Careful not rouse the attention of the doorwards on duty at the font of the Council Hall, he halted at its back corner and looked down towards the harbor. The city was alight as usual with no lack of movement along the lower streets and near the docks, but the sounds of the night were hushed as if enfolded in a heavy, muffling cloak. Menannon looked beyond, to the twin towers of the Crescent to see their lights shining bravely into the darkness, but beyond them there was no sign of the strange, all-encompassing mist of which Grandmaster Blackmore had spoken. Above, the sky blazed with the stars of the Bridge. Menannon was puzzled, for he expected the mist to be as visible from the island as it was from the sea, yet it was not.

Menannon quickly crossed the plaza, allowing himself only one quick glance at Nirna's darkened window. Tomorrow, he promised himself. Tomorrow would he call upon her and tell her the joyous results of his researches on their behalf. He had to force himself not to throw pebbles at her shutters now and blurt out his news.

Resolutely he forced himself to turn away, cross the plaza and run lightly along the Mathematical Bridge to the Equian and up the road towards his sire's villa, his pack bumping against his shoulder. The night was so still he could hear the passage of small animals through the bushes along his path and the muted sound of voices coming from the gardens behind the walls of the villas he passed, not unusual for this area of the city was normally peaceful at night. Yet there was a quality to the silence that was rather more like the muffled, waiting stillness before a storm.

Menannon quickened his pace. At the last corner below his sire's villa, he halted and listened. At first, he heard nothing save the beating of his own heart. He forced his senses past himself into the darkness beyond. Then he heard it: breathing and slight movement, a foot turning against gravel, sounds quickly hushed. There were others abroad this night watching Gorlanndon's villa for some purpose of their own, one which could not but bode ill for his sire.

At this thought, his heart began to pound painfully as his sense of dread increased. How could all be well with his sire if there were watchers in the night? Forcing himself to breathe lightly so that the sound did not carry, Menannon eased back away from the curve in the road and slipped into the bushes between two ancient walled gardens and circled around his sire's villa keeping well below the wall. It took him the better part of a half turn of the hour to reach the back wall hard by the hill enclosed within. Even here, there were parties of armed men stretched full length on the ground, watching the walls. Almost he stepped on one such, though by the High One's blessing, the monotony of the night had had its way with the fellow and he was snoring softly.

Forcing his racing heart to still, Menannon stepped over the prostrate figure and continued on until he reached the lowest spot in the wall and felt its face for a small line of shallow toe holds which made a set of crude stairs to the top. He had himself in his childhood chiseled them to ease his re-entry into his sire's villa when he had gone exploring without his sire's knowledge. The holes that had served well enough for the foot of a six-summers old child were barely adequate for the toes of that self-same child now grown. It was a chancy thing, but he made it and managed to roll soundlessly onto the top of the wall where he lay still once again, forcing himself to listen for sounds beyond the pounding of his heart.

Within were only normal sounds, a smattering of laughter coming from the kitchen where the scullery servants would be finishing up getting the kitchen ready for tomorrow's work. The rest of the house was dark and silent, the household having retired for the night. Menannon was struck by the difference in time between Aridion City, where it had been evening when he left, and Kalyria where it was closer to the mid-of-night, something he had never really thought about before this. Being further east, Kalyria was obviously several hours later than Aridion City, but it took the instantaneous travel of the Paths to bring this fact to his attention. Well enough. There would be occasion for rumination on the oddities of time later, but now he needed his wits about him, for danger lurked in the darkness without.

The sound of a lute came softly from the summerhouse which, though it was dark, was apparently in use with the windows closed and the screens lowered to ensure privacy. Who was playing? Menannon knew no lutenists among his sire's folk. There were also the muffled sounds of children's voices coming from an open, though dark, window in one of the bedchambers in the west wing of the house. Whose children could they be? Surely Firod's wife and family had not returned from Pedura so long as danger lurked here! Though danger waited without, he sensed a peaceful calm within. Well, whatever was going on outside the walls seemed to have no effect inside.

Menannon heaved a soft sigh of relief, his pulses quickening with anticipation as in moments now he would be with his sire and his questions would be answered. He rolled over and lowered himself from the wall, dropping lightly into the shadows behind the summerhouse. He started to stand, but the prick of a spear point at the hollow of his throat halted him mid-movement.

"So, what have we here? A spy? An assassin?"

The words were spoken in a soft murmur just barely above a whisper so they would not carry to any who might be interested without the walls.

"Or is it a blockheaded harper who should be hundreds of leagues away from this place in the safety of the royal city of the Men of the Long Ships? Perhaps Mid-summer's day has come early this season?" At this, Menannon jerked his head up and tried to see who held the other end of the spear, but all he could see was a dark shape. At his movement, the point dug in just slightly, drawing blood.

"Easy now, stand up and go into the summerhouse. You know the way and no tricks or I'll make sure Gorlanndon allows me your discipline for disobeying him. Now, move!"

From this last, Menannon realized that he was being confronted by none other than Skendrin himself for more than once in his childhood the steward had been tasked with his discipline. The one drawback to dealing with men who had helped to raise him was that they could all remember him as a child. The spear pricked again at his hesitation causing Menannon to follow the instructions given with alacrity.

He circled soundlessly around the summerhouse to its stairs and climbed them two at a time. The spear never ceased to be in contact with some part of his anatomy the entire way. He reached the door and found it locked.

"Knock twice, count to three and open it," Skendrin murmured from the vicinity of his shoulder.

Menannon did as he was bid. His knock was followed by the sound of a chair moving within, then the lock turned, grating softly. There was no other sound.

"Count."

Menannon began to count mentally.

"Aloud."

Menannon cleared his throat. "One..."

"Quietly."

"One...two...three!" he murmured, then gently pushed the door open on darkness though he could sense the presence of people within.

Skendrin gave him a slight shove inside and the door was shut behind them. He heard the sound of the lock grate again and the central Dwarf lantern was instantly unshuttered, its light nearly blinding him after the darkness of the night.

"What in all Hella is the meaning of this?" Gorlanndon's outraged growl demanded at his elbow.

"It would seem thou dost posses a most disobedient son, old

friend." The voice of Lord Lonier sounded from the far side of the table.

Menannon's eyes grew accustomed to the light and he looked up into his sire's face. After all the sevendays of worry and uncertainty, the sight of his sire sitting there at ease in his own summerhouse strong and in good health made Menannon's knees go weak with relief. Only the nearness of the table allowed him to keep his feet as he reached out a quick hand to its edge.

He glanced about to see that there were three other people in the summerhouse besides his sire and Skendrin at his back: Firod, Irenos and Lord Lonier. The Teluri was holding the now silent lute he had heard from the wall. All were staring at him with varying degrees of anger reflected in their eyes. Skendrin pushed him rather unceremoniously to stand directly in front of his sire. His reception was exactly as he had expected it would be.

At the sight of his son, Gorlanndon was instantly so furious his eyes began glowing slightly red and his face blanching white to the lips. More swiftly than Menannon would have credited, his sire lunged at him and had his right arm in a vicelike grip twisting it up behind his back nearly breaking it.

"No lies, boy! What in all Hella are you doing here and more to the point, how by the very throne of the High One Himself, did you get here? Your master's trials are not to be held for at least a sevenday yet!"

Menannon forced himself to ignore the pain in his arm and looked his sire eye to eye, his own anger rising out of his fear to nearly match his sire's.

"Suffice it to say, my father, I am here!" he snarled. "And I will not return hence without you! We swore an oath, you and I, the day we left Lornennog that we would ne'er be parted, no matter the cause, until the day Kaalamar is restored to the realms of this world. For my own good, you forced me to be foresworn and leave your side to train at the harper hall in Aridion City. That training is now complete and I am free to choose my path. I have chosen to leave the harper's guild and return to you. You may have chosen to be foresworn, but I have not!" Menannon's voice rose at the end and all present shushed him.

The elder Giant sat still a long moment studying his son's face, then he relaxed. He glanced at Skendrin beyond Menannon's shoulder and shook his head.

"As the High One is my witness, what can one do with such a son?" He released his hold on his willful son and very gently took Menannon's face between his hands and kissed his brow. "I love you, boy, more than I could ever tell you. I sent you away because I sought to keep you safe. I now know why you came back, but I still know not how you returned. There are no ships...."

"I came not by ship, though of how I made the journey I am not at liberty to speak, for it is not my secret to tell. Suffice it to say I am come and can go back the same way with any who desire to leave this place."

"That is a useful bit of knowledge, youngster," Lord Lonier spoke up, "but it is hardly wise to make plain that there is at least one other way on and off this island. So how shall we explain your sudden appearance among us once more?" The old lord looked around at the others only to see Irenos grinning slightly and glancing at Gorlanndon as though they shared some jest between them.

"I see nothing humorous in this, sirrah," Lonier snapped, giving the Teluri a sour look.

"I...." Irenos began, turning to his inquisitor, but Gorlanndon halted him with a hand on his arm and answered himself.

"Not humorous, yet it is ironic. Irenos is simply reminding me that one ne'er knows what useless skill will one day become useful and therefore any skill should be learned e'en if it cannot in all good conscience be practiced."

At this statement, Irenos began to grin outright.

"So, allow all present to enjoy this...irony," Lonier was not quite sure the Teluri was not having him on.

At the look the old lord gave him, Irenos swallowed and grew serious though his grey eyes still twinkled.

"Many summers ago, I discovered an ancient scroll containing many lost arts practiced by Gilarian, one of our most ancient kings. Among these arts was that of Distance Bending. I found this art fascinating and spent many summers perfecting its use much to the displeasure of my sire. Though my Lord Gorlanndon was ever encouraging to my studies." He glanced at the Giant again and raised an expressive eyebrow, which brought an answering grin.

Watching the exchange, Menannon realized there was much more in the relationship of these old friends than met the eye.

Irenos turned back to Lonier and continued. "In truth my sire has forbidden me to Distance Bend as it is a fey and dangerous practice."

"Unless one is a True-Vision Farseer," Menannon whispered to himself.

"Thou knowest of the practice then?" Irenos grinned at the youth's words.

"Aye, it is mentioned in several of the sagas." Menannon colored nicely at having been overheard.

"Thou hast been well taught," Irenos approved.

"What exactly is this practice and how can it aid us in this pass?" Lonier asked, bringing the conversation back to their immediate needs.

"Thy pardon," Irenos inclined his head to him. "Distance Bending as an art by which anyone with sufficient will power and concentration can step across any distance to any known place in an instant of time."

"What makes this art dangerous," Gorlanndon continued for him, "and why his sire has forbidden him to use it is this: should there be anyone or any object in the very spot to which he steps, there would be an detonation which would destroy the entire district and any within it!"

"But that would be only if he could not see ahead to know that the space was empty," Menannon interrupted. "Gilarian King was a Sunfire Golden, or True-Vision Farseer, and thus able to see clearly across space and time and could therefore step with impunity."

"True enough" the Teluri agreed. "Howe'er that may be, I am not a farseer of any sort, neither true-vision gold nor the vision-of-many-paths silver. Thus for me to distance bend can be dangerous beyond imagining."

Gorlanndon nodded at that.

"That being understood, though my sire would disapprove, may I propose that we find a semi-private place where we are sure to be watched by Azuron's spies and I shall distance bend with thy son in my company and thus seem to appear with him from the mainland and thou shalt have thy plausible excuse for his presence. What thinkest thou?" Irenos inquired of Gorlanndon.

"Can this be made safe?" Gorlanndon turned his troubled gaze upon Menannon who sat silently contemplating both of them.

The Teluri considered the issue in silence for a moment then glanced up and, with only the slightest hesitation, nodded. "If the place be chosen carefully and the timing perfect, there is little danger, but I will not say no danger, for there is always the possibility of a happening not looked for."

"Can anyone think of an alternative?" Gorlanndon glanced about at Firod, Lonier and Skendrin who but shook their heads. "As my muddle-headed son has necessitated this extremity, let it be done."

The elder Giant gave Menannon a slight wink which took some of the sting from his words, but he was still upset that his efforts to keep his son safe and beyond Azuron's reach had been brought to naught. "When shall we assay the attempt?" He turned his gaze back to Irenos.

"I deem now would be a good time, as under cover of darkness would appear to be an attempt to conceal his arrival and that would be well within our grasp." Irenos replied at which Lonier stood before anyone else could object and was followed by Gorlanndon who reached up and shuttered the Dwarf lantern plunging the summerhouse into darkness.

Gorlanndon's voice was soft as he issued his instructions. "Come, let us go to the Speakers Grove, as that place should be deserted at this hour and our walk there will give Azuron's minions ample time to follow us. Give us exactly one full turn of the hour, Irenos, and then come to us. The High One be with you both." Gorlanndon opened the door to the summerhouse, speaking softly to Menannon as he passed by, "You and I shall have some speech later."

They stepped outside before his son could reply. Firod left last, closing the door softly leaving the young Giant to face the Teluri prince alone.

Before the darkness in the summerhouse could become too oppressive, Irenos searched out a small Dwarf lantern from his belt pouch and set it upon the table as he opened it, as neither of them desired to climb upon the table in the dark to reach the one Gorlanndon had shuttered. The Teluri motioned Menannon to a seat. When both were settled to wait, Menannon turned to the Teluri and sought to apologize for placing him in danger.

"I am sorry—," he began, but Irenos cut him off, not unkindly.

"Knowest thou this: in thy situation I would have done the same. Our sires deem themselves invincible and we, their sons, of little use, yet little use is better than no use. Learn from this that nothing done out of kindness and love is ever ill done," he said.

"Perhaps not, but lacking in wisdom...." Menannon shrugged, causing Irenos to grin.

"Wisdom and the heart are ever strangers, lad, but enough. I deem that thou didst use the Straight Paths to gain access to us?"

"Aye, but how...?"

"All Teluri royalty know of their existence, but none save my father, Liélindar of Lilientharien and Lindren King of Gilaria use them with any regularity. The kings of the other four realms prefer not this mode of transportation. I myself know not their workings as my father has not deemed me ready for such knowledge." He grinned widely and continued, "And he is probably right. The temptation to, ahh, explore would be more than I could bear, I fear. Should I e'er have the misfortune of becoming king of Blue Hill, I shall no doubt need to seek out the Grandmaster harper and ask his guidance in their use, but until then, I deem this something best left to harpers." Irenos leaned forward and lowered his voice. "Howe'er, that said, the fact that thou dost know their ways is a blessing of the High One. There are those among us here on Kalyria who have made a pact to rescue as many as may be from the machinations of Azuron's Doomcriers and his twisted travesty of justice."

"Is my father one of you in this?" Menannon had to ask, although he already knew the answer.

"Nay, he and Lord Lonier are still convinced the rule of law will prevail." Irenos shook his head.

"And you deem it won't."

"It has already failed, as e'en now two of Kalyria's seven high judges are under house arrest awaiting trial on charges of sedition." The Teluri's face was grim.

"Surely you jest!" Menannon was stunned at this news, for the integrity of these seven judges was beyond question.

"I would that I did, lad." The Teluri raised his gaze to squarely meet the Giant's. "They were both arrested yestereve. Their crime is supposedly to have caused broadsides to be posted calling for the resignation of Azuron, though all know that it is actually because they refused to sign charges against thy sire and Lord Lonier for the murder of Lord Normanus. Thou hast heard about that, hast thou not?"

"Aye, the Princess Nirna sent me word of it through Paulus Muellen."

"There will be more arrests and assassinations now that Azuron has gotten away with these initial assays. Markest thou my words." Irenos shook his head and leaned back against the wall behind him.

"But...," Menannon began at which the Teluri held up a hand, forestalling him.

"On the morrow come to lowest level of thy sire's trade hall at the hour of nine. There will be time enough then for far too many questions and far too few answers. For now, let us relax a bit ere we join the others." With that, he closed his eyes and soon relaxed into a light drowse.

IN THE DARKNESS OF THE NIGHT beyond the summerhouse walls, Gorlanndon strolled amiably along with Skendrin talking softly as though they were in a long debated conversation, all the while keeping an eye out for any other Doomcriers who might be lurking about. They had at least one follower, of course, but that was not enough for their plan. Lord Lonier and Firod had departed surreptitiously one at a time from the villa, not wanting to be seen together just yet, Lonier to his home and Firod to the palace where he would be going on duty in less than a full turn of the hour. They had become quite skilled at evading the notice of their watchers.

The Giant and the steward were over half way to their destination before Gorlanndon finally spotted a group of Azuron's sycophants lounging outside a small pub. They seemed content to stay where they were, which did not serve the Giant's purpose at all. Their attention needed to be attracted so Gorlanndon raised his voice and spoke distinctly for their benefit.

"Azuron is...." he lowered his voice again and moved on knowing that the Doomcriers would be duty bound to follow them and discover what the Giant had been saying about their leader.

After a few more minutes, he glanced back to see that the Doomcriers had indeed disappeared from their bench. He listened carefully and heard what he expected to hear: the sound of people pushing their way through the undergrowth below the road. From the muttering, it was apparently not an easy thing to do in the dark. Gorlanndon could not help grinning to himself when he remembered the thorn bushes which in days of old had grown in profusion across the sides of the Aureun. Their descendants were apparently still here to judge by the language being employed by their shadowers.

Making sure that they did not outdistance their clumsy shadows, Gorlanndon and Skendrin attained the Aureun gardens and settled down on a bench in the center of the Speakers Grove. They had arrived perhaps a half turn of the hour ahead of the time appointed to Irenos. The Doomcriers could be heard settling down in the darkness as close as they dared to hear the conversation. Luckily, they had chosen to sit amidst the blackwood grove and were thus presented no obstacle to the prince when he bent distance. The Giant began to regale the steward with stories of debates held in the Privy Chambers which involved Azuron so that the Councillor General's name was mentioned often enough to require his henchmen to remain where they were, but nothing damning was said for them to report.

It was exactly on the turn of the hour when there was a loud sound like a crack of lightning and Irenos appeared in the middle of the Speakers Grove with Menannon held by the arm. Despite the fact he was expecting it, the suddenness of the noise and its volume startled Gorlanndon and nearly frightened the Doomcriers out of their wits as one of them let out a shriek almost at the Giant's elbow. The fellow was immediately silenced with a cuff to the side of the head to judge by the thud that sounded. Both Gorlanndon and Skendrin rose quickly and moved to greet the newcomers as though the Doomcriers had made no sound.

"You're late, gentlemen," Gorlanndon growled just loud enough for the Doomcriers to hear. "You were supposed to arrive this evening. What held you?"

"My lady mother wished to complete her order of sorak that I might bring it with me and give it unto thee for fulfillment," Irenos returned, not skipping a beat, though this part of their plan had not been discussed. "I have it here."

He produced a scroll from his belt pouch and handed it to Gorlanndon. He also withdrew his small Dwarf lantern and opened it as though to allow the Giant to see the contents of the scroll, but in reality, he made sure that the light shone on Menannon's face as well so that it could be reliably reported that the young Giant had come with him. Gorlanndon opened the scroll and perused its contents in a leisurely fashion. The fact that it actually contained a song Irenos had been writing was not something discernable to the Doomcriers.

"Your lady mother's list shows her usual exquisite taste, my friend and luckily all but one of these bolts lie in my main warehouse." Gorlanndon nodded and re-rolled the scroll, handed it to Skendrin, then turned to Menannon.

"Menannon, it is good to see you, boy," he said heartily his voice slightly louder than needed as he stepped up and took his son's face between his hands and kissed his brow with real feeling, then released him and stepped back. "How was your journey from Aridion City to Blue Hill? Uneventful, I trust."

"It was, my father. The weather held well and the roads were dry. Though I must say it took far longer to get there than it did to come here just now from Blue Hill via the good offices of the prince," Menannon added in hopes of reinforcing the idea that he had come by Mythrian Magic to the island, which in reality he had, though not quite in the manner they were attempting to insinuate into their watchers' minds.

"Come then, gentlemen, it is high time we seek our beds, for the morrow will be a busy one." Gorlanndon stretched expansively, the sound of his popping joints almost echoing in the silence.

All of them agreed and Irenos closed his lantern, plunging the grove back into darkness. Together, the four of them left the Aureun gardens and headed back to Gorlanndon's villa leaving behind them a small company of Doomcriers eager to get back to the palace and inform their lord that the Giant's son had returned along with the prince of Blue Hill by some arcane method. As they departed, Gorlanndon heard the Doomcriers whispering excitedly.

Well, so far so good. He laid his hand companionably on his son's shoulder. Despite his misgivings and all his plans to the contrary,

Gorlanndon could not help being glad of him.

※ C∙Ɔ※

THEY ARRIVED BACK AT THE VILLA and the great Giant led the way into the close, Irenos having parted from them at the crossing of the Equian Way to proceed to his own holding. Just within the gate, Gorlanndon halted and Skendrin took his leave. The elder Giant placed his hand upon his son's shoulder.

"There will be a meeting of the council on the morrow at the hour of two," he murmured. "Make sure you are there and appropriately attired. As you have returned, it is now time for you to take your rightful place as my heir, though Azuron will be greatly discomfited to find himself faced with two Giants rather than just one, as well as the vexing mystery of your arrival."

Gorlanndon did not wait for an answer, but gently squeezed Menannon's shoulder and headed for the villa's door where he halted with his hand on the handle.

"Welcome home, boy," he said over his shoulder before disappearing within.

Menannon resolutely forced his mind away from speculation as to how that council meeting would go and sought his own chamber. He would not sleep, as he needed to seek out Nirna before the day broke and rendered access to her tower impossible with its myriad folk moving about the palace and its grounds. He could use the few turns of the hour before then to think.

There was one Dwarf lantern open within when he entered his chamber, its light showing that the bed had been turned down in readiness for him. He set his pack on the hearth table and stretched out full length on the bed with a deep sigh, to rest a few moments before he got ready for the day. Despite his best intentions, he relaxed with the lifting of the tension of the last hours and his eyelids suddenly became leaden and he fell asleep almost instantly.

GORLANNDON HEARD MENANNON'S DOOR CLOSE and turned his
steps to the kitchen where even at this hour the kettle would
be on the hob. He entered the darkened chamber and halted.
Clarinda was sitting by the cooking hearth rocking in her favorite
chair, her long grey braid falling over her shoulder down the
front of her night robes and holding out to him a hot mug of tea.

"How do you always know what I am going to do even when
I don't know myself?" he inquired with a grin and a shake of his
head as he accepted the cup and sat down in the chair she had
already pulled up for him.

In return, she only smiled her enigmatic smile and picked up
her own tea. They sat in silence for many long moments sipping
tea and contemplating the dance of the small flames about the
embers of the hearth fire.

"So, he's come home," she said, breaking the silence at last as
she poured both of them another serving of tea.

"Aye."

"What would you be intendin' to do about it?"

"Nothing," Gorlanndon's reply was a thoughtful growl. "He's
a mind of his own and a will to match his lady mother's. Once
she decided on a thing, nothing in Kaalamar or Hella would turn
her and he's of the same mettle."

"Ya should have known that sendin' your collections and the
horses to him would be like wavin' the proverbial red flag. The
lad's not dense. Ya knew he'd immediately figure out things
were not well here and rush to your side whippity quick." She
could not help scolding the Giant a bit.

"Aye, there was that chance, but I had to do something. There
are irreplaceable things among my collections that all Linden
would be the poorer were they to be destroyed. And there were
the families of those working in the warehouses to be considered.
And how could I possibly leave Georgi Grimaxe to face the
machinations of Azuron? That Dwarf would burn down the
palace if one hair in the mane of one of his beloved horses was

harmed."

They shared a grin at the thought of the Horsemaster's volatile temper and his obsessive love for his charges. Gorlanndon quickly turned serious again.

"Though I would that Blackmore had been able to keep Menannon with him but a bit longer."

"Why is that?" She stopped rocking and looked up at him, a Dwarf's lust for battle glinting in her eyes. "Are ya finally goin' to assassinate the usurpin', blasphemin' ...!" She left the last word unsaid, but it still hung in the air between them causing him to grin down at her. Five generations of peaceful city living had not bred out of Clarinda the fighting spirit of her race.

"Nay," he said, setting his mug down on the warming shelf. "The High One forbids it." He hunched forward in his chair and steepled his fingers against his lips, his elbows resting on his knees.

"Humph,"she snorted softly and went back to rocking, her disapproval a palpable force in the chamber.

"You can't pick and choose what you'll believe in the High One's Word Hoard," he murmured thoughtfully. "Either you believe and follow all of it or none. Even in those times when parts of it become...*inconvenient*," he finished, raising an admonishing eyebrow at her.

She just sniffed and looked back into the fire.

"At least ya could be rearrangin' his torc a bit. Surely that wouldn't be displeasin' to the High One," she murmured piously, glancing at him out of the corner of her eye.

"I'd best not, as I know in my heart once I got my fingers around his scrawny neck I'd not be able to stop and I'd spend the rest of my life trying to convince myself I was justified in doing murder," Gorlanndon said with a strange look on his face the little cook could not begin to fathom.

There was a long silence again as each thought about the import of the Giant's words. At last Clarinda spoke, her voice as thoughtful as he had ever heard it.

"What you're tryin' to say is that the heart of the matter is blasphemy. This sorcerer has blasphemed the High One and turned against His will and if ya was after murderin' him ya'd be doin' the same." She glanced up at him then back to the fire.

"Aye! Basically to murder Azuron is to become Azuron. Not something that would please the High One in one of his true believers." Gorlanndon nodded reaching for his tea and settling back into his chair.

She filled their mugs again and sat watching him, her heart wrung with seeing his distress and indecision. Clarinda had loved and served Gorlanndon of Lornennog all of her long life and would until the end of her days. What ever decision he made in this pass she would abide by and defend to her last breath.

"This is not the first time I've been through this, Clarinda." He glanced at her over the edge of his mug then back into his tea. She kept her silence.

"Five hundred summers ago I was serving as the Council General to Boria and the eastern lands. It was the time of the Regency when the old king was ailing and his eldest son by his head wife was ruling in his stead. Yet there were other sons of the king by other wives who wished for the power of the throne and resented their brother. The situation would have been settled with the minimum of bloodshed and battle had not the Black Sorcerer come among them, seemingly out of nowhere. He was a Teluri possessed of a bald head, smoky eyes and a glib tongue filled with sweetness and venom."

"Azuron?" she more breathed the word than spoke it. He nodded and continued as though compelled now that he had begun to speak of the past.

"Azuron got the ear of one of the middle princes of the king's third wife. A boy of bright mind and little virtue. This lad he persuaded to follow him promising all manner of power and riches. Together they began to subvert the people, providing bread and circuses for them in exchange for their sloth and indolence. Betting on the races and games became the way of making a living.

"Is this sounding familiar?" Gorlanndon raised his expressive brow again and Clarinda nodded. "Yet still there were those who did not take well to the new scheme and sought to halt the Black Sorcerer's rise to power. The king's eldest son brought in mercenaries from all over the lands and began to fight for his land. I counseled that he should call upon the might of Kalyria but he sought to solve his issues his own way. A way which included the murder of Azuron."

Gorlanndon halted and Clarinda wondered if he would continue he was silent for so long. At last he did in a haunted voice.

"The king's son and his closest followers cornered the sorcerer in the royal box at the circus and the lad took the sword of his fathers and ran the Teluri through the heart.

"Azuron stood swaying for a few moments then, rather than dropping dead at the prince's feet he threw back his head and laughed and withdrew the sword from his own body and turning it, thrust it into the heart of the prince, saying *Reap what thou hast sown* as he did so.

The prince fell dead at his feet and all Hella broke loose in Boria. Clarinda, in full battle of true war, I myself severed Azuron's head from his shoulders only to see it attach itself back again. From that, I learned that he is warded by Khalandria and the only blade that can kill him is one that has been forgesung by the Teluri and thus imbued with the presence of the High One.

"I possess such a weapon now, but I had it not then, for my lady wife had made me swear to cease the practice of arms on our wedding day. It lay here in its sheath as useless as the ingot of metal from which it was forged. And wish though I might, I could not call it to me."

"The rest of the tale you know. The Black Prince of Boria won the day and turned his land and people over to the worship of Khalandria. And out of the ashes of their world arose a nation of brigands and pirates who are held in check only by the might of Kalyria's navy. And...now it is our turn."

This time, the silence in the kitchen was brittle. A thing to be shattered by a single breath like the peace of their land.

"Master, you must be after killin' him," Clarinda whispered, forcing her words past lips stiffened by her understanding of what they portended. Gorlanndon drew his thoughts back out of his memories of battle and destruction.

"Nay, lass. I'll not commit murder. Until or unless Azuron declares open war, his life is as sacrosanct as any other man's." The Giant tossed the last of his tea into the fire and setting the mug on the sideboard rose to go. Clarinda jumped to her feet and caught his hand, halting him.

"Master, what are we goin' to be doin'?" she whispered, eyes wide with horror at the vision he had painted. He knelt down on one knee and took her hand gently in his.

"I know not, lass. All I know is that all things turn to good for those who truly believe in and follow the High One and so we will await his time. In this as in all things, His will be done. Now get on to bed as I have kept you up nearly to dawn." He gently touched her cheek and stood to his full height, stretched a bit and turned towards the door where he halted with an impish grin.

"Who knows, Lady Clarinda, perchance the High One will let me rearrange his torque for him." With this last comment, he was gone, leaving her shaking her head and rolling her expressive eyes.

"Giants!"

CHAPTER 15

(SUMMER OF THE WORLD 6097)

THE CLOSING OF HIS FATHER'S DOOR woke Menannon with a start. The darkness outside of his garden window was noticeably lighter than when he had lain down. He should not have slept. Menannon lunged from the bed, grabbed his cloak and let himself out into the garden. He circled around through the kaleyard to the front gate to avoid passing his father's window.

The gatewarden let him out with a softly murmured, "Good morrow, young Master. Be ye welcomed home," as he closed the gate behind him.

Menannon swung on his cloak and ran lightly down the Equian Way even as the first birds began to chirp the dawn. Just as morning's first grey glimmer was lighting the eastern sea, he slipped silently into the palace close through a side postern normally used by the servants. He halted for a moment to survey the area. It seemed devoid of life, but he knew that the doorwards on the farther side of the palace's many-pillared portico would be alert at their posts as Firod brooked no dereliction of duty among his men. The young Giant took a deep breath and stepped out into the close and circled around the back of the huge building until he reached the base of Nirna's tower. There he stopped and reached into his belt pouch for the small stones he had quickly gathered as he went through the kaleyard.

With one last glance about, he stepped out away from the tower just far enough so that he could see the window at its top and launched a small pebble at the shutters. It struck with a soft thunk and Menannon jumped back against the stone and held still, barely breathing to make sure there was no reaction from any of the men on duty. There was no sound for several long moments, so he braved another throw. Again, the small stone struck the wooden shutters, this time with something of a clatter as it must have hit on the edge of two of the cross pieces of which the closure was made. Still there was no reaction from without or within. The eastern sky was lightening quickly. He must soon be gone. One more stone flew up and struck. This time there was a reaction. The shutter flew open and clattered back against the fabric of the tower and a voice called out.

"What do...!" it began snapping with displeasure. Mati stuck her head out far enough to look down, her grey hair, not yet bound up for the day, swirled around her with the suddenness of her movements.

Menannon glanced about and seeing no one, took the chance of stepping back into the gooddame's view.

"Here now what do you...!" she started to call down, then seeing who it was, turned back to call into the chamber without skipping a beat, "...think of that, my lady. The sun is already up and it promises to be a right gorgeous day for a walk in the garden behind the Council Hall this afternoon. 'Tis sorry I am that you'll not be being able to get out into the fresh air ere that as you've got too many duties this morning, but by the hour of four of the clock ye'll be able to get out there."

The gooddame raised her voice on this last sentence and Menannon heard Nirna's trilling laugh as the shutter clattered back into place.

The message was clear: Nirna would meet him at four of the clock in the garden! His heart had wings till then. Menannon glanced about quickly, then retraced his steps back out of the postern and fairly flew down the road to the Cokeyna to break his fast and listen to the gossip of the sailors.

A single pair of eyes tracked his movements until the postern gate closed behind him. Firod stood on the arch above the central gate which overlooked the yard below and had a clear view of the base of Nirna's tower. He shook his head half in understanding, half in vexation. Youth and stupidity were near kindred it would seem. Gorlanndon would have to put a leash on that one before the young fool got them all in trouble as it seemed the princess's nurse had no more sense than the youngsters, her words having carried clearly to him in the silence of the dawn.

A HALF TURN OF THE HOUR before the time appointed by Irenos discovered Menannon standing without his sire's trade hall facing its magnificent doors, his stomach full of victuals and his head full of sailors' discontent and strange tales. He had intended to enter the trade hall from the dock level, but had found it barred from the inside so perforce had climbed back up the Idrian to the public doors. He took a deep breath and squared his shoulders and entered, expecting to have to fend off the greetings and questions of his sire's serving folk but found himself brought up short in total surprise...the place was empty!

For the first time in living memory, there was no one there working or buying or even just strolling. Menannon walked into the center of the atrium, his footsteps echoing hollowly in the silence for even the fountains had been turned off. All of the decorations and plants were in their accustomed places, but there were no wares to be seen anywhere, not even on the balconies above. Menannon walked about looking into chamber after chamber and it was the same in each.

His path eventually led him to his sire's office where, strangely, nothing was missing, his mother's portrait was still in its accustomed place, even the scrolls were still in the pigeon holes behind the desk. Menannon wondered if there was anything in any of them to explain what had happened and stepped quickly around the desk and took out the first scroll that offered. He unrolled it and glanced at its contents. It was written in Giantish which surprised him as he had never known any of his sire's business transactions to be carried out in that tongue, since it was not spoken outside the Giant lands by any save a few Teluri and the folk of New Belitarra.

He briefly began to read and halted, shaking his head. None of the words were making sense as business, they were nonsense words and childish rhymes. He read it again sure that he must have misread it the first time as it had been many summers since he had used his sire's tongue. No! He had been correct. The scroll was gibberish. Carefully, he re-rolled it and returned it to its place then chose another at random, it was the same thing...pure Giantish gibberish. By the time the water clock in the atrium chimed the ninth hour, he had perused nearly a dozen scrolls only to find that none of them held any business information at all, only the doggerel and verbal doodling one might expect from a bored day schooler. As the clock finished chiming, Menannon returned this last scroll to its place and ran to the lift along the back wall of the atrium intent upon finding Irenos and getting some answers to even more questions.

With as desolate as the building felt, he was actually surprised when he pulled the lever that the grate lowered and he could step into the lift, where the Dwarf lantern was still shining. He quickly raised the grate and took hold of the descent lever. The lift glided into motion taking him down to the lowest floor above the dock level where Irenos had instructed he would be. The central hallway was dark beyond the circle of light provided by the lift's Dwarf lantern. Menannon stood motionless his hand still on the lever and wondered anew where everyone was and why, if there was no one working here any longer, the front door had not been locked? He listened intently, but heard nothing. Almost reluctantly, he let go of the lever and, taking down the lantern, exited the lift to explore the level and find the Teluri.

Menannon had but stepped out of the lift when his ear was caught by a slight sound. He halted and instinctively closed the shutters on the lantern plunging himself into total blackness. He held his breath wondering if the sound would manifest itself again. Almost instantly he heard a soft rumbling noise and then a muffled clank from along the back wall of the level. That was the side buried deep into the hill on which the trade hall was built. Then a door opened nearly beside him flooding the lift area with light, temporarily blinding him.

"Thou didst come," a voice spoke out of the light making him flinch with surprise. "I was afraid that thou wouldst change thy mind."

Before he could say or do anything, a hand took his arm and pulled him, nearly blind, into the light and he heard a door shut with a thud. When Menannon's eyes adjusted, he saw that it was indeed Irenos who had spoken and still held his arm to steady him. Behind the Teluri, in the chamber he had just entered, he could see several other folk standing and sitting around a table cluttered with scrolls, scroll cases and various maps. There were five others; two Dwarves, two Humans and another Teluri. Of these he recognized only the Humans, Turanio and Tullio, both stilt walkers of the Orlando clan, though he had never actually met them.

The chamber itself proved to be a small storage space possessed of an access door to the lower tunnels honeycombing the bowels of the Aureun. These tunnels had been used for centuries for moving the heavy marketables from the warehouses at the docks to the various shops and trade halls dotting the hill, as none of the other trade halls extended all the way to the docks nor possessed lifts as his sire's did. Menannon had not realized his sire had at least at one time made use of them as well, though why this surprised him, he was not sure.

"Join us, we have much to plan." Irenos indicated a tall stool at the far end of the table, cutting short Menannon's musing. The Teluri returned to his seat while Menannon took the indicated stool next to a tall Dwarf.

"Menannon, allow me to acquaint thee with the rest of our company. Conar, son of Corin."

Irenos indicated the Dwarf whose red beard was just barely reaching his silver-chased belt. His grey tunic and leggings were of fine brocade bespeaking his family's wealth and status, for his sire, Corin, owned a fine mercantile business of his own with trading posts both on and off Kalyria. Though the Dwarf was obviously young, he was already as broad shouldered and heavily muscled as any of his race and his deep brown eyes were studying the Giant speculatively even as he nodded to him in acknowledgment of the introduction.

Next to him was the second Dwarf, Dink by name, who was also young to judge by the length of his brown beard, which was only just tucked into the front of his tunic as it did not yet reach his belt. This fellow was small for his race with a thin face and a large beak of a nose which made him look rather like a ferret. His dark amber eyes were darting restlessly around the chamber while Irenos introduced him, as though he preferred to look anywhere except at the young Giant. His rusty red broadcloth tunic was a bit worn at the armholes and frayed at the hem and his woolen hose bagged at the knees. From his clothing, there was no way to know what trade he plied. That and his restless gaze made Menannon wonder if he were perhaps one of the sharps who made a living by separating the unwary from their money in the pubs near the docks.

On the other side of the table stood the two Humans, their stilts making it difficult to sit in so small a space. Though there was a full ten summers between them, the elder, Turanio having five and twenty summers and Tullio, the younger having only fifteen, the Orlando boys could have been taken for twins so strongly did they bear the stamp of their sire, Taratillo. All of the Orlando clan were of swarthy complexion and dark hair, ranging from black to red-brown, with green or blue eyes making it hard to ascertain in what part of the world the clan originated. The last member of the company sat beside the Orlandos, his fiery red head towering over his table mates.

"This is my swordbrother, Haalinoth of Taaliron," Irenos nodded towards the other Teluri whose bright grey eyes were regarding Menannon with undisguised interest. The fellow was far taller than Irenos, being slightly over eight feet in height and was of the long light build that the Giant normally associated with the fellow's race. His clothing and malinir were of a quality marking him as a member of the nobles of his land, a Teluri kingdom high in the southern Sythrin mountains above

Rhonndia. The fellow's name chimed a chord in Menannon's mind as it occurred in the family appendix to the Teluri king list. Haalinoth was consort to the youngest sister of Lindren, King of Gilaria.

"All of thee knowest Menannon, Councillor Gorlanndon's heir. He is a Journeyman Harper and has volunteered his services in our cause." At this, Menannon glanced quickly at Irenos who answered his unspoken question with a slight shake of his head. Apparently, the Teluri did not desire the rest to know that Menannon deemed himself recusant having abandoned his guild. Only Dink appeared to have caught this interchange and glanced rather suspiciously at Menannon. The introductions made, Irenos immediately came to the point of their meeting.

"As thou dost all comprehend, Azuron has pandered his position as Councillor General into being named head of the Courts now as well and has placed Lady Rhyland and Lord Bannor under house arrest on charges of sedition."

Menannon mentally shook his head but kept his own counsel as the rest exclaimed in protest, this being news to them, but not to him. Irenos held up his hand to still the indignant comments.

"The list is far longer than just these twain," he said, unrolling a scroll which already contained more than a hundred names of those who had been denounced by the Doomcriers. Most were folk of substance and placed to damage or even merely influence Azuron's plans, but there were a goodly number of humble folk as well. The last name on the list was a jongleur from the market near the docks who had been so ill-advised as to name his performing monkey "Azuron." Whether in honor or in jest no one knew, but the fellow was all of eighty summers old and nearly blind.

"Kha, is big threat, that one!" Turanio muttered glancing at his brother with a shake of his head, when Irenos read this last name.

"All of us are being observed by the Doomcriers with any activities being reported to Azuron," the Teluri continued, tossing aside the scroll. "We all stand in danger of being denounced and of those who have been denounced and taken...NONE...have been released!"

"How is this possible?" Menannon demanded, his stomach tightening in both anger and fear. "I have been led to believe that the Doomcriers were simply a disenfranchised sect that Azuron is encouraging!"

"As they were until a month since!" Haalinoth informed him with some asperity and the rest nodded agreement. "A riot broke out at the arena...."

"Is insult to family! Riot not in circus, she was outside!" Turanio interrupted slamming the flat of his hand down on the table. "Make no such affront to my papochka!"

"I intended no disrespect to thy esteemed sire, my friend," Haalinoth inclined his head to the red-faced youngster with a slight smile. When it seemed as though the fellow would take offence at the smile, Tullio took a hold of his brother's arm and began whispering in his ear at which point Turanio settled back with a "humph," but allowed the discussion to go on with no further interruptions.

"No matter its location," Haalinoth continued, "the riot allowed Azuron to countenance the organization of a group of the Doomcriers into a troop of his own personal 'peace keepers.' The ranks of that troop have swelled out of all imagining as countless numbers of men, from all walks of life and guilds, have rushed to join it. E'en some of Captain Firod's city watch and palace guards have turned their coats and donned the new colors. The greatest of its numbers have come from the lowest levels of society and they have brought their brutish ways with them."

Dink nodded to himself, but said nothing, his eyes taking in Menannon as though he did not quite think the Giant would be any use to their band.

"E'en me own cousin has gone an' joined 'em," Conar spoke up, his voice tinged with pure vexation, "though I'm after deemin' 'tis more to spite his da than bein' in sympathy with their cause."

"Many among thy wealthy worthless have joined for a lark,"

Irenos agreed with the Dwarf, then held up his hand halting further comments. "Be that as it may, the rest of the Doomcriers not of the troop will also turn against any save Azuron when they are called upon to so serve. Mistake not this threat. Now we must plan this night's campaign."

Without further comment, they set to work figuring out their ways and means of getting Menannon into the villa of Lady Rhyland and out again with the lady and her household, it having been determined to begin their efforts with this judge. It was decided that the distraction would be provided by the stiltwalkers and two Dwarves while the Teluri stood shadow guard and escorted Menannon and his charges to the harper hall. That this was his destination, Menannon readily admitted, but more than that he would not divulge though all save Irenos pressed him hard.

"It is not my secret to tell." Menannon replied patiently for nearly the dozenth time when Dink pressed him again for the details of what he intended to do with their 'guests.'

"If thou dost intend to bespeak Penor for sanctuary thou art sadly deceived." Haalinoth spoke softly, raising a warning eyebrow at Dink when that worthy seemed about to come to blows with the Giant.

"Oh, I intend to bespeak sanctuary, though not from Penor." Menannon informed them, almost grinning at the puzzled looks around the table.

"How— ?"Turanio began, but Irenos halted his words with an upraised hand.

"This is Menannon's concern. Our portion is to aid him in getting our guests to the hall. What the harpers do with them after is within their writ, not ours."

Irenos glanced about him quelling all other comment.

The next half turn of the hour saw the finalizing of their plans and the assignment of the duties of each. As the others sat back in various poses of relief at finally being set upon a course, Irenos drew Menannon slightly aside.

"I deem it would be well if thou didst reclaim thine harper's robes on thy trip to Aridion City as Azuron knows not that thou hast resigned from thy guild and it might just hold him in check a touch deeming thou dost still move under its protection." Irenos gave this advice quietly so that the rest did not hear his words.

"But—," Menannon began to protest, not wanting to claim a protection he no longer felt he possessed.

The Teluri halted his words with a slight shake of his head.

"In war, lad, all weapons are fair save those which would offend the High One. There are many kinds of armour and some is made of cloth and cords."

Irenos turned to the rest and raised his voice.

"Depart hence and we meet this night three turns of the hour past the mid-of-night at the back of Lady Rhyland's villa and the High One willing, we shall speed her and hers to safety ere the Doomcriers and their despicable master are any the wiser. Away until then."

As one, the small band filed out. The Orlando boys and Dink went out the back door into the tunnels while Menannon followed Haalinoth and Conar out into the hallway intent upon taking the lift. Irenos returned to his planning, closing the door softly behind them.

While the others took the lift down to the harbor level, Menannon stood silently in the darkness wondering how all of this would help as there were so few of them and so many in need. He stood quietly waiting for the rumble of the chains and their heavy counterweights to cease indicating that the conveyance had reached its destination. He waited several long moments more before pulling the lever to cause the lift to rise back for his use. The glimmer of the Dwarf lantern coming up the shaft announced its arrival. Just as the young Giant entered it to return to the upper levels, he heard the chiming of the atrium clock echoing down the shaft. It was half past the hour of twelve. He had just enough time to return to his sire's villa to prepare himself for the afternoon's council session.

Outside once more, Menannon began to make his way along

the Serpentine. The day was beautiful in the extreme with blue sky and sunshine highlighted with naught save a few white puffy clouds and birds winging about their business. All along the street, shoppers and strollers had emerged as though nothing were at all amiss in their land. And indeed, for many it was so, for Menannon noticed only a few who—like himself— wore no red. All shades of crimson and red adorned nearly everyone, be it a full robe or kirtle or just the wisp of a scarf adorning a lady's hair. How many of these folk were true followers of Azuron and how many were just following the new style out of a misplaced sense of fashion or out of fear? Indeed, that was the true question.

A short time later, Menannon was surprised to find himself back at the gate to the villa so deep had been his thoughts. He rang the bell and the gate was opened for him by one of the gatewardens whose grim countenance softened with a bit of smile for his master's son. Menannon nodded in return and made his way quickly to his chambers where he tossed his cloak onto the bed. Turning towards the bathing chamber, he was halted by the sight of a golden councillor's robe hanging on the front of the wardrobe. It lacked an indigo fringe which marked it as belonging to a cadet councillor, a rank the body heir of all sitting councillors was awarded at fifteen summers thus allowing them to educate themselves as to the council's work and even to participate in the discussions and debates, though not to vote, a privilege reserved for full councillors. At twenty summers, Menannon was indeed late in assuming his place. He briefly touched the robe, the sorak soft against his skin, then let it drop.

There had been a time when the very thought of sitting in Kalyria's council would have thrilled him beyond measure, but now his stomach almost tied into knots at the idea. A small voice in the back of his mind kept whispering that the council was no longer a voice of leadership and sanity, rather it had become naught but a hollow echo of Azuron's mind and voice.

The water clock tinkled softly in its corner, telling him that there was still over a full turn of the hour to the beginning of the council. His mind still spinning from all he had heard this morning, Menannon decided to take a few minutes to relax in his favorite spot in the garden.

He walked almost sightlessly out and settled onto the bench beneath the branches of a blooming wisteria which had been artfully trained into a tree attesting to the nearly infinite patience of his sire's gardeners for it represented a labor of pure love with its need for constant pruning to keep its shape. He reached out and took one of the blossoms between his long fingers and raised it into the sunshine where it fairly glowed with life and a sense of peace. A thought occurred to him then that perchance that same labor of pruning which gave such grace to the wisteria was what was needed in the council to take out the folk who were determined not to deem for themselves and replace them with others with more spine. He let go of the blossom and it swung back up with its kindred as his mind began to dwell once more upon all that was happening.

How could the council stand by while Azuron's followers denounced folk left and right and made them disappear without so much as a by-your-leave from the High Court? An aged jongleur with a bizarre sense of humor, for the High One's holy sake! A baker whose only crime was a cake shaped like Azuron served on Fool's Night! A sail merchant who had been complaining about the taxes levied to build the arena? The list was endless. Folk were being persecuted because someone, often out of spite or personal grudge, put the largest possible view on their actions and claimed they were besmirching the person and reputation of the Councillor General Azuron!

Then there was the rest of it. Lord Normanus stabbed to death in the council chamber! Lord Lanier and Councillor Gorlanndon threatened with arrest! And now, even two of the High Court judges had been denounced and placed under house arrest! Where was the Queen in all of this? Surely she could not be turning aside from the laws and traditions which had kept Kalyria great all these centuries? And why was his sire not acting? Gorlanndon was a king maker. He had ships, men and enough arms in his villa alone to outfit an army triple the size of Firod's guard and watch. He was arguably the most powerful person in the entire Kalyrian Empire—including the Queen— so why did he not step in and put a stop to the madness? Why?! Menannon shook his head in frustration and heaved a great sigh. This useless speculation was getting him nowhere. He had to talk to his sire.

The young Giant rose and re-entered his chambers to don the councillor's robe. He almost jerked it from its hanging place and draped it over his shoulders. It fell in perfect folds to his feet attesting to the fact it had been made specifically for him. He stopped for a moment and looked at his reflection in the peer glass. His sire must have known that he would come back when he sent his collections to Aridion City for it would have taken a fortnight and more to weave the cloth-of-gold to make this robe. Menannon found himself torn between love and exasperation at the thought of how well his sire knew him despite their summers of separation. He shook his head forcing the thought aside and left the chamber more determined than ever to make his way to the Council Hall and force his sire to talk to him, either there or in his seemingly abandoned trade hall.

That empty trade hall was another oddity. Why was the great Giant keeping his own counsel in public, yet moving all of his assets and employees off island in private? Nirna's letter apparently had not mentioned even the half of the wrongs here. Menannon found himself shaking his head again as he headed through the silent villa and back out into the courtyard. There were several grounds keepers and gatewardens about, but no one else, which was quite unusual, as Gorlanndon's villa was normally a hive of activity. As Menannon walked towards the gate, he caught a movement out of the corner of his eye and turned his head to see Skendrin come out of his own villa and head purposefully towards one of the storage sheds, a large scroll clutched in one hand. Menannon moved quickly to intercept him, but before he could even open his mouth to ask his questions, the steward held up his hand halting him mid breath.

"Don't e'en get started, young Master," he said shaking his head. "I know no more of your sire's mind than do you. I simply follow his orders."

"And what have those orders been?" Menannon demanded rather more curtly than intended.

"Until a sevenday ago, they were to load and send shipload after shipload of goods and folk to his off island trading bases which represent nearly every port of call on the Dawn sea and several more on the Dusk. I've packed his collections until I'm blue in the face!" Skendrin looked up at Menannon with a deeply troubled frown creasing his forehead.

"What stopped them?"

"That!" Skendrin pointed towards the bay. Menannon followed his pointing finger and saw nothing but the sun sparkling on the sea.

"What?" he asked.

"That!" Skendrin pointed emphatically. "Unfocus your eyes, young Master and look out there and ye'll see it."

Menannon did as he was bid, but still saw nothing despite Blackmore's assurance that there was some kind of magic shroud enclosing Kalyria. He was about to turn away when he caught a mere waver in the air as though he were looking through a sheet of bad glass. As soon as he caught it, he realized that the waver seemed to stretch across the entire horizon. "What is it?"

"That's a good question, but what e'er it is, it appeared a sevenday ago and no ship has been able to come or go since. We've been calling it 'Azuron's Fortress,' but other than the belief that our good Councillor General is somehow responsible for it, there is no real reason to call it anything save a total pain in the— !" Skendrin cleared his throat with something of a growl and turned his gaze back up to Menannon. "Is there aught else you'd be wantin'?"

"No that's more than enough," Menannon muttered ruefully and shook his head. "I needs must attend upon my father at the council, so I will take my leave."

He nodded to the steward, turned on his heel and strode across the courtyard to be let out the gate by the same gatewarden who had let him in only a little ago. Behind him,

Skendrin muttered something nearly inaudible which sounded greatly like "tell yer sire to get off the mark." Menannon glanced quickly over his shoulder, but Skendrin was already disappearing into the shed.

As Menannon walked up the steps to the portico of the Council Hall, he could not help the slight frisson of pride that crept up his spine to thus be here not as an observer, but as an actual part of this ancient assembly. Despite everything, he found himself walking a bit straighter as he strode across the portico to be bowed through the door into the outer hall by the duty doorwards.

The hall swept away in both directions lined all along its length with the doors of the offices and workrooms of the government which circled around the central chamber like jewels on a necklace. Directly in front of him were the great oaken doors of the council chamber itself. These, too, were flanked by two of Firod's doorwards, who likewise opened the door for him and bowed him through as had their fellows without. Menannon stopped just inside the entrance, stepping aside to allow two fellow councillors to enter and cross to their seats. The chamber was just as he remembered it.

The great council chamber of Kirith Kalyria was an architectural wonder well able to match all the rest of the wonders of the city. It was a long pillared hall whose finely painted ceiling rose well over eighty feet above the heads of the councillors gathering there. The east and west walls were mounted with long lines of clear windows to provide light in the day and there were three great chandeliers hung with Dwarf lanterns for nighttime illumination. All about its edges rose tier upon tier of marble platforms forming a long oval. Dotted evenly along their length were seats carved into the stone itself. Each seat was brave with multi-hued cushions set there for the comfort of those who would use them. Half way up the north and south walls great balconies ran, providing seating for those who chose to watch their governors conduct the business of state. Along this, high on the north wall opposite the entrance doors, was a special box for Kalyria's royal consorts should they choose to witness the proceedings.

The great paved oval of the speaker's floor filled the entire area between the rows of seating so that any who addressed the assembly could freely move about the chamber to see and be seen by all. Set opposite each other at the east and west sides respectively just above this floor were the king's throne and the huge seat provided for Gorlanndon seeming to embody in themselves the pillars upon which the stability of the kingdom rested. All was in perfect symmetry in the chamber's layout and space although rarely in its functioning.

Menannon glanced up towards his sire's seat and saw that Gorlanndon was already present and deep in conversation with Lord Lonier. Menannon stood still for several long heartbeats more taking in the scene before him. The arguing and shouting among the councillors hit him like a wall. He was not unused to the noise in the chamber as the council had always carried on its business rather loudly save when one individual was addressing the assembly, though he was not used to the strident tenor of it.

There was a sense of suppressed anger here that pressed against him like the coming of a thunderstorm. It seemed that this was going to prove a tempestuous meeting which, he sincerely hoped, would end before four of the clock, as Nirna had promised to meet him in the garden here at that time. At least, he hoped she had. For just a moment, he had a horrible sinking feeling that Mati had not really meant that Nirna would meet him, but no. Mati had been very clear in her words. Nirna would meet him.

Menannon turned his attention back to the chamber once more and noticed that here, as well as in the streets without, the predominant color was red. Not only had most of the visitors donned kirtles, robes and tunics of red, the vast majority of the councillors had replaced the indigo fringe on their official robes with an edging of red! The cadet level like himself who wore no fringe had added shoulder straps of the color. The few spots where a person or persons did not sport some vestige of red stood out like islands in a sea drawing his eye. The pure gold of the robes gathered around his sire's great chair positively glittered in their lack of crimson adornment. It was clear that those folk not following Azuron's lead were by far and away in the minority, even here. Obviously, things were getting out of hand rapidly and it was past time for Gorlanndon to act. Menannon could not help a quickly suppressed self-satisfied thought. At least he and Irenos and their friends were going to start doing something this very night.

With that thought to bolster him, Menannon made his way quickly across the speaker's floor to a point directly below his sire. Gorlanndon glanced down and smiled in approval at the sight of him. He waved Menannon to an empty seat so set that when the young Giant sat, his head was nearly on a level with his sire's, and so Menannon found himself seated next to Lord Lonier almost in the middle of the golden island surrounding his sire. Lord Lonier gave him a brief nod, but did not speak, as his attention was riveted upon two other councillors across the way who were arguing in voices so loud their words carried across the chamber despite the noise. Strangely, neither of them bore any red on their robes.

"I like not this idea of allowing Boria a place in our council and not just a place, but a voting seat and I deem Azuron is a fool for proposing it!" the shorter of the twain was shouting vehemently. "Borians have not been trustworthy since they served the Enemy in the Dim Times and nothing has changed...Nothing!"

In the sunlight streaming in the windows, the fellow's face was flaming nearly as crimson as his heavily jeweled red beard. His golden robe straining across his ample girth fairly threatened to split asunder with every wild gesticulation as he spoke.

The fellow to whom he was speaking so passionately was a

tall, spare councillor with a brown beard heavily salted with wisdom's pale color. His golden robe hung off from his sloping shoulders like a horse blanket adorning a scarecrow. Menannon searched his memory for names to fit the faces and found them in Siluc and Korkin. Korkin, the tall fellow, was from Kirith Kalyria itself and had ever served her in the Weights and Measures office while Siluc was from Kalyria's vassal kingdom of Hardura, near neighbor of Boria on the eastern shore of the Dawn sea. His family came from a long line of Marcher Lords ever tasked with the problem of keeping Borian interests beyond Hardura's borders and so could be well expected to hold a far more parochial attitude then Korkin.

"Now, Siluc. As a councillor yourself, you cannot let your own prejudice cloud your intellect," Korkin soothed, glancing around to see who had noticed their exchange. The answer to that was practically everyone, as nearly all eyes in the chamber were riveted on the twain. He glanced back hurriedly and raised his voice so that all could hear his reply.

"You must trust that Lord Azuron has reasons for what he is proposing and they are good reasons, I'm sure. His eyes see far more than ours and he has them focused on the future, not the past."

Korkin's voice was tight and squeaky with strain as he tried to verbally distance himself from his vociferous friend.

"His eyes are fixed on something alright and it's not the future! He's far too interested in our Princess and I, for one, like it not!" Siluc's voice cracked across the chamber stilling all other comments.

Beside Menannon, Gorlanndon made a small noise deep in his throat and shook his head. Menannon glanced over to see him turn to a councillor on his right and nod his head indicating the two arguing across the floor.

"A right lively debate, deem you not?" He chuckled as though enjoying the differences of opinion. "I've heard the exact same words about Boria from both his grandsire and his great-grandsire in their day as well. Hardura and Boria are like siblings scrapping with one another ere they come in for dinner."

There were answering chuckles from several parts of the chamber and not just from the Giant's own faction. For a moment, some of the tension was removed from the charged atmosphere. Across the way, the two councillors had turned their backs on one another and returned to their seats in a huff at the reaction of the chamber to their words. Siluc cast a rather hurt look at Gorlanndon and was rewarded with a slight shake of the Giant's head. The Harduran settled back in his seat much chastened.

"When did this Borian proposal come about?" Menannon asked softly of the old lord beside him. "It seems foolish in the extreme unless the Borians are prepared to give over slave trading."

"When islands fly!" Lonier murmured back and shook his head. "This particular proposal came about nearly a fortnight ago as Azuron seems intent on stirring up old sectional disputes with no better purpose seemingly than to make sure this assembly does not discuss anything of import. Divide and conquer, I should say. Unfortunately, a most effective device."

Before Menannon could make further comment, there was an imperial bang upon the doors and a general hush fell across the chamber.

The doors were thrown open and two guards dressed in Doomcrier red fish scale armour entered and took up their positions on either side of the opening. That their armour was red was startling to Menannon. Azuron had certainly moved rapidly since the riot or perchance even before it, as Dwarven armour was not the creation of a moment. Menannon glanced to his sire, but found no reaction visible upon his face from which he ascertained these crimson guards were nothing new. He settled back in his seat with yet another question added to his store.

The guards were followed in turn by three ladies in waiting attendant upon the Queen, all dressed in bright red sleeveless round gowns and crimson veils. One was carrying a tray with covered bowls, the other twain were burdened with fans made of rare albino peacock feathers. They stepped to the side and bowed low as Azuron followed them with Queen Norilendra on his arm. The Queen was dressed in a long-sleeved round gown of dark crimson while the Teluri wore his usual robe of many colors none of which, interestingly enough, was red.

At the sight of them, all in the assembly rose to their feet. With a slight bow, the Teluri escorted the queen across the chamber and up the stair to the heavily carven wooden throne and aided her to take her place upon it. He then stepped to a marble seat slightly lower and to the front of the throne.

He remained standing as the chamberlain stepped forth from the lowest row of councillors and rapped his iron shod staff upon the floor three times, then announced in a deep booming voice, "Our noble Queen Norilendra is before us. This session of the Kalyrian Council is now begun. Bring forth all ye the questions of thine hearts and be answered fairly and without prejudice."

Under cover of the noise of everyone again taking their seats a voice was heard to snicker, "Fairly and without prejudice? My beloved Aunt Loony's backside!"

At this comment, Azuron was stilled in his movement to take his seat and rose slowly back to his feet surveying the gathering for the source of the comment. At his movement, several folk in the far visitor's balcony stepped forward and scanned the councillors below.

Doomcrier guards...or informants? Menannon wondered, startled, and moved to lean forward to see if there were any such watchers on the gallery behind and above them, but his sire's hand on his arm stayed his movement.

"Welcome lad to your first council session as a member," Gorlanndon whispered in a stage whisper intended to be heard by all about them as though his movement had not been to keep his son from drawing attention to himself. With a slight warning squeeze he released his son's arm, Gorlanndon settled back with a mildly bored air ready to listen to this day's business.

The source of the comment being not immediately apparent,

Azuron sat down and spread the sleeves of his robes along the arms of his seat and leaned back nonchalantly. When he was settled, Norilendra signaled the chamberlain to begin at which sign the man once more struck the floor three times and returned to his seat.

The work of the council was slightly less mundane than usual as several traders stepped forward to inquire as to why they were unable to sail more than a league beyond the Crescent where they were forced to turn back. While the leader of the group did not come out directly and accuse Azuron of some sorcery, his words hinted of it. All eyes turned to the Councillor General to see how he would react to this. There was no change in him as he remained sitting easily in his chair eating from a bowl of grapes on the tray held by one of the Queen's waiting women who now knelt respectfully at his side, seeming to ignore the queen.

"I deem thou dost have captains that are indulging in too much volnaka ere they depart and find themselves unable to sail." Azuron quipped with a chuckle and his followers guffawed along with him.

"But all at once?" queried a voice from the farther end of the chamber where a contingent of councillors from the western vassal kingdoms was seated. Though all of them sported red on their robes, they were clearly not totally allied with the Teluri.

"Sailors are a superstitious lot are they not?" Azuron replied. "Let one be unable to complete his voyage due to his own error and the rest will claim ill luck and refuse to sail. But we are not bereft in this, not left to our own devices and speculations. Have we not among us the most able merchant in all Kalyria?"

Wiping his fingers delicately on a towel held out to him by the waiting woman, Azuron turned his attention to the Giant and addressed the ancient councillor in a voice that was almost gentlemanly.

"Lord Gorlanndon, have any of thy captains found themselves unable to sail in this last sevenday?"

The Giant looked briefly down at his hands then addressed the Teluri in all seeming innocence. "I have not found a need to send my ships forth in that time, so I cannot say if they would be able to sail beyond the Crescent or not."

At this blatant falsehood, Menannon caught his breath, but before he could speak, Lonier gave him a swift kick on the shin. He shut his mouth and schooled his face into a bland look of observation, but Azuron must have caught the movement for he instantly turned his attention to him.

"I see that thy son has been able to grace us with his presence again. Surely he can tell us about sailing beyond the Crescent."

Azuron glanced back at the queen as he spoke, for Norilendra had visibly stiffened at the sight of the young Giant. From the look on her face, the Queen was clearly not pleased with Menannon's return to his homeland.

"What say thee young sir? Can ships sail to and from our island?"

"I—," Menannon began, but Gorlanndon cut him off smoothly.

"My son came not by the sea, Councillor, as he came last night with Prince Irenos, who was instructed to bring him here by Ilenar King as a favor to me."

There was a slight tone in Gorlanndon's voice which clearly conveyed a warning to the Teluri to not interfere with the activities of the Blue Hill royalty should he wish to keep peace in the empire. With the mention of two such powerful Teluri, Azuron suavely changed the direction of his comments.

"In doing thee this favor, Ilenar King has also favored Kalyria, for we are the prouder by having thy son finally take his rightful place in this council."

At this, Norilendra leaned down to speak to him. What passed between them no one could hear beyond the royal contingent, but the queen sat back abruptly and Azuron turned again to face the assembly.

"Our lady Queen bids me welcome thee, Gorlanndon's son and body heir, to thy rightful place among us."

From the mutinous look staining the queen's face, she had bid him no such thing. Despite this, Azuron rose and inclined his head to Menannon. Everyone else followed suit leaving the young Giant rather embarrassed by it all, but his training came to his aid. As the rest of the council took their seats once more, he put his best Harper performance mask in place, rose and bowed to the queen and her Councillor General.

"I thank you, your highness, my lord and all my fellow councillors." He turned to include all in the chamber with a dramatic sweep of his hand. "Long and long have I looked forward to the day when I could stand with all of you in the service of our beloved empire."

With Irenos' words fresh in mind, he set out to remind the council and Azuron in particular the power that stood behind him by his next statement.

"The head of our guild, Grandmaster Blackmore, has given me leave to attend upon you and fulfill this, my bond and duty to my country and my people."

Amidst the round of applause started by Azuron himself and many shouts of "Hear, hear," Menannon returned to his seat with his mental fingers crossed that none here would fathom the real intent of his words and purpose. It was greatly to his advantage that Blackmore began pounding into his harpers from their first apprentice days the subtle arts of diplomacy. From across the floor, the Teluri gave him a slight nod as though acknowledging a touché. Menannon relaxed just slightly. He had managed to pass the first test with a whole skin. Beside him, Gorlanndon carefully changed a soft chuckle into a slight cough.

The council returned to other unimportant business and talked in circles for nearly two turns of the hour more before the Queen rose abruptly and swept from the chamber followed by her ladies, thus ending the council in the middle of a speech by a merchant from Boria extolling the virtues of allowing them into the council and in a voting capacity.

The fellow turned to the rest of his entourage totally nonplused at this action of the queen, his ice-blue eyes flashing with indignation. He was clearly going to make an angry comment when Azuron glanced his way and his mouth stilled mid-motion and changed its position. Menannon, who had been watching the interchange carefully, had never seen anyone able to turn a frown into a smile so fast.

"Clearly our gracious queen is fatigued by all our arguing. I shall return again anon, for I would not wish to discomfit her for all the world."

The Borian's gruff voice managed to almost be soothing in this little speech, but the fellow nearly ruined his own efforts by turning with a swish of his robe and stamping from the hall before the chamberlain could dismiss all. Behind him, the chamberlain's staff fell three times and all rose to stretch and begin talking among themselves as they turned to leave the chamber.

Menannon kept his eyes glued to Azuron during all of this and saw a brief look of distaste cross the Teluri's features as he looked after the Borian, then rose and swept from the chamber, the doorwards following him out like a guard of honor. Menannon found it a bit disconcerting that they had not followed the queen as was their normal duty.

Before he stood, Gorlanndon motioned Menannon to him. "Well done today, boy. We'll make a diplomat of you yet." He winked at Lonier over his shoulder. "I will see you at home, for I have a few things to attend to here ere I leave," he finished and turned purposefully to where a small group of councillors was standing by the north wall leaving Menannon silently fuming.

Once again his sire had smoothly prevented him from talking to him. Menannon heaved a heavy sigh and turned away, remembering the promised meeting and began to make his way from the chamber with a lighter heart.

Despite his great height, the young Giant lost himself in the crowd of councillors and courtiers and slipped back into a small side chamber until all was still.

The last of the doors along the hall closed and the main doors banged shut behind the departing councillors and guards and stillness returned once more to the hall. Menannon cracked the door open and peered out.

There was no one in the hallway, so he eased from his hiding place, closed the door with a soft click, turned and went silently down the hall. He willed himself to walk slowly and silently, though his thoughts flew ahead on the wings of emotion intent upon a meeting with Nirna too long delayed. He managed to reach the side door which led to the small garden without anyone being the wiser. The sun spilling through the door when he opened it was nearly blinding after the dimness of the hall. Once he had stepped through and eased the door shut, his impatience overcame him and he ran into the garden softly calling her name.

The queen's pleasure garden was a lovely tangle of flowering vines, lacy ferns, exotic shrubs and green leaves ranging from the size of Menannon's fingernail to one plant with leaves the size of an elephant's ears. All this nestled under the protective cover of the branches and leaves of a night-blooming peridüs. There was stillness within the garden as well as a peace which belied its location: only a stone wall away from the activity of the busiest building in the entire governmental complex. Nothing was stirring save a small bird whose green wings and red breast glittered jewel-like among the leaves of the lowest branch of the tree. It flitted about, stopping every now and then to peer down at the intruder with a dew-bright eye as though to make sure the Giant had the right to be here. Menannon held still, waiting for the little sentinel to finish his inspection. At last, with a happy chirp and a flick of its tail, the tiny fellow flew off into a tangled corner of the garden disappearing among the rose bushes and their attendant creepers. Menannon let his breath out slowly and began to circle the garden.

He had nearly made a full circle when a large-leaved shrub beside him erupted with a pink and gold vision which launched itself into his arms in a very unladylike fashion. He barely heard her words before Nirna began kissing him, torn between laughter and tears.

"Playfellow! You've come! I knew you'd understand my message."

Menannon was not loathe to answer her kiss for kiss, for his heart demanded nothing less. At last, the first storm of their emotions and pent up loneliness eased and she settled her head against his chest with a sigh. He rested his chin upon her sun warmed hair and held her close, breathing in the fresh scent of peridüs water wafting from her curls which along with the scent of the other flowers about them, was a heady brew. He would have been willing to stand thus with her for the rest of his life.

"Never has winter seemed so long, Playfellow," she murmured against the cloth of his robe. "I thought you would never come...and speaking of that...how did you come, for no ship has been in or out of the harbor in more than a sevenday." She suddenly jerked, half turning in his arm.

"Did you come hither from Aridion City a full sevenday since and not come to me until now?" she demanded, the purple of her eyes turning darker with hurt and suspicion.

"Nay, Faeori, I came but last night with Irenos Prince," he assured her, though telling her the story rather than the truth as he deemed it best for the nonce. "I would that it had been sooner," he added, giving her a quick kiss on the head as though to seal his words.

She came back into his full embrace with a sigh and raised her face to him for another joyful kiss in which he obliged her.

The time had come to tell his own news, yet now that the moment he had dreamed of for so many months had finally arrived, he found himself strangely tongue tied.

"Faeori...," he began, then halted, hot color suffusing his cheeks.

"What is it?" She opened her eyes and reached up to move a stray lock of hair away from his eyes. "What is troubling you?"

"I...well...I...."

He suddenly found himself stammering like a first summer apprentice being set a sum.

Knowing him well, Nirna kept her silence. He would find the words for which he searched in his own time.

At last he swallowed hard and spoke.

"My beloved, liege lady, when I reached Aridion City, I researched long and carefully as I did not want to err in this above all things." He had to stop and take a deep breath again before he could continue. "Faeori, I have found that it is not forbidden of the High One for Humans and Giants to wed. It was never common, but of old there were at least three such unions recorded on the books of lineage from my clan alone—."

"It is true then! We can be wed!" she whispered, interrupting him, her face shining with such happiness as he had never seen.

"The law will have to be changed," he reminded her, but she swept away his objection with a wave of her shapely hand. "Pooh to the law! I will be queen when I come of age and I will change the law, then we shall be wed in the most magnificent ceremony this city or any city has ever seen. The hundred bells will ring out for us, Playfellow! For us!"

She stood on tiptoe and kissed him long and passionately causing him to fervently hope that the eleven summers until she came of age passed quickly. When she released him, her smile was glorious.

Then, in one of her quicksilver mood changes, Nirna burst into a storm of silent weeping clinging to him as though her very life depended upon his presence. Not knowing quite what to do, Menannon simply continued to hold her and began to gently rub her back until her sobbing stopped and she was able to step back from him. He reached under his robe and withdrew a clean handkerchief from his belt pouch.

"Here, Faeori," he mumbled, handing her the cloth. She wiped her tear-reddened eyes and blew her nose like an obedient child then turned away to play distractedly with one of the huge leaves behind her.

"I'm sorry Playfellow. I didn't mean to cry all over you. It's just...." Her voice trailed off ending with a slight hiccough.

Menannon took her shoulders and gently turned her around.

"I took no offence, Faeori, and will take none if you will just tell me what has happened to cause you such distress."

There was a low bench a little along the path and he led her to it and settled her there then knelt on one knee in front of her.

"Speak to me Faeori."

He kept his voice low and gentle as he did when treating with Aridion City's orphans. She sat for several long heartbeats silently twisting the handkerchief between her fingers. At last she looked up through her lashes then ducked her head back down.

"I'm so happy with your news that I'm suddenly terrified that something will spoil it. It's just that I...."she started, then stopped and cleared her throat and tried again. "I feel like such a fool, Menannon, for there is really nothing I can mark and say 'this is the trouble.' Everything is wrong and nothing is wrong." She glanced up at him again then took a deep breath and straightened her shoulders. "It's just...there is in the very air here that which makes my skin crawl. There is an all-pervading feeling of something waiting to happen. Like a storm just over the horizon. It's everywhere. Conversations are halted when I enter the room. Furtive looks are cast my way from the serving folk and doorwards. Everyone is whispering and no one is talking. Do you know what I mean?"

"Sadly, my lady, I do," Menannon nodded. "For it's the same in my father's villa. The things not being said nearly roar in my ears."

"Aye, that's it exactly!" She said looking him in the eyes, her hand reaching out to clutch the sleeve of his robe. "E'en Mati just pats my hand and says that I'm imagining things when I say there is something wrong. Menannon, I am not a child any longer and I am tired of being treated as one!"

Nirna burst out, her sudden anger drying her eyes marvelous fast. She stood, nearly knocking him backwards and marched to the end of the garden and climbed up on the wall despite the delicacy of her gown and sandals.

This wall was tall enough that it still provided a bit of privacy simply due to its height above the surrounding plaza though should anyone be looking out of the windows of the Council Hall they could be seen to be in conversation, a thing which he doubted not was still forbidden them. Despite that, he followed her swiftly and stood below her on the lower reaches of the wall, their heads thus almost on a level.

"Do you see it out there?" she pointed to the crescent.

Menannon looked along her pointing arm, out across the plaza and the harbor and saw again the strange shimmer.

"It surrounds our entire land and the sailors are frightened. They are saying no ship can leave nor come, that all are turned back without e'en a turn of the steering oar."

"Do any speculate as to the cause?" Menannon asked, attempting to study the shimmer, but every time he looked straight at it, it disappeared.

"It's sorcery! It's him!" she almost snarled, her face hardening into angry lines.

"Him who?"he asked, keeping his voice level, despite the fact he was sure he knew the answer and it angered him.

She glance around suddenly furtive, as if she expected the very leaves about them to be listening.

"Azuron!"

Nirna spoke the Teluri's name as though it burned her tongue to say it. She looked over her shoulder at him. The deep purple of her eyes turning nearly black with suppressed anger and not a little fear.

"He is a sorcerer and he has cast a spell over our land...and my mother!"

"Why deem you that?"

"Because she dotes upon him and she, who has ne'er asked the time of day from a clock, now cannot e'en decide what gown to wear in the morning without first asking him his opinion."

Nirna fairly spat the words, so deep was her vexation with her mother's actions. Menannon had to agree that this new activity of the queen's was indeed out of character for her. He had never known Norilendra Queen to seek out any opinion save that of his sire and one other and even then it was only in a limited fashion and only when she had exhausted all her own devices.

The young Giant cast about in his mind for the identity of the other to whom the queen was wont to turn for council and found it in a name that bore ill tidings. It had been Lord Normanus, the aged councillor who had been assassinated in the very Council Hall itself! He swallowed a bit convulsively. What if Normanus had been killed because he had been a confidante of the queen? Would his sire be the next prey? The thought made his blood run cold.

"How did your mother react to Lord Normanus' death?" he hurried to ask though he already suspected the answer.

"She said he deserved to die a traitor's death and a quick knife had been too good for him...." Nirna's voice trailed off into a whisper.

"I have to agree something is indeed happening to your mother, for she was always one to set high store by the laws of this land and she would never have condoned murder ere this." Menannon raised a puzzled eyebrow. "But perchance she did not know the truth of how Normanus died," he suggested attempting to not let his own ill treatment by Nirna's mother color his reasoning.

The princess shook her head.

"She knew, for Captain Firod reported it to her exactly as it happened. I was attending upon my mother in the solar when he and Azuron sought an audience. The Teluri came and sat beside my mother as though he were her consort and faced the captain. Firod did not flinch or demur, but told her exactly how it happened and she looked at Azuron as if she wished him to confirm it. All that one said was that a cracked pot could not be mended and it is best to shatter it in the field and return its essence to the potter's mix to be made into something newer and better. As though there could be anything better than that good old man!" Nirna's eyes sparkled with tears again.

Menannon had to agree with her that Normanus had been a kind and intelligent man well known to the young Giant, as he had been his tutor when Menannon had first come to Kalyria. Normanus had done much to ease his transition from the Giantish world to that of the island without ever letting the youngster feel as though he were an outsider.

He could still remember Normanus setting him up on the top of the wall at his sire's villa the first afternoon he had come to tutor him.

"Look yonder, Menannon. What see you?" Normanus questioned, pointing out across the city.

"I see houses and ships and the sea and the sky and the clouds," Menannon answered, feeling rather puzzled by the question.

"Do you deem the High One can see as well as you can?"

"Of course! My father says the High One can see everything," Menannon assured him with all of his five summer's old wisdom.

"Is there anything down there that the High One cannot see?"

"I deem there is not." Menannon shook his head for emphasis.

"Can He see you?" Normanus looked down at him earnestly.

"Aye."

"No matter where you go?"

"Aye," the child replied solemnly.

"E'en if you go inside or it's dark?"

"Aye."

"Then you must always remember, Menannon, that anywhere in the world a person finds himself is his home because all places belong to the High One and nothing is out of His sight or reach. You are not a foreigner anywhere because this is the High One's world and he made all of it for us, his children."

Menannon wrenched his thoughts back from his memories and looked earnestly at Nirna.

"His murderer will not go unpunished! The High One will not be mocked. He will not allow one of His children to be murdered and do nothing."

"It seems as though He is doing nothing, for e'en now, our judges are being persecuted for performing their duties."

Nirna sighed and turned back to looking out over the garden wall.

"Remember that we must sometimes be the High One's hands and feet," the Giant observed softly.

She gave him a quizzical look, but Menannon only grinned and lifted her down from the wall. She started to go past him, but he took her arm halting her. Nirna looked up at him questioningly.

"We must go now, Faeori, for we have tarried over long and one or both of us shall be missed." He placed a restraining finger to her lips as she took breath to speak. "No. No more questions now. Meet me tonight at the mid-of-night in the brattice and you will get some answers."

He leaned down and gave her a long kiss then stepped away only to turn back with a grin. "Make sure to be dressed for an adventure and you will see one of the High One's answers." Before she could reply, Menannon strode away and let himself back into the Council Hall.

HE MADE THE RETURN TRIP TO THE VILLA walking on air. Despite everything, the world was alright, Nirna loved him and would one day be his. That thought alone gave wings to his heart and made the afternoon, spent in weaving beautiful visions of life with Nirna was his lady wife, fly by. Strangely none of those visions included himself as the Prince Consort of Kalyria, for what they would do in the future never intruded into his fantasies. He thought only that, whatever the future held, they would do it together.

Evening found him in the summerhouse still awaiting his sire's arrival. The elder Giant had apparently spent the rest of the afternoon and early evening talking to the few councillors still undecided about Azuron, although the thought uppermost in Menannon's mind was that he was avoiding conversation with his son. Reluctantly, he went inside and ate in the privacy of his own chamber the light dinner Clarinda had saved for him then went to bed, knowing he needed at least a little rest against the night's adventures.

It was a little over a full turn of an hour before he had intended to rise when he heard his sire walk past his chamber followed shortly by the sound of the closing of his father's chamber door. Menannon nearly rose and followed him, but stopped himself as he would not have time to pursue the conversation and still get to the meeting place on time. Reluctantly, he rolled back over and tried to sleep although it eluded him as his mind began to whirl with the what-ifs of tonight's undertaking. He finally threw off his covers and prepared himself for the quest.

As quietly as he could, Menannon donned his darkest kirtle and hose and a pair of soft boots, took up his old pack and let himself out of his chamber into the garden, heading for one of the sheds near the stables. He slipped inside as quietly as he could and cracked open the Dwarf lantern just a bit so that only a sliver of light was loosed. By that glimmer, he was able to find what he was looking for: two heavily bladed fishing knives. He slid the sheathed knives into his pack and slung it onto his shoulders, then closed the lantern.

He peered out for a moment making sure none of his sire's guards had observed him. There was no motion in the close. He eased his way back out of the shed and shut the door and quickly headed for the back wall of the close. The moon was full tonight, not very auspicious for a quest better performed in darkness, but it did make it easier for him to find the toe holds he had carved in this side of the wall and make his way over. He lay on top of the wall for nearly a quarter turn of the hour until he was sure that should anyone be watching the villa this night, they must all be on the more accessible side. The back of the close had only a few feet of level ground before it dropped off a goodly way down into a kind of saddle. It would have made attack from this side less than a desirable proposition. When he was sure all was as it should be, Menannon lowered himself down and disappeared into the darkness.

As careful and as silent as he had been, he did have one unseen watcher. Gorlanndon stood thoughtfully at his open window enjoying the warm softness of the night and watched his son's stealthy exit. Almost, he followed him, then decided against it, as the morning would be time enough to learn what the youngster had been up to.

CHAPTER 16
(SUMMER OF THE WORLD 6097)

MENANNON MADE HIS WAY to the near end of the Mathematical Bridge by following the outer walls of the villas for as far as he could before stepping out onto the road. He had apparently gotten past anyone who might be watching and so felt confident enough to cross the bridge and make his way to the back of the palace and halt in the darkness under the brattice. There was no guard on the wall as there had been no need for well over a thousand summers. Menannon eased from shadow to shadow until he stood beneath the ancient stone brattice which thrust out from the back wall of the palace close to cover any defenders who might have had to face a siege during the first summers of Kalyria's existence. It had never been tested.

He waited until he was sure that no one was in the plaza near him and then pulled out his fishing knives, unsheathed them and began to thrust them into the cracks between the great stones. They made a soft thunk as they went in and a slight scraping sound as they came out, but there was no help for it. He had no other way to climb the wall. Hand over hand, he managed to scale the wall and heave himself up through one of the murder holes into the brattice itself. He lay still, hugging the floor, his breath sounding excessively loud in his ears. Menannon looked around and saw no sign of Nirna, so he settled down in the darkest corner to wait.

It was perhaps a quarter turn of the hour before he heard the sound of lightly running feet coming along the wall. It was Nirna, but her approach was hardly stealthy. He wondered why, but had no time to speculate as she burst in upon him breathlessly.

"Playfellow?" she whispered. "Are you here?"

"Aye," he murmured back, rising from his shadow and coming into a patch of moonlight gleaming through an arrow slit. She ran to him and threw her arms around him and halted anything else he might have said with a kiss.

"I was afraid you wouldn't come," she said, pulling away to look up at him. "As you can see I can't accompany you," she indicated the heavily embroidered robe she was wearing. It shone silvery in the moonlight and chimed softly as she moved as there were small bells all along the hem.

"Mother has ordered a mid-of-night repast to be served in the solar to celebrate the full moon and Azuron is coming as the guest of honor. I swear, Playfellow, she would find it hard to e'en breath without his presence." This last she said with disgust. "I must go back ere they miss me, but I had to come so that you would not deem I had abandoned you."

"I would never." He leaned down and kissed the tip of her nose. "Perchance this is a good thing, as Azuron will be less interested in the happenings in the city tonight. Go then and the High One go with you."

"And also with you," she whispered. "Come and I'll stand watch while you use the stairs and the sally port in the side wall as you used to upon visiting me."

Before he could protest, she took his hand and began tugging him out of the brattice and along the wall. They reached the middle of the east wall and came to the staircase. Nirna pulled him down and kissed him again then pushed him on his way.

"Go! No one is watching." She continued to stand at the stair head until he had safely attained the shadows beside its base and found the sally port. With a last look up at her, he drew the bar free and slipped through the small door back out into the plaza.

Menannon made short work of leaving the plaza and crossing back to the Equian where, rather than going on up to his sire's villa, he took the right hand fork and began making his stealthy way down towards Lady Rhyland's. He was a good three turns of the hour early for the intended gathering time for the conspirators, but he was too keyed up to return home and wait.

Just above the judge's villa, he slipped off from the road and began making his way through the orchard surrounding it. At the very edge of the trees, he settled down to wait. From this position, he had a clear view of the front gate and the southwest corner of the close. There was movement here and there all across his field of vision. Azuron's Doomcriers were out in force making sure that no one entered or left. It was going to take quite a distraction to give him a chance to get the lady and her family out. Luckily there were only five members of Lady Rhyland's immediate family living there: the lady her-self, her eldest son, Rhys, his lady wife and two grandchildren: two small girls. Her own consort had passed away several summers ago and her other two sons and their families served Kalyria at off-island posts.

Menannon counted guards and moving bushes around the wall. There appeared to be someone at about ten foot intervals all along. The long night would hopefully dull their senses or else more drastic measures were going to have to be taken to get the folk out. The young Giant thought of and discarded a score or more of possible ideas until all he could finally think of was knocking out cold two or three of the Doomcriers on the backside of the close and having Haalinoth stand against the wall with Irenos on his shoulders to act as a living ladder for the folk to climb down. How they would get away after that was a matter of the wildest speculation.

The first birds were beginning to chirp and the air to smell of morning shortly after moonset, when at last he was joined by Haalinoth and Irenos, each dressed as he was in dark kirtle and hose. They nodded to him and signaled that they needed to withdraw and speak. Menannon followed the Teluri a little way back through the orchard so they could speak quietly without fear of being heard.

"What hast thou seen? Are there as many guards as was our fear?" Irenos murmured.

"Aye. They are as thick on the ground as caterpillars in spring." Menannon murmured back. "But I bethought me that if you twain would stand against the wall and let Lady Rhyland and her folk climb down you, we could manage this if we knocked out a few guards at the back. What say you?"

The Teluri exchanged a glance then nodded. "It is a good plan." Haalinoth murmured. "As soon as our friends appear to spread inattention amongst Azuron's stalwarts, we shall set it in motion."

"Come, they shall be here soon and we must be ready," Irenos urged, turning to lead the way back to the edge of the orchard and around it to the side well away from the gate.

They hunkered down to observe the Doomcriers and mark their positions. The fellow nearest them was not hard to find, as his snores were carrying quite well in the night air. Next to him, two of his fellows were intent upon a game of dice in a small space of packed earth they had cleared for the purpose. The two Teluri indicated that they would deal with the guards and the Menannon should ready himself to get over the wall as quickly as he could. The one aspect of their plan that was chancy was that they had been unable to alert Lady Rhyland as to their rescue attempt. With luck, the good lady would be quick to apprehend what was happening rather than raise an alarum.

While they waited the last few moments for the charade to begin, Irenos and Haalinoth faded into the darkness. Menannon barely heard three soft thuds and the Teluri returned as silently as they had left, bearing unconscious Humans, Haalinoth with two. They set them down and leaned them comfortably against the trunk of the tree and signaled Menannon to be ready. Again he took out his fishing knives and held them lightly, waiting for the disturbance to begin.

He had not long to wait, as suddenly a loud shout broke the stillness, startling a flock of starlings from their night's perch and threw the Doomcriers into confusion. The reek of Borian ale reached the villa before the riotous fools came into sight.

"Tiny catchrat, Dink! Bringing back now!" Turanio's voice cut the night air from just beyond the last curve of the road.

"Catch me if you can, you wooden footed goats," came a

cackling singsong reply and with that, the other four of their party burst upon the scene running down the road, the two stilt-walkers hot after the two Dwarves. Dink was waiving a full bottle of Borian ale and dancing about in and out around Turanio's legs. As soon as Turanio tried to lean down and catch a hold of it, Dink tossed the bottle to Conar who immediately started taunting Tullio in the same manner.

"Ye'll never catch me! Yer too tall an' clumsy, an yer head is after bein' made of wood just like yer legs!" Conar ran several steps towards the gate and stood waving the bottle above his head. "Here ye are, long shanks. Come an' get it!"

As the younger Orlando ran towards him, he tossed the bottle back to Dink and then ran after it to join him in a line dance around and around the two stilt walkers' legs. The Orlandos were making a great show of trying to stomp on the Dwarves as they danced and catcalled. These antics had the desired affect and soon all of the Doomcriers on guard at the front and most of them from the sides were standing around the gate rooting for each side and taking bets as to who would win.

At a signal from Irenos, Menannon broke cover and sped to the wall where he made good use of his knives and scaled it in a matter of seconds. He was up and over it into the back garden before anyone was any the wiser. Once inside, he spotted the kitchen door by its location fronting the kaleyard and made his way hastily to it, letting himself in. As the door clicked closed behind him, he whispered a brief prayer of thanksgiving that folk on Kalyria did not yet deem it necessary to lock their doors.

Though the kitchen was in darkness, there was a glimmer of light coming from the front reception hall declaring that at least someone had been disturbed by the noise from without. Menannon ran lightly down the hall and halted at the entrance to the chamber. Lady Rhyland and her son Rhys were standing near the front door in their night attire, listening intently. They had not noticed him. Menannon took a deep breath, said a brief prayer and stepped out of the shadowed hall.

"My lady," he murmured. They both whirled around in

surprise, she grabbing up a vase and his hand moving to where his dagger would normally be.

"Hold! I'm a friend." Menannon held out his hands showing that he bore no weapons.

"Menannon?" Rhyland quarried setting down the vase instantly recognizing the young Giant by his size and resemblance to his sire.

"Aye, my lady!" He inclined his head to her as was proper.

"What is the meaning of this?"

Rhyland was still tall and willowy despite her nearly seven centuries of life. Her white hair shone in the lantern light like a crown. She was a formidable figure even in her sleeping robe. Beside her, Rhys seemed to take in what was happening in a trice for his face cleared and a grin spread across it as he gave over reaching for his dagger and took his lady mother's arm instead.

"Mother, there is no time for questions," he said. "Go and dress quickly in something dark while I wake Missa and the children."

She turned to him, startled, and opened her mouth to question further, but he shook his head and propelled her past Menannon and down the hall, with a nod to the Giant. Menannon breathed a sigh of relief at the man's quickness and stepped to the window to look out and see how things were proceeding.

He could see through the lattice work of the gate that the chase was still going on and had now become something of a ball game with Dink as the ball. The little Dwarf had curled himself into a ball and the Orlando's were kicking him back and forth as though he were made of rubber. Conar was standing to one side waving the bottle and cheering them on. They needed to hurry, this could not go on much longer without Dink suffering some damage.

Menannon let the curtain fall back carefully and moved back along the hall to the family's quarters. Luckily the judge's villa was built along the normal lines of other fine Kalyrian homes and he found the family bedchambers with no trouble.

He could hear the soft sound of the parents waking and dressing their daughters from one of the chambers so he turned to the other that showed a light and knocked softly. The lady opened it, already garbed in a robe of black wool. She was just finishing tying up her hair.

"My lady, if you have a jewel box or treasury about, please give it me as you will need funds on the mainland and I know not what Azuron will do with your villa when he finds you fled."

She said nothing, only pointed to an iron bound chest about two feet square sitting upon her dressing table. She stepped out of his way and began gathering a few items of clothing into a satchel. Menannon took up the chest and put it into his pack. It barely fit. He turned back to her.

"Lady, is there anyone else in the villa who needs to be taken with us?"

"Nay. I let my servants depart as soon as I was accused for I did not want them tainted with my disgrace."

Menannon nodded and held the door for her. She threw a cloak about her shoulders and stepped out ahead of him, her satchel held firmly in her hand. Her son and his family were already standing in the hall waiting for them, the two girls wide-eyed with fear and uncertainty. Each bore a small satchel of clothing and the oldest girl held a basket with two cats in it. Menannon had not thought of that and whispered a prayer that the feline family members would recognize the need for silence as well as did their small mistresses.

Menannon nodded to them and led the way to the kitchen door and opened it a crack to make sure nothing was amiss. The sound of the chase was still floating from the front and he saw Irenos signaling them from the top of the wall. He pushed the door open the rest of the way and led his little band to the back wall.

"Is there a ladder anywhere?" he murmured.

Wordlessly, Rhys ran to a nearby shed and came back almost on the instant with a good stout ladder. This they set against the wall and Menannon climbed it and stood on its top rung, as it was not long enough to reach all the way. They would perforce need to climb over him to achieve the top of the wall. They handed the girls and the attendant basket of cats up to him and he set them on top of the wall with the soft admonition to "hold still." Lady Rhyland came next and Menannon braced her foot with his knee so that she could climb over him. Lady Missa followed quickly and then Rhys.

When all were up, Menannon followed and assisted them to climb down the living ladder on the other side. Rhys went first and then Menannon handed the girls down to Irenos one by one who then passed them to Haalinoth who in turn, passed them on down to their sire. The two ladies were a bit shaky climbing down the Teluri, but they made it and then Menannon simply jumped down and all of them faded into the darkness as rapidly as possible. As soon as they were well into the orchard, Irenos gave a high piercing cry which was a fine imitation of a hawk and they moved on knowing that the other four would soon head on down to the harbor and meet them back at the trade hall in the Serpentine.

As quickly as possible, Menannon led his little party around the face of the Equian and across the lower bridge to the Citadel thence to the Idrian, thence by circuitous ways to the back of the harper hall. Here they halted again to catch their breath and take stock. It was still too early for any of the day students to be about and a full hour yet before the dormitory bell would ring to awaken those who slept in. Only the kitchen staff would be about their business, so the likelihood of running into anyone inside the hall was slight.

"The High One's blessing upon thee. We will take our leave here shortly," Irenos whispered to Lady Rhyland and the lady inclined her head to both Teluri in thanks for their service.

"Be assured, I and mine shall never forget what all of you have done," she murmured and turned to Menannon who stood silently considering them.

"Ere we proceed any farther, each of you must all swear never to reveal to anyone what you see or hear tonight," he said, looking into the face of each person in the small group. "Do you so swear?"

Each nodded in turn.

Menannon took a deep breath and turned to open the secret door to the tunnel leading to the High Hall of Gathering and the gate to the Straight Paths.

"I shall return as soon as may be," he whispered to Irenos and Haalinoth and the two Teluri nodded and faded into the last of the shadows in the close, their part done.

With a quiet admonition to hold hands and follow him, Menannon herded the family into the darkness of the tunnel.

The floor of the tunnel was smooth and level and easily negotiated even in the total darkness that filled it, as none of them had a light of any description, an oversight in their planning to add to the list of things they needed to improve upon. He came to the spiral stair leading up to the door behind the throne and halted.

"We can still talk here, so listen carefully. We are going to ascend a spiral stair. When we reach the top, we will come out of a door in the wall behind the celebrant's high throne on the dais of the Hall of Gathering. You have all seen the throne, so you will know where you are. To the side of it, there is a mosaic that is actually a gate. I will open it and the chamber will be flooded with brilliant cobalt light, blindingly so, especially after this darkness. Close your eyes or squint as best pleases you, but you must hold hands as we move along. If your hands come loose, cease moving immediately and sit down. It is imperative that you move no further until I come for you.

"Know that you are safe now, but we are going to utilize Mythrian magic of a very powerful order to convey you to Aridion City and once there, you may bespeak Grandmaster Blackmore for sanctuary. Come! We must hurry ere the priest comes to prepare for the morning service. Remember: do not loose hands no matter the provocation."

It was strange giving orders and instructions in total darkness.

He hoped all had understood him. There was no way to read their expressions, for they were naught but faceless, bodiless sources of breathing and of body heat in the pitch blackness that was their resting place.

On second thought, he added, "Do you understand?"

Upon hearing murmured replies from his charges, Menannon turned and led the way up the stairs, feeling his way to the door. All followed him as quietly as possible. He eased it open a crack and the light of the presence lamp nearly blinded him. He waited a moment, listening to make sure the chamber was truly empty. There was a peaceful stillness within. He opened the door the rest of the way and ducked through. The family followed him closely.

Before anyone could say or do anything, he held a finger to his lips reminding silence and moved to face the mosaic. He turned with a silent prayer and spoke the word of command. The gate ground open, the sound of its opening strangely muffled. All his charges gasped at the brightness and beauty of the light, but held their tongues. Together, they stepped into it and the gate shut behind them, the grinding sound of its closing now faint and far away.

Menannon followed the pattern of steps Blackmore had provided him giving it all the single-minded attention only a Giant can, and they soon faced the gate to Aridion's harper hall. He took the last step and the gate opened on still starlit darkness. They stepped out and Menannon let go of Lady Rhyland's hand and crossed the chamber to light the cresset above Blackmore's desk. He turned back and his heart froze. One of the girls was missing.

The eldest, who had been carrying the cats, had been in the back of the group with her little sister next in line. Frantically he banged on grandmaster Blackmore's door then ran back to the Kalyrian gate and opened it before the family realized that they had arrived less one. Even as he stepped back through the gate, he heard Blackmore's voice welcoming the first of his refugees.

Menannon prayed fervently that the child had followed his directions and sat down when she became separated. He walked back along the path praying every step that he would find her, but he reached the Kalyrian gate with no sign. There he had to stop and take several deep breaths to still his racing heart. She had to be somewhere! He turned to retrace his steps with Blackmore's admonition ringing in his ears...*lost for all eternity unless you are found by accident...by accident...by accident.* He had not thought of the simple expedient of tying his charges together with a good stout rope and now a little girl was paying the price for his stupidity. He walked slowly back to the Aridion gate and still found no sign of her. There he almost stepped through to enlist Blackmore's aid, but suddenly felt that he did not have the time. He either found her now or she would be lost forever.

He turned back one last time and thought to call her name, but realized that he did not know it. So instead he simply called, "Sunshine, where are you? Sunshine, can you hear me? Sunshine!" Each time he stopped to listen in hopes that he would be answered, but there was no response. He reached the halfway point back to the Kalyrian gate and halted again at a crossing.

"Sunshine!" he called and his time there was a sound. Strangely, there was a slight rumble to his left.

"Sunshine!?" he repeated and the rumble got louder then a small black and white cat came out of a side passage. It was one of the cats the girl had been carrying in the basket.

"Sunshine?" he questioned. The cat purred loudly and rubbed his ankle. He dropped to on knee and scooped it up.

"Where did you come from and where is your mistress?" he asked, though he knew full well the cat could not understand him. It wiggled in his hands and he set it down. A soon as it was on the floor again it started back down the side passage out of which it had just come. It went a few feet then stopped and looked back as though it wanted him to follow it. Menannon took a deep breath and stood then looked about him to fix in his mind the passage he was now in and stepped out into new territory to follow the cat.

It led him a little way and then he heard another sound. It was the sound of soft crying, though there were words in it as well.

He stopped and listened carefully.

"Sunshine! Where are you?" a small child was saying. "Sunshine, come back. I'm scared."

It was all he could do not to run toward the sound, but he knew he did not dare as he would court the chance of losing his way and then they would both be lost. Menannon forced himself to follow steadily after the cat and he rounded a corner just in time to see it jump into a little girl's arms. She was sitting on the floor of the passage holding the basket with the second cat still inside, her face wet with tears.

"Hello there," he said softly, walking up to her and kneeling.

She looked up, her heart in her eyes and gave one last hiccuping sob.

"Thank you for sitting down when you got separated, sweetheart. That and your cat Sunshine helped me to find you." He smoothed his thumb across her cheek wiping away the tears. "Come, let us go find your family. Alright?"

She nodded and he picked her up, almost clinging to her in his relief at having found her. The High One be praised for having named a small cat Sunshine.

Menannon closed his eyes and retraced his steps back to the crossing by the vision in his mind so that nothing could distract him. He arrived back at the crossing and turned gratefully onto the path to Aridion. He opened the gate and stepped out, nearly colliding with Rhys who stood staring white-faced at it. When Menannon appeared with his daughter, Rhys almost tore her from his arms in his relief at seeing her again.

"Papa, Whiskers jumped out of the basket and ran away and Sunshine helped me find her, but I got lost," she told her sire as he carried her across to where the rest of her family sat talking to Blackmore in comfortable chairs near the newly kindled hearth.

Menannon stood watching them with a sense of near bone melting relief that the quest had been safely fulfilled then quickly left the audience hall and ran upstairs to his former chamber in search of his harper's robes as Irenos had instructed.

He opened the door as quietly as possible, not wanting to

awaken any of the other journeymen sleeping in the chambers near his. Long practice allowed him to find the cresset in the dark and light it with its attendant flint and steel. By its flickering glow, he crossed to his clothes press and had just opened its lid when a soft snore froze him in place. The sound was startling enough to his already raw nerves that he dropped the lid back with a loud whump and whirled to face the new danger. Across the chamber he found himself staring into the equally startled eyes of Lee, who until this moment had been blissfully asleep in the bed, under the watchful gaze of Pin, the stuffed puppy.

"What are you doing here!?" they both questioned at exactly the same time. "I thought...!"

The absurdity of speaking simultaneously, mixed with the relief at seeing only Lee, was enough to release Menannon from the strain of the last hours and he suddenly had to sit down on the clothes press as he began to chuckle, which turned into a guffaw, which in turn became a full side-splitting laughing fit. Lee could not help joining in. Between them, they twain made enough noise to cause the journeyman in the next chamber to bang on the wall in protest.

"My apologies!" Menannon called through the wall as soon as he got himself back under control. He stood and crossed to the bed.

"What are you doing in here?" he asked holding out his hand to the drummer in greeting.

"Well," Lee took the Giant's hand. "I...well, I..." he stammered, not wanting to admit he had changed chambers so that he would be on hand in the event Menannon came back for a brief visit or because he had forgotten something. He climbed out of bed to give himself a bit more time to think of a plausible excuse and in so doing, his eye caught Menannon's black harp resplendent on its stand.

"It's the harp's fault!" he blurted out in inspiration. "That instrument of yours is too heavy to drag around, so I found it rather easier to move myself than it, if you take my meaning," he finished with a rush, blushing to the roots of his hair.

"I do take your meaning and thank you for the care." Menannon inclined his head and turned back to the clothes press, but not before Lee caught the glint in his black eyes and knew that the Giant had seen right through him as always.

"So, what are you doing back so soon?" Lee asked, coming to stand beside the Giant and watching as he reopened the clothes press.

"I returned for these," Menannon reached out two of his harper robes and handed them to Lee as he smoothed the rest of the press' contents back into order and closed the lid.

"These? What do you need them for?" Lee demanded, nonplused. "Surely you're not planning on placing yourself under Penor's command!?"

"Perish the thought!" Menannon visibly shuddered as he took the robes back from the drummer. "Nay, I need them for another purpose. I've not the permission to tell you what, though I would that I might, for I could sorely use your singularly inventive mind."

Menannon nodded to him and let himself back out the door. Lee grabbed up his own harper robe and throwing it on to cover his nakedness, ran out the door after him.

"Whose permission do you need to speak to me?" he demanded, catching up to the Giant just as that worthy was beginning to descend the stair. He fell in step beside him, his bare feet making no sound on the cold flags.

"Blackmore's."

"Blackmore's? But you're doing something on Kalyria so why are you in need of Blackmore's permission to speak of it?"

"Because it concerns him most closely and is his secret, not mine," Menannon halted at the bottom of the stair and looked hard at his friend. "Were it my choice, I would tell you all and even take you along, though I know not if your sire would brook placing you in danger."

"Danger?!" Lee grabbed the front of Menannon's kirtle halting him as he started to turn away. "What danger are you in? Now I have to know what is going on!"

The Crenanocian's long line of warrior ancestors reared their spirit within him at the idea of danger to his dearest friend and sent Lee marching down the hall to the Grandmaster's audience chamber where he knocked peremptorily and entered before the echo of the knocks had died in the corridor.

Blackmore was seated at his desk alone in the chamber, having sent his guests to the refectory under the care of Jondlin. Lee marched up to him and took a position foursquare in front of his desk, the look on his face brooking no lies or dissimulation. Menannon followed a bit behind, not quite sure what was going on as he had never seen Lee in this martial mood before.

"Grandmaster, what danger besets Kalyria that has threatened Menannon and his sire?" There was no hysteria or wheedling in the tone of either voice or question, only a flat demand for knowledge.

The ancient Valinga set down his reading spectacles and studied the young fellow before him. Gone was all trace of the genial scapegrace who had scrambled about the harper hall and its environs passing his classes and learning his art by the seat of his hose. Leènoviilek had suddenly grown up and now in the place of the boy stood a man, a Crenanocian warrior with a mind like a finely forged sword who desired answers and who would receive them.

Blackmore studied him thoughtfully for a moment, keeping a fatherly smile to himself. One of the joys and frustrations of raising and training children was one never knew when the butterfly would break the chrysalis and emerge to stretch its wings demanding to touch the sky. For the drummer, that moment had come and thus for the first time in his life, Lee was beforehand of his friend, as Menannon stood beside him seeming still a bit coltish in comparison.

"To be honest, we know not the exact nature of the threats to Kalyria," Blackmore treaded softly, not knowing how much Gorlanndon had confided in his son. "All we know is that this Azuron is strengthening his hold on the reins of power by denouncing as many folk in high places as he can. He has them thrown into the dungeon and from thence we know not what is happening to them."

Raising an enquiring eyebrow to Menannon, he queried the young giant. "Have any yet returned, lad?"

"Nay, Grandmaster. None have been released according to Irenos Prince's latest intelligence."

"And how does this affect the Gorlanndon household?" Lee asked, glancing from Blackmore to Menannon and back.

Blackmore sat for a long moment, studying Lee, then nodded to himself.

"I have given Menannon permission to use the Straight Paths to rescue as many of these denounced folk as may be from Azuron's clutches."

Blackmore saw a slight flicker in the drummer's eyes. So, the existence of the Straight Paths was rumored in the hall as he had long suspected. That was interesting and not truly unexpected and that Lee should have heard of them while Menannon had not was also not unexpected, as the Crenanocian had spent far less time studying and far more time socializing than had his dearest friend.

"For the time being, the House of Gorlanndon is in no great danger as the councillor is too powerful to be yet assailed, though how long that will last, I know not."

Blackmore glanced at Menannon to see how the young fellow would take that bit of information and saw that Gorlanndon's heir had already come to that conclusion.

"Now that you are in on one of the harpers' great secrets, I have no recourse but to put your inquisitive self to work."

Blackmore turned back to Lee, all business now. He reached out a clean sheet of vellum and hastily wrote a few lines, sanded it and handed it to the drummer.

"From this point on, I am relieving Jondlin of the duty of escorting the arrivals as they come. This is a pass allowing you access to the king at any time and you are now responsible for taking the Kalyrians to the palace and seeing them settled into the protection of Gilderon King, fourth of that name. So be off with you. Go to the refectory and find Jondlin and his charges." The Valinga waved the drummer away and settled back to his interrupted business.

Lee glanced at Menannon to see that he had a very relieved look on his face.

"We will talk when next I come," the Giant whispered and stepped out of the way so his friend could take his leave of their grandmaster and depart the audience chamber. When the door closed behind the drummer, Blackmore raised his eyes once more to Menannon.

"Tell him all that you will save only the way to work the Paths. That I do not want him taught as it would put him at risk of being lost for I know that soon or late he will take it into his head to join you on Kalyria and that I do not desire. Is that clear?"

"Aye, Grandmaster." Menannon inclined his head in acknowledgment of this order.

"Good. Now hence with you. Irenos will be wondering at your long absence." Blackmore waved him away and picked up his reading spectacles.

Menannon crossed to the gate and raised his hand to open it.

"How did you find the child, lad?" Blackmore's question halted him once more just as he was about to speak the words of command.

Menannon turned and faced his grandmaster, his head lowered in shame that his thoughtlessness had nearly cost the girl her life.

"I was led to her by a cat named Sunshine," he said so softly he almost mumbled. "The creature answered my call and I followed it to the child where she had apparently caught her other cat and sat down to wait for me."

"Ah, so you were able to leave the path you were treading to find her and then retrace your steps. How very interesting. Well done, lad." Blackmore nodded his head approvingly then grinned at the look on his journeyman's face. "No one is perfect, lad. Only the High One, so don't be too hard on yourself. Just consider things more carefully the next time. Now be off with you." He waved him away with a nod and went back to his documents.

Menannon inclined his head again to his grandmaster and returned thoughtfully to the Kalyrian gate where he spoke the word of command and entered.

Blackmore looked up just as it was closing and smiled his secret smile. "Well begun, lad," he said. "Well begun."

⁂

Menannon made the trip back to the trade hall in a state of near utter exhaustion after the nervous tension of the quest wore off. He mentally berated himself the entire way for being such a fool and not planning better. The thought of the little girl lost on the paths and starving to death would haunt his sleep for many nights to come. The one good thing that had come of this trip beyond its dubious success was that Lee was now part of the quest. Menannon knew in his heart that this fact would be of the greatest importance at some stead.

He reached his destination and stood without the door of the small chamber listening to the sounds of laughter and celebration coming from within. He stood there for several long moments gathering himself and arranging his comportment to better fit the good humor within. There was no reason to spoil their well-earned good spirits because he had been a fool. He forced a smile to his lips, opened the door and stepped inside.

"Ah, here he is! How did it go? Are they after bein' in sanctuary?" Dink queried from where he stood upon the far end of the table.

"Aye, thanks to the cleverness of all of you, they are in sanctuary and need never more worry about Azuron's machinations." His reply brought relieved smiles all around.

"Three cheers for us" Dink shouted."Hip...Hip...Hurrah! Hip...Hip...Hurrah! Hip...Hip...Hurrah!"

Only Menannon and Irenos did not join in, but they applauded.

"Enough now!" Irenos raised his hand with a grin when Dink appeared to take breath for another round. "A little less noise, if thou wilt. We would lief as not have the Doomcriers without hear our cheer. Sit, sit and let us discuss our accomplishment."

When all had found a seat, the Orlandos on the side board to accommodate their long stilts and Dink cross-legged on the end of the table, the Teluri continued.

"Are there any comments that thou wouldst make to improve our endeavors?" He looked around the table enquiringly.

"Well, I fer one'll be after wearin' some paddin' on me nether parts!" Dink said, rubbing his abused flesh. "Turanio here has a powerful left foot!"

"Kha! Foot of ironwood. Sorry." Turanio reached over and ruffled the Dwarf's hair just as he would his younger brother's.

"I'll be attestin' to that, as I'll no be sittin' comfortable like fer a good sevenday!" Dink glared at the stilt walker and smoothed down his hair with a jerk. The others, save Menannon grinned at this sally.

"I vow there should be a good rope ladder added to our kit," Haalinoth chimed in rubbing his shoulder. "Irenos is not a feather to be born lightly."

"Aye. The weight was enough on thee ere we added the folk we were aiding," Irenos agreed seriously, but Haalinoth would have none of seriousness in the euphoria accompanying their success.

"It was the basket of cats which nearly over taxed us!" He shook his head and grinned.

"Cats in basket?" Tullio asked, glancing up in surprise. "Taking pets also, yes?"

"Of course, simple one!" His brother tapped him on the head. "You not leave Ponga if leave forever, no?"

"No, would not," the youth shrugged. "Not give thought is all. But not carry leopard. He walk." He sat back in a huff.

Before there could be any further discussion of the pros and cons of taking pets along, Menannon cleared his throat and everyone turned to him.

"I deem that we need to make sure that we find a way to inform our intended folk of our plans ere we arrive. They will be able to prepare and thus we will have a much shorter time in taking them from their homes. That would save more bruises to Dinks nether parts," he grinned at the Dwarf who preened, "and assure that we arrive at the harper hall while it is still dark."

Everyone agreed to this and set their minds to the task of figuring out a way to alert their quarry. It was finally decided that they would attempt to send a message to them hidden within a bouquet of flowers. Once that was settled, they chose their next party to rescue, set the time at just after the mid-of-night. Haalinoth volunteered to arrange the message and they went their separate ways feeling well pleased with the results of their night's work. Irenos held back and put a hand on Menannon's arm halting him. When the door had closed behind the others, the Teluri turned to him.

"What in this has caused thee disquiet, my friend?" he asked locking eyes with the young Giant. Menannon took a deep breath before answering him.

"I nearly lost one of the children," he said looking down at the Teluri and expecting to be censured, but Irenos simply looked at him, waiting for the rest of the story. "One of her cats jumped form the open basket and ran away. She followed. The High One blessed me and I was able to find her, but I ne'er want to go through that again. I did not bring this up earlier as I did not wish to dim their pleasure at our success."

"Ah. Of course. What dost thou deem is the solution?" Irenos asked. It was obvious he did not buy Menannon's excuse for not telling them earlier.

"I deem we must tie everyone together on a rope as well request them to hold hands and secure all pets so they cannot stray." Menannon rolled his eyes and shuddered. Irenos nodded in agreement.

"Consider this a lesson learned. Is there aught else?"

"Only a need for a light in the tunnel leading to the secret door. That is dark as the belly of a whale and caused much stumbling and frightened the children."

Before Menannon could say more, Irenos withdrew his small Dwarf lantern from his belt pouch and handed it to him.

"This should solve that," he said and stepped back, allowing Menannon to reach the door. Just before the Giant opened it his countenance lightened.

"Grandmaster Blackmore has informed Lee of our designs and has enlisted him in settling the folk with the king," he informed the Teluri with a grin.

"This is good news!" Irenos smiled back. "Now go home ere thy sire seeks thee," he said and turned back to his lists and maps.

Menannon departed, the door closing softly behind him.

CHAPTER 17
(SUMMER OF THE WORLD 6097)

T HE NEXT MORNING it began to be whispered that Judge Rhyland and her family had disappeared. At first, it was assumed that she had been taken prisoner and sent to the dungeons beneath the palace, but it was soon confirmed that this was not so, as none of Firod's guardsmen had seen her nor had any others serving at the palace, most especially the few gaolers. Where had she gone? Had she left the city? While Azuron made no overt accusations, the guards from the city's gates were called in and questioned, but they could give no clue. The Doomcriers on guard at the judge's home were stiffly warned and things appeared to return to normal.

At the villa, Gorlanndon heard the news from Firod who came to break his fast with the Giant each morning since his family had left the island. Of course the Giant immediately wondered at Menannon's odd exit over the back wall in the darkness. After Firod had left for his day's duties, Gorlanndon went to his son's chamber only to find it empty. He next resorted to the gatewardens where they were eating in the kitchen after they went off duty. Neither of them had seen the youngster since the previous evening…curious. Gorlanndon returned to his office and began to read his correspondence, patiently awaiting the truant's return.

It lacked a little of the ninth hour when he heard one of the maids in the long corridor leading to the kitchen chirp a happy good morning to someone. Gorlanndon cocked his head and listened for the footfalls. The stride length could only be Menannon. So where had he been this night? With Nirna, perchance? But no, the lad was too honorable to sully the princess' reputation by spending a night in her company. So was he involved in a clandestine rescue? There was one way to find out. He waited a full half turn of the hour then went into the garden and on around to stand outside Menannon's window. The boy had thrown himself upon his bed fully clothed and was fast asleep. From there, Gorlanndon went to the small back garden shed where the child Menannon had always hidden the treasures from his adventures. The great Giant knelt at its doorway and leaned down to look in.

There were still many treasures within its depths, a wooden sailboat and fine warrior and horse marionette whose every joint was movable with the strings tied to its crossed handles. Numerous other items from a broken chair to a collection of sea shells still lined the shelves amidst the gardening tools. Just inside the door to the left was a new treasure: Menannon's old pack hanging on a hook with a long length of fine strong rope, the kind used to climb mountains, looped over it and a small Dwarf lantern hanging on a nail beside it. Gorlanndon recognized the lantern as the one belonging to Irenos. So the boy was involved with the Teluri prince. That meant he was involved with this disappearance as the prince and several others, including Lonier, had been advocating passive resistance to Azuron. Gorlanndon quietly closed the shed door and returned to his office, not quite sure what his next move in this odd dance should be.

Having slept most of the day, Menannon was aroused by the smell of roasting meat and the sounds of singing coming from the kitchen where Clarinda and her staff were readying the household's dinner. He rose and went to the bathing chamber to make himself presentable. He heard the first gong announcing the food was served just as he was pulling on a clean kirtle and tying the laces of his boots. Dinner was served in the main dining chamber and attended by most of the household and several others, including Firod and a weatherbeaten old trader from Cromb who had come with the usual delivery of volnaka for the Cokeyna and had gotten stranded by the wall. He was enjoying the Giant's hospitality immeasurably and repaying it with the recitation of many a story. This night he was in fine form and kept everyone laughing and breathless by turns as he recounted the perils of sailing the high seas and trading in many a strange port.

While Menannon had spent many hours bemoaning his inability to speak to his sire in private, tonight he was rather glad of the crowd as he was not quite sure he liked the speculative glint in Gorlanndon's eyes nor the questions he feared it might represent. There would be time enough later to tell his formidable sire that he was involved in the prince's work. The dinner ended with the guests and their host repairing to the atrium for after dinner wine while the household staff returned to their work. Menannon announced that he was going to meet some fellow harpers at a pub near the university and bowing to all, took his leave before his sire could comment.

THE BLACK SWAN, more commonly known as the "Dirty Duck," was nestled along the outer wall of the university's close between two larger inns which were set there for the convenience of visiting scholars. It was favored by the locals and it was thence that Menannon repaired. He pushed open the door and ducked inside only to be brought up short by its lack of patrons. Where normally it was noisy with debating, arguing students deep in their cups and philosophies, tonight it was nearly empty boasting only a single table of journeymen members of the Bakers and Confectioners guild talking softly over large chalices of wine. Menannon made his way to the bar at the back and sat on one of the taller stools meant for the convenience of the Teluri scholars and instructors. The burly fellow tending the bar looked like an out of work fisherman, which he probably was.

"What'll ye be having?" the fellow asked, his eyes a bit rounder than was their wont judging by the myriad lines surrounding them at the sight of Gorlanndon's heir in his establishment.

"Honey mead," Menannon replied and set a coin on the marble top of the bar. He was served with alacrity. "What has transpired that the place is so empty?" he asked after taking a goodly swallow. The fellow stopped mid-scoop of the coin and stared at the young Giant.

"Why, haven't you heard? That Grandmaster Blackmore over on the mainland up and closed the university three months since and ordered all the students to Aridion City and the masters too. They moved everything, rigging, mast and sails."

"What!? Why?" Menannon was stunned that the Valinga would close the oldest university in the known world. It also amazed him that he had managed to miss that singular fact, as the students had landed upon his city all without him noticing, though he did vaguely remember that there had been quite a bit of building going on in the eastern district, a place he had not been to in several summers.

"There's none as knows why, save the Grandmaster his own self, as none of the masters could tell me when they came in for their farewell cup. 'Tis sure and certain a shock to business hereabouts. What with all them gone and the Councillor General telling folks as how they should be spendin' their coin at the circus rather than with the rest of us."

The fellow finished sweeping up the coin Menannon had set down and deposited it in his change chest. He set about wiping down the bar, probably for the thousandth time. He let Menannon drink in silence for a bit, then stopped his towel mid-motion.

"I don't suppose you'll be staying either?"

"Oh, I know not, 'tis rather peaceful here," the Giant smiled at him. "Do you mind if I take some of this mead over to the hearth?" He indicated a large lounging couch set beside a table with a small Dwarf lamp near the gently crackling fire.

"Suit yerself," the barkeep grinned back and took up an amphora with its iron stand and led the way to the couch where he set it near the raised end to be within easy reach.

Menannon handed him another coin and gave him a nod then

relaxed back on the couch. Its raised end fit nicely under his arm allowing him to sit upright enough to drink, but relax at the same time. His legs, from almost his knees down, hung off the end, something he was used to and this couch was more comfortable than most so he decided to stay until he needed to go back to the villa to prepare for this night's adventure.

The flames on the hearth were flickering nicely and a small bed of hot coals was forming at the near end. The sight of them took his mind back to the last day he had spent with Nirna at the cove dreaming about their life together. His pulses quickened and he took another swallow of mead. Then they had only been able to dream, but now he knew that their life together could happen. The High One permitted marriage between Humans and Giants and the laws of Kalyria could be changed to allow him to be the Prince Consort to Nirna. For nearly a full turn of the hour he let himself relax into a pleasant dream of a wedding and life with Nirna. They would keep her chamber in the tower as their bridal bower and after that it would be their retreat from the duties of court. She would rule with dignity and ease and he would be her first councillor. Together they would usher in a new golden age of Kalyria. Again he had a vision of a beautiful daughter with long black hair, the stature of her Giantish father and the graceful carriage of her Human mother. Once again, he saw her walking through a magnificent meadow rather than the palace where he had dreamed of himself and her mother. The sight of her filled his heart with awe as the vision was not of his making so it must be true then…he and Nirna would marry.

Before he could follow that thought farther a small party of lordlings banged through the pub's door and threw themselves noisily to a table demanding "Ale! Ale 'till we float!" The barkeep hurried to accommodate them and they settled down, but their presence put paid to any further romantic mood.

Menannon poured himself another chalice of mead and reluctantly changed his thoughts to tonight's adventure, which activity he was determined to carry off far better than he had the previous one. This time there would be nine folk to rescue, as

Irenos said the fellow had a wife, three children and three main servants who would be making up the cast of this night's desperate play. He settled in to spend the next couple of turns of the hour working out exactly how they were going to get the second judge to Aridion City. He found himself wishing, and not for the last time, that Lee was here instead of at Aridion City, as the drummer had always been the one who had masterminded all of their childhood escapades. The art of planning risky ventures was something the Giant would have to learn with alacrity, if at all.

THE MID-OF-NIGHT FOUND HIM again kneeling in the shadows of a wall with Irenos and Haalinoth listening to the antics of the other four of their team out in front of the gate. This time there were guards only at the gate, a fact he wondered about and found vaguely disturbing. He thought that Azuron would have doubled or even tripled the guards he had posted here since the disappearance of Judge Rhyland, but apparently he had not yet considered that as anything other than a random, if curious, act. At Irenos' signal, Menannon once again climbed the wall with his fishing knives and lay upon its top to study the garden. He held still, searching the darkness for any movement to show that there were Doomcriers on guard inside rather than without. There were none.

"Here, toss me up the ladder," he murmured and Haalinoth expertly tossed up a bundle of rope and boards. Menannon draped it over the wall and the two Teluri anchored it on their end and settled in to wait. Menannon dropped soundlessly into the garden, checking to make sure the ladder was long enough. He made his way to the kitchen door where he knocked twice.

"Page four and twenty begins with..." a low voice spoke from the other side of the door.

Menannon whispered the answer, "Thou shalt trust in none but the High One," and the door latch clicked allowing the door to swing open on a rectangle of darkness."

"Are you all ready?" he murmured, stepping inside to be surrounded by shadowy figures of various sizes.

"Aye lad, just as the little lady ordered. We are all dressed in dark colors and have our belongings gathered. Though I was much surprised and not a little baffled when the flower maiden told me your message as she presented my good wife with yonder bouquet."

The judge nodded to where a tall bouquet of lilies was silhouetted against the square of moonlight coming through the kitchen window. Menannon made a mental note to ask Haalinoth whom he had tapped as a messenger. Obviously, whoever it was had proven efficient. He turned his thoughts back to the task at hand.

"Here, tie yourselves together with this rope. Children in the middle."

Menannon reached out his rope and opened the small lantern just a crack so they could see what they were doing. The light showed the judge to be much younger than he expected. Then he remembered his sire saying that the man had been assigned to the bench but two summers since. He watched while he made quick work of tying his family together, then Menannon the took the lead and eased them out the door and back into the garden. At the wall, he anchored his end of the ladder and sent the judge up first. Just as the fellow reached the top there began a mournful howling from the direction of the villa.

"What is that?" Menannon demanded, instantly freezing into stillness his ears pricked for any sound from without other than that made by his own conspirators. There was none.

"That's my dog, Lily!" the tall lad whispered from his place behind his two sisters.

"What's it doing in the villa?' Menannon demanded, unable to keep the anger out of his voice. "Go get it, now!"

"But papa said we couldn't take her," the boy started to protest.

"Now!" Menannon growled, untying the lad and pushing him toward the villa.

The boy ran. The kitchen door banged and everyone winced. In a matter of moments the howling turned to joyful barking then silence. The door banged again and the boy ran back carrying under his arm a small black and tan spaniel with bright eyes and long silky ears. They all hunkered down in the shadows to see if there was any response to their noise. Apparently the antics of their diversionary team were still holding all attention without. Menannon tied the boy back onto the rope and then took the dog from him. She was just a pup and a very wiggly one with a tongue that could wash an entire face in a heartbeat—which she proceeded to do for him. He took an end of the rope, cut a piece as a leash and tied her onto the main line right ahead of her young Master and picked her up and handed her back to the boy with a grin and a shake of his head.

"Now go!" he murmured, sending the first child up the ladder after her sire.

Irenos had climbed onto the wall to see what was taking so long and so was there to assist all of them over and down. Even the old nurse made the climb with ease thanks to the strong arm of the Teluri.

There was a brief moment of trouble when the youngest girl started down the other side and found herself face to face with Haalinoth with his upswept eyebrows and pointed ears. She gave a little shriek which he instantly muffled with a firm but gentle hand over her mouth. He leaned to her ear.

"T'is alright for thee, sweet one," he murmured. "I only eat lads."

She stared at him big eyed and he grinned and winked and could feel her small mouth quirking up into an answering grin before he removed his hand and helped her on down the ladder. Menannon came last, tossing the ladder down to Irenos then dropping after it to land softly beside him. He took the lead and they faded into the darkness. The hawk called again and the party departed for the harper hall.

This time the audience hall in Aridion City was ablaze with lights with Grandmaster Blackmore at his desk, the sanctuary ledger already laid out when Menannon stepped through the gate. The old Valinga grinned and nodded approvingly when the rest of the party emerged, half blinded by the cobalt radiance, all tied together on a strong rope and each with a pack on their back and a satchel in their hand.

"Do you seek sanctuary?" he greeted them.

"Aye, for myself and my folk," the judge stepped forward as they finished untying themselves from the rope and gave Blackmore a flourishing bow.

"Come forward and be welcome to Aridion City."

Blackmore smiled and held out a brush already dipped in ink.

"When you have all signed, my assistant, Lee," he added, indicating the drummer who stood ready at the end of the desk, "will see you to the refectory for a repast, thence to your chambers."

Menannon wound up his rope and returned it to his pack then quietly stepped to Lee's side.

"We will have to plan a time for speech, but it is not now as I did not warn my companions that I would be overlong."

"Be careful," Lee murmured as Menannon crossed back to the gate and slipped back through even as the judge turned to speak to him.

"Where is Menannon?" he looked about hurriedly. "I wish to thank him."

"He has already returned to Kalyria," Blackmore informed him, having seen the Giant slip away. "The lad needs no further thanks than your safety, my lord."

Menannon made short work of returning to the small chamber in the trade hall and congratulating the others on their success. This time, it had gone off nearly without a hitch, the howling puppy notwithstanding.

By month's end they had not only rescued nearly five score of folk, but a seeming zoo's worth of felines, canines, birds, rabbits, squirrels, fish, reptiles and even a skunk, which last had garnered them the most interesting reaction when it arrived in Aridion City. The small boy whose pet it was had assured everyone that she did not spray unless she was frightened and she had behaved herself admirably, for which Menannon would ever be thankful, although Lee had suggested that one might have sent her to Azuron instead as that worthy was sure to frighten her, as he did everyone else, which comment was received with great glee by those who heard it, the mental image it conjured being most satisfactory.

AS TIME PASSED, it grew successively more difficult to find ways of distracting the Doomcriers set to guard the folk under house arrest and fewer and fewer people were being put under that same arrest when they were denounced. Most were now being taken straight to a holding area within the palace close before they were put through a mockery of a court trial and transferred to the dungeon itself. Menannon and the others were now forced to float the city in an attempt to hear who might be denounced before it happened in order to get folk away.

To aid in the gathering of information, Menannon took to stopping at the arena to try his hand at various games of chance as did all the other libertine sons of the wealthy. He also began to spend inordinate amounts of time in the less reputable ale houses along the waterfront frequented by the less discerning of Azuron's Doomcriers. Men will talk while in their cups and out of an ale cup more than one important piece of information was known to float. While all these activities would have done nothing to advance his reputation in normal times, they served his purposes now by giving him inside information while dulling the watchfulness of the run-of-the-mill Doomcriers who had been set to follow him. He wore his harper robes or not as the fit took him, which also seemed to placate his handlers, as they were perfectly content to have a harper dishonoring his guild by playing games of chance and consorting with unsavory folk in unsavory places in the robes of his office. Underneath his robes he always made sure to be wearing his most disreputable kirtle and particolored hose so that he could unfasten the robes at the front in a sort of semi undress to aid in the impression of feckless debauchery. He even let his hair and beard grow to unkempt lengths and began to wear beads and jewels in his beard. Though he was careful to so place them that they made no noise during his real business.

Based upon the bits and pieces of information all of them were able to gather, they had sent many floral messages to the folk about to be denounced and managed to carry many to sanctuary.

As luck would have it, Haalinoth had enlisted as their floral messenger the selfsame flower seller who had met Menannon on the dock on his arrival in the spring which now seemed so long ago. At ten summers old, Emma had proven more reliable and inventive than many an adult would have been and so far none of their messages had gone astray.

So many folk were being denounced that Menannon had even suggested to Irenos that they enlist Nirna's aid in finding out who would be denounced next, but the Teluri had forbidden the idea as it would put the Princess in grave danger. Nirna was being guarded more closely than ever and never left the palace without a troop of Doomcriers surrounding her. Only once had Menannon been able to speak briefly to her in the market before he had been muscled away from her by six fully armed Doomcriers. Firod had also previously appraised his sire of his son's visit to her on the second night of his unexpected return and Gorlanndon had expressly forbidden him to repeat the visit and to see that his order was carried out, he had informed his son that Firod had set a guard on Nirna's tower.

G REATLY THOUGH HE HAD PREVIOUSLY DESIRED to speak privately with his sire, now Menannon was doing everything in his power to avoid such a pass, something he could not help but find absurdly amusing. He spent as many hours away from the villa as he was able that he might avoid his sire's company, though he still attended the council sessions with him when full council was called, but that was much less often now. During these sessions, he had to literally grind his teeth to hold his silence as Azuron's adherents became ever bolder in their taunting disrespect of Gorlanndon and his faction. It was getting to the point that a few Doomcriers made bold to throw things at the Giant when he went about the city. Menannon was ready to burst with fury, but Gorlanndon told him that to react to such ill manners was to sink to the level of the perpetrators. The elder Giant simply ignored them all, both within and without the Council Hall.

As full summer came on, proof that their efforts were discomfiting Azuron came in the form of rumors being bandied about the pubs and whispered in the Council Hall that a gang of thugs was kidnaping and murdering folk.

Broadsides denouncing this disturbance of the civil order and demanding that any suspicious activity be reported to the office of the Councillor General were posted upon the street lamps and all entrances to the Circus. A growing reward was also being offered, a thing which Dink found particularly amusing though he would not vouchsafe his reasons to anyone.

Azuron appeared to be certain that the heart of these disturbances lay within Gorlanndon's holding as not a single soul could come and go from the villa without being followed wherever they went by their own personal guard of Doomcriers. More than once serving folk of Gorlanndon's had been waylaid and beaten, a fate which even Menannon had not escaped. This did not stop any of the rescues as Azuron had no proof that Menannon was involved with the disappearances else the Teluri would have arrested him and had done.

The activities of the Doomcriers had altered the pattern of the rescues as it was no longer possible to entertain those on guard at a villa or house. Irenos therefore had resorted to sending the other members of the group away from the rescue locations to draw off the attention of the Doomcriers. They had decided to make it appear that Menannon was spending a great deal of time in the company of Turanio, Dink and Conar crawling the pubs, including the Cokeyna and the Circus day and night. No one thought it odd that Tullio did not accompany them as he was too young to drink thereby allowing the younger stiltwalker to masquerade as Menannon in their little farce on those nights when a rescue was planned. By donning the Giant's harper robe and keeping the hood up, he passed for the Giant in the ill-lit ale-houses they habituated. Even though the hood was more of a long cowl and thus very deep and concealing, Tullio insisted on wearing a false beard to complete the ruse. At Menannon's asking, Clarinda had made the beard correct down to the matching jewelry attached. The old Dwarf had raised in inquisitive eyebrow, but asked no questions.

Thus their little band reveled all afternoon and long after the stars had sought their own beds and Tullio played the Giant on the nights of a rescue to make their watchers believe that Menannon was with them wallowing in Borian ale, while in reality he was escorting more folk to Aridion City.

To better play the role, the younger stiltwalker took to using a higher stilt than he was accustomed to so that his stature matched the Giant's. His were the special stilts that hinged as though they had an actual knee and thus, by walking stiff legged, the stilt broke at the right place and he appeared to be walking normally. Turanio liked not this arrangement at all as his brother had not obtained enough practice on the higher stilts and they were at times forced to run to get away from thugs. Each time the boy wore them, Turanio tried to dissuade him from using them, but Tullio would just laugh and start dancing. His brother would throw up his hands and they would set off on their quest.

While the others drew the Doomcriers' attention to the lower reaches of the city, Menannon, aided by Haalinoth and Irenos, was still finding ways to enter the homes and get folk away, though it was becoming more difficult with each rescue. Their greatest fear was that one or more of them would be seen in company with someone known to have been marked for denunciation.

The night it finally happened, they were carrying out the rescue of an old vegetable seller who had been denounced for talking negatively about Azuron and, strangely, assigned to house arrest. Irenos was of a mind that the gooddame being thus assigned, rather than simply sent to the holding chamber in the palace close, was setting a trap for her would-be rescuers and thought to let her alone, but the rest had voted him down saying it unfair not to at least try to carry her and her family to sanctuary. They had laid their plans, sent their message and set to work.

They had just gotten the gooddame over the wall and down to Haalinoth when a patrol of Doomcriers had rounded the corner of the next house but one down the street, heading directly for them. Irenos was still on top of the garden wall and Menannon on the inner side with the gooddame's two sisters when the Doomcriers appeared. They spotted Haalinoth immediately and began calling for him to halt. The Teluri just gave then a rude gesture, threw the gooddame over his shoulder and fled through the orchard behind the row of houses. The Doomcriers gave chase. Haalinoth went crashing through the trees making as much noise as possible to draw them off while Irenos and Menannon got her sisters and their belongings over the wall.

"You follow Haalinoth," Menannon whispered, "while I take the ladies to the hall." Irenos nodded and slipped silently into the moon shadows in search of the other twain.

"Come. He will find your sister. We must hence ere another such patrol comes." Menannon grabbed up their baggage and ushered the ladies as fast as possible in the other direction towards the harper hall and safety.

Irenos had not far to go before he found the gooddame hiding beneath an old log that had been left to show the boundary of the orchard. She was terrified, but none the worse for her strange ride. He could still hear Haalinoth running and catcalling the Doomcriers after him on down the hill.

"Come lady, quickly!" Irenos whispered holding out his hand to her. She took it, trembling with fear, but said not a word. He led her quickly to the back of the harper hall where Menannon waited with her sisters.

"Haalinoth?" Menannon made a question of the name.

Irenos just shook his head and departed.

Menannon led his charges on to Aridion City and unceremoniously left them in Lee's charge with no explanation. He simply retreated back through the gate before it had even closed upon their arrival, leaving the Drummer with a half-formed question upon his lips.

Once he let himself back out of Aridion's harper hall, Menannon kept to the moon shadows as much as possible and made his way to Haalinoth's small villa on the lower reaches of the Equian. There was no sign of life nor any Doomcriers surrounding the place, which made Menannon nervous that the Teluri might even now be being dragged before Azuron.

He turned hurriedly and ran up the hill through the orchards and vineyard to Irenos' villa, but here as well, all was darkness and peace. Menannon knew no where else to look at the moment, so he set off for the Cokeyna to find the brothers and the Dwarves before they became nervous and set out to find himself and the Teluri, as they had chosen that particular pub for this night's revels.

He reached the last vestige of cover across from the Cokeyna and knelt in the shadow of a net drying rack to study what was happening in the area of the pub. There was the usual small group of Doomcriers lounging about on the portico of the pub across from the Cokeyna. They were passing around a large chalice and paying little heed to anything besides the actual opening of the Cokeyna's door.

Menannon eased back into the shadows and moved around behind that pub before risking crossing the strand and coming up behind the Cokeyna and ducking into its small storage shed, Dink having procured for them keys to such sheds. None of them had asked him how.

He shut the door all but a crack, leaving a wisp of his kirtle sticking out. It was not much of a signal but one that Tullio would see. He took off his pack and hung it on the peg for the boy to find. He had to wait for perhaps a half turn of the hour before the young stiltwalker came out of the back door of the pub as though to get a bit of fresh air.

Tullio leaned nonchalantly upon the railing of the pub's small back porch and took several long breaths as though he were indeed in need of fresh air. The hood of Menannon's harper robe obscured his face nicely though anyone who knew the Giant well could see that the thing hung about the youngster's shoulders rather like a horse blanket upon a pony. After a few surreptitious glances about to see that no Doomcriers were near, Tullio stepped down from the porch and made his leisurely way across the sand to the shed and slipped inside.

"Menannon?" he whispered into the darkness there then nearly jumped out of his skin when he felt the Giant's warm breath upon his ear.

"I'm here." Menannon more breathed the words than spoke them.

Tullio instantly relaxed and grinned. "My life you almost shortened, my friend!" he whispered back as he began to loose the fastenings of the robe. When Menannon did not say anything in return the boy halted mid movement sensing something was amiss. "Something is wrong, yes?"

"Yes," Menannon let out his pent breath in a soft sigh. "Haalinoth has been compromised. Irenos was right, it was a trap. We had just gotten one of the ladies over the wall and into Haalinoth's care when a patrol came upon us. They were far enough away that he was able to run for it with his charge, but they saw him clear as day and gave chase."

"He was caught then, yes?" The mere thought of being caught by Azuron's creatures so discomfited the boy he almost could not say the words.

"By the High One's good grace, not then, but I know not if he has been since, as he came not to his villa nor that of Irenos, who also has come not to his home, as I went to both ere I came here." Menannon suddenly found he had to sit down on a convenient barrel. All of this had become distressingly real enough to make his knees weak.

Before this night, their activities had held an air of unreality, almost of play as though they were still children imagining themselves spies in the service of Telurion Firstborn in the wars of the Dim Times. Ever before it had been as though they were trifling with the Doomcriers, daring them to catch them. Thumbing their noses at Azuron's fools and stealing the prizes out from under them. Well, now the Doomcriers had stolen a march on them and what they were going to do about it was no nearer answered. Menannon could hear Tullio shuffling about, finishing removing the robe. He forced himself back to his feet and took the robe he felt being held against his arm.

"Wait a few minutes after I leave ere you venture out, then go not by the road, but down the strand until you pass the boats ere you emerge." Menannon turned and put on the robe. He laid his hand to the latch then hesitated. "Go carefully, Tullio."

"I will so." The boy's voice assured him from the darkness near his shoulder.

Menannon raised the hood of his robe and stepped outside. He waited a few more moments then walked around the end of the building and let himself back into the pub. The noise and normalcy of the place hit him like a wall. He glanced around and saw the others sitting near the back bar. Turanio sat on the end, his cloth covered stilts conspicuously stretched out towards the next table. Menannon mentally shook himself and walked over to the empty stool at the far end of the table and sat down, his legs folded under the table as Tullio would have been sitting.

Menannon took a swig from the chalice in front of him. It contained only water. A good thought that, as they needed to keep their wits about them. He wondered who had thought of it and how they were carrying it off. He glanced over at Davy, the turkeyesque barkeep, and thought he saw the faintest of winks as the fellow went back to serving a large group of fishermen. Menannon briefly wondered how many folk knew or suspected their activities and were going out of their way to aid them. That was an unsettling question for a group whose activities were supposed to be clandestine.

"Are ye after feelin' better?" Dink queried around his own large chalice.

Menannon nodded and took another long swig of tepid water.

"Am not believing!" Turanio brought his fist down on the table with a crash making the chalices jump. "You hide under hood all night so can not see you. Come out from hood and prove you better," he demanded loudly.

"No!" Menannon growled.

"Is not answer I accept. You take off hood or I take off hood!" Turanio raised his voice again to make sure they had an audience, several folk near them turned to look their way as it seemed as though there might be a fight which would add a touch of adventure to an otherwise dull evening.

"Oh, alright!" Menannon jerked the hood down and turned to glare at Turanio so that all those near them could clearly see his face. "There! Are you happy? I'm fine. Now leave me alone!" he jerked his hood back into place, drained his chalice and slammed it down on the table with a resounding thunk. "I'm going home. Goodnight!" Without another word or a backward glance, he left the table and stomped out of the pub.

"What's after bein' the matter with him lately?" he heard Dink asking.

"Oh, he's been fightin' with his Da again. Ne'er be mindin', have another drink. Davy!" he heard Conar's reply as the door closed behind him.

Outside, Menannon stood for a moment on the porch. What were they going to do now that Haalinoth had been seen? Menannon shook his thoughts away from the night's fiasco. There would be leisure to regret things later, after Haalinoth had been found. Not knowing aught else to do, he decided to return to his sire's villa to change his clothes then continue his search for the Teluri. He glanced over to the benches along the portico of the pub across from the Cokeyna. The Doomcriers were still there, waiting to follow and molest any they took it into their heads to harass. The sight of them suddenly made his heart burn. Thrice-damned fools with their red kirtles and pot metal swords! And their allegiance to a prancing fool. Among their number was the former strong man from Taratillo's circus.

As Menannon headed down the street, he saw from the corner of his eye that the strong man had suddenly come to his feet, intent upon the Giant. The fellow was tall, nearly seven feet, long legged and muscled like an ox from his long calling. The young Giant snorted with disgust. *It would appear I have acquired another keeper. Does Azuron actually deem such a man is a match for a Giant, even one with no fighting skills?*

Nearly shaking with fury, Menannon forced himself to continue on up the beach road towards the Citadel when he would far rather cross the strand and wipe the complacent smiles from every face among the Azuron's sycophants. Forced to choose physical action over righteous retaliation, he broke into a flat out run. Let this musclebound Human catch him if he could! He ran all the way to his sire's villa, taking a perverse pleasure in imagining the Doomcrier puffing up the Citadel in his wake.

He reached the gate breathing hard and tugged on the bell rope. The porter let him in and barred the gate behind him. His emotions still boiling dangerously, Menannon bid the man goodnight and walked across the courtyard. At the portico steps he halted, drew off his robe and folded it over his arm. For a moment he thought of going around to the kitchen and entering as was his usual wont, but then decided against it. For once, he was going to enter his own home through the front door rather than skulk in as though he had been engaged in wrongdoing.

He entered the atrium only to be brought up short in surprise. Despite the lateness of the hour, his sire was seated there, wine chalice in hand, talking softly with Irenos and Haalinoth! All of them looked totally relaxed. He stared at the prince, not sure whether to be relieved or furious. Here he had been worrying himself sick and searching for both Teluri only to find that they had spent the interlude relaxing here with his father. They all nodded to him and went back to their conversation.

Menannon mentally threw up his hands and went on to his chamber, hung up his robe and sat down on the edge of his bed. He slowly loosed his boots and let them fall. They landed with a soft thud to be followed by his clothing. Naked, he stood and went to the bathing chamber where he made quick work of showering and then relaxed in a hot bath. He lay back with his head propped on the edge of the tub and closed his eyes. Only then did he allow himself to begin to think about what had happened tonight. Haalinoth had been well and truly compromised. What were they going to do without him, for it was beyond question that the Teluri could not assist in any further rescues, else his life would be forfeit.

For the first time, he wondered for a moment whether what they were doing was actually making any difference. That thought was fleeting. All he had to do was bring to mind the face of the old jongleur who had disappeared into the depths of the dungeons for no other crime than naming his monkey Azuron. Firod had confirmed to Irenos that the old fellow had died not three sevendays after he was taken. How many others had been taken and were already dead? How many others were going to be taken? No! They had to keep going even if the numbers they were saving were but raindrops in the ocean, for some of those drops sparkled: any life saved was well worth the effort.

Menannon forced himself to clear his mind and just float in the water. He was not sure just how long he had been there when the door of the chamber opened and footsteps came in. His sire. He kept his eyes closed and listened as Gorlanndon disrobed and entered the shower. The water ran for a few minutes then turned off.

"Move over, boy."

Menannon opened his eyes to see his sire standing above him. Obediently he moved over and Gorlanndon stepped down into the tub and settled in with a long sigh.

"It has been long and long since we enjoyed a quiet soak together," he said as he reheated the water to nearly blood heat.

Menannon closed his eyes though he could not help stiffening as he wondered what his sire wanted to discuss.

"Just relax, boy. Nothing is wrong."

There was a smile in the elder Giant's voice. They soaked in companionable silence for nearly a half turn of the hour. Finally, Gorlanndon cleared his throat.

"Irenos came to me tonight to explain what all of you have been doing, though I already knew the gist of it, if not the details," he said quietly.

Menannon's eyes flew open. "Have we been that careless in our efforts for secrecy?" he queried in near panic. "Does the whole city know?"

"Nay, boy. There are probably a few who suspect who might be responsible for the disappearances, though their suspicions are unfounded. Most of the city suspects me."

Gorlanndon chuckled at the horrified look on his son's mobile face, reheated the water and settled more comfortably.

"Not to worry. It is only logical that they would suspect me as they know so little of you and virtually nothing of the prince other than that he is a smart trader and an honorable man—and one not to be trifled with. No, Irenos desired that I know everything as it is becoming more difficult with each rescue attempted. In the event something untoward happens, I will be able to move quickly."

When Menannon said nothing to this, he continued.

"He informs me that Haalinoth has been seen clearly and needs must go to Aridion City with you next time and remain there."

Menannon nodded. That really was the only answer. He wondered how long it would be before he would have to take the rest of them and their families to the mainland as Azuron was sure to include in his wrath everyone related to them. That gave him pause for the first time in this whole endeavor. He had never considered that Gorlanndon could be endangered by his actions. Menannon opened his eyes and found the elder Giant studying him thoughtfully.

"Father, I—" He began, but Gorlanndon held up a hand silencing him.

"I can take care of myself," he said. "It is you who worries me. Soon or late, you, too, will be seen to be clearly involved with one of these rescues and you Azuron will have no compunction in attacking."

Menannon nodded. That thought had occurred to him many times, though even now he would not allow himself to follow it to its logical conclusion. Again silence settled over the bathing chamber as both lay thinking about the other. At last they rose from the water and began to dry themselves and don soft sleeping robes. Menannon began to towel his hair then stopped mid-motion.

"How did you discern our scheme ere Irenos told it you?" he asked, truly puzzled.

"I did not know your scheme, boy, but I know you," Gorlanndon laughed softly. "When I saw you, night after night climbing the back wall and found your pack with its rope and Irenos' lantern in the small shed you'd always used to hide your childhood treasures, it was not hard to conclude that you had become involved with the prince's plans. I knew that you could no more sit by and see injustice being done and not attempt to right it any more than you could swim to Blue Bay."

Menannon grinned rather sheepishly and turned to the door. His sire's soft voice stopped him.

"Menannon, you must indeed take Haalinoth to Aridion City and any others you desire this one final time. After that, I forbid you to involve yourself in any more rescues. You are too closely watched and are suspected. I have seen the bruises you have sported and I know they are not being inflicted by the folk you are rescuing."

Gorlanndon raised a knowing eyebrow. Menannon left the bathing chamber and crawled into bed, his mind a-whirl. A few moments later, Gorlanndon emerged and headed to his own chamber. He came first to the side of the bed and leaned down and kissed Menannon's brow.

"I love you boy," he whispered and left.

The door closed quietly behind him.

CHAPTER 18
(SUMMER OF THE WORLD 6097)

THE NEXT MID-OF-NIGHT found Menannon walking swiftly towards his sire's trade hall headed for what he suspected would be a very difficult planning session. He held to the moon shadows as much as possible, though his Doomcrier guards were none the wiser, as he had left them guarding the villa having taken his usual way over the back wall. He was becoming more adept at climbing walls than anyone outside of an Aridion housebreaker should be. He shook his head in grim amusement.

Having reached the Serpentine, he halted next to the thick trunk of a night-blooming peridüse and surveyed the street. All was silent and peaceful as it should be this time of the night. Beside him was a small tea shop whose proprietor lived above and behind, its large windows giving an unprecedented view of the street and its flower boxes and trees now all silvery in the moonlight. Should he live there, he was sure he would spend most moonlit nights sitting in one of those windows drifting in the view. A slight breeze brought down to him the heady fragrance of the peridüs.

That was another thing for which Kalyria was famous: its peridüs trees. They grew nowhere else in the High One's world. There was an ancient nut from one of them in his mother's jewelry box at the villa, but that was the only one he had ever seen. Perchance one day he could persuade Blackmore to go ahead with his plans to build a conservatory at the harper hall and plant the nut there. Would a peridüs grow from such a nut or did they propagated by some other method?

The barking of a far-off dog brought him back from his thoughts and he shook his head, mentally chastising himself for wasting precious time. He took another quick glance about the still silent street and then set off for the trade hall some five and forty yards distant. He broke into a light run and darted down into the sunken plaza fronting its great doors. Here he halted once more to make sure no one was about. There was no sound, but still he circled the edge of the plaza and stayed in the shadows as much as possible, then almost dove through the doors pulling them to behind him. The slight thunk of their closing sounded in the darkness then all was silence again.

Within, his eyes had to adjust to bright light as, much to his surprise, the Dwarf lanterns in the atrium were open and the fountain at its center turned on and playing its own soft music of falling water.

"Come in and be welcome," his sire's voice hailed him from the office on the far side of the chamber. Menannon instantly relaxed from his stiff watchfulness and hurried across the atrium to find his sire seated behind his desk perusing a large stack of documents.

"Did you not retire for the night, sir?" Menannon blurted out in surprise at the sight of him.

"Aye, but I changed my mind," Gorlanndon chuckled. "I bethought me that I would accomplish a small amount of work as I was finding it hard to sleep. And what seek you here?"

Menannon was caught totally flat footed as he had no idea what to tell his sire as to his own business. At the look of consternation on his son's mobile face, Gorlanndon threw back his head and laughed.

"Fear not. Your companions are here awaiting you. I do but hold the bridge until all of you are gathered then we shall begin this night's planning. Go through yonder door and join them until all are assembled."

He indicated a side door near the back of his office and Menannon headed for it then halted to ask his sire a question, but changed his mind mid-breath and continued to the door.

It opened upon a smaller chamber which proved to be a combination bathing and sleeping chamber for beyond the soaking pool a low camp bed of huge proportions stood on its stout legs. At the moment it was occupied by his fellow conspirators. Haalinoth sat near the head with Irenos in soft conversation beside him. At the middle, the Orlando boys were playing at dice, their long stilts stretched out comfortably over the side. At the foot, Dink was sitting rather huddled, his arms wrapped around his upraised knees. Apparently, he was none too pleased with his nearest companion. Menannon was stunned to see Firod sitting quietly beside the young Dwarf, leaning back against the foot rest, his eyes closed in a light doze.

Menannon closed the door and stood looking in wonder at the gathering. He turned to Irenos, one eyebrow raised questioningly.

"With thy advent, we do but await Conar," the prince replied to Menannon's look. "Things have happened this day which have changed all and thy sire and the good captain are needed to aid in our planning this night. Sit thee down and relax until Conar attends upon us."

"If'n he does," muttered Dink.

Menannon turned his gaze to him quickly, but the Dwarf was staring at his hands and did not look up. With a mental shrug, the Giant crossed to the bed and joined the others, sitting beside Turanio, but refusing his silent invitation to join in the dice game, with a quick shake of his head.

From the office, they could hear the sounds of Gorlanndon arranging chairs then nothing more from that direction for the best part of a quarter turn of an hour. Just as the clock finished sounding there was the sound of the outer door closing followed by running feet. All in the small chamber stiffened, listening for the great Giant's reaction.

"They've arrested me da!" the voice of Conar blurted out before the sound of his feet even came to a halt. "E'en now their draggin' him an' me mum an' sister to the palace! They e'en took the wee one an' his nurse!"

At the words, Menannon could not help a quick glance at Irenos. Azuron was reaching high to denounce Conar's sire Corin, as that worthy Dwarf was a member of the inner Privy

Council. If *Corin, why not Gorlanndon?* was all he could think with a sick tightening in his stomach. Beside him, he saw the Orlando boys exchange a meaningful look and knew they, too, thought of their own sire.

"Sit down, lad and collect yourself." Gorlanndon's voice came clearly through the door. "Your compatriots are here. Allow me to call them forth so you need tell your story but once."

Menannon heard his sire's chair move back and the Giant's footsteps cross the office. The sound of that door closing and the lock clicking to was followed by Gorlanndon's voice.

"Come forth, gentlemen, our conference is begun."

Menannon instantly stood and almost bolted across the chamber, throwing open the door before any of the others had more than gotten to their feet. He walked into the office to see Corin seated upon an ingenious chair which was equipped with a small set of steps and a platform bearing a Dwarven sized chair, thus allowing its occupant to sit comfortably at the desk without being perched upon a chair many sizes to large for him. There was another such chair beside him for Dink. The young Dwarf's face was streaked with dirt and his clothing torn and disheveled, his breath still coming in ragged gasps. In his hand was a chalice of wine which he could barely hold for the tremors wracking him.

In moments, all were comfortably seated, even the stiltwalkers, as Gorlanndon had arranged more chairs meant for Teluri and thus were their stilts accommodated. Menannon sat on his sire's right hand, Firod on his left with the two Teluri at the desk's ends and the Orlando brothers and the Dwarves across its expanse from the great Giant. To give the young Dwarf more time to compose himself, Gorlanndon poured chalices of wine for one and all from the amphora sitting on a shelf behind him. These he passed around, then turned his full attention back to Conar.

"Now then, young sir, tell us what has transpired."

The Dwarf set his chalice on the arm of his chair in the place provided for such and sat forward clasping his hands together in his lap to stop their shaking. He took a deep breath and began.

"The whole household was after bein' asleep save for me alone as I was gettin' ready to come to this very meetin', when there was a great poundin' upon the gate. I had just slipped out into the back garden when it sounded an' so was able to scramble up into the big willow beside the reflectin' pond e'en as they used some blastin' fire to hurl the gate off o' its hinges. They'd not e'en waited fer the porter to be doin' his job. The old fellow was blown half way across the forecourt an' must be dead as I did'na see him move after that." Conar looked about at the tense faces of the others.

"I was after bein' sure they hunted me, so I hid. I'd no inklin' they were come fer me da, else I'd a stayed and fought!"

"It is well that thou didst not. Else wouldst thou have been taken as well and none there would have been to sound the warning," Irenos observed quietly, speaking for the first time.

Conar seemed to relax a bit and taking another deep breath continued with his story.

"Doomcriers flooded in, a score or more an' busted down the door an' were after roustin' the whole house. They dragged every one out into the forecourt, e'en the scullery girl an' she just a bit o' a child. Me da and mum had thrown robes o'er their night attire but the nurse was in naught but her night rail with the wee one in his blanket. The Doomcriers shoved them all towards the gate where their leader was still standin' an' lookin' at all o' them. He looked at each in turn then a scowl crossed his already bad-tempered face."

"'Where's yer son?!' he demanded, grabbin' the front o' me da's robe.

"'I'd not be knowin' the boy's after runnin' with scum of late', me da lied straight into that surly face as a'course he was after knowin' I was home. The fellow dropped me da and turned to his men. 'We've no time for this nonsense. Burn it down! That'll fetch the brat out. Bring these along!' He indicated me family an' marched out o' the gate, callin' to his men to bring me when they found me should I not burn. His men lit torches they were carryin' an' barged back into the villa an' set it all afire!"

Conar looked around the group again, a look of bewildered pleading on his face.

"Why were they after doin' that? Now our folk have no place to live an' they've lost everythin'! Why?!"

Menannon's heart filled with pity and anger at these further acts of brutality on the part of Azuron for there was no doubt in his mind that the orders in all their hideous detail came straight from that black-hearted Teluri himself. He looked to his sire to find the elder Giant exchanging a glance with Firod. Both were shaking their heads.

Gorlanndon turned his attention back to the Dwarf.

"Worry not for your folk Conar, they shall be succored, but as to the reason for the total devastation of your home it is sadly simple. Azuron is fighting a war of minds, not yet of weapons, though I doubt not that it will come to that. Folk are easy to influence if they do not find their self-worth in the High One. Most folk see themselves through their employ-ment, or talents or what their homes are like or their clothing and money, all of which can be threatened or denied them and they are then left with nothing save fear and hatred.

"By burning your sire's villa, Azuron is sending a message to all the rest of us living on Kalyria that we needs must do as he wishes else face the same fate as Corin, Privy Councillor. Only those of us who realize that our personal worth lies in the opinion that the High One holds of us and not in worldly things will be able to see this event for what it is—a terrible tragedy, but not a world changing moment. All Kalyria could disappear and we would truly be none the worse, for all things work together for good in the hands of the High One."

"How can that be?" demanded Dink suddenly speaking up, his amber eyes flashing. "How can fire an' death be after bein' deemed good?"

From the look on the young Dwarf's face, there was something more than just this incident behind his question. What it could be, Menannon could not guess, for Dink was a closed soul and the Giant knew no more of him than he had known at their first meeting despite all they had been through together. Gorlanndon's voice brought his wandering thought back.

"In the High One's own good time and in His own way, this will all be seen someday as the beginning of a blessing." Gorlanndon was assuring Dink and through him, Conar. "Perchance, none of us will see the time or the consummation, but it will come. Of that you may be as sure as you know the sun shall rise on the morrow."

Dink shrugged and sat back obviously not convinced, but somewhat mollified by the great Giant's answer. Beside him Conar was nodding his countenance more relaxed than at anytime since he entered the chamber.

"Now," Gorlanndon continued before anyone could bring up further questions that would be better answered at another time, "Councillor Corin's family is not the only one that has been forcibly detained this day for Sadram Joram, the elder of the House of Joram & Sons, and his entire family with most of their retainers were arrested just after nightfall. It was of him that this meeting was going to deal, but now we must consider of our intentions towards Corin and his folk as well."

Gorlanndon looked around the desk and then sat forward, his hands clasped in front of him.

"Earlier this day, a group of our most influential men held a meeting to discuss the new taxes and further depredations of Azuron's Doomcriers. They held this meeting in the Speakers Grove of the Aureun, a place held sacrosanct for all the millennia of Kalyria's existence. Any can voice their opinions there without fear of censure or consequences—."

"—until now!" Firod's low growl interrupted the Giant. Menannon glanced around his sire to see a look of pure disgust upon the captain's dour face.

"Aye! Until now," Gorlanndon continued. "This day, Azuron has broken one of the most ancient laws of this empire: the sanctity of the Speaker's Grove. He has arrested all of the folk who participated in that meeting and has them detained in a chamber on the palace grounds awaiting a trial which will be a mockery of justice as Azuron alone now sits upon the High Court bench."

"Are there not still five Kalyrian judges on the bench?" Menannon asked, astonished.

"There are, but we cannot count upon their opposing anything Azuron proposes."

Gorlanndon glanced around at Haalinoth and Irenos, then back to Firod. All were nodding in agreement with him. Despite this consensus, Menannon still could not bring himself to believe that the integrity of the Kalyrian judges could be open to question, but he held his peace.

"Now, Councillor Corin has been added to this group," Gorlanndon continued. "As he saw fit to decry this new tax of Azuron's openly in the meeting of the Privy Council this day. I feared there would be repercussions. I have been trying to convince my like-minded councillors to allow me to voice our opinions in the open as I still am sacrosanct. Howe'er that may be, an honorable man such as Corin chafes at this restriction and I can blame him not, though I cannot protect those who thus speak out. So!" Gorlanndon sat back and looked around the desk at all gathered. "Ere this trial can come to pass, we here must decide upon a course of action, for we cannot let our much-needed leaders be imprisoned or executed without so much as a whimper of protest."

"I'm after sayin' we should break into the palace close an' rescue them!" Conar spoke up immediately, which opinion elicited a quick grin from the great Giant.

"Aye, lad we all agree with you. The question is how shall it be done?"

This statement was followed by a thoughtful silence.

"Is there a way to enter the chamber in which they are held and get them out of it without arousing the suspicions of the Doomcriers and their master. For if there is, we could take them to the Harper Hall for sanctuary along with Haalinoth as he has been compromised and will be arrested soon if he stays here." Menannon reluctantly added the Teluri's name to the list of those needing to be rescued though it meant the beginning of the breaking of their fellowship.

"I believe there is," Firod spoke up, halting a murmur of negative opinions which had immediately begun to circle the chamber.

Everyone save Gorlanndon glanced at the captain in surprise. Conar sat forward, his young face stiff with concentration.

"It must happen this very night." Firod said.

"Impossible!" Both Teluri spoke out in unison.

"We are not ready to move such a large group without careful preparation," Irenos finished for they twain and Haalinoth nodded agreement.

"It is tonight or not at all, as the trials will begin on the morrow."

Firod looked them straight in the eye and none could doubt his sincerity. Seeing an impasse developing, Menannon cleared his throat.

"Can we but get them without the close's walls, I can escort them to the harper hall with a modicum of assistance from the rest of our fellowship." He looked meaningfully at the Dwarves and the Orlando brothers, all of whom nodded their heads in agreement. It was the older members of the group who looked skeptical.

"But how shall we be after gettin' me da an' the others out o' the close? There's but one gate an' it's guarded well." Conar raised the question all were thinking.

"Actually there are three gates," Gorlanndon spoke up with a decided twinkle in his black eyes. "We shall not be using any of them in this chance, as all will be guarded by Doomcriers."

"Art thou deeming of using thy special method?" questioned Irenos. "I can bethink me of no better way of leaving a sign pointing and saying 'Here passed Gorlanndon. Arrest me!' It is too dangerous my friend."

From the look on the Teluri's face, he clearly did not like what ever the Giant was planning. This immediately made Menannon dislike it, even though he knew not what it was.

"Knowing something and proving it are not one and the same thing." Gorlanndon actually smiled, but it was a smile that portended no good to someone.

"I like it not, either," Firod nodded to Irenos. "But there seems to be no other way, unless you can think of one. Can you?"

After several long, silent moments, Irenos shook his head, clearly unhappy with the thought.

"Alright then. It's decided." Gorlanndon sat forward again. "Now let us configure the rest of our plan—"

"Excuse you me," Turanio suddenly spoke up from where he and Tullio had been holding a whispered conversation. "We not understanding this talk. Explain please, how to get into palace close."

He looked expectantly at Irenos, as the prince had always been the leader of their small band. The Teluri turned to Gorlanndon, indicating that he should answer the question.

"We shall be going through the wall," the great Giant said simply, as though he were talking about a stroll along the Serpentine.

"We shall what?! The sound, she will give us away. Poof!" Turanio sat up straight his face alight with consternation. "Will not this say arrest all? Gorlanndon not alone?! Brother and I not go!" He shook his head emphatically and sat back.

"There will be no sound," the Giant assured him, much to Menannon's surprise. "We Giants have our ways, though I cannot tell you of them, as they are what you would consider *clan secrets*."

At that statement, the stiltwalkers both turned immediately to Menannon, but the young Giant could only shrug, for he knew no more of what his sire spoke than did they.

"Time grows on apace," Firod reminded them all. "We must finish our plan and then execute it."

As if to emphasize the need for hurry, the sound of thunder

rolled overhead. As the chamber possessed no windows and had many chambers above it, they could not tell if rain was included. Menannon could not help a slight shiver, the sound seeming to him a warning of some sort. He chastised himself, thinking he had been spending too much time with Clarinda lately as the old cook was chock full of superstitions which she only half believed.

"All right, you shall leave in one half turn of the hour." Gorlanndon instructed. "Turanio, Tullio and Dink shall go to the Cokeyna to play their usual parts. Irenos, Haalinoth and Conar shall go to the harper hall to make sure all stays clear for our coming. Should the Doomcriers get too thick there, Haalinoth, you and Conar go inside and hide while Irenos comes to warn us. Do try to make sure that does not happen." The Giant flashed the Teluri a significant look which Menannon was at a loss to read, though both Teluri nodded in under-standing.

"Menannon!" the great Giant turned to his son. "You and I shall go to the rear of the palace close just without the holding chamber and await Firod's signal. Against the time we shall act, Firod will go to the palace and replace the guards in the holding chamber with men of his own whom he can trust implicitly and who will spread the word of our intent among the prisoners. When all is ready, Menannon and I shall open the chamber and those within shall make their bid for freedom and sanctuary with the harpers. Any questions?"

There were none that anyone was willing to voice.

"Good!" Gorlanndon rose and signaled to Firod.

They walked to the chamber door together and unlocking it left the room. While they were gone, Menannon could not resist turning to Irenos with a question.

"What think you Azuron will be doing during all of this?" he asked raising one quizzical eyebrow.

The Teluri took a deep breath and a long swallow of his wine before he answered.

"Well, Firod reports that our dear Councillor General is hosting a revel this night in the palace and has posted an entire troop of Doomcriers within the close and along the outer wall."

He gave this news and then poured himself another chalice of wine and would speculate no more, though he did exchange another long look with Haalinoth.

Gorlanndon returned in a few moments and took his chair with a sigh. He, too, poured himself another chalice of wine and settled back to wait the required half turn of the hour. All waited until the water clock in the atrium had chimed two quarter turns of the hour and then Gorlanndon signaled them all to go their ways.

"Irenos," he said halting the Teluri as he was about to follow the rest. "Could you go to the villa and obtain Menannon's gear as he will not have the opportunity to do this. Skendrin will know where it is."

The Teluri nodded and left the chamber, closing the door softly behind him, leaving the two Giants to face each other.

"Does everyone at the villa know of my business?!" Menannon demanded, totally nonplused at the idea that his efforts at secrecy had been so transparent.

"Nay, lad, only those of us who have known you and raised you all your life," his sire assured him.

"Which means at least half the gardeners and three-quarters of the household staff!" the young Giant snorted disgustedly, causing his sire to laugh softly and slap him gently on the shoulder.

"Come, boy," he said, "We have our work to do."

Gorlanndon closed the Dwarf lantern upon his desk thereby plunging the chamber into darkness and taking his son's arm, led the way out of the trade hall, shutting down the fountain and shuttering the Dwarf lanterns as they went.

Outside, a cold, steady rain was falling, though the sound of thunder had diminished into the far distance. Menannon immediately wished that he and not Tullio had the use of his harper robe this night as its hood would be most welcome. Resignedly, he blinked the rain out of his eyes and followed his sire silently down the street.

They reached the lower bridge to the Citadel and were just

stepping out onto the span when a small troop of Doomcriers came marching around the corner. Menannon jerked back, looking frantically for somewhere to hide. There was a large tree just behind them with a deep shadow beneath it. The Doomcriers might just possibly miss them, with a huge amount of blessing from the High One! He turned to dive into the shadows, but Gorlanndon placed his hand on his shoulder and kept him moving on across the bridge in plain sight of the Doomcriers, who, strangely, did not see them and kept on marching up the street though the sound of their footsteps was a bit muffled for several moments. The only thing unusual in his sire's actions was that he leaned down and ran the tips of his fingers along the stones of the balustrade as they walked across the bridge.

Menannon glanced up at him, a questioning eyebrow raised, but Gorlanndon shook his head.

"All in good time," he whispered and stepped off from the bridge to move on up the Citadel. Puzzled, Menannon followed him.

They reached the back wall of the palace close without incident and settled down to wait at the base of a statue of one of Kalyria's elder heros. The noise of Azuron's revel pouring over the wall was almost deafening. There was some small chance, then that they would not be heard as they broke the wall.

Menannon glanced to where his sire was relaxing, his back against the plinth of the statue and wondered anew how they were going to fulfill this part of their quest. His sire was dressed in his usual kirtle, a dark chemise, hose and long boots. He had nothing else besides his belt pouch which was not large enough to hold any rock breaking tools. There were times he felt as though his beloved sire was a total stranger to him and this was one of them. He shook his head and settled back against the stone bearing the name of the elder above them and shivered. His own kirtle, chemise and hose were soaked through. He threw his arm across his face to smother a sneeze and wished the rain would stop. Beside him, his sire seemed to be perfectly comfortable despite the cold water dripping down his neck. Menannon rubbed his arms to get a bit of warmth back into them. Gorlanndon noticed the movement and cocked his head.

"Did I neglect to teach you that Giants can raise their body temperature at will, boy?" Gorlanndon murmured just above a whisper so the sound would not carry.

"I fear so, my father, as that is news to me," Menannon replied, his teeth nearly chattering.

"You warm or cool yourself in nearly the same way you make yourself lighter or heavier. It is along the same lines, only think of warmth and you will warm yourself."

Menannon concentrated for several minutes, attempting to think away the cold as he thought away his mass. At last, he did feel a bit warmer and tried harder. Of a sudden, his body temperature flew up into the bows and he found himself red faced and sweating. Beside him Gorlanndon chuckled softly.

"It does take some practice," he said.

Menannon only nodded, his mind too occupied with his efforts to manipulate his system to allow for speech. It was not long, however, before he was able to adjust his body to a nearly comfortable temperature, but he had to concentrate to hold it steady. At least it gave him something to do as they waited rather than worry about what lay ahead.

They sat quietly for nearly a full turn of the hour awaiting Firod's signal. Nothing appeared to be happening inside as the noise of the revel had not abated in any way. In fact, it seemed to get louder. Menannon finally screwed his courage to the sticking point and asked his sire the question he had been desiring to ask ever since he came back to the island.

"My Father, please be not affronted, but enlighten me if you will on something that has vexed me sorely."

Gorlanndon turned towards him with an expectant look in his eyes. Menannon suspected that he already knew what he would ask, but he plunged on anyway.

"My Father, you are the richest, most powerful man in the entire Kalyrian Empire. You are a king maker. In any other kingdom or nation, a person in your position would have long since overthrown the existing rulers and declared himself king and put an end to all of this. Why have you not?"

Gorlanndon sat in silence for so long that Menannon wondered if he had indeed offended him. At last, the great Giant spoke thoughtfully.

"Aye, I could have made myself king of Kalyria at any time after Kalyrinon the Elder went to join his long fathers. I have the resources, the prestige and the knowledge for such a pass." Gorlanndon murmured close to Menannon's ear. "Howe'er that may be, this is Kalyria, blessed of the High One and not just an ordinary kingdom or nation. It is the High One who rules here. It is not His will that one of his true believers overthrow a functioning and benevolent government anywhere, but most especially here. This is still a functioning, though increasingly questionable government, and until or unless the High One should withdraw his face from Kalyria, we have no right to interfere. Should the High One turn away, then and only then would it be up to us to step forth and right the wrongs being done here, either by open revolt or regicide. Or both, for you do realize, do you not, that such a revolution would have to assassinate not only Azuron, but Norilendra and likely Nirna as well, else would there e'er be unrest among the people."

Rain-drenched silence fell once more after these words as Menannon sat back to consider them. Once again, he had shown himself an inexperienced youth, for never had it crossed his mind that anyone other than Azuron would be executed in a revolution. For Kalyria to have a new king, without doing away with the old line, the thing needs must be accomplished by either marriage or procreation. There was no third way which led not to death. Despite his efforts to warm himself, a shiver went through him at the thought of what revolution would really mean and his respect for his sire raised higher.

But a few more rain-soaked minutes had passed when a small pebble came sailing over the wall above them. It was followed by three more thrown as though by a bored sentry. Firod's signal.

"All right then, stay behind me and learn," Gorlanndon murmured and stood, turning to face the wall.

The great Giant stretched forth his hands and laid them gently upon the stones before him and closed his eyes. He stood thus for a moment then, to Menannon's utter astonishment, he gently and quietly pulled a stone from the wall and handed it to his son.

"Set it down over there," he instructed. "There will be quite a pile, so leave yourself plenty of room."

With that, he turned back and began to create an archway in a solid stone wall as easily as if he were a small child playing with his mushy peas at table.

Menannon was so stunned by this display that he nearly got the wind knocked out of him when Gorlanndon handed back the second stone. He shook his head as though waking from a stupor and began setting stones aside as fast and quietly as he could.

As easily as a wave washes away a sand castle, Gorlanndon enlarged and lengthened his hole through thirty feet of core veneer masonry. Only once did he stop to survey his work and that was when he appeared to be considering which of two stones he should leave as the keystone of his new arch.

Less than a half turn of an hour found Menannon staring through a brightly lit hole into the startled face of one of Firod's lieutenants. The new archway and tunnel was only large enough to accommodate Humans, Dwarves and Teluri, if the latter bent nearly double, but not Giants, so Gorlanndon leaned down and called softly to the fellow.

"Come out as quickly and as quietly as you are able."

He stepped back, taking Menannon with him. Above them, Firod kept flicking pebbles down to let them know all was still well.

"Sir, you are going to have to teach me that little talent," Menannon murmured, nodding towards the hole, grinning up at his sire.

"I refrained from teaching it to you simply because I was the bane of your grandsire's life when I learned it as I was forever making arches and tunnels in the walls of our home and you are even more inquisitive than I. We shall discuss the technique when we have the leisure. You will find it most interesting."

Those were the last words they were able to exchange as a line of prisoners began to stream out into the storm and rain of a perfect night for clandestine activities. There was some soft rustling and bumping, but nothing Menannon felt could be heard by the guards within the close as the noise of Azuron's revel was still in full roar.

The group was led by Firod's lieutenant who came directly to the Giants.

"What is your will?" he murmured, looking to Menannon as Firod had apparently informed him that the youth was the leader of this little expedition.

"Have you informed them that they must stay together, hold hands, make no noise and follow where we lead?"

"Aye, sir."

"How many are there?" Menannon asked as he was already mentally calculating the length of time required to move a large group through the Straight Paths.

"There's near a hundred." the fellow informed him.

"What?!!" Menannon said, a near shout of surprise and consternation.

Gorlanndon slapped a hand over his mouth to silence him and everyone froze, waiting to see if the outburst had been heard. In a few breathless moments, a pebble flew over the wall and they all started breathing again.

"Surely, you jest!" the young Giant jerked down his sire's restraining hand, but managed to keep his voice under control this time.

"No, young sir. We counted them as soon as we entered the chamber and there are seven and ninety including the babes-in-arms. We'd no inkling the Doomcriers had denounced so many."

The fellow shook his head in dismay.

"We need more rope," Menannon locked eyes with his sire, totally nonplused by the situation.

"When you reach the hall, send Irenos to Skendrin for what

e'er you need." Gorlanndon told him and stepped back out of the way. Menannon turned to the growing group and signaled for them to follow him. He headed off into the wet darkness with nearly a hundred desperate folk and four of Firod's guardsmen at his back. He no longer needed to manipulate his body temperature to be sweating profusely.

He reached the back of the harper hall along with the head of the line without incident as far as he knew, for the people had continued to follow him without pulling on his arm, which he had passed along as the signal if there was trouble. If something happened they were to tug on the arm of the person in front of them and thus the message would be delivered to Menannon. No such message had been passed. Their silent arrival left Conar and the two Teluri awaiting them open-mouthed in alarm.

"There are seven and ninety," Menannon murmured to them before they could ask. "Go to the villa and get more rope from Skendrin," he whispered to Irenos as that worthy passed him his pack and lantern. "Haalinoth! Conar! Help me to tie these on and we'll start. Haalinoth, you will have to await Irenos' return ere you tie yourself on and follow. Conar, you follow me closely and when you get inside go to the great chamber doors and lock them. You will need to make sure no one enters from that way until the last of our folk have departed."

The red-haired Teluri and the Dwarf both nodded and began to assist the Giant in readying the first part of the line for the adventure of the Straight Path.

"Do not untie the rope until you are told to," Menannon whispered to the first person in line, a young lass of about sixteen summers, clutching hard to her little brother's hand. "We are going through a dark tunnel then there will be a brightly lit one and then you will be in sanctuary. If you come untied, sit down immediately and await my coming. Is that clear?"

She nodded wordlessly.

Behind her was Firod's lieutenant. Menannon pulled him out of the line.

"Stand here and inform all of the others of the instructions as they come and help Irenos Prince to tie the rest on. Then tie yourself on last. I will be back long ere the last of this folk reaches sanctuary, so worry not."

Menannon started to turn away then turned back.

"When your next guardsman comes along, send him into the hall to help Conar guard the doors from the inside, as we will not want any of the resident harpers disturbing our intents."

Menannon turned away from the man and took his place at the head of the line. He was reaching for the door handle to the back way into the harper hall when Conar stopped him.

"Were ya able to be findin' me da and mum?" Conar asked keeping his voice as low as his agitation allowed.

"I don't know! Ask him."

Menannon pointed to Firod's lieutenant and turned back to the door. He whispered a heart-felt prayer and opened it onto darkness and went in, the first of the folk following him as the rope pulled tight around them. At the spiral stair, Menannon opened the Dwarf lantern and hung it on the railing to light the way for those who would follow. He mounted the stairs wondering what was going to happen. Would the gate stay open long enough for all the folk to get through it? Would the knots hold or the ropes separate? Would any of the folk panic, as most of them would not see their guides, just those around them who also did not know of the Mythrian light they were going to be seeing? The what if scenarios ran through his mind like a river as he climbed the stair.

He reached its top and stopped, taking a deep breath and stilling his mind by sheer will power. All was in the hands of the High One and he must leave it there. He held still, listening intently, forcing his senses beyond the sound of all those breathing nervously below him.

There was silence from beyond the door. Praise the High One! Menannon took another long, settling breath then opened the door and signaled to the girl to follow. They stepped out from behind the celebrant's throne into the peace and silence of the Great Hall of Gathering lit only by the faint glow of the Dwarf lantern spilling through their door and the crystalline glitter of the vigil lamp hanging in the high vaults overhead. The peace of the High One still held here.

Hurriedly, Menannon saluted the lamp, acknowledging the High One, and stepped across the platform to stand in front of the mosaic of Kalyria. He spoke the words of command and the girl and several others gasped in wonder as the gate ground open, flooding the chamber with the intense cobalt light. Not giving them a chance to react further, Menannon tugged on the rope and led the front of the line in to the Straight Paths. They followed, stumbling, half blinded by the radiance and their own fears. Just as he stepped through the gate, Menannon saw Conar run across the great hall to lock the door and take up his position there. So far so good.

The Giant kept his pace slow and deliberate as he walked the needed pattern of footsteps to get his charges to safety. It seemed to take far longer than normal to reach the gate incised in its center with the runes for Aridion City.

At last, when he was beginning to think he had taken a wrong turning somewhere, the gate loomed out of the brilliance ahead of him. With a prayer of relief and thanksgiving, he stepped up to it and it ground open upon the darkness of an Aridion night. Only the cresset behind Blackmore's desk burned, bathing the chamber with a faint glow. Without the clerestory windows, the blackness of moonset pressed upon the glass. It was getting very late. It would be dawn soon on Kalyria.

"Grandmaster Blackmore!" Menannon called loudly as he led the first of the folk into the audience chamber. "Jondlin, get Lee now!" he called in a voice loud enough to waken half the hall, not waiting for the old Valinga to appear and give the order to his runner himself. He heard the runner's doors slam open in the outer hall and the sound of his feet disappear even as the line of Kalyrian outcasts grew longer.

"Form a line around the perimeter of the chamber, please. Someone will attend upon you in moments," he directed his folk.

They dutifully followed his directions, though in a bewildered shuffle as he had not had the leisure to explain to them where they were going and why. As they lined up, he hurried back to the gate, hoping that it would hold open for them all, as this aspect of the Straight Paths had not been explained to him.

Even as he reached the gate, the door to Blackmore's chambers opened and the ancient Valinga hobbled out. Despite the surprise of this late coming, his robes were immaculate and his demeanor unruffled. He halted but a small part of an instant at the sight of so many folk exiting Kalyria's gate, then stepped forward to greet them. If his six hundred plus summers of life had taught him nothing else, it had taught him that all surprises have a reason and a resolution.

"Welcome to Aridion City, my good folk," he called out to them, stepping up onto the dais beside his desk so he could be seen by all. "You have come to seek sanctuary here with the Harpers of Aridion and you have found it. Be not afraid. All will be explained and set to rights. Crowd in, there is room for all here. None are ever turned away by the High One."

With that admonition, he settled himself behind his great desk and smiled welcome to all of the half blinded, bewildered Kalyrians stumbling through the gate past Menannon.

"Grandmaster," Menannon hurried to the stand across the desk from Blackmore. "How long will the gate hold open?" he blurted out before the Valinga could even acknowledge him.

"It stays open or closes in its own good time," Blackmore informed him with a grin much to Menannon's consternation. The grin turned to a full smile at the young Giant's reaction. "Trust the High One lad to protect his own," he said and waved him to the door where Lee and Jondlin had just entered.

Feeling as though he was standing in the in the eye of a hurricane and would be blown to bits no matter which way he turned, Menannon took a deep breath and headed to intercept Lee and the runner.

"What's happening?" the drummer demanded as he clasped the Giant's arm in greeting. Menannon glanced nervously towards the gate where the line of folk was still streaming in.

"We had to empty Azuron's holding chamber," he said turning back. "They had arrested Councillor Corin, Sadram Jorum and their entire families. They were to be tried and executed on the morrow. We had no idea the Doomcriers had denounced others as well. We have nearly a hundred folk roped together this trip."

"High One preserve us!" Jondlin murmured beside them and Lee drew back his head like a shying horse, worry suddenly stiffening his face.

"Will the gate stay open long enough to get them all through?!" he demanded in a near whisper, not wanting to worry anyone standing within hearing whose family and friends might not have arrived yet.

"I know not," Menannon shrugged trying to school his face into a positive mien. "But I must go back and make sure all is well. Will you twain take over here and see to these as well as keep the line coming out?"

"Surely," Lee nodded and started to walk away, but halted and turned back. "How will we know that all have arrived rather than the rope parted?" he asked.

"Either I shall return with the final few or I'll send a peridüs twig with the last person. Fair enough?"

"Aye, that'll do, but I'd prefer it was you and not a piece of tree that brings up the tail of this serpent."

Lee grinned and turned away taking Jondlin with him.

"I'm here Grandmaster what is your will?" Lee called out affably even as Menannon began to make his own way past the folk coming out of the gate, preparing to reenter it.

He glanced back to see the drummer take hold of the young girl and her small brother at the head of the line and begin untying the rope. Menannon turned and dodged around a small girl carefully carrying her doll and stepped back into the cobalt light.

He immediately froze in horror. The gate ground closed leaving him alone! All about him was empty tunnel glittering clearly in the light of the Mythrian mages. His heart pounding in panic, he whirled, spoke the word of command and ran back through the opening gate into the audience hall tripping over a portly gentleman and landing headlong in the middle of the floor surrounded by the still roped line of folk. Menannon scrambled to his feet and looked to the gate where folk were still coming out in a steady line.

"What in the name of the High One is going on?" he muttered to himself and shook his head to clear it.

He glanced around the chamber to see everyone staring at him in surprise. He turned back to the gate and took a deep breath and plunged in again darting past an elderly granddame leading her small grandson. Once again, as soon as the cobalt light enfolded him, the gate ground shut and the tunnel of the Straight Path rolled away empty. This time, he managed to come back out of the gate with more decorum and cross to where Blackmore was watching his actions with interest.

"Grandmaster, I don't understand?" he said knowing full well the Valinga knew of what he spoke.

"When you enter through the gate, your fate is no longer tied to theirs." Blackmore informed him calmly. "Unless someone returns with you, you walk alone, your path your own."

"But they are still coming through from Kalyria...I understand this not!"

"Aye, they are and when you reach Kalyria you will rejoin any who have not already come through." Blackmore assured him, his good eye twinkling. "The Straight Paths have their own rules, lad and you are still responsible for your own actions. So go on and finish what you've started."

With that, the old Valinga turned back to the gentleman who stood beside him signing the sanctuary book. Menannon inclined his head to his grandmaster and went back to the Kalyrian gate.

This time he took a deep breath and tried to clear his mind the best he could. He stepped through into the empty silence and walked the pattern to Kalyria's gate and halted. It was closed. His heart began to pound and a trickle of sweat ran down his spine. Were the folk still moving or had they been stopped by the gate closing behind him? His heart in his throat, he stepped forward, the gate ground open and he stepped forth into the line of people.

The line still led around the throne and into the small door behind it. There was no way to tell how many were left to come. Menannon looked quickly towards the chamber's door to see Conar and a guardsman standing at post, their hands on the bar though they both looked towards the line. Menannon raised Conar a questioning eyebrow, not daring to call to him, and received a great smile in return. The Dwarf's family had obviously come through. He turned and slipped past the line of folk, a smile of relief lighting his features and raising their hearts for the outcome of this cast.

Menannon reached the back door only to come face to face with Haalinoth and the lieutenant tying themselves to the rope. Irenos stood watching not his fellows, but looking down towards where the harbor lay, his head cocked listening. He darted past them and took a sprig from the peridüs tree at the back of the garden. He returned to Haalinoth's side and took his arm in greeting and farewell.

"Thank you for all you have done for my folk," he said.

The Teluri gave him a swift embrace.

"It has been my pleasure," Haalinoth said stepping back. "Call me at need and I shall come no matter the ill-wind it may engender."

"It is to be hoped there will be no greater need. Please give this to Lee as a token that we are done and all is well."

Menannon handed the sprig to the Teluri, smiling his thanks and turned to the Lieutenant.

"Please close the door to the tunnel as you exit. Attach Conar and his comrade and go on through the gate. It will close behind you. They await you at the other end to welcome you into sanctuary."

The fellow nodded and the Giant closed the small door after

their retreating backs. Silence returned to the harper hall's close.

Menannon walked across to Irenos who still listened intently. He stopped by the Teluri prince's side and listened briefly, but heard nothing.

"What is it?" he murmured.

Irenos held up a hand for silence and closed his eyes the better to concentrate. Menannon waited silently, his stomach tightening in returning dread. Knowing the hearing of a Teluri was far better than that of any other of the High One's created beings, he doubted not that something was wrong.

The Teluri stood still a few moments longer then shook his head and turned to look up at the Giant.

"There was the sound of a banging door coming from the harbor area not but a matter of a quarter turn of an hour after thou didst leave." Irenos informed him softly. "Then there was yelling and scuffling and I heard Tullio's voice yelling... 'Give that back! It's mine I won it fair and square in a dice game!'... there were more words and I could hear blows exchanged then the sound of running feet following after the distinct sound of wooden stilts striking the ground. There was more scuffling and then a scream followed by banging and thudding as though someone had fallen a fair distance down into a lower courtyard, like as not from a higher street. Then Turanio's voice rose in a wail calling his brother's name. There has been no further sound I could discern as related to the happening since thou didst emerge from yon tunnel. I fear a tragedy has befallen our fellowship."

Menannon instantly turned to the wall and began to climb. Irenos took a hold of his leg halting him.

"Thou knowest not what awaits down there! It could be a trap!"

"I have to go!" Menannon jerked his leg from the Teluri's grasp.

"Then I shall attend thee." Irenos made to climb the wall as well, but Menannon halted him with a swift hand.

"Nay! If it is a trap, then both of us would be taken. Nay,

retrieve the lantern in the tunnel and go to my father's villa and await news. If I come not, bend distance to Aridion City and bespeak Grandmaster Blackmore's instruction as to the workings of the Straight Path so you can continue our work. My father will help you."

When Irenos looked as though he would not heed the counsel, Menannon shoved him back more roughly than he had intended and the lighter Teluri went flying several feet across the close and landed heavily. He bounced up instantly with only his dignity injured.

"One of us must be free to carry on!" Menannon hissed by way of apology.

Irenos nodded reluctantly, his grey eyes dark with worry and stood still.

The Giant climbed on over the wall, dropped silently into the orchard and moved swiftly down the hill. He stayed within the trees as long as possible then emerged onto a small side street and made his way from street to street down to the second level above the docks and there halted. Naught seemed amiss along the harbor front, for no untoward noise carried up to him, just the normal early morning sounds of docksmen and traders preparing for the new day. Dawn's light was brightening the strand and the lower road. Menannon could see the front door of the Cokeyna was closed and all seemed in order there. He could see no signs of a scuffle in the sand before it, though perchance such marks had already been erased by the barkeeps. Such signs were not good for business.

Menannon stood and moved easily down the last few switchbacks of the road to the harbor and stepped onto the strand for all the world as though he were simply out for an early morning stroll. He greeted several shop keepers setting out their morning wares and not a few fishermen putting their nets upon the drying racks after their night's work. Arriving at the door of the ale house he paused and looked inside. Davy was washing tables and waiting on a few early customers with the aide of a small pot boy. There was no sign of Dink or the Orlandos. At the sight of Menannon at the door, Davy waved him in.

"I've got yer sire's order in the back. If you'll give me a minute, I'll fetch it."

He motioned Menannon to a seat at the bar farthest from the other patrons and disappeared through the curtain in the back. The Giant sat as he was bid, doing his best to hide his consternation. His sire had ordered nothing from the Cokeyna and well he knew it. Something was indeed amiss. In a twinkling the barkeep returned with a sizable paper-wrapped bundle tied neatly with heavy string. He laid it on the bar.

"There ya are, tell yer sire it took a while to locate it, but we did it."

Davy's large adams apple was bobbing nervously, but his eyes held a meaningful look. "I deem you'll be wantin' yer usual breakfast," he said without skipping a beat as he turned to the stove and began frying up a hearty fare of fish and fruit.

Menannon could only nod and try not to look as surprised and worried as he felt. He rarely broke his fast at the Cokeyna and never since he had come back from the mainland this time.

As he worked, Davy began talking softly so as the other patrons and the pot boy would not hear.

"There was a great to-do here not but a bit ago. Yer friends Dink, Turanio and Tullio were sittin' at their usual table playin' at fox and hounds all night. Tullio had his hood up pretendin' to be you as has been his wont of late. Well, there was a table of Doomcrier's near 'em and one of that number, a little drunker than the rest, leaned over and snatched the hood from the boy's head."

Menannon's heart nearly stopped at those words and he glanced around to see if anyone else had heard.

"The High One Almighty!" he breathed.

Davy let out a guffaw as though Menannon had just told him a joke and then continued his tale.

"'I knew ya were a fake!' The Doomcrier yells at the lad. 'Where's the Giant?!' The lads were startled, but they aren't no slow tops them three an' Dink speaks up just as pretty as ya please and says: 'He's no fake, he's just after bein' a muddleheaded dreamer who wants to be a harper instead o' a stiltwalker. He's been pretendin' to be Menannon e'er since he won that stupid robe from him in a game o' chance at the circus. We've nay got the slightest idea where that stupid Giant is after bein' he's got his nose too far in the air to associate wi' the likes o' us anymore, now he's a councillor an' all.'

"'A councillor is he? Well then you riff-raff musta stolen this!' An the fellow jumps up an' tips Tullio out of his chair an' pulls yer robe off him. 'I'll just be taken it back to him!' An' he an' his mates start laughin' an' makin' rude comments an' march out the front door, waving the robe. Tullio jumps up on them great stilts of his an' starts after 'em, his face red as a coxcomb. The other two try to stop him, but he wouldn't have none of it an' runs out yellin' that he won the robe fair and square in a dice game and it's his! Dink an' Turanio runs after him an' so do the rest of the patrons as were not too drunk to follow. I got outside just in time to see Tullio snatch the robe back an' run up the road. I couldn't exactly see what happened next, but some of the Doomcriers an' Turanio ran after him and there was a to-do up above there an' then I heard a scream an' some crashin' and the boy landed over yonder in a heap of broken stilts. I ran to him, but Turanio got there first an' the boy wasn't movin'. He'd broken his neck in the fall."

"The High One's holy tears, it can't be! Are you sure?"

The blood drained from Menannon's face as the news sunk in. The boy had died for no more than a piece of cloth because it had belonged to his friend and he had taken it as a sacred trust to use it in their plans.

"I'm sorry, lad. 'Tis true. I helped a couple of the nightwatch pick the lad's body up to carry it to his father's house. An' Turanio gave me yon package contents an' said to give it to you. He said there was were gild owed fer his brother, but he did not say from whom." Davy looked long into Menannon's troubled face. "He followed his brother's body an' Dink slipped away on his own. Things ain't good, lad. News'll spread fast that Tullio's been pretendin' to be you an there'll be a lot of speculation as to why. Now finish yer food an' go home."

The barkeep slapped Menannon on the shoulder as though they had just shared a great joke.

"I'll be rememberin' that one!" he said and went back to cleaning tables, a merry whistle on his lips.

Menannon forced himself to smile and swallow the last of his food, though it tasted like ashes in his mouth. He quickly washed it down with a gulp of the ale Davy had poured him and, taking up the package, dropped some coins on the bar, called a bright. "*Good day!*" to Davy and left the Cokeyna.

CHAPTER 19
(SUMMER OF THE WORLD 6097)

ENANNON WAS ALLOWED NO TIME to mourn Tullio's death or truly consider its implications for their fellowship, as not an hour before the next mid-of-day found young Emma standing at the gate of the villa with a large bouquet of lilies for him. She was shown into the atrium by Skendrin while he was summoned.

The young Giant rose and dressed hurriedly and arrived in the atrium to find the flower seller perched on a chair drinking a glass of lemon twist and kicking her bare feet in slight impatience, the bouquet sitting on the table beside her. Skendrin and several of his father's servants were going about their morning chores of dusting and cleaning the great chamber a bit more assiduously than usual as all were curious as to who had sent their master's son flowers. At the sight of him, Emma jumped up and dropped him a very pretty courtesy.

"I've a gift fer ye, Master Menannon," she said. "There's a poem too." Emma quickly reached into the pocket of her oversized kirtle and pulled forth a folded sheet of vellum and handed it to him. He leaned down to take it from her and she murmured so none other could hear.

"Nirna Princess wishes to meet ye at the usual place at mid-of-night," she murmured then stepped back and spoke loudly. "I was told to tell ye not to give me any of the 'Specials' as I've already been paid a goodly sum." With that, she swallowed the last of her twist, dropped him another courtesy and skipped out of the villa intent on going on with the next phase of her errand.

Behind her, Menannon unfolded the vellum and found a simple love poem all Kalyrian children learned at their nurses' knees. This was not a message from Nirna, just an excuse for Emma to give him her real message. Puzzled and worried, he tucked the missive into the breast of his kirtle as he would with a real love message and taking the bouquet, retreated to his chamber to think. Skendrin watched him go and then left the servants to their efforts and proceeded to the summerhouse to confer with Gorlanndon.

Menannon closed the door of his chamber and set the bouquet on the bedside table then threw himself back onto rumpled surface of his bed. He took one of the lilies out of the group and held it to his nose, savoring its sweetness. His rational mind knew that this was just one of their messages and not a love token, still he could not help the quickening of his pulses at the knowledge that it was from Nirna. He carefully set the flower between the leaves of his copy of the Word Hoard of the High One and closed it gently. How Nirna had discovered their little group's method of communication, he knew not. But discover it she had and he fervently hoped that none other was as perspicacious.

He sat on the side of his bed and considered the implica-tions of this message. Something must be truly wrong, as he and Nirna had agreed not to meet in secret until the trouble on Kalyria was resolved, for such a meeting would endanger them both.

Menannon spent the rest of the day avoiding speech with his sire by feigning sleep each time someone looked in upon him. He finally arose at dinner time, changed his kirtle to one more suitable for a happy occasion and made his way to the dining chamber where he found quite a gathering in the huge chamber, which had been made even larger by the removal of all of Gorlanndon's collections and artwork save only the portrait of his mother. Among those gathered were a number of councillors whom Menannon recognized, but did not know personally and of course, Firod was there, as was Irenos. Menannon hoped the presence of the councillors meant there would be a meeting of his sire's faction this night which would allow him to slip away unnoticed. He nodded to all and took his usual seat at the foot of the table. At its head Gorlanndon nodded to him, but did not speak as Clarinda and the staff chose that moment to bring the repast to table. Amidst the bustle of serving and seating, Menannon took the opportunity to study Irenos.

The prince looked drawn and worried. No, not worried, but rather angry, for the Teluri kept exchanging fierce looks with Firod who kept answering with a slight shake of his head. Here was a conundrum. What had so shaken the Teluri's usual calm and how was the captain part of it? Unanswerable questions at the moment, but worrying nonetheless, especially in light of Nirna's message. Menannon's thoughts were brought back to the meal as Clarinda took her place at table and Gorlanndon spoke the blessing. Soon, everyone was eating the fine repast and the conversation was light and cheerful, replete with witty anecdotes by Gorlanndon who used merry stories from his past to entertain his guests. It was a ploy on his sire's part to keep the conversation from entering channels best discussed in private. Menannon had seen him use this many times before to great effect. It worked well this night, thus nothing of import was discussed at table.

As soon as the last sweet course had been removed, Gorlanndon stood to his full height and stretched. He looked around at his companion councillors and gestured towards the atrium.

"Gentlemen, if you would adjourn to the atrium, I shall join you there in a short while. There is good wine there to enjoy while you wait."

Knowing this to be as much of a command as an invitation, all of the councillors took their leave and proceeded to the atrium where they were attended by Skendrin and his staff. Menannon was thereby left at table with Firod and Irenos, both of whom were looking to Gorlanndon for his next instruction.

"Come. We four have much to discuss and little time to do so." The great Giant turned and made his way quickly through the kitchen and out into the kaleyard and thence to the summerhouse, the rest following silently. When they were all inside and the door locked, he turned to them.

"Irenos my friend, our good captain has a report for you I fear will not fall gently upon your ears." He motioned all to sit then took a seat himself as all turned their eyes to Firod.

"I was privy to a conversation not meant for my ears this morning," Firod began. He glanced at Gorlanndon then turned his gaze back to Irenos. "Azuron was talking to one of his closest confidantes and they were discussing you and your activities here on Kalyria. It seems that someone has reported that you have been involved with the disappearances of 'criminals'. Azuron has decided that this is an act of war as you are the Prince Royal of the kingdom of Blue Hill. He was saying that as soon as he has settled the situation here on Kalyria he will turn his attention to that kingdom. He also is going to have you arrested as a spy. He is only waiting for the next session of the Privy Council to enact his decision and get the warrants signed."

There was a deep silence following this announcement, finally broken by Gorlanndon.

"Apparently, the concept of diplomatic immunity is above Azuron's head," Gorlanndon stated dryly. "Regardless, it would seem that you need to depart for Blue Hill as soon as may be. We do not need a greater war than we already have, for it would not stop with your homeland, but would soon engulf all of the Teluri realms. The High King, Liélindar of Lilientharien, would not stand idly by and allow one realm to come under assault. Nay, he could not. You see the problem then?"

Irenos looked down at his own steepled fingers then back up to lock eyes with Gorlanndon.

"This doth confirm what I also have heard, how is no matter now. Dost thou think this is but a ploy to stop our activities or is the black one actually serious in his threats?"

"I fear he is serious," Gorlanndon said with a deep sigh. "He deems to kill two birds with one stone. Deprive Blue Hill of its Prince Royal and give reason to send Kalyrian troops against your sire, Gorlanndon said. "Yes, yes, he truly would dare that much," he added to forestall comments.

Firod raised a doubting eyebrow. "Must he have an excuse for that?"

"Aye! He is not sole ruler of Kalyria yet and needs must deal with the Privy Council and with me. The council will have none of it if there is no trial or execution. Without Irenos' presence here, there can be no charge of spying and thus no threat to our empire's security."

Menannon cleared his throat and the older men looked around at him.

"What you are saying, is that I needs must take the Prince to Aridion City as rapidly as possible else will he be arrested and executed, correct?"

"In so many words, aye!" Gorlanndon replied. "Though I would prefer you not be involved." He glanced at Irenos to see the Teluri was thinking hard.

"If we are to go to Aridion City, we should leave tonight," Menannon said.

Menannon looked hard at Irenos, wondering what he was thinking and how their work of rescue would get along without the Teluri. Irenos apparently felt all eyes upon him and raised his head.

"Thank thee, lad for thine offer, but I can step to Blue Hill as easily from here as from the harper hall." He squared his shoulders, the light from the Dwarf lantern gleaming from his ivory hair making him seem almost ethereal. "Dost thou all deem I needs must go?" He looked long from one to the other and all three nodded in turn. "It is done then." He stood and stepped around Menannon to the open space near the door and turned to look at them once more.

"It has been my honor to serve with thee. Should any of thee need me further or any aid that I or mine can give thee, send me word through Grandmaster Blackmore and I will come to thee no matter the cost." He inclined his head to them and before any more could be spoken he took one step towards them and with a loud crack, disappeared. Menannon could not help jumping back startled.

"Go with the High One, old friend," Gorlanndon murmured then turned back to his remaining companions. "Firod, go back to the palace and set the rumor mill to running that the Prince has returned to his own land, but none knows how or when. Make sure you hint well of Mythrian magic and the arcane powers of the Teluri. And Menannon," he turned to his son even as the captain nodded and left the summerhouse, "as of this moment, boy, no further rescue attempts shall be made. Is that clear?" he looked straight into Menannon's troubled eyes.

"Well, is it?" Gorlanndon demanded when the younger Giant did not answer.

At last, Menannon looked away, his shoulders slumping.

"Aye, my father. Your words are clear."

"Good!" Gorlanndon thrust himself to his feet. "At dawn, find Skendrin and he will set tasks for you that will serve our people in a different and hopefully safer manner. I needs must attend upon the councillors now. Good night."

The elder Giant leaned down and kissed his son's brow then he, too, left the summerhouse, leaving Menannon to ponder what he should do now and to wrestle with his conscience. He could not break faith with those who had been in the fellowship, particularly not with Tullio who had died for their cause, but for a Giant, a sire's word was absolute law. A law so inviolable as to be broken only by death. He smiled at the thought, for even so, not all that long ago, he had dared to disobey, but no longer. He was seeing things more clearly now. No, he would do as his father ordered. Yet, he admitted that this order troubled him.

Menannon shuttered the Dwarf lantern on the table, plunging the summerhouse into darkness. He opened the blinds and sat back down to think, the simple sounds of life coming from the villa washing over him like the gentle trickle of spring rain. He sat thus for several turns of the hour, pondering. Irenos was now safe in Blue Hill. Haalinoth and Conar were safe in Aridion City. Of Turanio, there had been no sign since Tullio had fallen to his death. Dink had disappeared as well. They had sworn at the beginning to continue their work to the last man and now he, Menannon, was that last man.

After long turns of the hour, the answer finally came to him in the splitting of legal hairs. His father had said *no more rescue attempts*. All right! There would be no more rescue *attempts*, only rescue *accomplishments*. Gorlanndon had not forbidden that.

Menannon rose to go change his clothing in preparation for his meeting with Nirna. As he left the summerhouse, he could not help grinning to himself. He was beginning to think like Lee, the great planner of mischief.

THE FINAL SOUNDING ofS the mid-of-night clock chime found him settled in the brattice awaiting Nirna's coming with his stomach tied in knots. What did her message portend? Perhaps—he fervently hoped it was so—she only sought to apprise him of Irenos' coming arrest and he would be able to tell her that such a chance had already been prevented. The sound of swift light feet put a stop to any further speculation. He forced himself to listen for any sound other than Nirna's coming, but heard none. She was not followed.

In a breathless moment, Nirna appeared through the opening in the brattice.

"Playfellow, are you here?" she whispered and again as he had done so many times before, the Giant stepped into the moonlight glittering through one of the arrow slits.

"I'm here Fæori. What do you require of me?"

Rather than answering, she threw herself into his arms. He could feel her trembling even through the heavily embroi-dered robe she wore. The sent of peridüs water wafted from her hair, She was again arrayed for a late banquet. He hugged her tightly then held her off at arm's length.

"Now tell me quickly what ill wind has caused you to send for me?"

She swallowed convulsively and tried to slow the beating of her heart. Menannon was here. he would know what to do. Nirna straightened her shoulders and took a deep breath.

"Mati was in the garden near the wall that adjoins the practice yard and she heard one of Azuron's lieutenants giving orders to his men. They are to come into the assembly on the morrow dressed as Borian traders and mingle with the councillors. He was telling them to get 'the old general' away by himself and 'deliver Azuron's greetings to him the point of which will tickle his backbone.' Playfellow, they mean to murder Lord Lonier on the morrow. There can be no other meaning, for the words were followed by as nasty a laugh as Mati has ever heard."

Nirna's voice faltered on these last words as she began to tremble again. Menannon turned to look out of the arrow slit down into the darkness of the Kidron gorge. How was it possible that pure murder could be so off-handedly planned in his own beloved land?

"What can we do, Playfellow?" Nirna whispered, taking his arm.

"I must take him and all of his family away." Menannon turned back and took her into his arms once more. "I must find a way to let Lonier know of this and get him away this night...."

"I already have," she interrupted him. "I sent Emma to him with a bouquet of lilies just after I sent her to you. She told him to prepare his family to leave and that help would come. Did I do wrong?"

She searched his face in the moonlight and saw there the indecision of going against his father's command. She sounded so like a little girl begging reassurance that he nearly laughed.

"Nay, sweet Fæori. You did exactly right in this. You are a true conspirator and a great friend in need."

Menannon shook off his doubts, his own resolve strengthened by her trust in him.

"You go back to the palace ere you are missed and leave Lord Lonier and his family to me."

"How will I know you have succeeded?" she whispered, still clinging to his arms.

"I will wear garnet beads in my beard if all is well when I come to the council meeting with my father. If I wear not garnets or come not at all you will know something went wrong...."

"No, nothing can go wrong. You have to stay safe, Menannon!" Nirna's use of his real name showed just how deep were her feelings and fears for him.

"Nothing will go wrong, sweet Fæori," he assured her and raised her chin with gentle fingers so that he could place a long, heartfelt kiss upon her lips. "Look for me in the council chamber on the morrow," he whispered stepping back. "I shall be there. Now go!" He gave her a little shove to start her on her way and himself faded back into the darkness of the brattice.

Nirna fled as swiftly as she had come, the sound of her feet quickly fading into the sounds of the night.

As soon as the sound of Nirna's feet disappeared, Menannon slipped out of the brattice and down the wall, returning to the villa by circuitous ways to wait until it was time to begin his rescue. He would be traveling light tonight, as he would have to make do without the ladder for that had been hidden somewhere at Irenos' villa and he knew not how to retrieve it. This night would test his mettle and prove whether or no rescues could be carried off singlehandedly.

When the hour to depart arrived, he prayed to the High One that all would go well and his rescue succeed. He then checked to be sure his father was still occupied in the atrium. Gorlanndon and the councillors were all well occupied, so Menannon slipped out the back of the villa via the usual route and headed for the lower Equian, equipment in hand.

The Giant attained the second level of the Equian's more spacious villas without any mishap, though he had almost knocked into a band of Doomcriers when he rounded a corner just above the docks, he having taken a long and devious route to his goal that took him first to the docks and then back up the Equian to Lord Lonier's villa. He was heading toward the villa's rear as Nirna had arranged and where the lord and his family would be waiting for him when he heard a scratching sound ahead of him. He halted for a moment, all senses pricked. The noise came again, then a large cat appeared from the alley's darkness, a fish firmly held in its mouth. Menannon sighed and moved on carefully past the mouth of the alley the animal had just vacated.

Out of the corner of his eye, he caught movement just an instant too late as a dark cloth was thrown over his head and strong arms began to wrestle him into the alley and onto the ground. When they finally wrestled him down by sheer weight of numbers, there were no questions asked, no explanations, nothing save fists, mindfully equipped with iron bars, and a length of cloth forced into his mouth to muffle any sounds he might make of either pain or protest. They methodically beat him senseless, a thing taking uncommon strength and skill to accomplish. Of his assailants, there was only one he was sure of and that was an Orlando, as just once he was able to grab a flailing leg and found it to be a cloth covered wooden stilt. The impression was there and gone as his moment of surprise caused just enough inattention on his part that another of his assailants was able to connect an iron bar solidly with his jaw and he knew no more.

Menannon came to himself in the darkness of the alley, his whole body aching from the beating he had taken. He lay still for a few moments trying to fathom what was happening around him and wondering why he had not been arrested, before he opened his eyes. He ached in every limb, but at least he was not spitting teeth, though a good deal of blood was dripping into his left eye from a nasty cut over it. He thought back over the incident and found that he could not countenance the thought that an Orlando had betrayed him. Could it have been Turanio, as Davy had told him that Turanio and sworn to collect were gild for his brother's death, but it was unthinkable that this event would so disarrange his loyalties he would turn against everyone, including his own family, and throw in his lot with the Doomcriers. It was unthinkable, yet the plain evidence of the feel of a wooden stilt among the appendages assailing him had been unmistakable. Some stilt walker was apparently now a Doomcrier. If not Turanio, then who? The question ran round and round

Menannon's aching head to no avail. At last he gave up the quest and determined to get on with the task at hand. He could search for Turanio later, but now time was pressing.

Carefully, so as not to arouse the notice of any who might be watching him, Menannon opened his eyes just enough so that he could look about through his eyelashes. The alley appeared empty. With a great effort of will, he sat up and then forced himself to his feet. He took momentary stock. At least nothing was broken, though his head continued to ring like a bell and ache abominably. Despite that, he had to get to Lonier's villa.

Retrieving his pack, Menannon managed to drag himself to the entrance of the alley and looked into the street. It was deserted. He stood, trying to gather his wits for several long moments. It was still velvety black overhead, but there was the distinct smell of morning in the air. He would have to hurry. With more resolution than he knew he possessed, the young Giant forced himself to move away from the wall and lurch up the street. He sincerely hoped his odd movements would be taken for drunkenness should anyone see him before he could blend into the shadows below Lonier's villa. Getting the lord and his family to the harper hall was going to be no easy task.

It took him the best part of a quarter turn of an hour to maneuver himself into position below Lonier's villa, the time allowing the stiffness to begin to work itself out of his ill-used muscles, but his head still pounded like a badly played drum. He stood still a moment and wiped dried blood out of his left eye with fingers that shook. The night about him was still, though there was a distinct prickle along his spine telling him that all was not as empty as it seemed. His need for haste warred with his need to make sure that all was well before he ventured to climb the wall. Despite his anxiety, he forced himself to stand still another quarter turn of the hour. It was the High One's own blessing that he did, as just as the first birds began to chirp the coming dawn, a harsh voice growled from almost beneath his feet.

"It'll be dawn soon an the captain said as t' how we're t' leave afore first light. So get yerselves up an let's hence afore we're spotted. They'll be takin' care of the old codger in their own way we was just t' make sure he didn't escape int' the night." At the sound of movement in the bushes all about him, Menannon froze, willing himself to be taken for part of the landscape. Almost, one of the Doomcrier guards discovered him as the fellow nearly fell over as he rose from the earth virtually at Menannon's feet and lurched a bit stiffly to follow his commander's orders.

"I'm gettin' too old fer this lying all night on the hard ground," the fellow growled under his breath and Menannon heard a soft sound of agreement from below and to his left.

The young Giant took as deep a breath as he dared and held it until his lungs were screaming for air to let as many of the Doomcriers get as far away as he could before he made any noise himself. The last of their footsteps died away even as Menannon had to breathe or pass out cold. He stood gasping for a few heartbeats then turned and made quick work of scaling the wall. Now that the watchers in the dark were gone, he had only to worry about not raising an alarm within the villa.

He reached the top of the wall and rolled onto it quietly stretching out full length and set himself to search the garden below for any sign of intrusion. There was none. The only warm-blooded thing in the garden below him was Lonier's old dog who sat with her head cocked, studying the person on the stones above her. He was eternally grateful that he had been to the villa many times and knew the dog so that she did not now consider him an intruder despite his strange method of entrance. Finding nothing amiss in the garden, Menannon lowered himself down and dropped into a crouch near the dog. Briefly, she sniffed his knee and seemed to be satisfied that he really was himself and began to wag her tail. Menannon scratched her ears and stood up motioning her to follow him. Together, they approached the servant's entrance in the kitchen wing of the villa.

He attained the doorway and halted again to take one last look about. The dog looked up at him curiously, seeming in no wise disturbed by either the Giant or the night around them. There was no one else about, then. Menannon breathed a sigh of relief and took hold of the door handle. With one swift motion he turned it and slipped inside. The dog followed closely. The back hall was dark, being lit only by the ambient light coming in the windows. Menannon hesitated, not quite sure where to find those he sought within the silent villa, but the dog suffered from no such quandary and quickly trotted off in the direction of the dining chamber located in the front portion of the building. With a shrug, Menannon followed, having no better course to set.

The sound of the dog's toenails clicking on the flags of the floor was the only sound he heard until he reached the dark dining chamber and halted in the doorway. The dog entered the chamber and apparently went to someone in the darkness, for Menannon heard a sudden hiss as though a person had caught their breath. The question now was whether that person was one of Lonier's family or a Doomcrier set there to trap him, although if it were the latter, surely the dog would not act so calmly, as if she were approaching one of her own, yet Menannon hovered in the entryway undecided for several long heartbeats, perhaps being overly cautious, then he heard the dog coming back. There was the sound of footsteps accompanying her. The dog came up to him and bumped into his leg with a soft whine. Everything stopped at the sound, then there was an in-drawing of breath almost at his elbow and a deep voice murmured softly.

"Page four and twenty begins with..."

"Thou shalt trust in none save the High One," Menannon finished and let his breath out in a heartfelt sigh. "Lord Lonier, we must go. Are you and yours ready?"

"Aye, lad. We busied ourselves as soon as Nirna's message came. I must say I was surprised by the message, but not its content. I knew I was going to be denounced or assassinated soon. So I've been contemplating what I would do should the call go out for me so when it did I was ready. The family are all by the rear door near the servants quarters awaiting you. Follow me. What took you so long? We had nearly given you up." Lonier took Menannon's arm to guide him through the dark villa.

"I had a little brush with some Doomcriers," he whispered as he followed the old lord.

Lonier halted and a group of shadows quietly surrounded them. There were fourteen in all, several of them children, and to Menannon's relief, they were already tied together on a single rope to which the old lord now tied himself at the farther end. Emma had not failed in her instructions despite having received her orders from Nirna this time. One of the children tied the old dog on with her which caused the Giant to give her an approving pat on the shoulder. Just before Menannon tied himself on at the near end, he murmured into Lonier's ear.

"Where is you treasury? You'll need funds to establish yourself anew on the mainland."

"Each of my children and grand-children bear a part of it so that all will prosper should we not all get to Aridion City and I have a sum I left with a merchant in Blue Bay some summers ago as an investment in his trade. One way or another, we shall not want."

Menannon nodded even though the old lord could not see him. The fellow was sharp. He tied himself onto the rope and eased the door open. There was no sound beyond the door save night sounds. The early morning twittering of birds was louder now, marking the passage of time. He led them quickly to the back wall of the close and led the way over the wall. Lonier's son and two sons-in-law aided the old lord to make the climb. All but the smallest girl and the old dog made it on their own and these twain were hoisted on strong shoulders. When all were assembled in the darkness without, Menannon led the way down through the bushes past the circling orchard and out onto the road below Lonier's holding. The group stayed together, the adults carrying the youngest children for the sake of speed.

They made short work of reaching the bridge to the third circle of the Citadel and halted there in the shadows of the lamp posts. The young Giant let out his breath softly and relaxed just slightly at having come so far without incident. He motioned for everyone to stay still while he surveyed the bridge and the road below. He saw no movement. He glanced down at the dog to see that she was showing no interest in the darkness around them. Menannon took that as a good sign and signaled for the rest to follow him. They crossed quickly and soon lost themselves in the twisting alleys of the lower Citadel.

Grey dawn was touching the eastern sky by the time they reached the close surrounding the harper hall. Menannon again halted in the shadows of the wall and listened intently. Once he managed to push his senses beyond the small noises made by his own group, he heard soft footsteps coming along the road behind them. He stood and looked around frantically for a place to hide, but there was none as the harper hall and its close were surrounded by a small plaza that was edged on three sides by buildings and on the fourth by the great cemetery of Kirith Kalyria. He turned to all and motioned for them to squat down and make themselves as inconspicuous as possible and above all to be silent and not to move. He pushed them together as closely as he could, then stood in front of them himself and rested his hand against the wall, willing its darkness and mass to cover them. He laid his other hand on the shoulder of Lonier's eldest grandson. He had never tried his sire's trick before now, and he had no idea if it would work for him or no, but necessity breeds inspiration. He held his concentration so completely that he almost lost sense of himself and began to feel like a stone. It was not until Lonier's grandsons touched his leg that he came back to himself with a start and a slight gasp. About them, the night was empty of footsteps, where the owner of them had gone, he had no idea. Menannon waited a few more moments then signaled everyone to follow him.

Together they entered the close and circled around the hall until they arrived at the back. Here he halted again and took the small key from his belt pouch and unlocked the door. It grated slightly despite its heightened use of late, but turned nonetheless and they were all able to enter the tunnel and shut out the night. He opened the Dwarf lantern and gave them a moment to breathe and relax a bit before he led the way up the stair into the sanctuary. Menannon stopped behind the throne and stood to his full height and looked quickly about. The great chamber was empty. He stepped around it and the rest followed him. One of the children started to say something, but Menannon hushed him with a gesture and led them to gather in front of the mosaic.

"I will open this gateway in a moment," he murmured, breaking his silence for the first time since they had left the villa. "There will be a cobalt light that is nearly as bright as the sun, so squint your eyes or keep them shut as you choose. All I need you to do is to hold hands and follow me. If the rope should break and we get separated, stop right where you are and sit down. I will find you so long as you don't leave the path. Don't be alarmed. We are safe now in the mighty hand of the High One and what is His, He does not lose."

Everyone nodded a bit nervously—even Lonier, though he seemed the calmest of all save for the old dog who was just content to be with her family. Menannon turned and spoke the word of command once more and the mosaic cracked down the middle and opened, flooding the sanctuary with cobalt light. Nearly everyone gasped in wonder at the sight.

"Follow me," Menannon commanded and stepped through the gate and all followed him. The mosaic ground shut behind them leaving the sanctuary to the shadows once more.

The stars were still shining through the clerestory windows of Blackmore's audience chamber when the Kalyrian mosaic cracked open and Menannon stepped through. When all had entered, the gate ground shut, plunging the chamber back into semi-darkness.

"Untie yourselves," he said using a normal tone of voice. "None can follow you here. I'll find the Grandmaster and, Lord Lonier, you may bespeak him to grant you and yours sanctuary. Come with me, please." Menannon waited for Lonier to untie himself, then crossed to the grandmaster's desk and gently tapped on the wall.

"Grandmaster, I have more visitors for you, sir."

He spoke to a seemingly blank wall much to Lonier's

puzzlement. Behind them, several of the youngest children began to cry with the after effects of the strain they had been under. The crying seemed to loose something in the fugitives for they all began to talk and laugh at once. Menannon glanced over his shoulder with a grin then turned back and knocked again. This time there was a response. There was a clicking sound then the section of wall sank in and moved aside. The small figure of Blackmore stood there silhouetted against the firelight from his bedchamber.

"You harpers," Lonier muttered at Menannon's elbow.

The Giant glanced down to see the old lord shake his head at another wonder thus revealed.

"Grandmaster, may I introduce Kalyrian Councillor Lord Lonier," Menannon inclined his head to both men and stepped back respectfully.

"It's been a long time, Lonier," Blackmore held out his hand to the lord who took it with fervent pleasure. "You've not been gettin' over this way as often as you did in your military days."

"Nay, I have not, Blackmore. Politics is a time-consuming profession," Lonier boomed in his usual manner, the discovery that his old friend Blackmore really was still the grandmaster of the harpers' guild having given him back much of his heart.

"You'll be wanting sanctuary, I assume?"

Blackmore glanced at Menannon, taking in the tears and dirt on his clothing and the dried blood on his face. He motioned to Lonier and hobbled to his desk, the door to his chambers closing with a soft swish behind him.

"Aye, I'm afraid it's come to that on Kalyria, with Azuron in full charge now," Lonier sighed, following him to the desk and took the seat the grandmaster indicated. He sat down gratefully. It had been a stressful night for an old man, even one as spry as Lonier.

Blackmore reached up and pulled his bell pull to summon Jondlin. Lee appeared nearly instantly with Jondlin following, proving that the runner had heard sounds in the chamber and divined their usual portent.

"Aye, sir?" Lee asked from the doorway. "You will be wanting chambers readied in the guest hall?"

"True enough, lad. Will you take Lord Lonier's family to the refectory and get them something to eat and then show them to chambers, please?"

"On my way," was the jaunty reply. The drummer immediately came to the side of Lonier's oldest son and bowed. "If you'll all follow me." He turned and led the way out of the audience chamber, Lonier's family in tow. The old dog padded happily along behind.

"Menannon...," Blackmore began, but even as he turned to address his journeyman, the cobalt light of the Straight Paths flashed across the chamber and the young Giant disappeared into it. The old Valinga shook his head with a wry grin for Lonier. "He doesn't take praise well," he observed

"Nor does his sire," Lonier nodded in agreement. While they continued to speak, Blackmore took out the large codex from a bottom drawer of his desk and laid it in front of Lonier.

"If you would be so kind as to list the names of your family," he said handing Lonier a brush and ink dish. "So how was the escape? From the look of the lad's clothing, there appears to have been trouble."

"He arrived at my villa in that condition and said only that he'd had a run in with Doomcriers. The escape itself was blessedly uneventful save for one close call." Lonier halted writing for a moment and pointed the brush at Blackmore. "We had arrived at the wall of the close of Kalyria's harper hall when we heard someone walking towards us. My heart nearly misgave me at the sound, but our Giant just told us to get down and then he leaned against the wall and everything went still. How, I shall never know, but a fully armed Doomcrier walked within three feet of us and apparently saw nothing, for he simply walked on past the gate of the close and out of the square by one of its lower roads. Then the boy told us to move and we all followed him." Lonier shook his head at the memory. "The High One only knows how the fellow missed us."

"Was Menannon touching the stone?" Blackmore queried, his good eye looking steadily at Lonier.

"Aye, I remember he had one hand on it and the other touching one of the children." Lonier tapped the handle of the brush against his lips thoughtfully. "I also remember that the sound of the fellow's feet was somewhat muffled though he was wearing hard boots. I thought nothing of it at the time...." He mumbled to a halt at the rather impish grin that was spreading across the Valinga's face.

"The lad is a Giant after all," Blackmore said by way of explanation, but said no more and simply held up his hand when Lonier would have questioned him. He pointed to the codex and settled back into his chair, a satisfied twinkle in his eye.

THE MORNING'S FULL LIGHT brought a heavy fist pounding on Gorlanndon's gate and an imperious voice demanding entrance. The porter opened the small embrasure to see who was without and a hand shot through, taking him by the throat.

"Giant! Show yourself, else this ratling dies!"

Gorlanndon came out of the house, walked over to the gate and simply took the fellow's fingers off from his servant's throat whether the man would or no. He moved the porter aside, but retained a painful hold on the outsider's hand.

"What is it you want? And be civil about it, else I may just keep your hand."

"I demand to know the whereabouts of your son," the voice snarled.

"You demand?" Gorlanndon's voice was soft, conversa-tional, but the pressure he began putting on the appendage he held was not.

"Yes, I demand...."

The pressure grew to just short of causing fractures to the fine bones of the wrist.

"Ahhhhh! Alright...alright! I would like to know where your

son Menannon is at this time." Then, following another slight tightening of the Giant's fingers, the speaker added, "Please?"

"A fair enough question, now that it is asked civilly. My son is in his chamber within. Why do you seek him?"

"Are you sure? For we have it on good authority that he was involved in another disappearance this night. A criminal and his family have disappeared while under house arrest and cannot be found, and your son was seen near the criminal's holding not three turns of the hour since."

"That is curious, as he has been within since early yestereve. He is unwell."

Menannon made good time getting back from the top of the Idrian and had seen no one on the way. He scrambled over the back wall and dropped into the shadows behind the summerhouse, when he heard voices. His sire was talking to someone at the gate. Silently, he deposited his equipment into the shed and dashed into the villa through the kaleyard only to find himself face to face with the old cook. Clarinda stood four square in the center of the kitchen, heavy skillet in hand, ready to defend her lord's home to the end. They eyed each other wordlessly, her dark eyes taking in the filth and blood begriming him and the multiple tears in his kirtle and hose. Very deliberately, she laid down the skillet and turned to the sink where she started hot water into a basin then turned to the laundry chamber and could be heard rustling about.

Menannon shook himself from the momentary paralysis her sudden appearance had caused him and went to the sink where he plunged his whole head into the warm water, washing away the blood and dirt of his night's adventures. That done, he washed the crusted blood from a gouge on the back of his left hand. The action of the water started the bleeding again. Before he could finish, Clarinda was back with clean hose and kirtle in her hands. Through the kitchen's open window he could still hear his sire arguing with someone. As quickly as he could, he changed clothes and wrapped his bleeding hand in a towel. She took the dirty ones from him and gave him a critical look.

Swiftly, she indicated he should lean down and she carefully toweled his overlong hair then arranged it across his forehead to cover the swelling gouge over his left eye. One last look seemed to satisfy her and she waved her hand indicating he should join his sire. All had been accomplished in intense silence. Menannon grinned his thanks and leaned to kiss the plump cheek offered him before he eased out of the kitchen and ran lightly down the hall past the dining chamber and through the atrium to the entrance hall. Here he stopped to listen. He heard his sire's voice rising in anger, but could not discern the reply.

"Nay, I will not call him forth to suit your fancy! This is my home and I alone make demands here. My son—."

"Your son and servant, sir," Menannon said, stepping out into the courtyard. "Have you need of me? I heard my name called." He walked forward into the full light of the rising sun. At some point, Gorlanndon had let go his captive and opened the gate so that their conversation could be carried on in some semblance of civility. The elder Giant knelt on one knee effectively blocking the further entrance of five armed Doomcriers, forcing all of them to stand just within the gateway. Menannon came up to stand a respectful distance behind his sire, being careful to keep his left hand and its damning towel hidden while trying to appear not to do so. The rough dried clothing Clarinda had chosen for him aided the impression that he had indeed lain in bed all day. Gorlanndon turned to look at him, his look replete with just the right touch of exasperation. He waved Menannon forward.

"Aye, aye! Come here so this fellow can look at you and see that you have indeed been ill and do not deserve to have been called from your bed by a fool who can't seem to keep track of the prisoners in his charge."

Scorn and impatience were writ large in Gorlanndon's tone and the look he was bending on his son. Catching sight of the towel wrapped around Menannon's hand he immediately and very naturally took a hold of his hand and pulled him forth to stand in front of him facing the Doomcrier. His large hand completely engulfed Menannon's much smaller one neatly covering the makeshift bandage.

The man stared at Menannon bitterly, clearly not believing anything being said, but also not daring to call Gorlanndon a liar. He turned with little grace and shoved the nearest of his men out the gate and followed after. The porter shut the wicket behind them.

"Menannon, you get yourself back to bed and stay there as you should not be out and about for at least another twoday!" Gorlanndon made sure to say this just loudly enough to be heard clearly on the other side of the gate where he knew full well the Doomcriers were listening. His voice was replete with all the aggravation of a parent confronted with a recalcitrant child.

A few moments later found both Giants in the summerhouse with the windows closed and the shades lowered. Gorlanndon whirled on Menannon took him by the shoulders and shook him hard. Menannon's ill-used body protested against this shaking and it was all he could do not to cry out in pain. Gorlanndon saw the pain in his son's eyes and let his hands fall away from his shoulders. He reached out gently and moved the hair from Menannon's forehead and shook his head in exasperation at the injury thus uncovered.

"You damn fool!" he growled. "I forbade you to effect any more rescues. Why have you disobeyed me? You are going to get caught and what then? Boy, I cannot fault you for your heart, but your brainpower is somewhat lacking."

"Brainpower doesn't keep these wolves from devouring the innocent, sir! Nirna warned me they were planning to murder Lord Lonier in the council chamber this very day. There was naught else I could do."

Gorlanndon visibly stiffened at the name Lonier, but then forced himself to relax and when he spoke, his voice was calm with no hint of the distress the information had caused him.

"You could have informed me and I would have dealt with it."

Menannon turned away from Gorlanndon's stare and pulled out the shade to look down at the harbor below, having no words to answer his sire's simple statement. Why had he not informed his sire? The answer to that came as clearly as the sunlight glinting from the harbor below. He feared the assassin's blade would turn on Gorlanndon instead.

"I did not desire you to be involved," he said letting the shade drop back into place and turning once more to look his sire full in the eyes.

"You did not des...." Gorlanndon growled shaking his head. "You did not desire! Menannon, how do I get it through to you?! This is not your fight!"

"Not my fight?!" Menannon blurted out, stunned, grabbing his sire's wrist as Gorlanndon started to turn away. "How can this not be my fight? This is our home!"

"This is my home, not yours!" Gorlanndon jerked his wrist out of Menannon's grip rather more roughly than he intended and sent the younger Giant staggering. Menannon tripped over the end of a bench and sat down hard on the flags of the floor. He staid there too stunned by his sire's words to move.

"Your home, but not mine? But where e'er you are, that is my home." Menannon nearly whispered this last, his con-fusion too great for full voice.

"Nay! Your home is where the High One sends you to serve Him, not where I happen to be living at the moment."

Gorlanndon sat down in his accustomed place and began removing scrolls from their cases and setting them out on the table. He purposely avoided looking at his son. This statement drew Menannon to his feet and his sire's side.

"Living at the moment? My father you have lived on Kalyria for over a thousand summers and my lady mother lived here with you." Menannon grabbed Gorlanndon's wrist again, halting his movements. "What are you not telling me?" he demanded, his voice low, almost dangerous.

"What I am saying is that the High One has plans for you that do not include spilling your blood for this island."

The great Giant looked long into his son's eyes willing him to listen to him this time. "Your blood is too dear to be left soaking into the sands of Kalyria."

"But yours is not."

"Nay, mine is not."

"Why?!"

The single word cut through the morning air loud enough to be heard in the villa. Gorlanndon instantly placed his hand over Menannon's mouth, stilling him. They waited to see if there was any reaction from the villa below. When there was none, Gorlanndon lowered his hand.

"Why?" Menannon repeated his question, but more softly now, almost a whisper.

"Because I am the past and you, my hard-headed heir, are the future. Now go away. I have work to do." Gorlanndon held up his hand forestalling any further discussion.

Reluctantly, Menannon turned and left the summerhouse.

CHAPTER 20
(SUMMER OF THE WORLD 6097)

THE COOK'S SOFT VOICE STARTLED MENANNON out of his dark thoughts later that night as she came into the kitchen to find her master's son standing by the cold kettledore, his arm wrapped over its caldron crane and his chin resting on the cold metal, as was his wont when troubled.

"Locked horns wi' yer sire again, have ya? Ah, lad, he survived near two thousand summers ere ya were born. You must trust him. He knows what he's doing."

"Mind my own business and leave him to his fate is what you really mean." Menannon ground out, his anger and frustration barely contained. "Why?! What is it about this land that holds him so hard? Yes, it is blessed beyond all others, but it is still only one land in the High One's world!"

"It's not the land, lad, it's the people. People who took him in when he had nowhere else to go in the civilized world. People who made him welcome when his own people had turned him away as a weirdling. This is your sire's home and he is fiercely loyal to it."

"Loyal unto death?!"

"If needs be." The very softness of her voice sent a shiver up his spine. It was as though that death were an already accomplished fact and he, Menannon, was the only one who did not recognize it.

"No!" he burst out far more hotly than he had intended and began pacing the dark kitchen. "This is not his home! It's just a High One forsaken pile of rocks in the middle of a High One forsaken sea and not worth dying for!"

"Your sire deems it is."

"My father deems it is—the High One in Paradise" Menannon nearly spat the words and whirled on her. "Yet he does not deem it worth my dying for. Neither the place nor the people. *Why?* Or is it that I am not worthy enough to shed my blood for this beloved land of his?"

"Or perhaps it is not worthy of *your* blood," she suggested mildly, bringing him to an inarticulate halt, staring at her uncomprehendingly.

"What do you mean?" Menannon came back to lean on the crane once more. "My father has said virtually the same thing to me, though not in so many words. He just looked me in the eyes and said that my blood is too dear to be left soaking into the sands of Kalyria. What is he talking about? Does he simply mean I am too dear to him as his son or does he mean something else? He said that he is the past and I am the future...." Menannon's voice trailed off into confused silence.

"Has your sire never told you of his vision?"

Menannon shook his head mutely, giving her a puzzled and questioning look.

"I thought not." She stepped around him, and went to the cooking hearth where the kettle was sitting on its warming shelf. She deftly stirred up the fire, until it burst into friendly flames then set the kettle back on the hob. Pulling up her rocking chair, she settled into it indicating he should bring up a chair for himself, before she spoke again.

Menannon watched her, torn between worry and wonder that here was something else that for some reason, his father had not shared with him. There was silence in the kitchen while he pulled up a chair and settled into it. The silence stretched until the kettle boiled and Menannon made them both a cup of tea, then settled back to await her pleasure.

"Though this be your sire's to tell, I deem it is time you heard it. I'm testing my friendship with your sire in the telling, but methinks it will survive the test. It happened when he was wandering the wide world after his people had, at the point of a polite spear, asked him to leave and not return until he had found a better mind," Clarinda said and sipped her tea thoughtfully, then set it aside on the warming shelf and rocked forward to study Menannon's face in the flickering light. She looked long into his troubled eyes then nodded to herself and relaxed back into her chair and began to rock gently.

Then softly, her voice sounding far away, she began speaking of a part of his sire's past far before Menannon's life and all unknown to him.

"When your sire departed Lornennog, he wandered far and wide, where'er his heart took him for many long centuries. No place claimed him. No vista fired his heart to linger. No living thing assuaged his loneliness. He wandered until at last he found himself in the midst of the great eastern desert at the end of his strength. There, beneath the merciless rays of the sun, he lay down ready to accept the gift of the High One to your folk and turn himself to stone. E'en as his sight began to darken, he heard a voice call his name telling him to go back to Lornennog that his son needed him.

"Out of the heart of his suffering and confusion, he called out a question seeking to know how he, who had no wife, could have a son. He was answered not in words but in a vision."

Clarinda ceased speaking and reached for her cup and took a long swallow of her tea. Menannon said not a word, his eyes following her motions with a deep frown furrowing his brow. She set her cup back on the warming shelf and turned her gaze back to the youth before her. She went back to rocking, cleared her throat and began again.

"In his vision, your sire was no longer in the desert, but standing on vast grasslands watered by a mighty river. He stood in a deep dale backed against the roiling waters of the river, amidst warriors much worn by long battle. There were among them folk of all races Dwarf, Human and Teluri, but no Giants. There were men, women and even children. The last defenders of a beleaguered world. Arranged all about them were the hordes of Khalandria, the dark god. From the blood on the faces and the terror in the eyes of all about him he knew this was the final stand of a defeated army. E'en as the horde began to move to make the ultimate rush upon them, the earth beneath their feet began to shake and a rumble as of thunder assailed their ears from behind the ridge to the west. A mighty cloud of dust rolled across its crest, then the thunder ceased. All movement on the battlefield halted as every combatant upon it, friend and foe alike, turned to look at the ridge top.

"As the dust cloud settled, there upon the ridge top was revealed a long line of huge figures on horseback, stretching nearly as far as the eye could see in both directions. Giants! Giants on battle chargers! In the very center directly above where your sire stood was the leader of this cavalry, in full battle armour, a banner cracking in the wind above his head. The standard was a deep crimson and bore a crest your sire never thought to see again outside of history sagas. It was a black stallion rampant above crossed swords: the battle standard of Lornennog!

"Your sire forced his eyes away from the standard and looked long at the face of the warrior general. It was fine-boned and sensitive with high cheekbones rounding smoothly into the shadowed hollows beneath them, a strong nose and well formed, full-lipped mouth. Unruly collar-length white hair curled about the high, broad forehead and a close-cropped white beard softened the edges of a finely sculpted jaw line. Thick, slightly arching eyebrows and long lashes framed midnight-black eyes. Great age sat lightly upon this man enhancing him rather than diminishing him. Wisdom enfolded him like a cloak.

"As the warrior general raised his arm to signal the charge a voice rang out across the battlefield, *Gorlanndon! Behold the generations of the sons of thy son, Menannon!* Your sire's heart nearly stopped beating. That warrior general was you, Menannon! And flanking you on either side were your seven sons and beyond them your grandsons and their grandsons unto the tenth generation. And all of them were like unto Giants of old, none taller than your nine feet and all able to ride horses! E'en as you and yours charged down the slope driving all evil creatures before ya, your sire returned to himself in the desert and the voice again said, *Go back, Gorlanndon. Go back to Lornennog. Thy son needs thee!* In that vision, your sire found the will to live and return to Lornennog where he met your mother and the rest is history."

There was a deep silence in the room when Clarinda ceased speaking.

"Are you attempting to tell me that my father believes that I am some messenger of the High One? Some visionary leader of our people?" Menannon whispered.

"No, lad, he does not. Rather, that is what you will become, in the High One's own time," she assured him, her dark eyes unwavering. "He told me of his vision the second night you were here when I had finally gotten you to sleep. He came into your chamber and sat beside your bed and spoke of many things, his vision among them."

"If I am to be some great warrior as in this vision of his, why has he not allowed me to train as one?" Menannon demanded, his voice holding all of his disbelief in this story.   Clarinda just smiled at him and continued to rock. "Your sire is a brilliant man and he knows that visions are not necessarily the exact truth of what will happen in the future. Only the True Sight farseers among the Teluri are blessed with the ability to see the future as it really will be. So he has chosen the path he most wishes for you and simply taken from his vision that you would be born and one day be of great importance to your folk."

"But this is ludicrous!" Menannon burst out, lunging back to his feet, beginning to pace again. "I'm only a recusant harper. I'm neither warrior nor statesman nor e'en much of a Giant. Look at me, Clarinda. I'm a small weakling who doesn't e'en have the ability to face my own father and force him to do right by himself. How could I possibly influence a race of people who would scorn me? A leader of the Giants?! Me?! I deem not! If I am the fulfillment of that vision, then someone must be seeing cross-eyed!"

"Don't be so hard on yourself, lad. No one ever said it was easy to be touched of the High One."

"Oh, I've been touched all right," Menannon shook his head and nearly bolted out the door, "in the head!"

The door slammed shut behind him, leaving his words

hanging in the air unanswered and unanswerable.

Clarinda picked her cup from the warming shelf and continued sipping her tea as she rocked gently, a knowing smile upon her lips. "In the High One's own good time, my lad, in the High One's own good time."

THROUGH DINT OF HIS SIRE'S COUNTERFEIT, Menannon was forced to lay low for another day and though his body was glad of the rest, his troubled mind was not. He slept most of the day under the influence of Clarinda's heavy sleeping droughts given to curb his restlessness. Despite his father's prohibition, he could not just turn away from the needs of the people of Kalyria. They were the only people he had ever truly known. They loved and respected him as one of them. Though his father thought otherwise, in his heart, this was his home, too.

The third day since Lonier's rescue found Menannon once again prowling about the city, wandering aimlessly, stopping here and there to observe children playing or to enter a pub and lift a few with the regulars, attempting to appear harmless to those whom he knew were following him even more closely now. He knew full well that not all would be fooled by his subterfuges, but he hoped enough would be to still allow him some freedom of action when the need arose.

Such need arose all too soon and more desperately than ever. It began a further sevenday later when the small flower girl Emma, approached him as he drank a companionable mug of ale in the Cokeyna with a small group of other loungers.

The small business girl walked up to his chair and cleared her throat for his attention. Menannon looked down, one questioning eyebrow raised. Her face was very serious and her grey eyes bore into his with an intensity uncommon for one of her tender summers. Strangely, she bore no flowers with her.

"Mother says you promised to meet her at the market in the Serpentine this morning. She waited two full turns of the hour for you and you did not come. She is not happy. She said to tell you that she'll come again this afternoon near two of the clock and you had best be there this time, else she'll have yer ears. An' you know full well Gooddame Matilda is not one to be crossed."

That was the message entire and as soon as she ceased speaking, she gave Menannon a very dark look, a perfunctory courtesy and flounced back out the door leaving behind her an extremely confused young man. Gooddame Matilda, the mother of Emma the flower seller? The only Gooddame Matilda he knew had no children of her own as she had nursed two generations of Kalyria's royalty. The closest she had to a daughter was the princess Nirna! Enlightenment suddenly dawned and Menannon looked after the child with a start, then instantly caught himself and finished his ale and called for another to cover his momentary lapse.

As the potboy served him, he glanced at his companions and shrugged. "Do a woman a good turn and she deems she owns you!" he growled, rolled his eyes and settled back to drinking.

His mind was spinning at the possible implications of this very odd summons by Nirna's nurse. A full turn of the hour later saw him no closer to any answers to what this summons might portend. He rose a bit unsteadily from his chair, mug still in hand.

"Where ya goin'?'" mumbled one of his very inebriated companions.

"I'd best be meetin' the Gooddame as there's no knowin' how much holy Hella fire she'll raise if I miss a second meetin' in one day," he said, slurring his words enough to make a convincing drunk and then, making a show of draining the last dregs of ale from his mug, made a wild flourish with it, and in a loud, unsteady voice added, "an' I value my ears."

This last was met with a round of guffaws from his erstwhile cronies. Menannon exaggerated his way to the door and any who saw—or heard—him would be certain he was far more tipsy than he truly was. At the door, he turned and broadly saluted his companions then staggered out into the bright sunshine.

He stood a moment, letting his eyes adjust to the light and to make sure where and how many his Doomcrier watchdogs were. Out of the corner of his eye, he saw two detach themselves from the deep shade of a large tree near one of the drying racks for the fishing nets and make ready to follow him. Good. They would bear witnesses to the fact he was doing nothing save a little shopping of a lazy afternoon. He turned and began to wend his way up the street away from the docks and into the city proper, staggering slightly and whistling off-key through his teeth. They followed him leisurely at a discrete distance, matching his pace.

At the entrance to the Serpentine, a group of children were gathered playing dice games, their laughter carrying happily through the afternoon air, an incongruous foil to his inner tension. Menannon stopped to watch, leaning on a convenient lamp post. The dice thrower looked up, his hand poised for the throw, to see whose shadow had darkened their play. At the sight of a harper standing over them, he blanched a bit, giving himself away. Menannon gave him a knowing look and the child glanced at his hand, then surreptitiously substituted a die he held for the one he had secreted in his other hand. He threw and won the toss without the loaded die. He looked up at Menannon in surprise and grinned widely. The young harper gave him a wink and moved on. Cheating was not a good practice, even if the winnings were only pebbles.

This day, the Serpentine was vastly different than it had been when he had been showing Lee its wonders just a few short months past. Many of the trade halls and shops were now boarded up and even the trees and flower boxes seemed dull and almost lifeless. The entire street was thus almost devoid of color or movement save for a few strollers and the loungers in front of the only pub still open. All the others had closed as Azuron had published an edict that all citizens should make use of the goods and wares at the arena and few people had the time or the courage to frequent aught else. Menannon reached the small plaza to find more signs of life. Though the plaza was nearly vacant of booths and those that were there were lean of offerings as

Azuron's wall had taken a great toll of the foreign goods for sale on the island, there were still some shoppers about. Menannon began to wander about, looking at the offerings displayed, his robes calling forth both honor and condemnation in the attitudes of the artists. He ignored the looks and tones, positive and negative alike.

He looked about quickly, seeing no sign of Nirna's nurse or of any other from the palace and for a moment, he thought this was some kind of trap set by Azuron and the child had been sent to lure him to his undoing. But no, Emma had spoken true. Menannon had no more reached a carver's booth and begun to look at the artwork both domestic and foreign displayed there than Gooddame Matilda appeared, moving through the plaza like a great-prowed galley making full headway, her white sorak veil billowing about the silver band which held it in place adding to the impression. Behind her trailed a small boy carrying a basket nearly as large as himself.

It took the good lady the better part of a half turn of the hour to reach the booth where Menannon stood contemplating an exquisite carving of a spiralhorn done by an artist from Boria. She had spent a great deal of time at each of the few booths before she added an item to the boy's basket. When at last she arrived where he stood, appearing to his observers to be utterly entranced by the Borian carving, her movements had long since ceased to be of any interest to the other shoppers in the plaza. Menannon glanced surreptitiously to see what the Doomcriers were doing. Both of them had settled on a bench in the shade of one of the Serpentine's great trees. One appeared to be taking a nap while the other was entertaining himself, flipping a knife into the dirt at his feet as though seeking to see how many times he could get it to stand point down into the ground without falling over. So long as he did not leave the plaza, they seemed to have little or no interest in him.

"Well! Are ye going to take all day to make yer purchase or will ye be getting on with it and getting out of the way and allow true shoppers in?"

Matilda's voice jerked Menannon's attention back with a start. Her question was couched with all the hauteur of the palace as though she thought him a great lump for his obvious indecision in choosing a piece of artwork. Taken a bit by surprise, he found no answer and so turned to the proprietor of the booth and hurriedly purchased the piece and placed the neatly wrapped carving in his belt pouch, a gift for Lee to commemorate happier times—if he lived long enough to return to the drummer's company. As he stepped back, she stepped forward to begin her shopping and thus put herself directly at his elbow.

"Meet me in the chapel." Her words were spoken without the movement of her lips, a handy skill to have!

Menannon in no way acknowledged her words and turned away from the booth. He walked slowly through the plaza, looking disinterestedly at another booth, then wandered on until he reached the steps of the small chapel. He hesitated, as though uncertain as to whether he would enter it or not. He made a small show of looking at the sun as though its heat was most disagreeable to one who had been drinking overmuch for this early hour. He finally shrugged and took himself inside. Once in, he glanced about quickly to see that the building was empty, which in summers past would not have been the case as Kalyria was blessed of the High One and her citizens had made good use of her places of worship. That seemed to be changing of late, a thing which troubled Menannon deeply and fed his fears for his beloved city.

One look back out through the archway showed him that his watchdogs had not moved from their comfortable bench beneath the tree. He moved away from the doorway into the cool darkness of the interior. The chapel consisted of one small circular chamber with a single altar directly in the middle, its vigil lamp showing brightly in the gloom of the rotunda overhead. There were marble benches surrounding it, but naught else. It was a simple chapel meant for private worship and needed nothing else. Menannon circled around the altar and sat down as though he contemplated the Almighty and set himself to wait for the gooddame to come.

In a surprisingly short time, the doorway darkened and he heard a stately tread, though he could not see past the altar to know who entered. He was soon informed as to that person's identity when Gooddame Matilda came to kneel at the High One's altar, almost at his feet, clasping her hands fervently at her breast. There was no sign of the boy who must be waiting without, basket at his side. She stayed thus for several minutes as a small group of day-schoolers were brought into the sanctuary and shown its ancient wonders by a low-voiced teaching harper. They left and peace was restored.

She remained positioned for prayer, though her attention now turned to Menannon and when she spoke, her words were low, angry and to the point.

"My ewe lamb is not going to be sacrificed on the altar of Azuron's ambition so long as there is a breath in my body—or yours! At tomorrow's dawn will her mother announce the marriage of Princess Nirna to Azuron and one dawn more will see it done!"

"What?! Surely you jest, Gooddame!" Menannon could not restrain his incredulity at this absurd statement. "Azuron is not of the blood royal! It's against Kalyrian law for him to marry Fæori!" Menannon nearly shouted, his indignation over-coming his sense of privacy—and propriety—in this sacred place.

Matilda hushed him with an upraised hand and a quick look about to see if his outburst had been overheard. It had not. The chapel was still empty save for themselves.

"Kalyrian law be damned as far as Azuron is concerned and Norilendra is as deep in his coils as may be. I heard it from her own lips at dawn this very morning when she entered my lamb's chamber to tell her of the great blessing she was to receive!" she hissed back, turning determined grey eyes upon him. "Azuron has made plain his intent to rule Kalyria and this is the best way, for Norilendra would have to step down as Queen Regent should she marry again and this would avail Azuron nothing. But if he marries Nirna, then e'en as her mother's rule runs, he will be lord of all by being the consort of the next queen. Azuron can afford to be patient since Nirna has twenty summers. He need only wait twelve more summers for her mother's regency to run its course and the princess to be of age to ascend the throne. And who's to say when a convenient accident will befall Norilendra or e'en Nirna herself? The widower of a childless queen is king by default." "The High One's holy tears!" Menannon breathed shaking his head. "I know from Nirna's own lips that our queen is besotted with Azuron, but to do this and throw our entire world into the hands of a conniving upstart? Why? No, she would not do this thing. It is unthinkable! It makes no sense!"

"It does, if your chief minister is an overly ambitious sorcerer."

Matilda's words hung in the air between them like a curse.

Menannon swallowed down their bitter gall, edified. "Are you saying he has her under some kind of compulsion?" he demanded, remembering Nirna's words that her mother could make no decision without asking Azuron's advice first.

"I'm saying nothing and fearing everything. I want my lamb out of it. Out of Azuron's reach, out of the palace, out of Kalyria."

She glanced furtively about the empty chapel once more then turned to face the Giant full on, taking hold of the front of his robe with frenzied hands.

"I know that people of yer sire's faction have been disappearing ever since ye came back. And I know also some folks as have proclaimed publicly against the Doomcriers have mysteriously escaped their machinations and Kalyria. I know ye can get my lamb to safety."

This last was spoken in a near whisper as Matilda's gaze changed from commanding to pleading.

"Ye are a harper, blessed of the High One. I know yer guild has its ways and secrets and ye have yer own. Tomorrow night will see the dark of the moon and Nirna's tower will be in shadow. Come not by the stairs, for Azuron has his Doom-criers guarding the halls and passages 'for the safety of the queen' and all. Get her away, Menannon, ere Azuron can get his hands on her!"

Abruptly, Matilda heaved herself to her feet, straightened her gown and veil and left the chapel, stepping grandly, a lady of consequence at ease with the High One, her task done, confident that the fate of her "ewe lamb" was now in good hands.

In the dimness of the chapel, Menannon sat stunned, his mind reeling with all that Gooddame Matilda had said—and everything she had not said as well. All he could sort out of the chaos was that he must rescue Nirna and he had only the few turns of the hour until tomorrow's darkness to find a way. Troubled as he had been before this, he was now near panic, for the fear had struck home with an intensity that surprised even him. He was shaking from head to foot, undone by the love he felt for Nirna, his beloved Fæori. That their love and marriage would also require a change in Kalyrian law was not the same in his mind, as he would be content to be the Prince Consort and aid his beloved to rule as the greatest queen in Kalyria's history, not simply manipulate her for his own access to the throne. The thought of what would happen to not only Nirna, but their entire land if Azuron was able to carry through his plot was absolutely terrifying.

G ORLANNDON SPOKE SOFTLY in a voice barely above a whisper, his words heard by Menannon alone as they sat in the summerhouse but a few turns of the hour later.

"I deemed Norilendra was planning something foolish, as she has been holding private conferences with Azuron and his chief adherents for the better part of a fortnight."

Over a private dinner with just the two of them for once, Menannon had told all that Matilda had spoken to him, keeping well in mind his sire's words after Lonier's rescue. This was too grave a situation to keep to himself alone.

Menannon spoke quietly, speculating. "This Teluri has been maneuvering himself and his faction into power in every way he can for just this purpose, but why? He disparages everything we hold dear. He has made it clear time and again that he deems this place to be nothing more than a pitiful, insignificant lump of rock, so why is he so intent upon ruling it? This could be the final step in his plan, for by marrying Nirna, he will become king. Matilda is right. Soon or late, there will be a regrettable accident and Nirna will die leaving no one to rule save her bereaved husband. But what does he want with Kalyria?"

Gorlanndon sat back with a sigh and looked long at his son as though he weighed what he would say. At last he seemed to come to a decision and sat up straighter.

"I had not intended to burden you with any of this, boy, but as you have seen fit to thrust yourself into all, I may as well enlighten you and so must start at the beginning."

Gorlanndon's voice was a soft growl and the look he leveled upon Menannon almost fierce. The elder Giant rose and moved to the door and windows of the summerhouse, listening intently. Satisfied that no one was without, he returned to his seat and reached out a scroll case from one of the carriers he had brought from his office. As Menannon watched, he carefully unrolled a scroll so ancient its writing was nearly invisible. Gorlanndon moved aside the remains of their supper and laid it out on the table and weighted its edges with various pieces of cutlery.

"This scroll contains the only known copy of the Lay of Kalyrinon the Elder. It is written in a ancient form of Giantish that I did not see fit to teach you as this is the only manuscript yet written in it and when it fades, the need for the language will be gone. I have, however, begun a translation. Mayhap I shall have the time to complete it."

Menannon swallowed this bit of news silently and continued to stare at his sire's intent face.

"As you well know from your studies and my teaching, the world was in total disarray at the end of the Dim Times. Though the Evil One had been defeated for a time, there was precious little left of the once blessed world the High One had created. The Teluri kingdoms were broken and scattered, their great city of Sharilandra left desolate. The Dwarf delvings were smoking ruins and their folk faced with the nearly insur-mountable task of reclamation. The Humans were reduced to naught but wandering, homeless vagabonds. Of our race, you know all that needs to be known."

Menannon nodded, as all of this was familiar to him from his student days and his own studies of the great saga literature of Linden.

"What you do not know from your studies nor have I taught you, for it is sacred knowledge known to only a few, is of the High One's Great Commission. Amidst this chaos," Gorlanndon continued, his eyes never leaving Menannon's face, "the High One saw fit to bring forth a single nation to create an empire and lead the world back to the peace and prosperity He meant it to have. For this purpose, he chose Kalyrinon the Elder and his people to build this empire. He called Kalyrinon across the Frostrill Stair to the very Throne upon which He Himself sits. In this meeting, the High One gave Kalyrinon the Great Commission and a tool of great power with which to fulfill it.

"With his own hands, the High One created the Orb of Making and placed it in the Scepter of Beginnings. This great jewel held within it the power to light the vigil lamps on the High One's altars whose light engenders a place of blessedness which the Evil One and his followers cannot enter.

"Through the power of the Orb, Kalyrinon founded Kalyria here on this island so that his city would not be part of any other land or nation, so that it could stand separate, a beacon of the High One's peace in the darkness that still enveloped the world. Kalyria has been blessed through the power of the Orb, for due to its mighty influence, the land is richer and more fertile, its people more gifted and creative and its efforts more successful than any other land in all Linden. Ere Kalyrinon returned the Orb itself to its Creator, he lit the Eyes of the High One so that the Orb's power remains ever present on Kalyria. E'en the great volcano which forms this island will never erupt nor e'en tremble to disturb the peace of this place as long as the Eyes of the High One shine upon the pediment of the Council Hall.

"For over six thousand summers, Kalyria has built, created and prospered, spreading the High One's peace and civilization by example, diplomacy and war. Our people have fought for and defended the High One's peace by setting up vassal kingdoms and outposts all across the known world on either side of the Dawn Sea. The empire was won with the blood and faith of the people of this land. The High One's will was obeyed and His peace has been established and prosperity grows across the known world. Our land continues to prosper because it is blessed of the High One through the power of the Orb of Making and shall remain so as long as we stay true."

Gorlanndon ceased speaking for a few moments, allowing Menannon time to think about all that he had heard. Menannon sat quietly studying the, to him, incomprehensible words upon the scroll in front of him. Finally, he raised a solemn face to his sire.

"What has been the price of this prosperity beyond the blood and faith of generations of kings?" he asked, knowing full well that there were always two sides to every agreement. While personal salvation was by the High One's good grace, His direct intervention in the lives of His children came with a price, for the High One is pure justice and one has to give in order to receive, an eye for an eye, so to say.

"You have gained wisdom, boy, with your learning. That's unusual for one of your tender summers." Gorlanndon smiled approvingly, but then he became serious again. "Aye, there was a price asked and agreed to. Kalyrinon was required to keep his bloodline pure. He and his brothers and all of their descendants were required to marry only within their own bloodlines. So long as this is done, the power of the Orb of Making will continue to be felt in this land, but should this pact e'er be broken, the blessing will be forfeit and all that we have created will fall."

"Is this what Azuron intends, then? To destroy Kalyria by breaking the compact with the High One?"

"He seeks not to destroy us, but to turn us to the worship of Khalandria, the Black God of Death, as he has many other nations before us. For a thousand summers, I have watched this creature bring death and desecration to the lands to the east, but Kalyria will be the jewel in his dark crown. Thus far, we have thwarted his plans to some extent, but this will bring a far greater doom upon us than even Azuron knows, for he is ignorant of the price we must pay for our existence."

A long silence followed and both Giants contemplated the meaning of the Commission and its breaking. Menannon sat staring into the future watching all his plans and dreams come down to dust and ashes, for if Nirna could not marry Azuron without breaking the pact with the High One, neither could she marry him no matter what the peoples' law of Kalyria said.

"So e'en were Azuron of some other royal bloodline, it would forever mar the bloodline of Kalyria's kings and to break this line is to doom our very civilization?" Menannon questioned. "She would not dare, would she? She does know of the Orb of Making and its ban, does she not?"

"Aye, she knows, as all of the blood royal are instructed in its lore when they come to the throne. E'en so, if she has turned from the High One as it appears she has, I fear she would dare to go through with this—and will—unless we can prevent. As you said, Matilda heard it from the queen's own lips. A twoday hence, Nirna will be wedded to Azuron and our land as we know it will cease to exist."

They sat quietly again, each contemplating the catastrophe that would befall their land and its people should this marriage come to pass.

"I have no choice then, my father," Menannon took a deep breath, blew it out determinedly and squared his shoulders. "I must take Faeori by the straight paths to Aridion City—"

"No!" Gorlanndon cut him off with a fierce hiss. "You're being watched too closely. You'd be arrested the instant your foot touched the palace grounds. Azuron expects nothing less from you." The elder Giant's eyes glinted slightly red as he glared at his son.

"What other choice do we have?" Menannon demanded. "You tell me our very world will be forfeit if Faeori is married to Azuron and then you say that I should not use the only way I have to prevent this catastrophe! What would you suggest? There is not a single hiding place upon all Kalyria that would keep her from him. No boat can leave our shores and Penor will be more than happy to perform this ceremony in the dawn so there is no help there! As I see it, we have but two choices: I take Faeori to Aridion City or we don our best clothes and join the celebration of our own demise."

Menannon's murmur was bitterly sarcastic. His troubled mind would not allow him to stand still, forcing him to pace back and forth across the summerhouse. Menannon had the freedom to pace his shorter stature gave him, but which was denied his sire in this small space. He paced for them both.

"You are right," Gorlanndon said heavily at last. "There is no other way. You must take her to Aridion City, but when you do, this time, you must remain there with her!"

"But—."

"No! I will not be gainsaid in this. It is your choice, boy. Take Nirna to the mainland and remain or leave her to her fate. I will not see you risked further, e'en to keep Kalyria's faith with the High One. I am still your sire and you will obey me in this."

Gorlanndon reached out to where Menannon had stopped and was staring sightlessly at the shades, took him by the shoulders and turned him around to face him. He took Menannon's chin with a firm hand and forced him to look up into his own stern face. There were tears of frustration sparkling in the younger Giant's eyes, but Gorlanndon hardened his heart and forced himself to ignore the anguish he was causing his son. "You will obey me, boy." The words were spoken softly, regretfully, yet Menannon knew them for the command they were.

"Come with us then, my Father! Leave this place! You have

lands and holdings scattered across Aridion. Move to one of them and be safe!" Menannon could not help the pleading note that crept into his voice.

"Nay, I am needed here—"

"Needed for what? To be treated with contempt by Azuron and the queen in the council and mocked by his Doomcriers in the streets?"

"—to help our people survive and keep Kalyrinon's accord with the High One," Gorlanndon finished, as though Menannon had not interrupted him.

"And how will you survive and get off this accursed island if I come not for you?" Menannon swallowed hard and demanded through clenched teeth.

"I will survive by removing the curse besetting this blessed island," was Gorlanndon's reply.

The words fell softly upon Menannon's ears and he was slow to grasp their full import. Then his eyes widened in understanding. "You and Firod intend to assassinate Azuron!"

"Let us just say that there are those among the chief men of this land who will not longer stand idly by and let our people die and our land be destroyed. How we intend to accomplish this is no concern of yours, as you will not be here!"

Menannon took breath to reply, but the look in his sire's eyes halted his words and he looked away, the frustration tearing at him. He began grinding his teeth so hard his jaw hurt.

"You will stay in Aridion City, my son. Your blood is too precious to be wasted," Gorlanndon repeated softly and, rising abruptly, quit the summerhouse."

LATE THE FOLLOWING NIGHT found Menannon clinging to the shadows at the base of the outer wall of the palace close and glancing about to make sure the near side of the plaza was empty. There was no one about, though the windows of the

Council Hall were ablaze, attesting to the fact that the last hope for Kalyria was being argued away. There was a quality to the silence this night which magnified all sound. He could hear the doorwards around the farther side of the wall as they shifted and stirred at their posts. A dog barked somewhere in the city and raucous laughter rang up from a street below. Down near the docks, he could see the huge bonfire which marked the festivities in honor of Azuron's coming nuptials. The wandering troops of Doomcriers would be focusing their attention there in celebration of this great coup. The thought of the sorcerer wedding Nirna and the consequences of such folly fairly burned in Menannon's heart, firming his resolve. He had to get her away and to safety and this night was his only chance, for the dawn would bring the wedding.

He'd had no opportunity for further speech with his sire as Gorlanndon had spent all of the day in the emergency council called even as Norilendra had made it public that she was giving her daughter, Nirna, the Princess Royal, into marriage with Lord Azuron, Governor General of Kalyria, Councillor General and Queen's Counsel. The announcement had been met with stunned silence by all, including the followers of Azuron. The queen was setting aside their most ancient law! All knew that this was the most sacred and inviolable law of their people and to put it aside? What would happen? All wondered in silence, though this wondering was not preventing a great host from forming down at the new arena where the nuptial celebrations were being held. The huge bonfire, free food, ale, wine and entertainments of all types were in the offing and few of Kalyria's fun-loving inhabitants were about to miss it. All but a few of the Doomcriers had left their usual rounds to join in.

Menannon had managed to give the slip to his own personal Doomcriers by once again climbing over the back wall near the summerhouse and keeping to the bushes until he reached the Mathematical Bridge. There it had been a near thing, as he had barely achieved the farther side when a group of more duty-oriented Doomcriers had come marching up the Citadel from the lower city. He had barely been able to dive into the shadows at the corner of the Council Hall before they came upon the bridge and marched across. Where were they going and in such force? Menannon watched from his hiding place to see that they reached the crossing on the Equian and turned right and down. He let out his breath—he had not realized he was holding it—with a great sigh of relief, his fears they had been heading to his sire's villa allayed for the moment.

Overhead, there was no moon as Matilda had reminded him would be the case and the stars seemed veiled by a high, thin layer of cloud. This night the clouds would give good cover as he attempted to gain the interior of the palace close and thence to Nirna's tower. When they were children, Menannon had always teased her that she was one of the princesses in the ancient sagas who'd been locked away in a tower by an evil sorcerer and was waiting for her prince to come rescue her. He had never dreamed that such a rescue would ever become a reality, or that the person performing it would be such an un-princely person as himself.

He glanced around one final time, then pulled out his fishing knives and began to thrust them into the cracks between the great stones. They made a soft thunk as they went in and a slight scraping sound as they came out, but there was no help for it. He had no other way to climb the wall. Hand over hand, he managed to scale the wall and once again heave himself up through one of the murder holes into the brattice. He lay still, hugging the floor, his breath sounding excessively loud in his ears. There was no guard upon the wall as there had been no need for such in well over four thousand summers. Matilda had said Azuron had placed guards about the palace, but not, it seemed, outside of it yet, though Firod was sure it was only a matter of time and a short time at that.

Menannon eased off from the floor and inched out of the brattice, circling swiftly around the wall until he could huddle in the shadows of the south east corner and study the great court below him. The mass of the palace itself hulked blackly within it, its veritable forest of pillars, archways and towers dark against the stars. There were lights spilling from the many windows scattered about its skin, but only one interested him and that was the light glowing at the top of the southeast tower, Nirna's chamber. He studied the glow closely and saw that it wavered from time to time as though someone were coming to the window and looking out. He wrenched his eyes away from that seemingly inaccessible spot of light and forced himself to study the close.

There were but a few folk moving about the close finishing their evening chores, all the rest having been given leave to attend the festivities at the arena. Menannon knelt and watched for a full quarter turn of the hour to be sure the last of the kitchen staff were finished. He stood and began to descend the stairs into the close itself. He had reached the final step when a side door of the palace opened and a group of staff newly loosed from their duties came eagerly out, intent upon joining the festivities below. Menannon froze, his hand braced against the wall, his face turned away, willing himself to blend in with the stones about him. The group walked within a few paces of him and passed by unconcerned, leaving Menannon alone and shaking in the darkness. When his heart stopped racing, he moved on across the close and nearly threw himself into the shadows at the base of Nirna's tower. It was the blessing of the High One that Kalyria's Princess Royal was housed in a tower at the first level of the palace rather than in one on the seventh level or this expedition would have foundered on the rocks of impossibility.

The bulk of the tower itself hid him from the searching eyes of the doorwards who stood their normal watch on the portico just beyond. Briefly, Menannon wished that Fæori had been housed in one of the back towers but, alas, that was not the situation. He could hear the doorwards shuffling at their posts and murmuring to each other. His knives would be too loud. He dared not use them. How was he to climb the wall? Nearly desperate, Menannon looked up the side of the tower searching for anything that would aid his ascent. In the blackness of the night, relieved only by a faint ambient light from other windows and the torches set at the portico, the tower wall was visible, but details were hard to see, yet he could see there were no balconies or ornamentation of any kind, leaving the skin of the tower as smooth as the stonemasons could contrive with hardly a chink between the blocks to force his finger tips into. The base and the side immediately above him were wrapped in deep shadow. Blindly, Menannon ran his hands across the face of the stones and his searching fingers touched something that was not stone. He froze for a moment until his mind could identify what his finger touched: ivy. Hidden in the shadows, there was a great vine of ivy running up the side of the tower. Menannon's memory brought back the vison of a living green mantle on the outside of Faeori's chamber that had always been home to song birds and so had not been cut down, though it threatened the stability of the tower. Praise the High One! He could see in his mind's eye the ivy running all the way to the roof.

Yet there was a problem: a small, light Human child might scale the vine with ease, but not a Giant, not even a small one. One touch of his weight and it would detach and come tumbling down in his hands. There was really only one way to do this, but it was something at which he was not adept. In order to make this assent, he would have to maximize the use of a skill few knew Giants possessed: the ability to lighten their mass. Menannon took a final glance about, whispered a brief prayer, closed his eyes, forced his racing heart to still and concentrated upon manipulating the life force within him to lighten his mass to a lighter state than he had ever succeeded in achieving, though he had tried many times.

To make himself the same mass as a Human or even a Teluri of his size had become so second nature to him that it was now his body's normal state and he could hold it even when he was asleep, but to go lighter? Theoretically, a Giant could so manipulate his mass that he could actually levitate, though what use this would be, Menannon could not fathom, as the mind would be so taken with holding that level of concentration, it could do naught else. To simply hang in the air to no better purpose than to hang in the air had always seemed a worthless exercise to him.

Pure desperation can do many things and this night, it aided Menannon to climb an unclimbable wall. He concentrated on his task so hard his face began to run with sweat, then suddenly, his body lightened almost to the point of levitation! He dared not lessen his mind control to even allow himself the luxury of feeling triumph. Keeping his eyes closed, Menannon reached out and felt for the ivy. His searching fingers once more touched the woody stem of the plant and almost convulsively seized it. He took a deep, settling breath, wrapped both hands about the plant and began to climb hand over hand. Using the ivy as a rope, he walked up the side of the tower.

He was close to the halfway point of the climb when his whole body began to shake as he neared mental exhaustion, his concentration slipping for but a single heartbeat. Instantly, his body returned to its normal mass and the vine began to pull away from the stones. Menannon grabbed wildly for some purchase and miraculously found a single joint that was not as fine as the others and sank the tips of his fingers into it. He clung to the stone by this slim purchase, his heart hammering in his throat. It took several moments for him to gather his scattered wits enough to try again, by which time his fingers, strong though they were, were nearly breaking. Forcing all else from his mind, he set himself to lighten again and almost had achieved this state when he heard a slight noise below him. He opened his eyes and glanced down to see one of the doorwards walking around the side of the tower. Perchance the fellow had heard Menannon's boots scrape upon the wall, attracting his attention. The fellow halted directly below him. Despite his predicament, he could not help the almost hysterical thought that if his fingers gave way as they were threatening to, at least the fellow would cushion his fall, allowing him perchance to do no more damage to himself than breaking both his legs rather than his neck.

The doorward stood in the darkness below, listening for several minutes while Menannon's fingernails began to tear from his fingers. Finally, he turned away and disappeared back around to the portico. Menannon nearly cried with relief and set himself to concentrate once more. With great effort, he reached the proper state and renewed his climb. He achieved the window at the top just as his mind was ready to crack. He was shaking so badly with both relief and exhaustion he could hardly hold himself on the windowsill long enough to see that the shutters had been left open and the curtains drawn aside.

The chamber beyond the glass was as he remembered: one large room whose furnishings were of the most exquisite styling, complete with a high platform bed, a tall wardrobe and a clothes press beside it. There was a night table with a beveled mirror adorning it along the wall opposite the window and two comfortable chairs drawn up to the fire, their damask upholstery catching the flickering light from the hearth beautifully. Each was accompanied by a footstool. The mantle above held several figurines and a tall decanter of wine with three gleaming goblets. There were two closed doors leading from the far end of the room. Menannon well remembered that one led to Matilda's small chamber and the other was the door to the princess' private bathing chamber. The stones of the wall were rendered less forbidding by the expedient of hiding most of them behind richly woven tapestries depicting flowers and spiralhorns. There was no light in the chamber save that which came from the fire.

He forced himself to hold still long enough to glance about to make sure that the princess was alone save for Gooddame Matilda. He saw Nirna sitting on one of the footstools staring into the fire with her back towards the window, obviously weeping, with Matilda leaning over her comfortingly. Thankfully, there was no one else about. He did not fear the gooddame's reaction to his sudden appearance, as she had as good as instructed him to come through the window when he came. Hopefully, Nirna would make no noise at his coming, but he had not the strength left at the moment to even call her name. Necessity drove him to simply slide one of his knives through the crack between the casements, lift the latch, open the window and let himself fall through it. He landed with a soft thud on a white tiger skin, a warm and reasonably soft surface upon which to land and much preferable to the cold, hard stone of the floor.

Both ladies whirled at the sound, and froze at the sight of Menannon suddenly lying on the floor of the princess' chamber. He was so spent that either of them could have stabbed him through the heart and he could have done nothing to defend himself.

"Playfellow!" Nirna breathed in a muffled gasp, her surprise drying her tears marvelous fast. She rushed to him while Matilda crossed to the chamber's main door and, opening it just slightly, checked to see that the guard at the head of the stair had not roused at the noise. He still sat on the stool half asleep, his halberd leaning against the wall beside him. She closed the door softly and turned with a quieting finger to her lips.

"The High One be blessed, Playfellow! What are you doing here? How did you get up the wall?" Nirna gasped as she dropped to her knees beside him. She took her handkerchief from her sleeve and dried his face as she spoke. In answer, Menannon could only shake his head, as at the moment, it was all he could do to just breathe. He closed his eyes, forcing himself to relax.

"Leave him be, lass," Matilda murmured.

"Mati, I don't understand. What's he doing here?" Nirna demanded softly, turning to her nurse, but refusing to leave Menannon's side. "This place is death to him if anyone finds him here!"

Matilda again shushed her then glanced at the door before crouching down beside the two young folk.

"He's here to take you to sanctuary lass, so ye don't have to go through with this travesty of a marriage," the nurse murmured fiercely.

"Sanctuary?" Nirna's eyes lit with hope and she turned back to Menannon and gently ran her fingers down the side of his face. "Do you truly deem the sanctuary of the Harpers will turn Azuron and my mother from their chosen course?"

"Aye, lass," Matilda whispered with utter conviction. "The sanctuary of the Harpers is inviolable as it is the sanctuary ordained by the High One Himself. Yer lad is going to bear ye away to that sanctuary and there ye'll stay until this upstart Teluri is put in his place and ye can return in triumph. So come now, hurry. Ye've got an adventure ahead of ye. Ye need to dress properly for it. Come, come, come!" She stood up with an "harrumph" and marched over to the tall wardrobe where she threw the wedding robes, hanging on the front of it, to the floor. She jerked the door open and pulled the lever on the back wall which opened Nirna's secret hiding place where she kept her boyish clothing.

"How long have you known?" Nirna whispered in awe, as she watched her nurse so easily open her most secret hiding place.

"Long enough!" Matilda pulled out the cote, hose and leggings and looked them over with a critical eye. "They'll do," she nodded to herself and turned to Nirna. "Azuron's bully boys will be looking for a lass, not a lad. Now get changed!" She handed Nirna the clothing and pushed her into the bathing chamber, then went to the mantle and retrieved a goodly goblet of wine into which she put a large pinch of herbs from the medicinals chest she kept in her side chamber. She went to the door one more time and put her ear against it. Silence reigned without. She came back and knelt beside Menannon.

"Here ye are. Now sit up and drink this. It'll help ye get yer strength back the sooner."

Menannon opened his eyes and struggled up onto one elbow. With a little help from the gooddame, he was able to take the goblet from her. Having taken this same herbal not a few months since, he knew it tasted wretched, so he took a deep breath and downed the whole in one go. He had remembered rightly. It was positively ghastly. With a slight shudder, in reaction to the vile concoction, Menannon set the goblet down and had to smother a coughing fit with his sleeve.

"Good on ye!" Matilda approved. "Now just lay back down and rest while the lass gets ready."

Menannon did as he was bid and nearly drifted off to sleep while he waited for the princess, though it was but a few minutes. Nirna came out of the bathing chamber and posed for her nurse who looked at her critically.

"Well, ye still look like the prettiest girl child that e'er I nursed but it'll have to do. Here. Put yer hair up under yer cap and get yer boots on." Matilda handed her a heavy pair of work boots and the large dock worker's hat under which she quickly hid all of her golden curls. That done, she was once again the "lad" who had begged Menannon for a ride on Kane, a rather feminine young lad, but passable as long as no one looked too closely. Matilda nodded her approval and went to wake Menannon.

The Giant sat up and shook himself back awake. While he did not feel like running a marathon, he did feel much better than he had upon entering the chamber. He rolled up onto his knees and held out his hand to Nirna. She came to him immediately, nearly throwing herself into his arms. He gave her a strong embrace then held her off at arms length and looked into her face.

"You have to climb onto my back and hold yourself on, Fæori, because I'll need both hands to climb," he spoke softly and without preamble. "While we're climbing, don't move or talk to me, for I shall be concentrating on staying e'en lighter than I did coming up as we will be heavier by your weight as well and we must get back down the vine. If I lose concentration for but a single second, we'll fall to our deaths." He looked into her luminous purple eyes, willing her to understand. She nodded silently.

"Do you deem Azuron will respect the sanctuary?" Nirna asked again as she settled her belt more comfortably about her shapely hips.

"Of course he will. He has to!" Matilda informed her with total sincerity though Menannon knew that the gooddame was fully aware the Teluri would do no such thing. Her answer seemed to reassure Nirna who nodded and went to her dressing table to gather a few things into a carry bag. The things she was taking were only those she most valued: a small portrait of her sire, a tiny phial made from a single huge emerald with a stopper of gold, a small conch shell and an ancient codex bound in leather and thin oaken boards. This last was small for a codex, only perhaps six inches wide and twice that long, and rather thin. It fit into the bag with no trouble and this she tied to her belt next to her belt pouch.

While she was thus engaged, Matilda went to the door again and listened intently. There was a new sound without—the guard was snoring. She breathed a brief prayer and turned back to the young people and studied them critically. Nirna had returned to Menannon's side where she clung to his arm looking terribly young and frightened in the flickering light. Menannon had aged summers uncounted in the last few months, his youth gone irretrievably. He locked coldly illusionless eyes with Matilda over Nirna's head. The likelihood that any of the three of them would survive this night was almost nil and they both knew it even if Nirna did not. This was a wild cast, but one that must be made for the sake not only of the princess, but of all their people and, as Menannon knew—though the others did not—their very land itself.

"Lass, you reach into my chamber and fetch me one of the red bags from my work table. The one with the strengthening medicinal." She stood aside as though listening again while Nirna stepped away from Menannon. As soon as the princess was beyond hearing, Matilda hurried to his side and spoke with soft urgency.

"Should ye get caught by Azuron and his bully boys, ye know what ye must do." Her dark eyes bored into Menannon's troubled gaze. "Freedom or death. There is no third way. Promise me!"

Wordlessly, Menannon nodded. Matilda took his hand impulsively and kissed it.

"Don't fail me, laddie."

"I—," he began, but Nirna's sudden reappearance put an instant end to their words and he finished with a solemn nod. The entire fate of Kalyria rested upon Nirna not marrying Azuron, no matter how that was accomplished.

"This is the only red one I could find, Mati." Nirna came back holding a small cloth pouch in her hand. Matilda quickly dashed away the tears blurring her eyes and turned back to her lass.

"That will do just fine. Now, put it in yer belt pouch and use it on yer playfellow if ye need to." Nirna did as she was bid, then returned to Menannon's side. He stood and looked out the window. The close was still empty, but they had to hurry. He quietly opened the window and turned to take Nirna's hand.

"Mati, come. We have to go," Nirna motioned her nurse to the window as well.

Matilda smiled and shook her head. "Nay, lass. While yer playfellow's a magnificent laddie, he can't begin to carry us both down the wall. When the coast is clear, I'll be coming to the harper hall and asking fer sanctuary, too. Now, hurry! Ye don't want to be here when yer mother returns from the festivities. You be makin' sure ye get her to the harper hall safe now and I'll meet ye there on the morrow." She growled in a rough attempt at sounding like her normal self, but there was a look in the gooddame's eyes that belied her cheer. Both she and Menannon knew beyond a shadow of a doubt when it was found that the princess had escaped, her nurse would die on the spot as a traitor.

"Would you not allow me to tie you to a chair so they deem I o'erwhelmed you?" Menannon offered, but the old woman shook her head.

"Ye've not the time and I need to be closing the window after ye so the guard won't deem to look there if he gets suspicious. I've served the House of Kalyrinon all my life and I'm not about to stop now! Now go!"

He could not resist reaching down and giving Matilda an embrace acknowledging her sacrifice, though his throat was too tight for further words. She returned his embrace.

"A word of advice for ye, dearest lad," she whispered for his ears alone. "Never let yerself grow too old and responsible to throw melons in the market. Ye'll live the longer and the happier. Promise me dear lad," she whispered

"I promise, Mati," he whispered, using the pet name they had always had for Nirna's nurse and their co-conspirator in adventure. He released her.

She stepped back with her head held high. "Go! Go, both of ye and the High One go with thee!"

"Make sure you come to me as soon as the doors are opened in the dawn," Nirna commanded her old nurse and gave her a quick hug and a kiss then turned to Menannon.

Menannon cleared his throat and forced himself to speak cheerfully, attempting to lighten the mood and keep Nirna ignorant of the truth. He knew that should she begin to have the slightest suspicion of the fate awaiting her nurse for this night's deed, she would never leave no matter what happened to herself and thereby, the rest of Kalyria. "Fæori, I would that you were the Teluri princess from the saga who possessed hair so long her beloved could climb it like a rope to her bower." He gave her a tired grin and knelt so she could climb onto his back.

"Yes, but while that would've allowed you to come up more easily, it still would not allow us to get down," Nirna reminded him with a wicked little grin.

"Ay, me! Thou art of too practical a turn of mind, my liege lady. Come, we must hurry." Menannon aided her to climb onto his back, all seriousness once more. When she was settled with her hands clasped about his neck and her legs locked about his waist, he nodded to Gooddame Matilda, stood and eased his long legs back over the window ledge, closed his eyes again and cleared his mind. His concentration was so complete it was almost pure in its intensity, for this time, he not only held his own life in his hands, but Nirna's as well. He took a deep breath, said a heartfelt prayer, took firm hold of the ivy vines and began the descent. Above them, Matilda quietly closed the window, fastened the shutters and drew the curtains, shutting out the black velvet of the night as she did so.

The High One was looking over Menannon's shoulder and he was able to reach the ground with only one slight misstep, though when he let go his fierce concentration, he crashed to his knees on the flagstones gasping and shaking. Nirna had closed her eyes and clung to him silent and still as a spectre, her heart racing. There were no sounds from the plaza, but the noise of the celebration at the harbor had risen to a fever pitch. She slipped from his back and stood still in the darkness, her heart in her throat as she waited for Menannon to recover some part of his strength. It took several minutes, but rather sooner than she expected, the Giant rose to his feet and took her hand.

"Follow my lead," he murmured. He turned and spoke loudly and cheerfully, as if they had every right to be where they were. "Come on then, lad, we're done with chores now and the festival is still a goin', so let's be joinin' em fer a tot."

"Aye, let's hurry!" Nirna attempted to make her voice deeper, more like a boy's and she turned with Menannon and strolled across the close in full view of the doorwards, making sure to walk flatfooted and swing her arms far more forcefully than normal. For just a moment, Menannon glanced at the doorwards. Both were looking at them and clearly were not fooled in the least by their ploy. Menannon's heart leapt into his throat as he readied himself to do what he must to make good their escape, but the taller of the two, the fellow who had come around the tower a seeming lifetime ago, raised his hand in a quick salute, but did nothing else.

Menannon gave the guards—Firod's men—a slight nod and they both turned back to their positions. It was all he could do not to run across the close, but that would only draw attention to them and force the doorwards into action, thereby ruining the silent pact he had just made. Through sheer willpower, he forced himself to take Nirna's arm and walk the rest of the way across the close. They reached the outer wall and he eschewed the stairs and the climb down the wall and walked non-chalantly out of the front gate right past the outer doorwards. Here as well, the doorwards made no sound nor raised hand, though either of them had plenty of time to raise the alarm or send an arrow into the fugitives. They sauntered into the darkness of the plaza and directly across it to the entrance to the bridge leading to the Idrian. Just as they reached the bridge, Menannon could have sworn he heard a soft voice behind them say, "The High One's good speed, harper." He forced himself to keep walking and not look back. *The High One's blessing upon you, sir,* Menannon returned silently.

At the entrance to the bridge, they looked down and much to their surprise and consternation, a long serpent of fire seemed to be wending its way inexorably towards them up the streets of the city. The Doomcriers were escorting their master back to his bed in preparation for the dawn.

"Too soon, too soon! Now it will be a race to see who reaches the Serpentine first. Come!" Menannon's deep voice sounded softly in Nirna's ears. Without another word, he took her arm and began to run. Fleet though she was, Nirna was no match for his long strides so without so much as a by-your-leave, he picked her up and fled across the bridge running flat out, his boots sending booming echoes across the night with every step. Nirna clung to him, her eyes fixed upon the line of fire that seemed to grow with impossible speed. It was a neck-and-neck race to see who would reach the Serpentine first—the Giant or the followers of the sorcerer.

They reached the farther end of the bridge and fled down the winding course of the Idrian Way. Menannon nearly careened off the corner walls as he threw himself down the steepest of Kalyria's four hills. If they could reach the Serpentine crossroads first, they would not need to cut across the city's ancient cemetery to the harper hall which stood on the far side. If not, they would have to break through and risk stumbling over tombs and headstones in the dark

Menannon was fast and they nearly made it, but both parties reached the crossroads at the same instant. He skidded to a halt in the full light of their torches to avoid running straight into the front line of Doomcriers carrying Azuron's sedan chair. Azuron himself twitched aside the curtains of his chair to see what had halted his bearers. Behind him, Menannon caught a glimpse of Norilendra's face pale in the shadows. Nirna's hat had flown off her head in the wind of their progress and the torchlight shone upon her golden locks, clearly identifying her. For just an instant, everyone stood frozen, then the Doomcriers' raised the cry and Menannon started as though he were coming out of a trance. He turned and fled across the square, his cargo holding on for dear life, and hurtled though the gate of the cemetery and into the darkness there, the Doomcriers hot after him. Behind them, Azuron's voice could be heard screaming for the Giant's blood and ordering his followers to bring back his wife.

Nirna clung to Menannon, her face buried against the cloth of his kirtle and prayed as she had never prayed before, praying that the enemy would not catch them, for she knew that Menannon would be tortured to death and she delivered into slavery and horror. Beneath her ear, she could hear the thudding of his heart and his breathing beginning to rasp as he hurtled around monuments and over headstones in a steeple chase without peer. With all of the exertions of the night, he was nearing total exhaustion despite the inhuman strength of his race. Only once did he misjudge the length of a memorial stone and land on it instead of past it. The miscalculation deposited them both into the deep grass hard against the base of an obelisk marking the last resting place of one of Kalyria's first councillors. Historic though the spot might have been, Nirna heartily wished it gone as she felt Menannon struggle back to his feet. Wondrously, he had somehow managed not to drop her and quickly regained his stride, though the Doomcriers had gained precious moments on them. Menannon clasped her harder against his chest and hurdled over the back wall of the cemetery in a beautiful high jump and threw himself across the square entering the close surrounding the harper hall just mere strides ahead of the pack hounding them. The noise and shrieking of the Doomcriers was deafening.

As he threw himself into the close, Nirna felt Menannon miss his footing and stumble slightly. He made a soft noise deep in his throat, but said nothing, only regained his stride and surged forward at even greater speed. The huge bulk of the harper hall loomed out of the darkness directly ahead of them. He took the steps three at a time and burst through the great doors, nearly taking them from their hinges in his haste. He crossed the entrance hall in three strides and smashed his way into the sanctuary, passing by the duty journeymen without so much as a by-your-leave. They called instantly for Headmaster Penor who appeared with amazing alacrity, fairly squeaking in outrage.

"What is the meaning of this?" he demanded, coming to stand at the center of the Great Hall of Gathering where he halted a nervous distance from the Giant, his breath wheezing like an ancient bellows. "Princess, journeyman! How dare you thus despoil the peace of this holy place?"

Menannon paid him no heed, but crossed determinedly to halt in front of the mosaic before Penor could even catch his breath. He set Nirna on her feet and took her hand. "Hold onto to me and don't let go no matter what happens," he almost snarled and raised his hand to say the command and open the gate to them. Despite the presence of witnesses, they had to go now or all was lost.

"Where are we going?" she demanded, her voice tinged with fear.

"Aridion City..."

"What? That's impossible!"Nirna gasped looking up at him in total bewilderment.

"Nay. It is very possible and must be done now!" Menannon looked to where Penor was standing, his face beginning to relax into an evil leer as he obviously heard the Doomcriers thundering up the front stairs in full cry. "I have to get you to safety now and the only way is through the gate...."

"Gate?! What gate?"she demanded, sure now that he must have knocked his head on the obelisk in the cemetery. He was speaking gibberish to her ears.

"This gate!" Menannon pointed to the mosaic, nearly frantic. "No time for this. They are nearly here!" The Doomcriers could be heard in the front hall.

Nirna realized that Menannon was in earnest and they were truly going to go to Aridion City by some arcane method. She suddenly felt betrayed and jerked her hand out of his and stepped back, her voice rising nearly to a shriek. "I am the Princess Royal! I do not run away like a craven and leave my people behind to die! I came here to claim sanctuary, not to desert my people!"

Menannon looked down at her desperately, his face strangely grey tinged. "Aye, you came to claim sanctuary, but not here, Fæori." The Giant's voice was a hard-edged low growl. "This fool will not stand behind the High One's sanctuary. When the Doomcriers enter, he will turn you over to them. He is recusant."

It struck him as he spoke that the man truly was recusant and therefore doomed and did not know it, and it saddened him. He shook his head, regretting the fall of a once good man. The thought rushed upon him and as quickly departed, for now was not the time for meditation.

Looking Nirna full in the face, he spoke with some urgency, "We must go to where sanctuary is real, now!"

"No! I'm the Princess Royal! He would not dare betray the High One in my case." She stood to her full height and looked down her nose past Menannon to the cringing excuse for a Master Harper standing beyond.

Menannon glanced over his shoulder and looked at Penor and could not help laughing, though the sound was tainted with an edge of hysteria.

"He'd turn in his own mother if they asked it of him," he said sadly. He turned back and held out his hand to her. "Come! We have to go." His voice was frantic with fear—not for himself, but for her. His eyes pleaded with her to understand.

She took a long look into Penor's eyes and with a sense of utter despair deep in her soul, knew then that Menannon was right. He would do as Menannon had said. The Master Harper stood there in all his pasty glory, be-ringed and pomaded, looking far more like a pudding than a man. Yes, he would indeed turn her over to the Doomcriers with but a single sniff of feigned protest and a dab of a scented handkerchief to his kohl-blackened eyes. She turned back to Menannon with a new understanding of the deep evil that lurks in the hearts of some men. She saw the pleading and the fear in his eyes and she was ashamed. She should have trusted him, for always was he her true friend and always would he protect her. She reached for his hand and stopped, this time in surprise and concern. There was blood dripping from Menannon's fingers.

"High One in glory," she breathed. "You're bleeding!"

"A bit. Let's go. They are coming." His voice was calm now, for he knew she would come with him with no further remonstrances, and would have smiled, but he was so near exhaustion that the act would have further drained what little energy he had left.

Now, as though for the first time, she heard the sounds of the Doomcriers at the door even as they spoke. Nirna looked up into Menannon's face and knew that he was far more badly hurt than he was admitting and she silently whirled at his side to face the mosaic. He raised his hand and spoke the word of command. To her great surprise and everlasting wonder, the glass in front of them cracked down the middle and opened with a grinding sound, flooding the chamber with near-blinding cobalt light. It truly was a gate to somewhere.

"Don't let go,' he commanded, his fingers closing painfully upon hers as he pulled her forward into the light. She glanced back just in time to see the first of Azuron's Doomcriers hurl themselves into the chamber and Penor raise his arm, eyes wide in surprise, pointing frantically to where they were just disappearing into the cobalt radiance.

The gate ground shut behind them.

CHAPTER 21
(SUMMER OF THE WORLD 6097)

NIRNA CLOSED HER EYES TIGHTLY and threw her arm across them to ward off the intensity of the light. She felt herself pulled several steps forward along what seemed to be a stone cut hall, then dragged two steps back, then several steps to the right, then two more to the left until she was totally confused, then Menannon halted suddenly and there was a grinding noise and she opened her eyes to find herself impossibly looking through another mosaic gate into a huge chamber filled with the darkness of an Aridion night. Menannon pulled her into the chamber thus revealed and the gate closed behind them, cutting off the light.

The details of the vast chamber slowly emerged from the darkness as her eyes adjusted to the low light. The chamber was eerily lit by the starlight reflecting off the myriad mosaics lining its walls. Menannon tugged her farther across the floor.

"Grandmaster Blackmore!" he raised his voice and called out the name, seemingly into thin air, his voice surprisingly weak. "Grandmaster...."

Nirna heard a clicking sound and a door opened from the left almost behind a huge desk, flooding the chamber with warm firelight. A small, bent figure stood silhouetted in it, dressed in a night robe and leaning on a cane.

"What is it, son?" Blackmore's voice was calm and reassuring. Nirna felt her heart begin to ease simply at its sound.

"This is Nirna i-Ronirinen, the Princess Royal of Kalyria. She seeks sanctuary. Will you grant it her?"

Menannon's whole body was stiff with the intensity of his need to be assured his task was complete. It took all he had left, and more.

"Granted."

Blackmore's instant response seemed to unlock something in Menannon's mind and Nirna felt him relax at her side. Then before anything more could be said, the young Giant measured his full length on the floor, senseless. The grandmaster hobbled forward to light the cresset on the wall behind his desk. He looked down at Menannon who lay on his side in a widening pool of blood, a black-fletched arrow protruding from his back.

"The High One's holy tears," Nirna whispered, stricken. She threw herself to her knees beside him, tears glittering in her eyes.

Blackmore knelt and touched the pulse point in Menannon's throat. It was steady. "Hush, child. He'll be alright."

The grandmaster called Jondlin who appeared with great alacrity and he instructed the lad to rouse the healers. "It will take more than a simple arrow to kill this one."

"But you don't understand! I stopped to argue with him when he was bleeding to death because of me." Nirna's tears spilled over .

"Fear makes all of us do things we later regret, child. Do not upset yourself. He won't hold it against you that you're a normal person."

As they spoke, the door opened to admit a short, somewhat rotund harper dressed in the silver robes of a healer. He was closely followed by his journeyman carrying a large harp. Along with them was a tall, dark-skinned harper dressed in the brown robes of a drummer. It was Lee and his face was a study in a fear that mirrored her own. Nirna remembered him from the holiday he and Menannon had spent on Kalyria a few months past. It was hard to imagine that so many horrifying things could have happened in so short a time. Before she could find voice to greet him, Blackmore took her arm.

"Come, child. You may observe, of course, but give space for my healers to work. Lee, you come over here as well. They don't need you hovering about, either."

Blackmore pulled her to her feet and led her to his desk where he sat her down in one of the chairs in front of it and then sat himself down in the other one to watch as his master harp healer and the journeyman set about tending to Menannon's wound. Lee reluctantly followed them and stood leaning silently against the desk.

With the ease of long practice, the healer cut away Menannon's tunic and the chemise beneath, laying him bare to the waist. The arrow had torn a ragged hole in his back under his right shoulder blade, made the worse by his exertions. It was seeping blood with every beat of his heart. The journeyman winced at the sight, but it did not seem to faze his master who calmly took up his harp and tuned it carefully. That done, he bowed his head in prayer. Everyone joined him.

"Guide my hands, O High One, to his good and Thy glory. Amen."

With that, he began to play softly. Nirna had heard of the harp healers of Aridion City, but until now, she had never actually seen one. There had been one in Kalyria once, but that was before her time. Despite her fear and emotional turmoil, the process fascinated her. The skilled fingers of the healer made the harp sing with a voice ancient and abiding as time itself. The music it wove was a tapestry of sound and spirit, a thing of deep and perilous beauty just beyond the range of understanding, commanding, soothing, healing. Beneath the imperious and soothing voice of the harp, Menannon's wound began to dry. When the blood had finally stopped flowing altogether, the journeyman took a sharp knife and cut off the fletching then with a long, thin instrument forced the arrow out through the Giant's chest. Nirna nearly retched at the sight of its metal barb piercing through the flesh. Blackmore laid his hand upon hers and held it there quietly. The healer picked up his harp and resumed playing, working with a fierce concentration. Miraculously, the wounds closed and smoothed until after nearly two turns of an hour's work, they had shrunk down to naught but thin white lines. Menannon breathed a long sigh and relaxed totally, his state changing from unconsciousness to deep, renewing sleep. The healer laid his hands flat upon the harp, stilling its healing voice.

"I thank thee, High One." A smile lit his round face from ear to ear as he turned to his journeyman. "Go and get help to move him to his quarters. He should sleep at least a three-day." The journeyman nodded and left to do as he was bid. The healer turned to Blackmore and the princess.

"Lady, do you bear any hurts?" His voice was calm and matter-of-fact.

She shook her head.

"No, he protected me." Her voice was almost a whisper.

The healer nodded and looked to Blackmore who dismissed him with a smile and a nod. He left the chamber as silently as he had come.

Nirna moved to kneel at Menannon's side once more and reached gently to smooth back his sweat-soaked hair. "I could not face his loss, Grandmaster. He is my be..."

She stumbled to a halt, her fear almost leading her to reveal their secret love. She swallowed hard and forced herself to change her words.

"He is as a brother to me and more. He is the only family I have left." She glanced up to see in Blackmore's kind eyes that the Valinga saw through her attempt at subterfuge and knew their secret. Nirna colored nicely and quickly returned her gaze to Menannon.

Blackmore came and stood beside her and looked down at his journeyman's still face.

"The road will be long and hard, child, but you must have faith. He is a rare treasure and the High One has great plans for him, though he does not believe it. In the fullness of time, you will have a family again and you will have your brother beside you, but not yet. Now, he must spend his time in the wilderness. Come, child. You are weary. Let me show you to a chamber where you can rest and await his awakening."

"I love you, Playfellow," Nirna whispered and kissed Menannon's cheek, then allowed Blackmore to help her to her feet and lead her from the chamber. At the door, he stopped for a moment and turned back.

"Lee, stay with him and accompany him to his chamber if you

would be so kind. He will need someone to watch him for any sign of discomfort or distress until he awakens from this healing. You are relieved from your regular duties until he is whole again."

The grandmaster hid a smile at the relieved look on his journeyman's face. He knew full well had he not given the drummer such instructions, the fellow would have been derelict in his duties anyway for wild horses would not have been able to drag him from Menannon's side in this, his hour of need. Blackmore allowed the door to close softly behind them leaving Lee alone with his friend.

The drummer almost threw himself to his knees beside Menannon and looked long at his still face. He was heartsick at how worn and tired he looked. Menannon had lost a good deal of weight he could not really afford to loose and his cheekbones stood out sharply against his skin. There were dark circles under his eyes and a decidedly grey tinge to his face.

"What in the High One's name is happening on that island of yours?" Lee whispered. "You look like the wrath of the High One."

Behind him, the door opened to admit eight stout journeymen bearing a large and equally stout litter with extra long grips. Lee stood and quickly got out of their way. They easily loaded the Giant onto it and picked him up, then turned and bore him out of the chamber, Lee close behind.

<hr />

UPON AWAKENING FROM HIS HEALING, Menannon threw himself into the work of the hall with frantic intensity. He taught, harped, illuminated, cared for the sick at the almshouse and entertained from the first light of dawn until well past the mid-of-night and spent many long hours in the library searching through ancient scrolls, only throwing himself onto his bed when he was too exhausted to move. He worked harder than he had ever worked before this, but nothing helped. No matter how little time he spent in bed or how tired he was, the dreams still came. Nightmares so vivid he could taste the salt spray of the raging waves upon his tongue even at waking. In them, he endured over and over the total destruction of Kalyria and they always ended with the pitifully few survivors huddled onto his sire's great ship with himself at the steering oar fighting for their very lives against a sea turned shrieking monster. It was as though the High One was telling him that he must return to Kalyria else there was no hope at all.

Only when he was with Nirna did he manage to throw off his concerns and relax for a small space. Yet being with her caused its own form of strain. For the first time, they were living under the same roof and seeing each other daily, sometimes hourly, as she was volunteering to aid with the children at the alms house and the younger day students. His love for her grew with each encounter and it was anything but brotherly. Yet with its growth also grew the terrible ache of knowing that she could never be his. So he both endured and reveled in Nirna's company for the small space of time allotted them.

Nirna insisted on staying at the harper hall until she was assured that Menannon was fully healed from his wound. After that, she kept finding excuses to stay on though chambers had long since been prepared for her in the castle as she was not just Kalyrian royalty, but heir to the throne of Aridion's overlord. Somehow, she could not bring herself to make the move, for in her heart Nirna feared that it would begin to form a wedge between herself and Menannon by reminding him again that she was of the Blood Royal and thus far beyond his reach. She was not going to let this be an impediment to their love and happiness. More than ever, Nirna was determined to find a way to allow her to marry the Giant, though by tacit consent they had returned to their hidden relationship, neither wanting the rest of world to know how they felt about each other. They managed to fool most folk, but neither Blackmore nor Lee were in the least deceived. To them, the love between the twain was patently obvious.

To the rest of the denizens of the harper hall, the two Kalyrians seemed to be clinging to each other rather like the survivors of a shipwreck seeking the companionship of their own kind as if to keep memories alive. Blackmore soon came to the conclusion that it was past time to insist that the Princess move to the palace before their love came to its inevitable conclusion, for their mere presence in the same room together caused the very air to vibrate even though they neither spoke nor touched. Blackmore finally insisted that Nirna move to the palace and ordered Menannon to escort her there and see her into the care of the Queen Mother. Having no other choice, the youngsters complied.

Menannon silently escorted Nirna to the palace in the soft rose light of a new day. She walked beside him equally silent, holding tightly to his hand. Mercifully, the way was short and they found themselves in the queen's receiving chamber before they could find word for speech. There Nirna was greeted with all the duty due her royal person and all the heartfelt warmth the Queen held for a lonely, nearly orphaned girl.

The young Giant left her there with a solemn inclination of his head and nothing else, for he had not the heart to tell her that their cherished plans must come to naught as theirs must be the abnegation that would keep the peace of their world else their love would shatter it. He returned to the harper hall to concentrate on his worries about the chaos of Kalyria and his sire's danger undistracted.

Almost three months to the day after Menannon's return and two since he had taken Nirna to the palace, Grandmaster Blackmore was awakened by a soft knocking on his chamber door. He rose, threw on his dressing gown and answered to find Lee standing there, a burning candle in his hand and a very worried look on his face.

"Grandmaster, sorry to wake you, but it's Menannon. There is something seriously wrong with him, but he won't answer me when I ask. Perchance you could talk to him?" The drummer kept his voice low and indicated the far side of the audience hall with a sweep of his candle. There was just enough moonlight coming through the clerestory windows for the Valinga to see that a tall figure sat huddled on the floor hard by Kalyria's mosaic.

"I'll talk to him, lad. You go on to bed. I'll not tell you to not worry, but I would advise prayer." Blackmore glanced up, a knowing look lighting his good eye. To tell the drummer not to worry about Menannon was about as useless as telling a bird not to fly. Born to two different families and two different races, they were brothers still, bonded by the long summers of childhood spent in a strange place far from home, and each worried about the other more than they worried about themselves.

"Go on, lad. It will be alright."

Blackmore waved him away and Lee went, though with many a backward glance. The grandmaster waited until the door had closed behind the drummer before he kindled the cresset behind his huge desk and hobbled across the chamber, his cane thunking hollowly on the flags of the floor.

Menannon was sitting with his arms clasped around his upraised knees and his face buried against them. The ancient Valinga pulled up a chair and sat wordlessly, reaching out a gentle hand to rest it upon the Giant's dark hair.

"This is driving you from yourself, isn't it son?" He spoke softly, not wanting to startle his hurting journeyman. "It's killing you by inches."

Menannon raised a face so wan and tired he looked decades older than his nineteen summers. "My father gave me an order and I must obey it," he whispered and buried his face back into his arms.

"Son, do you truly believe he has the right to order you to your own destruction?"

"His seed engendered me, Grandmaster. That gives him the right of life and death over me according to all law and practice. To disobey him in this would be to dishonor him in the sight of the High One."

Menannon's voice was muffled against his knees and Blackmore had to lean close to hear his words.

"And to not disobey him is to drive yourself to death or insanity, which e'er comes first. Och, Giants," Blackmore sighed, more to himself than to Menannon, as he sat thoughtfully considering the legalism of the lad's race.

Not for the Giants the shades of grey with which lesser souls had to contend. Black on black on one side and white on white on the other. Law, not justice nor mercy, had always ruled the Giants—even Menannon—hard though Gorlanndon had tried to bring his son up untouched by the tenets of the Giants via the teachings of the High One alone. Apparently, Law was bred in their very bones and could no more be set aside than they could cease to breathe. *Well, so be it! Let we lesser mortals find the devious ways. Why grudge the Giants their purity of vision? After all, that very purity is what has always enabled them to go forward against adversities when all others finally fall back.* Blackmore grinned slightly and took the lad by the shoulder and shook him gently. They would settle this situation *legally* later, but not now. Now, Menannon needed sleep.

"Look at me!!" He spoke loudly, his voice almost echoing in the silent chamber. For a moment, he did not think the Giant would respond, but then Menannon raised his head and stared at his superior, his black eyes nearly matched by the dark circles smudging them.

"How long has it been since you actually slept?"

"Uh...I know not," Menannon shrugged and went to lower his face again, but Blackmore caught a hold of his chin, preventing him.

"I do. You have been here the best part of three months and in all that time, you have probably slept fewer turns of the hour than a normal person sleeps in a sevenday. I think it's time you slept. E'en if you are virtually immortal, you are still vulnerable and can indeed die from lack of sleep and food just as can any other mortal, though it would take a little longer. I want you to return to your chamber and go to bed, then we will talk when you awaken and can think more clearly."

"Grandmaster, it will do not good. I'll only dream."

"Dream? What dreams come to you in place of rest, son? Tell me."

Menannon sought to lower his head again as it took all of his concentration just to hold it up. Blackmore let his chin go. After a short while, the young Giant spoke softly, recounting in a near whisper the many and horrifying visions of Kalyria's death throes his dreams had presented.

"Grandmaster, what am I to do? My father ordered me to remain here, but I would swear by my heart's blood that the High One wants me to return." Menannon raised his head to look pleadingly into Blackmore's face, his eyes glistening with tears of frustration. "How do I know that it is His will and not my own trying to find a way for me to get back to my father?"

"At this point, you don't." The Valinga's voice was gentle, but there was a knowing note in it that caught Menannon's ear, tired though he was.

"I don't? Does that mean that—."

"It means nothing at the moment," Blackmore snapped, cutting him off a bit more roughly than he had intended, but his own mind was roiling with a sudden unrest he needed to sort out.

Menannon returned his head to his knees and silence fell like a stone. After a few long breaths, Blackmore called Jondlin to him. The door opened and the freckle-faced boy entered, rubbing sleep from his eyes.

"Go to the infirmary and tell the duty journeyman to blend a sleeping draught strong enough to fell an ox and bring it back to me."

Jondlin's eyes jumped to the huddled figure beside his grandmaster and he nodded in understanding. There was not a soul in the whole hall who did not know of the young Giant's suffering—and worried about it, as Menannon was a great favorite. Fully awake now, he ran from the chamber, closing the door with a soft thud. In less than a quarter turn of the hour, he was back carefully bearing a large mug with both hands.

"He said if this doesn't work, he has one more thing that surely will," Jondlin whispered as he handed Blackmore the draught.

"Good. Now go and get pillows and blankets as we are going to put him to bed right here so we can watch over him while he sleeps."

The boy again departed.

Once again, Blackmore laid his hand on Menannon's dark hair. "Come, son, raise your head. I want you to drink this." Blackmore waited several heartbeats then at last Menannon raised his head and looked at him, one eyebrow raised questioningly.

"What is it?"

"Never you mind. Just drink it," the Valinga grinned at him rather mischievously and handed him the mug.

"As long as it isn't volnaka,' Menannon quipped, in a droll attempt at humor.

"Lee told me about that." Blackmore laughed outright, causing his journeyman to color nicely. "Sorry I missed it. But no, this isn't volnaka, so drink."

Menannon obliged him and downed the whole in one go and set the empty mug on the floor between them. The draught must indeed have been strong enough to fell a full grown ox, for in less time than it took to think about it, Menannon dropped into a deep sleep where he sat. A slight push from Blackmore and over he went onto the floor. At almost that instant, Jondlin returned accompanied by Lee. The runner was burdened with blankets and pillows and the drummer carried a feather ticking from one of the upstairs beds.

"I thought I told you to go to bed!" Blackmore scowled at Lee.

"I was...I mean you did...but—" Lee stammered.

"—but you just couldn't resist checking on him once more," Blackmore finished for him. "Boys!" He sighed and shook his head in amused exasperation. "Well, since you're here, you might as well help us get him comfortable."

"Yes, sir."

Lee's relieved grin lit his whole face and he and Jondlin set about making up a bed for the Giant and together rolled him onto it, pulled off his boots, loosened his clothing and covered him with warm blankets. During all of this, Menannon did not make the least sound so heavy was his sleep. When they had him settled, Blackmore sent Jondlin back to bed and glanced again at the drummer.

"I'll let you sit with him awhile as I have need of some speech with the High One."

Blackmore stood then and hobbled out of the chamber intent upon attaining the Great Hall of Gathering and having a word with the High One, for he had been dreaming nearly the same dreams as Menannon. Behind him, Lee settled down in faithful duty to watch his friend, alert for any sign of distress.

His vigil he kept until Blackmore returned and relieved him of it, although Lee left with great reluctance. Yet leave he did, as his friend was in good and capable hands. This did not, however, prevent him from checking in on the Giant whenever he could.

Menannon slept a full sevenday and more, aided by the infirmarer's sleeping draughts and his own near total exhaustion. When he was finally allowed to awaken late on the ninth evening, he felt immeasurably better in body though not in mind. Blackmore sat working late at his desk and waited for his journeyman to awaken. When Menannon did finally roll over and stretch, Blackmore said nothing, only watched him with mixed feelings. Sleeping, he could be kept safe and easy; awake, he would again be tormented and must be allowed to face a greater danger than any could imagine. It was the will of the High One, Blackmore knew, but that knowledge did not make it any easier to accept.

Finally, Menannon threw aside his blankets and sat up feeling a bit disoriented and ravenously hungry.

"I assume you are in need of sustenance."

The sound of Blackmore's voice from the semi-darkness startled him and he looked around, searching for the source, only to see the old fellow sitting at his desk, a single candle burning for illumination.

"There is a supper laid on the warming hearth in my chamber. Avail yourself of the bathing chamber there and bring out your food, for we have much to discuss." Blackmore did not wait for an answer, but returned to his work.

Menannon rose and entered his Grandmaster's quarters to do as he was bid. He returned in a half turn of the hour freshened and carrying a large tray of covered dishes and cutlery. Blackmore indicated he should sit at the end of his own desk to eat. Strangely, the Giant-sized chair was still drawn up there. Menannon sat and ate in silence, the slight noise of his own chewing and the soft swish of Blackmore's sleeves as he dipped his brush in the ink the only sounds in the chamber.

When his journeyman had finally finished his repast and pushed the tray away with a sigh, the Valinga put down his brush and lay down his spectacles and studied his charge. The signs of strain were fast returning in the tightening of his lips and the furrowing between his brows. Blackmore sighed softly and surrendered to the inevitable. If law was what Menannon understood, then law he would have. Blackmore cleared his throat and Menannon looked up.

"Now, pay attention, son, and don't interrupt. When your sire brought you here to apprentice you, he signed the standard contract for apprenticeship giving over his legal rights to you in my favor, for as long as you serve as a harper of this guild—"

"Yes, I—," Menannon began, but got no further as the Valinga shot him such a hard stare that he stopped instantly and was reminded that he had been bidden to remain silent and not interrupt.

The Grandmaster continued on, "—and in so doing, he gave me the right to command your obedience in all things. Do you understand?"

"Aye, but I'm not sure as to the point, sir." Menannon murmured, seeing now that speech was required of him. He turned his eyes from studying the candle's flame, his dark gaze slightly wary.

"And you such a bright lad," Blackmore said, shaking his

head. "The point is this: Your sire does not command your utter loyalty, I do. Should I choose to order you to go to Kalyria, you will go to Kalyria with no questions asked. Is that perfectly clear, you hard-headed, legalistic Giant?"

"But, my father—."

"Did you not hear my words?! Your sire no longer legally commands your obedience, harper, I DO!" the Grandmaster of Aridion's Harpers' Guild snapped, cutting him off with such finality that Menannon started. Blackmore glared him into silence. "Good, just—good. Now that we have settled that, I have a direct order to give you which you will obey without hesitation and without question. Will-you or nil-you, you are to return to Kalyria this very night and do what you can for the people there and most especially for Gorlanndon of Lornennog, as he is himself—by dint of having a son among the harpers—considered an auxiliary member of this guild and as such, will be looked after by this guild."

"But...." Menannon's face clouded with even more anxiety as his thoughts raced wildly about, trying to fathom what had just happened.

"No buts, young man. Either obey my direct order or resign from this guild."

There was such a depth of silence in the chamber as Blackmore had never heard while Menannon struggled with the legalities of this order. Almost, the Valinga thought he would actually refuse and resign in order to keep his word to his sire no matter the cost to himself, but at last, the young Giant's brow cleared and such a look of relief stole across his face, Blackmore's own heart was stilled. As always, the High One's will was perfect.

"So...as my Grandmaster, you are giving me a *legal* order to return to Kalyria?" Menannon nearly whispered, afraid that Blackmore would change his mind.

"Yes, son. As *your Grandmaster*, I am indeed ordering you to return to Kalyria and as a matter of fact, I am going with you."

"The High One's holy blood, NO!" Menannon burst out in horror, his heart suddenly hammering in his throat. "Kalyria is no place for you, Grandmaster. It would mean your death!"

"Take it easy, son. Think you that a Grandmaster of the Harper's Guild be without defenses?" Blackmore grinned, waving him to a halt. "Howsomever, as I do not intend to stay, I very much doubt me I shall have need of such things, but I do have words to say to my master harper there which cannot be said in a scroll. Were I a few summers younger, however, I would indeed stay and you would see what a Valinga can do with a sword, but nay. That time has passed."

Menannon's sigh of relief echoed through the still chamber causing the Valinga to grin broadly and the Giant to color nicely.

"Go on with you! Gather your things and report back to me in a half turn of the hour. But say nothing to Lee, else you will never be able to go alone as you must. I will tell him in my own good time."

Menannon nodded his understanding and rose, then stopped mid-step. "Grandmaster, I—," he began, but Blackmore cut him off with a shake of his head and a mischievous smile.

"Don't say anything. I am doing what is right for our guild and that which is the will of the High One. You just happen to be the tool He has chosen to use. Now, go!"

Menannon gave him a solemn inclination of his head and then nearly ran to the door, but there he halted again and turned back.

"Grandmaster, I have a small boon to ask of you," he said coming to stand at the desk once more. "I have a small present for Lee which I have forgotten to give him. Would you be so kind as to give him this?" He reached into his belt pouch and withdrew the carefully wrapped carving of the spiralhorn he had purchased the day of his meeting with Gooddame Matilda and set it on the desk.

"Of a certain, son. Now get you gone." Blackmore picked up the carving and set it safely into one of the pigeon holes behind his desk.

Menannon inclined his head and this time did leave the chamber at a light run. As soon as the door was closed behind him, the smile left Blackmore's lips and he shook his head.

"Were there anyone else I could possibly send, I would, son, and keep you safe, for this will break you. But alas! there is no other who can do what you can. The High One help us all."

Exactly one half turn of the hour later saw Blackmore and Menannon bathed in the cobalt light of the straight paths, standing still for a moment before opening the gateway into Kalyria's harper hall.

"Remember to give your sire that scroll as soon as may be, for there are certain things contained within which he, as a Kalyrian councillor must act upon. Stay behind me until I give you leave to move, is that clear?"

"Aye, Grandmaster." Menannon's voice was a bit hoarse with strain and he had to clear his throat. 'But—"

"Just do as I say, son and trust that I have my reasons." The old Valinga glanced up at his journeyman, his look unreadable. He turned then and raising his hand, spoke the words of command. The gate slowly opened and they stepped out into a scene of chaos.

The High Hall of Meeting was awash with people, very few of whom were harpers. There were Dwarves and even a few Teluri mixed in with the Human revelers. It appeared that Penor was allowing his most holy place to be used for entertainments and very dubious entertainments at that, as many of the folk there were obviously under the influence of strong drink and, judging by their clothing—or more precisely, the lack thereof—in the throes of emotions more properly belonging in the dens of the harbor district where such entertainments were bought and sold. Amidst this disporting throng were Doomcriers, their weapons drawn and at the ready, a thing unheard of in a place of the High One's peace.

At the sudden appearance of the Valinga and the Giant, all movement ceased for a stunned moment, then resumed as the commander of the Doomcriers recognized Menannon, if not the diminutive fellow in front of him. On command, all archers present raised their bows and let fly, the deadly shafts winging straight and true for Menannon behind whom the gate was just closing. In front of the Giant, Blackmore whispered something and held up three fingers. All arrows burst into cobalt flame and fell smouldering to the ground. Again, there was instant stillness as every one in the hall, including Menannon, looked at Blackmore in stunned disbelief. Silence reigned until the commander rallied and sent those of his men armed with swords and javelins speeding towards the two harpers. At the halfway point, Blackmore again whispered and once more raised his hand, the three fingers poised. Instantly cobalt flame licked along the attackers' weapons, turning them red hot. There was the sound of pain and the crash of weapons falling to the floor as their wielders had to loose their weapons or be fried alive.

In fury and desperation, the chief Doomcrier drew his sword and charged. Again the hand was raised and the words whispered and this time the charging man found himself turning around and running back to the place from which he started. Three times he started to charge the ancient Valinga and three times he found himself back at the beginning. He lowered his sword, his face a study in disbelief and confusion.

Thinking the fight was ended, Menannon moved to step past Blackmore, but his grandmaster laid a restraining hand on his arm.

"No, son, stay behind me. This is not over yet."

Obediently, Menannon stepped back and waited his grandmaster's pleasure. There was silence in the hall save for the idiotic giggling of the more drunken revelers. There was a slight movement from above and to the right of Menannon. He looked up to see Azuron himself standing in the doorway to the choir loft, his hand upraised as if to throw something.

Strangely, Blackmore did not look up at Menannon's slight catch of breath, yet he spoke to this new intruder as though they were comfortably ensconced in front of a companionable fireplace. "Dark One, you are before your time. The authority is not yet given those of your ilk to enter here. Run along now. Your tide will sweep all away soon enough."

The ancient Valinga looked up at the sorcerer and, smiling,

waved his hand as though he dismissed naught but a recalcitrant school boy, then turned away, not even bothering to see if Azuron heeded his command. To Menannon's utter surprise and disbelief, the sorcerer lowered his arm and did as he was bid and left the choir loft doorway and presumably, the building. The Giant looked down at his grandmaster in awe. What authority did he command that even servants of the Evil One obeyed him? Apparently feeling his journeyman's puzzled gaze, the grandmaster glanced up with an impish grin.

"One day, you will understand, but not this day." Blackmore turned away and hobbled up onto the dais below the altar, the tapping of his cane echoing in the stillness. Overhead, the crystalline white eye of the vigil lamp sparkled in the darkness of the vaults.

"Children," Blackmore raised his voice to address all in the hall, "gather your things and depart this place. You have been deceived. It is not pleasing to the High One to see you here in such a manner. Go and take all with you."

Again he waved his hand dismissively and all turned and began gathering their clothing, gear and drunken companions like mummer's puppets under compulsion. The hall emptied of all, save one. As the rest left, a single be-ringed and pomaded figure was revealed to be standing in the middle of the hall, dressed in naught but the kohl rimming his eyes. The final slamming of the door seemed to free Penor from the paralysis the coming of his grandmaster had caused him and the Master Harper of Kalyria made haste to don his robe and attempt to make himself seemly. While he was about it, Blackmore turned and beckoned to Menannon, who came to his side with alacrity.

"Be on your way, son. You need not fear Azuron this night, but he will regain his composure by the morrow, so be wary. Give my regards and my scroll to your sire."

Blackmore nodded in dismissal and Menannon turned away, but the grandmaster's voice halted him once more.

"Go with the High One, son. When the time comes, you will know how to find your way home."

Blackmore said no more and turned his attention back to his master harper. Menannon bowed and strode across the dais to the hidden door, his confusion at his grandmaster's final words drowned in his need to get to his sire. As the small door closed behind him, he heard Blackmore's voice.

"Penor, a word, if you please." Menannon was glad he was not the recipient of those words for they always boded ill for the one so addressed. The door closed and the stillness of the harper hall surrounded him. He hurried down the spiral stairs and into the stygian darkness of the corridor, his feet finding their way with ease after so many visits to this dark place and let himself out into the night.

The night was mild for this time of summer, its gentleness cast a soft feeling over the city. There was the sound of laughter carrying up from the dock area below. Menannon could just discern people moving about by twos and threes. From the twinkle of the moonlight on their gear, most of them were Doomcriers, but not all. There were still those of the citizenry who sought entertainment of a pleasant night.

Menannon made short work of attaining his sire's villa. He stopped in the darkness of the last wall of the neighboring villa to look over the land. He saw no one on the pavement in front of his sire's gate, but a sixth sense warned him that the way was being watched. Carefully, moving as silently as only a Giant can, Menannon circled around the enclosing wall of the villa and found the makeshift stairs up its back. By these, he mounted the stones and crawled along the top to the old willow where he dropped down behind the summer house beneath the cover of its ancient branches. There were a few lights spilling into the night from various windows about the place, but the one he was most interested in was the light coming from a window of the summer house where a screen was not quite drawn to. His sire was there.

Menannon took a moment to still his racing heart and prepare himself to face his sire. It was quite within the realm of possibility that Gorlanndon would either reject him or kill him as was his right, for all Blackmore's assurances to the contrary. The legal rights of a progenitor among the Giants could not be nullified, even by a signed contract. A sire was given the power of life and death over his children by the very act of procreation and nothing in the High One's world could change that. Menannon swallowed hard, straightened his tunic and kirtle and opened the door of the summer house, stepped inside and carefully closed it after him.

Gorlanndon sat alone, reading in the glow of the partially opened Dwarf lantern. He raised his eyes to see who had entered his retreat, but did nothing else. He remained sitting, holding his scroll and looking at his incorrigible son. The total stillness in the small chamber was broken at last when the elder Giant carefully rolled up the scroll and returned it to its case. Menannon stood nearly at attention, his heart thudding painfully. Gorlanndon laid his hands upon the table, palms down, and cocked his head as had been his wont when Menannon had been a small sailor on his trading vessel. The Giants studied each other for many long moments.

"Well," Gorlanndon took a deep breath and let it out slowly, "I must say it took you long enough. You have a deal more will power than I thought you did. I owe Firod a goodly sum. I was convinced you would return within a month, but he gave you three and that you have taken."

"You're not angry?" Menannon managed to force out of a mouth so dry he was sure he could spit dust.

"Angry? How can one be angry with the inevitable? I know you, boy. Since the hour of your birth, you have been as crystal to me, though all others find you complex to a fault. I knew you could no more stay in Aridion City while there was any danger threatening me here on Kalyria than you could sprout wings and fly to the very throne of the High One. I'm just surprised you were able to hold out so long."

"I could probably have held out a bit longer had Grandmaster Blackmore not ordered me to return to you. Though, I will admit, it was proving beyond my strength to stay away."

Menannon colored nicely under the knowing look his sire was bending upon him. Finally Gorlanndon simply held out his arms to his son and Menannon crossed the space between them in two strides and threw himself into that embrace.

"Forgive me, my father...." Menannon's voice was muffled, his face buried in his sire's chest.

"It's alright, boy. Love will always be more powerful than law, praise be to the High One!"

Dawn of the next morning saw a strange event occur in Kalyria's harper hall. All of the harpers and most of the day students and their families were assembled in the Great Hall of Gathering. They carried with them the hall's instruments, music scores, manuscripts and a few essential belongings and had formed a line, all holding hands. At its head, Blackmore stood facing the beautiful mosaic of the sea-girt island which represented Kalyria in the scheme of the Straight Paths. The Elder Journeyman Davin brought up the rear. Penor stood to the side, his head hung low upon his breast. When all were ready, Blackmore spoke the word of command and the gate opened with its usual grinding sound, flooding the chamber with the fierce cobalt light which challenged the newly risen sun—and won. The ancient Valinga stepped into the light and all the rest followed him one by one until none stood in the hall save Penor alone. The gate closed and daylight returned. It was perhaps two full turns of the hour when the gate opened again to reveal Blackmore, alone.

Penor ran to him and fell upon his knees, taking hold of the hem of his grandmaster's robe.

"Please take me with you!" he begged, crumpling to lie prostrate upon the flags. "Don't leave me here, I beg you!"

"You have chosen your way, Penor and now you must face the consequences of that choice." Blackmore looked down upon him, his face not unkind. "If you truly repent, then the High One will receive you at your journey's end, but you must—and will—stand the consequences of your actions in this world. Nothing can change that. Now rise and go. Join the rest of Kalyria and do what you can to right the wrongs you have done your people."

At last, Penor released his hold upon Blackmore's robe and rose. He stumbled away weeping, the kohl about his eyes running down his face like blood.

Blackmore waited until the door closed behind him. He hobbled out into the center of the great hall. He turned and faced the altar with its vigil lamp, a lamp neither mortal nor immortal could extinguish save by the will of the High One Himself. The ancient Valinga stood for several long moments, head bowed in prayer. He raised his head and looked full at the lamp, a long sigh fraught with sorrow escaping his lips, but he did not hesitate.

"By the Will and Word of the High One, I bid thee—extinguish!"

As he spoke, his soft words almost lost in the silence, he raised his right hand, the first three fingers extended, palm towards the lamp. High above him, there was a crystalline flash and a gentle chiming, then the lamp darkened and went out. A gust of strange wind blew through the hall. Blackmore shivered at its icy touch. He turned and without a backward glance, hobbled to the gate, spoke the word of command to open it and stepped through. The gate ground thunderously closed, its sound echoing hollowly in the hall and all was still. Then began a soft, almost inaudible rumbling that grew into a roar and a great fissure ran across the floor and up the wall. High above in the dimness of the vaults, the darkened vigil lamp swung upon its chain once, twice, three times, then the links parted and it fell, shattering upon the floor in a brilliant explosion of cobalt light. Upon its fall, the entire hall thundered down in ruins.

In Aridion City, in the Grandmaster's audience hall, the Kalyrian mosaic fell from its ancient place and shattered upon the cold stones of the floor. The way was shut forever.

Across Kalyria's four hills, a pall of dust floated and settled in a choking cloak, even as the thunder of the harper hall's destruction echoed and re-echoed across the dawn. Menannon ran out into the yard and up the hill to clamber to the top of the back wall to see what was happening. He could see the dust cloud rolling its way from the Idrian and knew in his heart that the harper hall was no more and so was its gate no more. The only way off the island now was by sea. He felt a moment's panic which quickly passed, but there was a hollow in the pit of his stomach that nothing could quite fill. He was on his own now. He had chosen and prayed for this homecoming; he could not now quibble over the cost. Menannon scrambled down from the wall and went in search of his sire.

"The harper hall has been destroyed!" he announced breathlessly as he pushed through the summer house door where his sire and Firod were breaking their fast. "The dust of its fall is e'en now headed this way."

"So, it is done," Gorlanndon nodded. "Our nation is now under interdict and no legal marriages, baptisms or funerals can be performed. All formal education has come to a halt and most of the higher level entertainments as well. The High One has officially turned his back on Kalyria. The rebellion against Him has been acknowledged."

"It is by our own fault," the usually taciturn Firod was the first to answer the elder Giant. "We have brought this upon ourselves by not facing and turning out this upstart Teluri." The captain's eyes snapped with anger. "We have let him and his ilk come between us and the High One and now we are paying the price. Are we to leave it thus or shall we act?"

"What exactly can we do, save stage a revolution and bring down Norilendra and the Blood Royal with her?" Gorlanndon mused, more to himself than to Firod and Menannon. "I have served the throne of Kalyria for over a thousand summers. Do I turn on it now?"

"Is going against the wishes of a mad queen really going against the throne itself?" Firod questioned as he rose and took his leave.

There was silence in the summer house then as each Giant considered the captain's words. At last, Gorlanndon shook his mind from speculation and turned to his son.

"Azuron has called a meeting of the Privy Council for this afternoon to discuss the succession as Nirna has disap-peared—as he thinks, for good—having been kidnaped and very possibly slain and Norilendra Queen being widowed and well past bearing age e'en were she not."

"Father, I—," Menannon began, but Gorlanndon halted him with an upraised hand.

"No, I do not fault what you have done. I only tell you this so that you can better understand what is happening here. Azuron is attempting to place himself on the throne e'en without a marriage to the princess. I will be attending this meeting and when I return we shall hold a conference of all who still side with our land and the High One and we will lay our plans, though we have waited over long. For this day, I will leave you with all of the reports my intelligencers have been able to glean." He indicated a huge stack of scroll cases on the side table. "Study them well. I'll need your insight as much as any other's."

Gorlanndon rose and crossed to the door where he halted with his hand on the latch.

"I am glad of you, boy. No matter what befalls, I'm glad you came back to me."

The elder Giant locked eyes with his son for just a moment then left, closing the door softly behind him. With a lighter heart, Menannon climbed up onto the stone table and reached for the first scroll case.

The day passed swiftly and the mid-of-night drew near to find Gorlanndon still absent and Menannon yet deep in his study. He had stopped only once and that was to eat the simple dinner that Clarinda had brought out to him. Azuron had laid his plans well, it seemed, as the sorcerer had made inroads into every guild and craft on Kalyria as well as the Royal Council. Now that the harpers had been withdrawn, there were only a handful of folk in any positions of authority who remained faithful to the ancient laws of Kalyria and truehearted followers of the High One. In his heart of hearts, Menannon felt it was already too late to save his beloved land. The images from his dreams had returned to him with the darkness and he could not shake the cold terror they laid upon his spirit.

The great bells of the carillon in the Council Hall chimed twelve times announcing the mid-of-night when Menannon began to roll up the final scroll. His hand froze even as the bells ceased sounding, for their calls had covered another sound which now rang loud and clear on its own: the sound of armoured men marching up the Equian way. He finished rolling the scroll and returned it to its case. Shuttering the Dwarf lantern, he opened the screen just slightly so he could see over the roof of the villa into the front court and watch the gate. Just as he feared, the troop or whatever it was halted at the gate and began banging upon it.

"Open up in there in the name of the law!" a harsh voice demanded from without.

"Doomcriers! Damn! What do they want? As if I didn't know, and my father yet absent," Menannon muttered to himself.

The arrival of this armed force was no surprise, really, as Azuron himself had witnessed his arrival in the night. The banging continued as Skendrin came out of the villa and shuttered the courtyard lamp, deliberately plunging the area into darkness. The steward waved the porter aside and signaled to the two gatewardens to flank him. Leaving the heavy bar in place, he reached to open the embrasure, being careful not to stand in front of it, lest something be thrust through and into his face.

"Who comes to the home of peaceable citizens thus bescreened by darkness?" Skendrin demanded, opening the embrasure wide. As he had expected, a spear was instantly thrust through and would have impaled him had he been so foolish as to be standing in the direct line of it. Beside him, one of the gatewardens grabbed the spear before it could be withdrawn and jerked it out of its wielder's hand, eliciting a short cry of pain thereby, and handed it to Skendrin. He nodded and turned back to the embrasure. "Again I ask: Who comes so rudely?"

There was some angry muttering without, then the same gravely voice spoke again. "I am Third Warden Noringar here by order of my Lord Azuron Governor-General of Kalyria to arrest the traitor Menannon who is charged with kidnaping and murder. Now open the gate!"

"Warn the master's son quickly," Skendrin murmured urgently to one of the wardens who made haste to the summer house at a run. Skendrin then spoke again to those without. "Who has been kidnaped and murdered?"

"That is none of your affair! Just open the gate!"

"This gate opens not, save on the word of its master, Gorlanndon, First Minister of Kalyria! If you want to bandy ranks about, take that one," Skendrin finished, although the final comment was muttered to himself. None without heard it, although several within did and they smiled in a supportive sharing of the sentiment.

"Open this gate by order of Azuron else we'll have it down and arrest all within!"

"You are welcome to try, little man, but you had better be more adept at gate breaking than you are at spear wielding."

"Well spoken," growled a new voice within and there was a low muttering of agreement. "If 'tis war they want, then let this be the first battle."

Skendrin glanced around to see that the noise had attracted most of the rest of Gorlanndon's household and all of his personal warband, save the four who would be awaiting him outside the Council Hall, who now gathered armed behind the steward. He grinned in his beard and turned back to the gate.

Above them at the summer house, Menannon stood listening quietly, torn between the desire to make his escape over the back wall or to turn himself in to keep his sire's folk from harm. The gatewarden rushed up the steps and opened the door on the darkness within.

"Young Master? Be ye here?"

"Aye," Menannon answered him and stepped into the square of moonlight let in by the open door.

"Ye had best be gettin' away, young Master, ere the battle begins. Yer da would ne'er forgive us if we were to lose ye to the dogs of Azuron."

"They'll get in then, you think?" He looked down to where Skendrin was still arguing passage rights through the gate.

"Most assuredly, in time, as they'll be usin' some implement of the sorcerer's to throw fire and burn the gate off its hinges, but once they're in, we'll be able to sort them out easy enough so long as we don't have to worry about ye," the old warrior assured him.

Menannon looked past him to see that there were a large number of curious women and children gathering below, refugees from several of the other villas nearby which had suffered the same fate as was now being proposed for his sire's. "Nay, I'll attend upon them. They will have to try me and in a court of law, I will be exonerated, as many folk know that the princess went with me willingly and that she yet lives."

Menannon knew the best witness to this, Gooddame Matilda, had died as a traitor the instant it was found that Nirna had escaped and thus could no longer vouch for his story.

"No, young Master! Don't trust 'em! They don't want ye in open court! They'll make sure ye disappear like all the rest!"

"Azuron would not dare! My father is still the First Minister. He will have to give me a fair trial. We still have laws and judges in this land." Menannon started past the gatewarden, but the old warrior grabbed his arm, pinning him to the spot.

"Our laws an' judges are bein' bent into twister cakes to suit the sorcerer!" the old fellow growled urgently. "Listen to me lad. Ye can't rely on 'em." Below them, the level of noise was rising to a fever pitch as the tempers of those without and within rose towards a violent climax. They were now yelling at each other, exchanging threats. Time was rapidly running out.

"Look down there, man, and tell me what you see," Menannon hissed at him, pointing to the courtyard below.

"I see our folk standing to defend what is ours. What else should I see?"

"Aye, you see our folk. Folk whom I have brought into this danger by my actions and I am going to get as many of them out of it as possible..."

"But it'll mean tha's life, lad!"

"I deem not."

Menannon was still young and inexperienced enough to foolishly trust to the underlying goodness of people, especially his own people of Kalyria. The true nature of the evil that was slowly eating the land from within had not yet revealed itself to his youthful idealism nor had he developed the discernment that would allow him to see it for himself.

"But e'en if it does, better the life of him who started the trouble than of those who had no part in it."

Menannon started down once more, but again the urgent hand on his arm halted him.

"The law be damned! Ye were only doin' what was right," the old fellow hissed.

"Damn not the law. If we have not law, we have nothing," Menannon said, pulling his arm from the gatewarden's grip and proceeding down into the front court at a light run.

In the courtyard, the noise was deafening with both sides yelling partizan insults and threats at one another through the closed gate. Menannon came up behind Skendrin and laid a quieting hand on his shoulder. At his appearance, the sound within instantly ceased as all turned to their master's son questioningly.

"Noringar! I am Menannon. Give me your word that none in this place will be harmed and I will come out to you. What say you?" The noise without hushed instantly.

"You have my word. Come out now!" the harsh voice answered, a note of triumph amongst its gravel.

"Nay! Young Master. Don't trust them!" Skendrin hissed at him, appalled. His words were echoed by nearly every person in the yard. "Once they have you, what's to prevent them razing this place anyway? All you're doing is throwing your life away for nothing!"

"Look there," Menannon muttered pointing to where a young girl was standing next to her mother who held another smaller child in her arms. "Are they nothing?" He pointed to where an ancient man stood braced and defiant, his cane gripped between gnarled hands, one of his sire's retired husbandmen. "Is he nothing?"

"That's not what I mean and you know it!" Skendrin snapped back a bit more loudly than he had intended. Everyone hushed him urgently. "But you are more important than all of us in here put together and we are not letting you go without a fight!" he continued in an angry hiss.

Menannon shook his head his mouth tightening into a grim line."My father's writ still runs here and therefore, as his heir, mine as well and I say you shall. I will not see one hair of one of these good peoples' heads harmed if there is any way I can prevent. I go. Tell my father when he returns and he can begin the legal battle on my behalf."

"Legal battle! There won't be enough left of you for a carrion crow to feast upon much less to do battle in court over. But," Skendrin raised his hand as Menannon opened his mouth to reply, "it's your life, lad, and I can't fault your honor or your courage, but your brains are seriously lacking."

"So my father keeps telling me," Menannon grinned a bit lopsidedly.

All further protest was stilled and the darkness hid the desolation writ large on the faces about him. To everyone's surprise, Menannon turned away from the gate and strode determinedly to the wall to the left of it.

"What are you about?"

Skendrin halted mid-reach where he had been about to help ease aside the great bar.

"I may be foolish, but I'm not stupid enough to open that gate and trust to their word to not come rushing in to take all of you along with me. Good fences make good neighbors, so they say, but e'en more so, barred gates make honest enemies and keep them that way."

He saluted his folk and turned to the wall and scaled it with the ease of far too much practice and dropped lightly down behind the waiting Doomcriers.

"You wanted me, gentlemen. Here I am."

The sudden, unexpected sound of his voice coming from behind them caused a moment's paralysis amongst the motley mob of Doomcriers and their thugs, a moment during which he could have made good his escape, but having traded for his people's continued peace, he would not be forfeit and run. He calmly glanced over the unsavory assemblage, their Dwarf lanterns revealing that they had indeed been prepared to rush the holding as soon as the gate was unbarred. For a moment, his stomach tightened, but he forced himself to relaxed and regain his composure. These were but the common rabble and not the imperial judges of Kalyria whose honor and integrity were beyond question. He need not fear them. Yet a small voice in the back of his mind whispered that there were but four of the seven judges left in the city, for one had been slain and he himself had led the other twain to safety through the harper's gate as his first rescues. He firmly clamped down on the traitorous thoughts and did not pursue them down that darkling path.

Noringar turned from the gate and thrust his way through his company. He was a heavyset, heavily jowelled Human of middle height with massive arms and muscles to match as Menannon soon found out when the Doomcrier suddenly reversed his war hammer and butted it full force onto the Giant's midsection, knocking him to his knees, his breath for the moment flown. With his quarry thus down and at his mercy, the erstwhile Guard proceeded to lock Menannon's hands behind his back with chain-linked iron cuffs with a loop of the chain around his throat, assuring if the prisoner tried to run he would choke himself into submission. He handed the loose end of the chain to a great lumpish fellow who stood nearly as tall as Menannon, but who was no Giant, as his whole face and form were stretched out of all proportion. He was obviously a Human who suffered from the affliction of gigantism and was simpleminded as well, but powerful for all that as he hauled Menannon to his feet and began shoving him back along the Equian way towards the Mathematical Bridge and the central plaza beyond. Save for a dog barking somewhere in the distance, the sound of the company's marching feet echoing back from the walls of the great villas was the only sound to break the silence of an otherwise beautiful night.

The simpleton was taking great relish in shoving Menannon along then jerking him back as he got too far ahead. From the men around him there were muffled derogatory comments and guffaws at his expense, but Menannon ignored them as he concentrated on not being knocked down and strangled by the fellow holding his chain.

They reached the plaza and made their way past the great bulk of the Council Hall whose many pillared portico was awash with light, attesting to the meeting still going on within. With all his heart, Menannon wished his sire would choose this moment to come forth, but alas it was not to be. To make doubly sure their passing went unnoticed, the simpleton clamped a meaty hand over the Giant's mouth, preventing any chance for a call for help. They moved on to the palace itself. The palace close was awash with the light of a full moon this night, a night far different from the last time he had been here. His captors thrust him up the stairs and brought him to a halt in front of the duty doorwards while Noringar sent one of their number back to the Council Hall to inform Azuron of their success and to receive his further orders.

Thoroughly tired of being half choked, Menannon took advantage of the halt to jerk his head forward suddenly, grab the chain that ran through his wrist cuffs and hold it fast to relieve the pressure on his throat. His guard started to grab the chain back out of his hands, but something in the look in the eyes of the taller of the two doorwards halted him and he stood back from his prisoner at a decent distance, though he did not do so happily. Menannon glanced at his defender and saw one of the same doorwards who had stood guard the night he had secured Nirna's freedom. The man gave him the ghost of a wink. Menannon dared not return it, yet his heart rose that here at least was one who would know where he was, should the need arise.

The respite was brief as the Doomcrier came back with alacrity and whispered instructions to Noringar. He entered the palace, indicating with a jerk of his head to the rest that they should follow. Menannon was instantly shoved roughly from behind, and he nearly stumbled, but regained his footing quickly. In this manner they crossed the great reception hall and turned left down a long corridor leading to the inner workings of the palace. Even in his current predicament, Menannon could not help but shake his head at the vagaries of fortune as he mentally compared this entrance into these halls with his last one: then as the pampered heir of Kalyria's First Minister and now as a disgraced prisoner.

There was no one about at this hour of the night. No curious eyes followed their progress. They had traversed perhaps half of the length of the hall when Noringar halted in front of a closed, plain door. He dismissed all his men save the simpleton then opened the door and stepped aside so that the latter could push Menannon on through and both followed close behind.

The door made a solid thunk behind him and Menannon found himself standing in the middle of a small, handsomely appointed, reception chamber. There were marble benches equipped with the softest of cushions scattered about, each with small tables nearby for the convenience of any who would sit there. Dwarf lanterns glittered overhead and the finely patterned damask curtains were drawn across the windows shutting out the night. The entire chamber was decorated in shades of cream and gold with blood red pillows and curtains for accent. Norilendra had obviously designed its decorations. She had always been overfond of crimson and gold leaf, though Menannon found the scheme ostentatious. It was, he thought, quite reflective of her character.

All this Menannon saw, and instantly forgot when he saw the sorcerer comfortably and carelessly seated upon a couch near the cheerfully burning hearth, a well-filled wine goblet at his elbow. *How did he get here ahead of us?* Menannon wondered briefly, but as now was not the time to speculate, he shook the thought aside and gave Azuron his full attention. The Teluri looked inordinately pleased with himself as he lounged there, the firelight glinting from his bald pate and immaculate dress. The only thing about him that did not glitter were his eyes whose shadowy depths seemed to swallow light rather than reflect it. Menannon knew not what to expect from this strange fellow. He tightened his mental guard and waited.

"Wait without," Azuron's voice was silky as he waved a negligent hand at his Doomcriers. Both men instantly quit the chamber with barely suppressed relief. Menannon felt a brief unreasonable tinge of regret at this departure, for with them went the last semblance of the familiar.

"I will not do thee the dishonor of bothering with the niceties," Azuron said without preamble. Lapsing into a relaxed silence, he carefully selected a date from a dish on the table beside him and ate it slowly, his white teeth clearly showing as he bit into the dark flesh of the fruit. Menannon waited silently, his mind carefully blank.

"Where hast thou taken my wife to be?" Azuron asked calmly while searching out another date. Receiving no answer, he glanced up with some surprise. "Oh, come, come. False heroics do not become us."

He spoke leisurely, yet there was steel in his voice.

Again, he received naught but silence.

"I desire a simple answer from thee and I will have it. I would not have need to treat with thee at all, but poor Penor is useless in this as in most things. He knows naught of the gate thou didst use in his own harper hall, a curious lapse I shall investigate later. Come now, young Giant, dispense with this irksome silence and answer me. I tire of this. Answer my question, then we can both seek our beds and forget this whole unnecessary incident. Where hast thou secreted Nirna?"

Menannon remained silent, having no intention of telling this Black Teluri anything.

"Come, now, tell me this one thing and thou mayest go. Is that so difficult?"

He spoke quietly still, almost affably, but Menannon was not fooled. The Teluri set the date pit delicately into a bowl with the other discarded pits, picked up his wine goblet and drank greedily. He set the goblet down, a single drop of scarlet liquid remaining upon the corner of his mouth which he delicately patted away with a handkerchief withdrawn from his sleeve, the red of the wine marring the white cloth like blood.

Many possible responses to all this entered Menannon's head only to be quickly discarded, for to even answer the Teluri's sallies with those of his own was to loose ground to him. In this case, silence was more than golden—it was priceless. The young Giant simply stood there, silently consid-ering the strange Teluri before him, his black eyes expressionless.

The silence dragged on for a quarter turn of the hour before Azuron sighed hugely and shook his head.

"So like thy sire: a great stubborn fool. The only laughter either of thee will hear in the end is mine as I wed Nirna and come to rule this puny insignificant little kingdom."

He shook his head slowly.

"Ay, me! 'Tis fools these Giants be."

The Teluri turned to his bowl of dates and delicately, leisurely, ate another. Dropping the pit almost gently into the waiting receptacle, he dipped his fingers into the finger bowl set beside the dates and dried his hands thoroughly, daintily, on a large table napkin. With a last simpering smile, redolent with malice, he clapped his hands, slowly. Once. Twice. Noringar and the simpleton appeared instantly upon the second clap.

Azuron looked squarely at Menannon and spoke. "I give thee one last chance to avoid unpleasantries. Where is Nirna?"

Menannon remained silent. Shaking his head, Azuron leisurely picked up a brush from the table next him, dipped it in the inkwell and briefly wrote something on one of the blank sheets of vellum placed there for the purpose. This he rolled up and sealed using the signet ring on his right hand. He gave this scroll to his lackeys carelessly, as if bored by it all.

"Take this young fool to the Chamber of Questions and ask him again what he has done with my bride. I would have thee do it here, but our lady queen so dislikes bloodstains on her rugs and so I shall have to wait yet further for my answer."   Noringar saluted his master and roughly jerked Menannon by the binding chain and pulled him out of the room. As the door closed behind them he heard Azuron sigh,

"Ay, me! Such a pity! I seem to be all out of dates."

Menannon's captors dragged him farther down several halls, finally halting to face an apparently blank section of wall. Noringar reached up and turned the bracket of a hanging Dwarf lamp and a section of the wall detached, sliding aside to reveal dark stairs spiraling down into the bowels of the palace leading to a dungeon carved from the living rock long and long ago during Kalyria's warring past.

Noringar took the lamp from its bracket and led the way down. They descended what seemed miles of stairs and sloping passageways lined with heavily barred wooden doors and gates behind whose anonymous faces lurked the cutpurses, thieves, murderers and all the other socially deviant folk of Kalyria. Some were here for but a few months, others for a lifetime, but all sentenced by the courts of Kalyria when all else had failed. But there were also many here whose only crime was to remain true to their land and oppose Azuron. For these, there would be no release. They would die here, their whereabouts unknown to those above who yet cared, forgotten by those who did not. Menannon was now to be counted among this number.

They came to a corridor that must surely be near the heart of the rock, an area not used in nearly a thousand summers. The coming of Azuron had pressed it back into inglorious service. The small party halted in front of a tall, metal-chased wooden door and Noringar knocked loudly, the resultant booming disturbed echoes that fled away into the darkness beyond the reach of their Dwarf lantern. For a moment, nothing happened, then bolts could be heard being withdrawn on the other side and the thick door swung inward surprisingly quickly for all it ponderous mass. The opening thus created was tall enough that Menannon could walk through it without ducking. Within was revealed a chamber lit not by Dwarf lanterns, but by fire.

Sconces filled with blazing torches were thick upon the walls and a large brazier lit the far end of the chamber nearly as brightly as daylight. Brilliant moonlight also spilled into the chamber through three great glassless archways piercing its side. Beyond them, Menannon could see the faint outline of the sea cliffs and in the night sky above the shadows surrounding Kalyria, a faint glitter of stars contended with the full moon, their sparkling brilliance almost veiled by its silvery luminescence. The dungeon of the palace was cut directly from the living rock of the peak upon which stood the Citadel and thus most of its length was windowless, but the questioning chamber was located on the outside overlooking the sheer drop of eight hundred feet into the rocky depths of the Kidron Gorge. During Kalyria's warring past, more than one prisoner had sought solace in the arms of death via the chambers three openings rather than face the torture within. From the outside, the three windows stared incongruously out at the sky, three black holes piercing the smooth, rocky skin of the cliff, the light from the torches and brazier dancing inside them giving them an eerie, evil glow that hinted at the horrors within.

Four figures stood in dark welcome. All were dressed in sleeveless leather tunics and hose, their feet encased in heavy leather boots adorned with spikes protruding from toe, heel and sole. Each of them wore a black hood over his head through which eye and mouth holes had been cut. All were thus rendered anonymous save for their size and build which bespoke their membership in the Human race.

Despite himself, Menannon had begun to realize that the rule of law no longer applied, for it had been replaced by the rule of

Azuron and the realization greatly saddened him to think that this once great empire had come to be ruled by such a one. What a fool he had been!

Noringar addressed himself to the tallest of these from whose stance alone leadership of this small band was obvious.

"The master wants an answer to this question," he said, holding out the rolled sheet of vellum sealed with the great seal of Kalyria. "He wants the answer yestereve, so take that as a guide to your activities."

He jerked Menannon's chain from the simpleton's hand and pushed the Giant over to the wall, to the left of the door, and exchanged the walking chains he had thus far borne for chains attached to the wall. This done, Noringar pushed the simpleton ahead of him and beat a hasty retreat.

The door banged shut, leaving Menannon to face the dark quartet of inquisitors. With slow, deliberate care, the chief broke Azuron's seal and unrolled the vellum. He gave it a quick perusal then tossed it aside onto a table littered with all manner of implements meant for one ill use or another, truly a table of pain. The four warders withdrew to the end of the chamber hard by the brazier and held a quiet conference while casting Menannon measuring looks.

While they thus talked, he took the opportunity to look about. This not only satisfied his curiosity, but served to keep him from thinking about what was to come. Scattered about the chamber were various things: a cage the size of a Human man whose clasping bands bore spikes—on the inside; a table with cranks at both ends obviously fit to stretch bodies out like thread; a whipping post; a breaking wheel to which a body could be tied and then hammered between the spokes breaking bones where the wood did not support them and all manner of other oddments. Many of them Menannon recognized as ancient instruments of torture as described in the saga literature of old, all long since outlawed on Kalyria as being inhuman and thus unfit for use in a civilized society. Obviously, Azuron came not from any civilized portion of Linden, as he had reintroduced these implements and many things to the people of this fair island and none of them were worthy of civilization.

As he waited for the four warders to finish their conference and turn their attention on him, he allowed himself one brief moment of thought to form a heartfelt prayer; *High One, if it is not against Thy will, help me in this to keep my silence. Let me not betray either Grandmaster Blackmore's trust nor Faeori's. Give me the strength to either endure or to die. Amen.*

He had no sooner finished his prayer than the four warders turned as one and approached him. The shortest of the four stopped just beyond his reach and looked at him. Menannon could see blue eyes looking out of the holes in the mask. They were actually not unkind. The fellow was simply doing his assigned duty, but that was exactly what made him so terrifying, for he treated torture and death as merely a job, a task to be completed and no more.

But then, Menannon thought, *I must not judge this man. That is for the High One to do when the time comes. Rather should I forgive him for what he is about to do and hold him no ill will.*

"You can still answer, boy," the man said reasonably. "Tell us where you have taken the princess and all will be over. Choose life or death."

Menannon cleared his throat and spoke for the first time since leaving his sire's villa. "Torture or a quick knife. Very little choice there."

"You have intelligence far beyond your summers, boy," the chief warder spoke quietly "but intelligence will avail you nothing in this chamber. Let us begin."

He picked up a heavy key ring and unlocked the chains holding Menannon to the wall and re-locked them to the whipping post where he proceeded to tear the Giant's kirtle and tunic down the center, baring his unblemished back to the flickering light. The warder—more accurately the torturer—picked up a scourge from the table of pain and carefully inspected it, making sure the nine long, braided leather thongs were clearly separated so as to allow the steel barbs braided into them to work their full malice upon Menannon's flesh. Satisfied, he began to wield the nine-tailed scourge with pitiless patience. One stroke: first blood. Thus began for Menannon an intimate acquaintance with the caresses of the Cat and a long education in the iniquity of mortals.

AZURON'S EDUCATION AS TO THE TRUE MEANING of the saying Beware the fury of Giants began on the ninth hour of the following day when Gorlanndon exploded into his audience chamber without so much as a by-your-leave and confronted him.

"Where in all Hella is he?"

Gorlanndon slammed his fist down on the desk separating him from the pinched faced Teluri, though in truth he would far rather have slammed it through that face and skull, sending the brains spattering against the wall behind it.

"Last night, while we of the council debated pointlessly over petty nothings, your creatures broke into my home and arrested my son illegally, without a warrant of the court and I demand that you release him NOW!"

"Calmly, my friend." Azuron looked up from his paper-work, his smoldering eyes hooded. As surreptitiously as he could, the sorcerer signaled to his clerk to go for help.   Gorlanndon let the man scurry away without the slightest qualm. Let them call whom they chose. It mattered naught to him.

"I sent no deputation to thine home to arrest anyone," Azuron continued. "I sent my chief investigator to ask thy son if he knew anything that might aid us in our search for the princess. Surely, thou dost not think I would so besmirch the good name of Gorlanndon to e'en intimate that his own son had aught to do with the disappearance of our beloved princess. Nay, my friend, I'm sure there must be some mistake. My investigator assures me that Menannon volun-teered to come to the palace and is e'en now assisting in our investigation."

Behind the Giant, the chamber door opened and four large Doomcriers entered fully armed. Once inside, they took a hard stance, swords drawn with their backs against the door. The Giant felt no need to even acknowledge their presence. Gnats would have been more important to him than the sorcerer's henchmen. He continued his words with Azuron without a break.

"If that is so, then you will have no objection to my having some speech with him." Gorlanndon's tone clearly indicated that he knew point blank that the Teluri was lying.

"Ahhh, were it in my power to do so, I most assuredly would call him to thee, but he and a company of my guards have gone inland to check out several reported sightings of the princess or her nurse and they will not return until at least tomorrow's eve. When they return, I shall inform him that thou desirest some speech with him. Does that suit?" The Teluri said this last with all but a smirk, his equanimity fully restored by the presence of his men.

"I shall await their coming then," Gorlanndon inclined his head to him and turned to leave the chamber. The Doomcriers braced to block his way as their master had not dismissed his visitor. Gorlanndon sighed and rolled his eyes then simply picked up the center twain of the four by the fronts of their cuirasses, his fingers bending the metal of their breastplates into perfect impressions of themselves.

"These are yours, I believe," he said and unceremoniously dumped them on Azuron's desk bringing the whole crashing to the floor in a splintered heap. The other twain scurried out of his way and he walked out the door, closing it softly behind him.

In the hall without, Norilendra stood with one of her ladies. He inclined his head to her and continued on down the hall. Her soft voice halted him.

"I miss my daughter as well, Lord Gorlanndon."

He stopped and looked back at her over his left shoulder in as near a snub for Kalyria's royalty as his nature would allow, "At least, my lady, your daughter is safe and well you know it. I cannot say the same for my son."

He gave her another curt nod and left her presence without her permission, a discourtesy which left her face blanched to the lips with suppressed anger. He stalked out of the palace and made his way to the guardroom within the Council Hall.

He did not knock, but slammed the door open and strode in, his black eyes edging with red. Firod glanced up at the intrusion from where he and his second were in close study of a map of the palace.

"Get out!" Gorlanndon hissed at the other officer who glanced at his commander. Firod nodded and the man fled, clearly not wanting to treat with the Giant in this mood.

"We will find him, Gorlanndon," Firod straightened and spoke, knowing full well what his visitor wanted. "He has to be within the palace. One of my men saw him taken in there and he did not see him come out."

"You damn well better find him, or I will be forced to search for him myself and I assure you that my method will not be polite!" Gorlanndon hissed, his eyes going full red and he turned without further comment and stormed back out of the building.

Once outside, Gorlanndon made his way to his trade hall where he composed himself to work. If there was one thing the Giant had learned in his more than two thousand summers of life, it was patience. Despite that skill, it was almost more than he could do to wait for Firod's most trusted men to find out where Menannon was being held. Once that knowledge was obtained, the High One alone could help those who held him.

TWO FULL DAYS AND MOST OF A THIRD had passed since Menannon's arrest and still his inquisitors had sent Azuron no word. The sorcerer paced the empty throne room, his anger rising steadily. Surely, it could not be that hard to extract a modicum of information from a mere boy. The question was simple: where had he taken his playmate? Simple, straightforward—and apparently impossible to learn the answer to. Finally, at high noon of the third day, Azuron's patience ended and he took himself to the dungeon to see what was transpiring. He quickly threaded the spiral flights of stairs and labyrinthine corridors leading to the Chamber of Questions.

Azuron halted in front of the metal-chased wooden door in the stony wall, marking the entrance to the place he sought. There was no sound coming from behind it. In stealthy silence, Azuron eased opened the great counter-weighted door to the torture chamber and looked within.

The high vaulted rock-cut space was awash with sunlight streaming in through the three great archways. Through them, the open, sunlit sky beyond the island seemed to beckon those within. A pure white albatross could be seen swinging about against that azure sky.

Azuron stood in the doorway and took in the entire scene with growing disgust. The bright sunlight clearly showed a site of futility. The floor was now liberally littered with broken implements and discarded oddments of torture, the bits and pieces of machines so effective against Humans, Dwarves and Teluri, but utterly useless against a Giant. Where they stood in conference hard by the wall openings, the inquisitors all looked far more harassed and spent than their victim, who sat cross-legged on the floor almost at rest, his dark eyes following the bird's flight. Only the chains about his wrists and the blood encrusted slashes on his back bespoke him prisoner. The warders looked up at the opening of the door and, as one, backed away towards the mental safety of the brazier and rack at the far end of the chamber, to a man their forms stiffening at the arrival of their master.

Azuron rolled his eyes and heaved a great sigh.

"Khalandria spare me from fools," he muttered and came the rest of the way into the chamber, his robes swirling around him with the tempestuousness of his movements.

Menannon rose warily to his feet to meet the Teluri, refusing to be deemed to be weakening. The sorcerer glared down at his cringing followers.

"Dotards!"

His strident anger sliced through the very air in front of them like a sword nearly cutting slashes across their sweating bodies. Before they could say or do anything, he whirled and pointed at the chained Giant.

"This thing is a Mythrian monster endowed with unlawful capabilities by its high one, not a Human thou canst question in any normal manner. Dost thou imbeciles actually deem thumbscrews and the rack will avail thee aught against a monster whose bones may as well be of stone?!"

He picked up a broken and discarded thumbscrew and threw it at the chief warder, hitting him on the side of the head. The man stood his ground out of sheer terror of his master, only slightly wincing with the pain of the impact.

"Thou must use the gifts of Khalandria to aid thee to extract words from a monster such as this."

With that, Azuron raised his hands to his mouth cupping them to form a hollow and spoke softly into them. He looked over at Menannon and, with a malicious smile, made a throwing gesture towards him. A ball of black fire streaked across the chamber and struck Menannon squarely in the chest with stunning force, hurling him back against the wall behind him, pinning him there, rigid with pain. The fire seemed to enter his body itself and speed along every nerve. His whole being writhed in pain so piercing he could not even scream. It stopped as quickly as it started and he crashed to his knees gasping. Before he could rise, Azuron began striking him with a positive rain of black fireballs, sending him into convulsions of agony so intense it was a wonder to the warders his back did not break.

A seeming lifetime later, the fireballs ceased, leaving Menannon motionless on the floor, bruised and bleeding, too spent to do more than breathe. The sorcerer came to him then and knelt beside him, reaching out a be-ringed hand to take his chin and turn his face so that he could be seen more plainly. Menannon was not a pretty sight. A broken wound at his hairline, caused by the sharp edge of one of the wall stones, was oozing blood. It dripped down the left side of his face to mingle with the sweat of his pain and the dirt of the floor. His left eye was already swelling shut, yet the right still glared black hatred at his tormentor. Azuron studied him for several heartbeats, then let go of his chin and rested back on his heels. When he spoke, his voice was calm, almost affable as though he but discussed a hypothetical question of philosophy.

"I have found it a fascinating study of summers uncounted, how much of pain and degradation of mind and body monsters such as thou canst bear. Thou wouldst be a particularly interesting study but, ay me, we have not the time. So! Shall we continue until we find thy breaking point or shalt thou find thy tongue and tell me what I desire to know?"

Azuron ceased speaking and removed a pristine handker-chief from his sleeve and, with deliberate consideration, wiped the blood and dirt from Menannon's left eye.

"Come, young sir, what sayest thou?"

It took Menannon three tries to finally gather enough strength to push words passed his pain stiffened lips. "I...say...your courage is marvelous much against...an unarmed man...chained to a wall."

The Teluri dropped the handkerchief and flexed his right hand whose little finger bore a sheath of serrated metal. This wicked object he laid against the bridge of Menannon's nose and thrust in. Blood started around it as he drew it slowly down from there across the Giant's cheekbone and ending near the hinge of his jaw beneath his left ear, leaving behind it a bleeding gash which clearly showed in its depths the bones of Menannon's face.

All the while Menannon continued to stare at him fixedly.

"Monsters deserve not the courtesies of courage."

Azuron reared back, fairly hissing and slammed a fireball directly into the side of Menannon's head, knocking him senseless. He stood and stalked to the table where he roughly sorted through the implements of torture thereon until he found a long tube of some strange, silvery metal. He scooped it up and thrust it towards the chief warder.

"When it awakens, use this on it and make sure that thou dost not fail me!"

This last was spoken with a dark look clearly stating should there not be answers extracted from the Giant, lives would be extracted from the warders and in the most painful manner possible. The thought of the ancient form of execution known as Death by a Thousand Slashes came to mind and seemed to hang in the very air about them. Azuron left the warders to their work.

The turns of the hour wore slowly on, consuming the afternoon and most of the night, their relentless march accompanied by the sound of inarticulate screaming whose endless echoes, carrying up from below, moved along the corridors of the palace containing no words but only pain.

The first light of the next dawn discovered the warders none the wiser for all their time and effort. They knew no more about the whereabouts of the Princess Nirna than they had when first they had set to their task. Hot irons, scourging and Khalandrian magic had availed them nothing save to finally drive Menannon's spirit so deep into itself that no further pain or word could reach him. In the dim light, he lay silent upon the blood-washed stones, his eyes half open, his breathing rasping in a throat long since made voiceless with screaming. Sometime during the endless night, his spirit had reached its core where only life or death impinge and nothing else is felt or matters, neither pain nor pleasure, joy nor sadness. Will he or nil he, Menannon was no longer capable of telling anyone anything.

Bone weary and frightened, the warders gathered once more beside the now cold brazier and held conference. Failure was not an option, but what alternative? There seemed to be three possibilities: one, admit defeat and throw themselves upon the mercy of a merciless master; two, drag their prisoner to the chamber's edge and throw him into the gorge and claim that he had broken free using Mythrian magic on them and again throw themselves upon the mercy of a merciless master, three: lie—tell that same master that the boy had finally broken and told them Nirna's whereabouts and volunteer to go and fetch her thereby departing the island never to return. All four stared at each other in consternation unable to choose their path. Which possibility would serve Azuron's purpose and which would actually save their skins?

CHAPTER 22
(SUMMER OF THE WORLD 6097)

A DIM, GREYISH LIGHT filtered into the deep cell wherein Walderan had been thrust in the late hours of the previous night, barely illuminating damp encrusted walls and an ancient door whose rusty grating opened upon darkness. High on the wall opposite the door, was a small air shaft whose upper end must be near some backwater or settling pool, for the miasma which passed for air that accompanied the light was nearly overwhelming. He knew he would become accustomed to the stench as he had become accustomed to all else in this gaol. To the dishonored harper, one cell was as good or as bad as another. It mattered little unless, one day, the powers that be deemed him worthy of one of the few cells whose outer wall overlooked the Kidron gorge and thus possessed a window. That was only a dream, but still it was a dream to be held to one's breast to keep some minuscule flicker of humanity alive. This move however seemed to put paid to that dream, for of the many he had experienced in his long summers of incarceration, this was by far the worst, as he now found himself in the kind of cell which you entered and the door was locked behind you, never to be opened again until the day came when the food thrust through its small opening remained uneaten. Then the door itself would be walled up and all forgotten. This was a death cell.

Well so be it. He had been sentenced to death, but that sentence had been commuted at the request of the Lord Gorlanndon out of respect for his calling as a harper. At the time, it had seemed a blessing of the High One, but now, some seventeen long summers later, he was not so sure.

Walderan stretched and sat up on the low stone ledge which served him as a bed and sitting place. At least he was unfettered and still had a bucket for his bodily needs and water to wash himself. That, plus a candle, flint and steel so he could have light or darkness as the fit took him, two harper robes—one to wear and one to wash—and another gift of the Giant: a much read copy of the Word Hoard of the High One—were all his worldly possessions.

He rose and lit his candle. It was a kindness of his long time gaoler that his candle was one by which the turns of the hour could be told, though why either of them had supposed that a good thing, he was not quite sure. Walderan hesitated a moment, his flint and steel still in his hand. Was it a good idea to light the candle when there was a modicum of natural light? He no longer knew if he would be provided with another when this one finally guttered out, for he knew not if his gaoler yet held his post or if he would still be able to bring candles, but then, nothing was truly certain in life, except death and so he kept it lit when awake and hoped for the best.

He reflected that he was not sure exactly what turn of the hour it might be, for from this new cell he could no longer hear the Council Hall carillon play the mid-of-day and the mid-of-night. Call it the ninth hour and have done. He shrugged, for it really mattered not anyway. One hour was as good as another in this hole.

By the soft golden light, he was able to see to relieve himself and wash, a thing he did scrupulously very morning. In his arrogance and overweening pride, he had made a mistake and was now paying the price for that arrogance and pride, but that did not relieve him of the responsibility to the High One to represent Him the best he might. He was determined to always show himself to his best advantage to any who visited him, though that had only ever been his gaolers. Yet even these deserved to see that a harper-priest of the High One was not a craven.

His simple morning routine completed, Walderan sat on the ledge once more and surveyed his new cell by the flickering light of the candle. It was the smallest he had as yet been in being no more than three paces wide and once again that long. It was high enough he could stand upright at his five feet and ten so long as he minded his head as there were stalactites crawling down from the ceiling stones. Someone had recently attempted to clean the floor leaving only the dust of old rushes. There had been chains set into the wall beneath the ledge which had long since rusted from their brackets due to the damp of the place. They had not been replaced. Three of the walls were solid rock, the fourth being of laid blocks whose mortaring was rotting away. It had so far gone that one stone at the bottom had actually fallen out, leaving a dark hole. How far back it went was a question he would sometime have to answer for simple curiosity's sake, but for now, it mattered not. At least there was no air coming from it as there was from the shaft whose wan light illuminated the cell.

Walderan turned his attention once more to the question of why he had been moved. It was passing strange, as he had been in the cell he had just left for five summers and a fortnight, so why had he been moved now and in the darkness of the second watch? Ever before this, such a move had been accomplished in the full light of day and due to the death or retirement of his gaoler. This time there had been no such provocation, as old Peter had been as hale and hearty as ever yestereve when he had brought Walderan's dinner. Had he been replaced? Speculation was fruitless, but tantalizing nonetheless.

It was two full turns of the hour by his candle when he at last heard sound from the corridor without and saw the flickering of a torch reflected upon the wall beyond the grating. He listened carefully and heard the sound of shuffling feet and the cracking of ancient knee joints as his gaoler came closer and squatted down to place something on the floor. There was a huffing sound and a bit of a grunt then the small metal slider at the bottom was opened and a tray thrust through. Walderan held his breath. The food was his usual breakfast of frumenty with currants and goat's milk and his daily flagon of drinking water, but would there also be a candle? There was a good deal of grunting and mumbling from without, then the slider did open once more and a large hour candle was indeed thrust through. *Praise the High One!*

"Peter, is that you?" Walderan asked a bit hoarsely, his throat oddly constricted. It amazed him how worried he had actually been about that candle. The High One almighty! How far he had fallen to find his heart so set upon a mere lump of wax! He shook his head at himself and stood to approach the door to better treat with the old man, his bare feet making no sound on the filthy flags.

"Aye 'tis me. Why they be puttin' tha clear down here? 'Twas mortal hard enough to keep tha's food even a hint warm where tha were an' now tha must be half way to Hella its own self an' now it be stone cold."

The old fellow grumbled as he dragged himself to his feet, his old body protesting at the cold and damp.

"I'll have to be bringin' tha a heat candle an' a pot, er tha'll ne'er be eatin' like civilized folk more. Bah! This place is mortal damp. Me rheumatics is flarin' up just comin' here. Why be they puttin' tha down here?"

"I know not. The second watch woke me near three turns of the hour past the mid-of-night and brought me down here. I can tell you no more," Waldron replied with a shrug even though the old fellow could not see it. The habit of body language was a hard one to break.

"Well, I be after askin' 'em why—an' don't tha think I won't."

"I would appreciate that for 'tis most curious. But ere you go, how is your good wife this day? And did you go to the herbalist and obtain the ointment for your knees I suggested?"

"Aye, master, that I did and it be helpin', else I could ne'er've walked so far as this benighted cell. Me wife's after usin' it on her hands an' says it be helpin' marvelous much," Peter informed him, the awe at the harper's knowledge obvious in the tone of his voice.

Walderan asked the old fellow no questions about what was happening on the rest of Kalyria and the wider world, as Peter's world went no farther than those sections of the prison that were his charge and his concerns were limited to the food he brought and the waste he took away, his small family and the creaking of his joints. But the fellow had a kind heart and a deep respect for harpers which made him deal more carefully with this prisoner than he did with most of the others on his rounds, a thing for which Walderan was ever grateful. Peter traded him a clean bucket and wash water for the used and picked his torch back out of the bracket.

"I be bringin' tha's laundry this evenin'. Is there aught else tha's needin'?"

An entire world of things came to mind at this question, but Walderan took no advantage of the old man and gave his usual negative answer, "No, thank you. I'm fine."

This had by now become a ritual between them—the question asked, the answer given—bringing a small bit of reality to an otherwise very surreal situation.

"I be goin' then."

"Go with the High One."

Walderan spoke the blessing and Peter shuffled away mumbling and muttering as he went. When the last echo of Peter's departing steps blended into silence, Walderan returned to his ledge and ate his breakfast slowly and then set himself to reciting another of the sagas he had learned as a school child in Tolgrin, a small mountain village in the north of Rhonndia. This one was "Niial and the Sand Drakta, a Traveler's Tale," one of the very oldest he had ever heard. Another day crawled slowly by.

The mid-of-night a twoday later must have been hard by when something more than the dripping of water and the scrabbling of rats in the corridor awakened him. He sat up, every sense alert. What was it? For many long moments he sat still, listening.

Nothing.

Just his imagination then. He lay back down and drew a fold of his robe over his head as was his wont to keep the rats out of his hair and beard at night. His hair was as long and full as a

Teluri's and his beard would have done a Dwarf proud. Both would have been far longer had he not discovered that he could control their length by carefully burning off a wisp at a time with his candle. Fire was a perilous and wonderful gift.

He had just dozed off again when he was brought bolt upright by a bloodcurdling shriek. The sound was quickly followed by hoarse screams and the sound of muffled thrashing. The cell was stygian. He could not see his hand in front of his face and had to grope for his flint and steel. His hands shook so badly he was barely able to light the candle. The light did not help. The entire cell was filled with the sounds of anguish and terror, but from where? The noise echoed and reechoed, directionless. Walderan moved to stand in the center of the space holding his candle high, his heart pounding, the sweat of pure terror drenching his face. Finally, the sounds diminished to a harsh, though greatly subdued, groaning.

"I warn you, I believe not in ghosts," he managed to mutter into the darkness, his voice almost a squeak.

The sounds instantly ceased. He cleared his throat and whirled around in a circle yelling, the flame of his candle guttering in the wind of his motion.

"What are you that thus be-screened by darkness comes to disturb my rest?! Where are you?!"

There was no answer nor further sound for seeming turns of the hour, but then the groaning and thrashing resumed, yet softer this time so they echoed less and the source was discernable. The sound was coming from behind the block wall! Walderan stood transfixed, staring at the dark opening at the base of the wall, for there was something crawling out of it. A large whitish thing was forcing itself out much as a slug oozing out from under a rock. It was just beyond the clear reach of his candle's light, so he was forced to take one reluctant, terrified step and then another to better see what ghastly creature penetrated his small domain.

In the light of the candle, the slug-like thing slowly resolved itself. It was a hand! A large, blood covered hand that groped its way with its fingers until it was much further into his cell and he could see it was a normal Human forearm creeping out of the hole. It kept coming.

"The High One's holy blood, what in all Hella *are* you?"

Between the blood and the darkness of the hole, it seemed as though the hand were disembodied, trailing a bloody stump behind it. Unknowingly, Walderan had come close enough so that the questing fingers touched him. They were cold as ice. In that instant, the hand grabbed his foot and he jumped backwards so fast that he crashed into the wall behind him. The candle flew out of his hand and fell, plunging the cell back into darkness. His own cry of terror was echoed by the other. Then all was silence.

Walderan lay where he had fallen, waiting for he knew not what. Finally, he screwed his courage to the sticking place and forced himself to reach out into the darkness and feel for the candle. He locked his thumbs together and spread his fingers running them in swaths across the floor. At last he touched it. Gratefully, he locked his hand about the still warm wax and went to pick it up only to find that something else held it as well! His heart was hammering so hard he was sure it must break through his chest. Almost, he let go, but then he stopped himself. He was being an idiot! There were no such things as ghosts, the dead did not walk and neither did severed hands. He was a harper and a healer, not a superstitious simpleton.

"Get a hold of yourself man," he growled under his breath.

Determinedly, he reached out with his other hand and felt along the candle until he felt the thing that was holding it. As he expected, it was the hand. Gently, he ran his fingers up the hand and over the wrist. The hand was cold, but not the cold of death. It was the cold of illness and damp. The hand flinched and dropped the candle. Instinctively, Walderan grabbed the candle before it could roll away, then crawled across the cell to the ledge. Groping in the blackness, he found the materials he sought, relit the candle and set it safely back in the niche he had scraped out in the wall for its use. He took a deep settling breath, firmly banishing his fears and turned back to examine the intruder.

What he saw was indeed a hand and arm, though one of mighty proportions. It was covered with dried blood and some fresh streaks as well, apparently caused by its being forced out of the jagged hole in the base of the wall. It was feeling around as though it searched for him. There was a certain frantic quality to the movements which bespoke agitation nearly the match of his own and perhaps more. He sat staring at it for several long heartbeats, then it penetrated the fog in his mind: That hand belonged to a living being! It was not just a disembodied thing on the floor. When the realization dawned, he threw himself down near the hole in the wall and took hold of the arm with both hands. All movement ceased.

"WHERE ARE YOU?!" he shouted at the top of his lungs into the darkness of the hole.

"Ow! You don't have to shout. I can hear you without that," a weak voice answered instantly and so close he jumped again in surprise.

"Again, I ask where are you?" Walderan modulated his voice this time to as near normal as he could manage at the moment.

"I'm not certain," came the reply in a deep, though distinctly breathy voice. "I seem to be in a small stone shaft and I can't move. Where are you?"

"I am in a cell in the gaol beneath the palace of Kalyria."

There was a brief silence, then Walderan could have sworn he heard a slight smile in the voice. "I must admit that is better than what I had assumed as to my whereabouts. Hella and eternal torture were coming to mind."

"Ah...no! We are both alive and this is not Hella—though there are some who might beg to differ with me."

"Can you contrive to release me?"

There was a brief silence accompanied by an indrawn breath, a response to the pain his unseen companion was obviously suffering. The sound brought Walderan back to an awareness of the condition of the arm he held. He looked again and found no sign of a door or any other opening in the wall between them.

Cold blank stone stared back at him.

"Nay! I am truly sorry, but you seem to be walled into a solid stone wall though how that is possible, I know not."

There was silence again as this news was received beyond the wall. The silence began to stretch and Walderan searched his mind for anything to keep the conversation going, as this was the first living person with whom he had spoken other than his gaolers in seventeen long summers. He was suddenly desperate for such contact.

"Who are you and how do you come to be inside this wall?" He tried to make his voice sound conversational, though he could not quite keep it from quavering. There was a brief spate of movement in the arm he held as though its owner were attempting to straighten. The movement ceased. Its secession was accompanied by a sigh that was more like a sob. When his unseen companion spoke again, his voice was a bit choked and it took two tries before words would come.

"I am Gorlanndon's son, Menannon. And as to how I came to be here, I know not. The last I remember, I was in the Hall of Questioning being attended upon by four of Azuron's more unsavory lackeys. They suddenly halted their efforts for what reason I know not. Then, I vaguely remember being dragged along a corridor so deep within the stone its floor was littered with slick, wet stalagmites alternating with stagnant black pools of foetid water. "

"Gorlanndon? The Giant? I knew not that he has a son. I owe him my life and my sanity."

"How long have you been in prison?"

"Seventeen summers and slightly more." Walderan admitted.

"Ah! That explains it. My father brought me to Kalyria only just over fourteen summers ago. None here knew of me ere that time." It seemed as though the lad was in desperate need of contact as well, for he continued the conversation though it was obvious that speech was difficult for him. "Now that you know me, may I ask who you are?"

Walderan hesitated. To tell this Giant his name was to tell him of his infamy and it was suddenly of great importance that the fellow did not scorn him, although he was well aware that he deserved the scorn of any right thinking person. At last, reluctantly, he cleared his throat and spoke into the darkness.

"I am Walderan, formerly the master harp healer of Kalyria."

He spoke reluctantly and was not surprised when there was a distinct silence from the other side of the wall. Then, just when he was sure that Menannon would shun him, there was a reply.

"You're the one who sought to heal Faeori's father..."

"Faeori?" Walderan questioned frantically running the list of royal names through his mind and finding none that matched the one spoken. Perchance this name belonged to someone born after his incarceration.

"The princess Nirna. My father has always said that the fault in Ronirinen King's death lay in the method, not the man." The words surprised Walderan and strangely, brought a mist to his eyes he had to blink away.

"Nay, your sire is over-kind. The fault was with the man, not the method. The Teluri master, Reuel of Blue Hill, is a great healer, perhaps the greatest of all time and his method is true. I studied many summers with him and had convinced myself that I could control the power of his method. So when the king was brought home sorely wounded from that hunting accident, I attempted to use Reuel's method to heal him rather than the harp healing I knew better and I lost him. I deserve to be punished for my arrogance and stupidity."

"But you did not willingly murder," Menannon objected. "My father sought to have you released, but the judges were adamant and would only commute your sentence to life in prison."

"Life in prison...that is something of a contradiction. In prison is true, but life? I deem not that anything in prison equates to life."

The only answer he received was a wheezing intake of breath followed by a deep groan. Instantly the healer's instinct came to the fore and Walderan carefully looked at the arm he still held. By the flickering candle light he could see a long gash filled with dried blood and dirt and the distinct marks of shackles that had bitten deep into the flesh of the wrist. It bore all the signs of torture. Walderan's heart lurched

"To judge by your arm, you are injured. How badly? Damn! I would to the High One I could see you and judge for myself!" There was a brief sound of movement, then a long sigh.

"There seems to be no part of my being that hurts not, save the tip of my nose. Though with my knees resting on that, it will soon join the rest of me, I'm sure," Menannon quipped, attempting a bit of levity despite his dire predicament. "Right now, I would to the High One I had obeyed my father and stayed in Aridion City."

"What were you doing there?"

"I'm a newly corded Journeyman Harper and I was supposed to be standing my Masters trials this summer and instead, I am wherever this is, getting far more intimately acquainted with my knees than I have ever thought possible...High One help me, it hurts." This last was whispered as though Menannon spoke to himself rather than the healer.

Walderan moved slightly so he could study the hand in front of him and he saw what he had missed before this. The gore encrusted fingers bore nails worn slightly longer than normal to aid in the plucking of harp strings and there were well-formed callouses on the ends of each finger, worn there by long playing. By the High One's grace, his unseen companion was a indeed a harper! He had to be the only harper of the race of Giants in this age of the world. A newly corded journeyman?

"How old are you?" he suddenly wondered aloud.

"I have twenty summers and would have turned one and twenty in a fortnight and a bit more had I lived."

"You're not dead yet!" Walderan's heart nearly froze at the thought of losing so soon what he had but newly gained.

"Nay. Still, I am like to be though it will perforce take longer than for a Human."

"No! We will find a way to get you out, as the High One is my witness. You will not die in a dark rathole. I swear to you!"

The only answer Walderan received was a strange, strangled gasping that bore the tinge of panic.

"What is it, lad?...Menannon answer me! What's wrong?"

"I...can't...breathe...it's too...small...." There was the sound of thrashing. The arm he held jerked and the fingers began reaching desperately for something. Walderan took it in both hands and the fingers closed convulsively over them as though to a lifeline. The sound of the breathing did not ease. Walderan felt something warm touch his elbow and he looked down to see a line of blood creeping along the crack between two flagstones.

"Menannon, where do you bleed?" He put on his best professional manner and managed to keep his voice steady and matter-of-fact, though in reality he felt like screaming in frustration at this entire untenable situation.

"The stripes on...my back...must have broken open..." Menannon managed to wheeze out the words between his strangled gasping.

"Menannon listen to me. I want you to stop moving. Lie as still as you can and change your breathing. I know you have been taught to breathe properly with your diaphragm through your nose, but I want you to do it wrong! Concentrate, lad, and breathe shallowly through your mouth. If your legs are against your front, there is more room between them and your chest than your stomach. Breathe shallowly" He could hear the youngster attempting to follow his instruction, but overcoming summers of training was not easy.

"Concentrate, Menannon. You can do this. Breathe shallow and steady."

At first, it seemed as though the Giant was managing to breathe more comfortably, but then, whether due to pain or panic, the breathing went back to the half-strangled gasping he had heard previously and it was not long before Menannon passed out, which perhaps a good thing in the circumstances. Walderan felt for the pulse point in his wrist and it was fast and thready but present nonetheless.

"The High One's holy tears, what a coil," he muttered sitting up, Menannon's hand still held between his own. "If I only had a harp!"

He sat still, trying to consider the situation in which he now found himself. This must be the reason he had been moved to this cell. To cover the fact that another life was hidden within it. This puzzled him, for it seemed to him it would have better suited their purpose to leave this cell empty and wall it up. Apparently, however, those responsible thought otherwise.

But the Lord Gorlanndon's own son?! What in all Hella was happening in this land that the son of its chief councillor should be incarcerated in such a barbaric manner? The lad had obviously been here since at least the mid-of-night a threeday since without the ability to move and without food and drink. To make matters worse, he had been the victim of torture before he was brought here and his wounds had not been tended and thus would fester. It had been intended by someone that the Giant should die and die horribly. This was not punishment, it was murder, ordered by this Azuron, whoever he might be.

WALDERAN WAS NOT THE ONLY ONE sleepless over Menannon's fate this night. Its darkness also found a single light shining in Gorlanndon's villa where the Giant sat late at his desk staring at nothing. He had neither eaten nor slept in the sevenday since Menannon's arrest despite Clarinda's pleas and Skendrin's arguments. At the sound of a knock on his study door, Gorlanndon drew his thoughts back from afar.

"Master?" Skendrin's voice came softly through the heavy wood, "Captain Firod to see you, sir."

"Come," was the only word he could muster from a mind gone suddenly inarticulate with fear. He watched the door turn on its hinges, his heart torn between hope that at last his friend had word of Menannon's whereabouts and the tormenting fear that they had found him too late.

The tall captain came briskly into the chamber and nodded to the steward who closed the door with a soft click. He turned and saw the look on the Giant's face and spoke hastily to reassure him. "No, old friend he is not dead, that I know for there have been neither burials nor stone masons called to wall up a cell, but how long it will be ere he dies I cannot say."

"Sit and tell me."

Gorlanndon straightened in his chair and indicated one across the desk from him. It was of normal human size though set high to ease its user in conversing with the Giant. Firod climbed up onto it and clasped his hands before him on the desk, his eyes never leaving Gorlanndon's face. He cleared his throat and spoke softly.

"Earlier this afternoon, I was duty bound to attend upon the execution of four Doomcriers branded traitor, though what their crime was, I know not for it was not published in the order of execution."

Gorlanndon shook his head in disgust and started to speak. "The law clearly states—", but Firod held up a hand forestalling him.

"Be that as it may, one of them was determined not to die ere he had a word with the High One and he demanded the right of Confidere which stayed his execution long enough for him to have some speech with the palace chaplain, but as there is no longer a chaplain at the palace, I stood as substitute intermediary. He seemed actually pleased to have ado with me alone instead. It was a queer business. He spoke no words to me, only handed me this piece of vellum and with nothing more than a nod, departed to his death. Yet, where ere then he had been in great fear of his impending doom as were his fellows, he now had upon his face the calmness of one whose mind was at peace, as if giving me this scrap somehow cleansed his soul and brought the Peace of the High One upon him, though how that could be, I cannot say. Yet the blue of his eyes was not darkened by any doubt when he climbed the scaffold."

Firod withdrew a much folded scrap of dirty vellum from his

belt pouch and spread it out on the desktop between them. As he unrolled it, a small piece of red sandstone fell out, thunking hollowly on the wood. The vellum's surface held a few odd scratches obviously drawn with the piece of stone. The scratches depicted what must surely be a cryptic code as they showed the drawing of a staircase with the number four beside it and then two parallel lines followed by a number seven. The last thing they showed was a rough doorway with a crown G in its middle.

"Your own crest, Gorlanndon." Firod stabbed a blunt finger into the vellum.

"So it is! Why would one of Azuron's Doomcriers place my crest in a code?"

Firod spoke softly, meeting Gorlanndon's eyes across the desk, "I believe he was trying to tell us where Menannon is being held. The man was a gaoler. This much, at least, was on the death order."

Gorlanndon returned the captain's gaze, then his eyes blazed with understanding, and both looked back to the drawing.

"Of course!" Gorlanndon tapped his finger against vellum. "This is some kind of code for a prison! So, then, this must mean that there are four staircases and seven halls that must be traversed to where his cell is located, but where is the building itself? This is an ancient city whose roots are deep and bones are old. He could be anywhere...."

"No!" Firod shook he head emphatically, reaching for the stone and holding it up for the Giant's inspection. "This, too, must be a clue. Why else would he have included it? I know the nooks and crannies of this city better than any living. I have to. It's my job. And this stone I know. It occurs in only one place—it is the very foundation of the Citadel."

In his mind's eye, Gorlanndon sought the vision of the foundations of the palace. He recalled an expedition he had made into the depths of the Kidron gorge nearly a thousand summers since. From its base, one could look up the east rampart of the Citadel at the top of which stood the palace. About half way up, there was indeed a layer of deep red sandstone topped by a shelf of white marble, overlain by the blackest of granite. Volcanic layering at its best. Yes. It was possible.

"But under which building does it lie, the Palace or the Council Hall, that is the question?" Gorlanndon's jaw tightened. "I have to know ere I can move!"

"I will find out old friend, my word on it." Firod departed leaving the Giant to stare at the rough map and wonder in what dark hole in Hella his son lay.

⚜

IN THAT SAME "HOLE IN HELLA" sought by the Giant, Walderan sat where he was for all the long turns of the hour until the dim light of day once more began to penetrate his cell. He had come to no conclusions other than he dared not tell Peter that another shared the cell with him, as he was sure the knowledge would result in his being moved and then all hope for Menannon's life would be extinguished. Yet he must contrive to get the lad food and water. But how was he to eat or drink if he lay in the position in which he seemed to be? Gently, so as not to disturb him, Walderan laid the hand he held onto the floor and stretched out full length beside it, so that he could insert his own arm into the hole next to the lad's.

His questing fingers began careful inspection of all Menannon's body he could reach. The main impression he had was of dried blood and dirt. The lad seemed to be liberally covered with swollen weals and gashes on his arms, legs and torso. He could feel no clothing in his inspection, but whether Menannon's modesty was completely outraged, he could not tell as his reach did not extend farther than the Giant's lower chest. Walderan was able to just touch the tips of his fingers to Menannon's face. There was a great swollen gash running from the bridge of his nose down to the hinge of his jaw. The edges of it were already warm with infection. As Menannon had said, he lay on his back, his legs folded up in front of him, his shoulder on this side hard against the near wall. So must his other shoulder on the other side be hard against the far wall. How exactly he had been able to thrust his arm through the hole was a matter of the wildest speculation. That he could not now move beyond turning his head was absolute truth and in such case, how was he to drink? Eating could be done by the simple expedient of Walderan's hand feeding him morsels of food. But life-giving water was another matter entirely. The jug his own daily ration of water came in would not fit through the hole and the lad could not raise his head to drink, even if it would.

Almost reluctantly Walderan withdrew his arm and sat up. How long would it take a Giant to die of thirst? For a Human, it would take but a matter of days. For a Giant, the ordeal would be prolonged, but yet inevitable. Shaking off his morbid thoughts, Walderan grabbed his candle from its niche and began a minute search of the wall enclosing the lad. He had nearly completed a search of its entire surface when he heard the shuffling tread of old Peter without his own cell. Quickly he returned to the center of his cell and straightened his robe.

The torchlight came through the grating accompanied by the usual grunting and crackling as the old fellow knelt down to push the food tray through the slot.

"Here tha be, Master." This morning, the food was followed by a warming candle and its holder. "There, Master. Now tha may warm tha's food. Is there aught else tha be needin'?"

"As a matter of fact," Walderan began, thinking fast. "The damp in this place has given me a cold and I'll be needing an extra ration of food for a bit and extra water to keep it under control."

"Aye, feed a cold, starve a fever, that be good sense, Master. I'll bring tha double food 'till tha gives me leave to quit," Peter assured him.

"You won't come to grief over this?" Walderan questioned not wanting to cause the old fellow trouble.

"Nay. None cares what I do as long as I be doin' me job. 'Sides the Dwarf in the cell beside tha's old one died yestereve an' none'll notice the extra food an' water as they've not gotten used to my takin' less on me rounds yet."

"I shall be forever grateful." Walderan sighed inwardly but immediately felt a twinge of guilt at being glad of another's ill fortune.

"Is there anythin' else?" the gaoler's creaky old voice broke in on his thoughts.

Walderan glanced about the cell, wracking his mind as to what it was he also needed for the Giant. His glance fell on the dark stain between the two flags near the hidden cell. Maggots! That was it! He needed maggots to clean the gash on the lad's face.

"There is one more thing. I seem to have gashed my arm on a stone in here and it is beginning to putrefy. I need maggots from the green bottle fly to clean it so it will obtain no further infection." Walderan breathed a mental prayer to be forgiven for lying.

"Maggots? Where would I be gettin' maggots?" Old Peter's voice was filled with surprise, but no suspicion, as nothing a harper said would ever be doubted by him or any of his. The High One forbid!

"The herbalist down in the Serpentine would have them. They are often used in healing."

"Well then I'll be after bringin' tha some as soon as may be."

"Thank you, Peter. Go with the High One." Peter began to turn to shuffle away when Walderan thought of something else. "A moment, Peter!" If he ever managed...no when he managed to release Menannon he would have to be able to clean him. "The floor in here is very rough and I nearly spilled my wash water this day because its small base is easily upset. I was wondering if you could bring me a larger vessel which will not upset so easily?"

"Aye, Master, that be easy." Peter's voice carried easily back to the cell and Walderan heard him turn and shuffle away, and the corridor without returned to darkness. He quickly picked up his food and water and returned to the hole in the wall. Now, how exactly was he going to feed his unseen companion? He sat and ate half of his frumenty knowing it would do neither of them any good if he let his own strength go down. When he had finished and washed it down with a goodly drink of water, he lay back down on the floor and reached into the hole. He found if he lay hard against the opening, his arm was just long enough for his hand to reach most of Menannon's face. He inadvertently touched the festering gash which elicited a hiss of pain.

"Menannon, are you awake?" he spoke quietly.

"Aye."

"I am going to try feeding you a bit of frumenty. I'll have to use my fingers, as I can't feel your mouth with my spoon."

There was a slight silence, then a sigh. "I know not how I will ever repay you for your kindness."

"It may not be kindness, as I am like as not to get the food in your ear instead of your mouth," Walderan quipped. There was a slight answering chuckle.

As carefully as he could, Walderan dipped his fingers into the bowl and scooped out a dollop of frumenty as though he were scooping up molding paste. This he proceeded to maneuver to Menannon's mouth where the lad was able to lick it from his fingers. It was rather like feeding a blind dog, but they managed it and all too soon the bowl was empty.

"I've not quite figured out how to get liquid to you, but there will be some way."

"At least there is a modicum of moisture in the frumenty, so I'm not as thirsty as I was," Menannon informed him softly.

"Aye, it will help some."

There was a long silence then during which Menannon seemed to sleep fitfully while Walderan began another minute inspection of the stone wall enclosing him. On the floor below there were strange scratches forming a shallow arc as though something had been dragged repeatedly across it. He searched the rest of the floor as well as he could, but saw no other scratches, so the arc had to relate to the wall. But how? Carefully lying down on his stomach, Walderan inched along the scratches following them with such an intensity that he banged his head into the wall before he realized that the arc ended there. He sat up rubbing his head consideringly. Well, it would seem that at least at one time there had been a door in this wall, as nothing else would explain the pattern of scratching. However *once was* and *still was* were entirely different matters altogether. Yet there must have been a door a threeday ago when the Giant had been shoved into the cell.

Walderan leaned close to inspect the mortar between the stones. It was old and rotten. He could dig out flakes of it with his fingernail. So this was not new construction so *still was* suddenly became a reality. There was a door in this wall and all he had to do was find it.

"Menannon, are you awake?"

There was no answer from within the cell. Almost, Walderan spoke again, but then thought better of it as he did not want to raise the lad's hopes until he was sure that the door really existed as his logic said it must. Resolutely, Walderan took up his candle and began to search every line of mortar in the entire wall.

Many turns of the hour later, he found what he was looking for. A keen eye could discern a pattern in the stonework that had an infinitesimal dark line of tracery around it. The door! Now where was the lock? There had to be a movable stone, since the lock was not to be seen and he had looked at literally every square inch of the wall's surface this day.

When Peter came with his evening meal and the extra food and water, he had already obtained the maggots.

"Here tha go, Master," he said, pushing a small glass bottle through the door's food hole. "The herbalist says these be the finest blue bottle fly maggots to be had. An' he wishes tha luck with them."

Walderan picked up the bottle and inspected the maggots wriggling about its bottom.

"Yes, they will do admirably. My thanks." He set them down.

"Get tha back from the door, as I've got an urn for tha's wash water and it won't be fittin' through this grate."

Obediently, Walderan retreated to the far side of the cell and knelt as was proper for a prisoner while old Peter opened the door, the key grating nastily in the lock. Though this seemed like an act of submission, what Walderan was really doing was kneeling over Menannon's arm to hide it from the gaoler's eye with the skirts of his robe. He need not have worried, as the fellow kept his face averted, as it always upset him to see the harper face to face in the cell and not be able to let him out. Somehow, the door locked between them made the job easier. Amidst much grunting and fussing, Peter wrestled a large urn into the cell and put it, and a clean bucket, down near the used one. This he took up and left the cell, closing the door behind him.

"My thanks, again." Walderan returned to the grate to retrieve the food Peter now pushed through.

"There. I'll be bringin' water in a regular jug and an extra empty bucket for tha to pour the used in."

"Again, my thanks," Walderan sat on the floor near the grate and ate his supper while the old fellow talked for a bit about his family, then departed. As soon as the gaoler was gone and the light of his torch dimmed again to darkness, Walderan moved back to the hole and set the second dish of food down. This was not going to be as easy as the frumenty had been, as this night's fare was mutton stew. With care, he washed the day's dirt from his hands and leaned down to speak into the hole.

" Menannon! Wake up lad. It's dinner time. I hope you like mutton stew."

"I never truly thought of sheep as something to eat," was the breathy reply, "but beggars can't be choosers, as they say."

Walderan grinned and shook his head and began the not inconsiderable task of getting the mutton stew through the hole and into the Giant's mouth. Luckily, it was a good thick stew and he had not warmed it so that it was rather stiff, so they managed the task without too many mishaps. When the stew was finished, Walderan reached across his cell and took up the wash water and cloth he had saved, having forgone his daily bath for the first time since he was incarcerated seventeen long summers ago. These he brought back to the hole and lay down on his stomach beside it.

"Lad, I'm going to try to wash your face so that I can treat that laceration, alright?"

"Do what you will, as I can neither help nor hinder you," came the reasonable reply.

"Prepare then for the attempt." Walderan wet his hands and taking the soap made a good lather. "Close your eyes, lad and keep them closed. This is going to hurt a bit, but it is for the best." So saying, he reached a soapy hand into the hole and as carefully as he could, began washing as much of Menannon's face as he could reach. When he had lathered it as well as he could, he wet the cloth and rinsed the soap back off. The whole process took perhaps a half turn of the hour.

"Now, lad, I'm going to treat your laceration the only way I can at the moment."

"That sounds rather ominous," Menannon said, which reply brought a grin to the healer's face.

"Not really, but my method will be a bit unusual. I am going to put maggots in your wound—."

"Maggots?!" Menannon interrupted him with a gasp then coughed. "Don't maggots devour flesh?"

"Yes, lad they do, but only flesh that is putrefying. They'll not touch clean flesh. Thereby they remove that which is bad and allow the healing to begin. Are you willing to stand the attempt?" Walderan well knew that there were those who could not brook the thought of having maggots touching them and this process had been known to drive folk from themselves.

"I would say that I have little choice," Menannon's deep voice was softly thoughtful. "I know that my wounds are turning putrid for my fever is rising and I can smell them over all the rest of the stench in here. As you have far more experience with this than I...." Menannon's words trailed off into a resigned silence.

"Let us begin then." Walderan quickly un-stopped the bottle and withdrew a few of the wriggling maggots. Care-fully, so as not harm the creatures, he reached through the hole and finding the gash in Menannon's face by feel and the hiss of pain that accompanied his touch, gently laid the minuscule creatures into the wound. There was a profound silence from the other side of the wall. Walderan waited a few minutes.

"Well, lad how goes it?"

He heard Menannon clear his throat then draw as deep a breath as he could. "I cannot tell you the extent of my joy that you warned me you were going to do this rather than waking up to find that you had done it. The feel of something wriggling in one's face is a sensation impossible to describe. Though there is little pain."

"Good. I will apply the rest and we will leave them to their work."

So saying, Walderan laid the rest of the maggots into the wound and settled back to rest for the evening.

Within a twoday, he would need more maggots if these had not finished their work, for as they grew satiated, they would crawl away from the wound as he had no way of holding them in place. But, if all went well, the twoday would suffice and see the wound cleaned and healing. He could hear Menannon move his head restlessly now and then, but overall, the lad took the treatment well. As he had done each night since his own incarceration, Walderan closed their evening by reading from the Word Hoard of the High One. The words had perhaps never meant so much to either of them as they did now in this extremity.

Thus was set the pattern of their hours for a further twoday. Menannon waited and Walderan searched. The healer's thirst for conversation after seventeen summers of near silence was insatiable and they talked together of everything imaginable from history to politics, art to music, the natural world to the spiritual world. Walderan was understandably most interested in the happenings on Kalyria since his incarceration and they discussed Azuron and his coming to power at great length for as long as Menannon could muster breath for speech. Nothing changed in this routine until, late in the afternoon of the second day, Walderan finally found what he sought. Under his prying fingers, a stone fell from its place to reveal a keyhole secreted beneath it. *Praise the High One!* The way to unlock it was no nearer, but at least the way could now be attempted.

Against the possibility of opening the lock, Walderan had been saving half his drinking water in the large urn so he would have plenty for Menannon. A third day passed as Menannon weakened physically and Walderan sought to pick the lock. He tried a piece of wood he managed to break from his food tray, but it was too soft. He tried bending his fork and using one of its tines, but it was too short.

He spent many precious hours of candle light in frustration grinding his metal spoon against a rock to make a pick long and strong enough for his purposes. He set himself to try again as soon as old Peter had left him for the morning. Menannon had made no sound since the evening meal the previous night and then he had been barely coherent, his fever raging to a terrible degree. Walderan could feel the heat of it coming from Menannon's arm as it lay against his leg as he worked to free the lad. He had to succeed soon, else Menannon would die.

Tirelessly, Walderan kept working the long day through and into the night. Time and again, he felt the tumblers click only to hear them fall back. Then disaster struck.

Near the mid-of-night, his makeshift pick broke. He pulled it out of the lock to see that the end of it was cracking off, barely hanging in place. With fingers that shook he took hold of it and the tip came away in his hand. He threw down the broken remains and turned away, defeated, tears of frustration and guilt flowing unchecked down his face. He threw himself down on the far side of the cell and sat with his back against the wall his trembling hands clasped to his lips lest the sound of his defeat alarm Menannon.

He sat thus for seeming turns of the hour. His frustration and fear grew until they drove him to stalk back to the wall and pick up the broken pick. He clenched it in his fist and shook it above his head at the ceiling, at the sky, at the very face of the High One Himself.

"High One, how can it end like this? How canst Thou let him die in a dark, stinking rat hole? Where is Thy justice?" Walderan growled under his breath, though in truth he wanted to scream the words at the top of his lungs.

Finally he dropped his hand to his side, his whole body slumping as he looked at the broken tool in his hand. Walderan reached out almost gently and slid the broken pick into the lock as far as it would go then turned away and threw himself onto his sleeping ledge where he extinguished the candle and lay down. Silence returned to the cell like the breath of eternity.

The healer lay still, listening to the scrabble of rats in the corridor beyond his cell's door and the steady drip of dampness from the ends of the growing stalactites. Yet something else was whispering beneath the rest, a soft sound. A sound which repeated itself twice. It was a very distinct click. Walderan lay still holding his breath and lo! there was a third distinct click, then a very metallic grating as though two parts of something metal were detaching from each other. There was no further sound. Walderan's lungs screamed for air forcing him to breathe. He took one convulsive breath and sat bolt upright. With hands that shook, he lit his candle and turned to search for the source of the sound. His heart nearly misgave him as his eyes fell upon the wall. The lock had turned and the door hung slightly open, its dark crack glaring sharply despite the flickering of the candle's flame! He sat frozen in dumb surprise.

"Praise Thee, O High One," he finally breathed in awe. "Thy ways are inscrutable."

He eased from the ledge and approached the door as though it might slam shut in his face. He reached it and stretched his finger towards the opening only to hold back in sudden fear. He had heard no sound from Menannon for a full day now. What would he find when the door opened?

LATE THAT AFTERNOON just before the evening rounds, old Peter's taking of extra food on his rounds was finally remarked by someone and the old gaoler was taken before his chief and questioned. It was the High One's own mercy that Firod was also talking with the gaol's chief warder that evening. Both men were sitting at the desk when Peter shuffled in and came to a creaking halt facing them. The meeting was brief and to the point.

"I've had it reported to me that you have been taking one more ration than you should be for several days now. Why?" The chief warder glanced through his stack of vellum then riveted the old fellow with a dark stare.

Peter shuffled a bit, but answered steadily enough. "One of me prisoners has the sickness these several days an' I've been takin' him an extra ration. Feed a cold, starve a fever as tha well knows."

"Has he recovered any?" the warder asked, more out of consideration for the health of his budget than the health of the prisoner.

"He's holdin' his own."

Peter shuffled a bit more and would not look his chief in the eye which action suddenly made Firod wonder whether the old fellow was feeding a sick Human or perchance a young Giant! Firod's heart nearly jumped into his throat at this thought, but he managed to keep his face still as he continued to listen.

"If he's no better in another day you will have to stop and he'll recover or not as he chooses. We can't afford to double feed any of our prisoners indefinitely." The chief warder waved his hand in dismissal and turned his attention back to the records he and Firod had been reviewing. Old Peter nodded his head and shuffled from the office. It was all Firod could do not to follow him on the instant, but he held his place and finished the interview so as not to raise any undue interest in the old fellow's prisoner.

FIROD REPORTED TO GORLANNDON a few turns of the hour later. "He was old and arthritic enough that I was able to overtake him ere he reached the kitchen door of the palace. I asked him where this prisoner was as he was complaining to one of the cooks how far he had to carry the food and how cold it was when he got it there."

Firod looked hard into the Giant's face as he spoke his next words.

"The prisoner he is double feeding lies beneath Nirna's tower! I believe the High One is directing us, as the most ancient part of the palace foundations lies beneath Nirna's tower on the southeast corner of the palace."

Firod quickly grabbed a clean piece of vellum and a stick of writing graphite and began to draw a hasty map.

"Here is Nirna's tower. It and the first quadrangle comprised the original palace. It was built when the need for a dungeon would have been most pressing. Here is the wall overlooking the Kidron gorge. I deem that somewhere directly below that tower lies an ancient cell into which your son has been thrown and left to die. It is the High One's own justice that the same tower which served as the path to safety for Nirna will also serve as the path to save Menannon. That old man is feeding Menannon! I would stake my life on it!"

Gorlanndon turned the vellum, his mind searching back for the ways of the palace he knew and compared it with the code. It seemed logical, as one needs must enter the current gaol levels by the western doors and descend two flights of stairs to reach the first corridor. Yes! It had to be there! Menannon had to be beneath the stones of the Citadel.

"It could still be just a Human whose illness has drawn on long...." Gorlanndon mused attempting to be logical about this.

"Not by your life," Firod snorted and Gorlanndon looked up locking eyes with his friend. He saw there total conviction and allowed himself to believe as well.

"I thank thee, High One," Gorlanndon whispered in heartfelt gratitude then turned his thoughts to the rescue.

It would be tonight, for he could not force himself to wait another moment should his own life depend upon it. Good! Stone, he knew. Stone, he could manage. Rock and stone, the Giant's demesne. Rock and stone, the Giant's delight! Gorlanndon took a deep settling breath. Though it had been long and long since he had seen battle, the skills needed were never forgotten nor blunted by disuse. Once something was learned by a Giant, it became a part of him and was his forever. He sat silently for a few moments considering his various options in this. Firod waited quietly.

At last Gorlanndon looked up. "I thank you for all your efforts in this my friend. I will attack the palace this night and rescue my son," he said as simply as he might say he was going to eat eggs for luncheon.

"Is that wise, old friend? Azuron has his Doomcriers on guard along with my palace regulars." The captain's face was tight with worry. "Giant though you are, you are only one against a hundred or more. What—"

"Clearly you are too young to have e'er seen a Giant in battle," Gorlanndon said, interrupting him, his smile grim. "Tonight will see my son set free or all dead." Gorlanndon cast a dark look at his friend. "I will not be stayed in this and there is naught that any mortal will be able to do to hinder me in any way. Only death will result if any assay to try."

Firod sat silently watching as Gorlanndon rose and opened an ancient, intricately carven wardrobe, withdrawing from its depths a set of arm bracers of some strange metal which seemed to glow soft green, illuminated by a light deep within them, giving impression of extreme depth and thickness though they were quite thin, not more than perhaps the thickness of a sheet of vellum. These Gorlanndon placed into his belt pouch and turned to the door.

"Are you taking no weapons?" Firod demanded, aghast.

"Against a palace and a middling small guard force I need none." The Giant's eyes sparked slightly red as he turned to go.

"I would there was a way I could aid you in this, old friend," the captain muttered softly, halting Gorlanndon with his hand on the door.

The Giant glanced over his shoulder. "There is one way."

"Name it!" snapped the captain, instantly ready.

"When I come, Firod, find some excuse to withdraw your men so I do not become a murderer of innocents."

With that, Gorlanndon opened the door of his study and disappeared into the darkness of the hallway. Firod sat for a few moments more, then left Gorlanndon's holding very thoughtfully. The gatewardens let him out the main gate and re-barred it behind him. He stood for a moment in the darkness there looking down at the lights of the city below. That it could have come to this in their beloved land was truly unbelievable. He shook his head and set off for the palace at a determined pace, intent upon seeing that his men were not involved in this night's doings. Let the Doomcriers face the Giant if they would, but his men would be no part of this.

IN THE CELL, Walderan swallowed hard, forcing his fear aside and with his heart in his throat, took hold of the edge of the covering stone and pulled. The door, which had taken the combined efforts of four full grown men to close, opened at the slightest touch and only a small whisper of scratching on the floor as it moved. He carefully threaded Menannon's arm back through the hole as he opened the door wide. What had been a hint of foulness before now struck him full in the face and made him gasp.

The low doorway revealed a cell built for Dwarves, a cell not more than three feet high and only slightly more than that wide. Within it Menannon lay stark naked and so covered with dried blood and dirt the true color of his skin could not be discerned.

The young Giant had been folded into a tight fetal position to push his long frame into the tiny space afforded. He lay perfectly still, his eyes half open, staring at nothing. Was he still alive? Walderan reached beneath his folded knees and felt for the pulse point in his throat. The pulse was there, barely tapping against the end of his fingers.

"Praise Thee, High One!" Walderan breathed, his eyes blurring with tears of relief and gratitude. He blinked hard and wiped his eyes on the sleeve of his robe then, with grim determination, set to work to free him from the cell. Menannon was so nearly unconscious that the task was almost insurmountable due to his sheer physical weight. It took well nigh two full turns of the hour to maneuver the Giant out of the tiny space and into the relative freedom of the larger cell. Yet still, the task of having to straighten his cramped limbs remained. The muscles in his legs were so cramped they were virtually paralyzed and thus could not move of their own volition and had to be straightened manually, a task that was both agonizing and slow. Walderan was forced to move the limbs mere fractions of an inch then massage out the new muscle cramps caused by the motion, then move them again.

He was less than halfway through the task when he heard the unwelcome sound of Peter coming down the corridor with his breakfast. Walderan experienced a moment's panic, then shook himself and threw himself to his knees in front of the grating so that Peter would hopefully concentrate on that point and not look within the cell to see that it had another occupant. He mentally crossed his fingers and prayed that Menannon would make no sound while the gaoler was there.

"Master, how be tha this mornin'?" Peter's gravely voice came through the grating soon enough as the old fellow put his torch in the bracket and knelt to slide the food tray through the grate. "Is tha cold still holdin' on?"

Walderan was taken by surprise by the question as he had all but forgotten his ruse to get extra food. "It's improving, but still there," he mentally crossed his fingers and said a brief prayer to be forgiven for still lying. "Are you getting into trouble for bringing me extra?"

"Nay, but the wife an' I be a bit concerned that tha's not feelin' well yet. Though how tha could be in this damp hole is more'n I can fathom." At that instant, Menannon groaned softly. "Master, don't be lyin' to me now. What's causin' tha to be groanin' such as that?" The old fellow was instantly concerned and began to stand to better see the harper.

"It's just a headache that has been plaguing me all night. I didn't e'en realize I'd made a sound. I'm sorry to worry you." Walderan quickly stood to block the barred window and prevent Peter from seeing in. He deliberately stretched, popping his back and neck as though he did indeed have the headache he claimed.

"Well, if'n tha's sure...." The old fellow stared hard at him studying his face as intently as the flickering torch light allowed. "Tha's not keepin' as clean as tha always do. They've done tha a great disservice sendin tha down here," he muttered darkly.

"I've not wanted to get wet here in the damp while I still have a cold lest it turn to a fever, so I've been saving up the wash water against the hour my cold subsides," Walderan replied, hoping this would satisfy his defender.

"That's a good idea, is that," Peter agreed, mollified. "I'll be on me way now, an I'll bring tha somethin' special for dinner. Make tha's headache go away." The old fellow shuffled off and Walderan turned to find Menannon awake and looking at him.

"I'm sorry, I nearly gave you away," the Giant whispered.

"It's alright lad, you've but given us an excuse for any noise we make getting your legs straightened out," Walderan assured him as he smoothed a tendril of dirty hair away from the healing wound on Menannon's face. Briefly, Walderan wondered what Menannon had thought at the first sight of him, though all the lad could have seen was his back as he treated with old Peter. Seventeen summers could not but have left its mark upon his visage as they had in the whitening of his hair and beard. At least the lad was not staring at him with revulsion. He quickly pushed the thought aside and set back to the work of straightening out the Giant's legs. Now that he was fully conscious, this was going to be an ordeal. Walderan looked around to find something soft to put in the lad's mouth to protect his teeth while they worked. The only thing he had was the clean cloth he had reserved for washing. Quickly he reached across the cell and took the cloth, rolled it up and came back to place it against Menannon's lips.

"Here lad, bite on this. It'll protect your teeth."

Menannon hesitated for a single heartbeat, then nodded and opened his mouth for Walderan to place the cloth, and when that was accomplished, the healer returned to the task at hand. A painful task, to be sure, and he was not relishing the prospect of adding to Menannon's pain, but there was no help for it. Full darkness had returned before the task was completed and Menannon lay out flat upon the floor. Walderan swore he would see himself damned to Hella before he would cause anyone such pain again.

The healer had to regain some of his own strength before he could muster the will power to retrieve some of his carefully harbored water and begin the process of cleaning the Giant. At last all was done as best as might be and Menannon's nakedness was covered as much as was possible with Wal-deran's second harper robe. The healer sat by Menannon's head, nearly exhausted, and leaned down to examine the wound on his face. The maggots had done their work well and all of the dead tissue was gone and the wound was actually healing. It would scar badly, but at least it no longer threatened the lad's life. For the thousandth time, Walderan found himself wishing for a harp. It would be so easy to heal the lad, but without one, the likelihood of his survival was remote.

Walderan dragged himself to his feet and went to his ledge where he had saved all of today's drinking water against the ending of his work. He took a long swallow then returned to Menannon and slid his arm under the Giant's shoulders and held the jug to his lips. Walderan ran his thumb across the fever blistered lips opening them for the life-giving water. He let a few drops of it moisten Menannon's mouth. At first there was no response, but then the lad began to drink thirstily.

"Easy, easy. Not too much or it'll come right back up," Walderan admonished him, holding the jug away. Menannon managed the slightest of nods as the healer eased him back down.

"Thank...you..." were all the words he could discern as Menannon's eyes closed and he sank into a deep though restless sleep. Walderan set the jug aside where it could not be spilled and laid his hand on Menannon's brow. The lad was burning with fever. With a deep sigh, Walderan laid down beside him. He left the candle burning and laid his hand companionably upon Menannon's chest knowing should the Giant awaken before daylight, he would be in desperate need of reassurance he was no longer in the dark rat hole and not alone. The healer fell into an exhausted sleep lulled by the sound of Menannon's steady though labored breathing. Peter came and went quietly, not wanting to disturb his prisoner's rest. The food he left was eaten only by the rats.

While Walderan and Menannon slept, Firod followed Gorlanndon back towards the heights of the Citadel, though he could not see him anywhere in all the dark beauty of the night. Ahead of him, the darkness stirred slightly as though it had taken on corporeal form and swayed with the breath of the night wind. A strange mist swirled and parted, only to thicken again farther along the Equian way until it flowed out onto the Mathematical Bridge. There it took more solid form, though what exactly that form was, Firod could not say, for its substance seemed to swallow light rather than reflect it. It might have been naught but a trick of the light, but Firod knew in his heart it was not. The staunch captain shuddered at what it might portend. A mighty shadow crossed the bridge and flowed into the darkness behind the Council Hall. Strange indeed were the ways of the Giants, and Firod realized that his friend had many secrets even from him. He lengthened his stride to a light run, intent upon reaching the palace before anything could happen. He arrived at the front gate of the palace close to find it barred and guarded by Doomcriers just as he had expected. Above on the wall, his own men stood uneasy watch.

"Let me pass," he commanded as he approached the gate, his voice was strident and echoed in the stillness. There was a slight hesitation, then one of the Doomcriers, a youngster who had until the sevenday before this served in the palace guard, turned and rang the entrance bell twice. The postern in the gate opened and he waved his former commander through, unable to quite meet his eyes. Firod nodded to him and stepped into the quiet close. The gate closed behind him. He stood still for a moment, surveying the area. There were armed Doomcriers everywhere, all along the great portico and along the walls as well as manning the newly erected guard towers at every corner of the walls on every level of the palace. Azuron quite obviously expected Gorlanndon to try something, but what that knowledge would avail him, Firod was not sure.

The captain strode out into the center of the close and placed his fingers into his mouth and whistled three sharp blasts and a final high piercing note, the signal for muster. Instantly his men began pouring down from the walls and out of the palace. There should be fifty and seven on duty this night and in short order all were assembled. They formed ranks and stood silently awaiting his orders.

"Gentlemen," Firod raised his voice so that he could be heard by all and impart his quickly concocted excuse for their departure, "there are reports of trouble down at the docks and the night watch there has requested reinforcements. As this area is so admirably guarded by our compatriots in the service of Lord Azuron, I deem it wise for us to march forth and answer this call."

He mentally crossed his fingers that his men would not find this order as peculiar as he did himself. There were a good many strange looks exchanged among his men, as all could hear that naught but laughter and a few dog barks were wafting in on the night breeze from the docks below. Despite this, no questions were asked. The time spent instilling strict discipline and in gaining his men's loyalty had been time well spent, it would seem. Firod gave the signal to march, at which they all turned as one and departed out through the great gate, for the first time in living memory leaving the Palace of Kalyria, as it were, unguarded. As they passed the Council Hall, Firod discerned a slight flicker of movement, something darker than the darkness of the night.

"Go with the High One, old friend," he breathed and led his men determinedly away from the coming battle.

Above them, Azuron stood in the darkness of the unlit throne room looking down across the close. He watched Firod and his men depart with a sense of consternation. Why were they leaving their posts? Firod never left his post even when point blank ordered to. So why was he leaving now and taking all of his men with him? It must mean the Giant was on the move. *Well so be it! This monster would not prevail against his Doomcriers and the powers of Khalandria. Let him come, let him rant, let him roar. It would avail him nothing.* Azuron turned contemptuously away to go to his chambers to sleep. His second-in-command would awaken him at need, though there was small chance of that.

In the darkness, Gorlanndon waited and watched as Firod led his men forth from danger. Good. Any fighting men left within the palace were the followers of the sorcerer and his fallen god and therefore deserved whatever happened. They had made their choice and turned their backs on the High One. Let Khalandria, the Dark One, look after his own! He waited until the guardsmen had the chance to reach the bottom of the hill before he made any further move. Then he detached himself from the shadows and edged around the back wall of the Council Hall until he stood between it and the overlook. From here in the light of day, one could gaze into the rocky depths of the Kidron gorge. There he halted and listened. Only the sounds of pacing guards and restless men within the palace close beyond him came to his closely attending ears. The outer wall of the close ran directly along the edge of the gorge, wrapping in the close within the solid protection of thick rock and stone. Azuron had doubled his watch. It would avail him nothing. For a moment, the wind ruffled Gorlanndon's hair and it almost seemed as though it bore with it the sound of Menannon's moaning. It was only a trick of the wind and his own emotional turmoil, but Gorlanndon knew that he must rescue his son this night or loose him forever.

He crouched in the darkness a full turn of the hour to allow any unrest among the guards at the leaving of Firod's men to settle back down. The great carillon chimed the mid-of-night.

"The time has come for this thrice-damned abomination to have ado with a man, not a boy," Gorlanndon muttered to himself.

He stood to his full height and pulled off his tunic, baring himself to the waist. With slow, deliberate movements, he took the bracers from his belt pouch and donned them, their strange flickering showing clearly in the darkness. For just a moment, he stood still, clearing his mind and concentrating on readying himself for battle. If any had been there to see it, they would have seen the Giant's skin darken and begin to glisten like mica in the moonlight as he applied one of the most basic gifts of the High One to his folk, the art of Stoneskin. Ready, he breathed a silent prayer, then let himself go heavy with the elemental heaviness of the great bones of the earth. Now invulnerable to all attack—even from Khalandrian Fire, as the bracers he wore were protection against that—he started forward. With each step, the earth trembled and groaned and a rumble echoed through the stillness of the night, causing many below in the city to start from their beds in fear. In three strides, the Giant crossed the intervening space and stood to face the lower wall of the palace close.

Rock and stone, the Giant's demesne! Rock and stone, the Giant's delight! Soundlessly, he laid his hands upon the stones, closed his eyes and concentrated on feeling his way into the very fabric of the wall. All about him, he could sense, then see the joins, the flaws, the cracks and weaknesses of the stones themselves. He flexed his mighty fingers, melding them with the crystalline structure of the stones, then as quietly and as inevitably as the workings of the elements upon a cliff, speeded up to the elapsing of a single heartbeat, Gorlanndon began to dismantle the wall. As effortlessly as a child tearing apart a snow fort, the Giant removed the veneer of the wall and began casting aside the core. Thirty feet of core veneer masonry melted away before him like spring snow in the sunshine. Nothing halted him, even boulders as big as small cottages were lightly tossed aside and others followed in a positive hail of destruction. A hole bloomed in the front corner of the wall, efficiently detaching the entire wall along the edge of the gorge from the stabilizing structure of its northern counterpart. With hardly any effort, Gorlanndon leaned his massive shoulder against the near end of this loose wall and shoved. With a long, grinding shriek, the entire wall along the edge of the gorge hurtled down into the depths below, leaving a great hole in the palace defenses that no number of living men could fill. Gorlanndon advanced through the breach with the awful inevitability of death itself into the palace close.

All about him, stunned Doomcriers stood or huddled in frozen panic as the very earth beneath their feet trembled and betrayed them, throwing them down before an advancing shadow which flickered with a strange green glow within like lightning seen afar. At the far corner of the close, Azuron's second in command shook himself from his stupor and began to drive his men with his short whip, forcing them to their feet.

"Shoot! Damn you! Shoot!" he roared at his archers. "It's the Giant! Kill him!"

All along the remaining wall, bows were readied and arrows flew, only to be thrown back from the shadow into the very faces of their masters as though deflected by a whirlwind. In the close below, men dragged themselves to their feet and drew their weapons then, with shrieks of fear and frenzy, threw themselves at the shadow. They entered it only to be deposited, dead and dying in heaps of mangled flesh in its tracks as it moved around the palace to the foot of Nirna's tower.

Nothing deterred Gorlanndon, as he once more melded with the stone before him and began to tear a great hole in the side of the tower. With the skill and art of a master stonemason, he dismantled the foundations, leaving only a single keystone to be removed from the center of his new arch in order to bring the tower tumbling to the ground.

Here he halted and for no other purpose than to give the warning his heart required, called out in a voice which thundered across the night, "MIND YOUR HEADS!"

With that admonition, Gorlanndon reached out as gently as though he but plucked a rare orchid and pulled that final stone, then jumped back, landing nearly halfway across the close, well out of danger. The same could not be said for those who had been attempting to thwart him. For them, the fabric of Nirna's tower became a rocky tomb.

The fall of the tower echoed through the night and shook the foundations of the city, drawing even Azuron from his bed. The sorcerer quickly rose and hastily donned his robes, intent upon seeing what was happening. He strode down the hall to the throne room, threw open the door and crossed to the windows once more and beheld the destruction. A veritable sea of rubble lay strewn about the close, glinting dully in the glow of the Dwarf lanterns.

"What is it?" The question came from the throne. He looked around quickly to find Norilendra sitting in the dark-ness there.

"What art thou doing out of thy bed? Thou needst thy beauty sleep!" he growled dismissively and turned back to the window, giving no further thought to she whom the rest of the world revered.

Almost, she began to stand, but then the ghost of the queen she had once been rose within her and she straightened, looking down her regal nose at this upstart Teluri.

"I will not ask you again. What is happening without, as I am assured that you have wit sufficient to answer me the first time!"

Almost, Azuron ignored her, but then he decided to humor the little Human. "The monster has come for its brat," he scoffed giving her a mocking little bow.

"Oh."

She sighed and stood, her steps nearly muffled by the renewed shattering of stone echoing from without and within the ancient palace. She reached the door and turned.

"You will find that love is stronger e'en than you, Dark One."

The door opened and she was gone.

Azuron stood a few minutes more listening to the shrieking and rending of stone and feeling the palace shudder to each new onslaught. Above all, he could hear the wails and screams of dying men as his Doomcriers continued to seek and fail to thwart the Giant.

"Useless, pitiful, Humans," he hissed and turned in disgust, his robes swirling about him, and stormed from the throne room intent upon reaching the cell where Menannon lay ahead of Gorlanndon.

"Love is a two-edged sword in this complex world of thy so called high one, little queen," he muttered as he went into the hall. Threaten the brat, control the sire! He would use Menannon to halt Gorlanndon, then both would die. The Teluri strode down the hall, his steps accompanied by the sounds of the Giant's progress.

IT COULD NOT HAVE BEEN MORE than a single turn of the hour past the mid-of-night when Walderan was awakened by a hideous rending shriek and a jarring which literally bounced him from the floor. Beside him, Menannon moaned in his sleep, but did not awaken. The rending shrieks continued with incredible regularity and the shaking grew in intensity until Walderan was sure that there was an earthquake going on, one that presaged the reawakening of Kalyria's volcanos. Down the air shaft came the sound of grinding, rending rocks mixed with the death screams of many people. Walderan hugged the floor, unable to grasp what was happening.

The jarring and sounds continued for what seemed to Walderan like many turns of the hour then there was a sudden silence. For just a moment, it held, then two things happened almost at once: the door of the cell slammed open to reveal a tall, bald person he had never seen before now holding high an open Dwarf lantern, the light of which nearly blinded the healer with its intensity and before his stunned mind could register more than the upswept eyebrows and pointed ears of a Teluri, the entire west wall shattered and the ceiling of the cell came off letting in a cloud of dirt and rocks and the smell of freshly plowed earth. The healer threw himself across Menannon's face attempting to shield him from the falling rubble. One large jagged fragment of ceiling crashed down from its place and careened across the space scraping across Walderan's shoulders as it went, barely missing the back of his head, though it did take a few of his long hairs with it to its final resting place in the far corner.

Walderan looked up through the choking cloud of dirt to find himself staring stupidly at a massive hole in the wall as a piece of the mountain seemed to crawl into the cell accompanied by rocks and dirt enough to fill half the tiny cell nearly to the ceiling. Walderan blinked dirt out of his eyes and stared at this strange apparition. Beyond all that was holy, it was a living breathing being, but so huge! The healer's whole being registered a shock as the apparition raised its head, barely missing a stalactite and he saw the face.

"Gorlanndon!" his lips formed the name, but there was not enough breath in his body to put sound to it.

The light filtering though the cloud of dirt showed the great Giant as plainly as full daylight. It could be none other. There was no doubt in Walderan's mind, though the last time he had seen him was as he himself had been dragged from the courtroom to be thrown into this very dungeon. Gorlanndon had looked after him, shaking his head in disagreement with the sentence passed.

Walderan opened his mouth to speak the name, but just as he did, there was a shriek from the other direction and a ball of black fire hurtled into his line of vision only to bounce off from Gorlanndon's dully glittering skin totally without effect and go careening around the small space causing more of the walls and ceiling to collapse as it exploded.

Having totally forgotten the other occupant of the cell in his surprise at seeing the Giant, Walderan turned his befuddled gaze towards the door where the Teluri had thrown down the Dwarf lantern and was spinning balls of black fire and hurling them at Gorlanndon so rapidly they were obscuring the hands that were forming them. For a man whose days for the last seventeen summers had passed in a blur of stultifying monotony, everything was happening too fast. All Walderan could do was hunch his shoulders, pull his head down like a turtle into its shell and cling to Menannon praying to the High One that he and his patient would not become inadvertent victims in this strange battle.

"You're efforts are ill spent, Teluri!"

Coming as it did amidst the hissing and crashing of the fireballs, the sound of Gorlanndon's voice startled the healer almost more than all the rest simply due to the sheer normalcy of it. The tone was as calm and offhand as one might have heard in a comment being made in a dining chamber rather than on a battlefield. Walderan forced himself to look up just in time to see Gorlanndon reach across the small cell and with total disdain shove the Teluri back out of the doorway and take a hold of the door itself and wrench the barrier shut in his face. As easily as another man might pick up a small block of firewood, Gorlanndon retrieved a huge chunk of fallen ceiling rock and wedged it with other rubble against the door, efficiently cutting off the Teluri's access and leaving the cell eerily lit by the strange green glow emanating from the bracers he wore.

Having dealt with the threat from Azuron, Gorlanndon turned back to the two figures stretched upon the floor and lowered his head until his nose was nearly touching Walderan's shoulder. In the uncertain light he could see that it was indeed Menannon who lay beneath the cell's other occupant. He heaved a gusty sigh of relief which turned again to worry almost instantly. He had indeed found his son, but was he alive or dead? With gentle strength, Gorlanndon pulled Walderan bodily aside as though the man were simply a blanket covering his son's body then reached out to touch the pulse point in Menannon's throat. His hand halted mid-movement as Walderans' voice sounded near his elbow, scratchy from a throat full of dirt.

"Lord Gorlanndon," the healer wheezed.

"Is he dead?" the great Giant asked, not turning his gaze from Menannon's battered face. His voice had a distinct quaver in it.

The healer cleared his throat and replied softly, "Nay, though he is like to die unless I can find a harp."

At the word 'harp', Gorlanndon looked around, startled. "Walderan? You're still here! I was informed you had died summers ago."

He looked hard at the healer and was not surprised to see his long hair and shaggy beard were snow white and his face pale and gaunt from which housing stared eyes filled with the light of reason. Despite all, the healer was obviously still sane, almost excessively so.

"Nay, the High One has ruled that I still exist," Walderan replied wryly.

"Come quickly then. We need to depart this pit ere Azuron gets his wits together enough to break the door. Menannon," Gorlanndon turned back and whispered his son's name, laying a gentle hand upon his chin to turn his face to him. His heart caught at the condition the boy was in, but he forced himself to push his emotions aside and concentrate on the task at hand: getting them all out of here.

"Menannon, come back to me. I can't move you if you are senseless." Menannon groaned and his eyes almost fluttered open. "Come on boy. You can do it. Come back to me."

Gorlanndon pleaded as the sound of explosions began from beyond the blocked door. At last, Menannon's eyes opened and he looked up in disbelief at the elder Giant leaning over him.

"Father?"

"Aye, boy. I'm here. Stay with me," Gorlanndon whispered as he slid his arms under his son's body and scooped him from the floor.

Menannon's fever was so high the touch of his skin nearly burned Gorlanndon's forearms and chest. The Giant hesitated for just a moment, then turned to crawl out of the cell, almost leaving the healer behind, but then remembered the Human and turned back.

"Climb onto my back," he instructed, turning so that Walderan could do so. "Stand on my belt and put your arms around my neck."

Walderan did as he was bid, though all he could reach was his fingers around the mighty Giant's neck. As soon as he was secure, Gorlanndon stood and climbed back out of the cell up the shaft he had so hastily created and into the clear night air followed dimly by the popping echoes of Azuron's efforts to break the cell door far below.

All around them was a scene of destruction. Gorlanndon had torn apart the entire south east corner of the palace and its foundations leaving a great gaping hole which yawned darkly in the night. All about amidst the rubble lay the broken bodies of men, strangely garbed to Walderan's eyes. They were soldiers of some kind, but none with which he was familiar. A few of their yet breathing fellows scrambled away from the Giant allowing him unhindered passage to the gates. Gorlanndon did not bother with the niceties of shoving aside the timber barring the entrance. He simply slammed the flat of his sandaled foot against it and broke the gate as efficiently as any battering ram. Watched by the remains of Azuron's Doomcriers, Gorlanndon walked out into the night and crossed the silent plaza in full possession of the treasure for which he had come.

Below them, the city lay in silence. Not even a dog barked or a voice laughed, its inhabitants apparently awaiting the outcome of all the noise and shaking. The soft night wind blew tendrils of Walderan's long hair across the healer's face and the deep breath he instinctively took almost overwhelmed him with its sweet purity. That he was truly free had not quite penetrated the fog still filling his mind. A nightjar whistled past them just above Gorlanndon's head, its call echoing eerily in the silence.

Before Walderan had time to more than glance at the passing bird, the Giant's long strides had brought them across the plaza to the entrance of the Mathematical Bridge where they suddenly halted. Menannon had nearly passed out causing Gorlanndon to almost drop him. The elder Giant laid him down as quickly as he could.

"Come on, boy. Don't leave me now. Azuron will be out soon enough and I can't lift you if you are senseless. You become heavy as the very bones of the earth." For just a moment, Gorlanndon nearly panicked.

"Lord, touch the wound on his face," Walderan instructed from his place on the Giant's back. "It will cause him sharp pain, enough to jar him awake, but not enough to make his senses flee."

Reluctantly, Gorlanndon did as he was bid and Menannon, hissing with pain, opened his eyes.

"Forgive me, boy, for getting you into this. I should have sent you home when you came back, but I had not the strength."

Gorlanndon picked Menannon back up and started across the bridge. At the farther end he saw the forms of armed men and stiffened. While he himself was invulnerable to attack neither Menannon nor Walderan were and in open battle both must be killed. He hesitated, not quite knowing what to do, when a voice rang out of the group and Firod stepped onto the end of the bridge.

"Come across, old friend, and be escorted home!" he called for all the world to hear, thereby openly declaring himself enemy to Azuron. Gorlanndon's heart eased and he quickly crossed the bridge and attained his own villa, the entire palace guard of Kalyria at his back.

Skendrin opened the gate just as his master reached it, having set a watch for this very event. The Giant entered his holding to find all his personal warband armed and in the courtyard. At the sight of them, Firod dismissed all but a company of his own men. These he set to watch the perimeter of Gorlanndon's villa and then turned and shut the gate himself. There was a great deal of muttering among the members of Gorlanndon's warband as they watched their master carry his son across the courtyard and into his home, Skendrin leading the way with Firod treading angrily behind. Just as the captain was about to close the door, he heard one old voice louder and angrier than the rest.

"I warned him, but the lad wouldn't listen, an wilt tha look as to what they've done to him."

"This upstart Teluri has been and gone too far this time!" another voice chimed in and there were many growls of agreement.

Even as Firod closed the villa's doors, Azuron emerged from the hole the Giant had torn in the side of the palace, his face and robes smeared with dirt and unseemly debris from the dungeon. With angry strides he crossed the courtyard, not even bothering to step over or around the remains of his followers that lay in his path. He entered the palace, calling stridently for his commanders, a clean robe and the queen to attend upon him in the royal bathing chamber.

He would sweep away all resistance to his plans, no matter what the cost. He would be king of this piddling little island and his first royal act would be to see that thrice-damned Giant beheaded!

CHAPTER 23
(SUMMER OF THE WORLD 6097)

ONCE INSIDE THE VILLA, Gorlanndon quickly made his way to Menannon's chamber and laid his son upon the bed. Almost as an afterthought, he knelt, allowing Walderan to climb down from his broad back.

Heedless of the fact the he was outside the dungeon walls for the first time in seventeen summers, the healer immed-iately came to the side of the bed and stooped over his patient as Gorlanndon and Firod opened the Dwarf lanterns about the chamber then both turned to look at Menannon. At the first sight, Firod made a low sound as though he had just been kicked in the stomach. He raised his glance to Gorlan-ndon's shuttered face and caught breath to speak, but before he could do so, Skendrin reappeared followed by Clarinda and two stillroom helpers bearing a huge cauldron of hot water and a mound of clean cloths. The cook carried a tray piled high with bottles and bags of herbs and simples and all other such equipment as would be needed. Gorlanndon and Firod retreated to the windows where the elder Giant leaned upon the sill, heedless of the dirt and gore that still begrimed him. Firod sat on Menannon's footstool, it fitting him better than the chairs in the chamber. At the bed, Clarinda and her assistants succeeded in assisting the healer to fully clean the young Giant, dress his surface hurts and array him in a sleeping robe of the softest linen.

"Alright, we have done as we can for him, now." Clarinda straightened up and gave a meaning glance to her assistants who instantly took the dirty cleaning cloths, Walderan's now soiled extra robe, sheets and cauldron between them and left the chamber. As they departed, the cook turned to Skendrin

"If ye would be takin' Master Walderan to a chamber where he can clean himself and rest, I'll be sendin' along a goodly supper in a nonce," she finished, this last to the healer.

For a moment, Walderan stood stunned into total stillness by hearing himself called "Master" in such a normal manner by someone other than a gaoler.

"Go on then, Walderan." Gorlanndon's voice broke into his thoughts, recalling him to the situation at hand.

"I should stay with him—." Walderan began, but the Giant cut him off with a shake of his head.

"You have all done what can be at the moment, so go with Skendrin and rest yourself. There will be great need for you later if he is to live."

Still reluctant to depart, Walderan leaned over the bed one last time, then straightened with a sigh and raised his gaze to meet the Giant's.

"I won't mince words with you, my Lord. Without a harp, I cannot be sure of his life. The infection has gone too deep and I fear there are other internal hurts I can only sense." The healer looked from Gorlanndon to Firod and back. "Is there a harp anywhere about? Menannon informed me of the destruction of the harper hall and, presumably, of all that it held."

Gorlanndon and Firod exchanged meaningful glances, then the Giant cleared his throat. "There is one harp of which I know, but whether we could obtain it is beyond my ken." A wry expression lit his features.

"What harp?" Walderan demanded sharply.

"It belonged to a dear friend of—." Firod began.

"Whose it is is of no consequence!" the healer growled again, interrupting him impatiently with a sharp glance at Menannon's still face. "All that matters is where it is and can we get to it."

"Whose it is is very much to the point," Firod informed him curtly and the Giant nodded.

"All right then. Whose is it?" Walderan ground out, holding onto his fraying patience with both hands.

"It belongs to the queen, for it was a prized possession of her late consort. Ronirinen King played as well as many a journeyman harper and took great delight in the art." Gorlanndon spoke quietly, crossing his arms over his chest, the glitter of his bracers bathing him in a strange glow. "She has treasured it all of these summers and let no one play it, keeping it ever in the treasure chamber."

"Surely she will allow its use by a healer!" Walderan stood up straighter and looked once again all of his rank and position despite his filthy hair and tattered robe.

"Under ordinary circumstances, she probably would," Gorlanndon agreed. "But we are talking about the healing of my son, a man whom she hates with a strange passion."

Firod nodded in agreement.

"Have things changed so greatly in seventeen summers, that a child of the High One would let a man die for personal spite?" Walderan frowned in bewilderment.

"Aye. She is a spiteful wench and no mistake," Clarinda informed him, taking his arm. "But now ye must to yer rest and I'll be sendin' ye some food and clothes." She motioned to Skendrin to lead him out.

"Come, Master." The steward inclined his head and held the door open, indicating that Walderan should precede him.

"I must allow as how you are right, then. If there is to be no harp, the crisis will come soon enough and we will all need our rest and strength."

Resignedly, he turned and preceded the steward from the chamber. The door closed softly behind them and Clarinda rounded on her master her hands placed firmly upon her hips.

"You need to clean yerself and rest as well," she scolded, looking him up and down as if he were a recalcitrant school boy. "You look like somethin' as the cat dragged in and yer gettin' dirt all over the place." With that, she turned on her heel and briskly left the chamber.

"Far be it from Clarinda to simply tell you that she has been worrying all night and is glad you are safely home." Firod shook his head and half grinned.

"She's a Dwarf," Gorlanndon replied knowing that was explanation enough for the captain to understand the words of a life-long retainer to her beloved master.

There was a brief silence broken only by Menannon's harsh breathing, then Gorlanndon stood and crossed to sit on the side of his son's bed. Firod came to stand beside him. Together they looked long at Menannon's battered face, each feeling the heat of his fever, though neither touched him. On the bedside table, a square of linen lay forgotten by the stillroom staff. It was dark with Menannon's blood in several places.

"Do you see what soaks this cloth?" Gorlanndon picked it up and held it for Firod to see.

Firod glanced down then returned a sorrowing gaze up to the face of his old friend and nodded.

"This is the life blood of my son." Gorlanndon spoke with a quiet deliberation that was far more unsettling than if he had shouted. "Every drop of this is dearer to me than all the riches of the High One's world. I warn you, Firod, should Walderan fail and my son die, I will tear this city apart stone by stone until I find that thrice-damned shaven-headed sea slug and I will destroy him and all who follow him!"

Gorlanndon threw the linen on the floor as though he threw down a gauntlet before Azuron. Firod's gaze followed the course of the cloth then turned back to Gorlanndon.

"In this, will I aid you, not thwart you, for I serve Kalyria, not Azuron or a queen gone mad."

His voice was low and earnest and he held out his hand. Gorlanndon took his arm in his great hand and they hand-fasted their pact, though there was no need. They were comrades lifelong and would not fail each other.

"Come, let us retire to the chapel and pray as neither of us has e'er prayed before … for Menannon's life."

"Right willingly, I come."

TOO RESTLESS TO SLEEP, Walderan determined to return to Menannon's chamber as soon as he had refreshed himself. He was dazzled by the chamber to which Skendrin led him with its tables and chairs, clothes press and wardrobe and soft bed, complete with sheets and pillows, and the High One be praised, windows! He could not help himself, but he had to dash across the chamber, as soon as the steward closed the door, and threw open the first window. He stood there for several long minutes, drinking in the moonlight and fresh, flower-scented air. Almost reluctantly, he turned back into the chamber, but it was beyond his strength to close that precious window. The cool air wafted around him as he examined the rest of the chamber, admiring the well-filled library shelves and wonder of wonders, a bathing chamber attached by an adjoining door.

He walked in to find that not only did the bathing chamber have the needed garderobe and shower, but a soaking tub as well. Without a second thought, he threw off his robe and almost ran into the shower and nearly cried when, with one twist of a dolphin, hot water rained down upon his upturned face. He washed himself until he was sure he had nearly washed his skin from his body and his hair from his head for the pure bliss of being able to do so.

A long soak took the rest of two full turns of the hour before he could bring himself to wrap up in a large towel and return to the bed chamber. He discovered that in his absence someone had entered and filled the wardrobe and clothes press completely full of clothing for him. They had even laid out on the bed a set of small clothes, a white linen chemise, a kirtle of light green linen and an over robe of dark green sorak much worked along its hems and front with threads of gold and silver and small beads of precious stones. Long hose and soft leather short boots completed the apparel. It was clothing fit for a king. Walderan donned it gratefully. He could not begin to articulate even to himself how good it felt to have taken an actual bath and be dressed in something other than just his harper's robe. There were soft leather thongs laid out to bind back his hair and beard. Skendrin had offered to call him the household barber, but he had declined, saying that there would be time enough for that when

Menannon's life was no longer in peril. He had just finished dressing when there was a soft knock on his door.

"Come" he called instinctively falling back into his old way as a master harper. The door opened swiftly and a young blonde housemaid entered bearing a try of covered dishes and cutlery. She was followed by a younger, dark haired girl who bore a large carafe and chalice. These they set upon the hearth side table and withdrew with courtesies and smiles, leaving the healer to eat in peace. Despite his concern for the young Giant, the appeal of a hot meal and wine after seventeen summers of abstinence could not be resisted and he ate his fill before returning to his self-appointed duty.

Walderan pushed open the door to Menannon's chamber to find Gorlanndon seated on the floor near the side of the young Giant's bed, close enough to reach him at need, but not so close that the light from the partially open Dwarf lantern by which he was reading would bother the youngster's sleep. Gorlanndon had bathed and donned a white chemise with a dark brown kirtle over it, tight fitting brown hose and soft leather tall boots rather than his usual bare legs and open sandals. In the dim light, it almost looked as though he were wearing armour. The healer nodded to Gorlanndon and stepped to the side of the bed where he laid his hand on Menannon's brow, though he did this more out of habit than necessity, for the heat of the young Giant's fever could be felt even as far away as the edge of his bed. With a sigh, Walderan sat on the side of the bed and turned to the lad's sire.

"Lord Gorlanndon, the chance of his survival is slim to none without a harp." He spoke softly. "E'en with a harp, it is not certain that I shall be able to save him, as the infection that has spread throughout his body is boiling him alive."

Gorlanndon set down the codex he had been reading. As Walderan had expected, it was a well-worn copy of the Word Hoard of the High One.

"I shall assay the attempt to get the harp you need, but I do not deem there is much of a chance that she will give it me. In fact I deem she would rather see it destroyed than used to save my son's life." Gorlanndon kept his voice soft enough that the healer had to concentrate to hear his words.

"What could have produced such a virulent hatred in her heart for the lad?" Walderan wondered, almost more to himself than to Gorlanndon.

"I know not, but it grows with each passing hour. Be that as it may, if you will stay with him, I will go to the palace."

Gorlanndon began to rise as he spoke, but Walderan halted him with a swift hand on his arm.

"Lord, the palace will be alive with guards after this night's work. Is there not someone else you could send who would be less...um...!" words failed him and he stammered to a halt under the slight grin quirking the Giant's lips.

"There are many less conspicuous than I, I agree." His grin turned into a brief smile at the look of chagrin on the healer's face. He quickly turned serious again. " Howe'er that is, there is none other who has the slightest chance of persuading her that we must have the harp else he will surely die."

Gorlanndon stood and leaned down to kiss Menannon's brow and whisper another in a long litany of prayers for his life. Then he straightened and left the chamber, leaving Walderan torn between relief that he might actually have a harp to attempt to save the lad's life and the fear that Gorlanndon would not live to bring it back.

Outside, the night was nearly spent, the darkness smelling of morning though the moon had yet to set. Gorlanndon made his way quickly and silently back the way he had come, across the Mathematical Bridge and into the plaza surrounding the government buildings. Oddly, there was no noise. No loud voices or furious pounding, nothing to indicate that Azuron had his remaining Doomcrier guards attempting to shore up the walls of the palace or dig their comrades out of the rubble. On the pediment of the Council Hall, the Eyes of the High One burned bright and steady, visible proof that the High One was still in control on Kalyria, hard though Azuron was trying to oust Him. Gorlanndon saluted the Eyes and glided past to the wall surrounding the palace.

He halted in the shadows between the two buildings and listened. The was no movement beyond the wall, no pacing of guards, no thunking of spears momentarily rested upon the ground as soldiers halted briefly in their endless rounds. No guards had been re-posted in the close to assure the safety of the Queen now that Firod's men no longer held to their posts. So much for Azuron's much vaunted care for the queen's person. Anyone could now walk unimpeded into the royal residence. Gorlanndon shook his head in disgust. The mere fact that there was likely not a soul on Kalyria who would wish to harm the queen was beside the point. There should be guards.

He detached himself from the shadows and walked quietly into the palace close, every sense alert in case this was a trap. Surely Azuron knew he would come for the harp. Norilendra must have told him of Walderan's skills and he would know of Menannon's need. Nothing could be more logical than to set a trap for him when he came. He was in full view of anyone looking out of the palace windows, but apparently no one was, for the Giant walked across the close and up the portico stairs without the slightest impediment. Not even a cat crossed his path. He gained the entrance hall and closed its great doors with the merest whisper of sound. The builders of Kirith Kalyria were legendary in their skill. There were no Dwarf lanterns open, no night lights of any kind. Luckily, there was just enough moonlight still filtering in the westernmost windows to allow him to see his was along the many halls and up the staircases to the treasure chamber where he knew the harp was kept.

Gorlanndon entered the last corridor as silent as a shadow and halted. Here at last was a light. A slight glow emanated from the crack beneath the throne room door; someone was within. Was it Azuron or the queen? No other would dare to occupy the chamber this late at night. Almost, he moved past and continued to the treasure chamber, but then he halted. Beyond all reason, he knew that the harp was in the throne room and he must enter there to retrieve it. Reluctantly, he opened the door and ducked inside.

There on the throne, Norilendra sat silently, watching the door. The light of a single, shaded Dwarf lantern glowed on a low table next the throne. She was dressed simply in a white linen sleeping robe, her dark hair an unbound river down her back. The rest of the chamber was lit by only the moonlight streaming in from the uncurtained windows, its corners dark with shadows and stillness. Beside the queen on a tall stand rested an ornately decorated whitewood harp, its silver strings glittering in the soft light. Gorlanndon halted just inside the door and they studied each other. Silence stretched endlessly until at last, she broke it.

"I knew you would come for it," she said softly. "I will give it you if you return my daughter to me and for no other cause."

Gorlanndon finished closing the door, crossed to the throne and knelt beside it.

"We are at an impasse then, my Queen, for I know not where she is. That knowledge lies with Menannon and he is dying and the harp alone can save him."

Following these words, a deeply troubled silence fell upon the room. When it had stretched beyond bearing, Norilendra rose and crossed to stand by the windows overlooking the harbor. Her movement released him from ceremony and Gorlanndon came directly to the crux of the matter.

"Why do you so hate my son?"

There was no heat in his voice, only a soft wistful quality that whispered in the chamber of summers gone by in which he had been the queen's confidante and mentor. Once, he had been second sire to a lonely girl sent here by her noble family to be raised as the consort of the Prince Royal. His tone echoed of those times.

"I must hate him," she said, not turning her gaze from the moonlit view without. Her voice was soft and passionless. "I must hate him, for she loves him."

When Gorlanndon did not speak, she turned her head to glance over her shoulder. They both knew the *she* of whom she spoke. At his silence, she felt impelled to explain farther.

"Your son is all that a man should be. He is magnificent of face and form, gifted and honorable beyond measure. The High One has placed within him the seeds of greatness which will grow to glorious fruition unless Menannon himself chooses otherwise. All this makes him fey and dangerous, for he attracts her like a moth to a flame. His very existence will mar her forever. Never will she be happy, for her heart will be in his keeping though her body belongs to another. I would that they had ne'er met or that he would die. For only then will she know peace. Mourn and go on is the way of the world, but with him living, she will never love another. I would have spared her the heartbreak of ever knowing him if I could have."

These words brought to Gorlanndon's mind a tall young man with hair the color of flame, a blue-eyed man with a strong arm and a ready laugh. The captain of the guard when Norilendra had been but a lass hardly older than Menannon was now. He had taught her to ride, to hunt and the use of weapons. Ever had the girl followed in his wake and loved him with all the fervor of her youthful heart. Cold duty and Kalyrian law, heredity and Gorlanndon's counsel had forbidden the girl's love. But nothing could forbid the woman's. An empty shell had stood at the back of Ronirinen King. A queen with a heart of snow.

Until this moment, Gorlanndon had not realized the full depth of feeling Norilendra had possessed for her shining cavalier. She had hidden it well, never letting even her consort suspect her heart was given to another. Was that why she was so easily manipulated by Azuron? Was her heart frozen and she cared naught for who possessed her body? Gorlanndon studied her where she had turned once more to look beyond the windows into history, the moonlight giving her white robe a slightly bluish cast as though she were truly made of ice. Many actions and reactions of Norilendra's over the long summers he had known her now made sense. As the silence grew again he wondered, was the fellow still in the world or had he passed out of it into the halls of waiting? When all this was set to rights and the balance restored to their land, Gorlanndon decided he would seek to know the answer to that question for her peace of mind, but for now Menannon's life was at stake.

The Giant cleared his throat and spoke calmly, knowing that he now tread a dangerous path.

"My son is not responsible that in his youth and strength he has attracted Nirna."

"No, he is not," she agreed much to his surprise, but her next words shook him to the core. "No, the High One is responsible for ruining her life as well and He is the one who should be punished."

The queen's words were spoken without heat as though they were a fact too settled to be disputed.

"Menannon's death will free her and punish the High One, for I deem He has great plans for your son and the youth's death will thwart them."

Gorlanndon struggled with the knowledge that Norilendra had, beyond all reason, grown to hate the High One. That knowledge made him pity her the more. She had done what was required of her for the good of their people, but in so doing she had sacrificed her own soul, for she had done it resentfully. In the hands of the High One, all things turn to good if we will but allow Him the freedom. Norilendra had not allowed Him that freedom and in so doing, had doomed herself and now the rest of them for in the end, her bitterness and hatred were allowing Azuron and his evil god Khalandria a foothold upon their shores and would force Menannon to die.

"Nori," he said using his pet name for the girl he had once nurtured. He kept his voice soft suddenly realizing that she stood on the brink of madness. "The High One will not be punished by Menannon's death, only the boy will. For the High One has time beyond all measure and He will but raise up another suited for His purpose. Nori, your's is not a heart of vengeance. At least let us try to heal the boy. Allow me the harp that Walderan may make the attempt."

"Walderan? Is he not the harper who sought to heal my

consort all those summers ago?" she glanced questioningly over her shoulder, her voice sounding suddenly young and vulnerable as though his use of the name Nori had touched some forgotten place in her spirit where the girl she once had been yet lived. "You pleaded for clemency, if I remember correctly."

"Aye."

She turned back and after a few moments, began to speak to herself as though she carried on both sides of an argument. It was an eerie thing to listen to.

"Menannon is young not yet one and twenty...he is old enough to know better. He is a fine boy... he is a lascivious monster who lures trusting hearts to their destruction. Were he mine, I would have great pride in him...there is nothing to be proud of in such a one as he. In a way, he is mine for he is one of my people and I his Dowager Queen."

She ceased speaking and seemed to consider her own words for when next she spoke, it was of herself alone, her voice no longer holding any trace of Nori.

"Queen of Kalyria....Queen of the greatest kingdom in all Linden...Queen by the will of the High One...Queen by the laws of the High One...Queen by the SPITE of the High One...!"

She nearly spit the last words, then grew silent once more. At last, she turned and faced Gorlanndon full on, the soft light of the Dwarf lantern casting weird shadows across her face and making her eyes look as though they were the color of obsidian and not their own lapis lazuli.

"By the High One's good offices and your strength, you have your pet healer on the leash again. Walderan, the charlatan who swore to heal my consort all those long summers ago." She suddenly threw back her head and laughed a horrible grating laugh. "What justice this is. The very harper who killed my consort will now kill your son!"

She came then and wrenched the harp from its stand and thrust it at him.

"May it bring you as much joy as it has brought me!"

Turning swiftly, she left the chamber, the door closing so

softly it was as though she had never been there at all.

GORLANNDON RETURNED to Menannon's chamber to find another sort of battle raging. Firod, Skendrin and four of the still room staff were fighting to hold Menannon down while Walderan sought to force water into his mouth by the expedient of dipping a cloth into a basin of cold water and dripping it into his mouth through his nearly locked teeth. From the looks of the bloodied faces of all, the battle had not been going well.

Walderan glanced over his should as the door opened and saw the Giant. "The fire has gone to his brain and he convulses! Get something to bathe him in and fill it with cold water!"

"I have the harp——," Gorlanndon began, but the healer cut him off, shouting over the sounds of Menannon's thrashing.

"The harp be damned! If we don't break this fever, he will be dead ere I can strike a note. GO!"

Without another word, Gorlanndon whirled and ran from the chamber, taking the harp with him. He set it on the long table in the kitchen as he bolted out the back door headed for the stables. There he wrenched a huge watering trough from its moorings and hauled it into the villa to the nearest bathing chamber where he broke the side out of the shower and shoved the end of the trough under the water tap and turned it on full force filling the container with water achingly cold from the depths of the Equian. When it was full, he threw the full force of his Giantish strength against it, picked it up and strode out of the chamber and down the hall to his son's chamber heedless of the water sloshing out at each step. Once there he smashed the door off from its hinges with one blow of his foot and set the trough down in the middle of the floor.

On the bed, Menannon was so far gone in convulsions that they had been forced to put the hilt of Firod's dagger between his teeth to keep him from swallowing his tongue. Gorlanndon swept the attendants aside with one thrust of his arm and took Menannon up in his arms and dumped him into the near freezing water. The youth fought anew at this onslaught, but the great Giant held him hard, forcing him to stay in the trough. For many moments, it seemed as though they were too late, but then by the High One's blessing and the temperature of the water, Menannon's body began to cool and the convulsions slowed, then finally stopped and he lay back limp with exhaustion.

"Get him out of the water and into dry clothing ere he catches his death from pneumonia," Walderan ordered as he rose from where Gorlanndon had thrown him in his haste to get to his son.

Everyone moved to do as he bid, Gorlanndon holding Menannon against his chest while the others fetched dry bedding, sleeping robes and towels.

"Where is the harp?" Walderan demanded, looking about and not seeing it in the chamber.

"I left it in the kitchen," Gorlanndon informed him as he sat down on the edge of the bed and drew the wet robe from his son's body and aided Firod in replacing it with a dry one.

Without a word, Skendrin dashed out of the chamber, climbing over the shattered door and went to fetch the instrument. By the time the steward returned with the harp and a few of the household staff to clean up the water and the remains of the door, Menannon had been returned to his bed where he lay as pale and still as one already dead. Skendrin glanced questioningly at Firod where the captain stood near the window holding a clean cloth to his bleeding nose. Firod held up his hand in a gesture of success, but said nothing. Gorlanndon sat on the side of the bed holding his son's hand and Walderan had drawn up a chair next the head. Skendrin held the harp while the healer removed his over-robe with its metal thread and loosed his hair and beard in preparation for the sacred ritual about to be performed. When he had done, the steward handed him the instrument and stepped back to help his staff set the chamber to rights.

Walderan took the harp reverently into his hands as though it had not been seventeen summers since he had last held an instrument. With not the slightest hesitation, he quickly tuned the harp and then glanced up, ready to begin. Everyone in the chamber removed any metal about their person and knelt in the High One's honor.

Walderan bowed his head. "High One," he said, his voice strong and sure, "guide Thou my hands to Thy glory and his good. Amen!"

With that, he struck the first chord which rang out true and clear then settled down to play as he had never played before. Out of respect for the ritual being conducted, everyone else hurriedly finished their cleaning and left the chamber, all save Gorlanndon who continued to hold Menannon's hand against his heart, his head bowed and lips moving in silent prayer.

It was nearly sunset when at last, and almost beyond hope, Menannon gave a great sigh and settled into the deep, renewing sleep of the newly healed. At this sound, Gorlanndon opened his eyes and glanced from Walderan to his son and back. The healer stilled the strings of his harp and sighed, relaxing back into his chair holding the harp loosely. Gorlanndon laid Menannon's hand down on the bed and touched his brow. By the blessing of the High One, it was cool and his breathing was deep and easy. Even the wound on his face had closed down to a jagged white line. The Giant blew out a breath that sounded like it came all the way from his toes and turned a huge smile upon the healer.

"I thank you with all of my heart," he said and inclined his head, giving the Master Harper his due.

"It was my honor," Walderan smiled in return and glanced at the harp. Only then did he realize that his fingers were bleeding and obviously had been for some time to judge by the amount of blood on the strings. "Well, you would think I'd not played in a while," he grinned and began to laugh. Gorlanndon joined him, both of them near hysteria after the strain they had been under.

The sound of their hilarity traveled through the villa and quickly told the tale of the healer's success without the need of words. Soon healer and sire could hear the sounds of cheering, even from within Menannon's bed chamber.

"What method did you use to accomplish this miracle," Gorlanndon asked, a twinkle in his dark eyes as he took the harp from Walderan and set it on the hearth table then sat back down on the edge of the bed and began to treat the healer's injured fingertips with salve and bandages from the bedside table supply.

"The only one capable of healing not only injury, but fever as well. Reuel's method." He stopped speaking, a questioning look in his grey eyes, clearly thinking to be chastised for risking Menannon's life by using a method with which he had so famously failed. Gorlanndon only smiled and nodded as he worked.

"I thought you might be, as there was about this healing an unfamiliar feeling.It was as though you reached out to calm my spirit as well as his. I commend your choice and skills."

Walderan relaxed with a grin and glanced at Menannon.

"I know he will never consider it a blessing that he was thrown into that cell, but for me it was and I shall always be grateful to him and to you for my deliverance." The healer looked up with a question writ large upon his face though he had not the heart to voice it.

"Nay, I shall not see you returned to the dungeon." Gorlanndon smiled knowing full well to what question Walderan sought the answer. "You are and always have been innocent of murder. Fear not you are free and shall remain so."

Gorlanndon finished his ministrations and stood holding out a hand to aid Walderan in rising from the chair.

"Come, then, old friend and let us seek our own beds as he should sleep peacefully at least a full threeday and perhaps more. Clarinda will set a watch upon him and call us at need."

The Giant motioned for the healer to precede him then turned and, leaning down, kissed his son's brow, rejoicing anew at the coolness of his skin against his lips. With another soft prayer of thanksgiving, he followed the harper from the chamber and sought his own bed nearly as exhausted as the healer.

Outside in the courtyard, Firod leaned against a pillar. Earlier in the day, Skendrin had called him to the gate to hear the words of the city criers as they made their appointed rounds along the Equian way announcing all the news of the city for the day. This noon they had sad news to cry indeed. Lord Azuron was announcing that there had been an earthquake in the night which had caused an ancient fault in the fabric of the Citadel to shift and the front right-hand tower of the palace to collapse. Sadly there had been considerable loss of life among those who served at the palace, but the Queen was unharmed and the hole in the side of the building was being walled up until the tower could be rebuilt properly.

Firod looked across the close and watched as a small girl, the child of one of Gorlanndon's servitors, played near a bench, dressing her doll and singing it a lullaby. Not for the first time, he thanked the High One that his own family had been gotten away to safety by the good offices of the Giants and wondered how all of this was going to end. Whatever the end, he stood ready to see it through. Evil must be confronted, no matter the cost, and he feared that this time, the cost would be high. At least his family was safe...for now.

GORLANNDON HAD BEEN EXACT TO THE HOUR in his estima- tion of how long Menannon would sleep, for at first light of the fourth day after his healing, Menannon opened his eyes in sense and health feeling a bit disoriented and ravenously hungry. He was stunned to find himself in his own chambers, the birds of the painted sky nearly flying about above him in their reality. How he had gotten here was something totally beyond his ken, for the last he could remember was Walderan lying down beside him on the cold filthy stones of the cell floor. He stretched luxuriantly for the pure pleasure of being able to straighten his body to its full length. Turning on his side, he discovered his sire dozing in a chair beside his bed. Menannon lay studying his sire with pleasure. Only the sight of Nirna could have caused him greater joy. The elder Giant was dressed in his loose fitting morning robe and sandals and an open codex lay face down across his chest. The High One was on His throne and he was back with his sire. All would now be right with the world, for together they twain could conquer anything that Azuron could throw against them. Had he not already been rescued from the worst the sorcerer could muster? Menannon almost laughed aloud with his joy at simply being alive and free once more. *The High One be praised with great praise!*

His movement alerted Gorlanndon and who yawned and stretched, dislodging the codex. Menannon caught it before it could reach the floor. He glanced at the title as he moved to set it on the bedside table. *The Way of Rock and Blood* had been carved into the oaken board of its cover with a sharp stylus. The title gave him pause. What would his sire be doing reading such a treatise? He set it down with a shrug and turned back to find his sire sitting up grinning at him.

"Welcome back my son. I have missed you these last few days." Gorlanndon held out a hand to him and Menannon grasped it with a strong grip of his own.

"I missed you as well, my father," Menannon colored nicely as he suddenly had to blink a mist from his eyes. "How come I to be here, sir?" he asked hurriedly to cover his momentary lapse.

"It was the work of many, most especially Master Harper Walderan," Gorlanndon nodded to where the harp still stood upon the cloths press.

"Ronirinen King's harp! She actually gave it to you to heal me?" Menannon looked at it stunned.

"Not exactly," Gorlanndon chuckled. "She gave it to me in hopes that he would *fail* to heal you. That, however, was neither in the High One's nor Walderan's plans and he wielded Reuel's method with mastery and here you are as good as ever, nay better than ever! Praise the High One with great praise!"

"Amen!" Menannon breathed, a little saddened at this further proof of the hatred Nirna's mother harbored for him. Gorlanndon must have read his thoughts in his eyes and slapped him gently on the shoulder.

"None of that now. It is too fine a day to worry about the ill whims of queens." He stood and held out his hand to draw Menannon up with him. "Come. Get you dressed and meet me in the summerhouse to break our fast in a half turn of the hour."

He started to turn away then turned back and gave Menannon a hug that nearly cracked his ribs and taking his son's face between his hands gently kissed his brow.

"Never give me such a fright as that again," he whispered and, taking up the codex, turned and left the chamber, his step lighter than Menannon had heard it in many a day.

With a smile, Menannon hurried to the bathing chamber to relieve himself and take a shower before dressing for the morning. He had never appreciated a shower more in his life and decided from then on he would take two a day just because he could.

As he washed, he looked down to discover his body was now puckered with numerous white scars, solid reminders of the time spent in the Chamber of Questions. He shuddered and forced his mind away from the dark memories that threatened to overwhelm him and went to the basin to use the polished glass mirror standing there to trim his beard. As he expected, the face that looked back at him was far thinner than it had been last time he saw himself in a mirror. His beard had grown out greatly, covering and softening the hollows of his cheeks and the edges of his jaw line. His beard was thicker and covered more of his face now, but this also hid half of the ragged white scar which now ran from the bridge of his nose, across his left cheekbone and on down into the beard. The mere sight of it recalled the memory of its infliction and his face burned and seared anew and he nearly screamed with the pain. He grabbed the edges of the basin to keep himself from falling to his knees and forced the memory from him with sheer will power. The pain in his face subsided slowly as though reluctant to leave. Breathing heavily, he wondered whether the scars on his mind would last as long as those on his body. Trying not to look at the scar, he finished shaving, leaving his new style of beard closely cropped to follow his jaw, but far less sculptured than had previously been his wont so as to cover as much of the scar as was physically possible.

That done, he returned to his sleeping chamber to don his clothing, resolutely pushing aside his memories, determined not to let the sorcerer darken his homecoming. Hastily, Menannon drew on his chemise and a kirtle of plain brown sorak over it and pulled soft leather boots over the feet of his hose and left the chamber to seek his sire in the summerhouse.

He walked a bit more hurriedly than usual through the villa and passed several of the staff. From most, he was able to turn his face so that they did not see the new scar, but there were enough who saw it that the news soon spread to the rest that the master's son's face now bore a disfiguring scar like the marring of a priceless work of art. Hatred for the sorcerer and his henchmen burned even brighter in the breasts of Gorlanndon's folk.

The sunshine of a beautiful day greeted Menannon as he stepped out into the kaleyard intent on making his way around the back of the villa to the summerhouse steps without any more people seeing him. In this, he was to be thwarted, as the oldest of Gorlanndon's gardeners was working away hoeing the weeds away from the young vegetable plants. As he came out, the old fellow straightened his back with a groan and turned to look him full in the face. Menannon stopped as the elder shook his head his lips pursed in disgust.

"We told ye tha shouldn't trust 'em, lad, and now ye've gone an' learned a hard lesson." The fellow shook his finger at him as though he were still the small boy who had begged him for rides in his barrow. Menannon started to turn his face away, coloring in shame.

"Now, none o' that! Look at me an' everyone else straight in the eye. That there scar is only a mark o' shame if ye let it be. He's blooded ye and now ye must blood him more. Understand?" The elder's rheumy blue eyes bore up into his.

"The Word Hoard of the High One says as an eye for an eye an' a limb for a limb an' yer honor bound now to carry that out."

The fellow saluted him and stepped back to let him pass. Menannon moved on, little knowing how often those words would come back to haunt him in the summers to come.

He found his sire in the summerhouse full of high spirits and good humor. Gorlanndon waved him in and served him a goodly breakfast from the covered dishes Clarinda had sent from the kitchen. Menannon made sure he sat so that the good side of his face was turned towards his sire and began to eat heartily, as despite all the happenings this morning, he was still ravenously hungry. Gorlanndon let him eat in peace while he himself drank a second mug of chocolate and studied him over its rim. The boy was so obviously self-conscious over the scar on his face that it was almost painful to watch him try to hide it. At last, Menannon finished eating and poured himself a third mug of chocolate, settling in with his arm along the back of the bench and with his cheek resting on his upraised hand. Though the pose was meant to look relaxed and natural, it was transparent as glass to Gorlanndon. Menannon was ashamed of the scar marring his features and did not want his sire to see it now that he was awake and could prevent.

"Enough boy. Do you really think I or anyone else cares that you now have a scar on your face? Many men bear scars far more disfiguring than that one. Your Grandmaster is one such. Have you e'er seen him hide his face as though he were ashamed of his missing eye and the old wound that deprived him of it?"

Menannon only shook his head, but still did not show his full face to his sire. A slight flush crept up his neck and he looked out of the window behind him.

"Well? Have you?"

"No," Menannon finally murmured.

"Then why should you?" Gorlanndon demanded not unkindly. "Look at me boy. So your face was scarred. Your life was spared and that is far more important!"

"But...," Menannon began then faltered to a stop. How could

he make his sire understand the shame he felt at the sight of the scar. It was a mark of ignorance and stupidity and anyone with half a brain would know it.

"But what?" Gorlanndon demanded, knowing full well that this conversation would have an affect upon the rest of his son's life. "A scar is a scar. What is the difference between them?"

"His was won in honorable battle. Mine was inflicted on the filthy floor of a dungeon by a mad man." Menannon finally turned to him and blurted out, "It is not the same!" His face went red to the roots of his hair making the scar stand out like a blaze on the face of a black horse.

"Is it not?" Gorlanndon straightened and took a hold of his son's face and forced him to raise his head and look him straight in the eyes. "Menannon, we are in the midst of a war here as much as though we were throwing javelins at one another. You went into that dungeon to keep our people safe. That was the act of a warrior, not a foolish child. Make no mistake boy. That scar is a war wound just as much as is this!" Gorlanndon let him go and rose to his full height and drew up his kirtle and chemise to show his bared stomach where a puckered red scar ran from beneath his right breast to disappear into the waistband of his hose. His sire readjusted his clothing and sat back down.

"That is a battle wound? I always thought it the result of some injury received at sea or during your wandering days. When were you ever in battle? You are a philosopher, not a warrior!" he burst out in surprise and consternation his own disfigurement forgotten in the moment.

"A man can be many things in a lifetime of two thousand summers and more, boy," the elder Giant chuckled then became serious again. "The very fact I have seen battle many times is the reason that I have refused you the same burden. You are more important to this world than to be used merely as a stone to fill the breach in some king's walls."

Gorlanndon's eyes darkened with some memory that Menannon could not share. They sat quietly staring at one another, each seeing the other as though for the first time, their perception having been forever changed by this morning's revelations. Finally, Gorlanndon sat back with a heavy sigh

"I have had a chance to think these last few days and I see now that in thus preventing you from learning the arts of war once practiced by our people, I have also robbed you of your heritage, for there is far more to the Way of Rock and Blood than just battle skills. To know these arts is to be a Giant in truth as well as in body. So against all my instincts, boy, I am giving you the rest of your legacy."

Gorlanndon ceased speaking and reached back to the table behind him and took from it the codex he had been reading in Menannon's chamber. He turned and set in front of his son.

"Within the pages of this book, you will find the secret lore of our folk as it has been handed down from sire to son since the days of beginning when it was penned from the mind of the High One by the hand of our longsire, Lornennir. Read it, boy, and take back your birthright. Use it wisely in the summers to come for it is a heavy burden to bear." Gorlanndon stood and nodded to him as he would to an equal. "One thing more I would give you, as it, too, is part of your birthright. Take this." He handed Menannon his signet ring which he had placed upon a strong leather thong. "It is the key to all that is yours. Keep it with you always."

Without another word, he left the summerhouse, leaving Menannon staring after him, too stunned to even think for a moment. While the sound of Gorlanndon footsteps had faded into silence, Menannon stared at both objects in wonder and some confusion. The ring with its thong he put around his neck for safekeeping. He knew it to be a key to many doors, for he had seen his father us it thus many times, but his sire's words came back to him with the peculiar emphasis upon the word all and he wondered what else it might be a key to.

He then turned his attention to the codex, opening its oaken cover with a sense of awe and wonder and not a little trepidation. The vellum was as crisp and white and the ink as black as the day it was made, though the writing was in an ancient script nearly unreadable to him, yet as he studied it, the form became more recognizable and he soon read with ease: *To my sons and all their sons until the end of time, I, thy sire Lornennir, do bequeath unto thee the words of the High One to the race of Giants. Into thine hands He has given the weapons and onto thine shoulders he has placed the mantle of Guardian of the World, protectors of Linden and all of creation therein. Thus sayeth the High One unto the Giants....*

GORLANNDON ENTERED HIS OFFICE in the villa to find Firod waiting for him with lists of men and arms spread out on the desk. He looked up expectantly.

"Did you give it to him?"

"Aye. Though I know not if I have given him a blessing or a curse." Gorlanndon sat down heavily at his desk and studied his friend. "To be a Giant with the full knowledge of our cal-ling is no easy thing."

"Yet to be a Giant without all of the skills bequeathed to your race is a dangerous thing, as we have already seen." Firod's expression was as thoughtful as Gorlanndon had ever seen it.

"Think you then he could have saved himself had I but taught him the Way ere this?"

Firod thought for several long moments before answering. "I think not, for as you have told me ere this, does it not take many long and long summers to master the Way? He is just a boy, no matter his skill and depth of mind. Had he known the Way, but not yet mastered it, Azuron would have killed him outright to rid himself of another practitioner, potentially the greatest of them all. No, you were right to withhold it from him until now. Now you have no choice, for he must have the knowledge ere Azuron begins his last moves for soon enough, the time for learning will be past and only the time of doing will be left."

Gorlanndon nodded silent agreement, then drew the plans they had been making around so they could both see them. They were now the self-appointed leaders of the soon-to-be rebellion that would hopefully force Azuron from his position and send him and his followers back over the sea or under it, depending upon how one looked at things. It struck Gorlanndon then just how far things had gone for Firod, loyal Firod who had been as a foundation rock to the Crown for all the years he had served it, from his youth as a palace squire until now as Captain of the Palace Guard, to be plotting treason against that same Crown. Yet, had not the Crown committed treason against the Land and the People? He shook his head, bemused by his thoughts. Let the lawyers sort that out!

As the two conspirators finalized their plans, Menannon began to commit his sire's codex to memory.

THE PEACE OF THE FOLLOWING DAY was interrupted by the bells of the great carillon which rang the hour at mid-day and then continued for another one hundred times, the traditional chimes of good fortune which always announced the weddings of their royalty to the people of Kirith Kalyria. As the bells continued to ring and the sounds of cheering and revelry grew in the streets, Gorlanndon and all his folk ran out into the courtyard in disbelief.

"As the High One is my witness, Norilendra could not be so stupid," Gorlanndon breathed even as his ears were assaul-ted by the ringing.

No bells ever rang sweeter than did the bells of the carillon, but this day they were as cacophonic as the screeching of the damned in Outer Darkness. Blood Royal could only wed Blood Royal, else Kalyria's pact with the High One was broken and doom was written upon all their foreheads.

Gorlanndon swung towards Firod standing next him, his heart pounding against his ribs in both fear and frustration. "Go quickly and find out if it is true!"

His fear was that it was indeed true that Norilendra had broken sacred law and his frustration was that they had waited too long to act. All of his folk including Menannon stood listening with him as they waited for Firod's return. It took the captain less than the quarter turn of an hour to return. Skendrin let him back in at the gate. There was no need for words, the look on the Firod's face was word enough. The pact was broken. Norilendra had wed Azuron.

"Stupidity is its own reward," Gorlanndon growled. "The High One will not be mocked."

REVELRY CONTINUED UNABATED throughout the afternoon and into the evening as Azuron decreed this a holiday and ordered that every pub, inn and eating house serve all foods and strong drink free to all comers. Blue fingered twilight saw all of the happy recipients of this largess who could still stand, struggle out to line the wide avenues leading up through the seven circles of the city as horns called from the top of the Citadel and the gates of the palace close opened. Out from the palace in majestic procession came the Queen and her new consort riding in an open litter carried on the strong shoulders of eight huge Doomcriers, accompanied by all manner of girls and women dancing along beside them throwing peridüse flowers and rose petals in front of them enough to make their bearers seem to wade to their knees in loveliness. Along with these were musicians and singers, dancers and acrobats and fourscore armored Doomcriers. Dozens of linkboys ran before and followed after, each bearing an open Dwarf lantern. Behind the entourage rumbled three dozen small carts loaded with all of the food stuffs, servants and materials the couple would need upon their month long honeymoon. Norilendra was taking her new consort to the nuptial palace on the eastern coast of the island as had been the wont of Kalyria's newly wedded royalty time out of mind. The city fairly rocked with the cheering of her people.

Children and the more spritely of their elders ran along beside the procession as it passed down the avenues, out of the city gates and down towards the crossroads. There they halted and stood waving in fair well as the procession turned onto the marble highroad even as true dark was falling. Amidst the tumult, few if any of the revelers noticed the small band of dusty, foot sore travelers who had stood to the side to allow the procession to pass and now returned to the road and the long plod still ahead of them to reach the city.

Slowly, though without hesitation, the little band made its weary way up the winding avenues and streets, passed the now quiet palace, over the Mathematical Bridge and on to Gorlanndon's holding where they halted at the gate and rang for entrance. The summons of the bell was answered by the duty gatewarden and Skendrin was immediately called for. Seeing that the band was lead by a white-haired patriarch and that there appeared to be no weapons among them, the duty guards allowed the group in and carefully surrounded them with weapons at the ready as they waited for the steward. Skendrin appeared with alacrity, having just returned to his home from the usual dinner with the Giants and not yet settled in for the evening.

"What seek you here?" he demanded.

"We be from Waterdeep an' seek an audience with the master of the house," the ancient one spoke, stepping forward. He was a gnarled old fellow with skin the consistency of boiled leather bespeaking him to be a fisherman by trade whose lifetime had been spent exposed to sun and saltwater.

"What do you want with him?" The hair on the back of Skendrin's neck rose and a shiver went down his spine for no reason he could fathom.

"We've been sent—," the fellow began, but Skendrin cut him off.

"I will not—!" he began, thinking to push the band back out, his sense of unease growing.

"It's alright, Skendrin. Let them come in and be at ease."

Gorlanndon's voice broke over them and the steward turned to see the Giant and Menannon had stepped out onto the portico attracted by the sounds from without. Behind them stood Firod with hand on the hilt of his sword and Walderan remained within the doorway listening intently. Gorlanndon nodded to Skendrin who immediately disappeared into the house to seek out Clarinda and ready food and chambers for their sudden guests. At the sound of the Giant's voice, all of the newcomers dropped to their knees and bowed their heads to the ground.

"NO! Never bow in such a manor to a man, only the High One deserves such reverence." Gorlanndon knelt on one knee and reached down and took the hand of the old man raising him to his feet. "What is your will here?"

"We were told to come here an' seek sanctuary, Master," the fellow looked up into Gorlanndon's eyes as he signaled his family to rise as well.

"Told? By whom?" asked Menannon, who had come to stand beside his sire.

"We aren't knowin', young Master."

The response came from a younger woman who stepped up to stand beside the old fellow, a small child on one hip. She pushed wisps of her long dark hair out of her eyes to look up at him. Her face was pretty, but dirty and tired from long travel. All of their clothing and footwear were worn and covered with the dust of the road.

"It were dawn a fortnight ago an' a bit more when me sons an' I an' a couple of our men were pullin' our boat out of the water when we heard it. An albatross flew o'er our heads nearer than I've e'er seen one fly an' then we heard a voice sayin' GO TO GORLANNDON. All of us heard it, save one of our men. He allowed as how he saw the albatross an' then saw us all start to have strange looks on our faces, but he heard nothin' "

"Is that fellow with you?"

"Nay, great Master. He wouldn't come though we sought long an' hard fer him to change his mind an' bring his family."

"Come, follow me into the house."

Gorlanndon rose and led the way with Firod, Walderan and Menannon following.

The group followed along behind, their eyes wide with wonder at the beauty of the Giant's home. Gorlanndon lead them into the kitchen and bid them to set their burdens down and sit at the table Skendrin had drawn to one of the hearths. All of them were bone weary and cold. Clarinda and her staff bustled around setting out cold meats, bread, cheese and fruit and putting kettles on to boil.

"Well, you are welcome to stay," Gorlanndon told them. "When you have satisfied your hunger, Skendrin will show you to chambers where you can refresh yourselves and sleep. We shall have more speech on the morrow. For now, know that you are safe and welcome."

"Bless you, great Master." The old fellow took Gorlann-don's hand and touched it to his forehead.

"I told ye, Grandsire. It was the High One as was taklin' to ye and Da, or the Giant woulda thrown us out," a small boy piped up around a leg of cold turkey, causing all present to smile and shake their heads, some in relief and some in wonder.

Over the group's heads, Gorlanndon signaled his fellow conspirators to sojourn to the summerhouse. When they were outside, Menannon glanced back in the kitchen window to see them looking relieved and eating hungrily, weary and famished from their journey. He hurried after his sire.

"Told to seek sanctuary?" Menannon questioned immed-iately upon entering the summerhouse and closing the door. Gorlanndon did not answer, but went to the sideboard and procured an amphora of wine with its stand and four chalices while the others sat down at the table. After pouring the wine for each of them he sat down himself and glanced around.

"What think you of this coming hard upon the heels of our Queen's remarriage?"

"The High One's ways are not our ways." Walderan shook his head after taking a long pull on his chalice. "Perchance he is sending his children to safety from what is to come."

"What is to come?" Menannon demanded looking from one to the other of his elders coming at last to his sire. "You have all gone white to the teeth and looked stricken at this marriage and spoken of breaking the pact with the High One, but none of you have told me what is to happen now that the pact is broken."

"That, boy, is because we know not." Gorlanndon shook his head. "The ancient saga tells us that the High One's blessing will be removed from Kalyria, but exactly what that blessing is it does not specify in so many words." Skendrin and Firod nodded in agreement. "It is useless to speculate. We shall know in the High One's own good time unless we can repair the damage e'er that knowledge is given us."

"Repair it how?!" Menannon sputtered almost choking on his wine.

"There are a brace of possibilities as there always are." Gorlanndon set down his chalice and looked long into its depths. The silence lengthened as all of them waited for him to elaborate upon that statement.

"Only two?" Firod finally coaxed. Gorlanndon looked up at him, a slight smile quirking his lips and he set his and Firod's chalices side by side on the table and pointed to them.

"Aye, two. Either Norilendra can be made to repent and annul the marriage." he pointed to Firod's chalice. "Or she can be forcibly removed from the throne." He pointed to his own. "Either possibility would satisfy the High One at this juncture."

Menannon looked at both chalices then glanced down at his own and set it beside the other twain. "There would seem to be a third possibility and that is neither possibility will come to pass and the High One will not be reconciled. If these fisher folk have indeed been sent here by the High One and sent over a fortnight ago, long before the Queen broke the pact, then the third possibility seems the most likely."

"And here I thought harpers are supposed to believe in miracles," Gorlanndon grinned and shook his head, retrieving his chalice and refilling it. "You've spent too much time around

Blackmore, boy. You're too practical."

Menannon colored nicely under his sire's grin.

"What think you?" the elder Giant asked turning serious again. "Is this deputation from the High One or have they come here for some purpose of their own?"

There was a deep silence for several long moments then finally Walderan glanced up then back to his chalice which he was spinning between his fingers.

"I deem we must wait and see if any more folk are coming, for if the High One sent these surely He will have sent more. Then we can decide our course." He glanced up and looked directly into Gorlanndon's eyes. "I do believe in miracles. That Menannon and I are both sitting here at this table is an act of the miraculous and no mistake."

"I deem then we should await what the morning brings," Gorlanndon agreed.

Later in his own chamber, Menannon could not help musing on the nature of miracles.

THE NEXT DAY AND EVERY DAY for the next sevenday and beyond saw a small but steady flow of folk coming from all over the island to seek sanctuary. It was the same story with all of them: they had heard a voice telling them "Go to Gorlanndon" and they had gone without question as the command had been so compelling. They came in twos and threes, small family groups like the first one and some alone as the rest of their family had refused to believe the command or had not heard it and claimed their family member daft. There was even one young woman who had not heard the voice, though her granddame had and the old woman had told her to go without her, for her bones were too old to make the trip, and she wished at least one of them to heed the High One's call, for certain she was that He had called them. There was one young farmer who had brought his three babes and no wife as she had called him a fool and refused to come hard though her husband had pressed her. By the end of the sevenday, there were nearly two hundred folk crowded into every spare corner of the villa and its surrounding buildings including the dormitory and Skendrin's house. Menannon had a family of seven sharing his bedchamber.

Another problem reared its ugly head. As Clarinda pointed out to her master as he broke his fast the end of the sevenday. Food was going to run short soon with so many extra mouths to feed.

"I've set about figurin's as close as I can and we've but enough provender to feed this army for not but a fortnight more," she said tapping her spoon upon the list of supplies she had laid out on the table between them. "We'll be needin' to be gettin' some more and soon."

"A fortnight you say?" Gorlanndon questioned, though he knew his cook was accurate in her summery for none knew the needs of the household better than she.

"Aye. We will still be havin' some from the kaleyard, but e'en that will be runnin' out soon." she nodded and returned her attention to eating her frumenty. No more was said, but then no more needed to be said for Clarinda had perfect faith that her beloved master could set right any state of affairs with ease.

SLIGHTLY MORE THAN A SEVENDAY after Norilendra Queen's marriage found Menannon seated on the high seat of a large farm wagon driving down the road from the city. The enormity of the situation was reflected in the smallness of the sack of touring victuals secured under his seat and that of the others. He was followed by Skendrin and members of his sire's warband, each seated upon the high seat of his own wagon. There were forty such conveyances in all. Behind these rode twenty fully armed men astride horses "borrowed" from the royal stables. At his sire's direction, they were headed for the largest of the elder

Giant's food storage sites located high on the shoulder of Kalyria's Crown. Gorlanndon traded in many types of goods, including foodstuffs from all across the known world and had no fewer than a score of such depots scattered across Kalyria. Several of these he had emptied when he began moving his business and employees off the island, but the largest he had kept intact against need closer to home.

On the first rise beyond the city gates, Menannon halted his wagon. Skendrin pulled his team up beside him while the rest held their teams in line behind. Not having been without the city wall since the breaking of the pact, none of them were prepared for the sight which met their eyes. What greeted them was devastation. The farms and once green fields rolling away across the Plains of Pelar looked for all the world like the aftermath of a war. The stone walls and farmsteads held their accustomed place, but were already falling into decay. The wood lots, orchards and fields were dying, rife with rot. Where there should have been activity and a riot of color, there was nothing. Silence and ruin ruled the land. It was as though all color had been leached from the world leaving the landscape a dull ashen grey dotted here and there with the blackness of rot as far as the eye could see. The wood lots and orchards held only the bare, dead skeletons of trees with nary a needle or leaf holding its accustomed place. Apple trees that should have been heavy with rosy apples bore only a few blasted pustules. The fields between were covered with the rotting remains of grain blackened and twisted beyond recognition. Over all, small wisps of strange vapor crawled.

"Smell that?" Skendrin raised his head and sniffed the air.

"What do you smell more than putrescence?" Menannon growled his stomach nearly rebelling against the odor wafting up to them on the sea breeze.

"I smell sulphur!"

"Sulphur?"

"Aye, lad! Now we know the first consequence of the removal of the High One's blessing. The volcanoes are indeed awakening. Look there!" Skendrin pointed across the rolling hills, to the wooded slopes of Kalyria's Crown and her seven sisters; all were enveloped with a vapor that drifted down their sides, shriveling any growing thing in its path. Nothing else moved upon the land.

"Come, we must hurry while the way to our destination is still open." Skendrin slapped the reins on the backs of his greys and they lunged forward their huge wagon jerking behind them. Menannon fell into line behind him.

They soon reached the floor of the plain and rolled through the land itself. Everyone had to cover their noses and mouths with scarves, for all around them was not only rotting vegetation, but the bloated carcases of livestock lay scattered upon what had once been rich pasture land, but was now greyish mud. Skendrin halted at a bridge across a small stream. He tied the reins to the brake handle and jumped down to better inspect the water below. Menannon joined him at the railing and looked down. Below them ran not clear, sparkling water as was usual state of rivers and streams on Kalyria, but a thick, greenish-brown sludge which bubbled and smoked along its path. Beside it and half in it lay the corpses of a large flock of sheep who had apparently attempted to drink from their accustomed watering hole.

"The poisons long kept safe within the volcanoes' hearts under the High One's blessing are leaching up and destroying all they touch." He shook his head in sorrow and disgust. "This by the will of a foolish queen and a soulless devil." The steward looked over his shoulder and locked eyes with Menannon. "It'll mean the wells in the city will soon go sour as some o' them are as deep as the plain." They regained their wagon seats.

"Don't let the horses drink any water on the land even if it looks clean!" Skendrin called back along the line and Menannon heard the order being passed along.

In his mind's eye, he could imagine the people raising buckets of putrid sludge from the wells in the courtyards and he had a vision of such horror running from the mouths of the dolphins in his sire's villa. He shook his head and clicked to his greys to send them after Skendrin.

Just before noontide, they rolled into the village where seeming lifetimes ago Lee and Menannon had stopped for luncheon. Near the corner of the inn yard, one sunflower yet stood, its multi-rayed blossom bent over as though in shame that it did not lay wilted and blackened as did all the rest of its brothers as far as the eye could see.

"Skendrin, halt for a moment," Menannon called. "I wish to speak to the innkeeper." Skendrin raised his hand in acknowledgment and Menannon turned his team into the yard, taking care to avoid the scattered rotting carcasses of chickens and pigs littering the place. His heart lurched at the condition of the inn and he hoped there was something he could do to help its proprietor and his family. Menannon jumped down from the high seat and started for the door only to have it opened with a bang as the innkeeper and his wife came charging out. Both came up to him anger writ large upon their faces.

Each of them had been more than pleasantly plump when last he beheld them, but now their very skin seemed to hang upon them like drapery. Both wore Doomcrier red from head to foot, a color which matched faces distorted with anger and livid boils.

"Don't ye come no closer!" The gooddame shrieked at him while she made frantic signs to ward off evil. "Yer sire has cursed us an' we don't need ye addin' to it."

"My father has what?" Menannon stopped, stunned at their words.

"Ye heard me wife, Giant!" The innkeeper chimed in. "Look around ye an' ye'll see we've been cursed! The whole village has an' 'tis yer sire as is responsible with his unlawful magics an' wicked ways."

"What makes you deem my father is responsible for all of this?" the young Giant waved his hand to indicate not just the inn yard but the fields as well.

"We all knows! Norilendra Queen has gone an' wedded a better man than he and yer sire is gettin' his revenge on all o' the rest o' us!" The fellow looked as though he would have punched Menannon had he stood a little higher than his belt buckle.

"We knows," the old woman shrieked. "An' if 'tis proof ye want, we've plenty and to spare!" She began looking wildly around until her eyes lighted on something. In a trice she had scooped up the carcass of a speckled hen and was shaking it at him. "See this? This be Lisby, me best layin' hen. Ne'er did she do nothin' to nobody. Not a scratch, not a peck and she's dead just by drinkin' the water out o' our well. An' everybody knows as how yer sire controls the waves. If'n a body can control the mighty sea, he can put a curse on our well an' kill me Lisby!" The gooddame's eyes were fairly bursting from her wrinkled face with her anger and indignation.

"But my father does not control—" Menannon began, thoroughly befuddled by the couple's accusations, but the innkeeper cut him off.

"An' he's sent us a plague o' boils! The whole village is sufferin' with 'em save one an' that one proves all."

"True, too true!" his wife shrieked in agreement. "That old fishwife ain't got boil one an' her chickens ain't died an' her well ain't poisoned an' her dogs ain't dead, an'...."

"What does her good fortune have to do with my father?" Menannon questioned loudly enough to get Skendrin's attention and the steward started to climb down from the wagon. Menannon caught the movement out of the corner of his eye and waved Skendrin to halt, knowing his size alone was preventing this strange couple from attacking him, an asset that Skendrin did not possess. The steward nodded and instead of coming into the yard himself, signaled for the armed escort to come forward.

Menannon turned his attention back to the couple just in time to get a clod of dirt thrown at him from someone near the portico. It bounced harmlessly off from the front of his kirtle. He looked over to see that the couples' daughter, the lass who had been so enamored of Lee, was standing there, her hands full of dirt, one hand just pulling back for another throw. Her face and form were exactly like her parents, matching them in every marring detail.

"Tis ye Gorlanndoners as are at fault!" The girl's shriek joined those of her parents. "That old fishwife worked for yer sire an' everyone knows as how the Giant takes care of his own! Now get yerself out o' here! We'll stand fer no more o' yer curses and magics! Get out afore we does fer ye like we're goin' to do fer her!"

Despite the armed and mounted warband directly on the other side of the wagon from the young Giant, all three of them reached down for more dirt clods and rocks and began pelting Menannon as fast as they could throw. Knowing not what else to do, Menannon turned his back upon folk his heart desired to help in their extremity, but whose misguided hate prevented him, climbed to his wagon seat and clicked to the greys. The riders gave way to him and he pulled out of the inn yard with a single backward glance to see his erstwhile attackers hugging each other as though they had just scored a great victory. What a world Azuron had created, where help was scorned and disaster was lauded.

As soon as Menannon's wagon was back in line, Skendrin moved off down the main street of the village. It was lined with all manner of other poor wretches whose condition bespoke the same ills as the innkeeper and his family. Here as well, they found themselves pelted with dirt and rocks, spat upon and cursed. The name "Gorlanndoners" was hurled at them like an evil epithet. None of the villagers followed them beyond the last house and when they turned the bend, all of the folk went back into their stricken homes and Menannon saw them no more.

There was another bend in the road where it circled around a blasted orchard and then it straightened out and they halted once again, stunned. Before them, glowing like a jewel in a queen's crown, was a stone cottage with its neat croft and small orchard. Even the sun was shining upon this single patch of ground, a thing which Menannon suddenly noticed was not happening to any other patch of ground as far as he could see despite there being no clouds overhead.

As one, they pulled to a halt at the gate and were greeted by a neatly dressed woman whose white hair and gently lined face bespoke her age and good health. In her hand, she held the hoe she had been using in her garden. All about her were living things: flowers, a healthy kaleyard with vegetables ready for the picking; an old horse looked at them around the back corner of the cottage while two fine hunting hounds sat watching them from its small portico.

"The High One's blessing upon ye strangers. Light down an' be welcome." Her greeting was all that was usual on Kalyria as was the grey, round gown she wore beneath her clean white apron. Menannon and Skendrin accepted her invitation and entered her small domain and came to stand before her.

"And also upon you, gooddame." Menannon inclined his head to her as he would to any elder. Beside him, Skendrin grinned and held out his hand to her.

"Long and long has it been since I served with your husband, Sara. It's nice to see you well."

"Skendrin, ye old crab! I am glad to see ye! What bring's ye so far from the sea?" she smiled and a dimple shown in her cheek. "An' ye must be the master's son." she said, turning to Menannon with a courtesy.

"Aye, Sara he is," Skendrin informed her before Menannon could speak. "But we've not the time for pleasantries much though I wish we did. We are just come from the village and they are plotting to do you ill."

"Well I know it," her grey eyes darkened with sorrow. "I have tried to ease their sufferin', but they're convinced their lives are bein' blighted by curses an' not their own poor choices. They'll not listen to me, more's the pity—."

"Gooddame," Menannon interrupted. "You needs must leave this place."

"But the High One has protected me—,"she began and again Menannon interrupted her.

"Aye, He has protected you from the ills leaching from the volcanoes, but not from the ills leaching from people." He indicated the obvious mud clots on the front of his kirtle.

She looked from Menannon's troubled face to Skendrin who

nodded agreement with his young Master's words.

"I see," she said almost to herself as she look about her small domain. "Where shall I go? I've naught but me memories an' this cottage."

Menannon glanced around and made a quick decision. "Skendrin, have one wagon and four guards fall out. Gooddame," he turned back to Sara. "We are on an errand for my father and will be coming back this way. So, if you will, allow my men to assist you in gathering your belongings into this wagon and when we return you can accompany us back to Kirith Kalyria where my father will find a place for you. Does that suit?"

She looked again from the Giant to the steward, bewildered by the swiftness of events.

"There is little time, Sara." Skendrin spoke softly, but urgently. "We must away and so must you. Will you accept our master's largess or no?" She looked around once more at her home and animals, then glanced towards the village. Menannon could see her internal struggle reflected in the way she clasped her hands to her breast. But when she turned back, her face was clear of worry.

"It be the High One's will, else ye would'na've come by this road to bear me witness. Aye. I will come. My thanks!" She gave Menannon another courtesy then turned briskly to the job of shooing her hens out of the way of the wagon Skendrin was signaling into the yard. As quickly as possible, four guards were chosen and their orders given.

A quarter turn of an hour saw the rest of the wagons on their way again. Menannon glanced back to see the gooddame leading her new champions into her small cottage to begin preparations to leave it forever.

The same eerie scenes played themselves out all across the land as they moved through village after village and past countless cottages and homesteads. Most were blasted ruins but some few were miraculously preserved against the poisons of the volcanos. Even a few villages were preserved whole. All along the way, they passed the warning that those whose lands were whole must prepare for more than just enmity from their neighbors. Twice more they left a wagon and guards to prepare a family to accompany them on their return.

Not even the wild creatures were being spared the evil stalking the land, a fact that was sadly proven when they rolled into the remains of the heavy forests on the slopes of Kalyria's Crown. Here Skendrin halted and pointed to the far side of a once thriving lily mead. There, its hind quarters still in the pool, lay a dead spiralhorn. Menannon could not help wondering what had been its demise, as the water here still seemed clear. He watched for a long moment then saw a bubble rise from the depths followed by another and the sulphurous fumes again assaulted his nose as it broke the surface. Skendrin had indeed been wise to order them not to water their horses from any standing water. Sadly, they moved on.

They reached their destination in the last twilight of a long day to find the gate barred and guarded. Strangely, there was a low rumbling sound that seemed to pervade everything, just barely audible, and it came in waves accompanied by a slight, if ominous, trembling of the ground. The volcanoes were indeed awakening.

"Ware the gate!" Skendrin called as they rolled up to the high enclosure surrounding the storage site. The embrasure immediately opened and a lantern was thrust through.

"Be gettin' down so's I can see ye proper!" came a sharp command from beyond the barrier. Skendrin and Menannon climbed a bit stiffly down from the high seats of their wagons and walked to the noses of their horses. Menannon took a hold of the bit of the nearest grey and stroked its soft nose as it sidled a bit, perhaps made nervous by the rumbling and shaking ground.

"Skendrin, ye old sea dog! So, the master really did turn ye loose fer a short snort. We were after receivin' word as ye were comin'. Hold fast there an' I'll be havin' the gate open fer ye."

With that, the lantern withdrew and the embrasure snapped

to only to be replaced by the opening of the entire gateway, which was high enough for Gorlanndon's use and thus comfortably accommodated the wagons and mounted riders. Menannon and Skendrin led their wagons through and the rest followed after. The gate shut behind them.

The courtyard into which they entered was a wide stone-paved affair surrounded by huge warehouses, a comfortable stone villa and dormitory and a large stable with an attached paddock. Here as well, there was no sign of the ills besetting the countryside below.

"Come in an' be welcome."

A Dwarf came around from where he had just closed the gate.

"As ye can see, we've already loaded all the wagons as we had here," he said without preamble. He was tall and lightly built for his race with a coal black beard just long enough to tuck into the silver chased belt he wore over his leathern kirtle. His dark grey eyes darted around, taking in all of their company. At the sight of Menannon, he nodded to himself and inclined his head.

"Tis been long an' long since I've had the pleasure of layin' eyes on ye, young Master. Not, as a matter of factuality, since we used to play together at Paulus Muellen's holdin'"

"Mikhal?"

Menannon studied the Dwarf in the uncertain light of the torches set about the courtyard.

"It is you!"

He held out his hand to his childhood friend, the eldest son of Georgi Grimmaxe, his father's master of the horse, which explained his stature, as his mother, Sandrina was a tall, willowy Human of no little beauty. The young Dwarf took Menannon's hand with a grin.

"Tis sorry I am that we be meetin' again under such circumstances, but come, unhitch yer horses an' settle 'em, then be comin' inside an' fillin' yer stomachs as supper is the best part o' bein' ready." Mikhal turned away signaling them to follow him to the attached stable yard.

They made short work of parking their wagons alongside the

seven that were already loaded and covered with oil cloth, then unhitched their horses and turned them loose in the paddock. Despite the circumstances which brought them together, supper that night was a riotous affair. Finding sleeping places for nearly sixty souls was another matter entirely, but it was accomplished with only one fellow left to sleep in the corn crib, which was rather fortuitous, as he had imbibed more mead than was good for him and would have fallen from any bed provided.

The return trip with wagons fully loaded was accomplished swiftly, as the villages they traveled through were now all but deserted, a new ill having been added to all the rest: con-tagion! There was not a single cottage, shop or villa of Azuron's followers which did not fly the white flag of death. The stench of burning carcasses wafted across the island, adding to the reek of the awakening volcanos, as the few still living tried to stem the contagion by burning the corpses of their own dead—too great in number for burial—and the carcasses of the dead animals around them. The Gorlann-doners, as they now called themselves with pride—the true followers of the High One—were being spared this new calamity as well, thus causing more conflicts between them and their Doomcrier neighbors. The folk who had agreed to join them on the return were packed and waiting as their growing train arrived. Menannon found himself looking once more into the first inn yard much sooner than he had expected.

This time, the door remained closed and a white death flag was attached to the door post. He caught sight of hate-filled eyes watching him from one of the upstairs windows, but there was no sound or motion beyond the listless flapping of the flag. There were two new-made graves near the kaleyard attesting to the need for the banner. Saddened, Menannon whispered a prayer for them and clicked to the greys. The wagon train rolled past on the last leg of the journey back to Kirith Kalyria.

Bong! Bong! The tolling of the city's death bell floated to them across the plain even before the city itself came into sight. Each toll was torture to Menannon, searing his soul with the reminder that he was witnessing what could only be the final doom of his beloved home. How could they possibly reconcile with the High One? Could Norilendra's renunciation of her unlawful marriage truly be enough to cure all of this?

What a change a single sevenday had made in the city. It was again late evening when they entered it through a now unguarded gate. Here as well, more buildings than not were grimly adorned with the white death flags and the stench of burning permeated everything. Just without the city wall, the ground was scarred with newly made graves by the hundreds and the dead were still stacked in piles waiting for the gravediggers to finish opening new mass graves. The hate ridden souls wielding the picks and shovels halted their work to watch the wagons roll by.

"Gorlanndoners!" one of the closest fellows growled just loud enough for Menannon to hear then spit at them before going back to his work. When they reached the crossing at the base of the Citadel, Skendrin reined his horses down the strand onto the road which passed by the Cokeyna and then around to the lowest level of Gorlanndon's trade hall, as it was impossible for the great wagons to make their way up the winding streets of the city. Strangely, light poured from the windows and noise erupted from the Cokeyna's open doors. There was music and laughter coming from it, slightly strained and hysterical perhaps, but laughter nonetheless. Menannon glanced down the strand in both directions to see that it was the same with all the pubs, but the great circus on down the beach was dark and empty, a death flag flying from the top of its main portico. No one had opened any of the Dwarf lanterns along the streets and avenues winding up through the city and that lack of light was more terrifying than all else for never before in the memory of men had Kirith Kalyria been shrouded in darkness.

Skendrin halted his wagon in front of the doors to the trade hall and signaled the others to gather 'round. All of the drivers parked their wagons side by each and jumped down to join their armed escort in a loose circle facing away from the building.

Though nothing moved in the twilight, the tolling bell was oppressive and set everyone's nerves on edge. Skendrin removed a small key from his belt pouch and unlocked the door and threw it wide. Just inside the dark maw of the warehouse was a signal bell pull and a Dwarf lantern. He quickly opened the lantern and pulled on the signal rope. Menannon heard the signal's clang echo somewhere deep within the building. Within moments, the sound of the lifts filled the night and a seeming army of Gorlanndon's servitors appeared to aid in the unloading of the wagons.

"Take all the provender up to the atrium level as from there we'll be able to shift it as needed to the villa and make sure you keep the personal belongings of our guests separate," Skendrin raised his voice to be heard by the newcomers as well as their own drivers.

"I'd prefer our drivers and escort stay on guard while the rest of us do the shifting," Menannon added, nodding towards where a shadowy group of folk were starting to form a silent ring a little way down the strand. "I know not the intentions of those folk, but I deem it is not peaceful."

Skendrin glanced to where the Giant was looking and nodded. "Aye, I fear you've the right of it. Do as the young Master says," he commanded then turned back to those folk who had joined them on their return journey. There were but four and twenty people, eight dogs, nine cats and one nag, Sara's ancient plow horse. All of the animals and the rest of the pigs, chickens and goats they had left happily ensconced with Mikhal, his family and a goodly number of volunteers at Paulus Muelen's empty holding on the way up to the city.

"Come all of you, bring what is yours and we will get your effects settled ere we see you on to the Master's holding." Skendrin commanded. All nodded and began gathering their belongings and found men at their sides ready to help shift them into the trade hall. Soon everything was well ordered chaos as the wagons of food and belongings were relieved of their burdens and their contents readied to move up to the atrium level.

"You go on up, young Master and report to yer sire," Skendrin spoke from behind Menannon's shoulder as the Giant was assisting in unloading. "I'll see to all this."

Menannon nodded and ducked past the line of folk shifting bags of grain and took one of the lifts to the atrium level. Even in the depths of the hall he could hear the death bell. It was more as a feeling in his teeth than a sound in his ears, but it was there nonetheless.

Menannon made short work of attaining the atrium level and crossing its vast emptiness and letting himself out of the doors. Here as well the city was dark save for the dim light that was filtering through cracks in hastily pulled curtains. He hurried towards the Citadel and its bridges as the last of the deep purple of twilight was leaving the western sky. When he reached the vast plaza he was surprised to find the Council Hall brilliant with light and folks running in and out as though intent upon errands.

As he got closer to it a new sound impinged upon him, a sound he knew all too well from the almshouse in Aridion City: the painful moaning and crying of the diseased. He ran lightly up the steps and dodged around two folk dressed in Doomcrier red at the door and entered the hall to be confronted by a small ocean of pallets and straw covering every possible floor space, from the halls to the visitor balconies above. In the great council chamber itself, Menannon looked for a familiar face among the folk attending upon the sick and spotted both Walderan and Clarinda bending over patients, lancing boils and pustules. He quickly crossed to the healer who was the closest of the two and touched his shoulder. Walderan looked up, a frown marring his tired face. His brow cleared and a smile touched his lips when he recognized who had interrupted him.

"You're back, lad! And successful I hope, as we're in dire need of victuals for all of these and more."

"Aye. We just brought in four and forty wagons of food stuffs; e'en now Skendrin is seeing it into my father's trade hall." Glancing around at the huge number of patients, he asked, "When did the contagion strike here?"

"A twoday after you left, a sailor came in from a night's fishing and dropped over on the strand in front of the Cokeyna." Walderan sighed and ran a tired hand across his brow. "He carried the pustules under his red kirtle. By dawn the next day, contagion was stalking the streets. There was hardly a Doomcrier house or business that did not have straw out about it to deaden the sounds from the street to ease the sufferers. 'Tis a cruel plague, for their bodies burn and boil and the slightest sound causes them excruciating pain. By that nightfall, the first of the death flags went up." The healer looked up at Menannon and shook his head. "I've ne'er seen so many bodies in one place save a battlefield. We've had to start making mass graves outside the city walls. E'en that is not enough and many folk are consigning the bodies of their loved ones to fire like a bunch of heathens. You can smell it."

"I know. We saw the graves as we came in. Has the contagion struck any of our folk?"

"Nay, the High One be praised! So far, none of ours have been affected. And unlike our poor neighbors, our wells are still clean. Your sire has organized a system by which we are aiding everyone to get a ration of clean water and food stuffs each day, but that has not prevented our folk from being attacked and cursed as your sire is being blamed for all the ills of Kalyria! Everyone's waiting for the end of the Queen's honeymoon and Azuron's return as if for a savior." Again Walderan shook his head.

"I know. It's the same throughout the countryside as well. Those of us who wear not the red of Doomcriers are being called Gorlanndoners and blamed for everything—."

Walderan held up a hand, halting Menannon's words as a scream suddenly cut across the atrium. "Another is dying. Go home lad, your sire awaits you and will tell you what tasks he has for you." Before Menannon could answer, the healer moved away motioning two other attendants to follow him.

Menannon began picking his way back to the hall's outer doors. He had gone but a few steps when the screaming stopped and all the attendants bowed their heads in prayer. Another of Azuron's followers had passed from the world.

Where, I wonder, goes a man when he dies if he believes he is his own god?, Menannon mused, though he deemed he knew full well and shuddered at the thought. *Another soul lost. I would that he had been saved.* Saddened, he closed the door softly behind him and went home.

"So FAR THE CONTAGION is only taking the youngest, the infirm and the old. The strong are not falling to it, but I'm sure it is only a matter of time," Gorlanndon informed Menannon as they sat within the summerhouse a few hours later, having just finished a cold collation left them previously by Clarinda.

"And of course, the more who die, the greater is the hatred among the rest for us," Menannon sighed. "Has there been any word from the Queen?"

"Nay, there has been no word from our new Prince Consort or our Lady Queen to say they even care about the suffering of our people. Yet the entire city and most of the council seem to think they will return as saviors and all will be set to rights." Silence fell then as both Giants contemplated all of the ills besetting their beloved land. From without, the ever-present tolling of the death bell continued monotonously, dulling their minds and ears until they became numb to it.

Menannon poured both of them another chalice of wine and then sat back staring into the amber depths of his as though somewhere within lay the answer. At last he looked up to see that his sire was perusing a heavy scroll he had taken from a case behind him. It was a list of weapons and men.

"My father, what are we going to do? We can feed the people for now. We can ease their suffering as they die, but that solves nothing." Menannon's voice trailed off in bewilderment.

"Armed bands of angry and hungry people are roaming the streets and alleys with nothing to do but fester with hate as even Azuron's circus has closed." Gorlanndon spoke quietly voicing his own thoughts aloud. "It is strange, though; the markets and shops have closed for the want of provender, yet the pubs and ale houses continue to have drinkable wares aplenty, though how this is being accomplished no one knows. Rumors abound of black ships with red sails bearing the sigil of a black sun all along the coasts beaching in the dead of night and unloading...something. There are rumors aplenty, but no witnesses. Of those who have tried to spy out the truth, none has ever returned, though a few mutilated and unrecognizable corpses have washed up on the shore from time to time." He drew out another scroll and unrolled it, leaving its spindles to weight it open.

Menannon said nothing, not wishing to break the thread of his sire's thoughts.

"Black ships...we have no black ships in any of our fleets on Kalyria...that means someone is able to get through Azuron's wall. Hmmm...." Gorlanndon suddenly turned the map so that it faced Menannon. He waved his hand over the entire face of Kalyria. "In your report, you said that the land without is poisoned by corruption leaching from the volcanos, correct?"

Menannon nodded, remembering the dead spiralhorn lying in what appeared to be clean water.

"Then there is no place upon the land we can find a sanctuary, so we'll have to look to the sea if our plan fails."Gorlanndon turned the map back and sat back, considering it while sipping his wine.

"What plan?" Menannon raised his eyes to his sire's troubled face.

"Firod, Walderan, Clarinda and I have discussed all angles and came to the conclusion that we need to await Norilendra's return and then I will confront her with the suffering of her people and try to persuade her to repudiate this marriage and restore balance. If she will not be persuaded then we will storm the palace and forcibly remover her from the throne and exile her to the mainland under Grandmaster Blackmore's keeping. I will then declare myself regent and will rule until Nirna can return and take her rightful place as queen."

Menannon noticed that his sire had said nothing about eliminating Azuron but then from the look in the elder Giant's eyes he did not have to. The bald headed Teluri would be eliminated.

"Must we wait until the Queen returns? Is it not a better plan to take the fight to her and storm the nuptial palace sooner rather than late?"

"If that were possible, that is what we would do but alas we cannot as there are ancient magics set upon that place and naught can open the doors from the outside until the month of solitude is accomplished." Gorlanndon took another long sip of wine. "Nay, we needs must wait until she returns here in all her glory...." He let his voice trail off into stillness, his mind's eye looking back to the girl he had once nurtured versus the woman he now was being forced to overthrow. Ah, the vagaries of power.

"So my father, what do you desire me to do in the mean time? Build more ships?" Menannon quipped, attempting to lighten the mood, as he did not like the look in his father's eyes.

"Nay, lad." Gorlanndon shook his head as though clearing it of a nightmare and smiled at his son. "Firod and I will take what care as can be taken of such details. I need you to assist Skendrin in doling out food and drink to our people for as long as our stores hold and pray that it will be long enough."

Later that night, Menannon awoke, drenched with the sweat of a nightmare in which a skeletal old hag had been waving the rotting corpse of a dead hen in his face and shrieking, "Ye did this! Ye killed me Lisby an' all the rest of us. Murderer...murderer...murderer!"

Thus was set the pattern of their days: Walderan and Clarinda waged war against the contagion in the makeshift almshouse in the Council Hall while Menannon and Skendrin doled out food and clean water from the trade hall atrium. All had to be done under the watchful eyes of Gorlanndon's warband, fully armed and ready to repel attacks. They were under orders not to kill or seriously maim any of their frantic neighbors, but they were to use any other force necessary to stem the growing tide of violence as the situation became more desperate and the death toll mounted.

IN GREAT CONTRAST TO THE POMP and circumstance of the Queen's exit from the city, her return was accomplished by stealth in the dark of the night. Only the gravediggers and stray dogs saw her closed litter as it made its silent way up through the city to the palace. The great doors boomed closed behind it with a sepulchral echo.

Yet despite that, dawn the next day found as many folk of the city, both Doomcriers and Gorlanndoners alike, as could crowded into the huge plaza silently waiting for the Queen and the Prince Consort to make their first official appearance. The full light of day was upon them before the doors of the palace opened and everyone took breath to cheer their royalty, but it was not the Queen and her Consort who came forth. Instead it was a phalanx of Dwarves dressed in Doomcrier red and burdened with the tools of their masonry trades and led by Master Mason Samlison, late of Starkhad, himself. The people gave way in whispering puzzlement as the Dwarves marched across the plaza to the statuary garden overlooking the sea. The great Dwarf bore a huge pry bar which he swung about and set to the joint of the nearest statue and with a mighty twist and shove brought low the statue of Kalyrinon King.

At his signal, his fellows set to tumbling the honored forms of the rest of the great ones from Kalyria's long history and tearing up paving stones at their feet. With the materials thus provided, they began to build an altar set prominently in the apex of the plaza directly across from the very Eyes of the High One. All this was watched in total bewilderment by the people of Kalyria. "Why has our Queen ordered an altar built? Why are they using the material from the statue gardens? Well, desperate times call for desperate measures. All will be well!" The questions and reassurances rippled back and forth across the plaza in a rising tide of anticipation.

It was nearing the tenth hour when Master Mason Samlison stood atop the altar himself and hammered the last stone into place while his fellow masons cheered him, then as one, they turned and marched back to the palace doors, where they hammered a tattoo, leaving their master standing on the altar.

As if on cue, Azuron himself came forth still garbed in his robe of many colors. Everyone gasped as they saw what circled his bald pate. The Prince Consort wore the crown of Kalyria's kings. He was surrounded by his personal guard. Everyone looked beyond him for the Queen, but she came not forth this day.

An aura seemed to surround the Teluri as he paced majestically towards the new made altar. The people felt their pulses quicken with anticipation believing that from his new position of power, he would call upon his own divinity and theirs, silence the volcanos and set all to rights.

At Azuron's coming, Master Mason Samlison dismounted from the altar, bowing so low his hooked nose nearly touched the ground. All watched as Azuron marched straight to the altar and climbed up onto it and stood to survey the crowd. Now he would prove Queen Norilendra justified in her faith in him. Now he would restore order. As the sun's light glinted from his robes and golden ornaments, Azuron, Prince Consort of Kalyria, raised his hand to signal to his commander who was still standing at the open doors of the palace.

At his leader's raised arm the man turned and re-entered the building only to emerge a few moments later escorting three councillors. At the sight of them, a strange stillness swept across the plaza. These venerable men were the oldest and most respected men on the entire council save for Gorlanndon himself. Down the steps and across the silent plaza, the Doomcriers escorted these men to the altar upon which Azuron stood. The councillors arranged themselves at the foot of the altar and stood looking up at the Prince Consort expectantly, though what they were expecting was unknown to the onlookers.

Above them, Azuron looked across the plaza, allowing his gaze to sweep all within it. Slowly as though performing the first gestures of a ritual he raised his be-ringed hands and pointed to the ancients before him. Now would these councillors be aided up onto the altar to stand tall beside their leader and order would be restored. The people of Kalyria were confident of this, but even as they watched Azuron's personal guards laid hands upon the councillors and did indeed place them upon the altar, not at Azuron's side as his equals, but forced to kneel at his feet, chain bound prisoners.

Contempt writ large upon his face, the new Prince Consort of Kalyria, the oldest and most blessed of all the High One's Human realms, raised his hands and his voice in an incantation not to his own spark of divinity nor even to the High One but to...*Khalandria, the Black God!* The people had been deceived though they knew not yet how completely.

There was but one spot of movement in the entire plaza now and that was the eddy caused by the crowd opening like waves before a ship, to allow a tall hooded figure to cross from the palace to the altar and climb upon it, mighty halberd in hand to stand over the kneeling councillors. Thrice Azuron's voice rose and thrice the halberd fell. The first sacrificial blood of the High One's followers spurted across the stones, sacrificed not to a brighter future, but to Khalandria.

All watched as Azuron accepted a golden bowl, offered him by his commander, then proceeded to fill it with the blood washing over his feet from the corpses lying on the stones beside him. With all the grace and self assurance of a great serpent, Azuron descended from the altar followed by his executioner and retraced the still open path across the plaza. Silently, he mounted the steps to the doors of the Council Hall from whose pediment still gleamed the sacred lights...the Eyes of the High One. He stood still for a moment, head bent in seeming prayer, then raised the bowl to arm's length above him, thrice. With a last word, followed by a mighty shout, he dashed the contents of the bowl across the doors.

As the blood touched the building—the lamps no mortal nor immortal hand could extinguish—flared, sending a flash of light across the plaza bathing the upturned faces of the throng with nearly blinding cobalt radiance. It held them entranced for an instant then went out as the High One turned his face away from Kirith Kalyria, leaving the transgressors to reap what they were sowing. The very fabric of the building seemed to shudder and shriek as great cracks and fissures spread across it radiating out from the darkened pediment. Many pillars fell and great blocks detached themselves from the walls. For a moment it seemed as though the entire building would collapse but the destruction halted with it still standing though battered. In the plaza there was total stunned silence, silence so still the gurgling of the waves around the pilings of the docks below could be heard, then one voice began to giggle.

BESIDE THE SOUTH PILING of the Mathematical Bridge and wishing his eyesight were not so keen, Menannon stood dumbstruck mute witness of the happenings in the plaza, too stunned to even return to his sire with the report of the progress the movement of the Queen and her Consort as had been requested of him when the first rumor of their presence had reached the villa with the dawn's breeze. In total disbelief, he watched Azuron turn from the doors and step to the front of the portico where the Teluri stopped and stood surveying the plaza. Azuron motioned the commander of his guards to him then waved his hand across the expanse before him apparently indicating any within it not dressed in red, as his words of command carried clearly across the silence.

"Bring them to the altar. Khalandria hungers!" With that

admonition, the Prince Consort of all Kalyria turned and re-entered the palace.

The banging of the great doors shattered the silence and with it the stillness in the plaza. Riot commenced there, a battle for survival as the Doomcrier guards began capturing any followers of the High One they could and dragging them to the altar to be sacrificed. Everyone began to either fight or flee as best suited their humor. Strangely, a goodly number of those in Doomcrier red fled the plaza as well, leaving behind them bits and pieces of their clothing as they abandoned their new faith and their hope together.

Even as the sounds of chaos and battle came to him, Menannon's attention was drawn away from the city to the ocean beyond the crescent where Azuron's invisible wall held all of them prisoners. Far beyond the wall, a small black dot had formed on the eastern horizon the instant the Eyes of the High One had been extinguished. Menannon strained his eyes to see that the dot was a fast growing cloud which quickly filled the entire horizon. Beneath it, a wall of water unlike any other wave he had ever seen, rolled inexorably towards the island. The young Giant barely had time to register in his mind that the far away dot was a cloud before the first drops of rain struck him in the face then darkness covered the face of the sun and the heavens opened.

Overhead great sheets of lightning slashed from cloud to cloud and thunder roared unchallenged. Rain fell in drenching torrents straight down from the roiling clouds above as a rock falls from the brow of a cliff, hissing and gurgling as it landed. Beneath this blackness of unnatural night the huge wall of waves crashed into the Crescent with hurricane-like force, its destructive power far beyond anything seen upon this seagirt island before. It snarled and crawled over the breakwater and across the mooring basin.

Wind could be heard screeching and screaming, yet there was no wind. Not a single breath—not even wind created by the force of the waves themselves—for this was not a storm of nature, but a sending of evil unchecked and unchallenged. Khalandria had answered his servant's call, for the wall of waves was lit by the seven red eyes of the Black God's most powerful demon, whose name among the follower's of the High One would ever afterwards be *Kalyria's Bane*.

As he watched, shielding his eyes with his hand to be able to see at all through the deluge, Menannon saw the darkness of the cloud above turn even darker in seven places. When all seven had become completely stygian they began to grow reaching down towards the land as stalactites grow from a cave roof. In less than a heartbeat they had grown to prodigious size then fell as one, like great mangonel loads trailing smoke-like pennants behind them. Three fell to the front of the city at the edge of the sea. Three fell towards the back beyond his line of sight, but he heeded them not, for the seventh and largest was falling towards the central plaza and the palace itself. The thing landed, throwing up a huge cloud of debris and bodies as it struck the plaza, crushing the flagstones beneath it. At its coming all other motion in the plaza stopped. As Menannon watched, the whirling thing seemed to drink into itself and become a solid mass which resolved into a huge figure almost as tall as his sire covered with black armour, bearing a huge sword and a blood red shield with a sigil of a black sun upon it. The figure turned towards him as though it knew he was there and looked squarely at him. The vizor of the helmet was thrown back revealing a face that was completely stygian, a black so deep it seemed to drink the light around it. At the sight of it Menannon's heart nearly froze. The thing was a Teluri! A black Teluri! The hair, the skin, even what should have been white in the eyes was black as were the teeth as it gave him a leering grin and turned to mount the steps to the palace cutting through any who stood in his way as easily as a scythe through grass, no matter the color of their coat.

The young Giant stood rooted in horror until the figure disappeared within the building. As the doors closed, the plaza erupted into battle again and his eyes were wrenched away to where the other three whirlwinds had landed. They too had resolved themselves into huge armoured black Teluri. Each was wielding its sword with abandon, at buildings and vegetation as well as people. Everywhere the swords hacked, gouts of flame leapt up in defiance of the drenching rain. Flames were soon licking hungrily at everything in the first circle including the hulks of the fleet that had been deposited there like toys in a child's bath by the pounding waves.

Thoroughly drenched and heartsick, Menannon fled back across the bridge and up the Equian way as the fighting poured down the sides of the Citadel and spread throughout the rest of the city. The entire city would soon be engulfed in bloodshed and flame. Menannon pushed past many curious people who had come out from the villas along the way to see what the noise and commotion portended. They stood staring and confused in the drenching rain knowing not what to do or to think.

Menannon's first impulse upon seeing these spectators was to shout "To arms! Death is upon you!" but he was neither sure who was a follower of the High One nor whether he would cause panic rather than rational action. Better report to his sire and let older, wiser heads decide their course. So he kept silent and ran on to the gate in his sire's wall where he halted, breathing hard, and pulled the bell rope. The embrasure opened instantly and Skendrin's hawk eye looked out briefly then it clacked to and the gate opened just enough for Menannon to squeeze through, then slammed shut and the heavy bar thudded back into place.

The steward saluted Menannon and returned to his work. Despite the rain, the courtyard was a scene of ordered calm as Gorlanndon's folk went about preparing the villa for a siege even before Menannon returned. The sound of battle had been heard. Skendrin already had his crews busily setting out stacks of arrows and javelins and filling casks of water ready to put out any fire which caught wooden surface. The steward was not one to deviate from precautions even if everything was already soaked. Luckily all of the roofs in the complex were slate or metal and would not catch fire if the rain had ceased by the time the battle reached them. Though from what he had seen issuing from the Teluris' swords, Menannon knew no amount of water was going to help.

Unsure as to where to find his sire, Menannon strode determinedly into the villa to look for him. Within, the staff went about their duties with their normal precision. The only thing which suggested that all was not quite as peaceful as it seemed were the furtive glances that were cast towards the doors or windows at each sudden sound from without. Menannon went out through the kitchen where Clarinda was overseeing the preparations for luncheon in her usual snappish manner. Praise the High One! She and Walderan had not gone to the Council Hall for the day and so were not there when it was nearly destroyed. As his sire was not within the villa, he must be in the summerhouse. Menannon rounded the kitchen wing and made short work of climbing the steps to the small structure. As he approached the door he could hear voices within especially the soft rumble of his sire's voice. What Gorlanndon was saying gave him pause even in his agitated state.

"There are weapons stashes here, here and here. When I give the signal, our folk will break out and take over the...." the voice lowered and Menannon heard no more.

He ran up the steps to the summerhouse three at a time and banged roughly on the door, then on the wall at either side, the prearranged signal. The door opened swiftly and Menannon slid inside pulling it to behind him. Inside, his sire sat at the table with Firod and Walderan all looking at a map of Kirith Kalyria laid out before them. An ancient scroll lay open beside it. Gorlanndon raised an inquisitive eyebrow. The others remained motionless looking expectantly at the youth, obviously seeing from his strained countenance that he bore ill news.

Menannon was forced to clear his throat twice before he could make his voice work. "The Eyes of the High One have gone out!" he blurted out at last. The statement settled into the small chamber like a stone falling into a well causing little noise, but deep ripples. All three men exchanged brooding glances then

Gorlanndon turned back and spoke softly.

"Tell us how this fell out."

Menannon told them all that he had witnessed hesitantly at first, but then his news came out in a torrent replete with his fear and incomprehension.

"And now there are seven huge black Teluri marauding the city, setting fire to all!" When he ceased speaking, Gorlanndon nodded and motioned him to take a place beside Walderan. The healer nodded to him wordlessly.

"It is as we feared then." Gorlanndon laid down the stylus he had been using as a pointer. He glanced at each of his confederates in turn finally locking eyes with Firod. "He has not only succeeded in breaking our pact with the High One, but has loosed Khalandria upon us as well." The great Giant's voice was calm almost conversational though his words announced the ending of the world as they had known it for nearly six thousand summers. He stood to his full height and stretched, the popping of his joints loud in the silence.

"Khalandria," Menannon whispered the dreaded name which to him had always been naught but a figure in the old sagas and the Word Hoard of the High One.

"Black God of Death...The sworn enemy of the High One and all His ways." Firod nodded, his voice echoed with the horror he felt. He turned back to Gorlanndon his hand white knuckled upon the hilt of his sword. "What say you old friend? Has the prophecy come to pass?"

There was a long silence in the small chamber as Gorlanndon considered his words his gaze resting sightlessly upon the scroll which still lay open before him. Menannon glanced at the surface of the scroll but could read nothing from it as it was written in ancient Giantish. One word alone stood out...Telurion. The author of the work was apparently the sire of the Teluri. At last the great Giant heaved a long sigh and sat down, gently removing the weights from the corners of the scroll. It whispered softly as he rolled it up and returned it to the case with its fellows. To Menannon eye his sire's movements had a deliberateness to them as though Gorlanndon were shutting a door which, once closed, could never be reopened. His sire sat still for a moment longer, then raised his eyes to lock with Firod's.

"There is but one chance left...Norilendra."

"Is it possible that all this can be righted by the Queen's recantation now that Khalandria has sent his demons?" Firod nearly whispered.

"It is the only hope for our beloved land." Gorlanndon's voice was calm as he spoke, but inflectionless and all the more troubling for that. "Norilendra recants or we flee there is naught we can do now. Since Azuron has found we would not go meekly into darkness and turn to the worship of Khalandria, he and his master have decided to destroy us. It has been conversion or death since his foot first touched our soil. If our Queen restores not our pact with the High One, Kalyria is doomed."

"Do you regret now that we did not assassinate this monster when the chance presented itself?" Firod queried, one eyebrow raised.

"No, I still say as I said ere this, one must abide by all of the Word Hoard of the High One or none of it, even when those things do not please you at the moment. It clearly says 'Thou shalt not deprive anyone of life save in mortal combat or in judicial execution to do aught else is murder and forbidden.'"

"Book of Telurion, chapter 57, verse 3" Menannon muttered to himself.

"To have assassinated Azuron would have been murder until now. Now he has gone to war against us and is free-game for mortal combat." Gorlanndon looked around the table and all were nodding, Firod with a slight grin as he had only asked his question to clarify their position to all. Gorlanndon straightened.

"Find Skendrin, boy," he said turning to Menannon. "Bid him raise the banner and sound the horn. Call all who remember or recognize the ancient summons to our side and if Norilendra fails us, we shall make our way to my flagship, for that is the only course now open to us."

"But surely...!" Firod began but halted when the Giant's black eyes swivelled once more in his direction.

"Nay! Now that the Seven Sons of the Bane have come, there is no other choice unless you can bend time as Irenos bends distance allowing us to undo the error of permitting the usurper to land upon our shores." Despite knowing such a thing impossible Menannon and Walderan found themselves glancing surreptitiously at the captain.

"Such is not my skill, nor that of any Human or Teluri," Firod sighed, shaking his head ruefully,"though I would that it were."

Gorlanndon glanced from face to face one black eyebrow raised in question seeming to silently inquire for any suggestions or other readings of their situation. There were none. He nodded, closing the interview.

"Then we must prepare to make our way to the lynne in case there is need. Gather all the folk the High One has sent here and all who come in the next few turns of the hour and if we go we shall collect those we can along the way still able and willing to join us and thus save as many as may be from this coil."

"Do you deem that the Queen will change her mind?" Menannon whispered the question to Walderan but all heard it.

"Norilendra will do as the sorcerer tells her," Firod growled in disgust. "Azuron has allowed her to retain nothing of her royal responsibility not e'en her responsibility to herself." His listeners noted his use of the Queen's name without the use of her title. The captain of the Kalyria's guard was thus subtly voicing his opinion of their queen's stupidity.

"Then the more fool she!" Walderan's voice was low and dangerous, his eyes were snapping with anger. To his mind, a queen who put her own desires ahead of the welfare of her people was forsworn before the High One and deserved the consequences of her actions.

"For that which was once between us, I will try once more to reach her better nature. She and the remains of the council will be clinging to the Palace so I needs must go there," Gorlanndon informed them. "Perchance she will listen to reason now that the results of her stupidity are playing out before her very eyes." At these words, Firod made a low disgusted noise in his throat, as he was unwilling to give voice to his thoughts.

Beside him Walderan just shook his head. "So doth a fool hope, my Lord."

"As to its foolishness, I must agree with you, but the attempt must be assayed for our people's sake. I will go, as there was a time when Nori listened to me. Perchance she will once more." Gorlanndon straightened his shoulders again and glanced around at all of them his eyes lingering on Menannon's tense face the longest. "Go, each to his duties as we planned it." All nodded as one and, as they turned to leave, Menannon whispered a question for Walderan's ears only.

"What of Azuron's wall? It's still out there blocking our way."

The healer glanced up at him and shrugged his shoulders. "We are highly unlikely to get that far, so I'd leave off worrying about the wall. If we actually do get that far, I have every faith that the High One will deal with it for the sake of his own," Walderan whispered back and preceded him out the door. Menannon could not but agree and followed him out.

Gorlanndon departed quickly.

Menannon halted in his search for the steward and watched him go with a brooding look, but made no attempt to stop him. As soon as the gate closed behind his sire, he resumed his search for Skendrin. He found the steward in one of the long storage sheds, slate in hand, taking stock of the remaining food stores. There was enough here to keep them going for yet a while. The Human looked up at the sound of Menannon's footsteps, his face a study in irritation which cleared at the sight of his young Master.

"My father sends instruction to sound the horn and raise the banner." Menannon imparted the order, not understanding in the least its meaning, but hoping the steward did. Skendrin stood stock still for half a heartbeat as though time had suddenly stopped, then he took a deep breath, hung his slate back upon its hook and time started again.

"So. It's come to that, then, has it? Follow me."

Saying naught else, Skendrin headed out of the shed at a fast lope that forced Menannon to lengthen his stride to match. Skendrin led him back into the villa and directly to Gorlanndon's office where he closed and bolted the door then drew all the curtains. Without a word, he indicated that Menannon should help him move the desk. Together and with great effort, they slid it aside revealing a long rectangle in the mosaic with a heavy brass ring at one end. In all the summers of his life, Menannon had never known his sire's desk hid more than just business transactions. He was surprised and puzzled. At Skendrin's nod, he heaved on the ring and raised a trapdoor which could not have been moved by Human, Dwarf or Teluri without the aid of a block and tackle. Thus opened, it revealed a set of stairs spiraling down into darkness. Skendrin took the Dwarf lantern from the desk, flipped open its shutter and plunged down the steps. Menannon followed.

The stairs were constructed at a riser length which suited Menannon perfectly, but caused the steward to thump down awkwardly as a child might. This stair had been built neither by nor for Humans. They went down what must have been at least two stories, then the stair ended abruptly in a narrow tunnel just tall enough for Menannon to stand upright. Gorlanndon would have had to bend nearly double to navigate it. The tunnel was lined with dark tiles imbedded with some glittering material on floor, walls and ceiling, giving the impression of being underwater. The young Giant had to force himself to not automatically hold his breath. There was a thin layer of dust on the floor denoting the lack of visitors to this place. In front of him, Skendrin closed the Dwarf lantern leaving them in total darkness.

"Why—," Menannon began, puzzled, but Skendrin shushed him.

"Wait," the steward murmured. They stood together in the blackness of a grave which gave Menannon the eerie feeling he was back in the small cell under the palace. He could feel his heart begin to pound and a fine trickle of sweat course down his spine. Just as he was about to panic, a strange flicker ran the length of the visible tunnel and then a glow softly surrounded them, growing ever brighter until the way was almost as bright as daylight. Menannon gasped in surprise and stepped to the wall to peer closely at the glowing tiles. They were embedded with fine chips of glowing crystal, similar to the crystals at the heart of the Dwarf lanterns. He had never seen anything like it.

Skendrin did not hesitate, but forged ahead, obviously knowing where he was going. Menannon had to actually run to catch up, so intent had he been in his inspection of the wall he had not noticed the steward move until the fellow was nearly lost to sight. He caught up just as Skendrin rounded a corner and the tunnel ended in a heavy metal door, its surface covered with intricate patterns of vines and leaves, obviously the work of the Teluri, probably Liliénthar himself judging by the quality of the work. He took a deep breath. and spoke a series of what seemed to be words in a strange, singsong voice and a line formed around the edge of the door. There was a soft click and it swung silently open revealing another spiral stair going upwards into darkness. Skendrin flipped open his lantern and began to climb in the same awkward fashion he had previously. Menannon climbed taking one stair at a time with a perfect stride length. Why had the way been built for Giants under a Human city, he wondered for in all the ancient records he had studied at Aridion City, there had never been mention of such a thing. Obviously, there were serious holes in the harper hall's collection which needed to be filled.

Menannon abruptly halted, stunned. Here was absolute proof that he, Gorlanndon's son, was a normal-sized Giant as of old, for all this was more ancient than even the original harper hall in Aridion City and it was sized exactly for him. Something finally clicked in his mind and he truly believed Grandmaster Blackmore's words at last. The thought left him both exhilarated and appalled. How far his people had deviated from the High One's design and intent! Menannon shook himself from his thoughts and raced on up the stairs to catch the steward.

Skendrin was breathing hard by the time they reached the top of the stair and stood on a wide platform facing another Teluri door. Here again, the steward sang the words of power and the door opened. They stepped through to find themselves in an empty circular chamber, walled, roofed and floored with glow tiles. They stepped into the chamber, the door closing soundlessly behind them. Skendrin shuttered the lantern and they waited silently for the glow to form while the steward caught his breath. Soon the chamber was as light as day despite its lack of windows as Menannon assumed they must have climbed up within the ancient tower on the farthest corner of his sire's close, as they had climbed at least twice as high as they had originally descended.

"What now...," Menannon began, but the steward shook his head indicating now was not the time for questions.

He handed Menannon his lantern and gently pushed him back into the doorway which resembled a small hallway of its own.

"Wait here, Young Master," he said and stepped to the center of the chamber.

There he knelt and removed the ancient torque he always wore and the signet upon his finger. These he placed into his belt pouch and tossed it to Menannon who nearly dropped the lantern in his surprise. Seeing Skendrin removing all metal upon his person, he understood that the steward was about to perform a sacred ritual, so Menannon hastily set down the lantern then removed his belt pouch and his sire's ring on its cord from about his neck, setting them on top of the lantern along with Skendrin's belt pouch. He, too, knelt and waited.

Skendrin bowed his head, then softly spake the sacred words.

"In the time of Awakening, Thou didst command a forging to be performed and a Horn created that would ever be sounded in warning in times of greatest peril to call Thy people out from among them. This day we ask to be allowed to sound thy Horn for Thy folk are in greatest peril. To their good and Thy glory, Amen."

Menannon murmured his own *Amen*, but remained kneeling as Skendrin stood. The Human squared his shoulders and began to chant in a language the Giant had never heard before this. It seemed vaguely Teluriesque, though none of the words made any sense to him. As he chanted, Skendrin began to circle the tower widdershins. Thrice did he so circle then, on the last note of his chant, he halted across the chamber from the door and knelt with his hands clasped and his head bowed.

Nothing happened.

They waited in a silence so profound Menannon could hear the blood swishing through his own veins. What was happening? Would the High One answer? What was this horn? These questions and many more chased themselves around and around in his head until he felt like screaming. When he was finally sure he would go mad with tension, there was a noise, a click and a slight grinding sound. He glanced around wondering if he had really heard anything or if his fevered brain had simply created the sound, for across from him Skendrin had not moved so much as an eyelash. But, no. Before him the tiles on the floor had begun to move. They were beginning to circle widdershins, slowly at first then faster and faster until they were spinning so fast they blurred into a mist.

The mist was a light aquamarine color at first then began to darken through emerald into cobalt then suddenly shot up to the ceiling in a column like unto fire. Its glow brightened until Menannon had to throw up his arm to shade his eyes or go blind. Even this was not enough and he bowed his head to the floor burying his face in his knees and arms as the glory of the High One shone around him so brightly he could see the bones dark within his hands despite his eyes being squeezed as tightly closed as he could get them. Everything around him seemed to fade away until even his perception of the tiles beneath his knees faded to nothing and he was floating in pure light.

How long this lasted, he would never know, but somehow it came to him at last that the light was dimming and going out. Gingerly, he opened his eyes and raised his head and saw that the mist had indeed disappeared and in its place stood an ancient horn nearly filling the entire chamber. Beside it, a rod rose from the floor and made its way through a roof which was no longer there, though something was, as the rain was pouring down without wetting either the chamber or the horn. Beyond this non-roof, a huge banner snapped at the tip of the rod, the sigil of the High One clear upon it. Lower, the wall was now filled with open archways through which no wind blew.

All this Menannon saw, then forgot, as his eyes were drawn to the mighty horn. Its coils, bell and mouthpiece were covered with the same vine and leaf patterns adorning the doors, but instead of being solid as they, it was made of some slightly aquamarine transparent substance for through it he could see the form of Skendrin still kneeling on the far side of the chamber. Not even the Teluri forgesingers possessed the skill to create such an object. Menannon found himself in such awe of the horn, he could neither move nor think. How could one play such an instrument? Apparently, Skendrin did not suffer from the same paralysis, for as the Giant watched dumbfounded, the steward rose and crossed to where he knelt and held out his hand to him.

"Arise, Giant, and perform thy duty. Son of Lornennir, sound the Horn Perilous." Skendrin spoke in the ancient ritual cadence heard now only during the rites of the High One in the great halls of gathering.

As though his mind and spirit were suddenly outside his body, Menannon seemed to watch himself take Skendrin's outstretched hand and rise to cross to the horn. The Steward remained where he was standing in the doorway. Disbelievingly, Menannon watched himself reach out and touch the horn, then instead of setting his lips to the mouthpiece, he saw himself reach up and untie the laces of his kirtle and chemise and bare his breast. He was the perfect height. Standing thus, his beating heart was exactly at the level of the mouthpiece. This truly was a task for Giants! Menannon watched himself in awe as his body stepped closer until the mouthpiece of the mighty horn nearly touched his flesh. How did his body know what to do when his mind did not? At that instant, Menannon's mind reunited with his physical self so suddenly, he actually jerked and in so doing touched his flesh to the High One's horn.

It sounded.

He knew with all his being that it sounded though he heard it not with his ears. His very soul vibrated with it. The call went forth, commanding, entreating, whispering, shouting …demanding that all come to the High One. It was not unlike the healing call of a harp as it ran through his blood and being, irresistible and comforting. Above them, the sigil on the banner kindled and a bright blue-white light flared out in all directions in defiance of the storm and darkness. Nothing could stand against it, for it was not of this world, but a rent in the fabric of creation, a gateway through which the glory of the High One Himself shone, an overwhelming explosion of holiness. Before it, Evil groaned and fled.

Thrice, the horn called out: *Come to me!* Thrice, the light flared its message: *I am here!* Thrice, Evil fled before them. The horn was silent, the sigil darkened, their work done. Menannon dropped to the floor, senseless.

He came to himself to find Skendrin shaking him. He sat up instantly, glancing around wildly. The chamber was empty and windowless again, its roof once more solidly above them, lit only by Skendrin's lantern. Had he been dreaming? Skendrin handed him his belt pouch and his sire's ring and waited until he had fastened it once more about his neck, then again gave him a hand up. Neither of them spoke a word as they left the chamber and made their way back to his sire's office. When they had closed the trap and returned the desk to its normal resting place. Skendrin laid his hand on Menannon's arm and spoke softly.

"It was real," was all he said. He handed the Giant the closed lantern and left the chamber.

Menannon found himself having to sit on his sire's great chair as his legs began to tremble too hard to hold him, his breath suddenly coming in painful gasps. He set the lantern back in its place as gently as he could before the trembling of his hands forced him to drop it. He sat there for a few minutes trying to come to grips with the fact that he had truly been in the very presence of the High One, albeit a small part. The sheer temerity of his actions suddenly appalled him. That he, a renegade harper, should actually have dared to enter a chamber so obviously made for his betters and touch the Horn Perilous! That the High One had not instantly struck him dead was beyond imagining. This thought alone petrified him so badly his stomach rolled and he had to bolt to the bathing chamber to keep from casting his accounts on the top of his sire's desk. It was the best part of a half turn of an hour later before he could trust his stomach enough to even consider going out into the courtyard to see what had been the result of the horn's call.

CHAPTER 24
(SUMMER OF THE WORLD 6097)

EVEN AS MENANNON SET OFF in search of the steward, Gorlanndon circled to the front where the guards let him through the gate and re-barred it behind him. Once again a seeming swirl of dark cloud appeared to cross the Mathematical Bridge as Gorlanndon made short work of attaining the central plaza undetected and stepped to the back of the palace. There he halted and glanced about. It was as Menannon had reported. The plaza was filled with battle as Azuron's Doomcriers were seizing and dragging to the altar as many of the High One's followers as they could. The new Prince Consort had had his throne removed from the throne room and now sat behind the altar watching as the blood gushed from its top and gurgled into the drains around the edge of the plaza, reveling in his success. Around the plaza all of the government buildings save the Council Hall and palace itself were wreathed in flames. Beneath his feet, Gorlanndon could feel the plaza tremble and heave as the storm pounded the island. Tearing himself away from the terrible scene, Gorlanndon lunged into the palace close and up the portico steps.

For the first time since is foundations were laid, the entryways of the palace were dark, lit only from without by the raging fires and the sporadic lightning. In the uncertain light, Gorlanndon could see the floor was rent and cracked, great fissures running across it into which the treasures of the ages had fallen. Nothing remained untouched. Even as he watched, the floor shuddered again to the pounding of the waves, sending another crack up the wall and another statue to oblivion. The fan vaulting high overhead was cracking, sending great chunks of stone raining down about him. A small, jagged hole tore open in the wall beside him, and a blinding light assailed his eyes. Through the gap thus formed came the sound of babbling voices, a frenzied caterwauling that increased in volume and intensity with every falling block. In the midst of this unequaled crisis the remaining council was reveling in the very throne room itself. A place nearly as hallowed as the Great Hall of Gathering in the harper halls. Never before this had it been so besmirched.

Gorlanndon wrenched open the still-solid door to the chamber and looked about him, stunned. Faces stared blankly back at him, expressionless, empty, mouths spewing gibberish. He stood frozen, barely able to wrap his mind around the sight. He felt an almost overwhelming desire to run away, to hide, to escape the insanity surging around him, but by main force of will he made his feet move and ducked into the chamber. The rest of the councillors swirled around him in their demented drunkenness, as though he were no more than a wraith in a fog. They milled about the chamber in full ceremonial robes, half drenched in wine, their bejeweled beards dripping the spittle of madness. The rich tapestries hung in shreds along the walls and the royal banners still suspended from the ruined ceiling were naught but tattered rags. All of the furniture and statuary lay broken and shattered about them save one long table holding the stuff of their revel. All around the edges of the central floor, a strange darkness seemed to crawl like a distant mirage in the desert which as it is approached retreats ever beyond reach.

Gorlanndon scanned the faces of his fellow councillors, desperately seeking some sign they knew or cared what was happening to themselves and their city. He was greeted by laughter and shrill yelling as if they only regretted they could make no louder noise. In that moment the darkness thickened and moved closer. Gorlanndon staggered as if by a blow, his head bowed beneath the weight of despair. "High One, forgive us, for we know not what we do." The words came from him as a sob of grief. He shook his head, feeling as though his lungs would burst. Again forcing himself to move, Gorlanndon pushed into the writhing throng.

One figure alone remained in place, lips tight closed. The queen, Norilendra, sat silently upon the throne, hands white-knuckled upon its arms. Gorlanndon inched his way past the crazed, howling councillors and knelt at her side, determined to make this one last attempt to get through to her.

"Oh, Lady, the ancient evil we have all feared since the depths of the Dim Times has been loosed upon us. Khalandria is here. His storm is upon us!" Even with the power of his great voice, he had to yell to make himself heard. "We must act swiftly. There is little time!"

Slowly, as if her mind was returning from some unfathomable distance, Norilendra turned to him, her face as white as alabaster and expressionless as a statue. She picked up a figurine lying in her lap, a talisman of…what? It was in the likeness of a Teluri child made of obsidian with diamonds for eyes that shone starfire in the chamber's light.

The queen's eyes burned brighter than those in the figurine, for the fires of madness now lit them.

"So, *Councillor* Gorlanndon, you have come again to gloat that you and your *creatures* were right!" she fairly hissed. "No! Deny it not, for did you not counsel that the compact with the High One must be obeyed and the blood line of the Kalyrian kings be kept pure? That to do otherwise would be to doom ourselves and all we hold dear?" She thrust the figurine into a pocket of her robe and stood, tall and darkly fair upon the steps.

"Go! Get thee gone! Rejoice in your wisdom, for around you, our city, our very world itself is dying by the spite of *your* High One!" The darkness now covered nearly the entire floor and had crept to the very steps of the dais upon which sat her throne, its blackness having becoming more solid, nearly oily in its appearance. Only where Gorlanndon knelt was there still a space of bare stone. The rest of the councillors were wading in the stuff up to their knees.

"Nay, my Lady, it is not by the will of the High One, but by the design of the Evil One. Khalandria is destroying our city!" Gorlanndon tore his eyes away from the darkness and countered her words. "The High One wills not our destruction, only our repentance. Despair not, my Lady, for there is still a way to save our beloved land."

Her answer was a high, hysterical laugh.

"Doest thou still believe in thy "high one's" justice just when he is doing so much for thee?!!! We shall burn or drown! Drown! Drown!" Her voice rose in a weird sing-song soon mimicked by the other councillors who crowded around Gorlanndon, pushing him back to the wall despite his great size, hands crawling over him, chanting madly those words of despair. With a lunge born of desperation, he broke free of them and caught his queen by the shoulders.

"There is still hope, Nori. Do not do this." He held her fiercely, desperately willing her to understand. "You can still live. You do not have to die." Slowly, his words penetrated the chaos of her mind and for a moment, she stood staring at him like a vulnerable little girl being offered a sweet, then her face took on the regal mien of old, from before the coming of Azuron. She drew herself up to her full height. His hands fell away from her shoulders.

"Do you really believe there is a chance?" she asked, turning to stare out the now glassless windows, a glimmer of hope in her eyes.

"Yes, I do."

"Why?" she snapped, turning back. "Why should High One see fit to devour this city and then turn his wrath for a few words of recantation?" Her desperation was plain in her voice.

"My Queen, this new destruction is by the hand of the Evil One, through the Demon who has become the Bane of this city. It is no work of the High One. Recant your unlawful marriage and the High One will welcome you back and our beloved land with you."

"But I am no longer one of your faithful. I truly believed the words of Azuron. We do have within each of us our own divinity. I have believed that this High One is nothing but a myth to frighten witless children." Her voice was soft, with an undertone of despair. "Why, then, do you expect the High One should believe me if I recant?"

"Never since the first day you came here to be Ronirinen's bride have I witnessed you guilty of an unworthy act save only this one. No matter what mistakes you have made, the High One only desires your repentance, not your death. Give up this forbidden marriage, repent you unbelief and the High One will forgive you. Let it go! Repudiate it as the abomination it is and the High One will grant us His blessing once again! And your daughter can return to you from the mainland." Gorlanndon held her gaze for a moment then she looked away beyond him, a child again, the longing in her eyes unmistakable.

"Is that where she is? Aridion? How?" she whispered.

"By the will of the High One and the craft of the Teluri was Menannon able to take her there and she longs to come home to you." Gorlanndon spoke quickly, a small spark of hope growing in his breast.

For a moment, and a moment only, the shrieks and screams of the dying city abated and silence reigned. Even so, had he not been so close to her, her words would have gone unheard. She turned pleading eyes of lapis-lazuli upon him, and spoke to him. "Help me." It was a plea wrought of deep despair, spoken as by a helpless child. The moment passed and the cacophony of sound again assailed them. The sea thundered and the city trembled, her plea buried under the sounds of destruction and battle.

As the cacophony returned, the darkness about her throne shot up around her swathing her as though in the folds of a liquid cloak until only her face showed untouched for a single heartbeat, then he saw in the depths of her eyes, a darkness like unto black pearls, as though something else suddenly shared them, then the lapis was gone, leaving only black pearl eyes blazing with fury. In that instant, all hope died.

"NO!" she screamed in a voice deep as the sea about them and not her own. "NO, by all the imps in Hella! No! I have no daughter! I shall not surrender! I shall not repudiate my CONSORT! I shall not go crawling to your puny high one. The high one who denied me my true love shall not defeat ME! I am Norilendra Queen of Kalyria! THIS TIME I SHALL HAVE MY

WAY!" The queen's body grew before his very eyes and the darkness moved out from her eyes until her entire countenance turned stygian. "Go! Go if you will! Run! Hide! Throw yourselves upon the tender mercies of your High One!" Her voice rose in mockery and mad triumph.

Gorlanndon forced himself to his feet and backed away from this thing which had been his queen and almost daughter, but it followed him, step by step, even as the city crumbled around them.

"GO! Never will I submit me! I am queen...QUEEN of the mightiest city in all the ages of Linden! Do you hear me? I shall never grovel before the High One! REPENTANCE BE DAMNED!" The stygian Norilendra-thing was swollen to twice her normal size and still it grew until it towered over the Giant. Suddenly its eyes blazed red with the demon light of Khalandria.

From the fold of its liquid robe, it withdrew the statuette Norilendra had been holding and hurled it onto his face, breaking his cheek bone.

"The one thing that gives us more pleasure than the destruction of this piddling little insignificant island is that you, Gorlanndon, shall die this night, for our Azuron, our KING, hunts you like the animal you are! You and your abominable seed."

To his horror, Gorlanndon knew this thing no longer spoke of a Teluri sorcerer with the word king.

"Go! Crawl to your High One! But we shall have our way in the end. The High One who has doomed us shall not rule the deaths of these creatures!" The thing which had been the queen of Kalyria reached down and tore a torch from its sconce, blew upon it a strange, black fire and skipped madly about the chamber, spreading black fire to all the tattered tapestries and banners, even the stone itself, until all was wreathed in ebon flames.

Gorlanndon backed through the door, his heart recoiling in horror and revulsion at the sight of his fellow councillors and what was left of their queen dancing a strange wanton dance among the hellish flames roaring to the roof vaults. Turning, he fled the palace, barely reaching the portico before the roof thundered down in ruins behind him. He staggered back to the plaza wall feeling its cold stones bite into the back of his legs as a pillar of darkness shot skyward above the flaming ruins. It coalesced into a solid thing and drew back, then hurled towards him. Just as it began to move, the night and chaos reverberated with a *call* and a bright blue-white flash emanating from the top of the Equian hill. At its coming, the darkness halted as though striking a wall. It started back then began to move forward again only to be halted a second time as the *call* and light flashed out again. A third attempt also failed and the darkness turned away and withdrew flowing down the Citadel like a shroud spreading madness as it went.

Gorlanndon fled.

STILL SLIGHTLY UNSTEADY, Menannon made his way out of the glass doors from his sire's office into the garden and thence to the back of the villa. The rain was still falling and the sound of the sea was louder now. He looked up towards the top of the ancient tower to see that it looked as it always had, windowless with a pointed circular roof unadorned by so much as a lightning rod. There was nothing about it to indicate that less than a full turn of an hour ago it had been the site of a miracle. Yet the sight of its solidity and normalcy did much to calm Menannon's rattled composure. If such a mundane structure could have been of use to the High One, then perchance he had not been as brazen as he felt. One day, he would have to discuss it with Master Blackmore. Even as he thought this, he looked beyond the tower to see that it was silhouetted against a background of flickering red. The fires devouring the city had grown so fierce they were reflecting from the clouds overhead. He could think of matters spiritual when he returned to Aridion City, if he returned. Now was neither the hour nor the place.

Menannon wrenched his eyes away from the ominous sight and hurried around the corner to where he could look into the main courtyard. It was filled with several hundred of His folk and more were coming in at the gate all the time. The horn had done its work and the High One's followers were making their way to Him as well as they were able. There were men, women and children from all walks of life. Most were Human, but there were a goodly number of Dwarves and even a few Teluri among them. They had all come as they were, bringing naught with them but what had been in their hands when the High One called. Some were divesting themselves of all trace of red upon their clothing, glad to shed the camouflage at long last; one gentleman was down to his hose, also red, but for the sake of modesty retained them. Mikhal the Dwarf was there, too, with his family. Menannon was both relieved and appalled by the numbers, relieved that there were so many still loyal to the High One on Kalyria and appalled by the number they would have to accommodate in their attempt to flee the island. He turned and ran up to the summerhouse in search of his sire.

He arrived to find Irenos in full battle armour, the single battle-braid wrapped around his neck, standing on the steps, his attention on the vast panorama of the city below. Menannon joined him, coming to a halt a few steps below the Teluri so that he could look him in the eyes as he spoke to him.

"What are you doing here? You were home, safe! Why did you come back?!" He demanded far more roughly than he intended in his surprise and consternation.

"I heard the Horn Perilous," the Teluri smiled. "I heard it as did all Teluri and I knew I needs must answer the call. So would others of my folk have done, had they the means, but I alone posses the skill to bend distance. I came to aid thee and thy sire in this, thy darkest hour."

"But, Highness, this is not your battle."

Menannon looked long into the Teluri's face, seeking understanding.

"The High One deems it is, else He would not have called

me," Irenos said simply and turned his gaze once more to the scene below.

Menannon followed his gaze and his heart sank. From there, the full horror of what was happening to the city was revealed. Already the warehouses and wharves were gone, torn from their foundations by the pounding waves. Closer, the second circle was wrapped in flames, an eerie background for black figures dancing in a frenzy of destruction. The demon-spawned flames were an inferno, already lapping at the third circle of walls and they would not take long to demolish the rest. There in the darkness, a deadly race was being run to see which would destroy the city first: the sea or the flames. Even as he watched, the sea won another round as a long section of the third circle's wall was breached. It crumbled and slid beneath the raging waves.

"I have had some speech with Skendrin and we needs must make our move soon if we are to have any possibility of escape," Irenos murmured almost as though he spoke to himself as he watched the destruction inexorably climb towards them.

"We cannot leave without my father. He has gone to seek the Queen and has yet to return." Menannon's voice was soft as well, but there was steel in it.

"We may well have to, lad. If that gets much closer, all escape will be cut off and this villa will burn just as the others are burning. Thine is one of the last ones holding." He pointed down the slope to where two others of the city's great villas could be seen wreathed in flame. "We owe it to the folk the High One has called into thy care."

"I know, I know, but if my father succeeds in getting the Queen to repent there would be an end…," Menannon tried to keep a tight rein on his fear, but his eyes were haunted.

"And what end might that be, lad? Is it honestly thy thought that Azuron and his demon could be stopped by such a simple thing as the Queen's repentance? While the High One would forgive her for her transgression, that which she set in motion must still attain its end. Our actions in this life have consequences, and though we would wish it, we cannot make them undone. Her actions allowed Azuron to do what he has done, and the god he serves is bent upon the perversion or destruction of everything ever created by the High One or in His honor and he's adding thine homeland to his clutch. Folly is Khalandria's tool as much as fire and water. This has gone too far to be halted now. Even if the High One were to restore his blessing, Kalyria as we have known it is doomed."

Irenos looked down upon the burning city, but what he saw was far older and more horrible.

"I stood upon the Delarian plateau nearly four thousand summers ago and saw this very demon leading the forces of the Evil One, Khalandria the Black God of Death. Its power was beyond imagining and only the combined strength of all the High One's followers and true-hearted creatures of Linden was able to hinder it. The folk of Linden were strong then. Those of the age of creation still walked among us: the Dawn Grey Beards, sires of the Dwarves; the twelve sons of Telurion Firstborn and his consort Sharilandra; the seven lords of thy folk as well as Beldronnen, tallest and mightiest of all Giants and his nine sons, mighty warriors all. And with us stood Gandomar Earthshaker, greatest of Draktas and his children in numbers uncounted. E'en then we could not defeat it, only send it back to Outer Darkness for a short while, though that cost the lives of over half our army.

"When all was o'er, all save one of the Dawn Greybeards lay dead. Of the sons of Telurion, none remained alive save Gilarian, Liliénthar, Rhindolier and Tanguroth. Of the Giants, Beldronnen alone still stood at day's end. His nine sons and all the rest of the Giants who had come forth to fight lay dead upon the stricken field. Nay, lad, neither water not fire nor or e'en force of arms will avail us against that which we now call Kalyria's Bane. The High One alone may one day give us the aid we need to defeat the monster. Until then, we can but try to mitigate its destruction and save as many of the High One's folk as we can."

"You are right in that, old friend," the softness of Gorlanndon's deep voice could not hide the note of sadness in it. "Azuron is succeeding in his master's demented plan."

Together, Menannon and Irenos whirled at the sound of the elder Giant's voice, startled at his sudden arrival. A short distance behind him, Skendrin, Walderan and Firod followed, having come from their several occupations to hear his report.

At their questioning looks, Gorlanndon simply shook his head. "Despite all, Norilendra refused to turn against her new consort and restore balance. She and the rest of the council are dead by the hand of the demon. Azuron now rules Kalyria. His Doomcriers are e'en now attacking the final strongholds of our folk led by the Sons of the Bane. They will be here in force in but a few turns of the hour."

Azuron! The very name of the Teluri sorcerer cut through Menannon's mind like flame and the image of the sorcerer with his emaciated face and shaven head was forever emblazoned upon his memory. Yes. Azuron was indeed the cause of all this! *By all that's holy, he will be brought to justice and made to pay for his crimes...!*

Gorlanndon broke the thread of Menannon's thoughts by motioning them all into the summerhouse for a final council. When they were all seated save Menannon who was too restless to sit, Gorlanndon began.

"Welcome back, old friend. Though I think you a fool for coming." Gorlanndon grinned at Irenos by way of greeting then turned to the steward. "Skendrin, you did well. The horn has sounded and the people come." Gorlanndon smiled at his steward, but Skendrin shook his head.

"I did but show the way, Master. It was your son who sounded the Horn Perilous, for only a true Giant can make it raise its voice."

Skendrin grinned at Menannon who had come to a halt behind his sire's chair. Every eye turned in surprise and approval to the younger Giant who colored nicely under the gaze. Gorlanndon turned and laid a hand upon his son's shoulder and gave it an approving squeeze, his smile wide and heartfelt.

"Prophecies are never fulfilled in the way you expect," the elder Giant whispered as though to himself and reaching down, kissed Menannon's brow then turned back to the table, his face growing stern again.

"The time has come for us to depart this island. The harbor has been destroyed with all ships within. Our hope now lies in my flag ship. She holds near six hundred normal-sized men in comfort, so all who are here will find room aboard, but I fear few others will. Unfortunately, someone will have to go to my trade hall in the Serpentine and get the key to the north water gate from my strong box where I foolishly left it and signal Waterdeep to ready the inclined plane, if it be unharmed."

"I'll go," Irenos offered instantly.

"Nay." Gorlanndon smiled at the Teluri, but shook his head. "I shall need you to aid me in escorting all these good folk to the lynne. Nay, someone else must be found."

"I...," Firod began, but there was that in the look on the elder Giant's face and his quick glance towards Menannon which halted the captain's words.

Firod raised one eyebrow in question, then his face cleared and he inclined his head and said no more. If they were forced to make their last stand here at the villa, Gorlanndon did not want his son trapped within. There were no words spoken in the summerhouse for a few moments. At last, Menannon shifted restlessly and took a long breath and let it out slowly before turning to look up at his sire.

"I will go, though I would lief as not leave your side until we are all safely aboard ship and out to sea."

Menannon reached into his belt pouch and withdrew a handkerchief and handed it to his sire to wipe the track of blood from his cheek where the figurine had broken it open. The cheek itself was already swelling and turning dark purple over the broken bone.

"I would we could stay together as well, but there is none other to whom I would trust this charge. All our lives depend upon it. Now," he turned quickly back to Irenos and Firod, "after Menannon achieves the key, he needs must bring it back to the head of the stair leading down to the lynne from the west side of the central plaza, for all other ways are below the Serpentine and, therefore, must be lost to us by now. Once on the sea, we shall make straight north so that we will escape this demon-spawned storm which came out of the east."

Gorlanndon ceased speaking and, laying the cloth he was still holding on the table, stood to his full height with such finality that all comment, should there have been any, was stilled upon the lips of his companions.

"Organize the people. We will be leaving in two turns of the hour." He nodded to Irenos and the other leaders. "Come, boy, I will see you gone."

Placing a gentle hand on Menannon's shoulder, he led him out of the summerhouse to the back wall of the close. In the darkness beneath the wall, he stopped and dropped to his knees to better treat with his son.

"There is much to say and little time to say it, boy," he spoke softly. "Know that all our lives are depending upon you and know also that I love you more than life itself and am prouder of you than I could ever hope to tell you."

Suddenly Gorlanndon reached out and clasped Menannon to his breast and held him hard. Menannon returned the embrace with a heartfelt one of his own, his stomach tightening again with dread, the slight sense of peace which had lingered in the back of his mind since the sounding of the Horn Perilous deserting him all together.

"Are you saying your final goodbye to me, my father?" Menannon whispered around a lump forming in his throat.

Gorlanndon held him off at arms length then took him by the back of the neck and kissed his brow.

"No, boy. If the High One wills it, we shall see each other again, but you have your duty and I have mine. Now come. I'll lower you over the wall and you must make your way down to the Serpentine. Stay in the shadows and off the streets as much as possible."

Menannon stood still for just a moment, but could not help himself and reaching up, threw his arms about his sire's neck and buried his face against his broad chest. "I love you, my father.

Please, please, please forsake me not," he whispered.

Gorlanndon said nothing, only held him hard for a moment more then unclasped Menannon's hands from around his neck and lifted him as easily as a Human sire would a small child and eased him over the wall. He held him by both hands for a moment.

Despite his own intentions not to further burden his son with the knowledge of how close was their doom, Gorlanndon suddenly could not let him go without first exacting a promise from him.

"Menannon, swear to me that no matter what happens to me or any of the rest of us, you will live through this holocaust. Whatever you have to do, you must live. Is that clear?"

There was suddenly such confusion in Menannon's mind that he could not answer.

"Swear to me boy! You will live no matter what it takes to do so. Swear it!" Gorlanndon hissed and shook his son slightly.

Menannon swallowed hard and spoke clearly, though softly.

"I so swear, my father."

Gorlanndon lowered him as far as he could reach, then let him drop the rest of the way.

Menannon landed with a soft thud amidst the rocks and bracken at the base of the villa's outer wall. He looked up for a moment, locking eyes with his sire, then turned and slipped away into the storm's unnatural darkness. Gorlanndon watched him until the darkness swallowed him then whispered the most heartfelt prayer of his entire life for his son's safety and turned back to his duty within the close.

FORCING ASIDE THE TUMULTUOUS THOUGHTS and emotions raging through him, Menannon concentrated on moving unseen, darting from one patch of darker shadow to another along the outer wall of his sire's estate. The brush and rocks at the base of it made for hard going, but provided additional cover for which he was grateful. He stayed below the outer walls of the other villas. At the crossroad, he would have to choose his path carefully, for from there the way would be open and visible to all until he achieved the cover of the back alleys of the city. Menannon scrambled up to the corner of the last villa's wall and surveyed the crossroad. Nothing moved to disturb the torrent of rain-water rushing along it.

Which way? His first choice, and by far the quickest, would be to go down the front road to one of the lesser bridges then across to the Citadel, thence to the Aureun and make his way to his sire's trade hall, which should still be above the rising waves, though barely. Menannon silently weighed his choices. From his vantage point, he could see the tops of the Idrian and Aureun hills beyond the Citadel. Both were wreathed in flames. The lower reaches of the city and the harbor were obscured by smoke and rain so thick he could barely see the tips of the twin lighthouses on the Crescent, soon to utterly disappear beneath the raging waves. Directly below him, having succumbed to the mob, the Equian was aflame as were all the estates gracing its side. Despite the torrential rain, the flames were spreading to the trees and shrubs covering the lands without the estate walls. Nothing could withstand or extinguish the demon flames.

As he looked, it seemed that the entire side of the Equian was rippling and moving. He brushed aside his rain-sodden hair and shielded his eyes and stared at the odd movement, which soon resolved itself into people silhouetted against the fires. The hill was alive with people fleeing the water and flames below, seeking the only high ground: the tops of Kirith Kalyria's four hills. It was rather ironic that they were fleeing upwards while he needs must make his way downward, for the key to life lay locked within the vault in his sire's trade hall. Or perchance they were answering the High One's call as well, a thought both heartening and horrifying. Heartening, in that there were so many still true to the High One and horrifying as to the fact that no more than those already at the at the villa could fit onto his sire's ship. Again, Menannon shied from such thoughts.

Resolutely, he made his way to the far side of the crossroad, wading nearly to his knees in the flood. The water made the paving stones so slippery it was little wonder people were eschewing the roadways and climbing the hill itself. He managed to reach the other side of the crossroads still on his feet, though he was already wet enough it would have made no matter if he had fallen. He rose to his full height and surveyed the hillside below. It was the same: seething with flames and fleeing people. The third way then, across the Mathematical Bridge to the Citadel whose central height was the only other hilltop not yet totally aflame. From the back of its central plaza, he could follow back-streets and alleys down to a lower bridge and cross to the Aureun and thence make it to the Serpentine.

He turned his attention to the bridge. It lay but a little way below him, blazing with light, both from the lightning flashing overhead and the torches raised high by its Doomcrier guardians who were holding the far end against the flood of people attempting to cross it to reach the central plaza, although why they should hold it against these desperate folk, many of whom were probably followers of the High One and therefore victims for their sacrificial altar, was a question Menannon found odd, yet where Doomcriers were concerned, nothing made sense.

There were twin phalanxes of people streaming up to the entrance of the bridge from both sides of the Equian and pouring out onto its airy span. Where those folk thought they could go from there, Menannon could not imagine. They should have been going down and not up, as the only way off the island was by sea. Perchance, not knowing she was already dead, they sought to force the Queen and her council to do something at this late hour or perhaps it was simply the life impulse, the desire to head for higher ground when threatened with flood waters. There must have been near three hundred people on the bridge: men, women and children all fighting and crushing each other in their frenzy. Even as he watched, bodies hurtled into the abyss as people lost their grip upon the stones, forced off the bridge by the sheer weight of those pressing about them. So, the third way was blocked as well. Yet he had to get down below and there was no fourth way.

Nearly frantic now, Menannon wiped the water out of his eyes with his sodden sleeve and looked back down the side of the Equian to see that the fires on the backside had joined into a solid wall. It must be the same on the front as well. The young Giant looked back to the bridge. It was his only hope. As there was no way to cross it in the normal fashion, Menannon turned his gaze to its underpinnings. The airy arches of the bridge might be a mathematical wonder, but as a crossing route, they left much to be desired as they were so slender and nearly vertical on their spans. His nine feet of stature and inhuman strength might just enable him to cross. Whether they would or no, he had to risk it. The people at his sire's villa were depending upon him. He had to reach the trade hall which meant he had to attain the Aureun.

Menannon breathed a quick prayer and began to make his way down the road to join the mass of people at the mouth of the bridge. They surged and crested there, a cauldron of mindless panic lit by the madly dancing flames devouring the city. He plunged into this seething mass of dementia, only to be pushed and buffeted away from his goal. Using every advantage of height and weight he possessed by increasing his mass enough to make him nearly immovable, Menannon slowly hammered his way to the entrance of the bridge, praying that none of the Doomcriers at its farther end would notice his figure towering over the people about him. Panting and bloody, he finally reached his goal and threw himself into the shadows of the buttresses beneath the span where he lay still as stone, waiting to see if an alarum would be raised.

From above, the sound of sheer pandemonium assailed his ears, screams and wails of terror, the swish of sword stroke and arrow flight, the shrieking and cursing of riot, but no alarum. Even as he waited, people hutled past him into the abyss in a seemingly never-ending fall of humanity, many alive and flailing, screaming and cursing on their way to meet Death who waited to greet them with fire and water, rocks and pavement, but many were already dead by the sword stroke or arrow of the Doomcriers. Menannon still could not believe that his own people could turn against their fellows and join the ranks of the Demon, but that they had was plainly seen upon that very bridge. Insanity was the hallmark of the Doomcriers, insanity in the guise of wisdom, justice and salvation. The light had clearly picked out the faces and forms of men well known to him standing among the ranks of the Doomcriers, wielding all manner of weaponry against their terrified neighbors and even in some cases, their own kinsmen. The sheer folly of it all sickened him.

Menannon forced his mind back to his task and waited until his pulses returned to as near normal as this night would allow and then he relaxed his mind and returned to his normal human mass and set about climbing up the treacherous stones of the bridge's supports. This state he could hold without effort, but to go lighter, even though it would make climbing across the bridge easier, would take too much mental effort and he had not the ability to shut out the chaos around him. The royal masons had been thorough in their work and had polished the surfaces of the stones until they were nearly as smooth as glass; add the rain water bathing them and crossing became an ordeal. He sincerely wished he had his knives right now, but he did not. That lack was going to cost him and well he knew it. Each movement was dictated by where he could dig in his fingertips alone and then pull himself up, for only the narrow joints between the stones allowed him any purchase.

By the time Menannon reached the center of the span, he was bathed with sweat as much as he was soaked with rain. His arms and hands were shaking so badly he could hardly hold himself in place, much less move forward. He managed to get a leg over the central beam and rested there for a few moments. The most dangerous part of the traverse lay ahead, as the wall of the central plaza curved outward allowing anyone who might wish to do so to look over its edge and view the understructure of the bridge.

For just a moment, he wished he had studied magic instead of music and could thus cover himself with a glamour. *Ah, well, the choices one makes certainly dictate the course of one's life...or death!*

Menannon shook his head and took a deep breath and forced himself to move on. Perhaps it was due to the interest the Doomcriers had in the activities on the bridge or by the blessing of the High One alone, but Menannon reached the other end of the bridge undetected and fell, more than climbed, down to the base of the plaza wall, safe from prying eyes from above for the moment. He lay gasping and shaking for several long heartbeats then staggered to his feet and circled through the bushes along the foot of the wall until he reached the side opposite the bridge in the shadow of the palace close itself where he carefully climbed up the wet stones and eased himself over and into the plaza. Once there, he knelt again in the shadows to catch his breath and consider his next move. The bulk of the ruined Council Hall blocked his view of the plaza and its turmoil. Seeing the ruins, he was guiltily grateful that none of theirs were within when those walls had come down and wondered how many of the sick had died. How little Azuron cared for life!

The only route open to him was the road leading down towards the Kidron gorge below the east corner of the Council Hall. At that corner, he would be exposed to the full view of Azuron and their minions in the plaza. There was no choice. Menannon took a great gulp of air and let it out slowly, then lunged from the shadows and fled across the intervening space and threw himself down the darkened side street.

The pitch of the waves' screaming rose a notch as he sped downwards. Time was running out. He reached the halfway point just above the beginning of the main business district, but here a ravine was acting like a chimney, concentrating the smoke and making it so thick he had to grope his way forward. He groped and fumbled his way around the crumbled corner of a building, moving faster than he really should in the nearly total darkness, when his foot stepped onto nothing but empty air! Frantically catching himself on a provident overhang, he realized the street had collapsed and he now dangled precariously over a thirty foot chasm to the courtyard below.

Carefully moving hand over hand, Menannon swung up and over the wet stones back to the relative safety of the remains of the street. He lay there panting for a moment, his heart pounding. He had to get to the trade hall! Menannon crawled to the edge of the precipice then lowered himself down as far as he could and dropped the rest of the way, landing hard on the flagstones at the bottom. He levered himself painfully to his feet and stumbled on. He reached the lower bridge to find it unguarded with but a few frantic people fleeing across it. Gratefully, he threw himself across it and on down the Aureun.

By the High One's grace, he met no one until he reached the western end of the Serpentine. Here, in what was one of the most refined of all the city's streets, madness reigned. Where not but a little ago, it had been wide and graceful, elegantly lit by street lanterns and adorned with trees and flowers of all descriptions, the street was now choked with the rubble of its paving stones and buildings. The stark, partially burnt skeletons of once lovely and graceful trees, lit only by raging fires and the storm's sporadic lightning emphasized the horror of it all.

He ducked into the shattered front chamber of the tea shop he had so admired, now naught but a gutted ruin. His nostrils were assailed by the acrid odor of the burnt remains all about him. He had to bury a sneeze in the sleeves of his kirtle else would he be discovered. He crouched down behind the shop's broken window to study the street. Strangely, the heady aroma of peridüse blossoms wafted through the night. Menannon glanced up to see a single spray of flowers still clinging to a charred limb of the streetside tree.

He turned his attention back to the street. It was alive with Doomcriers and folk of the city all dressed in red, both noble and common, smashing anything left whole and spreading the hungry flames in a kind of wanton frenzy. There were others here as well, tall figures cloaked and hooded, strangers armed with long, wickedly recurved bows and sharp, ugly swords. Who or what they were, he was not sure, for even Azuron's arrogant Doomcriers seemed to cringe away from them, but that they were set to watch for any who might have sought to escape—of that he was certain. If he had any doubts, the arrow one of them sent into the back of a sailor who broke cover about halfway along the street, bolting for the long stair to the harbor, would have put paid to them. They were not the seven black Teluri he had seen fall from the storm; they were but a little shorter than he, thus nothing near his sire's height. Who they were and from whence they came he could but speculate. Perhaps they came from the mysterious black ships that had been reported. That seemed the most likely explanation, but he still did not know who they were.

Menannon sank against the wall, wondering what to do, his near total emotional exhaustion causing a strange lethargy to overcome him. He felt as though he were trying to think and move through thick taffy. From where he crouched in the ruined window, he could see the bulk of his sire's trade hall near the first curve of the Serpentine, a distance of five and forty yards of open street away, street that lay under the watchful eyes of these hooded menaces, so close he could have hit it with a rock, yet the distance of death away from him.

If he stepped out onto the street, his height would instantly identify him for who and what he was unless there was some way he could disguise himself. He looked about the ruined courtyard, but saw nothing that would aid him. Naught was left here but ashes and stone, save in one corner of what had obviously been a small pleasure garden. A wisp of carmine caught his eye. Beneath a scorched and dying tree were the wilted remains of hibiscus blossoms tucked carefully in the dirt where some child had been playing gardener. Despite his desperate situation, the sight brought a slight smile to his lips for just such a garden had Nirna been planting the very first time he saw her. The memory lit the desolate courtyard for the briefest of seconds and nearly cost him his life.

In his moment of inattention, one of the hooded figures

found his hiding place. Menannon heard the swishing sound of cloth against rock and whirled back to find a large figure looming up directly in his face through the empty window frame.

Without thinking, Menannon reacted and threw his arms around the hood. A single, sharp twist, a muffled snap and the figure lay limply across the sill, nothing more than food for the carrion crows it resembled. Menannon dragged the body in the rest of the way and took it back behind the wall into the darkest shadows. He had the impression of dark hair and pointed ears...a Teluri of some sort with eyes like coal black marbles. He took no time to look closer to identify his victim, as he was trying not to think of what he had just done. He had never dealt death to anyone before and it did not sit well with him. Yet, he'd had no choice, for he had sworn to his sire he would survive at all costs. At this rate, the cost was going to be his immortal soul, but now was not the time to dwell on that. He quickly relieved the corpse of its cloak and pulled up the hood. It was a bit short , as its former owner had been about seven and half feet in height and of much slighter build, but it would have to do. With a soft prayer for the soul of his victim, he stepped out onto the rubble-choked street.

He hunched under the cloak and leaned over as though he searched for something and made his way down the street, stopping every now and then to look around some particularly large fragment of wall or into a burning building, keeping to the shadows as much as possible. There were hooded figures and Doomcriers everywhere. He had to dodge pockets of riot as well, as folk fought and squabbled over the remains of costly wares lying anyhow in the streets and falling from the shattered fronts of shops. Any value the wares had once possessed had long since become meaningless and Menannon could not help wondering why these half-crazed people even bothered with the stuff, much less tried to kill each other for it. Several times, he had to duck flying rocks and flailing fists from such a fight. One of the hooded figures was not so lucky and got knocked on the shoulder by a badly aimed rock. The reaction was swift and unexpected. A black-gloved fist shot from beneath the cloak and locked onto the throat of the nearest person, apparently not caring who threw the missile so long as someone paid the price. One squeeze and a loud crack and life departed the luckless wretch, his body tossed onto a pile of other such. The hooded one went back to patrolling as though he had simply dispatched an ant at a spring outing. Menannon swallowed the bile that rose in his throat at this act of casual murder and hurried on.

He had nearly achieved his goal when a phalanx of Doomcriers marched up out of a side alley with a group of twenty or so torn and bloody prisoners. His heart bled for them, but there was nothing he could do save let them be dragged to their fate. Hundreds of others were depending upon him. Menannon flattened back against a gutted shopfront and allowed them to pass. He glanced after them once, finding it totally incomprehensible that the Doomcriers would stick to their assigned duties despite the plain evidence on all sides of the pointlessness of their actions. Their entire world was ending in fire and water and yet they persevered!

With renewed determination, he stepped around more rubble and made the rest of his way down the Serpentine and attained the ruins of Gorlanndon's trade hall. He glanced quickly to see that no one was looking closely and fairly ran down the wide marble stairway into the plaza. Water was already surging about his boots as he made his way across. Whether it was sea water, rain water or both, he neither knew nor cared, but that it was there and obviously filling the lower levels was a matter of deadly importance. Could he still reach the vault and the all-important key which lay within?

He tore aside what was left of the doors, their marvelous carvings now but splinters underfoot, and entered the remains of the once great stone building. The water, the fires and the mob had done their work. The building was empty and gutted. The pillars supporting the upper floors were leaning dangerously, barely upholding the floors themselves which were still burning and raining hot ash down upon everything below, the cinders hissing as they hit the water. The flooring of the main hall had burned and been wrenched away, leaving naught but the bare floor joists and not all of those.

Menannon threw off the disguising cloak, draping it over the now headless statue just inside the doors and hurled himself across to the first of the solid joists. Only his great height and his strength—even if diminished by his prolonged exertions—allowed him to make the leap. He worked his way across the shattered remains of the floor to what had been his sire's office, his way dimly lit by the burning floors above. Here, the floor was totally gone and only the back wall that had stood behind his sire's desk remained whole. The portrait which adorned it was, oddly, untouched. His eyes were drawn to the likeness of his lady mother, the light peach of her sorak robe nearly glowing in the gloom.

In that moment, he had a flash of enlightenment as to why the folk outside could value things at a time like this. Some things are beyond price. Briefly, he looked about for something he could use to cut the portrait from its frame, but forced himself to stop. He was playing the fool, for he had neither the time nor the right to jeopardize the fragile hope of escape yet held by his sire and his people by attempting to rescue a pigment-covered cloth, no matter how dear to him was the subject depicted or incredible the quality of the work. Menannon turned away and began searching for some sign of the vault that should be in the chamber below the office. At last he saw it—half covered by beams, flooring and the end of his sire's massive desk directly below where it had once stood. The whole chamber was filled with water, complicating matters greatly. Yet there was nothing for it: he would have to attempt to un-bury it and force the lock.

He plunged into the dark, turgid water, swimming across the chamber to the point directly above the vault, then took a great breath and dove. The cold, salty water nearly crushed his chest, instantly sapping his strength and stinging his eyes. He managed to catch hold of one corner of the desk which proved to be precariously perched upon other debris and was thus readily dislodged, even by a swimmer, though with some effort. His lungs nearly bursting, Menannon lunged back to the surface. His head broke free and as he treaded water, his hand touched wood and he instinctively clutched it. He hung there gasping until he got his breath back, hoarding his remaining strength, then looked up to see what it was he was clinging to. It was the frame of his mother's portrait. Surprised, he looked to see that it had somehow departed its place upon the wall. Despite his dire predicament, the irony of that handhold struck him and he could not help a brief smile.

He took a deep breath again and returned to his efforts. A seeming lifetime and multiple dives later, he managed to uncover the vault. Luckily or unluckily—only the High One knew for sure—it had been opened and the contents spilled upon the floor. There were papers and rare cloths swaying in the surging water as though caught in some wanton dance. He could just make out the forms of empty cash boxes and broken porcelain by the dim light of the fires above. *Is the key still here?* Menannon had to search more by feel than sight. He had to surface again and again, clinging to the portrait for a little longer each time. At last, he finally found the key ring wedged into the crack between two flagstones. He nearly cried in relief as his groping fingers brushed the smooth metal. His fingers closed convulsively around the ring and he yanked. It came loose with a sudden jerk, knocking over a once-priceless vase in the process. He watched as though hypnotized as it slowly tumbled to the floor. It landed softly, undamaged, only kicking up a small storm of debris.

Breaking the spell holding him, Menannon kicked towards the surface and erupted out of the water, his lungs almost bursting, the key to the lynne's water gate—the key to life—clutched in one long-fingered hand. He clung to the portrait frame one last time as he caught his breath and secured the key in the breast of his kirtle, then reluctantly let go and swam back across the office. He pulled himself back out of the flood, dripping and shivering. Menannon stood for a moment gazing at the portrait, his mother's face floating so calmly in the water, oblivious to the horror and catastrophe around it. If he and his sire lived through this, perhaps they could one day return to Lornennog and find her. He said a silent prayer for her life and safety before gathering his wits about him, for he needed to focus every ounce of his attention on the task at hand, else a small chance of survival would turn into no chance and any dream of being reunited with his mother would remain a dream unfulfilled.

The next and final task would like as not prove insurmountable as the communication device to notify Waterdeep that the ship was to launch was located in Issilandur's office. Had that office been only one floor below his sire's it would have been an easier matter to make his way across the ruined floor he was on and dive down to the floor below directly outside of the Teluri's office. But as it was, the office was two floors below and half the distance of the hall away from the lift which was no longer functional. Menannon managed to cross to the wall opposite his sire's office and catch hold of the grating blocking the lift's entrance. Water was indeed sloshing almost to the lip of the opening.

The entire shaft and the floors below were filled with it. Menannon stood there debating what to do. In his mind he could see the device on the wall just inside the door of the Teluri's office, its handle in the up position. One tug on the handle and the message would be sent. He leaned his head against his arm, propped on the side of the shaft and looked down. It was pitch black down there, but he still had Irenos's small Dwarf lantern in his belt pouch so he could light his way. But could he swim that far and hold his breath that long? He had a greater lung capacity than most as he had trained for the past eight summers as a concert singer. He might make it, but then he might not and if he drowned, who would take the key to the lynne? On the other hand, if they got the ship to the inclined plane and the tank was not in place, how would they launch it? On the other hand, if the tank was not already in place, then there was no way anyone was going to get it there as the beach where the horses pulled it up was already under water. On the other hand, if he sent the message, then his sire's people would be there to come on board and be saved with the rest of them. Should he risk all and try to make the swim or turn back and deliver the key?

The answer to his dilemma came of itself as before he could make up his mind, he found his hands already reaching to untie the throat lacings of his kirtle. For the sake of his sire's people waiting at the other end, he had to try to send the signal. He knew he could at least swim to the office and pull the lever. Getting back would be another cast. If he had to, Gorlanndon could tear the gate from its hinges to free the ship at this end and hand winch the tank down at the other so long as it was in place. Menannon took a deep breath and pulled his kirtle over his head and stripped off his chemise and boots, leaving himself dressed only in his hose.

With careful precision, he set his clothing and the precious key as far from the edge of the shaft as the broken floor would allow. He took the little Dwarf lantern from his belt pouch and tied it onto the cord around his neck holding his sire's ring and opened its shutter bathing the empty hall in golden light. He stood for several long moments, breathing as deeply as he could to get as much wind into his body as possible. Then, with a brief prayer and as deep a breath as his lungs could hold, he dove in.

By the High One's holy blood! It was cold! Forcing all other thoughts from his mind, Menannon concentrated on swimming as fast as he had ever swum in his life. He sped down one floor, then two and out of the shaft and down the hall. One door...two...three...Issilandur's office. One more powerful stroke and he was inside. The signal box was there on the wall. A single pull and the message was sent. A turn and a mighty push with his legs, back towards the shaft. His lungs were beginning to ache and his arms to shake. Into the shaft and up, his body screaming for breath. The water pushed against him, his arms seeming to turn into lead. A quarter of the way up...half way up...the floor below his sire's passed by. He could swim no more, his lungs screamed and his vision began to go black around the edges. He could barely see the light above him. Breathe…breathe…shouted his mind and body! Water started to trickle from his nose down the back of his throat. His hand hit something even as his vision went black: the chain of the lift. With one last frantic effort even as his body began to breathe by pure reflex and water enter his windpipe, he grabbed the chain and threw himself up it. His head broke water even as he started to drown!

Menannon clung to the chain and the edge of the lift opening coughing, water running from his nose and mouth. He crawled out of the water and lay coughing and gasping and shivering uncontrollably, too exhausted to raise his body temperature as he had been taught. He lay there for the better part of a half turn of the hour before he could move to put back on his clothing. Even then, he was shivering so hard it was almost impossible to tie his kirtle and secure the Dwarf lantern in his belt pouch once more. He finally managed to put the key back inside the breast of his kirtle and attempted to rise. His legs were too weak and collapsed under him. He fell heavily and rolled onto his side. He lay there for a few long moments then forced himself to try again. He had no idea how long it was since he had taken on his quest. His sire would be waiting for him at the lynne. He had to get there!

Menannon pulled himself upright by the edge of the lift opening, overbalanced and almost fell back into the water of the shaft. He caught himself and stood still, his heart racing, then took as deep a breath as his aching lungs would allow and lurched back the way he had come across the ruined floor to the remains of the doors where he retrieved the cloak and threw it back on. Despite its own load of water, the wool of the garment felt wonderfully warm for which he was grateful. He looked about the plaza to make sure no one was watching, then staggered back up to the street.

Strangely, the street was now deserted. He glanced about quickly and saw the reason. The sea had risen to the level of the lower plaza, thus rendering the stairway to the harbor useless and no longer in need of a guard. All that was left was smoldering ruins. Menannon settled the cloak tighter about him, checking again to make sure the key was secure, then began to retrace his steps up the alleys and back streets leading to the bridge to the Citadel and the entrance to the lynne. Behind him, his sire's trade hall completed its collapse with a roar of tumbling masonry and wood accompanied by a great hissing as the final fires were met by the rising sea, the sound of it rushing past Menannon into the greater chaos. He looked not back. That part of their life was gone forever.

His path was littered with debris from falling buildings, broken wagons, fallen tree trunks and branches and abandoned belongings. The rain seemed to be coming down even harder than before, so hard he could barely see a few steps ahead of him. He turned a corner and found himself standing in the midst of the remains of a family, his foot on the cloth of a woman's kirtle. He jumped back and looked about. There before him on the pavement, in perfect order, lay the bodies of a young woman and three small children, one a babe in arms, all dressed in Doomcrier red. Beside them, in a less peaceful position, was he who had been their husband and sire, dead from his own sword thrust. In the despair and madness gripping the people of Kalyria, he had strangled his family and then slain himself. Menannon retched, his heart bleeding for his city. Nearly blinded with tears and rainwater, he forced himself to step over and around this human detritus of the holocaust and move on. Behind him, the sea was inexorably rising.

Menannon had made it across to the Citadel and nearly reached the halfway point of his journey when he turned a corner and walked into a group of Doomcriers he had neither heard nor seen through the rain. He stumbled, knocking those in front back against those in the rear. In the resultant scuffle, his cloak was torn off and all of them froze for an instant.

"It's Gorlanndon's spawn! Slay him!" the leader shrieked and lunged at Menannon who met his charge and picked him up bodily, hurling him into his fellows before darting into the darkness of a gutted building. He fled into the ruin, out across its blasted garden and through a gaping hole in its back wall.

The avenue upon which he emerged was empty, but not for long as the Doomcriers divined where he must have gone and gave chase. Menannon ran for his life, the pack howling at his heels and growing at every turn as the hue and cry attracted others of their ilk. He reached the east end of the avenue where it dipped downward before it climbed again and was brought up short by water. The sea had breached the third circle. He looked frantically around for some avenue of escape.

The only way was up onto the crumbling barrier wall which offered a slim hope that he could still make it to the upper end of the fourth circle. He scrambled onto the top of the wall and sprinted back west the way he had come, his boots slipping treacherously on the wet blocks. Behind and below him, the pack came to the same conclusion as he had and split, one half running back along the avenue, hoping to head off their victim, the other half climbing up onto the wall behind him. They were quickly closing the distance. Behind him, there was a triumphant howl as the pack closed in. Heedless of aching lungs and legs that were fast turning to clay, Menannon pushed himself to double his speed, but the Doomcriers were fresher and faster, driven by their frenzy.

He sprinted over the archway that pierced the wall and gave access to the street he had been climbing and ran on. Just ahead, the sporadic lightning revealed a huge crumbled section of this wall and he slid to a halt, barely able to stop in time to keep from falling into the raging sea below. He looked back to see the pack on the wall gaining on him, though the pack below in the avenue had been foiled by the curve in the street. He held his side, a fierce pain stabbing him, his breath sobbing in his chest as he stood torn between attempting to stand and fight or risking everything in trying to jump the chasm, but even as the thought crossed his mind, he knew fighting was hopeless. There were too many of them. He might take a few of them down, even in his exhaustion, but in the end, they would either tear him apart or bind him and carry him back up to the central plaza to mingle his with the blood already gushing from their altar. For a moment more, Menannon hesitated then he turned, drew on all that remained of his inhuman strength and hurled himself into the blackness.

He almost made it.

His fingers locked on the wet stones of the far side just as a huge wave smashed into the base of the wall, sending the section he had just attained hurtling down into the rocks and water below. Menannon fell with it, landing hard on what was left of a courtyard wall nearly forty feet below only to be hurled by the next wave up onto an outcrop of stone at the base of the wall above where he had started. For a moment—or a lifetime—he lay stunned, unable to even breathe, then his tortured lungs forced him to inhale. He had shattered several ribs, if not more, and when he inhaled, he breathed fire and blood. There in the darkness and storm Menannon passed out cold.

THE LAST TRUE GUARDIAN OF LINDEN stood silently in his chamber dimly lit by the light of a half-opened Dwarf lantern. Gorlanndon was dressed in naught but his hose and long boots, having doffed his kirtle and chemise. His bracers guarded his wrists. Crossing his arms at the wrist over his chest, head bowed, he spoke a soft prayer to the High One, a warrior's prayer, the prayer of the Guardians of Linden. He had last performed this act so very long ago it was ancient history to most, but once again, he was now prepared to do battle in the High One's name.

There was no sign of pending departure here in this chamber. All was straightened and in its place. Even his much worn copy of the Word Hoard of the High One lay in its accustomed place upon his bedside table. He looked about the chamber, then took up his abandoned clothing and opened the door of his wardrobe and hung them up beside the rest of his garments. That done, he opened a second door and stood looking at the small portrait of his lady wife where it hung within the depths of the wardrobe above the shelves lining it. She had been so young and beautiful on their wedding day, the only daughter of their deputy clan chief. Their love had been real and had not died for either of them, though space and time now separated them. He looked at the painting as he did each night before he went to his bed and for the first time, he was glad she had not returned to Kalyria after Menannon's birth. He considered her fine features and gentle smile and asked himself one last time if he had done rightly in raising their son by the ancient laws instead of Zilronen's teachings. Yes, he had. The peace in his heart answered him. It was the will of the High One and that was as it should be. Gently, he cupped the painted cheek with his hand and whispered the same prayer for her safety and happiness he had whispered each night for nearly sixteen long summers. He took the painting from its place and laid it on his bed then turned back and pulled the lever it had concealed.

With a soft click, a hidden door at the back of the wardrobe opened to reveal a long rectangular niche within which rested but a single item. An ancient sword stood in the darkness there.

Gorlanndon took it firmly in one hand and pulled it out into the light. The leather sheath was battered and scarred to the point that its ancient runes could hardly be discerned. The runes were such that none but the most ancient of Giants and a few scholars could yet read them. The sword had belonged to his sire's clan since the end of the Dim Times when it had been forged by Liliénthar himself, the first and greatest of the Teluri Forgesingers. It was a hand and a half for Gorlanndon and thus longer than his son was tall. It was long and long since he had used it in battle. Once, it had barely seen the inside of its sheath for months uncounted. With a quick motion he drew it, its blade flickering in the green glow of his bracers. It glittered and shone as though new-forged, its edge still as sharp as the day it was made. It fit his hand, its weight and balance perfect. For a moment he looked again at the now empty sheath then laid it gently down on the bed beside Julianna's portrait. He turned and closed the hiding place and wardrobe, then without a backward glance left the chamber, the door closing softly behind him, naked sword in hand.

He walked through the silent villa and out onto the portico overlooking the courtyard. All of his retainers and warband stood waiting for him along with the rest of the folk of Kalyria who had responded to the summons of the High One. At the front stood Irenos, Firod and Skendrin, the latter two fully armoured in the red kelandar armour of Gorlanndon's warband. Beside Skendrin, looking small and frightened, stood Clarinda, a basket of food clutched in one hand and her favorite kitchen spoon in the other. Her cloak was already soaked with rain, making her look even smaller. Gorlanndon gave her a slight wink which brought a bit of color to her pale cheeks. This was going to be hardest upon the old retainers who had lived and served here their entire lives. Clarinda had been born in the very chamber she now used as her own sitting room. As he had informed Menannon's friend Lee, the Dwarf had never even been without the city walls, much less in a ship upon the open ocean. It was going to take the full blessing of the High One to allow such as she to start anew in a strange place.

The great Giant raised his eyes to study the rest of the folk standing in the courtyard awaiting his word. They were all afraid, yet determined to trust in the High One, for in His hands all things turn to good for those who believe and follow His word. About him stood in excess of a thousand souls needing to be squeezed on board a ship which could hold naught but six hundred of them. Gorlanndon glanced about and sighed, leaving the mathematics of survival to the High One. He motioned for the Teluri prince to join him for a moment on the portico. Irenos came quickly, but was already shaking his head before Gorlanndon had even spoken.

"Nay, my friend, I shall not bend distance again. The High One called me to thy side. I am with thee until the end, whate'er that end may be."

"But this is not your fight—," Gorlanndon began and again

the Teluri shook his head.

"It is my fight, for it is the responsibility of all good men to attempt the defeat of evil where'er it lies. Should I go home and all here be lost," he glanced over his shoulder at the crowded courtyard, "ne'er would I be able to look myself in the face more, for my honor would be forfeit."

"Perchance it is better to forfeit honor than life?" Gorlanndon raised an inquisitive eyebrow knowing the Teluri would bridle at his words.

"Honor and life are one and the same. Thou and I learned that at our mothers' knees, old friend."

Irenos grinned, knowing he had taken the bait offered. He held out his hand and they clasped arms as brothers in arms as well as friends of old. Together they turned back to the courtyard, Gorlanndon to stand before them all and Irenos to return to Firod's side.

"Come, it is time," Gorlanndon's great voice carried easily to all corners of the courtyard. At the sound of his voice, those in the courtyard, both strangers and household alike, picked up the weapons and shields the Giant's household had provided, placed the children in the center of their number and stood ready to make the last attempt to save their lives. They carried nothing else with them, having determined that their only hope lay in moving as lightly and quickly as possible. Truly, it would be a crime against the High One to fill a place on the ship with things when it could be filled by life. For a moment, there was silence as Gorlanndon raised his hand and all bowed their heads in prayer.

"High One, we live and die by Thy Word and Thy will. This day and always, Thy will be done." Gorlanndon's words were soft, but heartfelt and an equally fervent "Amen" rose from the gathered folk. The Giant stood to his full height, his bracers glowing strangely in the dim light and circled his arm about his head, the sword singing its eerie death song. Then he cradled it in the crook of his left arm and raised his voice in one final command here.

"Open the gates and let us hence!" For the last time, the

gatewardens opened the gates to Gorlanndon's home and the Giant led his people forth.

Before them, the entire city was dying by flames and water. Nothing was untouched, for the sea had risen to the level of the final circle below the central plaza of the Citadel. People filled the streets and courtyards, surging in mindless pandemonium, too lost in terror or madness to comprehend what was happening. Here and there pockets of quiet reigned, but only because those within them were already dead or so resigned to that death that they simply stood and waited for it. Strangest of all were those who danced and sang in wonton celebration of—what?

From the shadows, a red-hooded figure came towards them, a Doomcrier by all indications, yet it was hesitant, uncertain, acting not at all like one of Azuron's bully boys. Still, such a one was a threat to them. Two of Gorlanndon's warband were preparing to feather him when he suddenly threw back his hood and shouted, "Stop! Not enemy! Not to kill me, please!" From behind the Doomcrier padded a huge leopard Gorlanndon had seen many times before with the boy Tullio at the circus...Ponga. He looked from the cat to the Doomcrier's face and recognition flared.

"Turanio?"

Before anyone could move or say aught else, the distraught stilt-walker was on his knees before Gorlanndon.

"Lord! Ponga and I join you now again, please. Have been great fool, thinking of self only. Hurt by loss of brother, I not think clear. Forgive, please. I fight with you, no?"

Some among Gorlanndon's own people would have had him skewered on the spot for his betrayal of Menannon, but the Giant stayed them in their course and spoke to the penitent in a surprisingly gentle voice.

"There is nothing to forgive, youngling. You are guilty of bad judgment, it is true, but so are we all. No lasting harm was done. The mark of wisdom is to learn from one's mistakes. Be wise."

With a jerk of his head, Gorlanndon motioned him to join their ranks.

"Thank you, my Lord," Turanio said as he slunk past the two warriors and joined the rest of the hopeful escapees, though not without some difficulty, as not all were as quick to forgive as was their protector. Ponga padded at his side and none could say him nay.

Gorlanndon moved forward, Irenos and Skendrin flanking him with Firod and his guardsmen bringing up the rear. The Red Death, Gorlanndon's warband, fully armed and armored for battle in their distinctive gear and livery, were scattered on both sides of the column ready to sell their lives dearly. The column found little actual resistance from those without until they reached the Mathematical Bridge. It was held against them at both ends as Gorlanndon had known it would be. At the near end were stationed Azuron's Doomcriers and at the far end were the huge figures of the seven Sons of the Bane, their great swords in their mailed fists. Beside them stood their hooded accomplices, hoods thrown back to reveal Teluri with hair black as the mid-of-night. It was true then: the eldest race was riddled with traitors to the High One as well, followers of Khalandria marked with the black hair, his Raven Mark, for no Teluri was ever born with hair of such a color. Gorlanndon glanced down at Irenos to see that he was staring at the black-haired ones, a look of pure loathing and hatred on his face. The Giant turned his attention back to the bridge.

Here now would come the fight of their lives. On the bridge itself a strange thing was happening. There were tens of dozens of people running back and forth from end to end as though they competed in a marathon which had neither beginning nor ending. It seemed to consist of just the mindless act of running as rats on a sinking ship will run back and forth from bow to stern as the craft settles farther into the waves. The only relief to this strange monotony was that each time the crowd reached an end so many bodies were scrambling to be at the same place at the same time that no few were forcibly ejected over the ramparts of the bridge by the sheer weight of numbers. In this wise, soon or late, the bridge would be emptied of its odd cargo by simple attrition.

Both Gorlanndon and Irenos saw the far greater problem at the same moment. The very plaza itself was fast being undermined by the sea. How long would it hold?

"Well, that changes things mightily," Gorlanndon observed softly. "I dare not go heavy, as my weight combined with the weight of all who follow us will prove our undoing."

"But if thou dost not, thou canst not armour thyself with Stoneskin through the Way of Rock and Blood. Thou shalt have no protection at all against their swords and arrows!"

"This is a good lesson in being careful what you wish for, as you just might receive it," the Giant smiled mirthlessly. "At the hour I first landed here I said to myself, *This is a good land. I could die contented here.* It would seem the High One has taken me at my word. But come, time fleets and my son will be waiting, we needs must get to him. I'll clear the way and then you lead the people across the plaza to the back of the Council Hall and there you will meet Menannon who will have the key. Get the people below and onto the ship."

"And you, my friend?" Firod's voice broke into their conversation as the captain had come forward to join them. Gorlanndon smiled again.

"I'll hold the passage as long as I can, for there is no way to block the stair to the lynne. It was constructed in happier times when there was no need for protection from within our own city."

Irenos and Firod nodded their understanding of the words not spoken. Someone was going to have to hold the stair until the ship was away or it would be stopped and all on board would die. Gorlanndon had chosen himself for the task.

Firod held out his arm and the great Giant took it in his large grasp. Nothing more needed to be said. With that, Gorlanndon stepped from the last shadows of the tree-lined avenue into the full light of the fires and sight of the Doomcriers.

"Why do you block the bridge so that honest folk may not cross?" he called.

His voice was not nearly at full volume, but it was almost deafening nonetheless for those closest to him. At his sudden appearance and the sound of his voice, all activity halted, even the mindless marathon. One of Azuron's lieutenants stepped towards him.

"We hold the bridge only against those attainted mad men who claim to follow the so-called 'High One.' We are determined that their madness shall not spread. Are you such men?"

Before Gorlanndon could answer, Azuron himself stepped out from among the Black Teluri at the farther end.

"This day all must choose whom they follow: the True Lord of Kalyria, Khalandria the Great, or the false god called the High One by his deluded followers." The Sorcerer's voice carried across the bridge, a raspy shriek. "CHOOSE!"

"Choose?" Gorlanndon's reply was replete with a contemptuous laugh. "Choosing between something requires something to choose between, does it not? As you are offering me a choice between the High One and nothing at all, there is no choice to make. I'm sorry, small terrapin, but nothing is still nothing, no matter what you call it or how you try to disguise it."

"Thou art blaspheming against the greatest power our world has ever known! Thou misbegotten monster...!" Azuron shrieked and the Black Teluri growled agreement.

"Blaspheming? Curious. Exactly how are you applying that word? It is difficult to blaspheme unless something is holy and as nothing is holy save the High One, I have not blasphemed. Again you mistake yourself. You can attempt to call anything holy. You can, for example, bow down and worship pond scum and call to it 'Oh, mighty Pond Scum,' but in the end it is still only pond scum and all your worship avails you nothing."

With that, the great Giant threw back his head and for the first time in summers uncounted, gave full volume to his laughter. Everyone covered their ears as the sound soared even over the roar of the storm itself and the very ground beneath them shook.

Gorlanndon raised his sword on high. "This is for you, High

One!"

Then he fell upon the Doomcriers, sweeping them away in a bloody rain. Behind him, his people forged across the bridge. So surprised were the defenders that they had nearly reached the farther end before the first flight of arrows was loosed by the hooded Teluri and the Seven moved forward to meet him. One moved too fast and came within the arc of Gorlanndon's blade before it was ready and the Giant's sword sliced it in half as easily as a knife through cheese. The strangest thing happened. For a moment, the two halves of the huge Teluri stood together then rather than falling, it disintegrated with a wail and turned into a black mist which hovered for a moment then dissipated as though blown by a great breath.

Taking heed of their fellow's demise, the other six retreated into the more open plaza where they could wield their fell weapons more easily. The arrows of the hooded ones felled friend and foe alike. Of those aimed at him, Gorlanndon blocked many, but not all, with the blade of his great sword. The few he missed soon bristled from the Giant's broad breast, but he did not falter, only laughed the louder, his great sword forcing all to retreat or meet their maker untimely. As the blocking Teluri fled the bridge, all the rest poured across it like champagne from a freshly opened bottle, sweeping Gorlanndon and his people along with them. All was blood and chaos.

COLD RAIN WATER slapping him in the face brought Menannon back to the realities of storm and pain. How long he had lain senseless he knew not, but by the High One's blessing, he had landed at the base of a wall not yet pounded by the sea and had therefore not been washed away. He lay still for a moment, his ears ringing and senses reeling, trying to breathe as shallowly as possible, for with every rise and fall of his chest his broken ribs sent lances of agony coursing through him. He opened his eyes, yet could see nothing save a slightly silvery mist that seemed to have formed where the sea met the walls of Kirith Kalyria.

"Menannon, takest thou my hand!"

A voice reached him as if from a great distance, as though the person calling to him was at the opposite end of a hallway. He was not sure if he was actually hearing a voice or was just dreaming.

"Menannon! Takest thou my hand," the voice came again, imperious and commanding, yet somehow gentle.

The Giant forced himself to ignore the pain and strained up onto one elbow. The sound of the sea seemed to quiet about him and for a single instant, he could have sworn he saw a tall figure standing on the wall above him reaching for him through the mist. Instinctively he reached out and felt a strong, warm hand close over his own.

"Goest thou heavy so thy ribs shall be caused no further hurt, then will I pull thee up," the figure instructed him.

"But if I go heavy, none but the High One Himself could lift me...."

"Trust me and goest thou heavy," came the soft reply.

Totally befuddled, but oddly reassured by the calm voice of his would-be rescuer, Menannon did as he was bid and allowed himself to go heavy. He found that, indeed, in this state his ribs were far less mobile and therefore, less painful. Before he could think about it further, Menannon felt a slight tug and twinge of pain, then the sensation of moving upwards. He was not sure if he passed out then, but when he gathered his wits about him, he found that the night had returned to its shrieking chaos of rain and sea, though slightly muffled. He forced his eyes open. Darkness once again surrounded him. The mist was gone and the figure with it.

He lay shivering on cold stone with water lapping about him. It had been a dream, then. Menannon forced himself to roll over and sit up though with difficulty as he found indeed he had gone heavy, a state to which his muscles were no longer accustomed. Perhaps that also explained the muffling of the sound, though he did not remember that going heavy affected his hearing as well as his movements. He sat still, feeling the water lapping about him far more gently than it should be and there was none falling on him.

Then it hit him. He was no longer at the base of the wall, but was instead within a dark chamber wherein echoed the sound of wood thunking against stone. By all that was holy, somehow he had gotten to the lynne and that was his sire's ship causing the hollow sound as it moved with the swells! *How?!* Yet even more importantly, *Who?* Who had saved him? What being could have possibly been strong enough to pull him from the wall and carry him all the way up the Citadel and down to this lynne when he was heavy? Despite his lack of stature, even his sire could not so pick him up in that state. None but the High One could. *None but the High One?* Impossible!

He refused to go where his thoughts would take him and the sounds of screaming and chanting coming through the grating above brought Menannon back to reality with a start. However it had been accomplished, he was here, and that was all that mattered. How long had he been here? He had no idea, but he knew he had to get up to the top of the stairs. His sire would not know he was here and was perhaps searching for him!

The darkness of the chamber, relieved only sporadically by lightning flashing overhead and the terrifying red glow of fire which found its way through the grating covering the apex of the central dome of the ceiling, made it difficult to see the path to the stairs as he dared not un-shutter the Dwarf lanterns for fear of calling attention to himself. He took as deep a breath as he could and dragged himself painfully to his feet. He was forced to go light again, as he had not the strength to pull himself up the stair which still clung to the north wall of the chamber should he remain in his heavy state. As soon as he had achieved his normal mass, the pain of his shattered ribs hit him full force and he retched. He could do nothing more for himself than press his hand against his side and stagger up the stairs.

He reached the head of the stair and halted. Above him, he

could distinguish the strangest combination of sounds. There was singing, chanting, thunder, the roar of the sea, screaming and the clash and ring of swords. Above all that could be heard the howling and shrieking of the wind that was no wind. Someone was fighting the Doomcriers at last! It had to be his sire and their folk. Instinctively, Menannon felt inside the front of his kirtle to make sure the key still rested there. His groping fingers touched metal and his heart eased slightly. Any of their folk who could win through to the stair would be able to get on board and set sail, though the High One only knew what would happen after the water gate was opened.

Carefully, Menannon moved up the last few steps to the plaza level and hunkered there, glancing quickly around. The stair came out on the north edge of the plaza where the ruins of the Council Hall hid him from the view of any in the main area. The ruins also blocked Menannon's view of what was happening without. He crouched in the shadows and listened to the howling crowd gathered around Azuron's altar.

The rock-cut drain running across the plaza spoke volumes of the atrocities being performed there as its contents steamed in the cold of the storm. The stony channel made for water was running with something far more precious: the heart's blood of the followers of the High One. The voices of parents pleading for the lives of their children and the cries of the children themselves kept rising and falling over all the rest, a composition of tragedy and terror. Menannon closed his eyes and leaned his hot forehead against the cold, wet stones, half paralyzed by the horror to which he was reluctant witness.

Do as you will. That is the whole of the laws of this world—the words of Azuron kept running through his mind as he had heard them coming from the sorcerer's followers the first time. *Do as you will...High One, if this is truly the will of the people of Kalyria, then all is lost and we do deserve to be swallowed by the sea. If this is truly the will of the people, then sweep us away, O High One, and cleanse the land of our stench!* "Papa? Where's my papa?!" A small voice reached his ears as it rose in terror above the noise of the night. "PAPA!"

There was a loud, sickening crack and the voice stopped. The silence it left was filled with the shrieking and cheering of the 'people' of Kirith Kalyria. Menannon threw up.

The tyranny of time forced him to raise his head and look about consideringly. He had to see what was happening. Carefully, he eased up out of the stairwell head and darted across the intervening space to crouch behind the half charred, crumbling ruin. There he waited, listening intently while he gave his aching ribs the chance to settle. The sounds of sword against sword were clearer now as was the distinct twang of flights of arrows being loosed. Each such flight brought with it more screaming and chaos. Menannon glanced up and saw through the roiling clouds a single star glittering. It had turned night during the time he had been on his quest and now that lone star would stand mute witness to a world's ending.

His heart in his throat, Menannon forced himself to straighten and step from behind the wall. The entire space was seething with moving bodies, some running mindlessly, some fighting and others—dancing? Just a matter of feet from where he stood, a strange group of adults and youths had formed a living chain and were dancing in and out and around the rest for all the world as though they celebrated the coming of Spring. They were led by a young girl of perhaps thirteen summers dancing crazily in the flickering light. All were dressed in motley and carried large baskets from which they were throwing things. Some threw flowers and others handsful of seemingly loose jewels to judge by the glitter and flash of the objects as they flew. A king's ransom was being played with this night. Here and there among the revelers were those who threw not flowers and gems, but handsful of some sort of powder at the crowd as they snaked in and out among them. The powder's granules sparkled in the lurid light, glinting rainbows as it fell into faces and covered clothes. Menannon watched in a kind of horrified fascination. Sud-denly, there was the incongruous sound of childish laughter beside him and he turned his head to look down only to be hit full in the face with a cloud of powder thrown by a wildy giggling little girl of perhaps six summers. The powder filled Menannon's eyes and nose and clung to his face, causing him to cough and blink, his eyes instantly beginning to sting and water. He wiped his face the best he could on his sodden sleeve.

"Praise to Khalandria!" the child almost sang, her small bow of a mouth pouting prettily, but her eyes were anything but pretty, as they seemed to be filled with living snakes of fire.

Menannon found his entire spirit recoiling from this lilliputian horror as she stood there laughing at him. In his mind, she suddenly took on an iconic quality seeming to embody all the evil in the hearts of Kalyria's people. Horror stricken, he turned and plunged into the crowd, forcing his way across the plaza towards where he knew his sire's force had to be though he could not see them through the murk and rain. His eyes continued to smart and run with tears as he reached the end of the palace's ruined portico and climbed up on it. From here he could see the battle. It was indeed his sire and all the last of the High One's folk.

By the lurid light, he could discern Irenos and Firod and the last of the Guardsmen and the Red Death, their swords flashing crimson. There were men and women using swords and shields inexpertly, but with determination all along the group as they fought their way towards the head of the lynne stair. Amidst the throng, he saw Walderan trying to protect Clarinda and two small children with his own body as he had nothing else to use. The healer, like Menannon, was no warrior trained. Beside the healer, Skendrin applied his sword in mighty arcs, his efforts telling upon the Doomcriers. In front of all, Gorlanndon stood, a mighty wall, hewing down hooded Teluri, Doomcriers and all, ten or more with each sweep of his sword. Menannon wondered where his sire had gotten this sword, for it was obviously his own and he wielded it with ease and skill.

Between the Giant's folk and the lynne stood three of the huge Teluri warriors Menannon had seen fall from the storm. All three stepped towards his sire, Irenos and Firod. As one, the two smaller men dropped and began hacking at the legs and feet of the outside two monsters as his sire crossed swords with the third. Green and red sparks flew as the magics imbued in the swords contended. Behind the three Teluri, Azuron was readying black fire bolts which he let fly at Gorlanndon. Their motion caught the Giant's attention and he deflected the first one with his bracer, sending it into the face of his opponent. It was enough distraction that he was able to reach under the monster's guard and cut it in half. Before Menannon's astonished eyes, it shrieked and turned to a cloud of mist which disappeared into the darkness. At their comrade's fall, the other twain lurched back and fled towards Azuron and the altar. Gorlanndon and his comrades did not give chase, but continued their relentless march towards the lynne stair. Menannon's heart swelled with pride as he watched his sire, then a fire flared up near him and his son saw the near forest of arrows protruding from his chest and abdomen. Gorlanndon was awash with his own blood as well as that of countless others. Instinctively, Menannon moved to go to him, to protect him somehow, even if with only his body and bare hands. Never in his life had the harper felt as useless as he did now, nor had he ever before this realized the full extent of what a curse it was that he had not been trained in war.

Menannon turned to run back down the broken steps of the portico only to find his way blocked by the shivering figure of a small girl. She stood looking at him obviously in shock. Half her hair was burned away and her tunica nearly torn from her small body. Her left arm hung down as though broken as well. He looked closer and found that she was Emma, the little flower seller. Almost, he shoved past her in his desperation to reach his sire, but he could not just leave her there. Despite his own frenzy, he managed to carefully scoop her up and knowing nowhere else to go, made his way back down to the lynne and set her on a coil of rope at the end of the gangway. She was shivering uncontrollably. There was nothing to cover her with save his own kirtle which though wet through would giver her at least a modicum of warmth. Ignoring his broken ribs he tore the piece of clothing off over his head and, as gently as he could, wrapped it around her.

"Stay here, Emma. I shall return as soon as may be," he told her, not knowing if she even heard him. Having done all he could at the moment, Menannon once more painfully made his way to the ruins of the portico. He quickly surveyed the plaza below.

Gorlanndon and his people had managed to force their way to the north side of the plaza and were readying themselves for the final dash to the stair head. Their path was littered with dead and dying, both their own and their enemies. Gorlanndon himself still stood between his folk and Azuron's hordes, his sword yet swinging in great arcs though more slowly now as the loss of blood was beginning to tell upon even him. Beside him, Skendrin and Firod held their ground as well, though both were obviously bloodied. They had been joined by Irenos, his single battle braid about his throat glinting almost red in the lurid light. Menannon looked quickly at the faces of the rest. Walderan still stood with the children, but there was no sign of Clarinda. Menannon turned his stinging eyes to look more closely at those who had fallen and among them found the cook. Her birth city, Kirith Kalyria had been her home life-long and now it would be her tomb. A memory flashed before his eyes of Clarinda, her blue eyes twinkling, handing him two large cookies in her sunlit kitchen and saying, "One for each hand child. Now go outside and play." More tears settled like stones in Menannon's heart. Beside them lay all save three of Firod's guardsmen. Next to Clarinda's body, Gorlanndon's retired herdsman lay, his heavy walking stick held cudgel-like in his gnarled hands. Death was preferable to slavery, the old fellow had said...*death*. Menannon had no more tears to shed. His attention was drawn back to the living by a sudden surge of motion. Gorlanndon's people were making their last cast.

As one, all turned and began running towards Menannon and the stair head, Skendrin, Irenos and Firod standing with Gorlanndon, as the Giant slowly followed his folk using his own body and blood to gain their survival. The four of them gave way foot by foot until they stood at the very head of the stairs their folk were now streaming down. Near the altar, Azuron was screaming at his Doomcriers not to let the blaspheming monster escape, his voice almost lost in the din. When only the four remained, Menannon broke cover and ran to them, narrowly dodging several sword strokes and not a few arrows. His sudden appearance nearly cost him his head as his sire swung at movement rather than a recognized target.

"Hold, my father!" Menannon shouted to make himself heard and Gorlanndon instantly raised his sword so that it narrowly missed the top of his son's head as it completed its stroke. The great Giant lowered his sword and thrust it through the back of a corpse lying at his feet and left it standing. His hands thus freed, he leaned down and laid his hands on both sides of Menannon's face and turned his face up to him. Gorlanndon spoke no word, only kissed Menannon's brow then thrust him bodily behind him into Firod's hold before he took up his sword again and went back to his bloody work.

"Come! Into the ship! We must get her away!" Firod spoke as he thrust Menannon after Skendrin and Irenos who were going down the stairs ahead of them. Below, all was chaos as everyone milled about, not quite knowing what to do.

"Get onto the ship…now!" Firod stopped on the stair to shout, calling all to order. "Make haste! They will be upon us in moments."

Skendrin and Irenos began pushing those standing nearest the gangway up its length and onto the ship. Silently, the whole of the survivors clambered up the gangway. Only one of Firod's guardsmen and two of Gorlanndon's warband had succeeded in reaching the ship. Menannon joined the flood, intent upon reaching his small charge. He found her exactly where he had left her on the rope coil. Emma looked at him with unseeing eyes as he reached down and picked her up. A kind of mental malaise had come over him, so much so that he no longer felt the pain of his broken ribs or the cold of the sea that was rising even here within the gate chamber. He turned and carried the child up the gangway amidst the rest and made his way to where Walderan stood with his group of children, grown now to more than a score as their parents had fallen in the battle. The healer looked around at him, equally as stunned as the young Giant. There was no emotion in his eyes as he took the child from Menannon and added her to his still growing group. Below on the flagstones, Firod had joined Irenos. They twain sheathed their swords and turned their attention to the mooring cables. Menannon stood on the deck watching them, his mind a total blank. They had loosed all save one rope when Irenos stopped, looked up and called his name.

"Menannon! Hast thou the key?" Irenos shouted to make himself heard over the din from above and the water sounding through the lava tubes. The question took a moment to penetrate the young Giant's frozen mind, but then it did and he reached inside his chemise and came back down the gangway.

"It was on the floor. I fear I nearly broke a rare vase getting it. I'm sorry—."

"Who in all Hella cares about a vase right now!" Firod interrupted him, his voice rough with determination as he pushed past Irenos and almost snatched the key from Menannon's unprotesting hand. "Wake up, boy!"

The captain turned as though to circle the ship and open the gate. Coming out of his trance, Menannon halted him with a swift hand on his arm.

"We cannot depart without my sire. He will be along any moment."

At these words, the older men exchanged a look which froze Menannon's blood. He stepped back a pace towards the stair, shaking his head.

"Oh, Hella, NO!" Menannon whirled and before any of them could stop him, fled up the steps taking them four at a time, Firod and Irenos hot after him.

Menannon emerged into the chaos above, the captain barely a pace behind him. Ahead of them, Gorlanndon stood foursquare against all the forces of Azuron, successfully holding the way until the ship bearing his people could make good its escape. His huge figure was silhouetted against the fires and lightning. The shriek of the not-wind and the roaring of the sea nearly drowned out the shouting and screaming of the people still alive in the plaza. Beyond his sire, Menannon could see Azuron and the last three Sons of the Bane where they stood on the stones of the altar, the sorcerer screaming orders to his Doomcriers to bring the monster down.

"Father!" Menannon shouted to no avail, as the elder Giant was bending all his remaining strength and concentration to hold his post as long as possible. "Father, come away, I beg you!" he took one step towards his sire and Irenos literally tackled him, wrestling him to his knees. Firod grabbed his arms, pinning him.

"Leave him, boy!" the captain yelled in his ear. "You can do nothing save die with him and he does not desire that. Come away!"

"NO!" Menannon struggled to break their hold, but they twain proved too strong and held him fast. "Father! For the High One's holy sake, come with us! Father!"

The elder Giant paid them no heed.

"GORLANNDON!" Menannon finally called out in fear and rage, his vocal cords nearly shredding with the force of his scream. Never before this had he addressed his sire by that worthy's given name. The strangeness of the call and its desperation penetrated the Giant's concentration and he glanced over his shoulder to see his son trying to break free of his captors. Against every order he had received, Menannon was there staring at him, his cheeks marked with blood from Gorlanndon's own hands as with war paint. The great Giant could not help a smile of triumph. *Yes, love is stronger than law! Praise the High One!*

"I love you boy!" he raised his voice in an exultant shout. "LIVE FOR US BOTH, MENANNON!"

With those shouted words he saluted Irenos and Firod, gave his son a final wink and turned to carry the battle to Azuron.

Against all odds, he nearly reached the sorcerer, but just short of the altar, Gorlanndon faltered, his great strength finally ebbing away with his blood and then the Doomcriers were upon him like ants boiling from their holes in the ground. By force of sheer numbers alone they brought him down, bound him and dragged him to the gore covered stone.

"NO!" Menannon's cry cut the night like a spear. In that same instant, Firod swung him around forcibly before he could see where the mob had finally been able to tie his sire to the altar. Irenos put both hands on the sides of Menannon's face, forcing him to turn his head away from the plaza. The sound of shrieking and chanting rose to a fever pitch beyond them. Menannon struggled, but Irenos held him fast.

"NO! Look at me! Look at me! LOOK AT ME! Look me in the eyes, boy! NO! LOOK NOT! Let them not taint your memory of your sire with this!"

Across the night the sound of the chant of the Doomcriers' sounded. Doom...Doom...Death and Destruction! Above their cries, Menannon could hear Azuron gloating over his sire.

"Dost thou change thy mind, monster?" the sorcerer shrieked. Gorlanndon's voice answered him as calm and peaceful as eternity itself.

"Pond scum is still pond scum, runt! And the High One is still the High One, ruler of us all and all is right with the world!"

"Blasphemy...blasphemy!" the crowd shrieked. Firod and Irenos watched helplessly as Azuron raised his blade for the final stroke.

Above the shrieking of the crowd Gorlanndon's voice rose in a last shout. "Praise the High One!"

Menannon nearly tore himself from their hold, but the captain and the Teluri proved the stronger as the young Giant was weakened and too far gone in terror and panic to coordinate his efforts.

Behind them, the chanting rose to a shriek, then the entire night went silent. The knife whooshed through the air and the thud of it striking flesh and burying itself deep in Gorlanndon's heart could be heard like a crack of thunder in the strange stillness. For just a moment, the world itself seemed to halt, then pandemonium broke loose and all sound returned. The crowed cheered and roared. The altar screeched and cracked, collapsing under the weight of the dead Giant whose body had instantly turned to stone. The sorcerer's voice rose in an exultant shriek. "Khalandria forever!"

A single sound cut across the noise. A sound wrenched from the very depth's of Menannon's soul. It was the sound of inconsolable grief that tore the hearts of those who heard it.

"Hush, lad! For the love of the High One, hush!" Irenos slapped his hand over Menannon's mouth and turned the youth's face against his shoulder attempting to muffle the sound of his grief with the folds of his cloak. "For the High One's Holy sake, silence! Azuron already knows thou art here somewhere, dost thou want to help them find thee? We are going to die with thy sire if thou are not silent!" Irenos was nearly frantic in his attempts to break through Menannon's grief and reach his rational mind.

Out in the plaza there was a stirring as Azuron signaled his Doomcriers to him. Irenos looked over Menannon's shoulder and saw the sorcerer pointing in their direction.

"Find it! It is an offence that it still lives! Find this abomination and bring it to die with its despicable sire else we are all doomed!" Azuron's voice rose again to a shriek. All began looking wildly about, searching for the source of the sound.

They were coming for him. Irenos pulled Menannon's head back and slapped him hard three times, then buried his face back against his cloak and held him close. There was nothing else he could do. He could not knock him senseless, his hand was no match for the bones of the Giant's jaw and even if he did, he would not be able to carry him anywhere. An unconscious Giant was an immovable object.

"For your sire's sake, be silent and live!" Irenos begged against Menannon's black hair.

Beyond hope, something in Irenos' desperation finally penetrated Menannon's grief and the bleeding of his heart changed to silent sobbing. He clung to the Teluri like a drowning man.

Someone must have caught sight of them there in the shadows, for the crowd suddenly drew itself up like an incoming wave then surged towards them. Firod tore Menannon loose from Irenos, dragged him to his feet and nearly hurled him towards the head of the stairs.

"Run, boy run! They are coming!"

Together they fled down the stair to the lynne. Irenos followed close behind. One thing only penetrated Menannon's howling mind: his beloved sire was dead! Were it not for the Teluri and Firod, he, too, would have been lost.

Down once more in the depths of the lynne, Menannon finally regained his reason and looked about. The roar of the sea and the lurid light of the fires above gave him a sense of having lived it all before this. Suddenly it hit him, he was walking the footsteps of his nightmares. It was true then. The High One had ordained that he return to Kalyria, but to what end, he did not know. He came to a halt at the end of the gangway. On the deck of the great ship, he could see no one save Skendrin and the three remaining warriors standing at the head of the gangway, scavenged arrows at the ready. Their folk had managed to squeeze below decks, though there was place only to sit and not lie down for the crush of bodies. All that was left of the true-hearted folk of Kalyria had actually managed to squeeze aboard. He was appalled. There were so few! Just over seven hundred out of a land of thousands. Nearly four hundred of those who had left Gorlanndon's villa lay dead along the way.

"They are all there is, my friend." Firod spoke hoarsely behind him, giving voice to his own thoughts.

Together Firod and Menannon looked about for Irenos then all three turned to the question of the water gate while Skendrin and the three remaining warriors kept the Doomcriers above at bay with a steady rain of arrows at any who dared to start down the stair. Water was now pouring through the grating at the top of the dome and leaks were showing all around as the stone chamber itself was being forced apart by the power of the waves battering the island. The water level in the lynne had risen alarmingly and the mighty ship was nearly ready to scrape the top of the lava tube. It was straining against the gate like a horse about start a race. It was suddenly clear to all three that whoever opened the sea gate would not be able to get on board before the ship surged away through the tube. For a moment, they looked at the gate, then at each other.

Menannon took a deep steadying breath, once again master of himself. Firod looked deep into his eyes, then nodded and turned away, but Menannon stopped him.

"Where are you going? You need to go aboard. Our people need your leadership. I will open the sea gates."

"Allow me, as thy people will need thee both," Irenos's steady voice interrupted them.

"No. I will open the gates." Firod shook his head with a slight smile. "Menannon alone has e'en a prayer of sailing this ship of his and this is not your land, my friend. You should not have to die for it. Now go!"

"I, however, can bend distance and thus escape," the Teluri pointed out earnestly.

Menannon however took his shoulder. "You need time to clear your mind ere you step and as soon as we depart, they will not give you that luxury!" he said, pointing to the frustrated Doomcriers at the head of the stair still being pinned down by Skendrin and his men. Irenos glanced up, but Firod took both of them by the arms and shoved.

"Enough debate! Time fleets! Get on board and prepare to get underway!" he barked in his best battlefield voice.

Irenos nearly said more, but the look in Firod's eyes halted his words. He only nodded his acceptance. Having won his point, Firod turned his full attention back to Menannon.

"Once you are clear of the island, head north as your sire instructed. Give my wife and children my farewell and tell them I am content, for I fall for Kalyria and the High One. No better cause can claim a life. Now, go!"

Menannon and Irenos ran up the gangway calling to Skendrin and the warriors to keep up their fire while they twain drew in the gangway. Together, Menannon and Irenos drew in and secured the gangway then turned to securing the deck and battening down all hatches. When only the main hatch remained loose, Menannon turned to Irenos and Skendrin.

"Come quickly, help me put the extension on the oar!"

Menannon crossed the deck to unlimber the great beam. Together, he and the other twain wrestled the extension into place and slammed the pins to.

Menannon started to take his place at the steering oar, when Irenos stopped him. The young Giant was still dressed in naught but his chemise, hose and boots. He was shivering uncontrollably and his lips had turned blue.

"Get thee into the cabin and fetch a cloak. Now! No arguments!" The Teluri gave him a shove to start him on his way.

Eschewing the stairs, Menannon stepped to the edge of the aftcastle and jumped to the main deck where he landed with a crash, scaring the passengers below. He turned and slammed into his sire's cabin, threw open the Dwarf lantern, strode across to the wardrobe and stopped short. The front of the wardrobe was a full-length mirror in which he saw an apparition staring back at him. Its face was sheet white with the prints of its sire's bloody palms on the cheeks. The eyes that stared back at him were so smudged with black they looked as though they were surrounded by paint. Tearing his eyes away from the sight of his own face, Menannon thrust open the wardrobe door where he withdrew the first cloak he came to and threw it on. It lay over him like a horse blanket on a small dog. Frantically, he searched around for another and surprisingly found one his own size. He thrust his arms through the arm holes and fastened it down the front even as he was rushing back to his post. Just as he reached the steering oar, he remembered why it had been in his sire's wardrobe. The last time Gorlanndon had brought the ship into Blue Bay to meet with him, his sire had gifted him the cloak, but in his hurry to exit the ship as it readied to sail, he had forgotten it. The vision of his sire standing on the deck with the cloak in his hand flashed into his mind. He remembered calling up to him saying, "I'll pick it up the next time I see you." The next time. Now there would be no next time until the world's ending or his own death. An arrow whistled past his ear, bringing him back to the present.

Below on the walkway Firod raised his hand in a final farewell. As Menannon watched, he turned and plunged through water risen nearly to his chest forcing his way to the sea gates.

Menannon called to Skendrin and the remaining warriors to get below. They retreated to the hatch, firing their few remaining arrows as they went. Seeing the last of them disappear below, Menannon glanced up at the stair head to see that some of the Doomcriers had realized that it was no longer defended and were attempting to come down it. So far they had not coordinated themselves as some were trying to let arrows fly while others were trying to push past them to come down to the ship. Even as arrows sang past his ears, Menannon turned all of his attention back to the task at hand.

Below them, Firod seemed to move unnoticed by the incoming attackers and managed to reach the sea gate. His hands were numb and fumbling and it was all he could do to get the key into the lock. It would not turn. The lock seemed frozen. It was as though all of creation stopped for an instant, then started again as Firod said a prayer. The key turned! The gates swung open and the waters of the lynne surged forth into the dark lava tube, carrying the Giantish ship with them.

The blackness was complete as the ship raced along. So strong was the current that Menannon was unable to keep to the center of the tube and thus the ship banged and scraped against its sides as they flew along at an incredible speed. He had no idea where the sea level would be in Watermouth bay. At this speed, he would be unable to stop their progress if the water was yet below the tube's opening above the inclined plane.

He did not know if he blacked out or the High One shortened

the tube or what, but long before it was possible the tube seemed to be lightening. Menannon strained his stinging eyes trying to see the end before they reached it. As the water was still rushing forward, he knew the outlet was yet above the sea, but by how much? He had no further time to speculate as the roaring of the water grew louder. At the speed they were going, there would be no way stop and take on more passengers. It was a moot point anyway, for there was no one standing on the towpath waiting for them. Unbeknownst to him, when his message had arrived at Watermouth, the folk there had taken stock of their situation and as the tub was in place and all else ready, they had decided not to wait for the great ship, but to take the stoutest of their fishing boats and set out on their own, their small boats nearly flying across the great waves.

Gorlanndon's flagship reached the end of the tube and raced across the tongue, barely giving Menannon a moment to glance and see that the inclined plane no longer stood! It had been torn from its mountings and shoved down the cliff face. There was nothing but pure air between them and the raging sea he could now see was still thirty feet or more below their keel. There was no stopping the juggernaut. Menannon clung to the steering oar with Irenos holding fast to the ropes beside him, helpless to do anything as the great ship leapt from the tongue and took flight. At the last moment and by the power of pure adrenaline, the young Giant wrenched the oar from its place and threw it onto the deck knowing if the ship did not break her back upon impact, the oar would surely shatter. The huge ship arced across the bay and beyond hope, just as it started to fall, a wave higher than all the rest rose up and took it upon its crest and drew it down into the maelstrom.

BEHIND IN THE NOW EMPTY LYNNE, Firod stood to his feet and faced the Doomcriers who stood as though dumbfounded by the empty lava tube. No one moved so much as a finger to stop him as the captain limped through them and dragged his battered body back up the stairs already beginning to run with seawater and into the destruction above. He ignored the chaos about him and bent his failing will to wade across the plaza once more and mount the crumbling steps to the remains of the portico where Menannon had stood. From this vantage point, he could see that nothing remained above water save the top of the Citadel, the other three hills having already succumbed. In the plaza itself was stillness broken only by the motion of the incoming seawater. There were people everywhere, followers of Azuron, standing about in the same dumbfounded manner as those below as though even their will to move had been taken from them. What was it? Were they all stunned that this should be the result of their actions? Firod shook his head, nearly laughing outright at their blindness and stupidity. What had they all thought? That they could do as they willed with no consequences?

He looked across at the remains of the altar. Gorlanndon's body lay amongst its broken pieces, a magnificent statue. Strangely, his great sword still leaned where Azuron's lieutenants had placed it against the end of the stone, its blade glowing through the murk, a talisman. Of Azuron and the remaining three Sons, there was no sign. Khalandria had rescued only his lieutenant and his three henchmen, the rest being naught but expendable, useful idiots. Firod raised his eyes to see that the single star still shown overhead and spoke one last prayer for the safety of the Giantish ship and all aboard her. His prayers for the future of his wife and children had all been said many times before this. By the blessing of the High One, his mind's eye was suddenly filled with a vision of Gorlanndon's great ship, riding the waves upon the wings of the storm, rounding the shoulder of Kalyria's Crown, its drakta headed prow cutting through the water like a sword!

He was brought back to the here and now as a final huge wave began to rise up over the remains of the doomed city, its crest alight with the red eyes of Kalyria's Bane. Firod, his heart at peace, watched as it rose, reached its apex and curled, crashing down onto the last remains of the city. Beneath its onslaught, all that was left of Kirith Kalyria shrieked, crumbled and slid beneath the waves. With his city, Firod fell into darkness and death.

CHAPTER 25
(SUMMER OF THE WORLD 6097)

AS THE GREAT SHIP PLUMMETED down onto the raging waves, the ghost wind that was no wind suddenly came alive and real, blowing like an insane thing in a madman's nightmare. Its added torment made it nearly impossible to raise the mast and set the mainsail. The niceties of untying ropes and raising the mast with its crank were beyond the scope of their abilities in this hurricane, so Menannon simply took the fire axe from its hook on the wall of the aftcastle and handed it to Irenos. Wordlessly, the Teluri took it and struggled to the mid of the mast where he set himself to chop the massive ropes holding it to the deck.

Skendrin appeared on deck to see if he could be of some assistance, but held back out of the way for the moment, clinging to the side ropes to keep from being washed overboard.

While the ship tossed about on the crashing waves, Menannon tied the ends of the sail's ropes around himself and went heavy so that when the sail was freed with the mast, it would not whip him around like a toy tied to a puppy's tail. He braced himself and took Irenos about the waist so the slender Teluri dared to let go of the rope to which he clung. At Menannon's signal, Irenos swung the axe, severing the ropes holding the sail furled and the mast down. The magnificent timber swung up into place and held despite the wind. With the help of both Irenos and Skendrin, Menannon managed to tie the sail off. It billowed and shrieked, but by the High One's good grace, did not tear. Together they dragged the steering oar back into place and Menannon wrapped his arms around it to begin fighting for their very lives against a storm that had turned the sea into more of a living, thinking creature than a thing of nature. It slammed and buffeted the ship, wheeling and turning it like chaff in a whirlwind. Despite using his natural weight, nothing Menannon did seemed to make any difference. The oar kept being torn from his arms and the ship turned broadside to the waves, almost capsizing at every surge. Beside him, the others were constantly tossed aside like dolls even as they attempted to aid him. It was to no avail. The sea was too powerful. The Human and Teluri could do little more than undertake to keep from being washed overboard.

The oar slammed into his broken ribs again and again and Menannon screamed in agony and growing rage each time until finally the near mindless fury of the Giants burst forth and for the first time in his life, his eyes took on the full red blaze of battle frenzy that out-shone the lightning flashing overhead.

"Get below and seal the hatch!" Menannon roared to be heard over the pounding waves.

"But—."

"Now!" The red of his eyes told Irenos there was no sense in arguing with him and Skendrin nodded. Old salt though he was, the steward knew when to say enough. So, clinging to the ropes, they made their way down the stairs and across the deck to the central hatch, Irenos coming last. Skendrin waited until a wave crashed over then threw it open and they dove in, Irenos pulling it to and dogging it down behind them. On the aftcastle, Menannon took the ropes and deliberately lashed himself to the steering oar then he went *heavy*, not just the weight of his own normal mass, but the true heaviness of the great bones of the earth. Despite the danger, he took on the elemental heaviness of creation without arming himself with stoneskin, as he dared not, for to become rocklike in his inexperience was to have the thought processes of a rock as well and he needed to have all his wits about him. Beneath his mass, the very skin of the mighty ship groaned and creaked. He became a truly immovable object and together he and the ship became a weapon to fight the monster.

Menannon turned the ship head-on into the savage waves and held it there, the huge oar bending almost to breaking. The waves tore at it like living things and the ship slashed back, a sword ever seeking the storm's heart. For many turns of the hour, the battle raged. The ship remained undaunted and Menannon held immovable, forcing it to hold fast though blood had long since begun to flow from his lips as his broken ribs were driven almost through him. Yet for all his effort, the ship made no headway. If he turned his head he could still see the top of Kalyria's Crown directly behind him. At times, they were driven so far back that he could see the mouth of the lava tube still above water. During the long battle, his anger and pain turned to pure hate. His desire for justice mutated into a thirst for vengeance against those who had done this to his sire, his folk, his very land itself. His fury finally turned against the High One and he began screaming at Him at the top of his lungs, pouring out the agony of his soul. Demanding answers from a voiceless void.

"Why, High One?! Why have You allowed this to happen?! What of the thousands of innocent people You have allowed to be slaughtered?!"

Through the crashing water and drenching spray, Menannon suddenly saw the ancient volcano that was Kalyria's Crown come alive again and begin to hurl lava and pumice bombs at them to add to the already mighty forces of the storm. Flaming boulders hit the sea and exploded around the ship hurling great gouts of steaming water crashing over him. Between the storm and the volcano, he was being alternately fried and frozen which did nothing to lesson his fury. Menannon turned his blazing red eyes to the clouds above.

"You are not worthy of the love of these people, High One, for You will not lift a finger to help them in their extremity, though they have done nothing, nothing but serve You and love You all the days of their lives! How dare You let them die like this! This ship contains only those who have remained faithful. Those whom You Yourself called to it and You are letting them die! What have they done to deserve this?!" Menannon screamed out his questions until his vocal cords nearly shattered, but only the raging sea answered him.

"Show me High One. Show me how much You love your children! Show me You deserve our love and loyalty! I dare You to be greater than Kalyria's Bane! Greater than Khalandria! Do You demand another life, High One? So be it! Take mine, then, but let these people live!"

A huge gout of boiling water washed over the ship at that instant, nearly blinding him and tearing away the mast and its precious sail. When it passed, his fury passed as well, spent against the inevitable. Without the mast and sail, they were doomed, for he was not large enough to scull the ship with just its oar as his sire would have been. One last time, Menannon's voice rose, only now his words were spoken softly, almost more to himself than the High One.

"Where is Thy justice, O High One? Where is Thy mercy?"

Over the shrieking of the storm, he heard the back of the great ship begin to crack and he let the oar swerve off and the ship's head came about so that they were wallowing in the bottom of a trough with waves rising so high above them their tops seemed to hit the clouds. This was the end, neither he nor the ship could withstand any more, the next wave would destroy them.

"Forgive me, my father. I swore to you that I would live through this, but I have failed you," he whispered as he waited for the waves to descend. "There is nothing I can do now save join you in the Halls of Waiting. I am sorry."

Even as the waves grew, there was a rippling in the bottom of the trough and suddenly a great scaly back broke the water, then another and another. All around the ship, the long serpent bodies of great hornéd orlandines broke the water, beasts no longer mythical, but very, very real. They rose up over her, their opalescent gill fringes billowing in the winds of the storm, their huge horns crackling with the lightning. At the sight of them, Menannon began to laugh in near hysteria. Justice and mercy? Well, at least they were going to die at the hands, or rather scales, of one of the High One's own creatures rather than the machinations of the demon, for orlandines were ship killers. They were said to twine their serpent bodies around a ship's hull and crack her ribs before they pulled her under the waves to lie in the cold and silence of the sea floor. A single orlandine could crush a full-sized war galley and here were three of them in full glory, their scaly heads rising to the very height of the waves above him.

As he watched, time itself seemed to slow down until a single minute became a lifetime. Everything seemed to stop. The waves, the orlandines, the very ship itself all hung motionless. Then a small white dot began to circle over them, closer and closer it came until it resolved itself into an albatross whose wings sparkled cobalt edged glory in the flashes of lightning, unaffected by the wind. She wheeled above him and turned to fly slowly away, straight over the ship and down the sea trough in which it wallowed. As the albatross passed each one, the orlandines seemed almost to bow and then curl down across the ship, their great heads coming nearly level with the deck. Even as Menannon watched, they seemed to grow until their huge gill fringes covered the entire ship in an opalescent roof. In that instant, time started again and the waves crashed down against the orlandines, but their great heads did not bow and instead of crushing her, the force of the waves raised the ship and thrust her forward in the wake of the albatross. The Giantish ship cut through the water at an incredible speed, but the orlandines somehow were able to swim with her and keep their strange protection in place. Menannon clung to the steering oar, helpless.

Ahead of the ship, he could suddenly see the clouds lightening and thinning, yet there was a solid line of something that lay ahead of them: Azuron's great wall. The ship reached just short of this strange barrier beyond which Menannon could see a cloudless sky whose light was causing his eyes to burn and ache. Before he could wonder what was happening, the albatross came again and flew over the deck. As he watched, she turned and flew at the barrier and the orlandines followed her. All three reached it and then, strangely, they dove into the waves and disappeared only to reappear at the barrier where their great scaly bodies rose up, creating a living tunnel in front of the ship which grew and raised the barrier itself until the ship could sail beneath it, had it the power. But it did not.

A final lava bomb hurled out from the dying volcano and exploded directly behind the ship, thrusting her forward and through the tunnel! She sailed out onto the open sunlit sea much as a stone skipped by a child sails across a lake. Just as her fantail almost cleared the tunnel, the lead orlandine closed down upon it and ripped the aftcastle roof with its steering oar from its foundations and hurled it and Menannon into the sea. The barrier slammed back down as the orlandines sank beneath the waves, leaving him in darkness. During all of this, the young Giant had forgotten to go back to light and so he and the mighty oar sank like a stone, his mass overcoming even the buoyancy of the great timber. As he sank, from somewhere he heard his sire's voice call to him. "Go light, Menannon and live, boy. Go light!" The only thing that penetrated the fog of his mind was the sensation of rising through the water and the wind of the albatross' wings caressing his cheek as he broke the surface and his lungs filled once more with air.

Against the darkness, the wings of the albatross glittered blue white as she circled over the dying remains of the island that had been Kalyria. Without the darkness, the day passed and night returned and still the sea boiled and great gouts of steam shot skyward as the cold water finally reached the ancient volcano's magma chambers. The resultant shuddering and explosions sent out huge waves in all directions, bursting Azuron's wall asunder and rolling unchecked across the sea. Great walls of destructive water were sent ranging far and wide about the Dawn Sea, redrawing coastlines, creating islands out of peninsulas and drowning lowlands to leave their inland hills the new headlands of a world forever changed by the fall of Kalyria.

The destruction seemed to go on forever, then at last the volcano cooled and the remains of the island sank, sending out a final bubble from where the city of Kirith Kalyria had once stood as a beacon of hope in the darkness of the chaos and disorder marking the end of the Dim Times. The bubble widened and spread until it encircled the entire land mass, then it rose up from the depths and broke the sea's surface only to keep rising, no longer a bubble of air but a dome of clear, cobalt light. The dome continued to grow forcing out the darkness of Khalandria, swallowing it as surely as the sun swallows the shadows of night. Within it, figures of light broke the water from points all across what had once been Kalyria. Glittering shades of animals and birds, of men, women and children, of Humans, Dwarves and Teluri and one great Giant seemed to dance and embrace and join hands in a long line of celebration, skipping and running up a flight of celestial stairs which rose as the dome rose farther and farther into a sky alive with stars. The bubble of light left the surface of the sea, moving ever upwards until it passed beyond the sight of even the albatross who made a last circling flight around a single dark figure floating on a great oar within a path of sparkling moonlight upon the now peaceful sea. Then she turned and flew away as well, a single flash of white and cobalt, into the sky higher and higher until she was gone and the night was left once more to the moon and the constellations circling her.

The stars of Telurion Wanderer, the Sky Hunter, glittered down from their frosty vault seemingly undisturbed by the need to contend with the light of the full moon. The three bright stars of his belt hung across the horizon as though he led the way, a starry guide for the ship sailing below him, the moonlight glittering from its bow wave. ❦❦❦

Typographic design by Richard L. Hardesty
at the Rising Wolf Press, Hungry Horse, Montana.
The title and chapter headings are set in Ringbearer.
For the drop caps, Golden Cockerel Titling Caps
was used. The text was set in 12 point Joanna
& Joanna Italic, Eric Gill's lovely design.
The regular Golden Cockerel
type was used on the
title page & a few
other places.
Various
decorative
fonts were
called up-
on for the
ornaments sprinkled
throughout the text. Gloria in excelsis Deo!

www.ingramcontent.com/pod-product-compliance
Lightning Source LLC
Chambersburg PA
CBHW070340030726
47504CB00001B/17